# THE LAST SEER AND THE TOMB OF ENOCH

By

Ashland Menshouse

Edited by
S. Christopher Francis
&
Sarah B. Fry

Illustrations by
Eric Losh

# Disclaimer

This book is a work of fiction, meaning it is not *real*. The characters do not exist, and are not based on anyone who does exist or has previously existed, and any resemblance to anyone who has ever breathed air is purely coincidental. The creatures of darkness may be real, but no one can be for certain, and yet again, they are not similar to or a depiction of anyone known to be living or dead, and, as previously stated, any resemblance, similarity, likeness or proclivity is, you guessed it, happenstance.

Buzz Reiselstein's inventions have never been created, tested or approved by any federal or governmental body or agency, and no one should attempt to reproduce any such instrument as described in this work of fiction as there may be dire consequences that include, but are not limited to, infection, bleeding and death. Also, other unique abilities which anyone in the book may display are fantasy and should not be recreated, reproduced or undertaken by anyone, especially those individuals who believe they have been abducted by aliens, lived a previous life on another planet, or folks who currently consider or have previously believed themselves to possess supernatural powers.

***Get it?*** It's fiction! Not real, but make believe. Not historical fiction or mythology, just straightforward, easy-to-disregard, home-grown, thunk-up, imaginary fiction. Simply meant to be read and enjoyed.

First published by Dog Ear Publishing
4010 W. 86th Street, Ste H
Indianapolis, IN 46268
www.dogearpublishing.net

ISBN: 978-145750-401-3

This book is printed on acid-free paper.

Printed in the United States of America

# Table of Contents

*For Dorothy*

# *Cornered Contenders*

Darkness shrouded the valley of Lake Julian as the sun's ruddy twilight rays disappeared behind the slopes of the aging, forest-capped mountains. Scattered along byways and creeks, pinpoints of lights streamed skyward from streetlamps and parking lots, which were nestled between hovels of pine and oak and patches of grassy fields. Ablaze with blinding beams of orange and white spotlights, a majestic white concrete dam held back the lapping waters of the sparkling lake as cars passed along the highway across the dam's crown.

Throughout the Appalachian town, yellowed beams from headlights crisscrossed streets and glinted through neighborhoods with retiring mothers and fathers arriving home to their families. Children gathered around dining room tables to grab an early taste of the evening meal. The blue glow of televisions and computers cast an electric glaze on windows, and a familiar foghorn blared in the distance.

The cooling air from the hills was still, and peace rested soundly over every house in town.

But peace wasn't paying attention.

In a forested, forgotten corner of Lake Julian, swirling wisps spun windy whirls between a mingling mesh of tree limbs and brindled bushes. The evening breeze whistled a warning atop the canopy. Blue jays and chickadees folded their wings and huddled low in their nests. Crickets ceased their chirping, and the cicadas' buzzing faded out. A somber chill settled over the wilderness.

A gray haze rushed through the woods. Transparent chains clinked through twirling leaves, and dust spewed into the air behind the racing mist. The haze slowed, and a face appeared. It turned its head and scanned the forest with its deep-set, sallow eyes. The misty form tried to wrench its body from the ground, but its chains pulled it back tightly to the ground. The ghost scowled at the silence, and an angry scar creased across its filmy cheek.

Deeper in the woods, charging stomps pounded the forest floor in the distance. Twigs crackled and large patches of grasses flattened under an immense weight. The ghost turned toward the source of the noise, acknowledging its hidden stalker, and fled in the opposite direction.

The long, hairy arms of the stalker swung quickly at its sides as it charged up the hill, its momentum building even as the steepness increased. The beast's jagged fangs dripped with spit, and its red, glowing eyes jolted and weaved through the darkness as it hunted its prey through the thick foliage.

The creature gained swiftly on the ghost. But the ghost found its haven.

Like wooden sentinels, a line of white pine trees lined the edge of the forest. The canopy opened up, and a thicket of gravestones jutted up from the ground at the crest of the hill. The ghost escaped the forest and rolled over the cemetery in smoky silence, sinking slowly into the earth.

The beast sprang from the edge of the forest and stopped suddenly at the sight of the partially buried, rusted iron wall that bordered the walled plots and tombstones of the cemetery. The stalker twisted its neckless head from side to side, searching for the ghost. A sour fog fumed from its stout nose while it trundled down the hill, glimpsing around walls and behind graves. The creature stopped at the lichgate. The front section of the iron fence was pitched forward, lured into the ground by erosion and time. The stalker eyed the circular figurine adorning the lichgate's crest. The beast now understood the plot of its prey.

The stalker took a single, mindful step inside the cemetery. A familiar slink of an ancient horror sifted between headstones. The creature jerked back quickly.

With heated breath, the monster howled fiercely, shattering the sleepy valley's sullen silence. A new refrain to an old battle filled the creature's heart.

## *Wide Awake!*

Aubrey's eyelids stood at attention. He did everything he could to try to force them shut, but they simply would not close. His eyes reminded him of a set of Venus fly traps, shuttering erratically, desperately attempting to capture a mischievous fly or a spindly spider that remained just out of reach. But the prey of sleep eluded his restless mind.

The morning was racing more and more quickly to the present, and the more Aubrey considered his rapidly evaporating time for rest, the more his anxiety energized him. He glanced at his alarm clock…

# 11:26

…and he sighed in exasperation. Why couldn't he simply lay his head back, relax all his muscles and unplug his brain? He had already counted sheep, thought of a happy place and drunk four glasses of milk without a hint of a yawn. Now he was left wondering why sheep counting would ever work in the first place, if there was a happier place than his favorite ice cream shop, and how long would it be before he needed to pee. The clock changed.

# 11:27

Aubrey felt the over-sized L.E.D. numbers mocking him. Even the tiny, alarm dot next to the 'P.M.' seemed to be shamelessly jeering at him. He briefly subtracted in his head the time until his alarm would buzz in the morning, and the result struck a deep fearful chord that only served to fuel his mounting distress. He now had less than seven hours of potential time to sleep before his first day of high school.

"Greeeaaat, "Aubrey murmured to himself. He wanted to surrender, but his frustration trapped his consciousness under its own weight.

*THUNK! Scratch. Squeak. Scratch.*

Aubrey's anxiety shifted gears. What were those sounds? He refocused his attention on the noises and waited.

*Squeak. Scratch. Squeak.*

Now sleep was unthinkable. Aubrey sat straight up in bed and investigated his room. His window was closed, but the drapes were fully open, providing him an easy view of the outside. He could see the neighboring house across his yard and the light and shadows cast by the street lamp through the trees out front, but there was no clear reason for the intrusive sounds. His closet door was open and his clothes hung neatly still on their hangers. His computer was turned off on top of his desk with his half-full backpack leaning over in his chair. The bookshelf stood quietly under the window and his TV screen was black with his hand-me-down video game controllers carelessly bundled on top of their console underneath. Nothing was out of the ordinary.

*Squeak. Squeak. Squeak.*

The unidentifiable racket was definitely coming from just outside the window, but there was nothing amiss. There were no birds, and it didn't sound like a squirrel or a mouse. There didn't seem to be any wind; in fact, there was no noticeable movement of any kind. His second-story location would have prevented most animals and pranksters from producing such a noise directly outside his window.

*Squeak. Squeak. Squeak. Squeak.*

The sounds were coming more rapidly now, and Aubrey's heart raced to match pace with the increased tempo of the hidden tones. Aubrey opened his mouth to try and catch his breath. He wanted to shout out at whatever was creating the ruckus, but his throat was already dry from breathing heavily, and the air sped past his vocal cords so quickly that they refused to move.

*SQUEAK! SQUEAK! SQUEAK! SQUEAK! SQUEAK!*

Louder the clamor came, as if the noise, already immediately outside the window, was advancing even more closely

*SQUEAK! SQUEAK! SQUEAK! SQUEAK! SQUEAK! SQUEAK! SQUE...*

Suddenly, the noise stopped mid-squeak. Aubrey closed his eyes. He was frozen in bed, and his legs cramped into knots at the stifling dread of the cause of the squeaks.

*Tap. Tap. Tap.*

The knocks rattled the pane of window glass, and chills ran up Aubrey's arms as a fine cool breeze wriggled across his nose and lips. He opened his eyes and saw a dark, bulbous face hovering just outside his window. His lungs convulsed in the anticipation of screaming, but suddenly he recognized the dark horn-rimmed glasses and the thick, curly hair that crowned the eerily suspended face.

"BUZZ! WHAT ARE YOU DOING?" strained Aubrey in a whispered yell. He flung off his sheets, a little angry but mostly relieved, and walked over to the window.

Buzz waved his hand ecstatically on the opposite side of the glass. Aubrey unlocked the window and slowly slid it up as quietly as possible.

"Are you nuts?" Aubrey asked a little more directly, now he was certain Buzz could hear him at a lower decibel.

"I couldn't sleep, so I decided to come see if you were able to sleep," Buzz replied eagerly.

"I'm obviously not sleeping now. You scared the saintly saut out of me! Seeing a disembodied head floating outside your second-story bedroom window at midnight is not exactly a visual lullaby."

"You were sleeping?" Buzz asked, regretful that he might have awakened Aubrey.

"No. Not really," Aubrey conceded, "Too nervous."

"How did you get up here, anyway?" Aubrey asked as he leaned out his window and looked below. A double-barreled metal pole about two-stories tall leaned against the siding of the house. It reminded Aubrey of a very long shotgun barrel, except there was a thin space in between, where a similarly long bicycle chain ran from top to bottom and back again. Fixed inside the thin space, two pairs of bicycle pedals were anchored to the chain. Buzz's hands clung to the top pair and he stood on the bottom set.

"So you just pedaled up?" Aubrey questioned in disbelief. He knew Buzz had a knack for mechanics and electronics, but lately his schemes had become more involved and bizarre.

"Yep," Buzz answered proudly. "It's slow going, but once you get your momentum going, it's not so bad. Gives you a bit of a workout. You would think carrying it would be awkward, but I made it retractable and it's really not all that heavy. I call it a *cyclevator*. It's sort of what would happen if an elevator married a bicycle." Buzz giggled sheepishly.

Dubiously impressed, Aubrey continued to gawk, hoping Buzz's part of the conversation would hang in the air longer and allow him more time to examine the contraption.

"When did you have time to make it?"

"I've been tinkering with it off and on all summer. Most of the pieces I lifted from my dad's junkyard. The idea first came to me when I saw the clowns from the circus practicing to stand on their unicycles. They fell a lot."

Buzz was amused by the memory. Then he realized why they fell a lot.

"Can I come inside? 'Cus if not, I need to cycle down. My legs are starting to cramp." Rivulets of sweat dripped down Buzz's cheeks. The strained expression on his face snapped Aubrey out of his haze of wonder, and he reached for Buzz's hands. Aubrey struggled to pull him inside. Buzz was easily twice as wide as Aubrey, and Buzz's rotund shape made it more difficult for him to squeeze through. He rolled more than climbed into the window. Buzz wiped the moisture from his face and leaned against the windowsill, relaxing his arms and hands.

Aubrey was surprised by Buzz's arrival, but Aubrey was grateful that Buzz was just as nervous as he was about tomorrow. Buzz was a different sort of kid, and although he was odd in nearly every way imaginable, to Aubrey, he was the best of best friends.

Aubrey laughed at his own anxiety, and then he noticed Buzz had a far-off look in his eye. Suddenly, Buzz's eyes flittered and his arms and legs stiffened straight as a board. He leaned back against the wall and trembled violently. Aubrey raced over to him and grabbed his arm as he slid to the floor. Buzz froze in mid-shake. He leaned forward and opened his eyes.

"Did you have a seizure?" asked Aubrey quietly.

"Yeah," said Buzz. "I'm all right." He crouched onto his knees and rubbed his forehead.

Aubrey sat down on his bed and watched Buzz closely.

Buzz shook his head and looked up at Aubrey. "High school tomorrow. Hard to believe. I'm so excited!" Buzz's chunky frame jiggled with glee.

"Excited isn't the right word," Aubrey dissented as he thought for a moment. "Scared…yeah…scared. That's the right word."

"But it's a whole new world!" Buzz's energy increased quickly as he forgot his aching limbs and remembered the reason they were both still wide awake.

"A whole new world, yeah right," scoffed Aubrey. "It's just another start of a school year where everyone else has grown leaps and bounds, and I'm still behind the curve. Another year where the subjects get harder and I feel dumber. And this year, instead of recess, we have P.E." Aubrey fell dejectedly on his bed and put his head in his hands. "You're really good at school…the book part anyway. So I can understand why you would be excited. But every day of middle school was a reminder of my lack of….of…everything."

"Aubrey, that's all off target. For one, the girls like you. They all think you're so cute because you're smaller."

"Yeah, and now they'll all be at least a head taller than me. And if they don't like freckled miniature boys with stringy red hair and asthma, then I'm really out of luck. And now I have these horrid braces. Just another reason to be picked on. And they cut my gums to pieces." Aubrey ran a finger along the jagged wires that imprisoned his teeth. "I think I have more wax than metal in my mouth."

Buzz shrugged off his sour chattering. "Secondly, you've always had good grades, and if you need help, just ask me." Buzz flicked a grin that hinted of a touch of arrogance.

"Psshhhh," Aubrey retorted.

"Three, we only have P.E. part of the year and it won't be that bad. Besides, I have more to worry about in that class than you." Buzz grabbed his gut and shook his flab.

"I still think P.E. is a government conspiracy to weed out the weak by publicly putting preteen inadequacy on display in an organized fashion under the guise of academic tutelage," Aubrey complained. "It makes my asthma flare just thinking about dressing out."

"But there is so much to look forward to! We'll have our own lockers. We'll move from class to class and not have to look at the same people all day long. School dances. We can play an instrument if we want. Basketball and football games. The world has gotten bigger and thus our part in it!"

"More homework. Less sleep. Less goof-off time. More anxiety. And bigger bullies! If you think Magnos and his thugs are bad, just wait till the seniors get their shot at us!"

"There you go. Wrong conclusion, again! Yeah, putting up with Magnos and his crew are a pain. But if it wasn't for them, we wouldn't even be friends!"

A hollow scream pierced the darkness outside, echoing inside Aubrey's bedroom. Both boys froze in silence. They turned stiffly and stared outside the window. There was no insect hum or cars passing by on the street. They could only hear the sound of the wind swooshing by. Aubrey stood up slowly and walked over to Buzz. They both leaned toward the edge of the window and peered stealthily into the backyard.

The nighttime breeze rustled the tops of the trees, and shadows danced across the moonlit lawn. The outline of a large, darkened shed in the back blotted out most of the view to the house behind them. A majestic old oak tree towered over everything else in the backyard and swayed gently as the fans of its foliage captured the wind. Its ancient trunk creaked quietly; its aching wood moaning under weather's strain.

From underneath the oak tree, two glowing red eyes flashed alight and glared up at Aubrey and Buzz. The pair of eyes squinted menacingly, and a dark form took shape around them.

Aubrey and Buzz gasped, jerked away from the window, and tripped backwards, landing hard on the carpeted floor in a crumpled heap of fright. Shushing each other as they untangled their arms and legs, they pushed themselves up onto their hands and knees and scurried to the back of the room, crouching low behind the bed.

Both of them breathed heavily through their mouths from the adrenaline rush.

"What was that thing?" whispered Buzz.

Aubrey shrugged, frantically searching his mind for a reasonable answer. "Bobcat?"

Buzz frowned at him. "A bobcat's eyes that are ten feet off the ground?" he questioned harshly.

"Maybe it was in the tree," guessed Aubrey

Buzz waved him off. "Maybe it was a reflection of starlight off Mars focused by satellites onto your dad's truck windshield?"

Aubrey shook his head. "Seriously creepy."

*Squeak. Scratch. Squeak.*

Aubrey and Buzz's eyes both widened, and they closed their mouths so they could listen more intently.

*Squeak. Squeak. Squeak. Squeak. Squeak. Squeak.*

Buzz pointed to the top of the cyclevator outside the window. The chain was moving.

"How do you turn it off?" squeaked Aubrey.

"You can't," whispered Buzz harshly. "It doesn't have a motor."

*SQUEAK! SQUEAK! SQUEAK! SQUEAK! SQUEAK!*

"That *thing*...it's coming!" Aubrey wrapped his arms around his head and cowered in the corner.

Buzz pulled Aubrey by the shoulder. "We need to defend ourselves." Buzz scurried over to Aubrey's desk. He jerked the mouse out of the computer by its cord and swung it overhead like a sling.

Aubrey crawled slowly over to Buzz with his head hugging the carpet. He groped the top of his desk and grabbed a stapler.

*SQUEAK! SQUEAK! SQUEAK! SQUEAK! SQUEAK! SQUEAK! SQUE!....*

Aubrey opened the stapler, business end out. They flanked the window, prepared to attack.

A baseball bat swung deftly inside the open window. Aubrey and Buzz jumped back. A short, wiry form somersaulted through the window and landed on its feet. The baseball bat flew through the air. With a thudded plop Buzz took the brunt of the bat to his plump gut. He moaned in pain and flopped down onto his side.

Aubrey raced over to the door and flipped on the light switch. "Rodriqa," shouted Aubrey through a whisper. "What are you doing?!"

Rodriqa turned her head quickly and scanned the room. Beads that cocooned her braided hair swished from side to side and clinked together. She held the baseball bat up close to her, ready to swing again. The dark skin of her thin athletic arms trembled. Her eyes twitched from the groaning Buzz on the carpet to Aubrey, who was holding his arms out near the door.

"I...I...I...thought you had a burglar," she stammered. "That contraption was sitting against your house. Your window was open. The lights were out, and I saw movement."

"*That contraption* is my cyclevator," groaned Buzz as he squeezed his belly.

"We couldn't sleep," said Aubrey. "We're too nervous about tomorrow." Aubrey crept slowly over to her. He wrapped his fingers carefully around the end of the bat and slipped it out of her hands.

Rodriqa balled up her fists and placed them on her hips. "Why are you guys having a sleep-over on our first school night of high school?" she demanded.

"We're not," insisted Aubrey.

Buzz sat up with his legs out and rubbed his tummy with care. "You haven't seen us all summer, and this is how you say hello?"

"Aubrey is my best bud, too," chided Rodriqa. "And if someone is after him, they have to deal with me."

"You smacked me with a baseball bat," growled Buzz. "You could have really hurt me."

"You were swinging a mouse," retorted Rodriqa. She twisted her neck and scowled at Aubrey. "And you were about to shank me with a stapler."

Aubrey's senses reminded him of his former fright. He flipped off the light and the room fell into darkness. "There's somebody outside."

"Yeah...me," countered Rodriqa.

"Unless your eyes glow red in the dark, I don't think it was you," argued Aubrey.

Buzz shimmied himself up against his knees. "He's being a glamour glitch. I think it was a trick of the moonlight."

"Something was there," fumed Aubrey.

"When did you get back?" Buzz asked Rodriqa nonchalantly.

"Ten minutes ago," replied Rodriqa.

Buzz shook his head. "Did you have a good trip?"

Metal clanging and a door banging echoed from outside.

Aubrey dropped down to the floor. "No...really...there's somebody out there!" He pointed out the window.

Rodriqa knelt down. The three of them shuffled over to the window and peeked into the yard.

"This reminds me of the time when we dug those tunnels under the old, vacant lot up the street and Mr. Jennings found us," Buzz reminisced.

"Shhhhhhhh," scolded Rodriqa.

The door to large shed in the backyard was wide open and light shone from inside.  Clanks and tings reverberated from outside.

"See," reprimanded Aubrey.  "I told you.  There's someone in the back-yard."

The shed shook and a deep rumbling flittered across the yard.

"Let's go down and check it out," whispered Rodriqa.

"It has to be some sort of wild animal," said Buzz.

"Are you crazy?" asked Aubrey.  "Who knows what's down there?"

Rodriqa stood up straight and leaned out the window.  "If we don't look, we'll never know."

The lights went out in the shed.  Aubrey and Buzz pulled Rodriqa down to the floor by the back of her shirt.  A tall, dark figure drifted out from the door.  It stood motionless in the shadows, and its head turned up toward them.

"HEY! *Brianna*, you should tell your girlfriends to go home!  It's past your bedtime!" bellowed a condescending voice from below.

Rodriqa's head shot through the window, and she squinted her eyes at the familiar voice.

Aubrey dropped his head and rubbed his eyes.  Their nighttime intruder hadn't been an intruder at all.  It was his brother.

"That's *NOT* my name," Aubrey howled in a wounded whine.

"And I'm *NOT* his girlfriend," protested Buzz and Rodriqa simultaneously.  They gave each other a curious look, and Aubrey ran his hand down his face.

Crowing with laughter, Gaetan walked into the yard between the two houses.  "Cry some more, you bunch of snail shuckers.  Morning's gonna come early in a few hours," he jeered as he sauntered toward the front door.

"Your brother's right," Buzz admitted as he stood up.  "Look at the time."

# 12:14

Rodriqa sighed.  "Yeah, he's got a point.  We need to get some rest."  She climbed out onto the ledge and scurried down the cyclevator.  Aubrey and Buzz were impressed by how quickly she made it down.

"Catch you two toad throwers tomorrow."  She smiled and waved at them before sprinting across the yard and disappearing into her house.

"I don't think I'll have much trouble sleeping now," said Aubrey

Buzz shook his head and laughed.  "See you in a few hours."

Aubrey grinned and helped him up onto the sill.  Buzz cranked the pedals back up and then spun himself clumsily down to the ground.

Aubrey closed his window and crawled back into bed, allowing his heavy eyes and his grateful heart to rest.

The colors behind his eyelids collided in reds and greens, fuming from above and below. The simmering myriad of kaleidoscopic phosphenes clashed into squares and swirls, tumbling in and out of sight. Aubrey felt the darkness wash away the colorful display inside his eyes. The colors faded but the structures remained, mingling in his mind. A face with wide set eyes collected in the dingy mist. A scar traced along a blurry cheek and lips tightened crisply across a foamy chin.

Then it grinned.

Aubrey's eyes cracked open, unsure of what he had seen. There was no face to be seen in his room and no reason to view a smile. He smiled at his own hyperactive imagination.

He closed his eyes again and surrendered to the intoxication of sleep. The phosphenes returned, and the colors stretched through the darkness. They wobbled side to side and finally faded out as before.

The same face reappeared, grinning more broadly this time, and eyeing Aubrey in his sleep.

Aubrey sat up in bed. Nothing was out of the ordinary. He could hear the wall-shuddering snores of his father in his room up the hall. He could hear Gaetan rummaging around downstairs in the kitchen. There was no explanation for the ghostly grin.

Aubrey's heart raced, and sleep fled from his mind. He knew it was going to be a long night.

**Monday.**

Tthe alarm clock's radio burst into a boisterous country remake of a 1980s metal rock song, yanking Aubrey out of a superficial sleep. His eyelids fought against him and the morning light shining into his bedroom window burned his already bleary vision. The clock sneeringly glowed

# 7:00

When he last looked at it, it read a quarter past five and that felt like five minutes ago. Aubrey yawned widely and stretched his arms and legs, but they spasmed wearily in revolt. The only upside, Aubrey thought, was perhaps the exhaustion would settle his anxiety about the first day of school.

Aubrey stumbled down the hallway into the bathroom, which had already been assaulted by his brother's morning melee with multiple grooming and hygiene products. A dried, cracking smear of tan acne remover stained one side of the faux marble sink. Paunchy clouds of disintegrating mousse clung to the mirror, leaving a filmy tail of gel as they slowly slid down its face. A nest of towels lay crumpled on the floor, nearly hiding a misplaced razor. Most of the shampoos, conditioners and soaps, which usually resided in the wire shelving that dangled from the base of the shower head, were scattered in the bottom of the tub, their tops partially open and their contents bleeding toward the shower drain in a shimmering multi-colored mess. And worst of all, the toilet was not flushed.

Aubrey wiped down the mirror and the sink with a damp washcloth. He closed the oozing bottles in the tub and returned them to their previous slots in the shower hanger. And after closing its lid, he flushed the toilet. This surge of tidiness was not typical for Aubrey, but anything he could do to avoid thinking about his inevitable first day, provided him some much-needed relief.

Aubrey brushed his teeth, paying particular attention to the gaps in between his braces. He combed his stringy red hair, which took the same, wire-brush shape regardless of how he fixed it, and washed his face, optimistic that he had lost a freckle or two over the summer.

He scrutinized his appearance in the mirror. The one thing he wished he could change more than anything was his height and weight. His nerdy looks made it difficult for him to fit in, but being short and skinny upgraded him to the category of misfit. He had tried to eat more over the summer, but it hadn't made any difference. Adding to his strained appearance, the whites of his eyes were bloodshot from a night of insomnia. He considered wearing sunglasses to school, but decided he wouldn't make it through his first class without an intervention.

Realizing the hour was passing quickly, he changed his clothes, stuffed his backpack with the essentials and ran downstairs.

The dining room table had one place set, and a plate of food was waiting for Aubrey. His brother and father had already eaten and left for the day, and his mother had cleaned up all but Aubrey's portion of the meal and escaped quietly to her bedroom. His mother's absence was routine, and except for the evidence of her household activities, he barely knew she lived under the same roof.

Aubrey devoured his over-easy eggs in two fork-fulls, drank a large swig of milk and grabbed a piece of bacon and toast for the road. He snapped on his helmet, slung his backpack over his shoulder, and rushed out the back door.

His ten-speed bicycle was secured to a hidden piece of metal plumbing behind a section of lattice work enclosing the side of the porch. He flipped the metal prongs of the combination lock into position and unwound his bicycle from the plastic-sleeved chain of the lock. After tightening the caps on the tire valves, Aubrey straddled the seat and pedaled for the sidewalk.

*Ten minutes and two miles until the first day of high school*, Aubrey thought to himself. He diffused his fear by forgetting his destination and, instead, immersed himself in his comfortable surroundings as he crammed the bacon and toast in his mouth.

He sped beyond Rodriqa's house and several other homes in the neighborhood, which ranged in size from three-story colonials to two-room duplexes. Aubrey had lived on Dalton Circle all his life, and although neighbors had come and gone, most of his childhood memories had been made in the yards, crawlspaces and hidden nooks along this road.

He passed an empty grass lot full of waist-high weeds peppered with young, spindly trees, where he, Buzz, and Rodriqa had dug for ancient artifacts and planted peach pits in the summer, and ate icicles and had snowball battles in the winter. Buzz would try and create some new invention out of rotting twigs, a hubcap, and some six-pack plastic rings to throw multiple snowballs at once. Slim on talent and body mass, Aubrey would simply use his small size to his advantage. He was the only one of the three who could fit in the stump and pelt Rodriqa and Buzz with snowballs. But it didn't matter. Neither Aubrey nor Buzz was a match for Rodriqa's fast pitch. Aubrey chuckled as he recalled how Rodriqa would beat the two of them every time.

Aubrey rode beyond the overpass at the top of the street, passed by **Ray Gene's Smart Mart and Finer Diner** at the corner and turned onto the Asheville Highway. It was still early enough that traffic hadn't picked up, so Aubrey had both right-hand lanes to himself. The brisk, late summer breeze chilled his cheeks, and he was more alert than he had expected with so little sleep.

The Lake Julian Dam crested at the top of the ridgeline. The concave wall of bleached white concrete twinkled in the morning sun, and Aubrey popped his bike onto the sidewalk so we could peek over the edge. He could hear the rush of the water from the spillway below as its spray fell deep into the gorge. On the opposite of the road, Aubrey waved to members of the maintenance crew atop the observation deck in the middle of the dam as they peered out over the crystal blue waters of the lake. This stalwart structure was the pride of the community, and Aubrey had always heard that if it weren't for the dam, there would be no Lake Julian.

Past the dam, Aubrey knew it would take little effort to arrive at the high school. The road switch-backed to and fro down the hillside, providing him with all the momentum he would need to make it there. He puffed out his cheeks and swallowed hard against his dry throat to force his ears to pop with the drop in altitude.

The road leveled out and he could see the school to his right, breaking through the dispersing trees. Bustling lines of cars vied for the best positions as they sputtered stops and starts in and out of the parking lot. Clusters of students migrated from sidewalks and reunion huddles through a series of double glass doors scattered along the periphery of the first level. The polished tan masonry uniformly plastering the outside of all three stories of the school and bars crisscrossing the lower windows reminded Aubrey of an industrial prison more than a supportive center for higher learning. Dread filled Aubrey's gut, and he slowed his speed.

A low rumbling to his left drew his attention with soothing distraction. The Berybomag Mine had started its digging operations just a couple of months ago, but over the summer the entire enterprise had grown to mammoth proportions. Lofty bucket-wheeled excavators trudged through hill-sized mounds of dirt. Two-story tall trucks with wheels as wide as a car drove slowly in and out of the mine's deep pit. A cloud of dust hung over the mine, draping the surrounding trees in a lining of gray, soily soot.

Aubrey pulled into the high school and stopped at the bike rack, which was nearly half-full. Exhaling his anxiety, he sighed deeply as he surveyed his new temple of torment for the next four years. He bent down to lock up his bike, and a familiar sputtering sound approached him.

Buzz rolled up next to Aubrey on his steam-powered bicycle, its cricket-legged pistons chugging in circles as puffs of steams spit from its central burner. Buzz hopped off the banana seat, blew out the pilot light, and the engine simmered to a halt.

He smiled at Aubrey widely and patted him proudly on his back. "Today will be a day of memory," stated Buzz with oratorical flair. "The day we transition from children...to giants. Our lives, our hopes and our dreams will never be the same. Are you ready for our first day of manhood?"

Aubrey shook his head at him, but he couldn't keep himself from grinning. "I think someone poured some liquid courage in your cereal this morning," countered Aubrey.

Buzz pushed his glasses up his nose. "Every person must face the daunting challenges that lay before them, no matter how treacherous or unyielding. History demands that fate pave our paths, but only we can choose to navigate toward peril or triumph."

"I would be satisfied with an easy, unremarkable and uneventful day," replied Aubrey as he hoisted his backpack high over his shoulders.

"Let the naysayers be heard," continued Buzz. "And may they be wrong!"

"I wish I could be as excited as you are," mumbled Aubrey.

"You set your sights too low, my friend."

"No, you set *your* sights too low!" A high-pitched voice squealed from behind them.

They turned around and Bates Hindenberg glowered at them, perched on his solar-powered bicycle. Wings of silicon cells jutted out from under the seat, nearly encasing his bike in a shell of reflective, dark blue panels. Bates' thick, black disheveled hair flitted in the breeze, and the weight of his thick-rimmed glasses pressed firmly on his nose and cheeks. He was no taller than Aubrey, but he was slightly more intimidating in the seat of his semiconductor-plated contraption.

"Still riding your second place project," badgered Buzz.

"You only won the County Science Fair last year because you used propane supplies from one of the judges," accused Bates, his voice now shriller than before. Although he was sixteen, puberty was a gift he had yet to receive.

Buzz waved him off. "Keep dreamin'."

"Oh, I never stop dreaming," replied Bates haughtily. "And this year, you haven't a prayer of winning any awards." He slid back three rows of solar panels and flipped them up, revealing the guts of his bicycle.

Buzz's jaw dropped. Aubrey squinted at the mess of electrical wiring and metal boxes.

"That's right," scoffed Bates. "In this year's science fair, I'll be entering my bicycle...*hybrid*!"

Buzz leaned over to examine the surging lines of electrical cord, fettered, whirling generators and metered lights of strobing greens and yellows. He shut his mouth to prevent himself from drooling enviously.

"Beryllium ion, baby," lorded Bates. He slammed the solar panels back into position, cutting Buzz off from any further inspection.

"I'm breaking up this geek convention," grumbled a voice from over top of them. Aubrey turned around and his throat tightened. The blue, beady eyes of Magnos Strumgarten leered from behind his mangy, blonde sheepdog locks, and he scowled menacingly. Aubrey gulped down a hard lump in his throat and marveled reticently at Magnos' new size. Aubrey barely reached the middle of his chest, and he guessed Magnos must have grown at least ten inches over the summer. Aubrey was grateful he was still wearing his bicycle helmet.

Flanked by the chubby, ruddy-cheeked twins, Lenny and Benny Van Zenny, Magnos pumped his ham hock-sized fists, eager for a fight. Bates scurried away fearfully on his bike with a surrendering yelp.

Buzz slotted his bike in the rack and locked it up. "How was your summer, Magnos?"

Magnos grunted from the opposite side of the rack.

"You're gonna wish your summer wasn't over," sneered Lenny. Benny snickered in tandem.

"Let's go," whispered Aubrey, nudging Buzz along toward the side entrance of the high school.

"Hi, Aubrey. How have you been?" The cheery voice caught him off guard. McCrayden Miller bounced in front of him and waved gently. Golden curls cascaded around her face and across her shoulders, and her rosy smile gleamed at him with unreserved kindness. Aubrey had had a debilitating crush on her since the sixth grade. Unfortunately, she had been Magnos' girlfriend since seventh grade. Aubrey's stomach flipped, and his heart raced uncontrollably at the sight of her. McCrayden rocked slowly back and forth, hugging her books against her chest, awaiting his reply.

"What's a' matter dude, your mouth full of mud?" scoffed Lenny.

Aubrey cranked his jaw to speak, but only unintelligible clicks and spits came out.

"He's just quiet. Aren't ya, Aubrey," she answered for him sweetly.

Aubrey nodded furiously in agreement.

"Be careful Magnos, or Aubrey might steal your girl," chuckled Benny.

Magnos snarled bitterly. "Take a hike, you orange-haired freak." Magnos shoved Aubrey out of the way. Aubrey felt like he'd been hit by a truck. He toppled off to the side and smacked head on into another student, landing them both face down in the dirt.

Magnos, Lenny and Benny guffawed proudly, high-fived one another and strutted toward the front doors.

"Magnos, that wasn't very nice," chided McCrayden, chasing after them.

Aubrey rolled over and sat forward. He glanced at the person next to him on the ground as she clumsily replaced a pair of honey-colored glasses on her slender nose. Her small, rounded ears peeked through her long, opalescent black hair, and her sorrel skin glistened in the morning light. Small patches of mud smudged her face and arms, and she slumped into a sitting position dejectedly.

"I'm sorry," squeaked Aubrey. "Are you okay?"

She nodded quietly.

An electronic chime dinged from the speakers on the corners of the building.

"Aubrey, we're gonna be late for class," pleaded Buzz as he ran toward the entrance.

Aubrey stood up and looked down anxiously at the girl. He was pretty sure he had never seen her before.

Books, pencils, and colored pens were strewn across the grass in front of her. She brushed herself off and raked the strewn contents back into her open book bag. The bell rang repeatedly, urging everyone inside.

"Sorry again," repeated Aubrey with as much sympathy as he could muster before he hurried after Buzz.

Aubrey burst through the side doors. Aubrey and Buzz had designed their schedules last spring so they would have most of their classes together. Aubrey rounded another corner and watched Buzz disappear into a classroom several doors down. Chasing him, Aubrey hurdled through the door just as the last chime rang.

A man only a few inches taller than Aubrey with a white, bushy mustache and a baldhead sized him up and closed the door abruptly behind him. He shooed Aubrey away from the door, and Aubrey scuffled toward the back of the room as he took of his helmet. Spotting an empty desk in the last row next to Buzz, Aubrey dropped himself quietly in the seat.

The squatty, aged man waddled behind a long, black lab bench up front. He half-turned away from the class and raised a piece of chalk in his hand, scraping it along the blackboard against the front wall. "This is Physical Sciences 115. I am Mr. Vandereff and I have three simple rules." He scrawled his name slowly in cursive and then listed a one, two and three below them, with a dot after each. "Number one, no gum. That includes candy, breath mints and other organic substances that induce saliva release. I won't be close enough to you to smell your breath, so chemically altering your halitosis here is not a priority.

"Number two, no cell phones. A missed text is not a catastrophe, and a web browser is not a brain substitute. Fortunately, the spotty service in the valley should help you keep this rule.

"Number three, no lip. Disrespect for me or your fellow classmates is not tolerated in my class. If you have a difficult time recalling these rules, remember this simple mnemonic. No G.P.L." He pointed to the rules again and then pulled a tall stool from underneath the black lab bench that separated him from the rows of desks. Mr. Vandereff laid out several stacks of papers as he pensively combed his mustache with his fingers.

Aubrey had focused all of his attention on Mr. Vandereff, but when his teacher stopped talking to hand out stacks of syllabi and course requirements, Aubrey's heart sank as he looked around the room.

Magnos sat several desks up in the middle of the room with Lenny and Benny on either side. The three of them whispered back and forth with Magnos occasionally chuckling loudly. McCrayden was a row behind and to the left, which put her diagonally to Aubrey. She waved to Aubrey when she noticed he was staring at her. Aubrey jerked his head quickly away and glanced at Buzz, who was feverishly studying the syllabus.

Mr. Vandereff cradled a final stack of papers and walked around the front of the lab bench. "It is my job to fill your minds fully with the essentials of chemistry and physics. Your indoctrination into the axiomatic world of the indivisibly unseen will begin with a detailed tour of the fundamental building blocks of all matter of the cosmos...an exploratory menagerie of the primordium, if you will, in the form of a comprehensive study of the Periodic Table of the Elements. You each will be given an element of study as well as explicit guidelines on the degree of elucidation you will be expected to provide in written format. And your first element report will be due this Friday." A collective moan leaked from the students. "Now, now," countered Vandereff as he passed a single paper out to each student. "The unknown is exciting! And I want the papers to be hand-written. Penmanship is a lost skill these days."

The classroom door slammed shut. Everyone spun toward the front corner of the room. A girl with sorrel skin, honey-colored glasses, and hair as dark as midnight stood meekly just inside, clutching her books to her chest as a book bag with a wide, jagged rip in one side dangled from her forearm. She watched Mr. Vandereff quietly, avoiding the sudden attention from every set of eyes in the room.

Buzz nudged Aubrey across the row. "Hey! Isn't that the girl you knocked down?"

Aubrey shrank in his seat and ignored Buzz.

Mr. Vandereff finished handing out the assignments and turned toward the door. "Can I help you?"

"I'm taking Physical Sciences 115," she murmured, pulling a slip of paper from between books.

"Well then...you're in the right place, just not the right time," Mr. Vandereff quipped.

"Excuse me," she asked, a little confused.

"The right time," replied Mr. Vandereff pointedly, "was five minutes ago."

She lowered her head. "I'm sorry. I had an accident."

Mr. Vandereff waved her into the middle of the class and pointed for her to sit in the last empty desk in the back corner next to Aubrey.

Aubrey feigned disinterest and glared at his assignment, rolling his eyes back and forth as if he was reading, when his honest attention was nowhere near the page.

"I have another rule against tardiness," said Mr. Vandereff as he walked back behind his lab bench. "I knew there was a 'T' in that mnemonic somewhere."

The girl slumped into her seat and set her ragged pile of mud-tinged supplies on the floor next to her. She pushed her glasses up on her nose and stiffened her lip. "Sorry. It's my first day," she whimpered.

"It's everyone's first day," Vandereff grumbled unsympathetically.

Aubrey glanced at her from the corner of his eye. He definitely had never seen her in Lake Julian before. She was small with a gentle frame and she repeatedly touched her finger to her glasses, even if they hadn't moved. She looked toward the front of the class and quickly buried her head into the stack of papers handed back to her. Mr. Vandereff was shuffling through more papers on his bench, but Magnos caught Aubrey's eye. Magnos looked over his shoulder over and over again at the girl. There was a curiously empathetic glint in his eye that he had never seen from Magnos before.

"Which one did you get?" whispered Buzz urgently.

"Huh?" grunted Aubrey in reply.

"Which element?" reiterated Buzz as he tapped on his assignment.

"Oh," answered Aubrey. He read his paper for the first time. "Magnesium," he replied, a little annoyed.

"I got silicon," he replied excitedly.

Mr. Vandereff cleared his throat to regain the class's attention. He counted heads up and down the rows. "Looks like everyone is here...now."

Aubrey looked over at the girl again. She glanced his way briefly and then returned to reorganizing her things. He was struck by how dark and penetrating her eyes were through her glasses. His stomach gnawed against his heart at how poorly he had treated her just a few minutes earlier. Aubrey ripped a corner from the blank edge of his assignment. He pulled out a pen from his book bag and scribbled on the scrap.

**HELLO THERE!**
**I AM REALLY SORRY ABOUT THIS MORNING**
**YOU HAVE REALLY PRETTY EYES**
**ARE YOU NEW HERE?**

Aubrey folded the note into a tight square. He raised his arms above his head, like he was stretching, and produced a gaping yawn. He gripped the note behind his back, and flicking his wrist at the last second, spun it forward. The note tumbled down the aisle between them, resting against McCrayden's foot. The girl grimaced at him disapprovingly and returned to reading the assignment, her shiny, straight hair forming an impenetrable curtain between them.

Aubrey's heart pounded hard in his chest. He scooted his desk forward and reached for the note with his foot. McCrayden leaned over and picked it up. Aubrey's eyes widened, and he grunted out in quiet protest, "No."

McCrayden didn't hear him. She unwrapped the note and read it several times. Taking a double and triple look back at Aubrey, McCrayden curled her eyebrows at him disdainfully. She tapped Lenny on the shoulder and handed him the note, whispering behind his back as he read it. Lenny chuckled and looked back at Aubrey with a sinister grin.

Aubrey shook his head and sighed. He knew this was going to be a long day.

# Rising Darkness

The bronze rays of the late summer morning sun warmed the crisp, dawn air of the Lake Julian valley. Dewdrops glistened on the forest leaves and meadow grass, casting final glimmering strands of rainbow light against the ground before they evaporated. The still waters behind the dam stretched calmly from concrete to shore like a sheet of fine silk, lazily juggling the single tugboat that broke its surface.

Soaring aloft billowing currents of air from the hilltops, a single black bird floated through the bright blue dome of sky overhead. It pivoted its slick-feathered head from shoulder to shoulder, surveying the landscape below. The teardrop shape of Lake Julian spanned a mile at its widest point and narrowed to a few hundred yards at the white, concrete dam at its tip. Beyond the dam a deep, flora-filled gorge sunk deep into the green earth, with misty runoff from the lake pouring into the dark abyss of the creek bed beneath. Houses and roads checkered most of the hills around the lake except for a gray, dusty crater that punched a yawning hole in the nearby forest.

The raven folded its wings and plummeted toward the lake, abandoning its graceful flight for the relentless pull of gravity. Only a few feet from water's surface, the bird suddenly snapped its wings fully open and curved sharply forward. It flapped furiously and bobbed its head into the wind, gaining speed as it hurled above the waters toward the dam.

The bird fanned its tail and rose steeply above the dam, soaring starboard above the canopy of the forest bank of the lake. It reversed the draw of its wings, and dagger-like claws extended from its open talons. It dropped through the tops of the trees. The coal-black raven gripped a white pine limb and hobbled to a stop with the knobby wood in its grip. Several seedling cones dropped to the forest floor below as the limb shook. The raven preened under wings with its shiny, saber-like beak and twisted its head in near complete circles, scanning the surrounding foliage. It cocked its torso to the side to gain a better view of the ground below with its single, dark eye, abandoning the use of its opposite white opaque eye.

The raven opened its wings and leapt into the air, gliding into a round, treeless opening in the woods. It rested on a dull, brick red cross hastily hewn from a block of stone that had irregular shavings cut coarsely in its surface. The grit in the stone marker sparkled in the morning light.

The raven peered at the weedy carpet of earth at the bottom of the cross and crowed loudly. Its hoarse and hollow cackle frightened several chipmunks into the brush at the edge of the forest.

A gray transparent hand slipped from underneath the undisturbed ground of the grave. Slowly a wispy human form rose and faced the raven. Thick locks of braided hair cloaked his head as dust swirled about him. A long, raised scar arced from his wide jaw to his cliff-like forehead. And chains locked its arms close to its sides.

"Theee Queeeeeeen haaasss preeepaaaaarrreeeddd eeeevvveeerrryyyythi-iiinnnggg aaaas yoooouuuu haaaavvveee detaaaaiiiillleeeddd," hissed the ethe-real man barely above a whisper. "Theee finaaaaal steeeeep iiiis uuuup toooo yooooooouuuuu."

The raven turned its body to the side and peered at the ghost from head to toe with its good eye.

"Whaaaaatttt yoooouu haaaaavvveee aaaasssskeeeed iiiissss doooonnnee," seethed the ghost angrily. "FREEEEE MEEEEE!"

The raven squawked a high-pitched caw at the ghost. It was not an admo-nition, but a cry of warning.

The ghost turned and scanned the stalwart battalion of white pines encir-cling the cemetery. Bushes and limbs shuddered in the distant depths of the dense forest. Red eyes, glowing between hidden shadows, glared back at the ghost and the raven.

The ghost heaved a raspy chortle. "Dooooon't wooooooorrrrry... theeeeyyy caaaaaan't haaaaaaarm uuuss heeeeeeeeeere."

# Cafeteria Blues

Aubrey stumbled down the long hallway from his Spanish class toward the cafeteria, passed easily by a rush of hungry, yet well-rested, students. The adrenaline rush from the morning had kept him fully awake for his first two periods, but now he was fading quickly as his disturbed night's sleep zapped him with debilitating exhaustion. He sauntered through the swinging double doors and absorbed the sight of a vastly different lunchtime than he'd grown accustomed to over the past nine years.

Throngs of kids clustered to clumps of tables crammed together in erratic configurations throughout the room. Students jockeyed for positions like bees swarming on a honeycomb. Two single-file lines stretched along both sides of the cafeteria's edge and extended deep into the central foyer out front. One kid after another whizzed by him either empty-handed and racing for a spot in line or fully loaded with food and hurrying to get the best spot at the busiest table.

Aubrey turned around and another student plowed into him, nearly knocking him off his feet. A flurry of black and white cell phones, pagers, and MP3 players bounced across the linoleum floor. Aubrey regained his balance and glanced up. Teton Bailston had rammed him head on with his fingers still in texting position while his phone fell from his hands and flopped face down on the floor. Teton had lived a couple streets over from Aubrey since they were toddlers, and they had been at the same school all their lives, but they hadn't spoken more than two words to each other since first grade. Teton was a member of the Mafisito, a local gang of kids who purportedly bought and sold the most advanced electronic devices at basement wholesale prices, although no one knew where they bought the equipment from, nor who they sold it to. Every member of the gang wore sunglasses, regardless of lighting or weather, and they always wore clothes that never fit. Today, Teton was wearing a white tank top that was so tight his shoulders thinned the fabric around the arm loops and khaki pants that were so large he had rolled cuffs to the middle of his lower legs.

Teton bent over and picked up his scattered milieu of merchandise. "Watch where you're going, Taylor!"

"Teton, you were texting," retorted Aubrey. "You ran into me."

Teton shoved the phones and pagers into his pockets, folded his arms and perched his sunglasses on top of his head. He gazed at Aubrey snottily, squinting his eyes while deciding his next, best course of action. "Tell you what," he said slowly. "I'm gonna let this go this time." A mischievous grin slid from ear to ear. "You know why?"

Aubrey shrugged glibly and rolled his eyes.

"Because you've got enough trouble of your own right now."

Aubrey scrunched his face together in confusion. "What do you mean?"

Teton chortled tersely and strutted off into the lunchroom crowd.

Furtive movements between stacks of irregularly-shaped instrument cases caught Aubrey's eye at the Marching Band table. A trio of kids were staring at him and whispering with their hands covering their faces. Aubrey glared at them, and they shifted away from one another in their seats. One of the girls glanced back and then, leaning forward, whispered to her friend again.

Aubrey shook it off. He decided he needed to eat and find a place to sit. He faced the Graham Cracker table, where neo-hippies and grunge rocker wanna-be's sat, slowly eating only vegetables and tofu while they listened to new-age music and drew pen tattoos on each other's arms. A girl with a spiky black Mohawk, fringed with bright blue tips, stared and pointed at Aubrey to her neighbor, a fair-skinned, shoeless boy with blonde dreadlocks.

Aubrey raised his eyebrows at her. She looked away, put her headphones in her ears and tapped her hand to the beat against her knee.

Aubrey turned toward the front of the cafeteria line. A sea of camouflage and bright orange safety vests blocked his view. Several members of the J.R.A, or Junior Rifle Association, sat clumped together around a table, leaning in and listening. Stew Parsons, a paunchy yellow-haired boy was telling a story with gesticulating fingers and adrenalized facial expressions. Next to Stew, one boy reclined in his chair with his arms crossed, glaring at Aubrey with beady eyes. Snakes McWhorter. Snakes was known to be the greatest hunter of game in the county, even though he was only a teenager. And it was easy to see how he'd gotten his name. His dark round eyes were so small, if he hadn't been facing Aubrey directly, Aubrey couldn't even be sure that Snakes was staring at him. And Snakes' hair was naturally multi-colored with auburn at his crown, brown in the back, and blonde on the sides. But it was the diamond patches of black at his temples, which gave him the appearance of a rattler. Stew turned to see what Snakes was looking at. Stew saw Aubrey and instantly, he closed his mouth and leaned back. Everyone at the J.R.A table turned toward Aubrey. Quickly, Aubrey turned around.

He felt lost in a dream. Aubrey looked back at the Marching Band table, and now everyone seated there was looking out him and murmuring to each other. His gut whimpered from unease and hunger. He decided to look for Buzz.

Since his best friend was the ultimate technogeek, Aubrey knew he would probably be sitting at the Wi-Chrome table. The Wi-Chromes were the self-pronounced group of high school nerds who touted the innate power of their 'Y' chromosomes to possess Wi-Fi, thereby imbuing them with an unnatural ability to manipulate all computers. Bates Hindenberg sat in the middle of the table and stared at Aubrey, his mouth chattering away feverishly to the kids around him. But there was no Buzz.

*What is going on*, Aubrey thought to himself. *Must be sleep paranoia.* He turned toward the center of the room where the tables were the most tightly grouped together, and around which the two most popular inner circles convened — the Rowdys and the Joxsters.    Freshman hopefuls smothered the tables for a chance to sit with the most coveted cliques of Lake Julian High. The Rowdys were the most exclusive group, as entry could only be achieved if your parents belonged to the higher echelon of tax brackets.   The dashingly well-fashioned Hamilton Miller, McCrayden's older brother, stood at the center of his table, addressing his doe-eyed flock of aspiring minions.   The Joxsters comprised the Varsity athletes and their groupies.   Aubrey's older brother was one of them.   He watched Gaetan give half-hugs and knock fists with old friends at the table of smarmy ballplayers.

Out of the milling crowd, the shaggy blonde hair and beady eyes that Aubrey had learned to fear emerged.   Aubrey's heart raced as he felt a new surge of adrenaline flush his cheeks and wet his palms.

Magnos stormed up to Aubrey and leered over him.   He ground his teeth and a growl rumbled in his chest.   "Did you give McCrayden a *love* note?"

"No," whimpered Aubrey.   He pulled his pasty tongue off the roof of his mouth. Magnos leaned over, nose to nose with Aubrey.   "Did you give McCrayden a love note?"

Aubrey looked down to avoid Magnos' glare.   "It wasn't a love note.   I wrote it for the new girl."   Aubrey could feel Magnos' hot breathe on his scalp.

"Did you give McCrayden a love note?" seethed Magnos.

Aubrey took a small step back, his mind racing with ideas.   He decided on a different approach.   "I would never try to come between you and McCrayden."

Magnos reared back and raked the hair from in front of his eyes.   He heaved deeply, squeezing his fists and puffing out his chest.   "I'm feeling generous today, since it's the first day of school and all."

"Really?" questioned Aubrey.

"Oh, yeah," replied Magnos.

Aubrey sighed deeply.   "I'm glad you see the misunderstanding."   He stuttered through his reply, slightly confused.

"I bet you're grateful.   And you'll be grateful to know I'm letting this go."

Aubrey's heart rose with elation.   He stuck out his arm to shake Magnos' hand.

Magnos shoved a crumpled piece of paper into Aubrey's hand.   "Since you'll be completing my element assignment for Mr. Vandereff's class."

"What?" muttered Aubrey.

"Oh, you don't have to thank me.   You can thank me by doing a good job."

Aubrey slowly pulled back his arm, blitzed by the conditional forgiveness.

"Make sure it's back to me pronto, so I can look over it first."   Magnos chuckled under his breath as he walked out of the cafeteria.

Aubrey flattened out the wrinkled paper. It was the same sheet he had received this morning in first period, except this one had "Boron" written at the top. His adrenaline rush faded. His energy was spent. All he wanted to do was sleep and forget this day ever began. He found an empty table in the back corner away from the hurried bustle of defamation and digestion. He laid his head on his books and his eyelids snuck together without him even trying. The din of the cafeteria faded, and he quickly dropped into unconsciousness.

*SMACK!!* The cafeteria table shuddered, and a lunch tray slid to a stop only a few inches from Aubrey's face. Rodriqa peered down at him from the opposite of the table with a wily grin. Her lively eyes and wide smile shone across her face. Rows of beads were stacked tightly around locks of braided hair, dancing and clinking against her richly dark skin as she threaded her legs between the table and the seat.

"Your mom told me I needed to watch out for you, so here I am," reported Rodriqa playfully. "Why aren't you eating? A growing boy needs nourishment."

Aubrey lifted his head and looked at her curiously. "When did you speak to my mom?"

"This morning," replied Rodriqa as she bit into an apple. "She was standing on your porch when I left for school." Aubrey felt a pang of jealously, as his mother hadn't spoken a word to him in weeks.

The newly familiar face from first period floated up behind Rodriqa and sat down next to her. The girl kept her head down and her honey-colored glasses slid to the end of her slender nose, covering more of her arching cheeks than her chocolate-colored eyes. She wore a ring on every finger, but they were all very simple; each one a stoneless band of polished metal.

"Aubrey, this is Jordana," introduced Rodriqa.

"Hi," he said as his voice cracked.

"We have Advanced Algebra together with Mrs. Makelroy in fourth period. That's gonna be a tough class."

Jordana smiled at him briefly, and then lowered her gaze to her tray, which was sparsely populated with only a cup of yogurt and a banana.

Jordana befuddled Aubrey. He thought she was picturesquely plain, yet organically exotic, and yet still the most beautiful girl he had ever seen. But when he examined her more closely, she was really no different than any other ninth grade girl. He also thought she was exceptionally charming, although she had never spoken a word to him. He chalked his meandering emotions up to insomniac's delirium.

Rodriqa waited a few moments for Aubrey to utter more than a pitiful greeting and then decided to intervene. "Jordana just moved here this summer. Her dad runs the mine across the street."

"That's great," Aubrey replied. "The mine must be doing well. Seems like it's tripled in size overnight."

Jordana nodded as she opened her yogurt.

"How was your summer?" asked Aubrey, searching for something to talk about.

"Did you miss me?" teased Rodriqa. "Aubrey is usually lost when I'm not around," she told Jordana.

"Where did you go?" Jordana asked quietly.

"My brother and I stayed with my grandmother outside of New Orleans. He's starting college down there next week. We had a blast. My brother taught me how to drive a car!"

"How is that legal?" questioned Aubrey.

"It was a beat-up jalopy that he let me run through the old fallow sorghum field on my grandmother's farm. No laws were broken."

A glint of polished pebble wound loosely around Rodriqa's neck drew Aubrey's attention. He knew Rodriqa rarely wore jewelry, which made him even more curious. "Where did you get that necklace?"

"My grandmother made it for me." She pulled several entwined strings of multicolored beads and stones of varying size, shape and contour from underneath her neckline. "She spent all summer working on it. They're called aegis beads."

It reminded Aubrey of a mineral version of homemade Christmas garland he used to string out of flavored cereals, caramel popcorn and gummy bears as a child. "It's sort of...unusual," he said with a twist in his mouth.

Rodriqa furrowed her brow. "My grandmother said it was supposed to provide me strength and protection...that I was destined to overcome adversity...."

Aubrey looked down at the table, unsure of what to say next.

"I think it's really pretty, and it was very sweet of her to make it for you," remarked Jordana quietly.

"Thanks," replied Rodriqa with a wide smile and a wayward perturbed glance at Aubrey. "So how was your summer without me?"

"Same as every summer," droned Aubrey. "There's this crazy high-tech circus in town, and Buzz made me go to it at least five times."

"Glad I missed it...the circus anyway. I hate clowns." Rodriqa mimicked a shiver. "And how were you classes this morning?"

Aubrey blew harshly against his pursed lips. "For starters, have you seen Magnos? He's the size of a load-bearing wall, and he and his flunkies have already started picking on me."

"Aubrey," stated Rodriqa authoritatively, "as duly instructed by your mother, it is my duty to inform you that this year, above all years, you must break the oppression that Magnos holds over you."

"And just exactly how am I supposed to do that. He weighs five times as much as I do and his hands are bigger than my head. He could probably dunk me like a basketball if he wanted."

Rodriqa thoughtfully examined the size of Aubrey's head, and then peered at Magnos in the center of the lunchroom, realizing she couldn't disagree.

"So, in first period this morning," piped up Jordana, "Did you really mean to give a note to the girl in front of us?"

"No," moaned Aubrey, "it was for you."

"It was a very thoughtful note, and I appreciate your apology," stated Jordana amiably as she took a bit of her banana.

Aubrey perked up and angled his head to the side. "How did you know what it said?'

"It's posted on the bulletin board out front with your name and another's girl name scribbled above it and large arrows pointing to it," she replied.

Aubrey dropped his head to the table and sighed with frustration. He couldn't wait for this day to be over.

# Curious Questions

Ray Gene Jennings flipped through a copy of the local newspaper in his convenience store at the top of Dalton Circle. He folded the paper several times edge to edge and laid it on the stool in front of him as he sat behind the cash register, tapping his foot to the beat of the music drifting quietly from the office in the back. He curled his sparse, feathery white hair back under his royal blue ball cap and dusted off the bleached white 'K' above the bill. Scrunching up his face, he took a sip from his coffee while he read a small local story entitled, *Shopping Cart Heist Continues To Stupefy Police.*

As the owner of the **Ray Gene's Smart Mart and Finer Diner**, the recent rash of unexplained thefts at several local merchants gnawed at his gut like a winter squirrel digging for acorns. His face, full of wrinkles that had been carved from a lifetime of laughter and worry, creased deeply across his forehead and down his cheeks as he pondered potential perpetrators and possible preliminary precautions.

The electronic doorbell chimed softly from the loudspeaker. He raised his head to greet the customer, but the door was closed and there was no one there. He craned his neck around the counter to look down the first couple of rows, but he didn't see anyone. He squinted his eyes and peered through the front wall of glass, but he couldn't see anyone outside, either.

He shrugged his shoulders. *Must be a short in the alarm*, he decided, and he returned to reading the paper. He turned the paper over, and the inky, black cursive heading, **The Lake Julian Mountain Lyre**, rose to the top as he skimmed for the continuation of the story in another section.

"May I ask you a question?"

Mr. Jennings jerked up and fumbled to his feet. He would have fallen to the floor if he hadn't caught himself with his hands on the stool next to him. Standing behind the counter a tall, shapely woman with pale green eyes and flowing bright red hair crossed her hands on the counter as she smiled gently at him, waiting patiently for his reply.

"Oh…uh…excuse me, Miss…uh…I didn't see you come in," spoke Mr. Jennings in startled spurts. He marveled at the unusual watch, which wrapped around her wrist. It reminded him of a sundial carved out of sandstone, with flecks of glimmering rock embedded in its surface. The woman's eyes and smile were chillingly stolid. Not a line on her face quivered or twitched, and she stood etched in the air like a living portrait. Yet her endearing smile and engaging eyes made Mr. Jennings' stomach putter with butterflies.

Mr. Jennings glanced at her several times, unnerved by her unusual affect. Her question quickly evaporated from his mind. "Can I help you?" he asked.

"I hope so." Her grin widened. There was a sweet song in her voice that made him a little dizzy. "Have you seen either an elderly woman posing as a beggar widow or an elderly gentleman working as a janitor recently?"

Mr. Jennings scratched his head. He was expecting a question about the price on a loaf of bread or what kind of battery her cell phone needed, not a missing persons roster. "As a matter of fact, I know everyone round these parts. Lived here all my life. The beggar widow sounds familiar, but I don't know any male housekeepers. Do you mind if I ask who's asking?"

She glanced down and her smile receded. "Magnolia Thistlewood," she replied tersely. "Can you tell me where I can find the widow?"

Mr. Jennings chewed the inside of his jaw, uncertain how much to tell her. "Welcome to Lake Julian, Ms. Thistlewood. Not a better place on the planet to live."

She chuckled smoothly. "I know...I've lived here for a while now. The widow's location, if you please?"

Mr. Jennings furrowed his brow incredulously, stunned by her persistent brusqueness. "I'm guessing you mean Old Widow Wizenblatt?"

She nodded.

"She usually roams all over Lake Julian. Difficult to know where she stays from night to night. Police chase her off if she's in one place too long, but occasionally she stays under the overpass down the street."

"Thank you," she replied, her eyes meeting his again. "I sincerely appreciate your thoughtful kindness."

"Anytime, ma'am," replied Mr. Jennings as he tipped his cap. "Can I help you with anything inside the store?"

"No," she answered directly. She turned and walked toward the front.

Mr. Jennings shook his head, perplexed and intrigued. "Ma'am, Can I ask you a question?"

She placed her hand on the silver metal door handle and turned her head over her shoulder. She stared at him with quivering eyes and tightly flattened lips.

"Where do you live in Lake Julian?"

"In the small stone cottage up the way," she spoke as she marched through the door.

Mr. Jennings scrunched his face in confusion and searched his memory. *There aren't any stone cottages in Lake Julian.*

# Widow Treatment

Aubrey lumbered through his afternoon classes in a fog of groggy stupor. The syllabi he had been given and the lessons he had learned were forgotten, and his most significant accomplishment of the day was remembering to collect all his homework at the end of his last class. Eager for bed, he threw his books in his bag and scuttled wearily out the side entrance of the high school.

He trudged over to the bike rack through the mass of exiting students. He strapped his bag to the back of the seat and bent over to release the lock. His eyes widened, and he plopped his rear on the ground in disbelief.

Both of his tires were flat and the caps to the tire valves were missing. He sat up straight and craned his head around, looking for potential suspects. No one else was close to the bike rack. He couldn't see Magnos or the Van Zenny brothers. He kicked the empty tires in disbelief, hoping they would magically re-inflate. He was ready to crawl up on the lawn and fall asleep.

A pair of eyes met his. An old man with bushy white eyebrows, wearing a forest green uniform, stood beside the outer brick wall of the high school. He beat a pair of dusty oil rags against the brick, wafting clouds of foamy soot into the air while he stared undauntedly at Aubrey.

Aubrey looked down, unnerved by his relentless gaze.

Buzz bounded across the lawn and stopped in front of Aubrey with a wide, ecstatic smile and rosy cheeks. Aubrey's gaunt face and heavy, swollen eyelids nearly frightened him.

"What happened?" Buzz asked with concern.

Aubrey glanced at the school again, and the janitor was still staring at him. "I think someone leaked the air out of my tires," mumbled Aubrey.

Buzz looked at his friend's bike, and then stared back at Aubrey. "No...I mean to you."

Aubrey sighed, "It's just been a really, long day." Aubrey covered his eyes with his hands, but despite his best efforts tears leaked down his cheeks.

"Can your dad come get you?" asked Buzz.

Aubrey shook his head. "He'd just tell me to walk home."

Buzz thought for a moment. He knew Aubrey's mom couldn't pick him up in her current state, and Gaetan would only laugh at his misfortune. "I'll help you take your bike home," said Buzz, as he patted Aubrey reassuringly on the shoulder. Aubrey pushed himself up and grinned thankfully at Buzz as he wiped off his face.

They rolled their bikes out of the parking lot and trekked up the side of the road toward the dam. Aubrey silently languished in self-pity. Buzz, on the other hand, felt the need to fill the quiet void with conversation. As exhausted as Aubrey was, Buzz was diametrically electrified by his day. He twittered energetically about his advanced placement classes, the academically oriented extracurricular activities he wanted to join and his new technologically-apt friends. At least Buzz's stories somewhat distracted Aubrey from the strain of walking up the switchback road to the dam.

Guiding the disabled bicycle home was more difficult than Aubrey had anticipated as it wobbled from side to side on its empty tires. A deep fatigue invaded his arms and legs, and a trouble-filled day had zapped his remaining reserves. Aubrey wasn't sure which needed more assistance, him or the bike.

"Sorry I missed you at lunch today." Buzz was so giddy he was babbling.

"We got to talking about second-order cybernetics in computer class, and the discussion continued way into lunch. Some of those guys have never even heard of cellular automata before. Can you believe that?! And most of them are in the Torquetum Club!"

"Wow," replied Aubrey, hoping he sounded impressed. Nearly too tired to care, his heart sank a little with the recollection of the highlights of Buzz's day. He stretched a smile across his face so Buzz wouldn't see his disappointment. "What's the Torquetum Club?" he asked, trying to act interested.

"It's the name of the Computer Club run by the Wi-Chromes," explained Buzz. "Torquetums were used by medieval sailors to calculate headings and are considered by some experts to be the world's first computer."

"Ahhh," replied Aubrey. "Fascinating."

"Here we are…what's this," interjected Buzz, as he stopped rolling his bike and flipped down the kickstand.

*We're not home yet*, Aubrey thought to himself. He slowed his pace, regretting the loss of momentum, and lifted his head. To his surprise, he had completely missed the dismantled car blocking the sidewalk only a few yards in front of them.

"Why is that here?" Aubrey asked impatiently. "And why are we stopping to look at it?"

Buzz ignored him and assessed with awe the 1970s Volkswagen Beetle carcass from behind. The red plastic taillight coverings were shattered, and its broken bulbs and wiring were exposed. The engine, which was visible from the back, had been gutted, and the remains rested unconnected to the frame under the back of the body. The outer dark blue, rusting shell appeared to be mostly intact and separated from any portions not yet pilfered, which further fueled Buzz's excitement.

"We might be able to teeter it on your bike. It shouldn't be too difficult to move to my house," suggested Buzz, unrealistically hopeful Aubrey would agree.

Aubrey gave him a dubious look, "I don't think there's any way we're moving this thing without a small truck."

"Your dad has a truck," Buzz fired back. "Maybe we could ask his help?"

Aubrey shook his head decisively, "I'm not asking him today…maybe tomorrow…."

Buzz thought intensely, looking upward as he mentally explored the materials readily available to him and weighing the Volkswagen in his mind. Aubrey waited for Buzz to move on, bewildered as to why Buzz would want a piece of junk like this dilapidated Volkswagen shell. Aubrey peered into the driver's side rear window, hoping to discover remaining parts, which might prevent further consideration of attempting to drag it to Buzz's house.

Aubrey's eyes widened. "Buzz! Old Widow Wizenblatt is sleeping in here!"

Buzz ran over and peered down through the open widow. The old Widow Wizenblatt had squatted in the most unlikely of places around Lake Julian for at least a decade. She was usually seen strolling up and down local sidewalks pushing a broken shopping cart that was clumsily melded together at the corners with duct tape and was missing a wheel, which had been replaced by an old, discarded inline skate. Her cart contained various items collected from the neighborhood trash, and at times had included an old sewing machine, pots and pans, bits of wood and occasionally a dead bird or rodent, which usually took premier position in the top of the cart. Most of the time she was harmless, and police allowed her to go about her business, except for a few mornings when she would be found sleeping on a neighbor's lawn and needed to be calmly ushered along.

Inside the dilapidated car, Old Widow Wizenblatt lay on the ground in a tattered floral print dress, which she had worn for more than a year. It was spattered with both mud and spaghetti sauce stains. She was wrapped in a tan parka that had several gapping tears in it, exposing its stuffing. Her arms crossed her chest, and her eyes were closed. Her gray, tightly wound, curly hair was riddled with flecks of dirt and sand, and covered most of her face, which was more wrinkle than skin. A rusted and disjointed walker stood upright next to her inside the Volkswagen. Aubrey and Buzz surmised she must have to have used it to get inside the eviscerated vehicle.

"She might be dead," proposed Buzz.

Aubrey winced. "I can't tell if she's breathing or not."

"Hard to tell."

"Ma'am? Are you all right?" Aubrey raised his voice, hoping to rouse her. The Widow didn't twitch or jerk.

"Maybe we could lift the bug up over her," Buzz offered thoughtfully.

"We can't just take it now. It might belong to her, and since she's inside, doesn't she have squatters' rights or something?"

Buzz shook off the suggestion. "Have you ever seen her drive a car? I doubt she has a license. It's not like she can move it, anyway. Only the frame is left."

"But what if she's a really good mechanic, or what if she knows where the rest of it is? Maybe she is related to the owner, who knows."

Buzz stared pensively at the motionless Widow. "Then let's find out," he said decidedly.

Buzz crept around the back of the Volkswagen and leaned into the rear window. Her face was closer to the passenger side, which gave him a better look. He still saw no signs of life.

"Good afternoon, Mrs. Wizenblatt!" yelled Buzz into the window.

No response. Aubrey gave Buzz an uneasy look. Buzz slowly reached his hand through the window and brushed a few of the curls from around her eyes. She didn't budge. Buzz raised his hand over her nose and mouth and waited for the warmth of her exhaling breath.

No air.

Suddenly, a tightening pressure sunk into Buzz's wrist.

"AAAAAAYYYYYYYYYYGGGGGGGG," screamed the Widow as she raved to life instantly.

Buzz's body slammed against the passenger side door as the Widow wrenched his arm down from around her face.

"HELP MEEEEEEEEEE! I'M BEING ATTAAAAAAAAAAAACKED!" The Widow yanked harder on Buzz's arm.

Buzz wrestled backwards against the Widow's grasp, but his feet couldn't find traction against the gravely ground. The Old Widow rhythmically jerked his arm up and down through the window. Buzz felt like a fish on a hook as the Widow tried to thread the plump Buzz through the window.

"Owwww! You're hurting my arm!" shouted Buzz. "Let me go!"

Stunned, Aubrey backed away from the car, vacillating between helping his friend and running away.

"HEEEEEEELLLPPPP MEEEEEEEEE! SOMEONE IS TRYING TO CHOOOOOOOKKKEEE MEEEEEEEE!" The Widow's unrelenting tirade was escalating.

"Let me go, you crazy old bat! I was only trying to see if you were still alive!"

Buzz's glasses flew off his face, and his pudgy torso dented the door.

"SEEEEEEEE! THEY WERE GONNA KIIIIIIIILLLLLL MEEEEEEE!" The Widow's trunk rocked violently inside the Volkswagen as all four of her limbs corkscrewed in the air with one of her hands securely fixed to Buzz's arm.

Aubrey watched the onslaught worsen and decided she must be having an epileptic fit. He jolted to the passenger side and wrapped his arms around Buzz's waist. His hands barely clasped together around Buzz's globular midsection. Aubrey pulled the lurching Buzz backwards, but his small size added little counter-traction to Buzz's struggle. Entwined together, they both bounced against the aluminum door, while the Widow shouted and convulsed.

"HEEEEEEELP!   OOOLD WOOOOMAAAN BEING ATTAAA-AAACKED!"

"We are not attacking you!  We simply want to take the car home!" yelled Aubrey.

Buzz and Aubrey collapsed to the ground.  The Widow had released Buzz and ceased her wailing.  Dust spewed up around the fallen pair, sending a small mushroom cloud of fine debris into the air.  Aubrey narrowly missed being crushed under Buzz's weight and landed only a few inches behind him.  Buzz picked his glasses off the ground and rested them back on his nose.

Old Widow Wizenblatt raised herself up inside the Volkswagen.  She opened the passenger-side door, carefully stepped outside, and closed it curtly behind her.  Addled by both the prior melee and the precipitous silence, Buzz and Aubrey spit dirt from their mouths as they dusted themselves off and stood up.

She pointed her finger at the boys with a stern accusing expression.  "You were going to steal my *house!*"

Buzz crinkled his nose in disbelief, "*House?*  It's the body of a 1973 Volkswagen Beetle and little is left.  You can't live in there?!  It will leak, and the bottom is completely open.  Besides, I'll fix it up and make something useful out of it.  If it stays here it will either rust out completely, or someone from the junkyard will pick it up.  Poor choice for a home if you ask me," stated Buzz with a decided lack of diplomacy or empathy.

"What may seem *old* and in *disrepair* to you, young man, may be someone else's last hope," countered the Widow sternly.

"But you already live under the overpass, and there is no way you can move it that far," retorted Buzz.

Old Widow Wizenblatt smiled eerily and said nothing in return.  A cold tingle trickled down Aubrey's spine.

"She's not going to let us take it," Aubrey besought Buzz under his breath. "There's no point in arguing with her. Let's go."

"But…but…she can't use it," whimpered Buzz.

Recognizing their futile position, Aubrey stared determinedly at Buzz. The Widow's austere expression never flinched, and her eyes dug deeper into them.  Buzz's attention flitted between Aubrey and the Widow as he searched for a new foothold on the Volkswagen's ownership.

Aubrey stepped away and lifted his bike from the edge of the road.  He wheeled it around the car to avoid further contact with the Widow.  Buzz's shoulders slumped in defeat, and he followed the cue, returning to his bike and toddling in Aubrey's direction.

"Sorry, Buzz. She'll probably forget about it eventually anyway.  Then you can pick it up." Aubrey's consoling words did little to elevate Buzz's demeanor. Aubrey gave him time to sulk while they finished their walk home from school.

"Oh well, we probably couldn't have carried it anyway," Buzz acquiesced softly.

"Maybe your dad can help us pick it up later. There's no way she can haul that by herself anywhere."

"That's an idea," Buzz's spirits lifted. "We could come back after dark. Although my dad isn't going to be thrilled that I want to bring more scrap home. Our backyard shed is still full of junk I haven't been able to use yet."

"Well, you can always store it at my place. I don't think my parents would mind, or even notice for that matter. We can tell them we're working on building a car for when we turn sixteen." Aubrey chuckled.

"I hope we can use it before then," Buzz laughed.

Aubrey looked at Buzz quizzically, and then movement out of the corner of his eye grabbed his attention. He glanced over his shoulder and took a second look. The Widow, with walker in hand, was scurrying up the street towards them.

"Buzz, don't look back, but I think Mrs. Wizenblatt might be following us."

Buzz stiffened. "Are you sure?"

"Not exactly, but she seems to be moving awfully quick in our direction." Aubrey forced down a gulp as he spoke.

Buzz turned around. The Widow glared directly at him, her lips chattering wildly, and her face straining with every step she took.

"I told you not to turn around," Aubrey chided through a strained whisper.

"Let's keep moving," Buzz replied. They plodded ahead more quickly, hoping to outrun, or at least outlast, the Widow.

"We're not far from my house. We should be good." Aubrey scanned the neighborhood to verify the validity of his statement. He thought he was correct, but something in the landscape up ahead was out of place. Something was not familiar, and he couldn't quite figure out what it was.

"If she's getting too close, we can always duck into Ms. Thistlewood's house," Buzz said.

"Who?" Aubrey thought for a moment. The name didn't register. He was confused and a little disturbed at his elusive sense of disorientation.

"You know, the real pretty lady who makes all those mouth-watering cookies and pies for everyone in the neighborhood. I think I can almost smell something baking now." Buzz sniffed the air and stepped livelier, invigorated by the prospect of delectable treats.

The more Buzz told Aubrey about Ms. Thistlewood, the more confused Aubrey became. Something was wrong, but he couldn't wrap his mind around it.

"Yes, we made it," Buzz announced.

Aubrey and Buzz were at the edge of the most impeccably manicured lawn in the neighborhood, and it was unlikely there was a yard in the city that could match its perfection. The deep green grass, thick and unnaturally level, carpeted the lot from edge to edge, without a single weed, bare spot or misplaced speck of dirt. Flower beds accented the yard near the road and along the edge of the house with crisp arrays of color. Roses, lilies, mums, and tulips exploded at the height of bloom, including those that should have already faded that late in summer. Intricately carved stone pots lined the walkway to the front door and were embedded with shrubs and small, gnarled trees, which were freshly trimmed to exacting figurine proportions.

The one-story house that sat about thirty yards back from the street was much more simplistic in nature and rustic in appearance. The exterior walls were a smooth, steely gray stone, interrupted only by two small windows on either side of red wooden door. The roof heaped over the cottage with large bails of thatched grass, bundled with thick rope underneath slotted tresses of cedar.

Aubrey was deeply puzzled. He was certain he had never seen this lot before, and it would be impossible to ignore or forget.

"How long has Ms. Thistlewood lived here?" questioned Aubrey.

"I don't know", responded Buzz. "A couple years, I think?"

Then Aubrey suddenly realized why none of this made sense.

"Buzz! This yard has never been here before. Remember! This is where the old, vacant lot used to be! We hollowed out that old, dead tree stump in the back just last week!"

Buzz looked to where Aubrey pointed. He could only identify a small cement figurine of an angel playing a pan flute. Buzz thought for a moment, and then looked at Aubrey mockingly. "Man, you are seriously sleep-deprived."

"No!" Aubrey objected. *This* was not here this morning!" Aubrey stretched out his arms emphatically to wrap the house and lawn inside his figurative grasp.

"If *this* is all make-believe, then explain the smell." Buzz inhaled deeply, enjoying every molecule his nose absorbed.

Aubrey sarcastically mimicked Buzz's inspiration and was instantly mesmerized by the bouquet of fragrances. Syrupy apples and walnuts roasted with cinnamon numbed his senses and nearly washed away all his baffling concerns. "That's incredible," he responded dreamily.

"Now, how could you forget Ms. Thistlewood's Chunked Apple-Walnut Delight," Buzz argued happily, satisfied with this conclusive evidence.

Aubrey shook his head. He knew he had never smelled anything this captivatingly blissful before, but now he didn't care either. The food, the lawn, the house and even Ms. Thistlewood were a mystery, but if they were all this beautiful, Aubrey decided his ignorance was inconsequential.

Through the left window Aubrey saw a woman inside brushing dirt from the ledge outside with a small hand broom. She had fair skin and bright red hair, just like Aubrey's. She looked up and took note of the boys, and then smiled the friendliest smile Aubrey had ever seen. She waved and then disappeared into her house.

Buzz waved blithely back.

"Where did she go?" Aubrey asked. He felt robbed by having experienced such a brief encounter with the lovely woman. Buzz didn't answer.

"Look at the mess she's made. I can't believe she decided to come here." The rough voice zapped Aubrey out of his trance. He froze and glanced quickly to his side. Old Widow Wizenblatt was standing next to him, the edge of her walker lightly brushing against his arm. Buzz covered his forehead with his hand, more annoyed than anxious. He grabbed Aubrey by the elbow and pulled him up the walkway, hoping to lose her. Buzz doubted the Widow would follow them any further.

The red wooden door opened, and the woman stepped out carrying a plate heaped with golden-brown, rectangular treats. Aubrey heard the Widow continue her ranting, but her words faded quickly into the background.

"Hi, Ms. Thistlewood!" Buzz greeted her with a crack in his voice. Her hollow, green eyes drew both of them to the door.

Aubrey stared at her intensely. She was indubitably the most beautiful woman he had ever seen. Tall and slender with curve upon curve, her red hair flowed over her shoulders, cradling her neck. Buzz stared at her figure and decided it would require a myriad of complex differential equations to recreate the series of parabolas and hyperbolas that defined her topographically.

"Hello, Aubrey and Buzz." She acknowledged both of them separately with a nod. "I just pulled these out of the oven. They stayed in there a little too long, I'm afraid. They look a little burnt. I hope they're still edible."

She handed a treat to both boys. Buzz's portion disappeared instantly behind his lips the moment it left her hand. Aubrey gazed at his muffin in wonder. Large pieces of steaming apple and dark shards of walnuts were condensed into crumbly bread, dusted lightly with cinnamon powder. He took a bite and moaned. It was perfection. His salivary glands flooded his mouth, and every taste bud stood at attention to allow every nerve ending maximal exposure. Each bite dissolved into plump, sugary dough that swallowed so easily he didn't even need anything to drink.

"May I have another, Ms. Thistlewood?" begged Buzz. "This Apple-Walnut Delight is your best yet!"

"Of course, Buzz." She smiled graciously, seemingly enjoying the compliment. She elevated the plate of treats in front of them. Buzz helped himself.

"You shouldn't be here!" The craggy voice lurched from behind them.

"Not in front of the boys," Ms. Thistlewood returned. "It's rude." The edge of her voice cut sharply in return.

"Rude," Mrs. Wizenblatt replied, "is manipulating the Earth's beauty like this." She nudged her walker up the walkway. Aubrey assumed the object of her statement was the potted shrubs she stood next to.

Ms. Thistlewood's calm and kind demeanor evaporated. "All beings of the Earth were created to be controlled and directed. I thought you of all people would have realized that by now."

Aubrey noticed his host's harsh tone and gazed up at her with a puzzled expression. Her initial soft, inviting face was now drawn and pointed. Careful of her audience, she gave Aubrey a reassuring grin.

"Some have toiled to show that just the opposite is true," retorted the Widow.

"Then they have wasted their time." Ms. Thistlewood's voice was now icy cold.

"*These* are a waste of time." Old Widow Wizenblatt lifted her walker over her head with ample grace and strength and slammed it into the nearest stone pot. It shattered like glass into dozens of small chunks of rock, spilling dirt and roots across the lawn.

Aubrey and Buzz's mouths gaped open. They considered running away, but they stood wedged between Ms. Thistlewood and the Widow. Aubrey looked closely at the injured shrub lying at the Widow's feet. Mixed in with the dirt, he saw small bones that to him appeared distinctly human. He wanted to examine the bones more closely, but the shouting from behind him jarred his attention back to the fray.

"GET OFF MY PROPERTY! GO BACK UNDER THE BRIDGE WHERE YOU BELONG!" yelled Ms. Thistlewood.

"I'LL TREAD WHERE I CHOOSE!"

Ms. Thistlewood took a moment to compose herself as she handed the platter of desserts to Buzz. Breathing deeply with resigned composure, she wrapped her hair in a tight ponytail. "Fine. Then you can discuss it with the Police Department. I called them earlier about the broken-down car down the street. I'm sure they will consider vandalism and trespassing a more pressing issue."

"That car belongs to me!" protested the Widow. "No one is taking it anywhere!" She swung her walker again, smashing another stone pot and scattering plant debris over the lawn. A broken femur rolled up the walkway.

Aubrey whispered to Buzz, "I think we should go."

"Wait a sec. I want to see what happens." Buzz grabbed two more Delights. He shoved one is his pocket and another one in his mouth.

A Poage County Police car pulled up next to the front of Ms. Thistlewood's lawn. Its shoddy muffler bubbled loudly as it clunked to a stop. Two policemen stepped out of the car and approached the yard's edge.

"Did you report a problem, Ms. Thistlewood?" The policeman from the driver's side was tall and lanky and spoke with a thick southern drawl, which was demonstrably more backwoods in origin than most heard in the area. His partner was shorter and rounder and had his pad and pen in hand, ready to take a statement.

Ms. Thistlewood nodded in Mrs. Wizenblatt's direction. "I called about an abandoned car earlier, but now there is a significantly more urgent problem."

"Yes, Officers, there is a problem that needs your immediate attention," agreed the Widow. "This woman has no right to be here, and she should be arrested immediately!"

The tall officer chuckled and glanced at his partner, who acknowledged his amusement. "Now why on Earth would we do that?"

"For multiple violations, both natural and unnatural," reported Mrs. Wizenblatt. "Look at her yard and house. They tell the entire story. And if you stand here long enough, you'll witness her true evil unveil itself as she tortures these two boys."

Ms. Thistlewood laughed with patronizing flair.

"You all bein' tortured?" asked the Officer, projecting his voice around the Widow.

"No, sir," Buzz answered quickly, shaking his head forcefully. He thoroughly enjoyed the opportunity to take a jab at the Widow.

"Ma'am, these boys don't look like they're in much danger of being tortured and, to be honest, Ms. Thistlewood's lawn is nothing less than a testament to her skill and diligence as a gardener. I see no violations here, natural or otherwise."

The Widow walked quickly up to the tall Officer and thrust her nose in his face. "You would be wise to listen to me." Her eyelids squeezed together intently as she glared at him.

"And you would be wise to move along, Mrs. Wizenblatt," responded the officer sharply.

"If you won't take care of the menace, then I will!" The Widow trotted back to her walker and swung it again, destroying another stone pot. She hopped over the scattering shards and marched up the walkway, carrying the walker in one hand above her head.

Ms. Thistlewood wrapped an arm around each boy and pulled them tightly to her chest. Aubrey felt like a human shield. He held his breath, fearing the wrath of the Widow's walker approaching. He could see the penetrating determination in her eyes.

"All right, Mrs. Wizenblatt, you're coming with us." The two officers grabbed her around her shoulders from behind, lifting her off the ground and pulling her back down the walkway.

"UNHAND ME!" the Widow shrieked. She struggled violently against the grip of the officers. "I've done nothing wrong," she demanded. Her feet clawed against the ground, and her arms gyrated as she attempted to free herself.

"Vandalism, threatened assault, trespassing on private property," recounted the tall Officer. "We've also received reports that several local supermarkets have been coming up short on shopping carts. And I have a sneaking suspicion we might have found our culprit." His huskier partner nodded in agreement. The handcuffs snapped a staccato series of clicks as they closed, and Mrs. Wizenblatt slumped to the ground in protest.

"You're arresting me?! You can't do that! I'm an old woman. My bones are frail. I might break a hip. I would never survive a night in jail," blustered the Widow.

"We'll take good care of you, Mrs. Wizenblatt. A night to cool off is just what you need." The Officers sat her in the back seat of the patrol car and slammed the door securely closed.

The tall Officer tipped his hat at Ms. Thistlewood. "Sorry for the disturbance, ma'am. We'll be by to take your statement later. Enjoy the rest of your evening."

She released the boys and sighed deeply with relief. "Thank you, Officer Kluggard and you too, Officer Kluggard! You've saved me again." She laughed heartily. As the police car drove away, Aubrey couldn't help but feel sorry for the Widow. He watched her sit motionless in the back of the car; her arms fastened behind her back, her chin dejectedly resting on her plump chest.

Ms. Thistlewood turned the boys around to face her and knelt down. "I'm so sorry you boys had to witness that scene. She's been such a nuisance for so long now. I hope she didn't frighten you." Her eyes slanted downward and her lower lip drooped.

"Nah," Buzz oozed with bravado. "We could have handled her."

She smiled broadly at Buzz. "Of course you could have." She touched him gently on the cheek.

"I can't believe she demolished your yard," Aubrey interrupted. "Can we help you clean up?" Aubrey's offer was more out of interest in investigating than genuine volunteerism.

"Absolutely not," she interjected politely. "You boys have been through enough today. And you probably still have homework to do. I wouldn't want to upset your parents." She walked into her yard, pushing Aubrey and Buzz in front of her. She stopped briefly to rake some of the dirt into small piles with her bare feet.

"You boys get home safely." Ms. Thistlewood waved goodbye to them as she attended to the yard. "Come by tomorrow and I'll have some chocolate drip cookies waiting for you."

"You mean chocolate chip," Aubrey corrected.

"Nope." She looked up from her lawn and smiled wryly.

Aubrey and Buzz stood at the sidewalk and stared at each other. Aubrey's body ached from exhaustion, and his mind swam with over-stimulation.

"This has been the most bizarre twenty-four hours ever," Aubrey concluded.

Buzz chomped down the last of the treats. "What's so weird about it?"

# Slippery Sleep

Buzz walked with Aubrey and the bikes a little further down Dalton Circle to Aubrey's house. Aubrey slumped down on the curb, gazing at his flattened tire, but too exhausted to care that he would either have to walk or take the bus to school in the morning.

"I'll fix your tires," offered Buzz.

"I don't think we have a pump in the work shed," moaned Aubrey.

"That's okay," said Buzz cheerfully. "I'll figure something out."

Aubrey relented hesitantly. Buzz had always come through for him, and usually there was nothing he could offer in return.

"Thanks, man," Aubrey muttered with aching gratitude, but Buzz had already wheeled his bike into the backyard. Aubrey marched slowly up the front porch stairs of his house and stumbled through the door.

Aubrey's dad sat at the far end of the dining room table with a fully unfolded *Lake Julian Mountain Lyre* newspaper in front of him. Aubrey glanced at the headline: *Vandals Strike Berybomag Mine: Local 'Green' Groups Suspected.*

"Aubrey?" questioned his dad from underneath the paper. "You finally home?"

"Yes, sir," he replied quietly. He dropped his bag on the floor and slumped into a cushioned chair at the table.

"How was your first day of high school?" The question sounded more perfunctory than inquisitive.

Aubrey sighed deeply. He folded his hands on the table and laid his head down. "It was fine," he fibbed, lacking the energy to provide further explanation or detail. This was the most comfortable position he had been in all day. He couldn't hold open his eyelids any longer. Fatigue swallowed him whole, and sleep blanketed his mind with instant dreams. Peaceful rest loosened his aching arms and legs. And a thin stream of drool crept from his mouth into a tiny puddle on the table.

*SLAM!!* Aubrey yanked his torso upright in his chair and nearly tipped over backwards.

"No sleeping at the dinner table! Isn't that right, Dad?!" Gaetan leered over him with a devilish grin. With his large, boney hands fanned out on the table, Aubrey's brother pushed himself up and laughed mockingly at the bewildered Aubrey.

"Hoaker Croaker, Gaetan!" Aubrey's father had crumpled his paper into a ball of sheets and was staring wide-eyed across the table. "Are you trying to wake the dead?"

"No, just reminding *Brianna* here that sleeping is for nighttime. If he slept then, maybe he wouldn't need to sleep when it's daylight." Gaetan chuckled at his own joke. He walked around the dining room table through the living room and quickly bounded up the stairs, taking three steps at a time. Aubrey caught his breath and sneered at Gaetan, but he knew if he fought back, he would be in trouble for Buzz coming over late last night.

Gaetan had always picked on Aubrey, and every memory of his brother that he held onto was either mischievous or mean. It didn't help that Aubrey was also jealous of his older brother. Gaetan was tall, dark-headed and athletic. Everything Aubrey wasn't, but wanted to be. *One more year*, Aubrey thought to himself. *He's a senior now, and then he'll be gone.*

Aubrey's father reached for a banana from a basket of fruit in the middle of the table and peeled off its skin, breaking the stem with a snap and pulling down all four sides simultaneously. His dad had always been proud of his nifty tricks. The widow's peak of his tightly cut, black hair narrowed to a point on his forehead and he kept his sideburns long to make up for it. It had only been in the last year that Aubrey had noticed how swiftly his father's hair was thinning.

Mr. Taylor's strong jaw and deep-trenched cheeks had passed to Gaetan, but Aubrey had his nose and smile. Unfortunately, Aubrey knew he was not nearly as manly as his dad was, and he was afraid he never would be.

Gaetan launched himself off the top of the stairs and landed, legs bent, in the living room with a house-shuddering thud. He straightened up slowly and smiled proudly.

"Don't do that. It's bad for the flooring," barked their father.

"Sorry, Dad. Just getting' pumped up for practice," he replied.

"Sounds like Chimney Falls has a strong team this year. That'll be a tough first game," assessed Mr. Taylor.

"Nah. We'll be division finalists easy," downplayed Gaetan. He walked around the table, carrying a wad of royal blue and gray jerseys. He grabbed a shiny, red apple from the mound of fruit on the table and chomped into it. "We got this new kid…he's a freshman but he's *HUGE!* He's gonna be my full-back." Bits of half-digested apple spewed into the air as he spoke.

Aubrey couldn't believe his ears. There was only kid in town they could possible be talking about.

"Who?" asked Mr. Taylor.

"Magnos Strumgarten," answered Gaetan.

"Unfortunately," Aubrey mumbled inaudibly. Gaetan glanced at him sternly.

"Hey, Dad, do you think mom could wash these tonight? Tomorrow's jersey day at school, and I'm wearing my last clean one for practice."

"You know your mother's not feeling well. We all need to pitch in to keep things going around here," replied their father.

"Then make Aubrey do it," griped Gaetan. "It's not like he has anything else to do."

Aubrey scowled at his brother.

"I'm sure Aubrey has homework to do, and he needs to cut the grass," countered Mr. Taylor.

"Fine! I'll do it when I get home." Gaetan stormed out the door, slamming it shut behind him.

Aubrey shook his head, relieved his brother was gone.

"You know he only means well, Aub," remarked his father.

"How is that?" questioned Aubrey.

"He wants you to grow up and be tough. That's why he's so hard on you." Mr. Taylor opened up his paper and disappeared behind it.

"What if I'm not meant to be tough?" rebutted Aubrey. "What if I'm not meant to be anything?"

His father didn't answer.

"AUUUUBBBBBBRRREEEEEEEEEEEYYYY!" Gaetan's shout echoed from outside. Aubrey and his dad stood up, raced through the living room, and clambered out the back door. No one was in the backyard, but the door to the work shed was wide open. Aubrey and Mr. Taylor ran down the porch steps and squeezed through the threshing of the work shed door.

"Hey, Aubrey. I fixed your tires," announced Buzz proudly.

Gaetan howled angrily. "Look at what this turd did to my car!" Gaetan's cherry red 1974 Pontiac GTO was his pride and joy. He loved it more than anything else on the planet, animal or mineral. Its sleek, polished doors were flawless, and Gaetan had completely refurbished the black leather interior himself.

Buzz waddled around from behind the car, dragging Aubrey's bike. "Hello, Mr. Taylor," Buzz said with a hearty wave. "It's good as new." Buzz held up the bicycle to show off its air-engorged tires. "They weren't punctured, just empty."

"He used the air from my car tires to inflate Aubrey's bike tires," squealed Gaetan. Everyone looked down at the car, and every single chrome-rimmed tire was completely flat.

"I needed the air pressure," said Buzz. "I was gonna fill them back up."

"Dad! This is a disaster! I've got practice in fifteen minutes!" Gaetan's cheeks were flushed, and he gripped his dark hair with both hands.

"Buzz, go home," commanded Mr. Taylor, his lips squeezed together tightly.

"Yes, sir," muttered Buzz as his cheerful disposition waned.

"Aubrey, upstairs!"

"But I didn't do anything wrong," Aubrey whined. His father pointed to the house mercilessly. Aubrey's shoulders slumped unevenly, and he stomped through the backyard toward the house.

"Gaetan, I'll take you to practice."

"But I don't want to be seen by *my* team with my *Dad* dropping me off! I'm the quarterback!"

Aubrey slammed the back door behind him. He wandered into the dining room, heaved his book bag over his shoulder and trudged up the stairs into his bedroom. Locking the door behind him, he dropped his bag on the floor and flung himself on his bed. He kicked his shoes off, rolled under the covers in his clothes and sank into the mattress.

The darkness behind Aubrey's eyelids swam with lights. Sound and light faded, and his mind wandered aimlessly away from consciousness. For a moment he saw the same grinning face from last night, but fear collapsed under overwhelming fatigue, and he drifted off to sleep.

# Refinancing Fault

**Tuesday.**

"Photovoltaic cells, transistors and semiconductors…." Mr. Vander-eff pointed with a long dowel to diagrams on the blackboard. "All are possible or improved by earth-shattering discoveries in the past few decades. And that is why silicon will be remembered as the most important element of the twentieth century."

Mr. Vandereff rested his dowel in the tray below the blackboard and dusted off his hands. The electronic bell chimed overhead. The students closed their books and rushed out the door.

"Don't forget about your element assignments due on Friday," Mr. Vandereff shouted after them as he patted the chalk dust out of his mustache.

Jordana politely waved at Aubrey and Buzz as she followed the crowd.

Buzz turned to Aubrey, who was still gathering his things slowly to give him more time to watch Jordana. "How did you sleep last night?"

"Hard," replied Aubrey happily. "I barely remember it. It felt like I woke up five minutes after I dozed off."

"Then you feel better?"

"Yeah, tons."

"Good, then you can go with me to the circus tonight. It's their last night, and they've supposedly got something really cool planned for their big finale," Buzz said excitedly.

Aubrey hesitated while he thought for a moment. "I don't think I can."

"Why not?" asked Buzz with an injured expression.

"I was supposed to cut the grass last night, and I feel asleep, so I have to do it as soon as I get home. You know how my dad is."

"That's fine. It doesn't start until seven," countered Buzz.

Aubrey slung his bag over his shoulder and marched toward the door. "Plus, I'm behind on homework."

Buzz chased after him. "You can do it after the circus."

Aubrey rounded the corner out of the door and stopped suddenly. Buzz bumped into the back of him.

Blocking the doorway was a massive, gray number '33' on a broad royal blue jersey. Magnos scowled at Aubrey. Lenny and Benny flanked him and held tight-lipped giggles in their mouths.

"Where's my element assignment, Taylor?"

"Aubrey's still working on his. Have you finished yours?" piped Buzz from behind.

Magnos ignored Buzz. "I'm not asking again."

Aubrey tried to invent an excuse, but he was never very good at make believe. He hoped the truth would work for now. "I didn't get any work done last night. I accidentally feel asleep."

"I see," grumbled Magnos. "I thought I told you I needed time to look over it before it was due."

"Yeah, but it's not due for three more days. I didn't think you needed it today."

"Wait a sec," interrupted Buzz, pushing Aubrey toward Magnos so he could be within the ring of conversation. "You're making Aubrey do your homework?!"

"Quiet! You Tub of Grub," barked Benny.

"Listen here, Meat Wagon," retorted Buzz, "Plagiarism is a serious offense at this high school."

"It won't be plagiarism. The homework Aubrey is doing will be mine. Isn't that right, Taylor?"

Aubrey gulped and nodded his head in agreement.

"Party outside of science class, boys?" A large boney hand clasped around Magnos' shoulder. Aubrey's swallowed hard and looked down at the floor.

"Gaetan, I have a little problem that I'd like to discuss with you," Magnos told Aubrey's brother with feigned thoughtfulness.

"What's up, Big M?"

Magnos heaved a deep sigh. "It breaks my heart to tell you this, but your little brother has wronged me."

"No," protested Gaetan. "That's simply unacceptable."

"I thought so as well," agreed Magnos.

"What did the little runt do?"

"He hit on my girlfriend."

Gaetan shook his head sadly. "Truly a slap to the face between gentlemen."

"Exactly, but I was kind and gave him a means to repay his debt."

"How exceedingly amiable of you."

"Thank you," replied Magnos in an appreciative tone. "Unfortunately, Aubrey has chosen to ignore my good will."

"So sinister." Gaetan scowled at Aubrey.

"What do you think should I do? I'm above simple retaliation."

"Up the stakes. Stoke the fire. Let him know who is in charge." Gaetan patted Magnos hard on the back and walked away chortling.

Magnos glowered menacingly at Aubrey. "You heard your older brother."

"Magnos, I'll have it done tomorrow! I promise!" clamored Aubrey.

"Yeah, you will," challenged Magnos, "and you'll have Lenny and Benny's work done for Vandereff as well." Magnos held out his hands, and Lenny and

Benny shoved their element assignments in his palms. Magnos smacked the ruffled pieces of paper into Aubrey's chest. "Tomorrow."

"And make sure the writing is different, since we won't have time to re-write it," added Lenny.

The trio turned and walked away. Lenny and Benny high-fived Magnos happily.

Aubrey stared down at the two other papers that read 'Gold' and 'Lead'.

Buzz fidgeted with his hands as he glared at Aubrey. "Guess that means no circus tonight, huh?"

# *Early Retirement*

Aubrey wiped his hand across his forehead and flicked droplets of sweat off his fingers. He kicked aside tiny mounds of trimmed green stalks and smacked at the early evening gnats and flies that bit at his ankles. He wished he could cover his ears to protect his eardrums from the loud vibration of the lawnmower. Scanning the backyard to examine his progress, Aubrey was despondent that he hadn't made it yet halfway.

Aubrey despised cutting grass. The wheels on his family's push mower were frozen stiff despite oozing gobs of oil over their axles. The motor died every two or three minutes without fail for no real reason. By the end of the backyard his strength was spent, and Aubrey knew he would have to ask his dad or Gaetan to restart the engine for him if it stopped.

Aubrey leaned into the handle, and the mower inched forward. He dug his heels deeply into the ground and pushed with all his might. The front of the mower edged upward as he walked over a swathe of uncut grass. He dropped the front of the mower and yanked it backwards to cut the piece he missed and then leaned into the handle again. Aubrey heaved with all his might, rolling the mower to the edge of the property line. He rocked the mower back and forth until he could angle it the opposite direction. The motor died. He huffed a sigh of frustration.

Buzz barreled around the corner of his house into the backyard, waving his arms up and down wildly. He had a white pole with a round, thick plate strapped to his back, which swung back and forth as he ran.

"What's going on?" Aubrey asked, grateful for a reason to take a break.

Buzz made an abrupt stop in front of the mower. "You're...not...gonna...believe...it!" He puffed out each word between deep breaths.

"What's wrong?"

"The...circus." Buzz leaned his hands on his knees and gulped in as much air as he could.

Aubrey sighed, a little annoyed. "I told you I can't go. I have too much to do."

Buzz flapped his arms again. "You...don't...understand."

Aubrey wiped the dripping sweat from his cheeks and waited impatiently.

Buzz sat down cross-legged on the grass. "The circus is gone."

Aubrey thought for a moment. "You know they were leaving soon. Did you get the dates wrong?"

"No...not the circus...the circus is still there." Buzz laid back on the grass to allow more air into his lungs.

Aubrey sneered in confusion. "But you just said–"

"The people are gone!"

"What?"

Buzz groaned in frustration. "The tent, the animals, the equipment…it's all in the same place…but all the performers have vanished."

"That doesn't make any sense," replied Aubrey.

"I know," agreed Buzz. "I was gonna surprise you and get us tickets and then come back and help you cut the grass and finish all the homework, but when I went to the circus grounds…the police were there and they were investigating the disappearances."

"What happened?"

"Nobody knows. They were there two days ago, and then all of a sudden, they weren't."

"But how do thirty or forty people just go missing without anyone noticing?"

"Fifty-six. The circus troupe employed fifty-six people and no one knows where they are."

Aubrey scrunched his forehead together incredulously. "How is that possible?"

Buzz shrugged. He picked himself off the ground. "It's a mystery. I want to go back and ask the police more questions once they've had time to figure things out." He swatted grass clippings off his jeans. "But, in the meantime, I brought this." Buzz pulled the long white pole from behind his back. A rectangular box was fixed to the opposite end.

"What's that?"

"It's a WASER!" Buzz trembled from excitement and lack of oxygen.

"A what?"

"Let me demonstrate." Buzz shoved a switch forward on the instrument's box. A bright, white light streamed outward from its crevices. He walked over to an area of uncut grass and pointed the round plate at the end toward the ground. He slashed an arc across its surface, leaving behind a patch of freshly cut grass. "It's a Weeding LASER! We'll have the yard trimmed up in no time."

"Cool," shouted Aubrey with excitement.

"And the best part," continued Buzz proudly. "It singes all the cut stuff, so there's no mess!"

"You're a lifesaver," said Aubrey. He shook his hand gratefully.

Buzz set himself to task. He pitched the WASER to and fro, cutting large portions of the backyard in seconds. Aubrey followed next to him, mesmerized by the speed and ease of the WASER.

"How did you make it?" Aubrey asked.

"It's a halogen car headlight," explained Buzz. "The light beam is focused down to a pin point with magnifying lenses in the shaft of the pole where it hits a mirrored spinner in the plate at the bottom. Convection from the heat produced at the bottom turns the spinner and light bounces off other tiny mirrors lining the inner edge of the plate. Light bounces back and forth within the bottom until its energy is dissipated, usually from material entering the open bottom. It rips through vegetable matter like a knife through hot cheese."

Buzz trimmed the area around the porch. They noticed a pair of feet on the porch as Buzz whipped the WASER from side to side. Aubrey and Buzz looked up. Mr. Taylor stood above them on the bottom step, jaw clenched and his nose flaring.

"Howdy, sir," greeted Buzz. "Sorry again about yesterday."

"And what about today?" grumbled Aubrey's father.

Buzz frowned questioningly.

Mr. Taylor pointed over top of Aubrey and Buzz's heads. They turned around and looked at the yard behind them. A fine, hazy smoke drifted over the lawn. Where the WASER had passed over the grass, the lawn was either turning brown or wilting into the dirt.

Buzz leapt back. "It's never done that before," he exclaimed. "I've used it to cut weeds in my Dad's garden, and it's always worked brilliantly!"

"Yard grass isn't a weed," denounced Mr. Taylor.

"Oh," muttered Buzz as he hung his head. "I'm really sorry."

Aubrey's Dad took the WASER. "Aubrey, finish the front yard…no more clever schemes. Just do as you're told!"

"But Dad, I didn't…."

Mr. Taylor stormed past them and walked into the work shed.

Buzz stared at Aubrey sorrowfully. "I didn't mean-"

"It's okay," relented Aubrey. "It's not your fault. I think what little luck I've had has run out."

# *Eye Candy*

Aubrey shoved himself away from his desk, mentally drained by the hours he had spent on his multiple assignments. Anions and cations, quarks and covalent bonds swam in his head in a myriad of letters and plus and minus signs. He examined the four sets of papers scattered side by side in front of him. They reminded him of newborn, monstrous pets that required incessant feeding and attention. All of the assignments were anorexic at best, each with little more than a page finished. He mused at the illegibility of his writing at the end of the pages, and the muscles in his hand ached in revolt at their overuse. He laid his pen down on the desk and rubbed his forehead, wishing he could massage his brain, which felt knotted up in one large cramp from the quadruple duty.

In the distance of the night, Mr. Osterfeld's horn bellowed outside. Aubrey looked at his bed and turned toward his dresser and then back to his bed. The clock on the nightstand read

# 10:48

He was too tired to change out of his clothes before going to bed. The energy wasn't worth the expense of lost sleep time. He walked over to his bedroom door and raised his hand over the light switch, but hesitated. Maybe, if the light stayed on, he wouldn't have the opportunity to see things in the dark. His eyelids resisted any further rational thought and repeatedly fluttered shut, blinking a five-minute warning until complete closure. He decided to leave the lights on. He unraveled his unkempt comforter and slid himself between the cool, inviting sheets.

He covered his head, obscuring most of the lamplight, and quickly relaxed into slumber.

Something jerked him out of unconsciousness. He felt like he had just closed his eyes. He peered out of his sheets and glanced at his alarm clock.

# 11:19

He had had a brief nap, and everything seemed undisturbed, but something made him edgy.

A car with a busted muffler roared down Dalton Circle, the sonorous clunking was so close it sounded like the jalopy was driving through his room.

Aubrey sat up. His bedroom window was wide open. The drapes fluttered in the wafting breeze from outside.

"Buzz?" he asked, reluctantly hoping for a repeat late night rendezvous. Aubrey's heart pounded anxiously. He tried to remember if he had left his window open, but his thoughts were so ragged, he was unable to recall it smoothly from his mind. He forced himself to mentally retrace his steps prior to climbing into bed. He closed his eyes to concentrate.

Suddenly, the form of a tall, hooded man took shape in the darkness of his eye grounds. The image tonight was full and dimensional, unlike before. Despite his fear, he succumbed to his curiosity and focused on the image, allowing it to become clearer.

The figure rolled its head backwards, and a protruding brow-line emerged. What Aubrey first thought was the hood of the cloak were, in fact, thick locks of long hair, which draped around the large, elongated head. The figure's eyes were small and buried deep within its sockets. The nose was long and thin at the bridge and sloped down into a bulbous tip. Its mouth scrawled a slinky, crooked line from cheek to cheek, and the angles of its jaw jutted out from its neck, like the gills of a fish. A thick, raised crescent-shaped scar ran from temple around the eye, and ended just before the corner of the mouth.

The figure was tall and dressed in a long, dark cloak that brushed the floor. A wide, ruffled collar ordained its neck, and long sleeves shrouded both sides of the lengthy torso like a theater curtain.

Too afraid to endure the sight, yet too awestruck to move, Aubrey held his eyes closed tightly, and the form filled out beyond its head and shoulders. A faint light glowed from behind the image, giving it a shadowy appearance, and small particles swirled in the space around it, shimmering in the light like a sooty halo.

The figure raised its arm slowly. A veiny, muscular hand stretched from underneath the sleeve, the fingers fanning out, reaching for Aubrey. Metal clinked as the figure moved, and a thick, linked iron chain bolted its elbow tautly to the floor. The particles whipped in ripples and vortices around the arm's movement, and a low, haunting whisper brushed Aubrey's mind.

"*Naaaaaaawwwwwwwwbbeeeeeeeyyyyyy*"

Aubrey convulsed instantly with the sound of his name and jerked off the bed with fright. He landed on his backside in the floor. His eyes snapped open. Lamplight flooded his sight. His bedroom appeared no different than before, but he couldn't see to the far side since his head was below the horizon created by the rumpled line of jumbled sheets.

He raised his head slowly and refused to blink. The whites of his eyes were stinging from tear deprivation. Nothing was out of place. The room was well lit, the window still open. The desk was littered with half-written pages, and his books were untouched. His computer was turned off, and his closet door was closed. Gaetan's hand-me-down television and video game consoles were undisturbed and covered in their unmolested dusty film of disuse.

Aubrey looked directly at the spot where the figure had stood on the opposite side of his bed. He saw nothing out of the ordinary. He slowly, deliberately squinted his eyes until the darkness closed in. No movement. No particles. No figure.

The desk chair creaked. Aubrey turned his head toward the sound, eyes closed. The figure towered over him, bending down with its hands reaching for Aubrey.

Aubrey launched himself backwards, his arms flailing, searching for the leverage to gain his feet. His hand found the corner of the nightstand, and he lurched up as it toppled sideways. The lamp and alarm clock tumbled to the floor. The lamp shattered as it made contact with the thin carpet, echoing a raucous *CRACK* as ceramic shards ricocheted across the floor. *FWUMP!* The room went dark, the lamp's bulb imploding with the impact.

In a frenzy, Aubrey scrambled to locate the doorknob behind him through the thick blanket of murky night. He flung open the door and bolted downstairs, his panic shuttling his clumsy feet forward carelessly.

On the last step, his ankles intertwined and he landed full force against the hardwoods at the bottom of the stairs. A resonant *THUD* shook the banister. Aubrey lay dazed on the floor, his fear knocked out of him as much as his breath.

He pushed himself up onto his hands and knees and crawled into the kitchen. Aubrey groped for the light switch above him on the wall. He slowly flipped on the light, grateful to be out of the dark.

Aubrey pulled himself upright, crawling up the cabinet underneath the counter. He panted heavily, his arms and legs begging for air. His inhaler was in his room, so he forced his lungs to breathe more regularly, desperately hoping he wouldn't need it. He grabbed a glass from the middle top cabinet and filled it full with water from the sink. He tipped up the glass and drank it dry in three large gulps. He sighed deeply, collecting his thoughts. His body was weary with fatigue, but his mind once again was wide awake.

Three pill bottles lay open on the countertop. His mother must have forgotten to put her medicine away before she went to bed. Each plastic, amber bottle contained pills of various sizes and shapes, from large white ovoid tablets to small green and blue capsules. He examined the names on the bottles and read the post-modern, alien-like words aloud.

"Boron Hydrogenax. Oxadallium. Carbonamide Litholeum."

Aubrey chuckled ironically to himself. One of the medicines his mother needed to remain stuporously therapeutic and absent from his life was the same homework topic he was being forced to complete by his lifelong bully. He felt like fate was mocking him. Then he reconsidered his thoughts of self-pity. He was his mother's son. Perhaps his hallucinations were merely signs that he was as disturbed as his mother. Maybe he needed to be on these medicines too.

A solid series of thumps bounded down the stairs.

"Aubrey?! What's going on?" barked his father.

Aubrey rummaged through his thoughts, piecing together possible scenarios which might provide a reasonable explanation for the commotion in his bedroom. He rested the palms of his hands against the edge of the counter and looked blankly into the sink. "I had a nightmare," he said, his voice as dull as his gaze.

"Must have been one heck of a nightmare," his dad grumbled, slightly incredulous. "You demolished half of your room." His father's midnight stubble gave his displeasured scowl a more ogreish appearance.

For a moment, fear erupted in Aubrey's throat as he remembered the figure. "It was the most real nightmare I've ever had," he said somberly.

"Why are you in your school clothes?"

Aubrey looked down at his wrinkled shirt and jeans and shrugged waifishly.

"Are you okay?" his father sighed.

"Yeah. I'm good," Aubrey replied. His monotonous response was meant more to placate his father than to answer truthfully. His dad's posture softened, and he walked over to his son

"Aubrey, you've not been yourself lately." His father placed his hand on his son's shoulder in a limp gesture of sympathy.

Aubrey's throat swallowed back a boulder of burden. He was clueless about the images he had been seeing behind his eyes and, what was worse, he had even less of an idea about what his father wanted him to say.

"You're staying up until the wee hours of the morning, and then you come in from school like you've had a day of hard labor. What's the deal?"

"It's been a rough first week," explained Aubrey. He avoided offering details, knowing it would only prolong this insufferable conversation.

"Son," his dad announced, "Are you doing drugs?"

"DAD?!" Aubrey squeaked loudly, the fullness of puberty betraying him.

"Aubrey, I'm asking you a serious question, and I need you to answer me honestly," his father rebutted.

Aubrey dropped his glass in the sink. It clanged loudly as it bounced around the stainless steel basin. He faced his father but took a step back, his father's hand dropping off his shoulder.

"Look, I've just had a lot on my mind lately, okay?! It's been a really stressful couple of days. My homework assignments are difficult, the other kids in school haven't exactly been friendly, and I haven't been feeling well. I apologize if things aren't as easy for me as they are for Gaetan, but I really need you to back off right now." His father's temper rose. He pointed his finger directly at Aubrey's nose. "We are *NOT* talking about Gaetan. We're talking about you and your odd behavior."

"Well, I'm fine! But a little understanding while I adjusted to high school would be great!"

They both stopped and glared at each other for a few moments, waiting for the other's mood to relent. His father looked down at the countertop and noticed the open pill bottles sitting out of the cabinet. He disconnected from Aubrey, grabbed the bottles, snapped on their caps, and shelved them in the top right cabinet. "Do I need to be counting your mother's pills?" he asked coldly, refusing to look Aubrey in the eye.

Aubrey exhaled a heavy sigh and rolled his eyes. He turned away and opened the door to the pantry. Brushing quickly past his father, he grabbed a broom and dust pan and rounded the corner into the living room.

Aubrey stomped indignantly up the stairs. Rounding the open door to his bedroom, he crouched down on the floor to allow the hallway light to brighten the room. He righted the nightstand and set his alarm clock back on top of it. Lifting the larger pieces of broken lamp and carefully avoiding the sharp, jagged edges, he placed them in the metal waste bin by his desk. He concentrated on blinking quickly and only when necessary to prevent further figure sightings.

Out of the corner of his eye, Aubrey sensed the kitchen light turn off. He kept his head down and focused on cleaning his room. Quick, soft footsteps passed in the hallway, and his parents' bedroom door clicked shut. Aubrey finished raking up the finer pieces of glass and plastic from in between the carpet fibers and emptied the dustpan.

The light from the hallway stretched long shadows across his bed and in front of his closet. His room and the house were quieter and more subdued than before. He walked over to his window, hoping mundane sounds from the outside world would alleviate the restless silence. The balmy autumn air whistled through the trees and cooled his flushed cheeks. He rested his elbows on the sill and leaned outside, appreciating the calm of the Auerbach home.

He turned to look toward the road for any signs of normalcy, a car passing by or a neighbor walking their dog in the damp, dark night. The streetlight in front of both houses burned an orange glow onto the sidewalk.

Aubrey noticed something behind the streetlight. He focused his eyes, so he could make it out more clearly. Old Widow Wizenblatt took a step forward into the light, staring straight up at him, without her walker.

Aubrey's heart jumped. He closed his eyes to clear his vision and then opened them again. The streetlight stood alone. His desk chair creaked.

Aubrey crumpled his sheets into a ball and ran downstairs to camp out on the couch for the night.

# Candlelight Confessions

**Wednesday.**

Aubrey curled up in the corner of a bright orange vinyl couch in the lobby of the high school library. He wrapped his arms around his legs and buried his face in his knees. He was embarrassed for feeling so frightened by so many things, but his embarrassment was tempered by sleep-starved apathy. He drifted between dozing and watching students walk in and out of the double-glass doors of the library, pushing the L-shaped turnstile as they encountered the entrance. He wondered how much of what he had been seeing was real. Was his imagination haunting him? Was the stress of high school more than he could handle? Aubrey stared at the unfinished homework lying on the round plastic coffee table in front of him. His frustration rose as he considered how much time he had invested in it. Anger multiplied in his heart at the injustice of Magnos' bullying, but then defeat drained him of all of that anger, as he knew he was powerless to change his circumstances.

Buzz bounded through the doors of the library. The strap of his book bag hooked over the arm of the turnstile, and he spun in circles to free himself from the metal prod.

Buzz loosened the strap and pulled away, unhooking himself and walking into several other students trying to leave. Buzz swung his book bag on his arm and walked over to Aubrey. "Why weren't you in first period?"

Aubrey dropped his legs to the floor. "I couldn't go. I don't have all the homework finished for Magnos and his clones."

Buzz sat next to him on the couch. "Mr. Vandereff asked where you were."

Aubrey shrugged carelessly. "I missed all my classes this morning."

"You can't keep doing this," urged Buzz.

"What else am I supposed to do?"

Buzz looked over the back of the couch and opened his book bag. "I've got a plan to put Magnos in his place." He pulled out a brown, thin plastic cylinder with a flame-shaped bulb attached at the end. Brandishing it proudly in front of Aubrey, Buzz uncoiled its long extension cord and plugged it into the outlet behind them.

Aubrey smirked at him. "A candle?"

"A candle...*pen!*"

Aubrey shook his head and moaned as he slumped back into the couch. "Not another contraption."

"No, wait," Buzz said. "This idea is foolproof." Buzz turned a round, flat knob at the bottom of the electric candle. The bulb flickered brilliantly at a rhythmic pace, like a miniature strobe light. "If you turn the dial underneath all the way, it lights up normally." Buzz rotated the knob underneath, and the candle burned solidly bright. "Touch it."

Aubrey reached his hand out and tapped the end of his finger on the bulb. "Owww!" He jerked his finger back quickly and stuck it in his mouth. "That's hot!"

"Exactly," replied Buzz. "But if I turn the dial down," Buzz rotated the knob in reverse and the glow slowly sputtered, "the incandescent light only has so much time to heat up the bulb, thus controlling the temperature. I put a rheostat in one of my mom's old menorah candles, so I can change the rate of the flash."

Aubrey shook his finger. "I really don't get how this helps me with Magnos...at all!"

"Watch this." Buzz knelt down next to the plastic table. He slid one of Aubrey's homework pages to the edge. He flipped the candlepen over and adjusted the dial again, so that it flickered with a rapid beat. He grasped the candle in his hand and scribbled across the page with the bulb. Buzz rested the candlepen on the table. He brushed off the paper and handed it to Aubrey.

Aubrey scanned the lines of text, turning the page over to inspect it thoroughly. "Nothing happened. It doesn't look any different."

"Precisely," announced Buzz. "You won't notice anything different...." He took the homework from Aubrey and held it high. "Until you look at it with light behind it."

Both of them peered at the piece of paper in Buzz's hands. The fluorescent light overhead filtered through the page. The inky lines of text popped out from the page like soldiers standing across a distant white battlefield. Buzz traced a line with his finger across the paper. A gray silhouette in cursive condensed across the darker writing. *Property of Aubrey Taylor*.

"You write your name with the candlepen on the homework, give it Magnos and Benny and Lenny, and after they turn it in, tell Mr. Vandereff!"

Aubrey shook his head. "This doesn't solve anything. He'll still find other ways to bully me."

"Huh-uh," challenged Buzz. "Did you read the Honor Code?"

"Is that a novel or something?" queried Aubrey.

"No, it's the Lake Julian Code of Conduct. We were supposed to read it this summer and sign it before we started Monday."

Aubrey shrugged sheepishly.

"Anyway, it says that cheating is grounds for expulsion."

"Really?"

"Yep! This little *light* is your opportunity for freedom from Magnos." Buzz unplugged the cord from the wall and handed him the candlepen. He tapped on the dial on the bottom. "Turn the dial to the red mark. It sets the blinking of the bulb to just the right temperature to denature the proteins in the paper and cause the watermark effect. If the dial is set lower, nothing will happen. If it's set too high, you'll burn the paper."

"Thanks," sighed Aubrey. Buzz noticed the dark circles sagging down Aubrey's sunken cheeks.

"You've looked tired all week," remarked Buzz.

Aubrey glared at him. "Because I've barely rested all week."

"But all you've been doing is chores, homework, then sleep, right?" countered Buzz.

Aubrey nodded sullenly and hung his head.

Buzz squinted his eyes as he scrutinized Aubrey's demeanor. "What's going on?"

Aubrey shifted positions in the couch and picked at his fingernails.

"Is Gaetan giving you grief?" Buzz asked.

"No more than usual," replied Aubrey quietly. Aubrey looked over the arm of the couch, avoiding eye contact with Buzz. "Can I tell you something totally crazy?"

Buzz laughed. "You think you have a secret. I'm your best bud, and you think there's something I don't know about you." Buzz leaned back in the couch and folded his arms behind his head as his smile widened. "Go ahead. Shock me."

Aubrey took a deep breath and exhaled it all at once. "I'm being haunted by a ghost."

Buzz's grin flattened. He eyed Aubrey warily as he thought for a moment. "Very funny. Now tell me what's really keeping you up at night."

Aubrey stood up suddenly. He stacked the homework pages on the table into a pile, folded them and stuffed them in his book bag. He dropped the candlepen onto the couch and slung his bag over his shoulder. Aubrey took a step forward and Buzz jumped up, blocking his way.

"What's your glamour glitch, dude?" Buzz asked.

"I knew you wouldn't believe me," Aubrey mumbled.

Buzz sneered in confusion. "You really think you're being *haunted*?"

"I keep seeing a face in my room, every time I close my eyes at night."

Buzz listened intently, uncertain what to say.

"I saw him for the first time Sunday night," continued Aubrey, "and each night I can see him more clearly. Last night, he said my name, or something like it. And the Widow was outside staring up at me from the street. I was so scared I slept downstairs."

"Maybe you should go to the eye doctor," Buzz said, trying to be helpful.

Aubrey rolled his eyes and pushed Buzz out of his way. He stormed toward the door.

"Wait," hollered Buzz. He chased behind him. "At least take this." Buzz handed him the candlepen. "Maybe your ghost is afraid of the light?"

Aubrey thought for a moment and chuckled darkly. "I don't think he's that kind of ghost."

## Shiny

Mr. Osterfeld's booming horn blew in the distance. Aubrey capped his pen and rested it on the three homework assignments in front of him. Each was written in a different colored ink, each had a slightly different slant of lettering, each was finally complete. He sighed deeply, rubbed his hands, and glanced over each page once more.

Aubrey was bitterly proud of the quality of work he had created for Magnus and the Van Zenny twins. He was hopeful his own homework would be as good. He meticulously slid each assignment into an individual folder and stacked them together carefully before slotting them into his book bag. He leaned over and spotted the candlepen in the bottom of his bag. Aubrey picked it up and stared at it pensively. He didn't want to use it. He knew if something went wrong, Magnos would be even more conniving and sinister. However, if he did use it and decided at the last minute not to say anything, no one would ever know, not even Buzz.

He unraveled the extension cord and plugged it into the wall. He turned the candlepen over and turned the dial to the mark as Buzz instructed. The bulb's glow danced to life. One by one, he slipped the pages of the forged homework assignments out of their folders and traced 'Aubrey Taylor' diagonally across the paper. He replaced the pages and returned the folders to his bag.

Aubrey turned to look at his clock.

## 10:39

He grew concerned about the return of his nightly visitor. Squatting on the floor, he crawled quietly over to his window. He peered over the sill and gazed at the lamp-lit street below. Aubrey felt silly for being so paranoid. No one was there.

But in the corner of his view he could see something in Ms. Thistlewood's yard. He scooted over to the edge of the sill and raised his head for a better look. He couldn't quite see what it was.

Aubrey leaned away from the window and stood up. He ripped the sheets off his bed, flipped off the lights, and ran downstairs to the living room. Dropping his bedding on the couch, he knelt on the cushions, craning his neck through the drapes to look outside. The moon was full in the cloudless sky, and the street was nearly as bright as daylight.

Ms. Thistlewood sat on her lawn between a bed of tulips and a round setting of potted shrubs. She sat cross-legged with her head hung low and her bright red hair wrapped behind her head in a ponytail. Something shiny sparkled in her lap, but Aubrey couldn't make out what it was.

Aubrey popped up and raced into the kitchen. He rummaged through several drawers without turning on the lights. Once he had found what he needed, he slunk back to the couch and resumed his spur-of-the-moment stakeout.

Ms. Thistlewood flipped through something silvery and golden, like a gleaming container of metal. The item sparkled in the moonlight. Part book and part box, whatever it was, she seemed deeply engaged with. Aubrey strained to see more detail.

Ms. Thistlewood's head snapped up, and she stared straight at Aubrey. He fell backwards onto the arm of the couch and slipped below the window's edge. *Did she see me*, he wondered.

A light upstairs caught his attention. He gazed up at his bedroom. A dim, yellow light blinked in his bedroom. He stood up and walked toward the banister, watching his open door with cautious intrigue. The light faded then brightened, and flickering shadows drifted along the wall of the upstairs hallway, casting darkened forms from inside his room. Caught between two frights, Aubrey slowly backed up and buried himself under his covers on the couch.


Upstairs in Aubrey's bedroom, the candlepen hovered daintily in mid-air. There was physically no hand to guide it. No form took shape. Gently and deliberately, the candlepen rose and spun without a tangible grip. It turned upside down and the tip of its bulb drug along the desk, scrawling letters of a specter's intent.

# Through the Rooking Glass

**Thursday.**

Jordana tapped her pen on her notebook. Paying attention in the last period of the day was always difficult. At least her English teacher, Mrs. Staum-Pierre, battled to enliven the end of the day. Her chirpy voice warbled between contrasts and comparisons of current and historical literature, but it was her unusual appearance, which was the most engaging. Jordana was intrigued by her looks so much so that she hadn't heard a word her teacher had said for the past ten minutes.

Mrs. Staum-Pierre's loopy locks of black hair helmeted her head like a bouquet of wrapping bows. Clumps of air-filled curls were held tightly in place with a potpourri of ornamented berets and hair clips that dangled precariously from winding wisps of hair as she spun from classroom to blackboard. She wore a red yarn sweater vest that depicted puppies and kittens tussling about across her back. By the looks of it, she had obviously knitted it herself. One dog had five legs and several cats were missing ears.

Her long, smooth black skirt dragged the ground, and dust clung to its fringe. Her bright red lipstick extended just a smudge beyond her lips, and her square-shaped, rose-tinted glasses bounced at the end of her nose as she lectured. Jordana wondered if her teacher's glasses would look just as good on her.

She slid her honey-colored glasses off her nose and rested them with its arms extended on her desk. Massaging her eyes, she squeezed the dull ache of monotony out of them. She clenched her lids tightly together and pulled wayward strands of her long, straight black hair behind her ears. Jordana had worn her glasses for so long, she was afraid to see what the world looked like without them.

Eyes closed, she reached for her glasses, but all she could feel was her notebook and the wooden table top of her desk. Concentrating on keeping her eyes securely shut, she patted the space in front of her, gently searching for them. They weren't there. She angled her head to the side and allowed a glimmer of light to slip through her eyelids. They weren't on the floor, and her desk only held her pen and notebook.

"Nice glasses," drifted a voice back to her. She glanced up, and Benny Van Zenny, who was sitting in the seat in front of her, was tinkering with a beam light from the window as it filtered through her glasses.

Jordana swallowed a dry lump in her throat. She could feel her palms moisten and tremble. She took a deep breath to calm herself. "I need those," she whispered harshly. "I'm blind without them."

Benny chuckled. He slid the glasses up his nose. "These aren't real glasses," he teased. "I can see through them just fine."

"I need them back," chided Jordana.

The electronic chime binged overhead. Students shuffled for their belongings and scooted out of their chairs. Jordana lowered her head and stared at the floor.

"Hey, Lenny," jeered Benny. "Look at me! I'm a movie star!" Benny held his open hand to his ear and jiggled to and fro. Lenny cackled wildly.

Benny and Lenny stood up and walked toward the door, posing like runway models.

Jordana chased after them, holding her head down. She grasped Benny's portulent arm. "Please, let me have my glasses," she begged.

Benny pulled away and handed her glasses to Lenny. He donned them as if he was royalty.

"Hi, I'm the new girl in school, and I wear these glasses so everyone will know how important I am," Lenny mocked. Several other students giggled as they ambled toward the door. Benny guffawed loudly and ripped the glasses off Lenny's face.

Jordana's gut knotted up, and a sorrowful anger flooded her heart.

Benny shoved the glasses up to his forehead. He stifled his own laughter and rested his hand on his chest. "Don't be jealous of how beautiful I am. I only wear these to block the pain I bear inside."

Jordana stiffened straight up. Her eyes widened as she glared demandingly at Benny. "GIVE THEM BACK NOW OR *ELSE*!"

# Dam Time

Rodriqa fell into the chairs lining the wall outside the high school's gym. She unwrapped her ponytail holder from the back of her head, and strands of beaded and braided hair clinked around her shoulders. She heaved her gym bag off the floor and pulled out her street shoes and a towel. Droplets of sweat were still beading up on her arms and forehead, despite having dried herself off three times already. She tore off her gym shoes and stretched her feet to knead out the cramps.

*The first volleyball practice of the season and I'm exhausted*, she thought to herself disappointedly. She attributed her lack of stamina to lack of rest, a full day of classes and poor training over the summer. The first two reasons returned some of her confidence, and the last convinced her to consider taking up kickboxing.

She took a few moments to relax, enjoying the chance to breathe without exertion. She placed her dry shoes on the floor and, in her usual superstitious fashion, put them on and laced them up. Left foot first, tying the laces right over left; then right foot, tying the laces left over right. This was her routine since her grandmother taught her how to tie her shoes when she was four, and her grandmother's words echoed in her mind every time she tied them. *A solid foundation always keeps you from stumbling.*

Rodriqa collected her sportswear and school bags and draped her towel on her shoulder, certain she would need it for the walk home. She walked away from the gym and rounded the hallway towards the front doors of the school. A muffled clamor from ahead slowed her pace. Two men were shouting from around the corner, but the distance in between muted the clarity of their exchange. She assumed the verbal reprimand was most likely due to the indiscretion of a wayward student. She chuckled to herself and thought, *nice way for that kid to start off the year.*

The light from the main entrance of the high school angled into the end of the hallway. The yelling intensified. Rodriqa quickened her step so she could bypass the oratorical melee swiftly, saving the involved student from the least amount of embarrassment possible. She bolted around the corner with her face forward to prevent any interaction with the scene.

She stopped before she could reach the doors.

The silhouette of two men facing each other and waving their arms darkened the fogged glass of the administrative office to her left. Jordana sat hunched over in a metal chair outside the closed door. She cradled her honeycolored glasses in her hands. Both lenses were shattered within the frames, with one of its arms mangled into a crooked zigzag. Her long, dark, shiny hair draped the sides of her face and heavy tears dropped from her cheeks, leaving splattered water stains on her jeans.

"There is something *REALLY* wrong with that child!" More shouting bellowed from inside the office with perfect clarity, the words now clear to Rodriqa. "And you better figure out what it is, or she is going to end up just like her mother!"

"Jordana, what's wrong?" Rodriqa approached her cautiously.

Jordana raised her head and wiped her face with the back of her hand. Her eyes darted left and right, and her lower lip quivered.

"That is my daughter you're talking about!" Another voice roared from the office.

"Do you have any idea how many phone calls from angry parents my staff has had to field today?"

"What would you have me do?! If I could fix it I would. No one knows what to do! Least of all...*YOU*!"

Rodriqa waved Jordana to her feet. "Let's get out of here."

Jordana wavered for a moment, but Rodriqa's kind offer of escape was too good to pass up. She shifted forward in her seat and reached for her book bag. Rodriqa walked over and flung Jordana's bag over her unoccupied shoulder. She placed her hand under Jordana's arm, gently lifting her up. Trembling, Jordana slid her broken glasses on her nose and stood up. Quickly, they both walked out the front doors.

"Tough week, huh," sympathized Rodriqa. Jordana didn't respond. They marched briskly across the parking lot and steadied themselves along the brim of the highway. Rodriqa gazed curiously up at the Berybomag mining entrance across the road, wondering if that's where Jordana was headed, but Jordana kept her head down, plodding forward and away from the mine. The silence hung around them like a thick fog. Jordana matched her steps, but Rodriqa felt miles away. Rodriqa held her tongue, fearful to say anything that might worsen the tense sadness.

Rodriqa crossed the highway, and Jordana followed. They climbed the hill down from the school to avoid walking the switchback path of the road up to the dam. Rodriqa held back tree limbs and stomped down brush to clear their way. Jordana never said a word.

The stifling silence frustrated Rodriqa, so she decided to end it.

"Look." She hesitated at first, and then fully emptied her mind of words. "I've heard the principal can be a total jerk. So I wouldn't take anything he says too seriously. I know I have no idea what's going on, but it's the first week of school. It can't be that bad, can it?!"

Jordana snorted sarcastically in protest. She stopped walking and turned around.

Rodriqa spun to face her. "I didn't mean to salt your celery. I'm only trying to help."

Jordana shook her head and pointed a finger toward the sky. "That's not it."

Slowly, the birds stopped chirping, the bugs quit buzzing, and the air froze. A chill raced down Rodriqa's spine. A thunderous percussion of shouting echoed from the mine below. They both stopped and stared down the hill. A group of men yelled frantically as they ran out of one of the huge pits at the edge of the excavation.

"I wonder what happened," asked Rodriqa softly.

Jordana shrugged. They both took a couple of cautious steps leeward to gain a better view. Snapping tree limbs and swishing twigs hurdled up the hill. A dark figure ran with breakneck speed through a patch of forest a couple of hundred yards away. His dark red eyes glowed and he was covered with a thick mat of shaggy hair. He glanced at Rodriqa and Jordana and ducked behind a swathe of dense foliage, disappearing instantly. Both of the girls ducked down to avoid being seen, a little too late.

"What was *that?*" whispered Rodriqa.

"The mine's been under attack from a bunch of tree-huggers lately," whispered Jordana. "It was probably just a protester fleeing from the mine workers."

"Funny, it didn't really look...human to me," retorted Rodriqa.

"What do you think it looked like?"

Rodriqa knew what she thought she saw, but she didn't want to sound crazy. "Nothing," she mumbled.

"Where are we going?" asked Jordana as she turned back up the hill.

"To the dam," replied Rodriqa. "My parents are the chief engineers there. It's a fun place to hang out after school sometimes. Something different anyway. Might help take your mind off things."

Jordana nodded, and Rodriqa returned to climbing the hill.

"Do you want to talk about what happened?" Rodriqa asked.

Jordana shook her head decisively.

Rodriqa nodded. "If you need a place to get away, you're welcome to stay at the dam or my place. My family's pretty laid back."

A small smile curled at the edge of Jordana's lips. "Thank you," she murmured.

The hill leveled off, and they picked up their pace. Jordana saw a clearing ahead and straightened her course for a direct line out of the trees and brush.

Rodriqa stuck her arm in front of Jordana. "Wait. We don't want to walk through there."

"Why not?" asked Jordana. "I'm getting all cut up from the branches."

"There's an old, abandoned cemetery up there. Pretty creepy if you ask me. I always avoid it. Besides sometimes the Mafisito hang out there, and they're usually up to no good."

Jordana hated superstition, but she was in no mood to argue. "Which way, then?"

Rodriqa pointed ahead to her right. "We curve around the edge of the clearing, and the tourist entrance to the dam is just at the lake's edge."

They plodded through the forest's ring of white pines, careful to wedge sticker bushes under their shoes and avoid slipping on mossy rocks. They broke through the tree line, and Lake Julian spread out before them, its glassy waters glistening like wrinkled blue foil between marshy, emerald banks. Cattails and sea oats waved in the breeze, and Rodriqa pointed out Mr. Osterfeld's white tugboat drifting in the distance. She raised her hand to her forehead and looked up. Jordana followed her gaze to the white brick tower rising several stories above the highway over the dam.

"It's the observation deck," commented Rodriqa. "It's a great place to do homework."


Rodriqa and Jordana marched up the hillside, abutting the side of the dam. Its bleached concrete shone a brilliant white, which twinkled with sparkling flecks embedded in the walls, glinting in the sun. Jordana glanced at the tall, bronze statue of a man with outstretched arms, dressed in military uniform positioned in the middle of the entranceway. She guessed he was someone important, but didn't bother reading the plaque under his feet on the monument's pedestal, as Rodriqa was already approaching a row of mirror-like glass doors several yards ahead.

Rodriqa gripped the handle of a heavy steel-trimmed door and tilted all her weight backwards. It swung open slowly, like a pendulum. Jordana slipped through the crack of space created, and Rodriqa lunged forward to slide inside before the door closed.

Jordana gawked in awe at the spacious, marble-lined foyer and all its accoutrements. Inset in the walls were tablet-like tarnished brass plaques that told the history of the dam and the workings of its hydroelectric power mechanics. Busts of local politicians, who were responsible for procuring resources for the dam's construction, rested regally on miniature marble columns. Rodriqa smiled at Jordana and her awestruck expression as she took in the design of the foyer.

Rodriqa trotted over to the security desk and slumped her torso against the countertop. "How's life treatin' ya?" Behind the desk a young man with olive skin and straight, slick black hair lifted his head up from underneath the security desk.

"Rodriqa," he said, smiling broadly. "I haven't seen you all summer. How's high school?"

Rodriqa shrugged flippantly. "Just like middle school except all the really cool people have graduated."

The man smiled widely.

"Jaime Kontrearo, meet Jordana Galilahi," said Rodriqa, waving her hand between the two. "Jaime and my older brother are best friends. They graduated from high school together last year."

Jaime nodded and took a second glance at Jordana, noticing her glasses were broken. She could tell he was staring. Brushing a few strands of her straight black hair from behind her ear, she covered her shattered eyeglass lens.

Jaime smiled uneasily. "How is your brother?" he asked Rodriqa.

"He hasn't started classes yet, so he's doing pretty good so far," joked Rodriqa.

Jaime chuckled in reply. "It's good to see you, little sis number two."

Rodriqa grinned gleefully. "Are my mom and dad here?"

"Yeah, they're down in the control room. There's been a lot of activity down there today. I'll buzz you in." Jaime leaned over and pushed a large red button on the panel under the desk. Rodriqa pushed the turnstile next to the desk, and she and Jordana walked through.

"We'll take the back stairway. It's faster and less noisy," directed Rodriqa. Jordana nodded agreeably.

They passed a group of tourists perusing the upper galley. Dressed in attire ranging from summer chic to Sunday's best, the small ensemble crowded around a small plaque behind the security desk.

A soft, sweet voice echoed from the group off the marble walls of the galley. "How many levels make up the dam?"

A high-pitched canary-like voice responded robotically. "The top two levels are for security and exposition. The third and fourth levels house the command center of the dam and employee offices. The fifth level holds the turbines, and there is structurally a sixth level that forms the dam's foundation."

"And what does the sixth level contain?" asked the sweet voice.

Rodriqa stopped and glanced at the clump of tourists. The question was curiously intrusive as it was not something many visitors asked about. And something about the voice prickled Rodriqa's skin. A woman with bright red hair and pale, flawless skin stood out among the group. Rodriqa listened to the tour guide intently as she squawked her well-memorized spiel. The redheaded woman glanced at Rodriqa, and then she quickly redirected her attention back to the tour guide. Rodriqa touched her aegis beads, almost instinctively, as if she needed to protect herself.

"What's wrong?" asked Jordana, as she stood at the door to the stairway.

Rodriqa shook her head and pushed the metal door handle open.

Jordana surmised they had entered a maintenance stairwell, as oily smudges darkened the walls, and bits of gravel filled the corners of the floors. Water beaded on the brick like industrial sweat, and noxious fumes from burning fossil fuels stung their noses. Rodriqa grabbed hold of the railing and led them down. As they descended, Jordana could feel the stirring, mechanical guts of the dam vibrating through the concrete slabs around them.

Rodriqa stopped next to another door several flights below. "Cover your ears. We're gonna run through to the control room," she instructed Jordana, who was now slightly nervous to be buried in the belly of this noisy beast.

Rodriqa slammed open the heavy metal door, and a blast wave of thumping hums washed over both of them. Jordana cringed and slapped her hands over her ears. Rodriqa raced around the corner with Jordana following closely behind.

Jordana glanced around the massive, concrete-lined rhomboid room. Pipes and wires, varying in diameter from electrical cords to the width of a trash can, ran for miles above, layering every inch of the ceiling. Panels of blinking buttons and flickering lights blanketed the walls, and a long thin grate intersected the middle of the room. A slim, dark-haired man wearing earmuffs pushed a metal cart hung full of electrical tools and wiring. He paused and waved at them. Rodriqa dashed past him and wiggled her elbow in reply.

Rodriqa stopped suddenly at another door that held keypad on its left edge. She shrugged her shoulders over her ears and punched in a number with her outstretched fingers. The door snapped open, and the two of them rushed inside.

As it closed, the deafening drone of the dam dampened to a soft thrum. Both girls sighed, grateful for the door's soundproof thickness. Rodriqa rubbed her ears to reset her dulled hearing.

Jordana scanned the metal-walled, hexagonal room they waere now in, which was furnished with rows of computer panels and wide TV screens, lining most of the wall's free space. Several screens pictured rotating images from both inside and outside the dam. Jordana watched brief video clips of gears turning in the guts of the dam and men and women walking up and down hallways of the upper levels. A central, round desk flashed and bleeped with a display of green and red lights, and needles flipped and spun in circular gauges.

From the back of the room, a colossal, bald-headed man stomped toward Jordana and Rodriqa with clenched fists, as a scowl rippled across his face. Dark green tattoos scrawled up and down both sides of his forearms, and his chest heaved to twice its size with every breath. Jordana gasped and leaned back against the door.

"I can't believe you!" The man's deep baritone voice startled Jordana. "I haven't seen you all summer!"

"Charlie!" shouted Rodriqa with joy, and she leapt into the air. Charlie caught her in mid-flight and swung her around like a tiny doll.

Rodriqa hugged as much of his chest as she could put her arms around. Jordana relaxed and smiled happily at the reunion.

"You've been back how many days now?" Charlie asked as he set Rodriqa back on her feet.

"Only a handful," replied Rodriqa softly.

"And you haven't been to see me," Charlie playfully scolded. He patted her on her shoulder, and Rodriqa grinned sweetly.

"Hey, Charlie, this is my friend Jordana," introduced Rodriqa. "Jordana, this is Charlie Buckswaine. He's head of security at the dam.

Charlie clicked his heels together and saluted officially.

Jordana returned his salute half-heartedly.

"Has Jaime been toeing the line?" Rodriqa asked.

"Yes, ma'am," replied Charlie. "Jaime is a good listener and follows the rules. I like that."

"Good," stated Rodriqa with approval. "Where's my dad?"

Charlie pointed to the far corner of the control room where a small group of men wearing stiff white lab coats huddled together, murmuring to each other.

Jordana followed Rodriqa to the corner of studious engineers. Rodriqa reached into the middle of the crowd and tapped a man on the shoulder. A tall, stately, dark-skinned man stood up, straightened his tie, and brushed off the front of his suit. He leaned over and kissed Rodriqa on the cheek. "Good afternoon, sweetheart."

"Hi, Dad." Rodriqa tried to sound tough, but everyone around her could hear her voice soften into an endearing tone. "I brought a friend from school. Remember me telling you about Jordana?"

Rodriqa's father smiled and shook Jordana's hand. "Jamison Auerbach," he introduced himself. "Pleasure to meet you."

"Thanks, you too," replied Jordana quietly.

"Any chance we could get a tour from you?" Rodriqa asked. "You always know all the cool stuff the regular guides miss."

Rodriqa's Dad rubbed his forehead and glanced down. "It's not a great time, Driqa."

"Did you feel that?" blurted out one of the lab-coated men.

"Yep," agreed another. "It's minor, but I definitely felt the vibration this time."

The clump of men glared intently at a lined piece of paper running horizontally as a needle furiously scribbled a wavy line across it.

"There's some…unusual activity," explained Dr. Auerbach to his daughter, "that requires my attention at the moment."

"There it goes again!" shouted the engineer. "Another vibration!"

The rest of them conferenced amongst themselves in low whispers.

Jordana was a little confused, not only by the polygraph-like instrument that they were all glued to, but also by the talk of vibrations. To her, the whole place had been shuddering the entire time she had been inside the dam.

The needle jumped high up the page, and everyone staring at it lurched backwards.

Charlie Buckswaine inserted his meaty arm though the small crowd and raised a finger at the high mark of the jagged line. "Dr. Auerbach, I think we should evacuate the dam."

# Circle Shock

Aubrey held his head in his hands as he sat on the railing of the overpass at the end of Dalton Circle. Not that he expected the first week of high school to be exemplary, but it had certainly been quandarously memorable in a menagerie of unusual ways. Hopefully, now he could resolve one portion of the weirdness.

Puttering down the street on his steam-powered bicycle, Buzz peeled into the gravel on the edge of the bridge and stopped abruptly. He hopped off his bike and capped the propane tank, and steam hissed out its edges. He tiptoed over to the railing and leaned over cautiously.

"Is she here?" he whispered.

Aubrey nodded.

"Remind me why we're stalking her again?"

"We are not stalking her. She is stalking *me*," insisted Aubrey.

"A homeless woman, who lives in your neighborhood and stands outside your window at night, isn't stalking you...she's begging," countered Buzz.

"She was watching me and the ghost through my window!"

Buzz squinted at Aubrey skeptically. "Are you sure you didn't break into your father's secret stash last night?"

Aubrey rolled his eyes, stood up and stormed off the bridge. He turned the corner at the railing and disappeared quickly down a dirt trail that followed the embankment below. Buzz sighed and chased after him carelessly.

Aubrey stretched out his arm anxiously to slow Buzz down. Both of them peered around the concrete abutment, completely speechless at the scene under the overpass.

A white refrigerator lay on its back in the dirt, missing its doors and brimming with murky pond water. A mallard swam lazily in circles in the makeshift water feature, and ringlets of tiny waves broke the surface just in front of the duck's breast. A wooden park bench, wrapped in a plastic-couch cover, sat next to the refrigerator alongside the Widow's shopping cart, which today was full of crushed aluminum cans, empty milk jugs and hubcaps. Jaggedly hewn tree stumps sat on their sides in a ring at the edge of the bench. Strings of hand-carved wind chimes dangled from a concrete ledge, and Old Widow Wizenblatt stood behind it all in her tattered floral dress, with her back to them.

"What's she doin'?" Buzz whispered. Aubrey shook his head and put his straightened index finger up to his mouth. Aubrey leaned further in to gain a better view, with his hand gripping the ledge.

The Widow's bushy crown of white curls bobbed up and down as she rocked back and forth on her feet. Her arms gyrated rhythmically, and she hummed peacefully. The hollow pegs and marble balls of the chime twirled in the wind and seemingly tinkled along to her quiet song. Smoke billowed from in front of her, and a pungent mixture of rotting flesh, sour milk and mildewed cheese wafted from under the bridge. Aubrey's lip curled as the stench slapped his face, and he opened his mouth to avoid breathing through his nose.

Buzz angled his torso against Aubrey to look around him. Aubrey tipped at the edge under Buzz's weight and pushed back to keep from falling. Aubrey's feet slipped in the crumbling dirt. He clung to the ledge as his legs swung from underneath him. Buzz tripped and tumbled down the path, landing tummy up at the bottom next to the refrigerator.

"Dinner's almost ready," called the Widow without turning around.

Buzz sat up quietly and slowly dusted himself off. The sweat gathering on Aubrey's fingers loosened his hold on the ledge, and he dropped to the concrete below.

The Widow turned over her shoulder quickly and spotted Aubrey crouching down behind the abutment.

"Visitors aren't welcome," she snarled.

"What's for dinner?" Buzz asked, as he sat down on the plastic-covered bench behind her. Mrs. Wizenblatt swiveled on her heels and slapped a smoldering pan of fish on the stump in front of him.

Buzz's stomach lurched into his throat. Boiling in the skillet, a bulging, bubbling eye popped out of its socket, and scaly skin dripped off the flesh of a fish, exposing its boney ribcage. Buzz covered his mouth and closed his eyes as the steam from the pan blew past him.

Aubrey shuffled over to the edge of her camp and peered over Buzz's shoulder. She had being frying the fish on a conventional stove which had a wood-burning fire crackling in the oven. She opened the door and slid a piece of chopped wood into the fiery blaze, and the flames licked up through the open, soot-lined burners.

"Where's my house?" the Widow asked Buzz.

Buzz choked back tears of nausea. "Where's my appetite?"

She walked over to the refrigerator and plunged her arm in the water. The mallard burst into flight and disappeared into the sky over the bridge. The Widow dredged her hand through the water and wrenched out a catfish. For a moment, Buzz thought the Widow was wearing a black leather glove, but then he took a second look. The fish had swallowed her forearm halfway. The catfish's tail flailed and flopped as it munched further up the Widow's arm. She ripped the catfish off her arm and pulled another frying pan out from the mess of items in the shopping cart. She dropped the fish in the pan over the fire, and the squirming catfish slowly sizzled until it stopped writhing.

"Where's my house?" she asked again.

"Aubrey and I came to ask you a question," replied Buzz as he scooted away from the steaming pan on the stump.

"I need my house," she muttered, flipping the fish on the stove.

Aubrey slunk over to Buzz and sat next to him on the bench. "What's she talking about?" he whispered.

"The Volkswagen Beetle chassis," murmured Buzz.

"What happened to it?"

"My dad picked it up and drug it to his junkyard after I told him about it."

Aubrey rolled his eyes. "You mean you told your dad you wanted it, and he came and got it."

"Details," uttered Buzz carelessly as he waved him off.

"House stealer," muttered Mrs. Wizenblatt. "It's an outrage, really."

Buzz continued. "Aubrey saw a ghost with a big jaw and a long scar, and he thinks you were outside of his window watching the whole thing."

Aubrey glowered at Buzz angrily. Buzz shrugged. The Widow stopped rotating the pan over the fire. She turned around slowly and raised a pointed finger. "Ignore it!"

She turned back around to the stove and flipped the fish again.

Aubrey and Buzz looked quizzically at each other. "But the ghost keeps coming back. I've seen it every night this week," replied Aubrey.

"Ignore it," she replied tersely, with a tap to the 't' at the end of her sentence. "It will go away eventually."

"I want it to go away now," complained Aubrey.

"What offense did you create to bring about the wrath of this spirit?" she asked.

"Huh?" Buzz grunted.

The Widow turned around and placed the hot pan on a nearby stump. "Have you disturbed anything sacred or accursed lately?" she asked.

"No." Aubrey and Buzz mused as they responded.

"Ever been to the Circle of Circles?" She squatted on the ground and snapped the head off the steaming, slimy catfish.

"The what?" Buzz asked, completely enthralled.

"Not a what, a where." She tore a piece of greasy meat from under a cooked pectoral fin and shoved it in her mouth.

"Where is the Circle of Circles?" Buzz asked.

"Nevermind," replied the Widow as she chewed her food. "Ignore your ghost."

"Please tell us," Buzz begged.

"If you don't know, you don't need to know," she crooned as mealy bits of fish spurted from her mouth.

"What is that supposed to mean?" asked Aubrey with a sharp edge to his tone.

"Someone has cracked the piper, but the piper was already half-cracked."

"Excuse me?" said Buzz. He didn't know whether to feel sorry for her or insulted.

"Why is there a ghost keeping me up at night?" insisted Aubrey.

"Ask him," spouted the Widow through a resounding guffaw.

Aubrey and Buzz glanced at each other with puzzled expressions.

"All we are asking for is a single clue to direct us to this Circle of Circle's you mentioned?" said Buzz calmly.

Mrs. Wizenblatt pushed herself up slowly, her hips and knees cracking as she straightened her back. She swallowed more chunks of fish and stared upward, musing through ancient thoughts and undisturbed wisdoms. "When the irregularity and entropy of nature is interrupted by a forced and focused geometry, then something or someone has intervened. Creation dislikes its boundaries." The bags under her eyes darkened and her cheeks grew sallow.

Aubrey shook his head and gritted his teeth.

Buzz stood up. "She's one patient short of an asylum," he whispered. "Let's get out of here. We got what we need." Buzz marched out from under the bridge.

Aubrey stood up, glared at the widow and then yelled after Buzz, "Wait! We don't know what to look for."

"Yeah, we do," hollered Buzz over his shoulder.

Aubrey furrowed his brow and ran to catch up with Buzz.

"Where are you going?" asked the Widow sternly.

"To find the Circle of Circles, of course," sang Buzz as he turned up the trail with Aubrey close behind.

She chased after them. "Be wary, boys. There is more to our world than your eyes can see, and more horror than your imagination can conceive. You are surrounded by spirits eager for power, and they'll do anything to get it."

"She sure is a loony ol' goat, isn't she," teased Buzz loud enough for the Widow to hear.

She screamed at them up the trail. "If you find the Circle of Circles, and you chose to open the door, it can never be closed. The creatures hidden in dark places will never let you be."

Aubrey and Buzz rounded the top of the overpass. "That's some serious creepitude," commented Buzz nonchalantly.

"I'm glad we made it out without landing in the frying pan," Aubrey agreed. "Although I still have no idea where my ghost comes from or what's she's talking about."

"It doesn't matter," answered Buzz triumphantly. "She gave us what we needed to know. We need to find the Circle of Circles…and what she doesn't realize is that you can find anything with the Internet!" He laughed proudly at himself.

"But what about everything else she said?" Aubrey questioned thought-fully.

"She's crazy! It's all just hocus-y pocus-y gobbledygook."

Aubrey leaned against the railing, watching the cars pass by. "What if she really knows more than we get?"

"What are the chances?" challenged Buzz. "She's a homeless woman that lives under a bridge."

"Maybe I should follow her advice and just ignore it."

"You ignore it. I'll find the Circle of Circles."

"I don't think you should, either." Aubrey stood up and frowned at Buzz. "I'm tired of everything being weird…nothing about me has ever been nor-mal…or average…or typical…the last thing I need is to embark on some silly goose chase that proves I'm even more abnormal that anyone thought."

Buzz rolled his eyes. "You worry too much about what other people think."

Attempting to place a decisive period at the end of their conversation, Aubrey turned toward his house and strode forward.

"You're the one who wanted to know why the Widow was standing outside your window last night," Buzz yelled after him.

"Well I don't want to know anymore," shouted Aubrey over his shoulder. "Whatever is trying to drag me into its own mess, I'm not interested!"

Suddenly, the ground shuddered and shifted under their feet. Houses along Dalton Circle creaked and leaned to and fro. Buzz fell against the bridge railing and clutched it tightly to stay upright. Aubrey was toppled to his rear. A rumbling roar echoed throughout the valley like a monstrous subway train racing underneath them.

People poured out of their homes, covering their heads and ducking vac-illating beams and boards. Aubrey gripped the ground, desperately hoping not to fall off the flat asphalt. The bridge shook Buzz like a rag doll.

After a few moments, the ground stiffened, and the world stopped trem-bling. Aubrey clasped his head between his hands and crawled up onto his knees. Buzz steadied himself cautiously on his feet and surveyed the neigh-borhood. Mothers hugged their children in the street, and many examined the outside of their homes for structural damage.

What had seemed like an eternity of upheaval had lasted only a few sec-onds. Buzz marched down the road and offered Aubrey his hand.

"That was amazing," Buzz whispered in awe.

"Scary is more like it," replied Aubrey as he took his feet.

"I don't see much damage though."

"Was it an earthquake?"

"It has to be. What else would shake the ground like that?" critiqued Buzz.

A trickling stream of water percolated behind them.  They both turned toward the Highway at the top of the street.  A thin wave of black water spilled down the road and washed into Dalton Circle.

Both of the boys glared at each and murmured, "The dam."

Buzz ran over to his bike, lit the pilot light and climbed on.  The pistons hissed and recoiled under the building pressure.  Aubrey jumped onto the back of Buzz's bike and stood on the foot pegs.

The bike lurched forward.  They sped up Dalton Circle and turned onto Asheville Highway with the bike's wheels wading through inches of water as they raced forward.


At the ridgeline, a murmuring crowd of tourists, local folks and dam employees stood on the grassy, high ground on either side of the dam, watching maintenance workers scurry in and out of the side entrance.  Small waves of lake water sloshed rhythmically over top of the dam, spreading out along the road and spilling over into the deep ravine below.  Directing oncoming traffic to turn around, security officers set plastic yellow road blockades at the edges of the dam in the middle of the road.

Buzz and Aubrey hopped off the bike and clamored up the hill to the closest crowd.  They weaved through clumps of individuals sharing near-death experiences and theorizing explanations regarding the incident as they headed toward the front, hoping to get a better view of the dam.

Rodriqa grabbed Buzz's arm and wrenched him around.  "Children have been asked to stay in the back."

Buzz smiled at her and waved his hand wildly.  Jordana stood next to her, biting her lip and still slightly shaken by the quake.

"Then why are you up front?" Buzz asked.

"Clearly, I am not a child," she replied as she popped her neck and held her chin high.

Buzz chuckled and then noticed something odd about Jordana.  "What happened to your glasses?"

Jordana brushed a lock of hair forward and stumbled to explain.

"Ummm, Captain Amnesia, did you just forget about what happened five minutes ago?" jeered Rodriqa.  "Her glasses were crushed in the rush to get out of the dam.  She was lucky to save them."

Jordana smiled gratefully at Rodriqa.

Aubrey noted Jordana's uneasiness.  "Are you okay?" he asked her.

Jordana nodded quickly and flashed him a brief smile.  "Thanks."

Buzz rolled his eyes and returned his thoughts to the developing scene, examining everything around him and searching for casualties of the event.

"Did the earthquake damage the dam?" Aubrey asked with concern.

"They're not sure, but they can't find anything obvious yet," replied Rodriqa, who was now distracted by the activity of the dam workers. "But my dad doesn't think there was an earthquake."

"Really?" questioned Buzz. "What does he think happened?"

Rodriqa shook her head and shrugged.

# *Footy Call*

Jordana pulled herself up the wooden stairs to the back porch of her house, dreading the impending conversation she would have with her father with each step. She pushed up on the black metal handrail, hoping to dampen the sound of her feet on the steps, but the cracked and peeling wooden planks under her refused to be silent.

The glass and metal wind chimes, hanging from the corner of the porch, danced lazily in the soft summer evening breeze and sang a soothing melody of tinks and dings, welcoming Jordana home. At the top of the stairs, carved oak rocking chairs tapped gently against the house's siding as she walked across the creaking floorboards. The chairs brought warm memories of summers past, when her father and grandfather would chisel furniture from the downed trees that fell that year during springtime thunderstorms. She wondered if those secure and carefree days would ever return.

She opened the flimsy screen storm door and lunged at the back door with all her weight. The main door was obviously a little too wide for its frame and required a great deal of effort for Jordana to open. She pushed against the door repeatedly. A muffled rubbing vibration shook the side of the house until the door finally gave way, eliminating any possibility for a discreet entrance.

Jordana and her father had just moved in a few weeks ago, but she couldn't avoid noticing how quickly this house reminded her of their old home. Her dad had spent most of his free time decorating every last corner to the almost exact configuration of their previous residence. The furniture in the living room, the stations of cabinets and appliances in the kitchen, the paintings and pictures on the walls; all were carefully placed in precise positions, perfecting the arrangement of the house in which she had grown up. Jordana was convinced her dad wanted them to feel like they had never left.

She dropped her school bag in the kitchen floor, stripped her rings from her fingers and rested them on the counter. She dumped her broken glasses in the trash and rummaged through several of the drawers around the sink. She found an identical pair with honey-colored lenses, slid them on her face, and pulled her hair back, composing herself for the imminent parental discussion.

She knew he had to be home. Mining blueprints, office memos and several legal affidavits layered the kitchen table. She was hopeful that the act of cooking dinner would be a reliable distraction.

"Jordana," bellowed a voice from the living room.

"Present," she replied stoically. She removed several small plastic containers from the refrigerator and unwrapped produce, which had ripened on top of the microwave.

"I was worried about you." Rugged and tall with features worn by years of heavy labor, Mr. Galilahi leaned against the doorway into the kitchen, eyeing his daughter cautiously. He knew he would have to choose his words thoughtfully. Crossing his arms and resting his head leisurely against the doorframe, his short, dark thick carpet of hair splayed against the wood. Several irregular craters carved out portions of flesh on his forehead, jaw and nose, leaving his previously handsome face grossly disfigured, with sagging eyes and a mouth that couldn't fully close. He spoke clearly, although each arduous articulation strained the muscles in his face. His left ear held mostly to its expected form, but his right ear consisted of only a few small flaps of skin jutting out from the side of his head, with scars stretching the intact portions into unnatural contortions.

"As you can see, I'm perfectly fine." Jordana turned around and raised her arms out to her waist, sarcastically presenting herself for inspection. She quickly returned to the kitchen sink, diligently rinsing off several carrots and a head of lettuce. "And no one else was harmed on the way home either," she added.

"Where have you been?" he asked, nonplussed by her mockery.

"I was with a friend." Jordana filled a pot with water and set it on the stove. She lit the fire underneath it, pulled a cutting knife from the drawer, and chopped the celery and carrots into bite-sized pieces.

Mr. Galilahi's eyes lightened. "Oh, wow, that's great, Jordana! You've made friends already, and it's not even been a week!" He walked over to the kitchen table and rolled up the blueprints to clear space for the cooking meal, his left hand exerting most of the force since his right hand had no thumb. "What's," he paused, unsure of the most appropriate pronoun to use, "*her* name?"

"Rodriqa," Jordana returned. "Her parents are engineers at the Lake Julian Dam. She showed me around, and we hung out there for a while. It's really close to the mine, so I figured it would be okay. Besides, I knew you would be busy at work, anyway."

Jordana's father shrugged off her suggestion of his lack of parental concern, but the comment's sting lingered. "Were you at the dam when the earthquake hit?"

"Yeah," Jordana replied nonchalantly, downplaying her response to hide how frightened she had been. "It seemed like a lot of concern for very little consequence."

"Yeah," agreed her father, grateful she hadn't been addled by the quake. "We didn't really feel much at the mine, which is odd, considering how close the dam is to the mine. Was anyone hurt?"

Jordana shrugged. "I don't think so, but it washed a lot of water out of the dam."

Her father pursed his lips and rubbed his jaw in thought.

Jordana changed the subject. "It sounded like there was a lot of commotion at the mine today before the earthquake. Did something happen?"

"Just some environmentalist rabble rousers inciting trouble again. No harm done. There's still some local dissent with the mine being so close to the dam, but for the most part, the municipal officials are on board."

Jordana mixed the diced vegetables and the prepared meats from the plastic containers into the boiling pot and stirred the brew gently. Her father returned to the subject at hand. "How was your day at school?"

"As good as any day in public can be expected," Jordana replied.

"Jordana-" her father chided.

"Can we *not* do this," said Jordana in a biting tone.

"I just want to know what happened," consoled her father.

"You know what happened. I'm sure you heard all the details from uncle."

Mr. Galilahi sighed deeply and searched for the right words to say. "Can't you just let me help you?"

She slammed down the mixing spoon and glared at her father. "*What* do you want me to say? Today was great! Most wonderful experience of *my* lifetime! Couldn't have been *any* better! Will *that* make you feel like a better father?" She yanked a couple of plates from the shelves and slammed the cabinet doors shut. Her dad walked over with his head lower than before, took the plates from her, and placed them on the table.

"I want to hear what happened to *you*." Her dad's voice softened. "You're the most important thing in the world to me, Jordana."

Jordana bit her lip and rubbed her cheeks under her glasses. "There's not a whole lot to say, really. It's not much different than what's happened before. Some kid at the end of my last class decided to be cute and took my glasses. I kept my eyes shut, like I'm supposed to, and quietly asked for them back. He continued to taunt me and passed the glasses to his brother to look through. So I asked a little more assertively and he refused. Then I simply insisted he return them."

"And how did that evolve into thirteen students being injured with one needing to been seen at the hospital?" Her dad forced his voice to remain even.

Jordana sensed the rising tension in her father's mood. "They were teasing me, okay?! So I did what I had to do to get my glasses back!"

"What did you say to him, Jordana?"

Jordana looked down at the floor. "I told him to give them back…or else."

Mr. Galilahi nodded, imagining the scene unfold in his mind. "So this kid, who had your glasses, fled for his life, I'm guessing."

"Yes," Jordana murmured. She sniffled and blinked back a few developing tears. "He was standing about ten feet from the door and there were a bunch of other kids leaving class at the same time. He was a big kid and he barreled through them, knocking most of them down, like a stampede." A single tear rolled down Jordana's cheek. "I couldn't do anything to stop it. It happened so quickly." Jordana quivered. Her father wrapped his arms around her, but she pushed him away.

"I'm turning out to be just like mom, except I'm worse," she whimpered.

"There was nothing wrong with your mother, and there's nothing wrong with you."

"Mom couldn't control how she affected people, and look how she ended up," Jordana insisted. "I don't want to be like that. It would be better if I just stayed inside, away from other people, so I'm not a danger. To others or to you."

Her father frowned. "You're not a danger to me."

"How many school conferences will you have to go to, how many different places will we have to move to, until you realize how much of a problem I am."

"But it's been almost six months now since anything has happened. You're making progress." Jordana glowered at her father. He thought twice about his words. "*We're* making progress."

Jordana set dinner on the table and sat in the chair closest to her. Her father followed her cue. Jordana tightened her lip and avoided her father's gaze.

Mr. Galilahi cleared his throat. "Look, it's not going to be easy, but you're much more aware of your," again he paused, searching for the best phrase, "influence on people than your mother ever was. It's going to take some more time. You need to be more patient with yourself."

"And while I'm being patient with myself, will everyone at school be patient? Will Uncle be patient?"

"I can deal with the school," her father asserted carefully, "and your uncle." Mr. Galilahi looked at her and grinned. "Besides, he's just jealous."

Jordana chuckled sardonically through as she lifted her spoon to her mouth. "Sure, he is."

The mood through dinner lightened as her father spoke about the day's mining operations and the various foibles of the men he was in charge of. Jordana listened half-heartedly, nodding and grinning at the appropriate times throughout the conversation, but her focus was scattered. Facing the next day weighed heavily on her mind. Her dad asked about her classes and teachers, and Jordana offered him more pleasant glimpses of her day. Occasionally, while they ate, she thought she might interject the odd 'hairy man' sighting she and Rodriqa had experienced on her way to the dam, but she decided her dad had dealt with enough weirdness for one day.

The dimming light of dusk withdrew from the valley while they talked. They cleaned up the table, and Jordana rinsed off the dishes and set them in the dishwasher. By the end of dinner, her dad's eyelids formed thin, fatigued slits, which he struggled to hold open.

Mr. Galilahi kissed Jordana on the forehead. "Get some rest. You deserve it," he told her. He walked out of the kitchen and up the stairs to his bedroom, closing the door behind him.

Jordana sighed with exhaustion. Her mind replayed the scene at the end of school, searching for a better outcome. She hoped her classmates would simply ignore her or simply not realize she was truly responsible.

She was grateful she had already finished her homework and decided to leave her school bag in the kitchen, since she wouldn't need it until morning. She locked the backdoor in the kitchen and drug herself to her bedroom, eager for the fleeing peace of sleep.

Music bathed Jordana's ears, more melodious than a lark, sweeter than a lullaby and softer than water bubbling over moss-covered rocks in a hillside stream. Her head rested against her crossed arms on a cloth-covered table. The music gently woke her, and she lifted her head, heavy with sleep, to find its source.

In front of her rose a darkened theater stage with two spotlights illuminating its middle and rear sections. Front and center stood her mother with a toddler's grin, her mouth moving to the music. Her long, dark shiny hair, shimmering in the spotlights' rays, hung like a curtain down the side of her face and neck. Her dark eyes danced in the spotlight as her tall, sleek undulating figure swayed to the music's beat.

Jordana's heart engorged with excitement. Time had stretched out into eternity since she had last seen her mother, whose death spiked a deep chasm in her heart and left her feeling desperately empty. Her mother was just as Jordana had remembered her on stage: a mesmerizing enchantress. But the music was not in her voice, and the song was missing words. Four men with unrecognizable faces stood behind her mother in an amber light, each playing a different instrument. But the music had no piano, drum, bass, or guitar in it.

Jordana leapt to her feet and raced to the stage. Her mother's tight embrace was the closest feeling of home she had ever known, and she couldn't keep herself from it any longer.

Jordana stopped abruptly, the orchestra pit deepening as she neared the front of the room. There weren't any musicians in the pit, and she couldn't see the bottom. She looked for a way around the pit, or across it, but the pit enclosed the entire base of the stage. She looked up to her mother, pleading for help. Her mother returned her gaze, but continued her smile and song, uninterrupted by her daughter's longing. Jordana tried to scream, but she was unable to make a sound that could rise over the din of the music. Her voice was low and rough, and she nearly choked at the attempt.

She scanned the space behind her, searching for help. A large nightclub full of people sat at endless rows of tables. Couples, large groups and a few singles were all facing the stage, enjoying the music, drinking and gregariously talking with one another.

Jordana walked over to the nearest table, where an elderly couple sat. The man had white hair, slicked back over his head, thick with oil. He wore a blue button-down shirt that was open a little too much at the top, exposing his ample chest hair. His brown tweed jacket was worn and shrunken, with a large amount of his blue sleeves exposed at the end of his forearms. He had obviously had more than his fair share of drink, as multiple empty glasses with melting ice claimed the table space in front of him. In contrast, his company was elegantly dressed, with a long red evening gown and perfectly coifed gray locks rolling down her shoulders.

Jordana stood directly in front of them, hoping to get their attention. They stared through her, hypnotized by the view from the stage. She stood next to the man and grabbed him around his wrist. The elderly gentleman laughed, but never looked at Jordana. His laughter loudened, and his mouth opened wider. The woman beside him also chuckled and was covering her mouth politely, seemingly unable to contain her amusement. Jordana backed away, confused by their reaction. She looked around and noticed everyone else in the club was laughing uncontrollably as well.

The music stopped.

Jordana turned abruptly toward the stage. The guitarist's hands were pulling her mother's hair and covering her mouth from behind her. The bass and drum players were lying on the stage with their arms wrapped tightly around each of her legs, anchoring her in place. The piano player clasped her wrists, pulling her toward the orchestra pit.

Jordana raced to the edge of the pit. *No, not again!* She thought to herself, *this cannot be happening again*! She tightened her gut with all of her strength to scream, but only a murmur squeaked out, "Please, no!"

A blast of searing heat blew up from the orchestra pit, forcing Jordana backwards. Orange embers spun in the currents of the heated plume as it rose. She tried to move forward to the edge of the pit, but each attempt burned her skin and stung her eyes and nose, repelling her each time.

More than twenty black humanoid figures crawled out of the pit stage-side. Each one had long talons extending from their reptilian arms and legs. Their heads were small and pointed with simmering yellow eyes, and their bodies were twisted and missing large portions of their torsos, as if they had been carved out of a larger whole. Jordana thought she could almost see through some of them, like shadows, but their darkness absorbed most of the light onstage.

Swiftly the dark figures overran the stage. Three of them encircled the guitarist and lifted him off his feet. The guitarist flailed to free himself, but the relentless grip of the figures only anchored him more tautly, the more he struggled. They drug him to the edge of the orchestra pit. He freed one of his arms and reached for Jordana's mother, wrenching his elbow around her neck pulling her to the side of the pit. She bellowed a piercing scream. Struggling to free herself, she backed away to the middle of the stage. The guitarist lost his hold and was drug into the pit by the figures, disappearing instantly into the darkness.

One by one the accompanists were overcome by the dark beasts. Each struggled against their captors, but their fear and fight only made the figures' hold stronger.

Jordana's mother stood alone center stage. Jordana again yelled for her mother, but her throat refused to open. For the first time Jordana could hear her mother speak. Her mother looked at her serenely and said, "Look inside." Slowly, she mouthed the words again.

A single black figure, larger than the rest, leapt from the pit and faced her mother, blocking Jordana's view of her. Her mother screamed, and then her cry ended abruptly.

Jordana turned around and saw everyone in the nightclub in a fit of uproarious laughter. She searched for a single gaze that would meet hers, but they all stared at the stage. She waved her arms, pleading for help from anybody. No one would look at her.

She turned back toward the stage and watched the black figure carry her mother down into the pit on its bony back. Her body was motionless, her eyes closed and dark. Jordana wept. She knelt down at the edge of the pit, enduring the waves of blistering, ash-laden air. She reached helplessly for her mother. Jordana's mother and her dark captor evaporated into the darkness below.

Jordana stood up and covered her face. She sobbed uncontrollably, the grief of losing her mother again tearing her heart apart. Out of the corner of her eye, she saw the man in the brown tweed jacket stand up. He was no longer laughing, but now his face was cold and still like stone. He stood up and walked forward. Jordana pivoted toward the tables, and she saw everyone in the nightclub stand upright and walk deliberately in her direction.

The elderly gentleman strode passed her. Jordana edged cautiously away from him. He stepped off the edge of he pit and plummeted into the darkness. Jordana's stomach dropped, and she covered her mouth in disbelief.

A crushing pressure grasped her ankles. She looked down at her feet and long black claws had encircled both her calves, levering her backwards. She tried to right herself and catch her balance. The dark creature was too strong. She leaned forward, but it was too late. She fell into the pit.

Jordana thrashed awake in her bed, her sweat-soaked sheets wrapped fit-fully around her, like a damp cocoon. It took her a few moments to shake the strength of her dream. The vision of her suffering mother draped a haze of remorse and longing over her. She scanned her bedroom as her consciousness settled, looking for pieces of reality for her mind to cling to. She focused on her alarm clock, which, like an anchor, drew her back to the present. The clock glowed a scarlet

# 2:48

Illuminated by the fiery red glow of her clock, Jordana grabbed her mother's picture on her bedside table. She pulled the picture close to her face, studying her mother's features. Her chest pounded painfully as she relived the dream over and over in her mind, the memory of her loss ripe in her heart again. She had been so elated to see her mother, only to have her taken away so quickly. She laid the picture face down on the bed and sat up, too awake to sleep.

A thin line of darkness outlined the opening edge of her bedroom door. She felt certain she had closed it tightly before she lay down, desperate as she was for privacy. She was worried she had disturbed her father, but she knew his hearing had been poor since the mining accident. *Perhaps I screamed during my dream*, she thought to herself. Jordana's thoughts shifted. *I don't need to be giving him reasons to want to put me away*, she chided herself.

She raised herself out of bed, flitted to the door and closed it, examining it for instability. *After all, the house is old and the foundation is probably settling*, she considered. The bedroom door shut easily and held its position without strain. She decided it was unlikely the door had opened from faulty mechanics.

She reopened the door slowly and peered into the hall at her father's bed-room door. It was closed as well, and there was no sign of recent movement upstairs. Unconvinced, she wanted further proof of her father's slumber. She would do anything to avoid another 'what's going on' conversation in the morning. She mustered all her grace and tip-toed carefully toward her father's bedroom. She leaned in and listened intently. Deep rumbling snores echoed on the far side of the door. Her anxiety drained away, and she sighed deeply in relief. If he had been awakened by her dreaming, hopefully he would not remember it in the morning.

She turned slowly to retrace her steps in the hallway. Her hair danced around her neck, tossed in a breeze that floated up the stairs. She stopped, unsettled by the cool nighttime air that brushed against her face. Jordana rum-maged quickly through her memory of the evening's events. She couldn't recall leaving any windows open before heading to bed, and she and her father had rarely opened the windows, since none of them were protected by screens.

Dread flooded back into her gut. *Dad has been awake and was downstairs*, she decided ruefully. She rubbed her eyes and debated whether or not to investigate. The crisp wind raised the fine hairs on her arms and she was too afraid to ignore it.

Jordana leaned over the railing and hunted for the open window. Jordana could see most of the living room from upstairs, but all of the visible windows appeared to be firmly flush to the bottom of their sills. Shadows from the tree limbs outside twitched in the streams of streetlights, which beamed onto the slats of the hardwoods like skeletal fingers playing a ghostly tune on a floor-sized piano. Small tinges of panic pinched her spine. She concentrated on her desire to know how much her dad knew about her nightmare.

Turning on the lights was her first instinct, but she was afraid to wake her father. She decided to wait until she was downstairs. Jordana forced herself to place her right foot on the next step down. If she focused more on simple concrete thoughts, such as her quiet motion down the stairs, she could control other irrational, imaginary thoughts more easily. So she hoped.

Her toes curled in protest as she fixed her left foot on the step below her right foot. *Baby steps*, she told herself.

She plodded silently down the stairs, arriving at the bottom with a sigh of relief. *No injuries, no noise, I'm set*, she thought, rallying her sensibilities. She cupped her hand over the light switch and victoriously flipped it to the 'on' position.

Nothing happened.

She tried again. No lights, no flicker of a bulb's final demise, no static pulse in the switch plate.

She furiously flicked the tiny plastic arm up and down, but again there was no response.

She frowned as her anxiety heightened. The power was still working upstairs; her alarm clock was alight. And maybe one bulb in the living room had burned out, but several at once would be unusual, unless there was an electrical surge. *That's it! The breaker*, she reminded herself, relaxing again. A hypothesis formed in her head, fighting to explain all the oddities' collusion. A brief thunderstorm must have tripped part of the breaker and broken a piece of one of the old windows. That theory satisfied both her need to keep her dad asleep and her fear of a malevolent intruder.

The cool air blew with a renewed chill. Suddenly, a noxious invisible blast slapped her in the face. A sensory-searing stench of odors ransacked her nose, reflexively halting her breathing and inciting a wretch that squeezed up from her stomach. She tasted and smelled what in her mind could only be described as a combination of burning landfill and boiling formaldehyde. Tears pooled in her lids as the putrid aroma stung her eyes. Lightheaded from the nausea and lack of air, she remembered to breathe, this time through her mouth.

The porch door creaked as it swung, and Jordana could hear the wind rush into the house. She covered her face with her hands. *Certainly a burglar couldn't stand the stench*, she thought. She rounded the corner of the kitchen to close the door as quickly as possible.

Jordana's muscles contracted in mid-stride, frozen with terror. Between her and the outside stood the most massive man she had ever seen. His head was the size of a normal man's chest, and the top of his scalp brushed against the ceiling, even though he stooped over. He was looking down at the kitchen table with his broad shoulders hanging forward, their width nearly matching the table's length. He had unrolled the mining blueprints and held them open on the table with his catcher's mitt-sized hands.

Jordana's entry had not startled the man, which allowed her more time to study him while she stood stiff with panic. His true height was even more frightening, as she realized she was eye-level to his waist. From head to toe he was covered in soft, downy hair, but unlike an animal's coat, it gave the man more of a fuzzy than a furry appearance. The kitchen door stood fully open, resting along the edge of the countertop. As the nighttime air floated by him, his fur didn't move, and he continued peering at the documents below him.

Jordana hoped to escape while the man's attention remained focused on the table. She slid her front foot backwards as silently as possible. The man's massive head turned, and deep-set red eyes fixed on Jordana. Her heart exploded with alarm. A moment masquerading as an eternity passed, and neither person moved. Jordana fought the need to close her eyes and remove herself from her surroundings, and instead forced herself to gaze directly at the man. Then familiarity walloped her mind with the sudden realization that she had seen this same man earlier in the day, on the hillside between the mine and the dam. The man slowly angled his head to the side, as if examining her from a different point of view, resembling a dog trying to understand an owner's query. He seemed to recognize Jordana. He took a small step toward her.

Jordana's trance broke. She backed up, rounded the corner and raced up the stairs with all her might, her calves burning with the rapid change in her step. Halfway up, she could feel her lungs expanding freely. She screamed with her diaphragm's full force.

She turned right into her bedroom. Slamming the bedroom door behind her, Jordana crawled over her bed to her window. She clawed at the rusty latch, but it would only move a few millimeters with each of her attempts to slide it over. She hammered against it with her fist, and it jerked open as it unlocked. Jordana slid the window up with her hands against the pane and placed her foot on the ledge outside. She hesitated at the twelve-foot drop to the ground below, but there was no other route of escape. She had to jump.

"JORDANA!"

The words shocked her out of her frenzy. Her father stood in the doorway and turned on the lights. Jordana blinked at the brightness.

"Jordana?! What's going on?" her father demanded.

Jordana breathed in and out at an exhausting pace, her lungs trying to recover from her sprint upstairs. She trembled uncontrollably as she replayed the downstairs events in her mind.

"There's someone...downstairs." The words eked out, barely audible.

"In the house?!"

Jordana nodded. "In the kitchen."

Mr. Galilahi turned from her bedroom doorway and disappeared into his room. Jordana could hear him rummaging recklessly through his chest of drawers. She walked cautiously to the hallway, concerned about her father's safety now as well as her own.

Her father rushed down the stairway, revolver in hand, turning on all the light switches he passed on the way. The lights and lamps brightened effortlessly. Jordana was puzzled at the switch's obedience. She slowly walked down the stairs, anxiously anticipating a scuffle, or worse, a gunshot. She heard her father open and close the kitchen door without any sounds of a fight.

"Jordana?!" He called for her just as she peered around the corner into the kitchen. The kitchen was well lit, and her father walked in circles searching for evidence of intruder.

"My blueprints? Where are they?" Mr. Galilahi asked.

Jordana shrugged as she trembled. Her father walked over to her and hugged her tightly, careful to keep the gun an arm's distance from her. "Are you okay?" he asked.

Jordana looked down at herself, unable to trust her own senses. "I think so," she muttered.

Her father walked back to the kitchen table and examined the floor closely. He opened the kitchen door again and walked onto the porch. "My blueprints are gone, and so is one of the chairs on the porch." He squatted down and looked under the table. "Did you take my blueprints upstairs?"

"No," Jordana uttered in confusion. She walked over to the sink and ran her fingers along the countertop. "My rings...."

"Where are they?" he asked.

Jordana shook her head. "They're gone."

"Who was here?" demanded her father. "And what is that smell?"

Jordana stared at him with a dumbfounded expression. She didn't know what to say. Her dad lifted the phone from the receiver and dialed 9-1-1. "I need you to tell me what happened!" His tone was insistent.

A mechanical, feminine voice came from the receiver. "9-1-1. What is your emergency?"

Jordana strengthened her jaw. "Dad...it was a Tsul'kalu."

Her father hung up the phone.

# *Homework Intervention*

**Friday.**

Aubrey rushed for the closing door. He planted his hand in the middle of the cold metal, bracing it open. He slipped through the crack, and Mr. Vandereff's mustache twisted as he scowled at him. Aubrey lowered his head and raced toward his seat in the back.

The room was eerily quiet. He sat down and leaned over to say hello to Jordana, but her curtain of black hair blocked her face.

Aubrey pulled out his notebook and glanced around the room. Everyone had their heads down. He looked twice at Benny. Did he have a black eye?

"Pretty quiet for a Friday in first period," commented Mr. Vandereff sarcastically. "That must mean your weekly element assignments are due!" An air of glee wafted through his tone. No one responded to his exaggerated joy, so he dropped his smile. "Okay, pass them forward."

Aubrey pulled his folder out of his book bag, watching Jordana out of the corner of his eye. She gathered the pages of her homework together and handed it to the student in front of her. Her face never escaped the cover of her hair.

"I searched the internet for 'Circle of Circles' for over two hours last night. I couldn't find anything," whispered Buzz in a rankled vent.

Aubrey glanced at Buzz, nodded briefly and then returned to handing in his homework.

"Did you use it?" queried Buzz.

"Huh," grunted Aubrey, intentionally daft.

"The candlepen!" Buzz rocked in his seat, vying for Aubrey's attention. Aubrey reorganized his notebook.

"Well, did you?" Buzz insisted.

Aubrey shrugged and rolled his eyes. "Yeah, I guess so."

"Awesome," hummed Buzz jovially over the shuffle of papers throughout the classroom.

"But I don't think I'm gonna say anything about it," countered Aubrey.

"You're just getting cold feet. You did the right thing."

"Just the same, I think it's best if I lie low for a while."

Buzz sneered at Aubrey. Buzz's hand shot straight into the air, and he waved it back and forth.

Aubrey glowered at him. "Don't!"

Mr. Vandereff cradled the stacks of homework in his arm, turning pages right side up as he collected the pile. Buzz cleared his throat boisterously. Mr. Vandereff looked up and furrowed his brow at his most overly eager student. "How can I help you, Mr. Reiselstein?"

Buzz stood up and interlaced his fingers pedantically around his belly. "Sir, I apologize for the interruption, but I fear there is something that must be brought to your attention...*immediately*."

Mr. Vandereff paused impatiently. "Please continue, if it is that important." Scattered chuckles echoed throughout the room.

Buzz took a dramatic step forward. "A crime has been committed, and I feel it is my duty to expose the perpetrators."

Jordana looked worriedly up at Buzz. She bit her lip and listened intently.

"Buzz, sit down," shouted Aubrey under his breath.

Buzz took another step toward the front and continued. "Three members of our student body...nay...our very own Physical Sciences class have transgressed the Honor Code, and I must bring light to this incalculable offense in order to protect the sanctity and justice nurtured by this institution of learning."

Mr. Vandereff sighed and rested the stack of homework on the lab bench behind him. "Make your point, but make it brief."

Buzz nodded thoughtfully, closed his eyes and focused his composure. "There are three knowledge charlatans in this class." The other students murmured amongst themselves in bewilderment.

"Buzz, please!" pleaded Aubrey.

"What?" questioned Mr. Vandereff harshly.

"Cheaters," reiterated Buzz. "Plagiarists...swindling shysters who would abscond the due diligence of another to ease their own burden and force the lowly to suffer!"

Magnos, Lenny and Benny turned over their shoulders and scowled at Buzz. Magnos balled up his fist and rubbed it into his chin

"Those are pretty serious accusations, Mr. Reiselstein. I hope you can prove your allegation."

Buzz chortled. "Proof will present itself in due time. In that stack of assignments, there are four texts that are the work of a single individual."

"So three of them wrongfully belong to other students," replied Mr. Vandereff.

"Yes," charged Buzz with the flare of a courtroom prosecutor.

"And which students are responsible for this supposed infraction?"

The three bullies growled quietly at Buzz.

"They are...." Buzz took a deep breath and blurted out the names in quick succession. "Magnos Strumgarten, Benjamin Van Zenny, and Leonard Van Zenny."

Magnos jumped out of his desk and loomed over the class. His nostrils flared as his chest heaved. He mouthed 'You're dead' silently at Buzz and faced Mr. Vandereff indignantly. "No way!" yelled Magnos. "I worked hard on my assignment!"

Aubrey laid his head down on his desk in defeat and covered his ears.

"Mr. Reiselstein, the ball of proof is now in your court," said Mr. Vandereff.

Buzz marched up to the lab bench at the front. He pointed to the pile of homework. "May I?"

Mr. Vandereff relented and took a step back, raising his hands in accession.

Buzz sifted through the pages and picked out what he was looking for. He gave the alleged forged homework to his teacher.

Mr. Vandereff looked at Buzz quizzically.

"Hold them up to the light, and you will know the truth," Buzz asserted.

Mr. Vandereff lifted the papers one by one up to the window, scrutinizing each page with a focused eye. His eyes widened and he held the papers closer to his face. He saw something, which he didn't expect. Carefully, he followed unseen words across the page. Buzz paced pensively up the aisle of desks, awaiting his perusal.

Mr. Vandereff dropped his hand to his side. "This is not proof," he barked.

"Can you read the hidden writing?" patronized Buzz.

"I believe you're referring to the translucent writing scrawled across the ink letters," Mr. Vandereff replied.

Buzz nodded decisively.

"Then yes. I can read it."

"What does it say?"

Mr. Vandereff raised the homework up to the light and flipped through them. "*FREE ME*...on every single page."

Aubrey gasped and covered his mouth. Buzz's jaw dropped to his chest. The class erupted in laughter.

Buzz raced back up to the lab bench and ripped the homework out of Mr. Vandereff's hand. He sifted through the pages holding each one up to the light, searching for the amateur watermark. The lucent writing read just as his teacher had said.

"Satisfied?" Mr. Vandereff asked, reaching for the assignments.

Buzz nodded and scurried back to his seat.

"Now if we're down with the early morning antics, I would like to continue with some actual teaching," grumbled Mr. Vandereff.

Magnos barreled toward Buzz with fists held high. Buzz whimpered and wrapped his arms around his head to protect himself.

"Mr. Strumgarten, take your seat, or there will be no football for you tonight," ordered Mr. Vandereff.

Magnos stopped suddenly and huffed at Buzz. He walked back over to his seat, sat down, and folded his arms.

"Let's talk about your weekly assignment due next Friday," addressed Mr. Vandereff.

Buzz tapped Aubrey on his shoulder and frowned at him. "Why did you write that on their homework?"

Aubrey raised his head and moaned, "*I* didn't!"

# Friday Night Football Strife

Aubrey pedaled home from school slowly. Traffic was messier than usual, since it was Friday afternoon, and his mind wandered away from the road as he mulled over his repeated bad luck at school.

Magnos, Benny and Lenny had taken every opportunity both during lunch and between classes to taunt him with tales of unspeakable retribution. Not to mention that he had already promised them he would complete all their weekly assignments for Physical Sciences for the rest of the year, hoping for some small amount of clemency. Unfortunately, his graciousness only opened the door for more torment.

He pulled into his driveway on Dalton Circle and rounded the side of his house. Something was different. He unsnapped his helmet, locked his bike against the lattice on the side of the back porch, and walked back toward the front of the living room. Two long planters full of spiky, germinating sprouts lined the front banisters. Had his mother been outside gardening today?

Aubrey bumbled through the front door, carelessly loosening his book bag, and it slammed to the floor. Aubrey took a deep whiff, and a soothing wave of deliciousness washed over him. The entire downstairs swarmed with smells of melting chocolate and roasting almonds.

His father sat at the opposite end of the dining room table, hidden behind his newspaper. **NO FAULT FOUND FOR SUSPECTED EARTH-QUAKE** entitled the top of the front page.

Gooey mounds of nut-laden chocolate rested on top of the table in a silver platter. Steam rose from their curlycue tops, and their sumptuous bases were dusted with powered sugar.

"What are these?" Aubrey asked.

Mr. Taylor folded his paper and sized up his son. "A woman from down the street, Magnolia Thistlewood, brought these by today. She said she knew you were having a rough week and wanted to cheer you up. She called them chocolate drip cookies…or some such nonsense. She also brought your mom two planters full of begonias. Very thoughtful," he said, but then mused about his encounter, "yet kinda odd."

Aubrey nodded in complete agreement. His mouth watered at the culinary delights, but his mind fearfully restrained him.

"Worn out by your first week?" his dad asked, less than sympathetically.

Aubrey shook his head and carefully eyed the morsels on the table.

"Time to be a man, Aub. It only gets worse from here," said Mr. Taylor. Aubrey looked at his feet, avoiding his father's stare. In some ways he knew his dad was right, but Aubrey wasn't ready to take that step. Mr. Taylor unfurled his paper and disappeared within its pages.

A loud knock rapped repeatedly at the door.

"Get that, will ya," mumbled Mr. Taylor. Aubrey leaned forward and plodded for the door.

He cracked it open. "Whatchya up to?" asked Rodriqa on the other side with a shrewd smile. Jordana stood beside her with her eyes fixed on the ground.

"I just got home," replied Aubrey.

"Jordana and I are heading to the football game. Wanna come? I called Buzz. He's gonna meet us there."

Aubrey rubbed the back of his neck dejectedly. "I'm tired. I think I just want to stay home and get started on homework."

"Ahhh," protested Rodriqa. "You should come with us. It'll be fun."

"I don't know," languished Aubrey.

"Aubrey," grunted Mr. Taylor. "You should go and support your brother. It's his last year of high school football."

Jordana glanced up and smiled at Aubrey meekly. Aubrey's gut tingled with a wince of hopeful joy.

"Okay," he relented.


"Thanks for driving us, Mrs. Auerbach," Jordana said as she slid out of the back seat of the car. Aubrey smiled at Mrs. Auerbach, and she waved kindly back to him.

"I'll be back in a couple hours to pick you all up," offered Mrs. Auerbach.

"Thanks, mom," replied Rodriqa, closing the door.

Rowdy cheers erupted from the Lake Julian High football stadium on the opposite of the school's expansive parking lot. Aubrey, Jordana and Rodriqa scurried around the slow, but steady traffic toward the jumbled beat of brass and percussion, spilling out of the stands.

"Hurry up...the game has already started," urged Rodriqa as they dashed through the lot. They wove between tailgaters and late-comers, hurrying toward the thinning crowd that was piling at the last minute into the front gate.

Buzz stood at the ticket counter with arms crossed, tapping his foot.

"You're late," he chided as his three friends walked up to him.

"Don't blame me," Rodriqa retorted. "I'm not the one with the glamour glitch."

Buzz glared at Aubrey. Aubrey shrugged apologetically. "I needed time to get ready."

The four kids bought their tickets at the gate and pushed through the fork-tined turnstile at the entrance. Buzz made a beeline for the concessions stand to the left where five lines of students, parents and small children clumped up against a small wooden counter.

"Do you really need to eat right now?" cajoled Rodriqa.

"I'm hungry," protested Buzz.

"Fine. We'll save you a seat."

Aubrey, Rodriqa and Jordana filed into the stadium among the massing mob of spectators. Above, the orange-tinted sky of dwindling daylight cast a wide shadow on the lush green field. Below, a ring of huddled blue and gray Lake Julian football players circled in front of the cheerleaders, who clapped and tumbled at the track's edge, rallying the crowd. The green and yellow Chimney Falls team lined up at their twenty-five yard line with the ball.

"Wow…it's a packed house," remarked Rodriqa, as she spun and gawked at the congregation of high school football fanatics filling the bleachers.

"No kidding," agreed Aubrey. The three kids scanned the stadium for a seat. Aubrey glanced across the field. The visitors' stands were awash with yellow and green.

"I see a free bench," said Jordana. She pointed to a vacant spot high up to their left.

Rodriqa sighed. "Behind the marching band, it is."

The three friends climbed a thin set of concrete steps to the top and walked across the landing in front of the press box. They careened though cliques of students and dodged elementary kids playing tag. Jordana glanced twice at a familiar blackened eye. Benny peered through a circle of students, narrowing his eyes as he glowered at her. He murmured loudly to Lenny next to him. Everyone in the circle turned and glared at Jordana. She turned away, pushed up her glasses and followed quickly after Aubrey.

Rodriqa, Aubrey, and Jordana turned past the band boosters section and marched up a set of rickety bleacher stairs to the back of the stadium. Hobbling over fans and ducking the swaying golden bells of tubas and baritones, they climbed toward a patch of empty seats. Aubrey sat down, relieved to have made it past the squirming obstacle course of legs and metal. The girl sitting in the bleacher in front of him swiveled awkwardly around in her blue and gray band uniform and peered at Aubrey.

"Howdy, Aubrey," she greeted him gleefully.

"Hey, May," replied Aubrey. May O'Klammer grinned happily at him, as her thick arms clutched her euphonium. May was the only other redhead he'd ever known who had more freckles that he did. Her wiry hair, stuffed under her cylindrical hat, twirled frantically in every direction, trying to escape its constricting captor.

"How've you been?" she asked, leaning backwards into Aubrey's personal space with her round, chubby face and torso.

He straightened his knees to keep her at a distance. "The usual," he remarked glibly.

"Where's Buzz?" she asked eagerly.

"Oh, he's coming," replied Aubrey with a smile.

"Hey, Aubrey, your best friend is on the field," choked Rodriqa with a chuckle, while she stood up and pointed down the stands.

"Really?" Aubrey replied. He thought Buzz had won a prize or got lost. He stood up and scanned the stadium. The ominous number '33' caught his eye.

Magnos had his arms outstretched, blocking two Chimney Falls football players at once in his generous wingspan. Aubrey dropped in his seat and huffed angrily at Rodriqa's jibe.

**"Turn over...Lake Julian ball!"** shouted the announcer over the loud speakers. The Lake Julian stands roared. Every member of the marching band set their instruments to their lips, as Gerty Noriega, the drum major, jumped up on her box at the bottom of the stands and clapped time. The school fight song blared across the stadium. Aubrey cupped his hands around his ears, protecting them from the blasts of May's overpowered embouchure, resonating in every direction. A pack of blue and gray football players rushed the sidelines and exchanged defense for offense, but Magnos stayed on the field. Coach Kaniffy slapped his players' helmets with praise as they knelt down in front of the track, listening for the next plan of strategy. Cheerleaders bounced and flipped in triumph. A student, adorned in a beluga whale costume, rocked jeeringly back and forth at his opponent mascot, the Chimney Falls Chimney Sweep. The velour whale punched and clapped his pectoral fins together, while pretending to spew water out of his spout at the visitors' side.

Aubrey glanced up at the scoreboard. Zeroes lit both competitors' point totals. Three minutes and thirty seconds remained in the second quarter. The green LED football glowed under the 'Home' side of the board, and '1st & 10' flashed at the bottom.


Ten blue and gray-jersied Lake Julian football players raced toward the middle of the field at the forty-yard line. They filed into their positions, and Gaetan, with a blue number '2' emblazoned on his chest, handed the football to his center, Treywick Compton. A wall of hulking, Chimney Falls linemen hunkered down and growled across the line of scrimmage. Compton leaned forward and clutched the ball against the grass.

Gaetan readied his hands and shouted down both lines. "Sunshine, 14, 37...hike!"

Compton snapped the ball to Gaetan, who stepping backwards glimpsed his wide receivers, as rows of linemen slammed into each with a thunderous clap of colliding shoulder pads.       Gaetan swiveled and weaved, searching for a hole. Suddenly, he stiffened, pulling the football to his chest. A massive yellow '55' was barreling toward him with lightning speed from his left side. Gaetan closed his eyes, preparing for the split-second impact.

A quick wind breezed passed Gaetan's arm, and the ground shuddered in front of him. Gaetan peeked through squinty lids. Number '33' had pancaked '55' helplessly to the field, with his arms and legs flailing underneath the hefty fullback.

"Nice job, Magnos!" yelled Gaetan. He bobbed and turned through another potential sack and tossed the ball to his halfback a few yards downfield.

The scoreboard flashed '2ⁿᵈ & 7.'

The scoreboard flashed '2**nd** & 7.'

The Lake Julian crowd clamored raucously.

"Who's winning?" shouted a voice across the stands. The entire row glanced to their left. Buzz clung to a box of popcorn, two hot dogs, a bag of candy and a bladder-buster-sized soft drink as he climbed clumsily over Lake Julian fans to reach his friends.

Rodriqa cupped her forehead and shook her head.

Jordana nudged Aubrey. "Is he always so forthright?"

Aubrey snorted. "Always."

Buzz sat down next to Aubrey and quickly lost his smile. "Did we have to sit behind her?" groaned Buzz softly.

May stopped playing and turned around quickly before the band's peppy jazz number was over. A crooked toothed smile creased her face from chin to nose. She reached up and yanked Buzz down to her. His head banged against the bell of her euphonium, and a sonorous ring hummed down the stands.

"Ouch!" Buzz squealed, as he rubbed the growing bump on his forehead.

"Sorry," replied May gleefully. "I was just so excited to see you, I couldn't help myself."

May O'Klammer had stalked Buzz romantically since fourth grade, and her intentions had never been less than overt.

"I missed you this summer," she told him, as she twirled a wiry sprig of her hair. "I thought about you every day."

"That's nice," Buzz grunted tersely. He shoved a hot dog in his mouth so he wouldn't be able to speak. Aubrey felt a little nauseated as he watched the coarse, chubby May flirt with his equally stout best friend.

May readjusted herself on the bleacher so she could speak with Buzz more easily. "So I was thinking…we should go to the Homecoming Dance together this year."

Buzz inhaled a piece of hot dog in shock. He choked and sputtered, and he knocked over his tub of popcorn as he jostled about. Aubrey righted the half-empty box and kicked the dirty kernels under the bleachers.

Buzz coughed and gagged, and Aubrey giggled at him. Suddenly, Buzz turned red and white, like a turnip, and he went silent. May dropped her instrument and shook Buzz by the shoulders. Aubrey beat him on the back vigorously and lifted his arm high above his head. Buzz gasped, and a hunk of half-eaten frank plopped out of Buzz's throat into the wide mouth of his soft drink.

Aubrey cringed as droplets of soda splashed against his jeans. "I think Buzz is allergic to dances," said Aubrey. May scowled at him.


Gaetan jerked Magnos to his feet. Magnos victoriously high-fived and exploded knuckles with several other teammates, taking his time to return to his position. The other players filtered between one another across the field and lined up. Compton leaned forward, and Gaetan readied his stance.

"49, Chicken bog, 23, hike!"

Gaetan pulled back with the ball. The linemen crashed and wrestled for advantage. The halfback rushed through a hole in the defense. Gaetan passed the ball to the halfback, who reached up to catch it. Deviating from his route, Magnos picked it out of the air and leaped over two tumbling linebackers. He switch-backed between another pair of tussling lineman, and suddenly Magnos was staring at the sky. His back pounded the field, and the ball spilled across the grass. A scrum of players dove for the free football. Hands, helmets and feet jutted and rolled in a mangled mess of bodies as each player scurried for control.

The referees blew their whistles and waved their arms, signaling the end of play. One by one the umpire ripped the kids off one another. At the bottom of the pile, Compton grappled the ball between his knees and chest in the fetal position.

Magnos jumped up to his feet. Gaetan grabbed his mask and shook it. "Mag...Know you're route! That was the halfback's ball! You're a fullback! Don't be a hero!"

**"Fumble by Strumgarten! Lake Julian ball!"** blared the announcer over the spectators' din.

Standing behind Gaetan, Number '55' was grinning arrogantly. Magnos scowled vengefully in reply. Number '55' turned around and walked back to his position. For the first time Magnos could see the name of his opponent on the back of his jersey.

"Hey, Wastokowski!" shouted Magnos. "Hit me again and see what happens!"

"Go back to the flag football league where you belong, you overgrown baby," jeered Wastokowski over his shoulder.

Magnos clenched his fists and stormed toward Wastokowski.

"Strumgarten!" yelled Gaetan. "Get back here!"

"Magnos, get in position!" ordered Compton.

Magnos stopped and slowly stomped to back to his place on the field.

The scoreboard flashed '3rd & 7.' Half of the Lake Julian fans groaned. The other half cheered. Buzz coughed hoarsely as he continued to clear his throat. May had offered him her water bottle, but he quickly refused.

Aubrey watched as a police car slowly drove up to the wire fence outside the end zone. Ned and Fred Kluggard stepped out of the car in full dress uniform. The tall lanky Fred strutted toward the fence with authority and leaned against the fence to watch the game. Ned waddled up behind him, pulling his leather belt over the edge of his gut.

The bushy-haired janitor walked from behind the stadium and stood next to the officers. They seemed to be talking to one another in harsh tones with quippy gestures. A twinge of worry forced Aubrey to watch them more intently.

"That's odd," he muttered.

"Yeah," agreed Buzz as he grabbed a fist full of popcorn and munched on it out of his palm. "I can't believe Coach Kaniffy is putting up with Magnos' foolishness."

"No." Aubrey shook his head and leaned his head toward the end zone. "That."

Buzz looked in the direction Aubrey was staring and furrowed his brow. "I wonder what they're saying...."


The janitor brushed the dirt off the front of his forest green, industrially-designed uniform and coughed as the floating debris formed a cloud in his face.

Fred Kluggard looked at him briefly and sneered with contempt.

"What are you fellers up to?" asked the janitor, as he leaned next to Fred on the fence.

Fred shook his head and continued watching the players line up on the field. "Just watchin' the game, gramps."

The janitor nodded and swiveled his head slowly at the sky. "Nice night for it," he commented peacefully.

Ned whispered to Fred, and Fred chortled. "Don't you have something you need to clean up, old man?"

The janitor grinned mischievously at Fred. "Why do you think I'm here?"

Fred and Ned looked curiously at each other.

The janitor pulled an oily rag from his back pocket and polished the glass plate on his watch. "Seems like you boys have gotten yourselves wrapped up in a bit of trouble."

"We're the law," touted Fred. "If we're involved...it ain't trouble. And if it is trouble, then we'll haul it to jail."

Ned elbowed Fred, giggling in agreement.

"Guess you've been slackin' off on the job, then," the janitor chomped back.

"Move along, ya crazy ol' loon," charged Fred angrily.

The janitor sighed and replaced the rag to its rightful place. He crossed his arms and cleared his throat. "You've only got one soul, son. You might not want to sell it off so early."

Fred pulled out his nightstick. "And you've only got one nose. You should keep it out of other people's business!"

"74, 96, Sailor Raver, hike!"

Compton snapped the ball to Gaetan. Gaetan rolled out around the edge of the linemen. The Chimney Falls safeties surged after Gaetan. Magnos barreled in front of Gaetan and knocked one safety to the ground. Magnos ducked two battling linemen and ran toward the other safety. He stopped suddenly, and then made a ninety-degree turn back toward the line.

Gaetan lobbed the ball to his receiver a few yards away. Gaetan was sacked at the same time the receiver was pummeled to the ground. Magnos ran up behind Number '55' and blind-sided him so hard his helmet popped off. Wastokowski moaned. Magnos pushed himself up and leered over him.

"Wastokowski...shouldn't your name be WASTE-okowsy?" Magnos chuckled and walked back toward the new line of scrimmage.

"No more games, Strumgarten," chastised Gaetan. "Either follow the play or sit on the sideline!"

Magnos shrugged with disinterest. He had claimed his revenge.

Both crowds hollered and moaned loudly. The Chimney Falls fans cried foul at Magnos' roughhousing. Some of the Lake Julian fans did too, but mostly they were jeering childish replies at the visitors' whining.

Aubrey turned his head toward the opposite end zone. Old Widow Wizenblatt sauntered down the lanes of track from the concession stand. Aubrey's stomach quivered with unease. Something wasn't right.

The scoreboard flashed '4th & 2.'

"Coach Kaniffy says to go for the throat," ordered Gaetan.

The players lined up on the field amidst the noisy ruckus from the fans. The referee placed the football on the line of scrimmage, and Compton leaned over and gripped it. Gaetan walked up behind Compton and waved his arms like a flapping bird to quiet the stands. The rest of the players readied themselves.

The barraging banter slowly died down, except for an occasional yelp from the visitor's side. Gaetan angled his hands under the center.

A gut-wrenching screamed echoed through the stadium from behind the Lake Julian stands. Everyone turned toward the howling cry. The Chimney Falls players straightened up and looked over their shoulders. Gaetan took advantage of the distraction.

"*Hike!*"


Aubrey, Buzz, Jordana and Rodriqa stood straight up. Spiky tingles raced down their spines. They turned around and leaned over the back railing of the stands. Members of the marching band filled in behind them on the bleachers, anxious to see the source of the screaming. Aubrey searched the scrambling horde of adults racing back and forth on the asphalt below.

A woman with dark, disheveled hair dashed out of the restroom.

"BIGFOOT!" she shouted frantically. "There is a *BIGFOOT* behind the woman's bathroom!" She crumpled to the ground and shimmied on her hands and knees away from the small cement brick structure.

Gasps and shouts followed her cry as a few people helped her to her feet. Steady streams of spectators trotted toward the parking lot.

"That's Teton Bailston's mom," whispered May over their shoulders.

Jordana leaned over the railing, scrutinizing every shadow meticulously.


Compton snapped the ball to Gaetan. Gaetan reached back and handed the ball off to Magnos. Magnos hurdled forward, dodging legs and arms. He leaned into the wind and, with no other players in sight, drove toward the goalpost.

"Take it all the way, Magnos!" Gaetan yelled after him.

Wastokowski launched himself through the air at Magnos. Magnos spun and ducked quickly. Wastokowski's helmet beamed Magnos in the head, and Number '55' silently dropped to the ground. Magnos gulped in air and forced his legs to stiffen, steadying himself to stay upright. The world spun like a top, and he closed his eyes to refocus his route. He could see open field in front of him. He lumbered forward, and then ran with all his might. His ears rang loudly, and he knocked his helmet against his shoulder to clear the clutter from his hearing. The goalpost moved closer and closer.

Fifteen yards left. The crowd exploded to their feet, shouting loudly. His heart raced, and he pumped his arms up and down his sides. He put his head down and plowed forward.

Ten yards. He could see players coming up behind him in his periphery. He heaved harder for breath, gripping the ball more tightly, and jammed his legs into the ground.

Five yards. Blue and gray lurched forward at him. Magnos jumped into the air and a player slid beneath him. He bounded into the end zone triumphantly. He spiked the football and turned to face the cheering crowd. He raised his arms high above his head, ready for his team to celebrate his touchdown

Green and yellow flurried around him, scurrying for the ball. A Chimney Falls lineman erupted through the scrim with the football perched within his squeezing grip. Several of his teammates raised the victorious lineman aloft on their shoulders and paraded him around the end zone.

Gaetan, Compton and several other Lake Julian players were gathering angrily around Magnos, shouting indecipherable snubs and rebukes. Behind them, more Chimney Falls players clapped and high-fived each other as Wastokowski pointed and laughed at Magnos. Coach Kaniffy slammed his clipboard on the ground and yelled at the direction of the end zone. Every Lake Julian player at the sideline was on their feet with faces full of contempt and disbelief.

Magnos glimpsed the scoreboard. The visitor '0' flashed to a '6'. He looked around. He had run back to his own end zone. He couldn't believe it. He had done the unimaginable. Dread and anguish washed over him. Wastokowski was cheering at him grandly.

Magnos ran toward the fence behind the end zone and vaulted over it. He stomped up the hill, ripped off his helmet, and flung it across the parking lot. Embarrassed rage filled his heart. He slammed his fist into a metal light pole, denting it. He wandered between the cars and trucks, hunting for the exit. The lot was full, and he was so confused. The lights and sky twisted around him, and his heart pounded harder and faster the further he walked. He leaned against a car and held on tightly to try and right himself. He felt as if he would topple over. He slipped to the ground and lowered his head between his knees.

A tall, shapely woman with bright red hair strolled up quietly behind him. Her sweet, gentle voice strummed through the air. "May I ask you a question?"

# Electric Shock

**Two months later.**

Aubrey stood up on the pedals of his bike, shoving all of his weight downward to force the wheels to turn. The last switchback curve before the dam was the steepest, and it was only in the last year that he had been able to make it all the way up without having to stop and walk the last curve to the top. His thighs burned like they were being branded with fired irons, and sweat dripped down his nose onto the asphalt below as the road passed underneath him at an achingly slow pace.

Adding to the challenge was his chronic lack of sleep, but Aubrey fought hard to ignore that obstacle. He kept his head down, so that how far he had remaining to the top was a mystery, in the hopes of deceiving his body into continuing to pedal.

Suddenly, Aubrey felt the pedals release and spin with ease as the rushing wind cooled his face, as he crested over the edge of the highway that topped the dam. His legs relaxed, and he looked up to see that he was coasting along the flat brim of the highway. The dark blue water behind the dam on his right sparkled in the afternoon sun. The gorge below the dam to his left glowed with leafy greens peppered with the oranges and yellows of budding autumn.

The tall, white observation tower rose on the lakeside of the dam. Formed of glistening, bleached stone brick, lichen and moss marred its grouting and crept up the full height of the tower. Aubrey saw Buzz's bike locked to the stair railing at the bottom of the tower. He stopped, listening to the muffled voices of Rodriqa and Buzz spilling over the top. Aubrey linked his bike with Buzz's and headed up the stairs.

He paused as he ran up the first flight of steps. A familiar face met him on the landing. A brown corkboard placard nailed to the stone wall overflowed with advertisements of homes for sale, dog-sitter phone numbers and offers for rafting guide lessons. The visual litter of flyers and business cards crowded around a central wrinkled, photo that was entitled "**MISSING**". Below the lettering, a square-faced young man with shaggy blonde hair and deep-set, blue eyes smiled with his cheeks bunched up into tight, ruddy balls. Although it was an older picture, Aubrey recognized his former bully instantly.

Aubrey felt sorry for Magnos but didn't miss him, and for feeling that way he felt guilty. He rounded the corner, but took his time, since his legs were still stinging after his ride up the hill.

A mind-splitting scream echoed from the top of the tower and reverberated off the block walls of the stairs. Aubrey winced and covered his ears. He could still hear the conversation above, albeit unintelligibly, but now the sentences were shorter, and the banter more rapid. Aubrey quickened his pace.

"OH, NO!" screeched Buzz from above. A shuddering thud battered the top of the tower, its aftershock rippling down the stairwell. Despite his ribs searing in piercing pain with each breathe, Aubrey forced himself to run in full gallop up to the observation platform. He collapsed onto the top deck on all fours.

Aubrey looked up and saw Buzz rolling on his back along the platform's floor, flailing like a turtle flipped onto its shell, and chortling so hard his face was bright pink. Rodriqa sat with her fists on her hips on a bench opposite Buzz, smirking at him unappreciatively.

"What's…going…on," Aubrey eked out between gasps. He unzipped his backpack and reached inside, digging around desperately between his books and papers. He pulled out his asthma inhaler and shoved the end of it in his mouth. Depressing the canister and inhaling deeply, he sighed with relief.

"She's taking *Taxi*," guffawed Buzz amidst his comic convulsions.

Aubrey's confusion and the sudden return of oxygen to his brain made him dizzy. "Huh?" he grunted.

"Andy Anacker asked Rodriqa to the Homecoming Dance this morning, and she said yes," explained Jordana softly. "Buzz is apparently amused." She folded her hands on the open book in her lap. Aubrey stared at her, enchanted by her words and fumbling to look beyond her beauty to understand what she had said. He breathed faster, and his heart pumped harder, even though he was no longer running. Jordana flashed a faint, whimsical smile at him and pushed her glasses further up her nose, uncovering the dark circles underneath her eyes.

Buzz inhaled harshly and squalled, "She's taking *Taxi* to the dance." His raucous, gleeful fit resumed.

"Buzz is about to die of laughter, and if he doesn't, I might kill 'em," responded Rodriqa spitefully. The beads in her hair clicked together tersely as she snapped her neck from side to side.

"Why do they call him 'Taxi'?" asked Jordana.

"Because," Buzz answered through howling snickers, "his ears are so big…when you look at him from straight on, he looks like a taxi cab with its doors wide open." Buzz crowed so loudly a flock of pigeons resting on the upper guardrail flew away in a frightened frenzy.

Aubrey and Jordana chuckled.

"That's mean," retorted Rodriqa. "It's good to know you find yourself to be the epitome of physical perfection."

"I am pretty irresistible." Buzz leaned himself up on his elbow as his round belly flattened against the ground, agreeing with a haughty grin.

Rodriqa grimaced. "At least May O'Klammer thinks so."

Buzz lost his grin. "She has too many freckles."

"What's wrong with freckles?" asked Aubrey.

"Nothing...unless you want to look like a human star chart," argued Buzz. Aubrey scowled at him.

"Okay. That's enough disparaging the foibled features of others for one day, Reiselstein," ordered Rodriqa. Jordana nodded in agreement.

"Why did you scream a second ago?" asked Aubrey, still bewildered by the mundane scene in front of him.

"A pigeon almost pooped on my homework," replied Rodriqa. She pointed angrily at a speckled, white dot on the stone bench next to her.

"You all scared me to death." Aubrey stood up with a forceful heave.

"You're the scary one," returned Rodriqa. "You look like a walking corpse, man. What's wrong with you?"

Aubrey hung his head and plopped down on the bench. Buzz sat cross-legged on the platform and answered for him. "He hasn't had a decent night's sleep in two months."

"Is that ghost still bugging you?" asked Rodriqa. Aubrey nodded solemnly.

"It's more than bugging him," countered Buzz. Aubrey furrowed his brow to try and silence him, but Buzz took no notice. "It's writing on stuff in his bedroom and keeping him up all night."

"Really?" responded Rodriqa. She and Jordana leaned forward to hear more.

"Buzz is exaggerating as usual," Aubrey waved him off. He noted Jordana's interest, so he didn't want to down play it completely. "But at this point, I guess you could say my room is haunted."

"Do your parents know?" asked Rodriqa.

Aubrey hung his head again.

"No," scoffed Buzz. "And he's had to throw out all his stuffed toys, because the ghost keeps pulling them apart and spelling words out on the floor with the stuffing."

"Shut it!" reprimanded Aubrey. "Look, it's not that bad. I've decided to take the advice of a *friend*, and I'll just ignore it until it goes away."

"Looks like you and Jordana have something in common," said Rodriqa snidely.

"What's that?" asked Aubrey. His heart pounded a few beats more quickly.

"You're both sleep-deprived from your own personal nightly visitor," contended Rodriqa.

Jordana twisted toward Rodriqa and frowned at her.

"Really?" Buzz inquired. "The Bigfoot visits causing you to lose sleep, too?"

"*Tsul'kalu*," corrected Jordana.

"Oops, my bad," replied Buzz.

"It's just the local loonies trying to get at my dad, since he's the mine fore-man." Jordana glowered at Rodriqa.

"What's a Tsul'kalu?" Aubrey asked.

"It's what the Cherokee refer to as the 'forest giant'," answered Jordana. "Our legends describe the creature as a hunter, more human than beast. I grew up hearing about how he saved small children from animal attacks and pun-ished greedy trappers for their overindulgence. Very different from some shaggy half-breed who throws rocks at hikers and terrorizes campsites in the middle of the night."

"So he's like an invisible hero?" inquired Aubrey.

"More like vigilante," replied Jordana. "Most Native Americans see him as either a guardian or an omen. Problem is you never know which, until it's too late."

"Well, guardian or omen, he sounds more like a nuisance to me," added Rodriqa.

"So there's just one Tsul'kalu," questioned Buzz.

Jordana shrugged her shoulders. "Supposedly."

"I don't know," mused Buzz, "there's been a lot of Bigfoot...I mean Tsul'kalu sightings around town lately." Jordana shuddered at his comment.

"And now I have a mystery of my own," reported Rodriqa proudly.

"I hope it's better than ghosts and Sasquatch," teased Buzz. "Or else, we'll just be bored."

"Probably not better, but I think it might be related," Rodriqa hinted. "Remember that earthquake that wasn't *really* an earthquake a couple months back? And how everyone was worried about what it would do to the dam and the mine, but everything turned out okay, no major damage or problems?" Aubrey, Buzz and Jordana nodded. "Well, it turns out, everything is not okay.

"A couple weeks ago, water started oozing up from the bottom level of the dam, the old closed down section where no one goes anymore. They figured there must be a small crack above the intake grates that was letting the water seep in.

"My parents organized a crew to pump the overflow out. They deter-mined it was a slow leak, because after a week or so the lines had drained about half of the water out of the entire sixth level. So they decided it was safe to send crews down to patch the problem. Up to this point, my parents couldn't stop talking about it. Planning what to do, picking who should fix it. On and on. They chatted about it everywhere, at home, in the car, at the store, and it seemed like everything was going well."

Rodriqa leaned in, and her voice softened. "For the past four days my par-ents have refused to say anything about the dam leak. Even when I asked about it over supper, they would change the subject. So I decided to do a little inves-tigating."

Aubrey shook his head. "You're too nosey for your own good."

"Hush it," she replied. "I talked to the guards and maintenance guys, and they were tight-lipped too, so that made me even more curious. But Jaime Kontrearo spilled the beans."

"He's the dude that graduated from Lake Julian High School last year, right?" asked Buzz.

"Right! He's been a security guard for about five months, so he hasn't quite figured out who not to talk to yet." Rodriqa grinned mischievously.

"Earlier this week I cornered him. He told me that a construction crew went down there to patch the leak. Everything seemed to be going according to plan, and everyone was in good spirits that day, knowing that the dam would be fixed soon.

"The crew was in the bottom level for less than an hour when one by one the workers started bolting up the stairs, screaming and swearing. Each one of them was white as a sheet. They had crazy far-off looks in their eyes and could barely speak. They all ran out of the dam and refused to come back in. They even left some of their equipment in the basement." Rodriqa looked down into the stairs, looking for eavesdroppers.

"Just before they drove away, Jaime said one of the other guards asked them what had happened. Supposedly, one of the workers said that they had been attacked by ghosts and large, ape-like monsters. Jaime said they were acting like a bunch of kids scared by the boogey man." Rodriqa snickered. The other three kids listened intently. "My parents haven't been able to hire another crew to go down there. Apparently, word has spread that the lower level of the dam is haunted, and no one is willing to take the job."

"So you think it's related to what Aubrey and Jordana have been seeing at night," surmised Buzz.

Rodriqa raised her eyebrows agreeably. "What else could it be, except a really farfetched coincidence?"

"But how is that possible?" questioned Aubrey. Jordana leaned forward, eager to hear the answer.

Rodriqa shook her head. "I don't know exactly, but that's not all." She stood up on the bench, turned around, and pried a crumbling piece of stone from the ledge's corner. She leaned over the edge of the tower, staring down through the barrier fence at the water sixty feet below. It was calm, and there was only a gentle ripple on the surface from the soft, flowing breeze.

"Watch this," said Rodriqa. Aubrey, Buzz and Jordana joined her on top of the bench and looked down at the lake. Rodriqa stuck her fist, palm down, through the fence's grating and released the rock over the lake. It fell swiftly to the water and splashed through the surface, disappearing from sight. Small waves curled away from where the rock hit, which rippled against the dam, and then bounced back out into open water, fading quickly over lake.

The three of them looked up at Rodriqa, confused as to what they should be watching for.

"Wow," remarked Buzz sarcastically. "Now, that's exciting."

Aubrey held back a laugh. Jordana chided him silently with a frown.

"Wait for it," murmured Rodriqa, mesmerized by the water.

Without warning, crooked, electric arcs of blue lightning flashed deep underneath the murky water, like a miniature thunderstorm below the surface. Sparks zipped back and forth between the dam and open water, lighting up the bottom of the lake. A massive, oval-shaped boulder, embedded with yellow, jagged crystals, glowed under the flickering array of scattering bolts.

"Whoa," exclaimed Aubrey. "What was that?"

"I'm not sure," replied Rodriqa. "But some tourists' kids who were skipping rocks along the shore last week told the guards about it, and I bet whatever it is, is also in the same spot as the leak in the dam."

"How do you know that?" queried Buzz.

"Because the guards didn't want me to know about this either," reported Rodriqa smugly.

"What could it be?" asked Jordana. "Do you think someone put it there to cause the leak...like sabotage?"

Rodriqa shrugged. "You mean like someone from the mine?"

Jordana nodded slowly, studying the water.

"I think it would be pretty difficult to move something that size without someone noticing it."

"Regardless of who put it there, we can easily hypothesize what kind of material is causing the underwater fireworks," rattled Buzz.

"Oh, really?" questioned Rodriqa jeeringly. "Do tell, professor."

"In order to create a display like that, the responsible material has to be piezoelectric."

"Pizza- electric?" questioned Aubrey.

"Nooooo," corrected Buzz. "P-I-E-Z-O-electric. Remember, Mr. Vandereff mentioned it about a month ago in class."

The three of them stared at him blankly.

"It's a rare property of certain compounds, usually either gemstones or ceramics. Piezoelectricity allows mechanical energy to be converted into electrical energy and vice versa, depending on the stress placed upon a material."

"Huh?" moaned Aubrey, still confused.

"It has to do with how the atoms are arranged in a substance. If the atoms are lined up, then it allows the material to produce electricity when movement or pressure is applied."

"Still not following you," said Jordana flatly.

Buzz looked around, exasperated by his failed attempts to explain the phenomenon. "Rodriqa, give me your watch."

Rodriqa scowled at him and slipped her arm behind her back.

"Fine, don't give it to me. But let me see it," bartered Buzz.

Rodriqa slowly stretched out her forearm and twisted her watch's face plate-up, so everyone could see.

"Does it have a battery, or do you have to wind it?" asked Buzz.

"Battery, I think. I've never wound this watch before."

"Perfect," said Buzz as he examined it.

"Look at her watch. See the second hand tick?" The three of them nodded in agreement. "The battery doesn't make the hands move directly. There are still gears that cause the hands to move at different rates of speed. There is a small piece of quartz inside her watch that, when excited by a small electrical pulse from the battery, moves one of the levers just a tiny bit, resulting in the motion of the hands. The quartz is piezoelectric. Whenever it gets a shock it moves, but it also works the opposite way. It can produce electricity if it's pushed on."

All three of them uttered a faint, comprehending *Ahhhhhhhhh*.

"That's what's going on under the water. That's what caused the sparks in front of the dam. Driqa dropped a rock. It applied stress to whatever was down there, and it created a shower of electricity.

"Now the odd thing is, piezoelectricity is a rare quality, it's even rarer in naturally occurring materials, and the amount of material needed to cause that much electricity is probably pretty staggering," calculated Buzz.

"How much material?'

"Several tons, I would think. Maybe more."

"Enough to cause a leak in a dam if it hit it during an earthquake?" asked Rodriqa.

Buzz nodded thoughtfully. "Jordana, is your dad's mine digging up quartz or silica?"

"I don't think so," she replied. "I've heard him talk about boron and beryllium ores and some other salts, but not quartz."

"Then it's probably safe to say, the mining personnel are not responsible."

"But tons of quartz crashing into a dam might feel like an earthquake," surmised Rodriqa.

Aubrey scratched his head. "I've missed something."

The other three looked at him curiously.

"I get what you're saying about the electric rock, but I still don't get how that relates to my ghost, or Jordana's Bigfoot, or what the construction crew saw at the bottom of the dam."

"The crew probably got shocked, or saw the sparks flying through the air, and got so scared they didn't know what to think," offered Buzz.

"Or whatever is causing the sparks is also what your ghost and Bigfoot are after," countered Rodriqa.

"But there's no way to know that," argued Buzz.

"Which is why we should go look." The sliver of a wily grin slid across Rodriqa's face.

The five friends all glanced at each other with curious expressions.

"Not me." Jordana stepped off the bench, attempting to physically remove herself from any involvement in Rodriqa's idea.

"No way," stated Aubrey firmly and joined Jordana. "All of this craziness will go away if we ignore it. I'm sticking to my original plan of...Don't React...Don't Tell."

"We should definitely go down there," countered Buzz. "If there's that much quartz down there, we could make a clock the size of a house!"

Rodriqa rolled her eyes. "But if we figure out what caused the leak, we could be the talk of the town. And just maybe we could get your ghost and your Bigfoot to leave you two alone."

"This is a bad idea," retorted Jordana.

"She's right," said Aubrey. "Someone could get hurt, and if we got caught, we'd been in serious trouble."

"You're just afraid of the ghosts," hounded Buzz. "Besides I doubt the bottom level of the dam is haunted or harbors over-sized orangutans."

Rodriqa raised her hands, palms up. "In one hand I have two friends that see unexplained creatures of the night. In the other hand we have random strangers who see the same creatures in the bottom of a dam with some massive *thing* causing a leak." She hovered her hands over one another. "There has to be a link."

"But people have reported seeing ghosts and Tsul'kalu for centuries," argued Jordana. "Maybe it just means Aubrey and I are crazy." She chuckled half-heartedly. Her careless jibe jilted Aubrey a little.

"I think Rodriqa is on to something," rallied Buzz. "What if it is *all* connected? What *if* this over-sized battery is exactly what *your* ghost and *your* Bigfoot are after?"

"I think you two have too much time on your hands," grumbled Aubrey. "None of it means anything."

"But what if you're wrong?" Rodriqa jumped down and walked over to Aubrey, with her nose in his face. "How many more nights are *you* gonna spend cowering before the boogeyman, Aubrey Taylor?"

# Underwater Otter Barter

Aubrey stood at the edge of the gorge downstream from the dam, overlooking the deep valley that captured the runoff from Lake Julian. The river below appeared serene and idyllic, like a picturesque brook perfect for a Sunday picnic, but the rapids were more than a thousand feet nearly straight down, and the distance beguiled many to see this raging torrent as a timid stream. Lush grasses and small, supple trees carpeted the valley walls, but their exposed roots and crumbling soil warned that only the most experienced of climbers should ever dare hike to the bottom. Like a brewing thunderstorm in the night sky, the gorge was beautiful to behold, but deadly if trapped within, and it carved a trench in the earth for miles south of the dam.

Twilight embraced the valley, and the orange and white lights from the dam sparkled from sky to sod. The weeds were already wet with dew, and Aubrey knew the combination of dusk and dampness on the hillside could be dangerous, if he wasn't careful.

Rodriqa had asked Aubrey and Buzz to meet her and Jordana on the west side of the dam at one of the rarely-used maintenance doors around eight o' clock that evening, when the security at the dam was thinner. Buzz thought it was a great plan, but Aubrey continued to have his doubts.

Mr. Osterfeld's horn blasted over the lake and echoed through the valley. Aubrey shook his head and chuckled at his erratic timing. When he was younger, Phineas Osterfeld would signal the town that it was nine o'clock every evening. Without fail, on the dot, at 9 p.m. his tugboat's horn would sound. People would set their watches by his audible beckon. Age and liquid proclivities had affected his sense of timing, and lately the high-pitched toot blared over Lake Julian at much less predictable times.

Aubrey bent his knees and scooted one foot at a time down the slippery grass toward the dam's face, cautiously checking his traction with each step. He peered down into the gorge and leaned back, a little fearful of the steep decline.

"HEY!" shouted a voice from above.

Aubrey's feet slipped out from underneath him, and he slid on his rear down the embankment. He kicked his feet and clawed with his hands, desperately searching to gain traction. Dirt and loamy rocks tumbled between his fingers and fell quickly into the crevice below. He glided faster on top of the wet foliage into the gorge. He propped up his foot and aimed for a rock at the cliff's edge.

Aubrey's body came to a jarring halt. The rock, congealed within the mud at its base, held firm, and he stood up and dusted off his quivering hands. He turned around and looked up toward the top of the ravine as his heavy breath fogged in the moist air.

"Are you okay?" bellowed Buzz from above.

"I was before you scared the saintly saut right out of me," replied Aubrey in a harsh whisper.

"Sorry," mumbled Buzz.

Aubrey shook his head in frustration and walked in tandem tightrope fashion along the step-off toward the dam.

Buzz rubbed the bottom of his shoe along the grass. "Slippery, isn't it," hollered Buzz down the gorge.

"Yeah, figured that out, thanks," barked Aubrey back.

Buzz sat on his rump and scooted diagonally in short bursts down the embankment.

They arrived at a set of narrow, leaf and mud-plastered metal stairs at the edge of the dam. They both steadied their way up the steps, avoiding piles of rank-smelling muck and bundles of twigs, trapped within the grating. At the top, a heavy steel door, built into the side of the dam, bulged from its threshold, warped by years of weather and settling concrete walls that surrounded it. A sliver of light sliced through the edge of the door, and Aubrey and Buzz peered into it, hoping to see Rodriqa. The crack was too small, and all they could hear from the opposite side was a whirling hum that vibrated the door and the stairs underfoot.

Aubrey tapped on the door with his index finger. The door creaked painfully as the hinges' dry rusting metal pivoted against oil-starved pins.

Rodriqa slipped her head through the small opening. "Don't knock!"

The reverberating shudder of machinery from within the dam startled Aubrey and Buzz.

"Why would it matter if we knocked?" asked Buzz, raising his voice. "Who would hear us?"

"What?" Rodriqa yelled in reply. Buzz shook his head as to say, *Nevermind.*

She grabbed Aubrey's shoulder and pulled him through the half-dozen inches of open door. Inside, Jordana took a hand briefly off her ear to wave hello. Aubrey squinted under the noise. He screamed, "How are you?" but Jordana only shrugged, unable to hear anything.

Rodriqa slammed her shoulder into the steel door and forced it open another couple of inches. "Suck in your gut," she screamed at Buzz.

She tugged at his arm, squishing his doughy pudge between the door and its frame. Buzz's mid-section popped through, and he self-consciously straightened his shirt and pulled his jeans up. Rodriqa jerked the door closed and motioned the other three to follow her. They rounded an inset, brick enclosure, and the room opened up, exposing the dam's three turbines. The massive gray blocks, each the size of a house, throbbed violently as water rushed from the lakeside of the dam through large-bore metal tubes. A prickly draft of hot air flowed ceaselessly through the room, quickly drying out the kids' eyes and forcing them to blink rapidly.

Rodriqa led them along the outer sheet-metal wall to a security door in front of the middle turbine. Aubrey thought his ribcage would rattle out of his skin. He wrapped his arms tightly around his torso and buried his ears between his shoulders, hoping to hold himself together. Buzz gritted his teeth together to prevent the battering hum of the turbines from chattering them loose.

A keypad with number buttons like a telephone jutted out from the wall next to the door. She punched in four numbers and pulled the curved, cylindrical handle on the door. A red light glowed on the keypad, and the handle stiffened tautly. Rodriqa frowned and punched in the numbers again. She wrenched the handle clockwise and the red light flashed angrily three times. The handle refused to move.

Buzz pushed Rodriqa out of the way impatiently. He bent over and examined the keypad closely. He punched a small, unlabeled button in the top corner and motioned for Rodriqa to enter the numbers again. She dialed the same four-digit code, and then a steady green light blinked on. The door clicked, and Buzz turned the handle with ease. He shoved the door open wide, and all four of them ran in quickly, slamming the door shut behind them.

"Hoaker Croaker! That's loud," sighed Buzz with relief.

Aubrey shook his head, trying to drive the ringing from his ears.

"What did you do to the door?" asked Rodriqa, both miffed and grateful at the same time.

"Reset button," explained Buzz. "All number pads have a reset button in case someone before you hit an extra button, so you can start the sequence over automatically."

"How did you know that?" Rodriqa asked incredulously.

"Video games...lots of video games," replied Buzz proudly.

Jordana walked in front of them to the edge of the landing and looked over the railing. "What is this place?"

A narrow corner in the ceiling across from them opened into a wedge-shaped arroyo that delved several stories down into the dam. Dripping from large-bore, vertical pipes, gentle trickles of water dripped onto the floor of the deep room and snaked into black, circular mesh grates.

Rodriqa leaned over the railing and peered into the arroyo. "It's the spillway. It redirects water that escapes from the turbines and redirects it to the bottom level, and then drains slowly into the gorge."

"What's in the bottom level?" Jordana asked hesitantly.

"Empty drainage chambers that haven't been used in years," replied Rodriqa.

"And that's where the electric rock is?"

"Pretty sure." Rodriqa held onto the railing and stepped quickly down the metal spiral stairs that led to the bottom of the vaulted room. Buzz galloped down the stairs behind her. Jordana and Aubrey followed cautiously.

Rodriqa turned the corner into another room. The concrete walls ended, and masonry brick lined the walls and butted jaggedly against the door. Yellow rubber suits lined three of the four walls, hanging from thick, rusty nails in the brick. To the right, an oval submarine door was ajar, with its central turn wheel wound out. Everyone followed Rodriqa into the brick room.

Buzz ogled the submarine door and groped the lining of the suits. "They're waterproof," he commented.

"Yep," agreed Rodriqa. "Anyone who goes into the bottom level is supposed to wear them. It's usually pretty damp down there." She pulled a suit from the wall near its edge, and a face appeared from around the corner.

Rodriqa screamed and jumped three feet back, then swatted the air in front of her. The other three kids gasped and lunged backwards.

"JAIME!" yelled Rodriqa. "Why are you spying on us?!"

Jaime Kontrearo stepped out from around the corner, dressed in his security guard uniform, and tapped his nightstick against the aluminum badge on his chest. "I was starting my shift tonight and noticed that door number three in the turbine room had been unsuccessfully accessed twice and successfully once, so I decided to check it out."

"You've checked it out," scowled Rodriqa," and now you can leave us alone."

"What are you all doing down here?" questioned Jaime, less than officially.

"We're just looking around...nothing to be worried about," reported Rodriqa condescendingly.

"Your dad would be so not happy, if he knew you were down here."

"He doesn't need to know," Rodriqa chided.

Jaime stepped curiously into the middle of the room, checking everyone and everything out. "So what's the plan?"

"We just want to check out the leak," sassed Buzz. He lifted a pair of waterproof pants off the wall and slipped his feet into the leggings.

"So what really happened down there?" Rodriqa asked.

Jaime scratched his head. "Don't know."

"Such a toad thrower," mocked Rodriqa.

"No...really," Jaime replied. "No one is really saying anything, and I'm at the bottom of the ladder when it comes to information."

"Then we're gonna find out what's really going on." Rodriqa handed pants to Aubrey and Jordana and jumped into her own suit. Buzz's belly peeked out from under his top, and he couldn't quite button the pants.

Jaime walked over to the submarine door and flipped open a small black box on the wall. He mused at the lights inside and shrugged his shoulders. "Water meter reads green-four."

"What's that mean?" Rodriqa asked.

"Every green bar is six inches of water...so it should only be two feet deep."

"So what's it gonna take for you to not tell my parents?" gambled Rodriqa.

Jaime chuckled and rubbed his forehead. "It's not your parents I'm worried about."

"Then what's your glamour glitch?" challenged Rodriqa.

Jaime rolled his eyes. "Mr. Buckswaine. I've seen him become pretty unpleasant when he finds out someone broke the rules."

Rodriqa waved him off. "I've got ol' Charlie wrapped around my finger."

Jaime twisted his mouth as he considered what she had said. "You don't rat on me, and I won't rat on you." He disappeared around the corner and rushed up the spiral stairs.

Rodriqa leaned over and picked up a flashlight, flicking it on. Its hazy beam brightened the dimly light room. She tossed it to Aubrey, who nearly fell over in his partially-donned pants trying to catch it.

"You first, Aub," charged Rodriqa.

"Why me?" Aubrey's voice cracked.

"Because you're the one with the flashlight!"

Aubrey scowled at her.


Rodriqa, Buzz and Jordana followed Aubrey through the submarine door and traipsed down the mold-encrusted stairs leading from the spillway. Moisture beaded to every surface, from the red brick and gray mortar walls to the irregularly poured cement steps. Half-century-old incandescent bulbs glowed with trembling white balls of light within thickset, wire cages at the top of each stair landing. A hand rail, which had deteriorated into a crumbling pole of rust, was bolted into the bricks of the wall, and Aubrey steadied a single finger along the rail while he clumsily clomped down one foot at a time in his yellow, waterproof rubber boots and pants.

The four friends stepped slowly in a single-file line more than a dozen flights into the bowels of the oldest portion of the dam. The only reminder of current technology in the stairwell was a bright orange extension cord that traced down the stairs in the bottom corner. Buzz reached down and picked up a frayed piece of twine from underneath the electrical cord, wound it through a belt loop of his waterproof pants and tied a knot. He exhaled deeply and sucked in his globular gut, strung the twine through the buttonhole and pulled it tautly. He tied the opposite end into another knot and relaxed his bulging tummy onto the fold at the top of his pants.

After eight stories, the four kids reached the edge of a pool of brown, murky water lapping against the steps in a large brick-walled room at the bottom. Bits of wood and plastic jetsam floated in the water as tiny insects skated on its surface. Aubrey tried to calm himself by thinking of it as nothing more than lake water.

"This is the basement level," described Rodriqa. "It looks like the water is knee high. Hopefully we won't get too wet, if we're careful." Jordana curled her lip at the sight of the room and pinched her nose. Aubrey and Buzz slowly waded down into the flooded room, carefully planting each squishy step for solid footing. Two hallways led in opposite directions from the room.

"Wow! The work crew really did leave in a hurry," remarked Buzz as he scanned the room. Half-submerged stacks of metal buckets were scattered along the floor next to shovels and axes that were propped up against the moldy walls. A cement mixer stood at the center of the room, already rusting along the edges of the waterline. Squalid droplets of water coalesced from the drain grates on the ceiling and splashed ringlets in the standing water.

"How do you know which way to go?" asked Jordana as she followed her friends and peered down the dim hallways.

"I've been down here a few times. It seems like a big maze, but it's just a series of interconnected drainage ways," replied Rodriqa as she thought out loud.

"That doesn't make me feel better," muttered Aubrey as he shined the flashlight down each hallway.

Rodriqa scrunched her nose at Aubrey. "Fortunately, the work crews left their lights here, too." The extension cord snaked along the walls and forked in two, heading in opposite directions down the dimly lit corridors opening away from the room. Silver-belled canisters cradled tiny pin-points of light at regular intervals along the extension cord, like a makeshift string of industrial Christmas lights. They could see to the end of each hallway until the corridors disappeared around corners into darkness. The kids looked each way grimly, one route just as forebodingly quiet and gloomy as the other, like looking into a cave full of starlit midnight.

"Which way?" asked Buzz. He wiped the sweat from his forehead before it trickled down his face. The humidity and his nerves had soaked him through.

Rodriqa mused for a moment. "It's been a while since I've been down here...but if we want to go lakeside...we should go this way...I think." She cinched the loose waistline of her waterproof pants in her fist and marched forward, careful not to slip on the slimy cement floor.

Jordana followed behind her hesitantly, yet anxious not to loose sight of her. "What do we do if the lights go out?" she squeaked.

"Grab the extension cord and follow it backwards," explained Buzz.

"Exactly," agreed Rodriqa. "I'm hoping the lights will lead us to the leak in the dam, and that should be where the rock is."

Buzz and Aubrey followed them down the hallway. Aubrey pulled his suspenders tighter to pull his pants up as high as he could. He scuffed his foot along the slippery floor below the inky water, unsettled that he couldn't see any more than a few inches below the grimy surface.

Aubrey glanced up and forgot about the water. A large slab of concrete hung directly over him from thick rusting, wrought-iron chains. Like a drooping hunk of driveway it loomed over them from a recess in the ceiling. Several yards ahead, Aubrey saw another monolith of concrete hanging over Rodriqa.

"What is that?" Aubrey squawked as he pointed upward.

Rodriqa turned around and looked up. "Ballasts," she replied. She faced forward and kept walking. "The lower level was once used to re-route dam runoff, and they controlled the flow with those."

"Can they fall?" asked Aubrey.

"I doubt it. They have to be rusted in place by now. They haven't been used in ages."

The friends turned the corner, and the corridor ran a score of yards before splitting into three other directions. The extension cord beaded with lights turned left ahead at the top of a corridor ahead.

"Shouldn't be too much further," comforted Rodriqa as she led them down the hallway and rounded another corner. She tried to change the subject. "So Aubs...why do you think this ghost is haunting you?"

"I don't know," murmured Aubrey.

"Do you think it's haunting anyone else?"

"How am I supposed to know?" he responded.

"When did you first see it?"

Aubrey thought for a moment. "The night before the first day of school. I saw his face for the first time...when I closed my eyes."

Rodriqa thought for a moment. "Jordana, when did you first see your Bigfoot?"

"Tsul'kalu," she corrected quietly. "First week of school."

Rodriqa rubbed her chin. "They both showed up about the same time, then...maybe there is some connection between the rock and the ghost and the Bigfoo...I mean Tsul'kalu."

"Is anyone else bothered by this?" remarked Buzz suddenly.

"By what?" asked Rodriqa

"All of it bothers me," replied Jordana.

"No...I'm talking about the otter," said Buzz.

Aubrey and Jordana paused for a few seconds and stood still in the water, looking around them for anything out of the ordinary. Rodriqa glared at Buzz, and then kept moving. She turned another corner, following the extension cord.

"I don't understand," said Aubrey, both a little confused and nervous.

"The otter," reiterated Buzz as he pointed down into the water.

"Did you see a rat or something?" asked Jordana.

"I know the difference between a rat and an otter," scoffed Buzz. "I'm talking about the otter swimming around me right now."

Aubrey and Jordana examined the water around Buzz, and it was completely still, like a sheet of glass covering a bog of silt. They gave each other a curious glance and turned around to follow Rodriqa.

"What's he talking about?" Jordana whispered to Aubrey.

"I think he's trying to be funny," replied Aubrey quietly.

"The water's getting deeper," hollered Rodriqa from up ahead. "Be careful. We should be almost there."

Aubrey and Jordana adjusted their waterproof pants and leaned into the water as they walked.

"Did you hear that?" Buzz asked from behind them.

"Hear what?" Aubrey said in an annoyed tone. He continued walking forward without looking back.

"The otter is talking. Can't you hear it?"

"What's the otter saying?" asked Jordana with a chuckle. Aubrey nudged her jeeringly on.

"He's saying we really shouldn't be down here," answered Buzz with a sharp edge to his tone. "Bad things will happen if we keep walking forward."

"Do you think you could be any more obnoxious right now?" Aubrey replied.

Buzz ignored him. "Hey, Rodriqa," he shouted down the corridor, sloshing through the water to catch up. Aubrey and Jordana turned another corner. Rodriqa leaned with her back against the muck-covered wall with her hands high above her head.

"What's wrong?" Jordana asked.

"I saw a snake," breathed Rodriqa hoarsely.

Jordana yelped. "We have to get out of here."

"The otter says it's too late," Buzz said.

Aubrey sighed angrily. "And why is that?"

"The otter says a ballast is about to fall," replied Buzz, his voice trembling.

"That's ridiculous," rebutted Rodriqa. She slid her torso along the wall, traveling slowly back the way they had come.

Aubrey trudged around Buzz and turned back into the hallway they had just walked through.

"Wait!" yelled Buzz. "The otter says it's not safe that way."

"Cut it out, Buzz," growled Aubrey. "You're not scaring anybody, and it's not funny any more!"

"I asked him to go away, but he said no," whined Buzz.

A knocking creak whined from overhead. Aubrey stopped and glanced upward. *SNAAAPP!* A concrete ballast fell into the water a yard in front of Aubrey. A wave of gritty water washed over him, knocking him to his knees. He scrambled to push himself up against the brick floor and right himself. His stomach lurched in disgust, as he engulfed mouthfuls of stagnant, rusting rot from the dingy water. He spit and sputtered to clean his nose and throat from the slimy spray.

"Groooooosssss," whispered Buzz. "I can't imagine how many bacteria you just swallowed."

"Are you okay?" Jordana asked from down the hallway, afraid to move any closer.

"Yeah," replied Aubrey as he wiped his face off and stumbled back toward the group. "What's your otter saying now?" He decided being miffed with Buzz would help stave off the nausea from the putrid water rolling in his stomach. The flashlight bobbed up in the water and flickered out. Aubrey moaned as he picked the flashlight off the rippling surface and shook it. The faceplate was cracked and the bulb shattered. He dropped it back in the water.

Buzz rubbed his temple. His left eye twitched and his mouth twisted into a curve. "Is someone buried down here?"

"No, why?" asked Rodriqa.

"The otter keeps talking about some tomb...it doesn't make any sense."

"Would you stop?" Aubrey pleaded.

"I'm trying," insisted Buzz, "but he won't leave me alone!"

"Is there another way out of here?" Jordana asked, slightly panicked.

"Yeah," replied Rodriqa. "It shouldn't be hard to find our way back. Let's head this way and stick together." Rodriqa pointed down a dark corridor straight ahead.

"But there aren't any lights," reeled Aubrey as his voice cracked.

"As long as we hug the walls and hang to the right, we'll find our way back." Rodriqa led the way and placed her hand against the right wall. Suddenly, she jumped out of the water and screamed wildly.

"What's wrong?" asked Jordana.

"I felt something rub my leg. It felt scaly, like another snake!"

"Let's hurry," urged Jordana.

The four of them huddled together and slowly scuttled down the corridor.

"Why don't we follow the lights...maybe we'll meet the other set from before," offered Jordana hopefully.

"I think that's an excellent idea," murmured Aubrey. They turned the corner and followed the extension cord, each grabbing hold of the other.

"Is it just me, or is the water getting warmer?" asked Jordana.

"I'm freezing," replied Rodriqa as her lower lip trembled.

They traced the path of the electrical cord around another corner, and a bright light shone up ahead. Aubrey broke from the pack and hurried forward, the water spilling over into his waterproof pants as he waded through.

Rodriqa kept her head down. "I think I see more snakes."

"I don't see any snakes," replied Jordana, "but I feel like I'm boiling in these pants." Buzz had his fingers in his ears and was humming to himself.

Aubrey stopped at the next cross-section. "Look at that," he said in a voice full of wonder.

Several yards in front of him, an expansive, another brick-lined room opened much wider than any they had encountered before wide, and a single, beaming fluorescent light on a metal stand illuminated every corner. The dark water stood chest high, reminding Aubrey of an indoor swimming pool that had never been cleaned. On the far wall, Aubrey discovered the cause of the dam's leak.

Above the waterline, a large circular stone protruded through the dam wall, and kudzu wound up its face, like a curtain of green foliage. Round shimmering pebbles of various sizes ensconced the larger stone, and jagged quartz crystals of pale yellows, rosy pinks and ashy greens jutted out from the edge of the circle. A pile of concrete rubble had settled at the bottom of the stone, and rivulets of water trickled from small cracks around the large stone in the dam's face.

The other three kids waded up to the entrance of the room. Buzz slapped at the water erratically. Jordana breathed heavily through her open mouth and wiped rills of sweat off her forehead.

"What is it?" Rodriqa asked.

"I don't know, but it's beautiful," replied Aubrey.

"Hey, I think I found the way out," Jordana said excitedly. Buzz and Rodriqa turned right and looked down another dark corridor. At the end, a string of tiny lights were wrapped around a shovel.

"Yep, that should be other end of the extension cord. We've completed half of the loop," agreed Rodriqa.

Rodriqa, Jordana and Buzz edged into the dark corridor.

"Wait!" exclaimed Aubrey. "Don't you want to get a better look at the rock?"

"Not really," spurned Jordana.

"We saw it…it's cool…now let's split," quipped Rodriqa.

"I want to get closer," Aubrey said with fascination in his voice.

Aubrey sloshed hurriedly through the water. The others stood waiting impatiently. He shaded his eyes as he walked past the blinding fluorescent light and climbed up on to the broken crags of shattered dam below the stone.

"Amazing," whispered Aubrey. The shards of quartz were the size of his forearm and pierced the shell of the stone. Copper wire snaked in circles around the smoothly ground pebbles and glistened with the light's reflection. Thin flakes of gold and silver layered areas between the pebbles, like a metal varnish.

"This thing has to be some sort of artifact," surmised Aubrey as he yelled back at his friends.

"Probably," agreed Buzz, distracted by his own thoughts. "Kind of looks like a geode, but turned inside out." He slapped the water again.

"I think I see another snake," cried Rodriqa.

"I wonder where it came from. This can't be a geological formation. Someone had to make this." Brushing back a vine of kudzu, Aubrey rubbed an orange-glazed pebble in wonder. It was completely smooth, without a single defect or blemish.

Everything went black. Aubrey was sucked into a distant world that hauled him in by his heart. He saw faces, contorting, mouths misshapen and eyes pulled to the sides. Heads twisted around their necks. Sharp teeth grinded and mouths screamed without sound. Aubrey's hand burned fiercely. He fell backwards into the water. He swam furiously to reach the surface, sucking in water as he tried to control his breath. The air opened up against his face, and the light returned.

"Are you okay?" hollered Buzz.

"Did you see that?" asked Aubrey, dumbfounded.

"Yeah, I can't believe this otter can do that many back flips in a row," replied Buzz across the room.

"No...I mean the faces in the dark, trying to scream. They came at me, pulling me toward them."

"What are you talking about?" Rodriqa asked incredulously.

The room moaned like a drowning ship about to sink beneath hungry waves. The stone slammed forward through the dam's face. Concrete boulders from the damaged dam's wall splashed into the water in the room and Aubrey tumbled underneath a miniature tsunami of displaced water. Buzz and Rodriqa took several steps in to catch Aubrey and realized the huge wave was heading quickly toward them.

The wave rushed toward the back of the room. "Hold on," ordered Rodriqa as she clamped her hands around a metal handle in the wall. Buzz braced himself, and the wave smashed over them. Water raced into the corridors behind the rom. Buzz and Rodriqa plopped up out of the water like fishing bobbers and wiped off their faces. Lake water gushed into the room with the pressure of a score of cracked fire hydrants. They swung their arms fervently under the water, searching for Aubrey.

A splash broke the water behind them. Aubrey coughed violently as he clambered to stay above water.

"Let's go," Rodriqa said as she pulled Aubrey onto his feet.

The kids turned down the dark corridor and waded as quickly as they could toward the lights ahead. Buzz took deep breaths to fight off the claustrophobia from the darkness of he air meeting the darkness of the water as it rose chest-high. For Rodriqa, the water was shoulder high. She tore off her waterproof pants and swam furiously.

Rodriqa drifted first into the soft angle of light, followed by Aubrey, who was now doggy paddling, and then Buzz, who floated more than swam. Aubrey and Buzz peeled off their waterproof suits and watched the yellow rubber float back into the darkness.

"Where's Jordana?" asked Aubrey.

The three of them looked at each other fearfully.

"JORDANA!" hollered Rodriqa down the corridor. The echo died quickly under the rush of moving water. "She was just here. Where could she have gone?"

"What if she drowned?" asked Buzz.

Rodriqa smacked him on the arm. "You're not cute." Buzz reared back away from her as she swam into the darkness. "JORDANA!" she yelled again.

Rodriqa's dim voice crept out of the black corridor. "I keep feeling something touch my legs. Dive down and see if you can find her." Rodriqa disappeared under the water.

Aubrey and Buzz were treading water.

"We don't have much time left," cried Buzz.

"We can't leave Jordana," insisted Aubrey. He gulped a deep breath of air and sunk down under the surface.

Rodriqa re-emerged in the lit hallway, breathless. "I...can't...find...her."

"We're losing air," Buzz bawled. "We have to get out now."

Aubrey came back up and spewed water out of his nose. "I don't feel anything...where could she be?"

Another wave of water pushed the three of them against the wall and the lights above them flickered.

"We're gonna loose the lights too...then we're dead," howled Buzz.

Aubrey and Rodriqa looked at each other frantically.

"We have to go," Rodriqa decided quietly.

In a frenzied dash, the three of them swam with all their strength up the corridor, following the extension cord. Aubrey realized how deep the water was now, as he could have easily reached up and touched a ballast overhead. The rumbling water licked the extension cord, and sparks zapped sections of wire that were exposed, causing the lights to flash erratically. Corner after corner, the raging water pushed them faster onward and closer to the ceiling.

"We're in the first room," hollered Rodriqa.

"Where are the stairs?" replied Buzz, thrashing about and gasping for breath.

Rodriqa clung to the walls and felt for an empty space under the water. "Here," she shouted. She ducked under the water and disappeared.

Buzz and Aubrey dove down and chased after her. Under the water, Buzz's knees skidded across the irregular steps, and he pushed himself up. Aubrey grabbed the chipped railing and pulled himself to the top. When both of them resurfaced, Rodriqa was squatting on the landing above them, holding her head and sobbing loudly.

Jordana was gone. Rodriqa knew there was no way she could be alive. The pressure from the water was too great and, by now, all of the oxygen in the bottom level would have been forced out. She had drowned in the bowels of the dam. And the brick-faced hallways, gorged with lake water, were her grave.

Aubrey and Buzz crawled up the stairs, savoring every precious breath of dry air. Their limbs barely moved under the weight of their waterlogged clothes. Their ribcages cramped with sharp stabs of pain, and their eyes stung from the dirt in the water.

They sat next to Rodriqa on the landing silently. Numb by the inexplicable thought of Jordana's death, they replayed her disappearance over and over in their minds.

"I still don't understand," murmured Buzz hopelessly.

"What's not to understand?" squealed Rodriqa through her tears. "Jordana is dead...and it's my fault!"

"No," consoled Aubrey weakly.

"Yes," shrieked Rodriqa. "It was *my* idea to go down there."

The water had crept up to last step and was spilling over onto the landing. Buzz stood up and grabbed Rodriqa under the arm. The three of them marched slowly up the stairs, lost in their astonished grief.

"It's about time you made it," crowed Jaime from the top of the stairs. "I was about to come get you all. You've been down there quite a while."

"Call my parents!" squalled Rodriqa from below.

Jaime furrowed his brow and stared at her with confusion. "Why?"

"Jordana," She crumpled onto the stairs, crying relentlessly.

"What's wrong?" Jaime asked.

Buzz clamored up the stairs. "The whole basement level is flooded," he told Jaime frantically.

Jaime cocked his head sideways and shook his head. He walked back inside the antechamber and shouted out to them, "The water meter reads the same as before...two feet."

"That meter is wrong," Buzz replied manically. "The water is still rising...it'll be in the upper parts of the dam in minutes."

"Are you sure?" Jaime asked as he scratched his head.

"Absolutely," asserted Buzz.

Aubrey lifted Rodriqa up the remaining steps. "Jordana is still down there. We need help to get her out."

Jaime chuckled.

"It's not funny!" insisted Aubrey. "This is serious!"

"Yeah, seriously stupid. Did you all find an opened bottle of some crew-man's flavor of the month down there and take a sip?" Jaime asked.

"No! This is no time to be cracking jokes!" yelled Aubrey. He handed Rodriqa to Jaime and ran into the antechamber.

Suddenly, Jordana stormed up to him and pointed her finger straight in his face. "You should never have gotten so close to that rock! You could have gotten hurt!"

Aubrey gasped. "You're alive?" he asked in disbelief.

"What took you all so long to get back?!"

Buzz jumped to the top of the steps. "You're here?!"

"Of course, I'm here," chided Jordana. "I told you all I was coming back. It was too hot down there."

Rodriqa flew through the door and raced at Jordana, knocking her to the floor.

"I...I...I...didn't hear you tell us you were leaving," stuttered Buzz.

"You were too busy playing with your otter, I guess," replied Jordana through Rodriqa's tight squeeze on her torso. "What's wrong with you all?"

The three of them spoke at once.

"Aubrey touched the stone, and it fell forward, and water came rushing into the corridors...I knew we should have never gone down there...we were asking for trouble," charged Buzz.

"It wasn't my fault...and I wasn't even close to the rock when it dropped into the room...you're the one who kept distracting us with your ridiculous otter...and I actually *tried* to save Jordana," retorted Aubrey.

"We had to escape, but we lost you...we walked through the dark hallway to get to the lights...but I kept feeling snakes and thought maybe it was you, but I couldn't find you... I would never have forgiven myself if you had died," Rodriqa exclaimed.

Jordana looked at them all wide eyed. "Everything is fine."

Rodriqa walked over to the water meter and checked it. Four green bars were lit. Twenty-four inches. Two feet deep.

"Wait," interjected Jaime. "Buzz saw an otter, Rodriqa saw snakes, and Jordana was burning up in the coldest part of the dam?! Wow! That's some serious imagination overdrive." Jaime laughed as he clapped in amusement at their story. "Play time's over. I need to lock up down here."

"But the dam is flooding," pushed Buzz. "We nearly drowned!"

"If you nearly drowned, then why aren't your clothes wet," argued Jaime.

Aubrey, Buzz and Rodriqa looked themselves up and down. They were completely dry.

"Then it was just a dream?" asked Aubrey in a fog of doubt.

Rodriqa stiffened her upper lip. "...or a trick."

## Nepotism

Jordana hurriedly ran through her yard, worried her father would be upset that she was back so late without calling. Lately, he had been out late himself. With all the attacks from environmental groups and the consequential bureaucratic unrest, he often didn't finish up until ten or eleven o'clock at night. Tonight, however, every light in the house was on. Her dad was home.

She ran up the stairs to the back porch and dropped her shoulder, preparing to force open the back door.

"Your continued involvement is what's making this worse!" The shout came from inside the kitchen. Jordana shrank away from the door and listened.

"You're blowing this out of proportion," said her father in a patronizing tone.

"Oh, really! Then why are your miners quitting left and right?!"

"Every business has a certain amount of turnover, especially early on."

"There hasn't been activity like this for centuries! Maybe even millennia!"

"There is no way for you to really know how often the Tsul'kalu pop up. Maybe they come and go in cycles."

"But so much of the general public is suspicious about what's going on now! What will you do if others find out about your indiscretions?!"

"They won't! Besides, I'm sure the police have more pressing matters to attend to than random sightings of Bigfoot. They still haven't found out what's happened to the Strumgarten boy…or the circus."

There was a long pause from the kitchen, and Jordana inched closer to the door.

"Do you know where the boy is?" asked the other man hesitantly.

"Of course not!" roared Mr. Galilahi. "Your superstition doesn't interest me. I'm doing what's best for my family!"

"Your obstinate refusal to accept the obvious is exactly what is destroying what's left of your family!"

Jordana barged through the door. Arturo Galilahi and Principal Lequoia abruptly stopped speaking. Their creased expressions of rage softened, and the principal turned away from the door. Jordana walked into the kitchen and set her book bag on the table like nothing was out of sorts.

"Hi, Dad," she greeted him, overly cheerful. "Hello, Uncle." Her tone darkened, and she refused to look at them.

"You're late," her father accused sternly.

"Sorry, Driqa and I had a long study session." Jordana turned her attention to the countertop. She turned on the water in the sink and dropped dirty dishes into its basin.

"We're not finished with this conversation, Arturo," muttered Lequoia.

"No, I believe we are," responded Mr. Galilahi.

"Then you leave me no choice." Principal Lequoia stormed out of the kitchen, and Jordana could hear him stomping, heavy-footed, up the stairs. She looked at her father, and she watched him waver between walking toward her and chasing after her uncle.

"What are you and Uncle fighting about?" she asked him.

"Where have you *really* been?" her father countered.

"I've been with Rodriqa, like I said," she reiterated rigidly. "I'm being honest with you. Why can't you return the favor?"

Arturo looked down and scowled. "I've never been untruthful to you."

"Then why won't you tell me what's going on?"

Arturo's voice lightened, and he smiled at Jordana. "There are some things that children need not be privy to."

Jordana marched up to him and spoke face to face. "I am *not* a child!" Angry tears swelled up in her eyes, and she clenched her fists in frustration. Her father returned her gaze, his eyes quivering with tortured adoration for his daughter.

Jordana took off her glasses. Her father covered her eyes with his hand and looked away. "Please, not now, Jordana."

The principal charged down the stairs and walked past Jordana and her father. "You have no right to use *this* any longer. I'm taking it back to where it belongs!" He carried a hefty, leather-bound tome under his arm and Jordana glimpsed the writing on the cover, although its title made little sense. *Anathagraphia*.

Lequoia raced through the kitchen and out the back door. Arturo chased after him hastily into the backyard.

Jordana returned her glasses to her face and sprinted for the door. She watched as the two men tussled on the lawn, lit only by the lights shining from inside the house. Arturo grabbed the book from behind Jordana's uncle and tried to wrench it free from his grasp. Lequoia spun and lifted the book out of Arturo's hands, and sped up toward the tree line.

"How dare you steal from my home?" shouted Arturo.

"Steal?! It doesn't belong to you, and you have abused it," rebutted Lequoia.

The two men disappeared into the forest as they wrangled over the book in Lequoia's hands.

Jordana ran down the stairs of her back porch and into the yard. "Stop it!" she yelled. "You're acting like children!" She could hear her father and uncle arguing, their voices moving further away.

Without warning, the stench of scorched decaying meat seared her nose. The heralding smell chilled her with frightening memories of the monstrous burglar.

"GET OUT OF THE WOODS!" she screamed. The odor grew stronger, and she backed up toward the house as she trembled, hoping to escape what she knew was coming.

Jordana could no longer hear her father and uncle fighting. The forest noises halted abruptly as they smell of burning flesh grew stronger. There were no animals rustling through the leaves. The cicadas stopped chirping. The landscape and all its inhabitants were deathly silent. Jordana turned to run into the house.

The Tsul'kalu loomed over her from the steps of the back porch. Its red eyes followed her, like a predator tracking its prey. It drew back its lips and a low, hungry rumble gurgled from deep within its throat.

Jordana panted in terror, the creature's odor stinging her lungs. She was trapped outside and alone. She tried to scream, but she couldn't speak.

"STAY AWAY FROM HER!" shouted a voice from behind her. Mr. Galilahi leapt in front of Jordana and waved his arms, trying to attract the Tsul'kalu's attention. It leaned forward and howled fiercely at him, like a lion about to attack.

"DON'T MOVE!" commanded her uncle from behind them. Her father and the creature stood only a few feet apart, face to face as if daring the other to make a move.

"Jordana, how much ancient Cherokee do you remember?" asked her uncle urgently.

"A little," she whimpered.

"Repeat after me."

Jordana and her uncle spoke a prayer in tandem.

*Unalogas woon ehisdov*
*Udodlades sivun aliwiloston*
*Wo osdevdos be telo*
*Doda, Nolonegev wo*

The creature softened its posture, and its red eyes bounced between Lequoia and Jordana. It tilted its head as if mesmerized by their words. The Tsul'kalu rounded its lips and whined a gentle, whimpering cry that sounded like something between a dulcet whistle and a baby's coo. It even appeared less hairy, like the edges of its body were sharper and easier to see.

The Tsul'kalu stared at Jordana, and it dropped a tiny, round object in the yard. The Bigfoot turned and ambled fluidly into the forest.

Arturo nearly fainted as he fell onto his hands and knees. He hadn't realized how long he had been holding his breath. Jordana ran to the spot where the creature had been standing. She waved away the smell and searched the ground for what it had dropped, sifting through blades of grass and dirt with her fingers. The hard round item glanced against her palm. She picked it up and blew the dirt off of it. It was one of her stolen rings.

"What did you tell it?" Mr. Galilahi asked.

"It *wasn't* from this book, I can assure you," barked Lequoia.

Arturo laughed darkly as he pushed himself back up on his feet. "A child's lullaby won't keep the Tsul'kalu away."

"Then I guess you'll need to undo what you have done."

# Ghostly Centerfold

Buzz yawned with a gaping yawp. His vision doubled as his eyelids drooped, and he shook his head, hoping to muster some concentration to watch the bright, familiar picture on the white board ahead.

"What all did you trash at the dump this morning?" he asked Aubrey to him keep himself awake while Coach Kaniffy, the football coach, who also substituted as their history teacher, lectured monotonously over slides of the American Revolution.

"So, you see, the crossing of the Delaware River by Washington on Christmas night in 1776 was really the turning point for the Americans during the war. This early-morning, strategic move in a horrible snowstorm put them in the right place and the right time in order to defeat the Hessians in Trenton, New Jersey, and gave them the upper hand."

"Comforter and sheets," Aubrey responded nonchalantly. They sat together in twin desks. Aubrey flipped lazily through his history textbook as he stifled a yawn. He looked at page after page, scanning the pictures for something engaging to hold his attention and keep him awake. Buzz nodded, attempting to look like he was responding positively to something Coach Kaniffy said.

"Washington's victory that fateful day was like the 1999 season of the St. Louis Rams, when a team that had only won a handful of games in nearly a decade had an unknown quarterback with no playoff experience. With a killer offense at just the right place and time, they came out on top, winning the XXXIV Super Bowl."

Buzz and Aubrey looked at each with confused expressions at Coach Kaniffy's statement. They looked around the classroom for signs of similar bewilderment, but no one else seemed to be paying any attention.

"I have no idea what he is talking about," complained Buzz. "It's like he's speaking a different language half the time."

"It's called E-S-P-N-eese," retorted Aubrey. Buzz chuckled. Aubrey was less amused, since he was surrounded by jocks both at home and at school.

"He wrote on your sheets last night," whispered Buzz sympathetically. "Your ghost must be really hard up for something to do."

"When you've got all eternity to do nothing, I guess torturing children brings some much needed spark into your life," Aubrey replied.

"Did he write anything new?"

"Nope. It's all the same. Never changes. 'Help me,' 'Monsters nigh,' 'Free me.'"

"I thought you removed all the pens and markers from your room?"

"I did. I've removed any conceivable writing utensil. I've trashed any scrap of paper, including books, all my encyclopedias, and anything else he could write on. I took out my desk and TV. I've kept my backpack and schoolwork downstairs at night so he can't get to those. I have one blanket left, which I've stain-guarded. Now all that's left for him to write on is the walls."

"How did he write on your sheets, then?"

"He opened my lava lamp and used the oozing goo inside for ink. It leaked it all over the sheets. I didn't hear anything last night. I just woke up with my sheets covered in sticky, red writing."

Lenny Van Zenny turned around from two rows ahead and mockingly shushed Aubrey and Buzz. Buzz puckered his lips, balled his fists, placed them knuckle to knuckle, kissing the back of his hands. Lenny looked back toward Coach Kaniffy, fully understanding Buzz's butt-kissing jeer.

"Your dad still giving you grief?"

"Oh, yeah," Aubrey replied in a comical tone. "We're not really speaking at the moment."

"Pretty serious, huh?"

"It's been serious." Aubrey's mood darkened. "But there's nothing I can do about it, except continue to ignore it and hope that it will go away, like Mrs. Wizenblatt told me to do."

"Why don't you tell your dad what's really happening?"

"Sure, and give him more fuel for the 'Aubrey is crazy' flames. No thanks. Besides, he's already thinking about sending me away to boarding school. I found pamphlets sitting out on the kitchen table this morning."

Buzz's urgency rose. "Jeez, dude. There's gotta be something we can do. We should call a paranormal investigator...or an exorcist!"

"Maybe," said Aubrey as he flipped over another page in his textbook. Suddenly, Aubrey froze, his eyes fixated on the page. He scanned it repeatedly, convinced that the picture was an illusion, or a cruel trick of his mind. Aubrey leaned forward and buried himself in his book to examine the page more closely. He couldn't deny what he was seeing. His arm shot vertically into the air.

Coach Kaniffy droned on, unabated.

"And thus Washington's army slaughtered the Hessians handily, giving him his first great victory of the war and turning the tide, much like how our own Belugas defeated the Panthers last Friday, giving us the conference championship and a bid to the post-season."

Coach Kaniffy chortled at his own analogy, overly pleased with himself. He was slightly disappointed at the lack of humorous response from the class, and was mostly annoyed that the only sign of life in the room, among drooling, blank faces and students tapping their pencils, was a raised hand.

"Taylor, what's your question?"

"Mr. Kaniffy, can I go to the bathroom?" blurted Aubrey.

Mr. Kaniffy grimaced at the request, irked by Aubrey's apparent disinterest in sports or the history lesson. "Class is almost over. Can't you wait a few minutes?"

Aubrey realized he needed to be more compelling. He stood up and stooped over, gripping the textbook tightly around his stomach. He groaned and grunted, moaned and flexed, doubled-over in colon-wheeling pain.

"No! I really need to go now! The chili I had for lunch is about to make a reappearance." Aubrey twisted his trunk frantically as he waddled slowly up to the front of the class.

Coach Kaniffy upturned his lip. "Well, then go. Reiselstein can share the rest of his notes with you after class." Buzz nodded fervently in agreement, unclear of the reason for Aubrey's shtick, yet careful not to give him away.

Aubrey stumbled to the door and raced out of class.

"He looked like he was dancing with a boa constrictor," Benny Van Zenny joked. A few scattered chuckles bounced around the classroom.

"Why'd he take his history book with him?" Lenny asked.

"Probably for a little light reading while he's riding the dingleberry express," replied Benny. Most of the students in the classroom giggled, but not Buzz. He knew something was afoot.

Outside the classroom, Aubrey stood upright and rushed away from the room with renewed purpose. He passed the bathroom without a glance. His finger bookmarked his page of interest as he rounded a corner and aimed for the next hall on his right.

He turned down another hallway and opened one of the large, heavy double glass doors to the library. He passed through the security turnstile, and the student worker at the curved, faux wooden information desk nodded a greeting. Aubrey ignored him and instead directed his attention to the ceiling, acting enthralled by the mobiles hanging from the ceiling wires.

A blue, oval poster with yellow writing, embellished with shimmering silver streamers for trim, announced the Homecoming Dance this weekend. Like spokes from a wheel, several smaller lime-green posters radiated out from the larger one stating dates, times, and cutesy quotes from last year's dance. Another mobile with an orange background was cut into the shape of a Jack O' Lantern and advertised the upcoming, annual Paddling Pumpkin Raft Race and Parade. Autumn-colored leaves floated up and down on curved wires in orbit around it. Aubrey sneered enviously at the mobile-makers' obvious abundance of free time.

He walked beyond the brief foyer and scanned the library as it opened up into three main sections. The lounge area was immediately to Aubrey's left, furnished with large puffy, vinyl chairs and couches in bright oranges, dark browns and dull greens.

Directly behind the lounge, a state-of-the-art amphitheater descended with widened stair steps into a miniature stadium, set deep below the main floor of the library. Semicircular rows of desktop computers perched on rounded cafeteria-style tables faced a small, rounded stage at the bottom, where Mrs. Kapodophalous, the school information specialist, was teaching class. She cycled through various diagrams and algorithms on an overhead projector that was displaying images on a projection screen behind her. Most of the computer seats were occupied by students, and Aubrey decided he needed more privacy. He changed course and turned right into the block of gray shelving holding the hardbound volumes of the library, anxious to be invisible and uninterrupted.

He snaked through rows of reference books, wound around the edge of the research journals and bulleted between the modern fiction racks. Aubrey emerged on the far side of the library, where a train of double-ended, tan cubicles ran end-to-end along the back wall. Here, he felt certain he would find an available computer and wouldn't be disturbed.

He sped down the walkway between the shelving and the cubicles, searching each desk for signs of use. The Study Hall students occupied most of the cubicles toward the front. Further back a few of the cubicles appeared empty at first, but when he walked in to sit down, a backpack or purse filled the seat.

Aubrey's last hope beckoned from the back corner next to the restrooms. From the angle where he was standing, a single cubicle appeared to be vacant; no body, no bags and no homework. He rushed down to the end hastily. Opening the book to the marked page, Aubrey rested it next to the keyboard. He stared in wonder at the history text, his mind gleaning every fuzzy, archaic detail of the picture on the page. He reached down to turn the computer on, and he noted a small note card, which was taped over the power switch.

Requisition Order # H-406
Monitor Bulb is blown

Aubrey sighed disgustedly. Defeated, he stood up and retraced his steps.

Back at the amphitheater, Aubrey spotted a single open computer in the top back corner. *Not ideal, but it'll have to do*, he thought to himself. He stepped gently down onto the first platform and eased into the chair, careful not to disrupt the class or catch Mrs. Kapodophalous' attention. Out of the corner of his eye, he peeked at the student sitting next to him, hoping to avoid her notice as well. She was typing on her computer, oblivious to his presence, and only glancing up briefly to look at her screen. He pressed the main switch on the hard drive to his computer and waited for it to boot. He was relieved when the green LEDs flashed across the bottom of the monitor.

Once again, Aubrey leafed to the unnerving page of his American History book and studied a grainy, black-and-white family portrait. The background was flat and amorphous, and the picture was pockmarked by fading flakes of artifact that resembled a layer of snowfall on the print.

In the print, the children were upright and stiff like toy soldiers, their faces stoically void of emotion. On the left, three young girls, each only a dozen months apart in age, stood in long, dark pleated gowns with laced collars and sleeves. A single older boy stood on the right dressed in a short jacket and knickers, with his hand on the back of his father's chair. His brow and cheeks were full and adult in contour, but his mouth and chin were slight and thin, revealing his youth.

The mother and father sat in between the standing children, their wrinkled faces worn by hardship. Aubrey surmised they were younger than their age-riddled faces credited them. He could barely divert his gaze from the face of the husband. It was as familiar as a best friend or a close relative, he had seen it so many times. His long, heavy hair was pulled back, clearly exposing his face. The father's deep-set eyes made it impossible to know whether or not he was looking at the camera. His long, bulbous nose, crooked mouth and prominent jaw were distinct, but not absolutely identifiable due to the poor quality of the reproduction. But the scar...the thick crescent-shaped scar that ran from his forehead to his mouth was unmistakable. This man was Aubrey's ghost. He read the caption at the bottom of the picture.

"Primitive Daguerreotype of the Trottle Family, Charleston, South Carolina, circa 1852. Courtesy of the South Carolina Historical Registry."

Aubrey studied the lines intently, scanning them repeatedly. His desperation and chronic exhaustion spurred his need for liberation from his taunting phantom.

The computer screen flickered through its loading sequence and rested at the Lake Julian High School homepage. Aubrey clicked on the browsing tab and typed "Trottle daguerreotype and South Carolina Historical Registry" in the search engine field at the top right hand corner of the web page. A handful of appropriate references filled the screen, followed by links to throttles and tourism sites for the southern United States. Anxiously, he clicked the first link at the top of the page.

"S.C. Historical Registry," penned in golden cursive, traced across the top of the page. The screen glowed with a list of antique pictures on the left and brief counterpart explanations on the right. Aubrey scrolled through the series of family and individual portraits and images of historical buildings until he reached his target. His pulse raced as he studied the synopsis next to the Trottle family photograph.

"This daguerreotype was produced in the Charleston home of the Trottle family in the winter of 1852-3. Reverend Hovis Trottle (second from the right), a prominent Anglican priest in the low country, migrated from Great Britain in the late 1830s and was appointed bishop of the area diocese in 1849. Shortly after this print was taken, the family, by record, relocated to the North Carolina Mountains to establish a new church, where after their legacy becomes cryptogenic."

Aubrey pulled a pen from his pocket and jotted notes above the picture in his history book.

A burst of compact air roared by his ear. Aubrey jumped two inches skyward and spun to the edge of his chair, his hand covering the side of his head in self-defense.

Behind him stood the janitor in his forest green, button-down industrial-style shirt. A silver, rectangular nametag, pinned to the top of his pocket, traced the name 'Griggs' in black lettering. His pants, which matched his shirt in both color and texture, were hemmed a little too high, exposing his bright white socks, which nearly glowed above his black leather postal shoes. He held what appeared to be a miniature acetylene blowtorch in his hand and was adjusting the control knob at the end of its limb.

"Sorry," said the janitor nonchalantly. "I was testing my new keyboard cleaner." He held the apparatus close to his face and repeatedly hit the trigger. Wisps of rushing air blew past his face. The short, curly white hairs of his unkempt beard shuddered with each truncated blast.

In the depths of the amphitheater, Mrs. Kapodophalous paused and stared in the janitor's direction. In turn, several students in the library looked over their shoulders, rubbernecking to find the source of the blasts of noise.

The janitor held up his cleaner with pride and addressed the class, "No one likes a dirty keyboard, do they?" Mrs. K shook her head and returned to the overhead projector.

Aubrey turned back to face his computer and lowered his head, hoping to disappear behind the monitor. "Could you please do that somewhere else?" he asked. He closed the web browser and tried to look busy studying his text-book. He wrote down the name 'Hovis Trottle' next to the picture.

The janitor leaned down over Aubrey's shoulder and asked, "What you workin' on there, son?"

Aubrey was both miffed and bewildered at this intrusion. "Extra credit for American History," he mumbled quickly as he slammed his book shut.

"Lookin' up famous faces and places are ya?"

"Not really," Aubrey retorted.

"Funny things…names that is," continued the janitor. "A potpourri of knowledge…and power in a name."

"Excuse me?" Aubrey asked, sliding to the edge of his seat and angling to end the conversation.

"For example, if I call you Mr. Taylor, then you're just another student. No one special. One of a crowd of other kids without any significant distinction. However, if I call you Aubrey or by a nickname, like Aub, then I am familiar with ya in a less formal manner, and you may respond to me more amiably. But, if I were to speak your full name in its entirety, then it can be used as an imperative, a request or command, said with authority. It becomes an expectation that must be answered."

The janitor pulled an oily rag out of his back pocket and polished his duster. "You see, knowing someone's name, not only clues you in to their parentage and heritage, but it also gives you a certain amount of…control over their behavior, and most importantly, it affects how they react to you." The janitor grinned. "Do you understand, Aubrey Taylor?" He blasted a wave of air across Aubrey's keyboard with his cleaner. Bits of food, dust and debris sprayed across the desk, showering the student next to Aubrey in a cloud of dirt. She scowled at Aubrey and the janitor as she resumed typing.

Aubrey stared at Griggs, dumbfounded. "How do you know my name?"

The janitor's grin widened. "It's on the front of your book cover." Aubrey glanced down at his history text. His name was written in black marker in the lower corner.

"Mr. Griggs, sir," Aubrey addressed him clumsily.

"Griggs is fine, boy. I'm not a teacher and I work for a living. 'Mister' and 'Sir' are unnecessary."

"Um, then, Griggs," Aubrey said less sure of himself. "I would like a little privacy, if you don't mind."

"Sure, son," Griggs answered. "Besides, class is over."

"What?" asked Aubrey.

Griggs stretched out his wrinkly, crooked index finger toward Aubrey. The white hair of his knuckles circled in forested hoops that blanketed that top of his hand. He raised his arm over Aubrey's head and pointed down toward the bottom stage. Aubrey turned to look, and Mrs. Kapodophalous had turned off the projector and was gathering her books and teaching aids. The students were standing up one by one and shuffling down the curved aisles and exiting the stairs out of the amphitheater. He turned back toward Griggs once again to request solitude, but the janitor was gone. He craned his neck to look back at the rows of reference shelving and to his left at the foyer, but he was nowhere to be seen. It was like Griggs had disappeared.

Aubrey pondered briefly what the janitor had said as he stared at the computer screen. The student next to him stood up and walked away. He turned off his computer, clutched the history book to his chest, and followed the class out. He mingled among the students, hoping to blend in with the crowd as he walked toward the double glass doors.

"Hey, Aubrey!" The familiar shout from the lounge shocked him. Buzz was sitting on the orange couch with both of their book bags at his feet. Aubrey lowered his head and walked over to Buzz.

"How did you know I'd be here?" Aubrey asked, surprised by Buzz yet still mystified by his encounter with Griggs.

"I figured the whole *bowel emergency* scene was a charade, and if you found something of interest in your history book, then I guessed you'd be here," Buzz deduced soundly.

Aubrey nodded quietly, but said nothing.

"So what's up?"

"Look at this," Aubrey held open the textbook and pointed to the daguerreotype of the Trottle family.

"It's a picture of some old dead folks," Buzz responded flippantly.

"But not just any old dead folks. The man in the middle is the guy who's been haunting me for the past two months."

Buzz's eyes widened, and he examined the picture intently. "Are you sure?" Buzz questioned hesitantly. "How do you know?"

"The scar," replied Aubrey resolutely, tracing the man's face with his finger. "And I've learned a few things about him."

"Like what?" Buzz asked, engrossed in the picture.

Aubrey hesitated, his thoughts elsewhere, but his tone sternly quickened. "I'll tell you later. I need you to cover for me for the rest of the day. I want to be home when my dad and brother aren't there."

"What are you going to do?"

"Just meet me after school. I'll fill you in then, okay?"

Buzz nodded anxiously. Aubrey closed the book, jumped to his feet, and headed for the exit with his backpack in tow. For a moment, Buzz blinked out of his contemplative stupor.

"Don't do anything crazy," Buzz counseled him as he raced away.

Aubrey paused and looked over his shoulder at Buzz. "Things can't get any crazier, can they?" He didn't wait for Buzz's response as he slipped quickly through the turnstiles.

Buzz didn't know why, but he couldn't disagree more.

# Hovis Exposed

Aubrey dumped his bike in the front yard of his house, and his backpack tripped off his shoulder into the grass. The house and lawn spun dizzyingly with his rapid transition from pedaling to standing, and his chest hastily squeezed air in and out of his lungs to catch up with his fatiguing flight from school. He was grateful the school security officer Mr. Berdun and his canine crony, Sonya, had already been preoccupied with what the hired guard called a T.I.P., or truancy-in-progress, or else his escape wouldn't have been so smooth.

Aubrey ripped off his helmet and dug through his backpack. Grabbing his inhaler, he held it to his lips and pressed the cartridge as he inhaled deeply. His anxiety from skipping the second half of his school day ebbed now that he had made it home. He plodded up the stairs to the front porch, unlocked the door and flung it open.

Aubrey froze. Across the dining room, he met the eyes of his mother as she leaned against the kitchen sink.

"Aubrey," she asked him meekly, "Are you feeling better?" Her knee-length, pink nightgown, buttoned haphazardly down the front, was at least two sizes too big and was peppered with holes from years of wear. Aubrey decided this type of garment needed an expiration date, as it had clearly outlived its life expectancy. His mother looked at him and smiled warily, like she saw him through a fog.

"Huh?" he grunted in reply.

"Didn't you stay home from school today?" she asked.

"No," Aubrey responded. "I just got home."

His mom stared at him, and her expression darkened, lost in delirious comprehension. "Oh," she said. Her face was as flat as her response. "I thought I heard you upstairs earlier." She abruptly opened the cabinet door and pulled a pill bottle from the top. She flipped it open clumsily and dry-swallowed several tablets.

"What did you hear?"

She glanced at him, but ignored his question. She rounded the counter and walked impatiently through the living room and up the stairs. Aubrey chased her slowly, but he knew the opportunity to speak with her had ended.

At the bottom of the stairs, he heard his parents' bedroom door close softly with a click of the lock, sounding his mother's return to her emotional hibernation. He sighed dejectedly, saddened and confused by the brief encounter.

Aubrey walked up the stairs slowly, pacing himself so he didn't disturb his mother or give her the idea he was following her. He paused at each of the three wooden sconces along the wall of the stairs to create the illusion of more time passing. New cream-colored candles had been set in each of the sconces recently. He recalled how the old ones had been burned down to stubs from years of evening power outages, and how upset his dad would be when the lights would go out. As one of the head managers at the power company, Mr. Taylor always took blackouts personally, and repeatedly mentioned how the neighbors were probably talking badly about him whenever a transformer blew or a heavy lightning storm disrupted the grid. Aubrey always thought his father's paranoia was unreasonable. After all, who could be held responsible for things out of their control?

He stared down the hallway at the top of the stairs and waited for more time to slither by. His thoughts of bewildered concern for his mother waned as anxiety squirmed to the front of his mind. He considered the possible explanations for the sounds his mother heard coming from his room. His bedroom door was closed. He couldn't remember if he had closed it that morning or not.

Aubrey walked cautiously toward his room and listened intently for any clues that might explain his mother's odd line of questioning. He heard nothing. He pressed his ear against the door and stood motionless. Everything was still. He gripped the doorknob tightly in preparation as he inhaled deeply. Something was burning.

He thrust the door open. The door battered the inside wall and shuddered backwards with the force. Clouds of smoke billowed from the ceiling of his room into the hallway. A white haze drifted through the room, which was thickest and a milky gray at the top but cleared a few feet from the floor. He covered his mouth with the top of his shirt and ran through the silty vapor.

CLUNK! Aubrey toppled to his hands and knees. He inhaled a lungful of smoke on the way down and coughed violently as his lungs spasmed from the noxious air. Tears pooled at the bottom of his eyelids as the smoke burned his eyes. He closed them tightly, blinking only as much as he needed to see his way through his room. He crawled over to the window and took in a deep breath at the carpet. He pulled himself up by the sill and searched for the latch. He flipped it to the unlocked position and slid the window open, hanging his head outside. He gasped furiously, desperate for the fresh afternoon breeze to wash the smoke from his face and lungs.

The room cleared quickly as the air rushed between his bedroom door and the window. He pivoted slowly and sat down inside the room to look for what had changed.

His bed, desk, empty TV stand and bookshelves were clumped together in the center of his bedroom in a tight circle. He had tripped over his chair, which had skidded across the floor during his fall and now rested several feet from the rest of the furniture. The chair seemed out of place to Aubrey. It didn't look like it did before. Then he realized why. His chair was missing a leg.

A small, thin plume of white smoke drifted upwards from the center of his bed. He heard a crackling pop as a tiny blue spark shot like a miniature firework from the center of his bed. He lifted himself up so he could see the rest of the room. The alarm clock was broken and lay in two pieces on his sheet, its electrical guts frayed and tangled like a bionic hairball. Flickers of electricity jumped between the wires, fueling brief, orange firelets between torn bits of insulation.

Aubrey ran to the opposite wall and pulled the alarm clock's plug from the outlet. He cupped the smoldering alarm clock gingerly from underneath and rushed to the bathroom. He dumped the clock in the sink and turned on the water, dousing its singed, electronic entrails. It drowned to a sizzle. *At least the source of the smoke is gone*, he thought to himself. *No harm done. Now all I have to do is clear out the smell.*

He returned to his bedroom, grateful he had come home early and had the rest of the day to clean up the mess. He stopped at the doorway, and his chin fell in horror at what he hadn't been able to see before.

Black letters scarred all four walls from ceiling to floor. Horizontally, vertically and diagonally, phrases in thick, dark letters marked every spare space like graffiti.

**FREE ME. MONSTERS NIGH. OPEN THE TOMB. GREAT DANGER. HELP ME. RELEASE ME. YOU ARE THE KEY. FREE ME.**

Aubrey circled the room slowly, examining the full vandalistic scale of the writing while reading every word. He touched the wall, unsure if it was real or a dream. A fine, dark dust powdered the pads of his fingers. The black ink was chalky and gritty as he rubbed the ends of his fingers together. He raised his hand to his nose. It smelled like charcoal.

He raked his hand across the writing in a disgusted, angry sweep. The letters faded in his hand's path, but the charcoal remained thick across the wall. He stepped backwards and scanned the room again, his fear losing ground to his frustration. His father's patience had been wearing thin with him since the beginning of school, and he knew this would be the last straw. He had no other choice but to fix it.

As the air continued to clear, he walked over to his bed, and could easily recognize the offending utensil. The missing chair leg lay under his pillow, shortened, charred and blunted at the tip. Aubrey replayed the fiendish act in his head. He imagined his unseen visitor constructing a crude lighter out of the broken alarm clock to fashion a large, scorched pencil with which to write this ghostly, yet elementary, manifesto. In a bizarre way, Aubrey considered the specter's inscriptions quite brilliant, really. His room's defacement would result in a terminal grounding that would give Hovis a captive audience. This ghost was more capable and cunning an adversary than Aubrey had previously thought. Aubrey surged with determination to clean up the mess, hoping to disappoint his ephemeral bully.

Aubrey decided he wouldn't have to be quiet since his mother had just taken her medicine. He rushed downstairs and out the back door. He ran into the shed and collected two plastic buckets with flimsy metal handles, a dried-out sponge and several raggedy towels, permanently marked with dried oil and grease stains. He ran back into the kitchen and set the buckets in each side of the sink, and he turned the faucet to the extreme end of the hot side. Aubrey filled both of them to the brim with near boiling water and squeezed a full bottle of dishwashing liquid into the right bucket, creating a soapy soup of bubbles.

Aubrey struggled to lift each bucket out of the sink and onto the floor. He drug them out of the kitchen with a towel and sponge wedged under each arm. Cautiously he lifted the buckets, balancing them as he slowly plodded through the living room. Occasional droplets of tap water and the bubbly mix would peak over the edge of one of the buckets and fall to the carpet, leaving a trail of moist, round imprints behind him. Each step was calculated to keep as much of the swirling water inside the bucket as possible.

Aubrey stopped halfway up the stairs to rest his cramping hands briefly and regain his grip on the thin handles that had cut into the palms of his hands. At the top, he decided to shuffle the buckets the rest of the way to his bedroom to save his strength.

After he had made it though his door, he shoved the buckets against the far wall of his room. Aubrey rolled the towels into long rolls and laid them at the bottom of the far wall, snug to the baseboard to form an absorbent, protective barrier for the carpet. He drowned the sponge in the murky suds and slammed the hot loam against the wall, scrubbing relentlessly to erase the embered writing.

Patch by patch, the charcoal stain slowly cleared. After the sponge was caked with muddy grime, Aubrey doused and wrung the sediment into the clear bucket and then reloaded the sponge with soap. Splattering the wall again with the sudsy lather, he would scrub, rinse, refill, and repeat. In a few areas, he scoured the wall with enough force to flake off a few bits of drywall, but it didn't matter. The writing was slowly washing away. Aubrey was tremulously pleased with his progress and, by his estimation, he could have his room back in order before sundown.

At the end of the first wall, Aubrey's arms were burning from all the fervid scouring. He paused to survey his progress and felt a twinge of success.

Where he had already cleaned, the mess was almost completely wiped away. The cleansed area reminded him of a large puffy cloud in the middle of a nightmarish sky. Below that, the dripping suds, running down the wall like dark foamy tears, were washing away the charcoal for him. His heart rushed with joy. He was going to beat his ghost.

Intent on changing out the water in the buckets and switching walls, Aubrey walked over to the middle part of the wall and grabbed their handles. His toes sloshed in cold, moist carpet on the floor. He glanced down, and dark flecks of dirt clung to his feet. Frothy black foam rolled slowly out from the wall through the fibers of the carpet, like a tiny tsunami of muck gently advancing toward the center of his bedroom. Quickly, he lifted one of the towels at the bottom of the wall. The towel was dry. The milieu of soap and charcoal that dribbled down the wall had run underneath the towels and over the baseboards, staining the carpet. Aubrey's heart dropped and all his toil's happiness drained through his stomach. He dropped the sponge lifelessly into the bucket. The mess he thought he had washed away had simply seeped across the floor.

Aubrey backed up slowly and viewed the far side of the room. The entire length of carpet at the edge of the wall was inky black. He slumped onto his bed with his head in his hands, completely defeated and demoralized. Tears streamed down his charcoal-smudged face and between his fingers as he sobbed softly.

His father would yell. With all that had happened, he was afraid his father might hit him. He would certainly call him crazy, and might even make references to him being like his mother. He had done everything he could to cover up his intruder's destruction, despite each encounter being worse than before.

"Why me?" he begged in moans. "Why did you have to ruin *my* life?" The guttural words croaked from the back of Aubrey's throat.

Anger, frustration and pain swelled inside him. He had been picked on, pointed out and laughed at his entire life. Now that a world he couldn't see was against him, this new victimhood was more than he could stand. It was time for his attacker to face him or move on.

"Why are you here, and what do you want with me?" he yelped. He addressed the air around him, expecting the haunter to hear his protest.

His lower lip trembled with rage and resentment. Aubrey choked back on his tears as he filled his lungs fully to speak.

"If you want me to help you, then show yourself!"

The air didn't respond, and the only sound in the bedroom was his own tearful breathing. Aubrey punched his pillow violently in an explosion of exasperation.

"SHOW YOURSELF!" he screamed. The inanimate world around him stood still. He wrenched the pillow to his face and wailed into its cover without restraint.

"Show yourself, Hovis." He felt silly when he thought about what he was doing, speaking a dead man's name out loud, but at this point, what did he have to lose? He remembered what Griggs had said.

"Show yourself, Hovis...Trottle." Hearing the name out loud for the first time chilled Aubrey and forced his despondency to kowtow to his fear. His thoughts morphed from mournful outburst to cautious alert, and he watched and listened attentively for any changes in his surroundings. He scanned the room, eager for a response, yet hoping for nothing to happen.

Moments passed slowly at first, but his trepidation deflated as time returned to normal with the lack of response from his ghost. The reality of his ruined room returned and suffocated him with futility. He allowed himself a pity chuckle. Why would he believe some random old fool of a hall sweeper? *Desperation spurs regression*, he thought to himself.

"Hovis Trottle, meet Aubrey 'the Gullible' Taylor," he uttered self-mockingly in a sing-song tone. He shook his head in disappointment. Aubrey stood up and dried his hands off on his pants. He walked over to the buckets, unrolled the towels from against the wall and pressed them deeply into the bubbly mire at the edge of the carpet, hoping to tidy up some of the new mess he had created.

The bedroom door slammed shut suddenly. The walls shuddered from the force. Aubrey froze with fright. He lurched forward and slipped rear-down into the boggy floor. He gasped so hard it felt like the center of his chest grazed his backbone.

Aubrey hunted his room for the source of the unexpected movement. No ghost. No new furniture changes. Nothing unusual. And all he could hear were the limbs and leaves of the trees swimming in the breeze blowing outside the window. *Ahhhh*, he thought to himself, *the wind must have drawn the door shut.*

Sharp aches from his tailbone reached his brain, and he grimaced with discomfort. He exhaled slowly to try and calm his heart from pounding against his shirt. Aubrey gently secured his hands on clean flooring and lifted himself out of the damp carpet.

The desk chair skidded across the floor, almost like it had been kicked. Jarred with fright, Aubrey jumped sideways, avoiding the tumbling chair.

It rocked to a stop directly in front of him. The blood drained from Aubrey's face, and he stood there frozen, staring at his supernaturally-abled, yet handicapped, desk chair.

"Hovis Trottle," Aubrey eked out with a nearly inaudible voice.

A haze of darkened shadow flashed instantly around him and then, as quickly as it fallen, disappeared. Aubrey jumped back and dropped against the damp wall. He forced his eyes to stay open and watched the daylight from the window for an explanation for the shadow. The darkness fell again, obscuring his vision.

Aubrey's jaw clenched, and he grunted out the name, "Hovis...Trottle!"

The darkness lifted, and the full view of his room returned. Aubrey wanted to figure out more about what was going on and ask why he was being haunted, but the fear from this new level of intimacy with his ghost was too much for him. He needed to run.

Aubrey launched himself forward and fell onto his bed. All four of his limbs flailed to propel him out of his bedroom. The single bed sheet twisted around his bicycling legs like a rag caught in the blades of a fan. He slumped over the opposite edge of the bed to the floor. The room blackened again. He ripped manically at the sheet, scrambling to pull his feet from the thick knots of cloth.

"HOVIS TROTTLE!" he shouted, and the darkness faded.

Aubrey stood upright, clawed at the doorknob until it released, and ran into the open safety of the hallway. He turned around and faced his bedroom, bracing himself against the opposite wall. The smoke had completely cleared. He worried that maybe he was having a stroke, or worse, hallucinating. He rubbed his eyes with his thumb and index finger and pressed in deeply, hoping to reset his vision, and scrunched his upper face into a tightly wrinkled ball as he squeezed his eyelids together. The dark figure coalesced behind his eyes. Aubrey released his contracted face and opened his eyes, but the darkness hung in the doorway. But now it had a face, the same thick-browed, wide-jawed face Aubrey had been seeing and dreading at night for months. For the first time, he could see it in broad daylight with his eyes open.

Aubrey was mesmerized by the intense detail of the image. The chains that fastened Hovis' arms to the ground, his laced collar, the deep-set scar on his face, were now all solid and three-dimensional. This figure transcended phantasm; it was real, and he was undoubtedly the man in the antique photograph.

"GO AWAY! HOVIS TROTTLE!" he yelled in a firm but shaky voice.

Thick clouds of dust crested upwards from the floor and spindrift swirled around the ghost's head. Hovis' jaw craned open, and his lips strained and warbled.

"Naaawwwwbbbbeeeeyyy...Taaaaaaaayywwwoooooorrrrr," hissed Hovis in a faint, soft whisper. Aubrey easily recognized his name in the utterance. He bolted frantically down the hallway.

Aubrey stopped abruptly at the top of the stairs. The candles along the descending wall were burning brightly, the flames several inches high with dark, wavy streams of smoke rising to the ceiling. He clung to the right side, opposite the wall, and walked briskly down the steps, cautiously monitoring each sconce as he passed it.

Midway down the stairs, the bottom candle ejected itself from the sconce and bounced along the living room floor, smoky wisps rising from its tip as the fire extinguished. The air at the bottom of the stairs clouded up. The husky voice Aubrey heard was louder and more succinct.

"Aubrey Taylor."

Aubrey bolted through the darkening space at the bottom of the stairs and arrived at the front door in four bounding steps. He had made it. He could escape. He flung open the door and catapulted himself through it.

Hovis Trottle stood on the porch in full, physical form, like a mobile statue etched in darkness. Hovis raised his arms into the air, blocking Aubrey's forward movement. The chains wrapped around Hovis' elbows, now clearly visible, tautly pulled downward against his arms, extending deep into the wooden porch flooring. The soot around Hovis swirled violently as he moved forward toward Aubrey, like he was kicking up dust from a dirty floor.

Aubrey panicked. His thin frame scarcely slipped between Hovis' arm and the exterior wall as he jumped over the railing onto the side lawn. He unsuccessfully dodged two large flowerpots of red, bristly begonias on the ledge, which tumbled to the ground with him. They shattered in an array of clay shards, potting soil, and pulverized plant parts. Aubrey rolled along the ground with the exploding vegetation, and a root ball pierced by a bone landed next to him. Repulsed and frightened, he gained his feet and raced toward his bike. His feet landed on the pedals with all the force of his weight, jolting him and the bike onto Dalton Circle. As he left his yard, he looked back over his shoulder and saw several large bones lying scattered among the pot wreckage, bones of appropriate size and shape to be human. Hovis had disappeared from the porch, but Aubrey had no intention of learning his new whereabouts.

# Fading and Abetting

Relieved by his narrow escape, Aubrey raced to the top of Dalton Circle. His new burst of energy sent him sailing up the road carelessly. The shadows around him lightened, and he had no intention of speaking Hovis' name again any time soon. He passed Ms. Thistlewood's house before he realized he didn't have a destination, and he couldn't think of a place of refuge, since he was still supposed to be in school.

Aubrey slackened up on the pedals. He looked over his shoulder at his house in the distance. There was no new sign of disturbance, but with all that had happened, he couldn't bring himself to turn around. He closed his eyes and scanned the road behind him, but the phosphenes quickly faded, leaving only darkness behind his eyelids.

Aubrey looked at Rodriqa's house, but, as was expected, no one was at home. Mulling over possible pit stops, he swerved toward Ms. Thistlewood's cottage. Something about her made him unquenchably uneasy, but at least there he could cover up his truancy and maybe ask some questions that desperately needed answering. Buzz seemed to trust her, and he trusted Buzz. Why couldn't he trust her?

The shutters to her cottage were closed tightly over the windows, and no smoke rose from the chimney. Aubrey quickly surmised she was not available and gratefully resigned the option of stopping there.

He sped forward again and pondered his predicament. Aubrey needed a place to hide and to think, somewhere could he go and avoid authority and responsibility.

As he approached the Asheville Highway, a sign of sanctuary came into view. The familiar site helped him relax.

***Ray Gene's Smart Mart & Finer Diner*** could be the perfect place to rest without intrusion. It was a simple, safe and secure solution. He could look like he was shopping around, avoid school, and have time to evaluate all that had happened that day. And better yet, the parking lot was empty.

Aubrey pedaled around to the backside of the store and wheeled his bike into the thin space between the wall's stuccoed exterior and the brown metal dumpster to keep it out of sight. He rushed around the corner of the store and kept his head down until he pushed the glass doors open. An electronic *bing-bong* chimed from overhead.

"Well, hello there, Mr. Aubrey," boomed a voice that was startling and a little too loud, but friendly and familiar, and Aubrey was desperate for both at the moment. Mr. Jennings folded his newspaper and waved Aubrey in.

Mr. Jennings had solely owned and operated his self-christened corner market for as long as Aubrey could remember. Although the premises were a civic institution, nearly eligible for historical site status, the inside had radically changed over the past several years.

A couple of decades ago the **Smart Mart** was nothing more than a simple local vendor, providing a venue for area farmers and ranchers to sell their produce, dairy and meats with little middle-man involvement. With the advent of corporatized megamarkets, Mr. Jennings couldn't compete, and was forced to adapt and diversify. The grocery section shrank and crept to the rear of the store with each new addition of shelving occupied by the latest and greatest hot-ticket, retail items. Rows of hardware and automotive parts, sporting goods and electronics filled most of the right-hand side of the mart now. And the left-hand side made way for a miniaturized fast-food restaurant that sold hot dogs, hamburgers, renamed *harmburgers* by the locals since they were piled with every fatty topping available, along with abundant assortments of potato cuttings and daily, unique desserts.

After Mr. Jennings had installed the electronics section, he experienced a string of thefts during operating hours from some local high school hooligans. He was completely blind to the shoplifting until he realized all his MP3 accessories were missing, and no one had paid for them. In order to plug his widening financial leak, Mr. Jennings installed the entrance door chime and four concave silver security mirrors in the top corners of the ceiling.

Waving, Aubrey walked up to the rectangular counter isolated in the center of the store and flashed Mr. Jennings a smile. Aubrey felt awkwardly safe standing in front of Mr. Jennings while flanked by two plump, plastic barrels filled to the brim with icy sodas and fruit drinks. Aubrey scanned the headlines to the **Lake Julian Mountain Lyre** sitting on the countertop, feigning interest and hoping to kill time. *Leader of the Shilac: May O'Klammer blasts away competition at regional band festival.*

Uncomfortable with the silence, Aubrey asked, "How have you been?"

Mr. Jennings' deeply creased face beamed with genuine cheer. As much as the market had changed over the years, its owner had remained steadfastly kind and helpful, especially to the loyal locals. His hair was mostly white now, and fewer sprigs of it sprouted from beneath the ball cap he always wore. Even the cap revealed its age, its bright royal blue dulling from wear.

"I can't complain," replied Mr. Jennings. "Been a slow day today, but the tourists should be rollin' into town soon."

Aubrey rested an elbow on the counter and stared past Mr. Jennings to the pictures displayed prominently on the brown paneling behind him. The three black-and-white photos, framed in corkboard, hung in a triangular formation overlooking the cash register. Yellowed and wrinkled with time, they attracted the attention of nearly every customer.

The top center photograph showed a much younger Mr. Jennings standing in front of a 1958 Ford Fairlane, holding a gleaming metal trophy over his shoulders. To his right, a beautiful young woman with dark curly hair wrapped a congratulatory arm around his back. She reminded Aubrey of a brunette Marilyn Monroe. To his left another gentleman, who Aubrey didn't recognize, was in mid-stride toward the couple with mouth agape in laughter. It was clearly a happy day, as everyone had excessively boisterous facial expressions. Aubrey couldn't decide which was brighter, the chrome bumper of the car, the trophy, or Mr. Jennings' wide smile. Beneath the photo a caption read,

1959 Stock Car Racing Rookie of the Year
Ray Gene "Ragin' Jennings

The picture to the lower left was a wedding picture of Mr. and Mrs. Jennings. Mr. Jennings was dressed in a traditional tuxedo and bowtie. Mrs. Jennings looked like a fairytale princess. She wore a simple but elegant strapless white gown, and her hair was swept upward into a beehive with small white flowers wound within it. Joyful innocence glowed from the photograph. Its happiness was so infectious, most couldn't look at the picture without returning a smile. But Aubrey always thought it was odd that the woman from the top photo was not the same one as Mr. Jennings' wife.

The third photograph at the lower right was an action shot of a series of antique cars racing on an inclined curve. Dirt sprayed from behind each of the vehicles' wheels, and all the cars appeared finely blurred from their forward motion. The focus of the picture in the center appeared to be the same Ford from the top photo, except this car's chrome fittings were caked in mud, and the hood and doors were painted with the number "74."

"What's buggin' ya, kid?" asked Mr. Jennings. His broad grin curled downward, and his brow furrowed into a concrete spasm. "You don't seem yourself."

Aubrey's daydream spilled wide open, and he was forced himself to look directly at Mr. Jennings, instead of beyond him. "How so?" he inquired in turn.

"For starters, you're as pale as a frost-covered whippoorwill in the dead of winter. Plus, you're not your usual cheerful self. Are you feelin' okay?"

"I'm fine," Aubrey muttered as he shifted his gaze downward. Aubrey was becoming more annoyed with everyone asking about his well-being, although he knew he was not 'okay.' He figured it was some sort of karmic penance for stealing out of class earlier today.

"I think you might need a little more meat in your diet, son. You look like you've seen a ghost," offered Mr. Jennings.

Aubrey opened his mouth to refute both claims, but then realized he couldn't disagree with either of his proposals. The empty silence was uncomfortable, for the both of them.

Mr. Jennings leaned in toward Aubrey. "Did school let out early today?" he whispered cautiously.

Aubrey grew anxious, and his tongue tripped over his lips. All he could do to interrupt the silence was utter a few stuttering 'um's" and an arduously awkward "ah."

"Tell you what, you don't tell Mrs. Jennings that I eat more of the crescent cream puffs than I sell, and I won't tell Mrs. Taylor that you needed a," he crinkled his brow to think, "what do they call them these days...oh yeah...a mental health day. Deal?" Mr. Jennings' grin stretched wider than before, and he placed his open hand on the counter.

Aubrey returned a smile, and his eyes lightened. He grabbed Mr. Jennings' hand and shook it firmly.

Mr. Jennings inhaled deeply. "How's your mom and dad doin'?"

"Fine, I guess," Aubrey replied unenthusiastically. "Same as usual."

Mr. Jennings hunted for conversation. "Amazing high school football season this year. You're brother's done mighty well. I've heard he's the leading quarterback in the region. There's even talk of the Belugas making it to state."

Aubrey's head dropped. "Yeah, it sounds like they've done well. I hear about it every night. My dad's real proud. It's all he talks about...almost."

Mr. Jennings was perplexed with Aubrey's shifting mood. He leaned forward and grabbed two sodas from the ice bin next to Aubrey, cracking them both open and handing one to Aubrey. With a deep sigh, he said, "Sounds like it might be a lot for you to live up to." Mr. Jennings took an obliging sip from his can.

"Yeah," replied Aubrey in a somber tone.

"So what brings you in today?" Mr. Jennings decided the direct approach might be less painful.

Aubrey searched his mind for a quick way to evade the truth, but the mental energy to concoct a meaningful, believable ruse just wasn't there. He gave up and let his heart speak.

"Honestly, Mr. Jennings, I just needed a break."

"A break from what?" Mr. Jennings pursued.

"Everything," Aubrey answered. Mr. Jennings creased his eyebrows together, unsatisfied with the response, and Aubrey knew he expected a clearer reply. "It's been a really rough year so far, and everything just seems turned on end. There's no good explanation for it. And no way to fix, I don't think. I wish things were the way they used to be, and being here, at least, life feels...simpler, I guess." Although the brief catharsis felt good, hearing the words out loud left Aubrey a little ashamed of himself.

Mr. Jennings squeezed his lips together and mused at Aubrey empathetically. "Welp, you're always welcome here, no matter what's going on." He smiled at Aubrey comfortingly. Aubrey nodded his head in appreciation.

"You're a good egg, Aubrey. You've always been a good kid. Don't let anyone tell you otherwise. Besides, seems like a lot of folks around here have been having a tough year. Lots of strange goings on, too. The circus. The weird earthquake that messed up the dam. Bizarre Bigfoot sightings all over town. The missing football player from Lake Julian. Did you know him?"

"Yeah," Aubrey affirmed grudgingly. "He was in a couple of my classes. I've known him for years."

"Such a shame," said Mr. Jennings, shaking his head. "And now I hear there's been ghost sightings up at the Circle of Circles Cemetery-"

"The *what*?" interrupted Aubrey. He shook with such a force from hearing the name that he nearly jumped over the counter.

"Yeah," Mr. Jennings explained, happy he was able to finally invigorate Aubrey, "Mrs. Napier, you know her, right?"

Aubrey shook his head impatiently, unconcerned about who she was but desperate for more information about the cemetery.

"You know," Mr. Jennings continued, "She lives over off 4th street. Real nice lady, kinda looks like a schnauzer in the face and walks with the bad limp. Anyway, she was walkin' her dogs up above the picnic area at the dam, and they caught a whiff of somethin'. They started barkin' and chasin' whatever it was, and she couldn't get 'em to calm down. They ended up draggin' her all the way to the top of the hill.

"But when they got close to the cemetery, the dogs stopped runnin' all of a sudden and started growlin' and almost moanin', so she says. Then she saw two dark figures standing in a plot, like shadows you couldn't see through. They were yellin' at each other."

"Really?" reacted Aubrey with intrigue.

"Yeah. Strange, huh?" replied Mr. Jennings. "At first she thought it was some goofy kids staging another attack on the mine, but when she walked to the opposite edge of the cemetery to get a better look, they were gone. No noise. No movement. Nothing. They hadn't walked away. They just disappeared."

Aubrey stood there as still as molasses, spellbound by the story. "Whoa," Aubrey replied in awe. "I didn't realize that old graveyard had a name."

"That's what they used to call it when I was a kid. No one's been buried there in years, though. People stopped using it when the dam was built, afraid the higher water levels might wash away the coffins. I'm surprised it hasn't been relocated, especially with all the activity at the mine. I think families and folks in the area just forgot about it. And thankfully so. It's always been kinda spooky. Never liked cemeteries much, myself."

A car engine with a shoddy muffler roared up to the front door of the mart and cranked to a halt. Startled by the unwelcome patron, Aubrey wrenched his head around quickly to see who had arrived. He could easily read the block letters painted on the side of the car. Icy shivers speared down Aubrey's spine, and his heart dropped into his stomach.

The two Kluggard brothers emerged, one from each side of the police car. Fred wiped off the top of his cap and primped in the car side mirror, combing the hairs of his temple into place. Ned's gelatinous frame poured from the passenger side, bouncing between the edge of the seat and door as he heaved himself upright on top of his stick-figure legs. Large crumbs from a car-ride meal tumbled to the ground off his chest. He brushed down the front of his uniform shirt, but he couldn't quite press out all the wrinkles. He looked like he had recently log-rolled down a hillside.

"Mr. Jennings, please don't tell them I'm here," Aubrey begged in a high-pitched panic. He didn't wait for Mr. Jennings to reply. He sped toward the back of the store and crouched down behind a row of breakfast pastries in front of the dairy refrigerators.

The computerized *bing-bong* sounded from overhead. Aubrey peered toward the counter between the cereal boxes on the top shelf. Fred strutted in slowly with his hand on his holster. Ned waddled in after, barely avoiding a collision with the front door before it closed.

"Howdy, officers. How's the day treatin' ya?" Mr. Jennings greeted them merrily. Fred flipped up his clip-on sunglasses and surveyed the entire store in a panoramic head sweep.

"Not too shabby, Ragin'. How's business?" Fred asked.

"Typical weekday," Mr. Jennings offered. "Not much goin' on, but it'll pick up soon, I suspect." Mr. Jennings pulled several stacks of papers from underneath the counter and flipped through them, feigning distraction. "So what brings you two out on such a calm day?"

Fred walked up to the counter and watched Mr. Jennings intently. "Just makin' the rounds," he replied. Ned sauntered up behind Fred, pulling his belt over his rotund mid-section, trying to stabilize his extra poundage.

Fred leaned over to catch Mr. Jennings eyes. "Seen anything *unusual* lately?" he asked suspiciously. Mr. Jennings paused for a moment and stared briefly at Fred, considering his question, and then returned to his paperwork.

"Nothing out of the ordinary," Mr. Jennings replied. "Why do you ask?"

Fred smiled half-heartedly and watched while Mr. Jennings filed through his papers. Ned spied the wire shelving next to the checkout counter. It was stocked full of packaged doughnuts. He walked over to it and fingered through the vast varieties: powdered sugar, strawberry coconut, chocolate glaze, and blueberry oatmeal. Mr. Jennings gave Ned a cursory glance and frowned. "Why? Should I have seen something *unusual?*" he replied to Fred, without looking at him.

"Well, there have been some strange goings-on around here lately," Fred said, straightening up to his full height. He stretched out his shoulders and popped his neck, like he was preparing to engage the enemy.

"Uh-huh," Mr. Jennings agreed.

"We got a call from Mrs. Habershum this morning. She reported a disturbance at the old abandoned cemetery between the Berybomag Mine and Lake Julian Dam." Mr. Jennings looked up at this unexpected news. Ned turned briefly toward Fred and scowled, displeased with his brother sharing so much information, but his attention quickly returned to his doughnut hunt.

"We came to check it out," continued Fred. "Was just curious as to if you had heard anything about it...or related to it." Fred spiked an eyebrow, trying to mentally pump Mr. Jennings for information.

"Really," responded Mr. Jennings, mystified. "What did she see?"

"It's most likely nothing," Fred sighed, frustrated that his precious time was being squandered. "It's probably just a couple of kids playin' hooky and causin' trouble with nothin' better to do than to scare an elderly woman enjoying a fall afternoon."

Mr. Jennings' cheerful demeanor melted into an assertively grave calm. He paused and formed his words carefully. "I wouldn't take anything Mrs. Habershum said lightly. I've known her for many, many years, and she's not one to overreact or allow her imagination to get away from her. I would take her at her word. Besides, she's only in her sixties. That's not exactly elderly." Ned grunted and smirked in disagreement as he tore open a clear plastic bag of white-powdered doughnuts. "What did she report?" asked Mr. Jennings directly, ignoring Ned.

Fred chuckled. "If what she said wasn't so far fetched, we wouldn't have such a hard time believing it." Ned shoved two doughnuts in his mouth and munched down on the sugary-laced, crumbly mess. "Maybe she went off her medication," Fred added, laughing. He looked at his partner for a reciprocal response to his off-color joke. Ned guffawed awkwardly. Several more doughnuts had disappeared within his cavernous jowls, and a pasty white film of foamy saliva crystallized around his lips.

Aubrey marveled at the spectacle from the rear of the store. He strained to make out their words, tilting his head so that his ears could catch as of much of the conversation as possible, while simultaneously turning away to avoid the sight Ned's barbaric dining habits.

Aubrey's tight grip on the top shelf slipped slightly, and he knocked over a box of cereal. The cardboard box bounced down the shelving and slammed into the floor in front of the aisle.

Fred jerked his head to the back of the store. "What was that?" he asked through his snickering.

Aubrey sank to the ground, and his heart pounded fretfully. He formed the tightest ball his body could make, hoping to stay out of sight, and crawled slowly toward the back corner of the store.

"It's probably just a mouse. Sometimes they like to scurry along the shelves and look for crumbs," fibbed Mr. Jennings. "So you think Mrs. Habershum was hallucinating?" he asked, in an attempt to redirect the conversation.

Fred grimaced at the thought of rodents running rampant in a grocery store. "I'll tell you the report we got, then you decide," he chortled. A shower of moist, doughy particles spewed from Ned's mouth as he crowed loudly at Fred.

Fred recounted the report through his giggles. "Mrs. Habershum called downtown around noon, and said she was out picking blackberries on the hill atop the dam when she reportedly saw a dozen of the darkest shadows she'd ever seen rolling over the tombstones at the old cemetery up there." Ned squinted his eyes tightly together and large chunks of moist donut spilled to the floor as his mouth gaped open in uproarious laughter. Fred's laughter intensified as he watched Ned. Mr. Jennings peered at them both disconcertedly.

"Then she said they swarmed together like a group of bodiless bees." Fred pursed his lips tightly to contain his merriment. "And this is the best part," Fred continued, snorting in between his words, "She said they started swirling in and out like couples as if they were dancing. She said it reminded her of a *ghost cotillion.*"

Fred put his head down on the counter in a full onslaught of laughter and beat his fist against the Formica. Ned bent over and covered his mouth with his hands to keep himself from vomiting between his shrieks of amusement. Fred stared up at Mr. Jennings, whose face was solid and still as stone. Tears streamed down Ned's scrunched up face, and he struggled for air as his torso squeezed outbursts of thunderous gut-wrenching howls. Fred turned over his shoulder and looked at the mirror in the rear corner. His laughter suddenly stopped.

"I think I found your mouse," said Fred sternly.

Aubrey turned his head to look at the mirror above him and met Fred's eyes across the store. Fred grinned slyly. Aubrey bolted for the front of the store and escaped through the door, the overhead *bing-bong* announcing his departure.

Fred jerked himself upright and pivoted to catch the eavesdropper. He took a quick step forward, but his shiny officer shoe slid on the slippery wet doughnut cud covering the floor. His foot shot straight for the ceiling. The back of Fred's head slapped against the linoleum with a sharp crack. Ned's snickering halted immediately, and he fumbled to his brother's aid, sliding through his own egested mess. He spun and twirled like a brawny ballerina, finally landing firmly on his well-cushioned rump.

Mr. Jennings leaned over the counter and chuckled, "Now *that* was funny."

## Real-ly Chill-ly

Pearly gray clouds, heavy with glistening arctic moisture, whisked hastily across the sea-blue sky, dissolving and breaking apart from the reckless barrage of slaloming winds. The late summer sun glowed low in the horizon, flickering behind the herds of passing clouds, its brightness slowly dying earlier and earlier each day. Chevrons of squawking geese flew high above the foggy fray, heading south for their winter holiday. The seasons were changing, and today everyone knew it.

Aubrey pedaled his bike in a frenzy up the grassy hillside between the dam and mine, but the increasing slope made it nearly impossible for him to gain any momentum. He jumped off his bike and huddled between a cluster of trees. Crouching down, he surveyed what little he could see of the Asheville Highway below. He breathed a deep sigh of relief. At this point, if the Kluggards hadn't caught up with him, maybe he could take a quick peek at the cemetery before they made it to the top to take a look around. *Not like Ned would be an agile climber anyway*, Aubrey chuckled to himself.

He laid his bike on its side and covered it haphazardly with twigs and dying grasses. Aubrey faced the cemetery at the top of the hill and walked cautiously toward it. The air was cooler than when he left school, and the rush of brisk, whirling breezes iced the tip of his nose and raised goose pimples on his bare forearms.

A thin layer of dried auburn and burgundy leaves danced in the wind along the hill, like wax paper gymnasts tumbling head over heels on their brittle ends. Aubrey's feet shuffled through the leaf litter, fearful of what he might find, yet anxious to catch a glimpse of what Mrs. Habershum had seen.

The abandoned graveyard's front gate crested over the top of the hill as Aubrey approached the summit. Little of the original perimeter fence remained, but most of the intricate wrought iron entranceway stood sturdily, despite its precarious forward lean. Its black metal bars were heavily pitted with jagged craters of devouring orange rust, and the double-swing lichgate was frozen ajar. Many of the fleur-de-lis ornaments that topped the posts were broken off or missing, but the single large adornment atop the gate remained largely intact, as if challenging the elements to destroy it like a stubborn captain determined to hope against hope on a sinking ship.

Its elaborate pattern struck Aubrey, and he felt daft for never noticing its significance before. An outer thick ring bearing on its inner side a series of smaller circles which were connected by three wired globes that formed a three-dimensional Venn diagram, that were also united by a central halo.

"Circle of circles," Aubrey murmured out loud. He shook his head in disappointed triumph. He and Buzz had wasted so many hours hunting for something that was so close and so simply marked. Yet they had been dumbfounded about where or what it was. They simply hadn't asked the right person the right question. Mr. Jennings had known all along, and he didn't need a book or Internet access to tell them.

Aubrey walked up alongside the cemetery at the edge of the forest to inspect the gravestones from a distance. Many of the trees at the top of the hill had lost most of their leaves, especially higher up, where the sap's retreat had left a collage of fading greens in the canopy. Only the evergreens stood untouched by summer's farewell. A row of pine trees outlined the graveyard's perimeter, their plush, green needles standing out amongst the waning background foliage. Their branches stretched broadly and straight into the air, parallel to the ground, like sentinels positioned for a century's long attention. Aubrey recognized these trees as white pines, all oddly the exact same height, as if they had started to grow within a season or two of each other. He stopped and turned around. He realized they were all about the same distance apart around the cemetery...forming a circle. And the limbs radiated out at regular intervals from the cylindrical trunks of the trees...creating circles. Aubrey turned and, in awe, appraised the panoramic view around the summit.

"Another circle of circles," he remarked to himself. But what did it mean? Aubrey furrowed his brow as he tried to connect all the odd relationships. Then something Mrs. Wizenblatt had said flooded back into his mind. He concentrated so he could remember the quote as accurately as possible.

"When the irregularity and entropy of nature is interrupted by a forced and focused geometry, then something or someone has intervened. Creation dislikes its boundaries."

Some of the Old Widow's babble was starting to make some sense. Question after question blitzed Aubrey's brain. If someone had planted these trees here, what were they trying to do? Did the circles make the ground more sacred? Did they want to keep someone out? Or in? And what does that have to do with Hovis? And why he is haunting me?

Aubrey was grateful for the tiny spark of hope. It was like a glimmer of understanding amidst a rumbling sea of uncertainty. Now, he had a clue...a lead to follow for answers. This was no ordinary cemetery, and he had to find out why.

Aubrey stared across the graveyard to the opposite tree line, positioning as much of the plot in his field of view as possible. He closed his eyes and waited. Green and red counter-images faded, and the phosphenes swirled behind his eyes until only darkness remained. There were no weird figures. No movement. And, most importantly, no Hovis. Aubrey wasn't sure if he could see any ghost, or just Hovis, or perhaps only those that wanted to be seen, but he decided it didn't make him crazy for trying. If Mrs. Habershum had seen a horde of specters earlier, they didn't appear to be here now.

Aubrey walked up to the graveyard's old fence line and stepped over the crooked, corroded remnants that spiked upward, careful not to impale his feet on hidden points lying under the fallen leaves. The cemetery was several acres in size and irregularly shaped, as if additions had been devised in various arrangements throughout its history. Not a single tree grew in the graveyard's lot. And although the entire hilltop was covered with old timber, only small grasses and weeds grew within the cemetery's borders, leaving a clearly demarcated oval in the woodland dome that exposed an unobstructed sky.

Aubrey plodded forward with guarded scrutiny. The ground was no longer the firm topsoil of the hillside, and Aubrey's feet sank several inches into the soggy, graveyard peat. It hadn't rained for a week, but the thick ground debris trapped the moisture within the sodden muck beneath. Man-made rubbish, mostly evidence of prior adolescent pandemonium, was also scattered about the plots, mingling among the damp twigs and leaves. Torn plastic bottle rings, half-bent bottle caps, remnants of faux flower stems and leaves, and triangular shards of opaque brown glass littered the ground around collections of gravesites with taller tombstones. Aubrey figured the larger gravestones would be easier to hide behind if someone was up to something nefarious. At the bottom of one of headstones, Aubrey stopped to examine three gunshot beer cans lying on top of a yellow piece of paper. He cautiously shimmied the paper out from underneath the cans so he could read it.

The page was ripped through its middle, shearing off the upper part of a clown's face. Only the swollen, red smile, purple-blushed cheeks and chin, and the lower portion of its blue, bulbous nose could be seen. Below the half-face, the word CIRCUS was embossed in pink, bubbled letters along with the dates July 17th to August 22nd. The flyer was wrinkled, damp and dirty, and was decorated with a couple of bullet holes of its own. The disappearance of the circus had perplexed the entire community, but in light of other events, it had become more of a background nuisance. Aubrey dropped the paper on the ground, lacking the energy to take on another mystery at the moment.

Aubrey tried to tread around the gravesites as best he could out of tacit respect for the deceased, but the plot lines were less clear the closer he walked toward the center of the cemetery. Some of the tombstones did not reside at the head of a grave, and many of the foot markers had been moved or were missing.

Aubrey scanned the cemetery for any clues that might give away where Hovis' grave might be located. He marveled at the ample variety of gravestones that had been planted more than a century ago. The rounded tops of several pairs of tablets that were bound at their edges, like marbled mimicries of the Ten Commandments, crested throughout the cemetery. The handful of lined obelisks broke up the forest of large ornate crosses, which paused seemingly in positional protest at their pagan counterparts. A statue of a human-sized angel had fallen face down in the dirt, its head and sides splattered with mud and its wings jutting awkwardly skyward from its back. A cloaked, stone vase on top of one tombstone had split in two under the stress of the seasons, leaving a cragged-edged remnant behind and the casualty half-buried in the ground in front of it.

Aubrey had little idea as to what he should be looking for, and even if he found Hovis' grave, would he know it? Aubrey examined the headstones more closely. Most of the writing on the tombstones was nearly impossible to read. The smaller, elaborate cursive writing had worn flush with the stones, making birth and death dates illegible. The epitaphs were scarred by lichen and tiny insect infestations, and most of the block-lettered family names didn't form a decipherable word without guessing several letters in between.

Aubrey sighed dejectedly, exasperated that he had come this far, and now time was being frittered away by the microscopic vandalism of an era's worth of rain, wind, bugs, and bacteria.

A scraping scuffle in the trees broke Aubrey's attention. A flock of noisy birds flapped wildly in the canopy. Several robins and a blue jay in the surrounding woods hopped haphazardly from tree to tree, precariously leaping from one limb to the next, barely making their landing. A wren flipped upside down and grappled nearby twigs, nearly losing its fight against gravity before it righted itself. A redheaded woodpecker climbed a trunk with its wings fully extended, flapping clumsily to maintain its balance.

At first, Aubrey thought they were agitated, like they sensed a nearby predator, or maybe the change in seasons had interrupted some communal migration instinct. But as he watched them more closely, he realized they seemed more confused, as if they couldn't remember how to fly.

An inky black raven swooped down from the top of a white pine and landed adeptly a few feet in front of Aubrey. He was mildly frightened at its considerable size. From tip to tail, the raven was easily as bulky as a small dog, and could probably make a meal out of a housecat. The raven faced Aubrey head on and cocked its head from side to side, studying him inquisitively. It dropped its beak twice in succession, giving Aubrey what appeared to be a salutatory bow. The gesture sent a searing sense of unease down his spine.

Aubrey dropped his guard a little when he saw the bird's eyes. Its right eye was coated in a foggy gray film that stood out brightly against the dark, downy head. The raven's left eye was as black as his feathers, and easily missed on that side of the raven's midnight-stained face, except when it glared straight at him.

The raven had angled its body perpendicular to Aubrey, examining him with the full view of its good eye. Its thin, black eyelid squinted tightly, focusing directly on him. The raven side-stepped toward Aubrey. Aubrey took a slow step backward, unsettled by such a seemingly perceptive fowl. Startled by his movement, the raven flapped its wings in agitation and lofted quickly in to the air overhead, soaring effortlessly to a lower branch on another white pine outside the cemetery. The raven's wings folded, and its gaze returned to Aubrey.

Aubrey tried to watch the raven without looking directly at it, but his eye was drawn toward a tombstone it had flown over. Tucked in a lower corner among a grove of raised family plots, an earthy red, rough-hewn cross stood out from its dusty, gray peers. It appeared carelessly sculpted, with large shavings removed from its edges to form rudimentary arms and stem, as if someone was in a hurry to create and erect it.

Aubrey walked over to the unusual gravestone. He gazed back at the trees behind it and looked for the precocious raven, but the bird was no longer there. He scanned the surrounding trees, but only the oddly behaving jays and robins remained.

As he approached the tawny cross, the cemetery floor beneath him crunched. He looked down, and saw the sod of dead leaves and weeds had been overrun by a mangled trellis of spiky lichens. It felt like stepping on Styrofoam peanuts. With every step closer, the cemetery floor thickened, and he cringed. *I'm walking on eggshells*. The sensation was unnerving, and the scour of his shoe against the carpet of stiffened, floral scrag caused his legs to quiver.

Aubrey jumped onto the foot-tall stone perimeter wall that enclosed the ruggedly-cleaved cross to avoid the tactile feel of the surrounding ground. Unlike the other family plots, which were square or rectangular, this one was circular, and a tight mortar held the miniature wall firmly intact. It contained five smaller, blocked headstones, arranged in a ring at the edges of the stone wall. These crudely fashioned wedge markers were shrouded by fallen leaves and growing shrubs, but the site was absent of human rubbish. It was obvious that great care had been taken by most to avoid this plot.

Aubrey surveyed the elevated earth in the plot. Except for the lack of upkeep, nothing seemed unreasonably out of place. He stepped down cautiously onto the raised earth.

The ground rumbled with a menacing *HISSSSSSSSSSSSSSSSSSS*. Aubrey instantly retracted his foot to the safety of the stone wall.

The hissing stopped.

Alarmed and a bit confused, Aubrey knelt down on the wall to examine the plot more closely. The dirt was difficult to see. He leaned over the outside edge of the plot and wrenched a dead twig free from under the craggy lichen.

Aubrey stabbed the ground inside the plot with the stick. The damp dirt gave way as expected and bits of mud ejected upward, splattering Aubrey in the face. He wiped his face with a rub from inside his elbow and bent down to get a better look.

Suddenly, a black-winged form with globular maroon eyes catapulted up from underneath the brush and bombarded Aubrey's face with its multiple appendages. Thorn-sharp, spiked legs scratched his nose, and its stiff paddle-shaped wings stung his cheeks as they slapped him abrasively. He could feel its angry buzzing vibrate in his ears. Aubrey closed his eyes tightly together and batted at the creature with a flurry of swats.

Aubrey dropped back onto the wet soil outside the plot, and his alien assailant dropped to the ground as quickly as it had emerged. His heart pounded furiously as he held his breath tight. Aubrey gently massaged his face and peered through his fingers to gain a guarded look at his newly-discovered foe.

The air was silent. Aubrey surveyed the plot for clues, but nothing moved. No claws grappled against the foliage and no wings thrashed about.

A brown locust leapt from the site onto the short stone wall and stroked its folding wings with its barbed, hind legs, aiding their furl. It ignored Aubrey and bounded through the air, landing on the crest of a dull, white gravestone a few yards away.

Aubrey sighed with relief and snickered at his own anxious fear of the tiny insect. He stood up and wiped the waterlogged ground clutter from his rear. He took a thoughtful repeat step into the family plot. No more hissing. *Bugs I can handle*, he thought to himself.

Aubrey tip-toed over to the closest headstone and brushed away the moss and dirt from its front slope. Faint lettering labeled the marker, but it was too weathered to read. He placed his hand on the stone and ran his fingers along the outline of the shy indentations, like a blind man reading Braille. The first letter felt like a "G." He grazed his hand rightward until he could feel another, sparse divot. The next letter formed a "J", followed by another "G" and a "T", "E" and finally an "R."

"Gjgter." Aubrey pronounced the word aloud phonetically. He shook his head, knowing that wasn't right. He fingered the stone again concentrated to try and form a coherent word. He could discern distinct, minuscule curves off the main body of the letters.

"Cursive," he deduced. "The 'G's' were most likely 'S's' and the 'J' is probably an…"I.'"

"SISTER!" he said triumphantly. "Now that makes sense."

Aubrey hopped from headstone to headstone reading the headstones the same way. Sister, Sister, Brother, Mother, Father. *Just like the picture from my history book*, Aubrey mused.

The sun broke through the clouds and lit up the plot, seemingly joining in the jubilation of Aubrey's discovery. The heat warmed Aubrey's back and renewed his determination. The dark red, feral cross at the center of the plot glittered in the light as the sun shone over it. Flecks of silica in the carved stone reflected the sun's rays, and it radiated with an unusual glow. Aubrey walked up to the tombstone and looked at it more closely. Four plantless, unmarked stone pots, packed full of dirt, were wedged in the dirt in front of the cross. Aubrey winced with a twinge of recollected dread and decided to leave them alone.

He looked for a family epitaph, but the crudely crafted cross stood laconically without a name or any dates. Aubrey brushed the ground litter away from its base and felt the stone skin of the cross's leg. There was no broken marker lying in the soil and no hidden epitaph worn with time. He needed confirmation, but the tombstone was not revealing its occupants.

Aubrey backed up and sat on the plot wall, unsure of what to do next. There was no sign of the Kluggards yet, but he knew his free time at the cemetery was nearly gone. He stared at the cross, hoping for an answer.

The sun faded again, darkening the gravesite. A few moments later, the light returned with brighter beams as the clouds raced across the sky. The rays danced along the plot and then retreated again, darting in and out like a slowly cycling strobe light.

The minuscule quartz-like flecks in the cross flickered in time with the fickle sunlight. To Aubrey, as the sunbeams intensified, more light reflected from the center and arms of the cross than its upper and lower limbs, as if the specks were concentrated in some areas more than others.

Aubrey angled his head to the side and stared perpendicular to the cross, hoping to catch a clearer glint from his peripheral vision. Daylight gleamed across the plot and Aubrey jumped up off the wall, pumping his fist in the air with excitement. The sunrays blanched again and he fixed his eyes on the cross where he had seen the letters.

The sun shone on the cemetery, its brightest all afternoon, as if daring the clouds to defeat it. The letters "T-R-O-T-T-L-E" glistened amongst the specks, sparkling across the arms of the cross.

Aubrey deliberately marched along the ground in front of the Father's grave marker and leered over it. "Now I know where you live," he said brashly to the empty dirt underneath him. Perhaps now he could both free Hovis…and himself.

The chill in the air sharpened as the sun dimmed behind the clouds and fell below the top of the trees. The wind blew furiously and cut deep through the knit of Aubrey's shirt and jeans, bringing winter's bite to his unguarded skin. Goosebumps raced from his neck to his toes. His left arm was so cold it tingled, as if an army of ants was marching up his arm. He stretched his left sleeve past his fingers and briskly rubbed his hand over his left forearm, hoping the warming friction would bring back feeling.

The prickly pins vanished, and he lost all sensation in his hand. Aubrey shook his hand vigorously and beat it against his leg, trying to restore blood flow. Fear filled his chest as he could no longer move his fingers. He squeezed his left hand with his right, and it was icy cold, like touching the hand of a dead man. He pulled on his fingers and wrenched his left hand around on its wrist, hoping to force it back to life. The frigid numbness crept up to his elbow.

Aubrey didn't know what to do. He was afraid that he might lose his arm. He his arm paled, and he could barely hold it up. Frightened and out of ideas, Aubrey took a deep breath and held his dying arm out in front of him as he closed his eyes.

The phosphenes flashed and slowly washed away, and the imprint of his arm faded into the background. A sparkling, undulating form corkscrewed up Aubrey's arm like a dark python writhing around its prey. The shadow churned and twisted, crawling around his forearm as it squeezed the life out of it. About half of the figure still hung off the end of Aubrey's fingers, hungrily reaching for his flesh.

Aubrey clutched his left elbow and raked his hand down his forearm, hoping to free his limb from the ghostly serpent's grasp. He jumped backwards, and his legs fumbled between the empty stone pots. Aubrey dropped flat on his black. A pot see-sawed between his legs and spun into the air, smacking the cross in its center. Rock shards and dirt scattered across the plot. Half of a rib cage landed on his leg.

Aubrey scrambled to his feet and held his dying, left arm against his chest. He ran out of the cemetery and, in a flurry, tumbled down the hill to the clump of trees where he had hidden his bike.

Warmth and feeling returned to his arm, and suddenly he regained control of his hand. He couldn't recall ever being this happy to wiggle his fingers. He brushed aside the leaves and twigs in the middle of the wooden copse. His bike was gone.

Aubrey scanned the hillside for another gang of pines or oaks where he might have hidden his bicycle, but no other grouping matched the same location he was in. He was certain this was the spot. He looked down at the highway, and the Kluggard's patrol car was parked in a ditch several hundred yards down. They had found him.

He crouched down behind one of the thicker trees, hoping to stay out of sight. The days' events swirled together, and one individual came into focus more clearly than anyone else. At this point, he knew there was only one, living person who could tell him what he really needed to know.

Aubrey needed to visit the old, vacant lot.

# *Sore Bruiser*

Buzz barreled out of the side entrance of the high school with his book bag flapping violently against his back. He weaved in and out between the throngs of students, who were also scurrying to leave school premises, but all the counteractive jiggling of his extra load made it difficult for him to stay on course.

Buzz slipped on a small patch of wet grass and plowed into the back of the McCrayden Miller. She stumbled over her feet but righted herself quickly, and her purse dropped to the ground in the balancing act. A screeching *YEOW!!* echoed from inside the purse.

"Watch it!" yelled McCrayden, shoving Buzz back in reply as he raced past her. Buzz glanced quickly over his shoulder at McCrayden, waved briefly and responded, "Sorry." Disingenuous though his reaction seemed, Buzz had more important matters on his mind.

McCrayden lifted her checkered, leathery purse gently, caressing it as she raised it to her chest. She slowly unzipped the top compartment, and a flailing bezoar of hair and tiny sharp claws spun out of the bag.

The kitten fastened itself to the sleeve of her cashmere sweater and marched its way up her shoulder, clutching her neck and hiding beneath her locks of blonde hair.

"Owwwwww," cried McCrayden as she tried to twist the kitten's claws free from her skin. The cat anchored down more tightly with each attempt. "GET IT OFF!" she screamed. McCrayden's friends, Jon Harney and Pam Trank, looked at each other, bewildered as to what to do. They glared at the kitten, which promptly seethed a menacing, warning hiss in their direction. Her friends decided McCrayden was doing just fine all on her own.

Buzz fell to his knees in front of the bicycle rack and fumbled with the combination of his bike lock until it snapped loose. He shoved the lock in his bag and sparked the pilot light. No flame appeared. He tapped the propane tank and moaned. It was empty. Buzz straddled his bike, and pedaled out through the school parking lot, barely avoiding a collision with three different cars as he swerved from side to side.

He felt a little guilty about leaving school directly after his last class, and he hated missing Torquetum Club today, but his curiosity surrounding the reason for Aubrey's odd behavior earlier was overwhelming.

Buzz raced onto the highway in front of the school and headed west along the road. A booming *MWWWWAAAAAAAMMMP!!* from a semi's horn shuddered him from behind. He had cut off a large dump truck loaded with a toppling mound of rubble as it turned out of the mine entrance, opposite the high school. Buzz waved his hand, gesturing for vehicular forgiveness. He was lost in the myriad of possibilities as to what Aubrey had figured out, and he wavered across the entire right-hand lane.

As he rode past the mine and up the switchback curves to the dam, several cars honked, closing in on his bumper.

"I HAVE THE RIGHT OF WAY!" he shouted at one green sedan that swerved as it passed, nearly side-swiping him. A red mini-van pulled up along side him, and Andy Anacker's mom rolled down the passenger side window and bellowed, "GET OVER, FATTY!" Andy hung his motionless head to the floorboard, his cheeks like ripe, bulging tomatoes, red from embarrassment.

"HELLO?! CHILD RIDING A BIKE!" cried Buzz, but Andy's mom accelerated angrily around him. Traffic was heavy since school had just let out, and Buzz wasn't used to biking on the road with so many vehicles competing for the lane. He teetered his bicycle carefully on the grassy line between the ditch and the asphalt, fearful that one small bump on the road could result in peril.

*THWAP!!!*

A sharp, agonizing sting throbbed against his skull, and flashes of tiny white lights briefly twinkled through his sight. The world twisted around him in a dizzying stupor, and Buzz struggled to maintain control of his bike. He swiveled his handlebars side to side, trying to compensate for his disorientation, but he turned to the right a little too far. He crashed face first in the ditch.

Buzz lay there for a few moments in complete bewilderment. The cool, fall grass cushioned most of his fall and soothed his head wound. He reached up to massage his forehead, but winced as soon as he touched it. A warm, bulbous knot was rising quickly, stretching the skin with a pounding ache that was pulsating underneath. He reset his glasses on his face, pushed himself up, and lifted his bike off of his back.

"Pssssssssstttt," floated a muted, yet conspicuous whistle down the hillside. Buzz thought it was most likely a woodland creature or an echo from a passing car's dying radiator and paid no attention. He sat up in the ditch and surveyed his body for further injuries. He noted how fortunate it was that his bike landed on him instead of vice versa, or else it might have taken substantial damage.

A louder, more directed, "PSSSSSSSSSTTT!" hissed from above. Buzz searched the hillside and noticed a dark form crouched down between several young mountain laurels.

"Who's there?" shouted Buzz.

"Come here," replied an anxious whisper in a familiar voice.

"Why are you hiding?" questioned Buzz.

"Would you get off the side of the road? Please?!"

Buzz thought for a moment and rubbed his forehead gently. "Aubrey? Did you throw a rock at me?!"

The wind whipped through the mountain laurels, and Aubrey's face was exposed. He leaned down and faced Buzz. "I'm sorry, but I wanted to get your attention with out being, you know, obvious."

Buzz stood up and waved his arms sarcastically. "You don't think a fat kid falling off his bike on the side of a major thoroughfare is obvious?!"

Aubrey sighed loudly in frustration. "Could you just come up here, and I'll explain?"

Buzz pulled his bike out of the ditch and marched begrudgingly up the hillside. He kneeled down in the small thicket of mountain laurels where Aubrey was hiding and gave him an expectant look.

"Dude, why is your face all torn up?" asked Buzz as he nursed his own head wound.

Aubrey shook his head scornfully, "I was terrorized by a wayward locust and that's been the *least* interesting part of my day."

Aubrey quietly explained everything that had happened from the discovery of the photo and his ethereally vandalized bedroom, to his run-in at Mr. Jennings' store and the discovery of Hovis' gravesite. Buzz's demeanor changed from irritation to fascination with the flood of details.

"Ahhh…I can't believe we missed the cemetery," mused Buzz, rubbing his swollen forehead. "Of course! It makes perfect sense, and it was right under our noses."

"Shhhh," chided Aubrey. "The Kluggards are still up here snooping around. They'll hear us." Buzz nodded, mesmerized by all he had heard.

"But why would the Kluggards care if you were here? Yeah, you were skipping school, but they're technically here investigating a disturbance."

"They're in league with Ms. Thistlewood, and they're involved with Hovis somehow too. I'm sure of it," argued Aubrey.

"That just doesn't make sense."

"Then why would they steal my bike?"

"They wouldn't *steal* your bike," Buzz concluded, trying to reason with him.

"There was no one else around," pleaded Aubrey, his voice cracking two octaves higher. Buzz shook his head in disbelief. Aubrey decided to take a different approach. "I watched their so-called 'investigation.' Don't you think it's weird that they came up here to check out the cemetery, and they never stepped foot in it?!"

"No," countered Buzz, "I don't. Because they're incompetent!"

"I think there's more to it than that. If they at least wanted to look like they had investigated the cemetery, they'd walk through it or do something to prove they had been there. All traipse around quickly and walk away." Aubrey's debating manner collapsed into a sullen, pensive tone. "They sulked around kind of squeamishly. Like they were afraid of something."

"I think you're giving the Kluggard brothers way too much credit," Buzz rebutted. "I really don't think there's any connection whatsoever between Ms. Thistlewood, the Kluggards, and your ghost."

Aubrey stared at Buzz intently. "You're wrong...remember the bones," demanded Aubrey. Buzz rolled his eyes at his friend's over-active imagination.

"Ms. Thistlewood is at the center of all of this, and it's time for me to call her on it." Aubrey stood up and made his way out of the thicket.

Buzz grabbed him by the shirtsleeve. "And what exactly is your plan?" he asked.

"I'll try the direct approach...and I'll be nasty if I have to, but all this insanity has to end. Besides, it's not like I can go home, not with the way my room looks and my dad coming home soon." Buzz could see the determination in his face. Aubrey looked down the hill away from Buzz.

"You shouldn't come," Aubrey told him. "It's not your fight."

Buzz stood up and sighed with frustration. "Well, someone's gotta make sure you don't do anything stupid."

# *Tight Fit*

As Buzz and Aubrey rode up to the front of Ms. Thistlewood's cottage, Aubrey leapt off the front of Buzz's bicycle and marched up the front walk determinedly. Buzz rested his bike between the shrubberies at the entrance and raced to catch up with him.

"What are you going to do?" asked Buzz from behind.

Aubrey paused for a moment and turned around. "I need to look around the place. There's gotta be something in there that will clue us in to what's going on. I need you to keep her busy."

"How?" Buzz questioned.

"Ask her questions. Tell her you've been seeing ghosts. Distract her. Anything so I can get a better idea as to how she's involved, then I'll ask her what I need to know."

Buzz shook his head and muttered, "It won't work."

"Why not?" he demanded.

Buzz was quiet and looked down to avoid answering.

Aubrey faced forward and stared at the red wooden door to the cottage. He could see space between the edges of the door and the stone walls, but there was no light or movement noticeable on the other side. Aubrey knocked on the door forcefully.

They waited several moments, but there was no response.

"Well, I guess she's not home. Let's go," announced Buzz as he turned away from the door.

"Wait," responded Aubrey in a firm tone. He knocked again more forcefully. They could hear distant footsteps crescendo towards them and the click-lock sound of a shutting door from the other side.

The front door opened slowly, and the radiant Ms. Thistlewood appeared from behind it. Her bright, auburn hair was wound in a ponytail tied at the back of her head, lifting the wrinkles up from around her eyes and cheeks. Her cherry-colored lips, porcelain skin and crystalline, pale green eyes were warmly inviting and terrifyingly intimidating all at the same time. Aubrey noticed that her lime green shirt had either been washed and dried at the hottest setting too many times or she had gone shopping in the children's department, as it was pulled paper-thin tight around her torso, leaving no curve hidden. She held the door half-open and stood in the threshold.

Ms. Thistlewood forced a smile. "My day just got a thousand times better," she chimed.

Aubrey and Buzz were stunned, unsure of what they should say. They stared at each other, and then Aubrey's wits returned to him. He nudged Buzz and subtly peered around Ms. Thistlewood into the foyer.

"Um, hello," bumbled Buzz. Aubrey gave him a stern, visual reprimand.

Ms. Thistlewood edged the door closed slightly and wedged her body into the doorframe. "Mercy me," she said, rolling her head whimsically, "where are my manners."

"Huh?" grunted Buzz. Annoyed, Aubrey glared at Buzz and then craned his neck to see between her body and the door.

"I've been so busy today with tidying up, I haven't had any time to bake. But if you give me a couple hours, I'm sure I could scrape together a few things. Maybe a peach-pecan cobbler," offered Ms. Thistlewood.

A small string of spittle leaked from Buzz's open mouth. "Okay, Ms. Thistlewood, we can come back later," agreed Buzz. She winked at him and slowly swung the door toward its frame. Aubrey flinched, shocked at Buzz's easy deviance from the plan. He popped Buzz in the stomach with the back of his hand and stuck his foot just over the threshold, keeping it open a crack.

"Oh…no…we can't do that…we need to talk to you now," sputtered Buzz back into reality. Startled by the unexpected intrusion, Ms. Thistlewood's inviting expression washed away and her lip curled.

"Yes, it's very important," murmured Aubrey.

"It is?" she asked incredulously. "Then let's hear it." The soft melody in her voice was replaced with flattened accusation.

"We need to discuss it inside. It's personal," Buzz appealed.

"Yeah, personal," echoed Aubrey.

Ms. Thistlewood didn't budge.

"Besides," Buzz entreated, "I can't stay out here. My room has been sacked by a…uh… homeless person…um… and if my dad gets home, he's gonna blame me and we won't be able to prove who really did it."

"What?" she barked. "*Your* room?!" Ms. Thistlewood's eyes widened slightly and looked Buzz up and down, like she had a built-in lie detector. Buzz returned her gaze with limp eyes and a protruded lower lip that reminded Aubrey of a pouting bulldog. She loosened her ponytail, rewrapped it and sighed. "If you insist," she relented. She spun on her heels and walked tersely down the hallway behind the door. She disappeared around the corner, and Buzz was at a half-run to catch up.

Aubrey chose to plod along, examining every speck of her house he could lay his eyes on. The inner walls were painted stone, similar to the outside, and there was little decoration. The foyer was small and sparsely adorned, with only a small triangular table in the corner. The lighting inside was low, and the afternoon sun from behind him illuminated the hallway. The floors were planks of unfinished, knotted wood with large gaps in between the adjoining pieces, as if someone had chosen rejected parts to construct it. Directly opposite the entrance was a closed door, larger than he would have expected for a typical closet or small washroom. Aubrey assumed this was where she had been before they came, and that it was most likely the entrance to her root cellar.

To the right of the foyer was a small bedroom, meagerly furnished with chest of drawers at the front end of the room, upon which sat a white ceramic washing bowl and matching pitcher. A padded, delicately woven straw mattress lay in the middle of the floor, surrounded by several large clay pots full of dirt. Nothing grew from the pots. A chill tingled down Aubrey's spine.

Aubrey walked into the foyer and made his way slowly down the hallway. To his left, a cavernous sitting room opened up that reflected light from the open door. Two-dozen rainbow-colored, cuboidal crystals hung from the ceiling, each on a braided twine like stalactite chandeliers. A single folding chair stood in the center of the room, and under each icy, quartz-like rock sat plates covered with oily, metallic stains. It looked like Ms. Thistlewood had been making giant pieces of rock candy.

"Don't dawdle," barked Ms. Thistlewood, her head craning from behind the corner at the end of the hallway. A fearful jolt thwacked Aubrey, and he picked up his pace. He rounded the corner tightly, and multiple, dense objects smacked him in the face. *CLANG! TINK! BANG! TINK! TINK! CLANG!* Aubrey raised his hands to cushion the blows from the swinging shards of glass and strips of metal piping encircling his head.

"Why do you have a wind chime in the kitchen?" questioned Aubrey, startled by the commotion he had made. Ms. Thistlewood scowled at him condescendingly and lit a match. "Why don't you have a seat so we can find out more about Buzz's vandal?" She opened the front grating to her wood-burning stove at the edge of the kitchen and threw in the match. The kindling flashed alight, and Aubrey could feel the heat from the fire across the room. "I'll make some tea. Tea soothes the soul, you know." Her tone softened, but there remained a fine tremor in her posture.

He joined Buzz, who was already seated at the round, oak dining table. Several rows of pine shelving hung on the near wall to their left, stair-stepping from a thin board near the ceiling and increasing in width toward the floor, where larger bowls and jars were kept. The top shelves were stocked with various spices and dainty, decorative ceramics. A row of clay pots sat in the windowsill at the back of the kitchen with a few small sprouts peaking out of them. Ms. Thistlewood turned to a large basin next to the stove and pumped a handle behind it, releasing pulsating streams of water from the spout into the sink. She filled her antique, silver teapot halfway and placed it on top of the stove.

Aubrey noticed her watch, which was nothing more than a sundial on a small, flat pedestal. There were no visible gears or electronics. Only a leather strap snapped into sandstone that glimmered in the light from outside.

"So tell me, what is so private my shrubs can't hear?" she giggled and smiled crookedly at the boys.

They sat like statues opposite Ms. Thistlewood, petrified by their fear of what she might do, and even more frightened by what she might say. Buzz remembered it was his job to stall. Buzz focused his mind, sucked in his gut and spit it out. "There's been a lot of weird things happening lately." Regret washed over him as he watched for her reaction.

"Really," she replied. "What sorts of things?" Her grin twisted into a sinister pucker.

"First off, I know most people think the Bigfoot sightings are simply tree huggers protesting the new mine, but then why are people seeing them away from the dig site? And what's up with the Old Widow Wizenblatt? She's been acting creepy lately, but smart creepy, and she shows up at random times and places that sometimes aren't so random. Aren't hobos just supposed to sleep on your lawn and pick through your garbage?"

"Agreed," Ms. Thistlewood nodded thoughtfully as she furrowed her brow. "She's probably the cause of a lot of problems around here."

Buzz shifted forward in his seat, continuing his analysis. "And lots of people have disappeared. Magnos Strumgarten…sure he was a bully, but he was *huge*…who could ever take him, unless he ran away, but why? So what that he made a bad play at a football game? He's one of the most popular kids in school." Buzz's momentum heightened with every word he spoke. "I think it all started with the bizarre, *en masse* vanishing act of the circus this summer." Ms. Thistlewood's eyes widened and her forehead flattened. Aubrey watched her intently as she stiffened her lips. He knew they were onto something.

"And now Aubrey's being haunted by a ghost," spilled Buzz.

"GHOST?!" she exclaimed. "I thought you were going to tell me about Ms. Wizenblatt breaking into your house?"

Aubrey sat up rigidly and glowered at Buzz. Buzz fumbled, "Uh yeah…um well… that's what I meant." Ms. Thistlewood bent over the table, squeezed her eyelids together tightly, raised her finger and pointed it at Buzz.

"*WHEEEEEEIIIIIEEEEEYYYYYYYYYYYW*," announced the steam from the teapot with a scalding scream. All three of them jerked, surprised by the piercing sound. Ms. Thistlewood regained her upright posture and wiped her brow. She took three cups from the shelving and removed the teapot from the stove as she calculatingly brewed the Earl Grey.

With her back turned, Aubrey kicked Buzz in the shin and stared at him with a stern, crumpled face. Buzz squeaked out a muffled yelp and shrugged his shoulders apologetically.

Ms. Thistlewood interrupted the silent squabble calmly. "A few out of the ordinary circumstances in a rural town, such as this, can easily be blown out of proportion when connections are made that don't really exist, especially from a small-minded perspective."

Buzz frowned at her slight.

Ms. Thistlewood pulled for her sugar bowl off the shelf. "How many lumps would you like?" Aubrey was afraid she was talking about more than sweetener.

Buzz stood up and lifted a cork-stoppered glass vase filled to the brim with a thick, yellow-tinged liquid from the lowest shelf. He walked toward the water basin and extended the vase toward her. "I think I would prefer honey. I've read that fructose provides a greater nutritional benefit than refined glucose," he offered in a pedantic tone.

Unexpectedly the jar was slippery, not sticky, and the tighter his grip on the vase, the faster it slid through his hands.

"That's *not* honey," charged Ms. Thistlewood. Buzz fumbled his hands down the vase faster and faster, but he was losing the race. "It's sunflower oil." Ms. Thistlewood scrambled to reach the falling jar.

*SKAAAACRAAAASSSSSH!* Greasy, glass shrapnel ricocheted off the floor and onto the sides of the basin and wood stove, and a pool of oil lapped against Buzz and Ms. Thistlewood's shoes. "Sorry," mumbled Buzz. Ms. Thistlewood's face tightened, and she clenched her fists as she glowered at Buzz.

A few small drops that landed on the stove's open front grating burst with tiny flickers of yellow flame, and the fire hopped from drop to drop down the iron facing.

Feeling the warmth of the back of her legs, Ms. Thistlewood turned around quickly and gasped at the sight of the growing fire. She flipped the top open on the teapot and doused the front of the stove with the hot water.

"NOOOOOO!" screamed Buzz. The flaming emulsion raced down the stove onto the floor. "That's a bad idea," he remarked solemnly. "Smokey would not approve." Buzz shook his head.

"Who?" she asked, annoyed at his condescending tone.

"Smokey the bear," he replied.

Buzz and Ms. Thistlewood jumped back out of the puddle of oil as the fire spread swiftly with the running water across the hardwoods. Aubrey jerked out of his chair and stepped back toward the hallway at the sight of the growing blaze.

"Then fix it, if you're so smart," ordered Ms. Thistlewood. "This is *your* fault!"

She waved her arms at the burning slosh.

Buzz hastily examined his surroundings and ran to the back of the kitchen. He lifted a clay pot from the window and flung it toward the fire. Ms. Thistlewood reached for the pot, but she was too late. The pot shattered, and the fire in the middle of the oil slick dampened as the dirt formed a muddy mixture with the oil. A shoulder blade stuck up from the cindering soup. Buzz took a double-take at the bone in the mix and looked at Aubrey, aghast in disbelief.

Waves of burning oil fanned out as the implosion of the clay jar forced the uncovered slick outward, and flames licked the bottom shelving on the wall. Aubrey burst down the hall.

"Thanks for leaving us," she announced, hoping to catch Aubrey's ear.

"We need more dirt," commanded Buzz. Ms. Thistlewood sneered in return. She hoisted a massive clay pot from below the windowsill and launched it over the table into the fire. Buzz was amazed how easily she threw the hefty load. The flame puttered out and only a few small embers glowed at the edge of the wall.

"There," Ms. Thistlewood said, "it's out," as she sighed with relief. Buzz heaved from the stress of the accident, but was grateful the damage had stopped. Ms. Thistlewood walked over to the pantry behind her, pulled out a broom and a mop, and handed them to Buzz.

"I believe this is your mess to clean up," she said.

Suddenly, the bottom shelving on the wall creaked and groaned. With a loud snap, the weakened shelf dropped to the floor. Several glass jars shattered, ejecting their slimy contents across the floor. The flame seared back to life with a fury.


Energized by his chance to perform a more thorough investigation of Ms. Thistlewood's house, Aubrey bolted down the hallway and ran into the sitting room. He carelessly kicked a couple of the plates, and they scattered across the wooden floor, clanging as they skidded into other plates. He reached up and pulled one of the faux stalactites from the ceiling. The twine tore at the top, and the glistening rocks fell hard to the ground. Aubrey realized it was heavier than he had thought and way too much for him to carry. There was no way this could be candy. He pounded at the crystals with his heels until the top part cracked away from the rope, leaving only a few small, coalesced rocks intact at the bottom. He shoved the unpulverized portion into his pocket.

Aubrey bounded into the foyer and stopped at the door to the basement. He heard frantic shouts from Buzz and Ms. Thistlewood shudder down the hallway, and he looked back toward the kitchen. He could hear crackling from the growing blaze and saw a thick, black smoke rolling toward him. He knew if he wanted to make it out alive, his window for snooping was closing quickly.

Aubrey opened the door carefully and peered around its edge down the stairs. Stone steps angled steeply down into a murky darkness. Two plump roaches scurried deeper into the darkness away from the light of the foyer. At the bottom, a faint, gray light flirted from around the corner. Cool, moldy air wafted up from below, and it felt refreshingly damp on his skin. His pulse quickened, and his hands trembled with anticipation. He hesitated as he took his first step. He decided to think of it like hopping into a cold swimming pool in spring. *Better to just jump in and get the shock over with.*

Aubrey felt like his feet only touched three stairs. The mid-stair darkness engulfed him, and he passed through it so quickly he barely had time to blink. There was only one way to go at the bottom, to the right, where the light angled from around the corner. He rounded it, and a soft, blinding daylight dazzled his eyes. He squinted to give them time to adjust. The early evening sun inched its way down over homes across the street and shone straight into the basement through a small dirt-speckled window near the ceiling.

The basement reminded him of a glorified crawlspace with a low ceiling, dirt floors, and rough-hewn stone walls. Several mirrors hinged to the walls crisscrossed the room, spreading the window's light. Antiques and artifacts were strewn along the bottom of the walls, like a museum's junk room. He surveyed the items quickly, careful not to touch anything. Chipped brass urns, broken pieces of inscribed tablets, rusted swords and bejeweled chalices filled the corners and were nestled by packing straw in opened wooden crates. Matted burlap sacks spilled over with carved runes and antique texts along the far wall. A white, chalky circle, intersected by two perpendicular lines, had been drawn in the middle of the room on the floor. Tiny stone shelves jutted out of the walls midway up, a few holding half-burned cream-colored candles. The room emanated a hum, like a radio stuck between stations or a television without a signal.

Toward the back of the room, a large opened crate full of sand rested between a black curtain that hung against the wall and a dilapidated roll-top desk. Aubrey wanted to look behind the curtain, but a glint of light sparkled between the slats of the desk's curved top and caught his attention. He walked over to the desk and rolled back its shutter, revealing a rectangular, golden box. He thought he saw a gleaming hue around it, but as quickly as the wooden slats slid anyway, it disappeared. Aubrey guessed it was a trick of the sunlight behind him. He bent over and examined it more closely.

The cover of the box was a dense, metallic golden plate intricately stenciled with undulating forms, which were fine and barely noticeable. Pointed stars and ringed-planets were clustered around the edges. In the center lay a morphed composite of a blazing sun and a crescent moon in the shape of a face. An eye was carved in each portion and the mouth crossed over both. The sun had a mischievous grin and the moon a menacing grimace.

Aubrey was utterly mesmerized. The pictograph seemed more like a mirage or a memory than a real image. He ran his fingers along the top of it gently to prove to himself that it was real. It felt cool and hard like metal, and yet tingly, like sticking your tongue to a nine-volt battery. A thick, platinum hinge bound the box at its side. Aubrey lifted the top effortlessly, although it felt heavy, and another golden plate lay underneath. He fingered along its edges and raised it to the side. The second plate turned like a page in a book with another stiff, leaflet beneath it. He thumbed through the pages to the end, and they all had the same look and feel, smooth and electric, but each one was blank.

Aubrey scooted the desk chair back and sat down to give himself a moment to examine the empty encyclopedia. A spot of sunlight glowed against the wall from a mirror above him. He reached up and adjusted the mirror, directing it onto the desk. The sunlight flitted across the open, golden plate. Delicately elaborate arching and bowing lines scrolled across the page. Aubrey thought he could make out a word. Then it formed a sentence. The page flushed with writing and, in an instant, an entire scroll lay before him.

When angles walked on Earth with men
And forsook their souls to clad fleshly skin,
The Watchers engaged the hearts of human wives
And taught young maidens the secrets of heaven's lies.

Begotten forms born of daughters' stolen wombs
Grew to giant men who wrought blood-thirsty doom,
That sparked the fire of man's most gifted hour
By unleashing the Clockmaker's hidden, unbridled power.

The Seven Archons bemused the plan unfold
And helplessly feared the Watcher's corruption take hold.
Uncertain how best to intercede,
Time all but lost against the giants' greed.

They sought the counsel of 'he who once knew blood',
A one-time human, now bequeathed angelhood.

They charged young Enoch with the task at hand
To thwart the earthly angels and their sons of men.


Quickly the angel-man replied,
"Entomb the Watchers deep inside.
Drown their children in the mud
And restore the Earth with a suffocating flood."


He engineered a living shell of broken rock,
Sealed in sand and shut with an uncompromising lock
Entrapped to snare any trespassers who admire,
With merciless sufferings from the threat of death's fire.


The Archons deftly interned the Watchers in Enoch's
tomb
And imprisoned them inside with a quartz's voltaic
plume,
Securing their graves deep within the crust's domain
And washed the Earth's pain clean with Noah's rain.


Enoch left a simple clue to break the unbreakable mold,
A single key to open the Watchers' eternal hold:


The arm of wine, an ivy thread
Slowly opens the sepulcher's head.
The cipher grows but does not truly eat,
Except to sift the dirt beneath its feet.
Winding its arms toward the beckoning light,
This be the key to free the buried night.

Below the text, a figure of the tomb was etched into the gold. It was an egg-shaped coffin of rock, embedded with shimmering stones. Its flattened door face, secured with a metal grating, was carved with precious stones in a familiar arrangement of circles. *Could this be the object stuck in the dam*, he thought to himself.

Aubrey marveled at the page, both bewitched by its verse and dumbfounded by its secret.

"Please, no more. I can't take it," echoed a raspy voice through the room. Aubrey jerked out of his trance and flipped around in his chair. He stood up to look around the crates, but no one was behind him. He closed his eyes and stared behind his eyelids. The phosphenes faded, but nothing was there.

"Please," begged the voice, softer than before. Aubrey craned his neck to look behind the black curtain, but all he could see was the stone wall disappear beneath it. He picked up the dregs of a burnt candle lying on the floor and threw it at the curtain. The curtain dimpled in where the candle hit and then swung back and forth from the impact, further than the wall should have allowed.

"I'll do anything you want, just leave me alone," the voice pleaded, its will to fight nearly lost.

Aubrey stood in front of the curtain. "Who's there?" His muffled voice cracked with fear.

There was no response. Aubrey took a deep breath and pulled the curtain to the side, standing as far away from it as his arm would allow.

The stone wall gave way to a shallow cave, gouged out of the rock. The hum in the room throbbed louder. Within the depression, a yellow, wire-latticed cage held a ghostly pale man, who lay limp against the floor. Except for its oblique shape, the metal enclosure reminded Aubrey of an oversized birdcage, completely enclosed with a locked door at its face. Empty, muck-lined bowls sat in disarray, and clumps of moldy gruel and scattered mouse skeletons lined the floor of the cave. The light from the basement window washed across the human form.

"PLEASE, NO!" screeched the man as he pushed his body away in protest. Aubrey gasped at the sight of him. The limbs of the moving corpse trembled under the weight of his cachectic frame, the meat of his flesh quivering in gelatinized agony. His blonde shaggy hair and his massive, bony hands were familiar to Aubrey. His voice was weak, but reminiscent of someone he knew.

"Magnos?" He asked in disbelief, stunned by his appearance and startled that he was oddly part of Aubrey's living nightmare.

The figure lifted up his head and shielded the oncoming light with his fingers. "Do I know you?" he asked. The form's blue eyes met Aubrey's and recognition of the other overwhelmed them both.

The boy in the cage heaved a haggard sigh. "I thought you were that awful woman again." His voice shuddered, and Aubrey could hear the sobs backing up in his throat. "Did you...come to save me?" He begged more than asked, his tone giddy and sorrowful at the same time.

Aubrey's brain froze. That Magnos was missing was no surprise, but that he was here, in *her* basement, only yards from his own house, without someone else finding out, and that he was unable to escape through a few flimsy metal bars was unfathomable. For a moment, the world spun, his mind swimming for answers.

"Um, I guess so," was all he could say, less than valiantly. Aubrey reached mechanically for the cage's door.

"NOOOOOOOOOO!" screamed Magnos hoarsely. Aubrey stiffened in place, petrified by his hollow roar. Magnos pointed meekly to the side of the cage.

Aubrey was so captivated by Magnos and his enclosure that he had failed to see the contraption that actually held him prisoner. A dull gray, vibrating aluminum cylinder sprouted thick braided copper extensions that were plugged into an electric socket protruding from the rough, stone wall. A set of red and black jumper cables led from the top of the cylinder toward Magnos, their gator-like clamps secured to opposite sides of his cage.

"If you touch it, it will kill you," Magnos muttered in defeat. Aubrey saw that all the wiring was exposed from the cables to the wires plugged into the socket. There was no way to disconnect the circuit without being electrocuted. Magnos rested his face against the bottom of his cage, the exhaustion and dismay too heavy for his will to fight.

Aubrey charged over to the desk and lifted the encyclopedia over his head. It was solid but easy to lift, and its static electricity tickled his fingers. He ran over to Magnos and dropped the book on the plug. Sparks bounced against the stone wall into the metal cage, and Magnos flinched as they burned him. The socket was wrenched from the wall under the weight of the golden box, and the hum died.

Aubrey kicked the jumper cables' grips off the cage and twisted open the lock to its front door. Magnos breathed out a lengthy sigh. Aubrey pulled him by his arms and dragged him out of the metal enclosure. Magnos pushed against the floor, but his muscles trembled more than gainfully contracted. Magnos looked up at Aubrey, and clean pale tears streaked down his dirt-mottled face.

"Let's get you out of here," spoke Aubrey. Magnos bobbed his head in agreement. Shouting ricocheted off the stone walls from the opposite side of the room.

"I CAN'T BELIEVE YOU SET MY HOUSE ON FIRE!!"

"WHY ARE YOU RUNNING INTO THE BASEMENT WHEN WE SHOULD BE RUNNING OUTSIDE?!"

"BECAUSE I NEED TO GET…" Ms. Thistlewood jarred to a stop as she rounded the corner at the bottom of the stairs. Buzz bumped into her back. "…something important," she snarled.

"Aubrey! We have to get out of here! The whole place is burning down!" Buzz screamed. "Who's that?" he asked, pointing at the anorexic Magnos lying on the floor in front of him.

"No one's going anywhere," she seethed. Her eyes glowed red with anger. She reached behind her, grabbed Buzz by the neck of his shirt and flung him to the ground like a rag doll. His face hit the dirt floor with a screech. She pressed her foot into the nap of his neck, pinning him to the ground. Buzz squealed in pain.

"If you want Buzz to be able to walk again, both of you need to get into that cage," Ms. Thistlewood ordered, her face pinched taut.

Aubrey reached from behind him and pulled the encyclopedia forward, drawing it under his arm. "If we go in there, so does this," he demanded.

"That's fine with me. The book will survive the fire," she snickered spitefully. She leaned more of her weight onto Buzz and he moaned frantically.

Magnus crawled feebly backward. Aubrey boiled with revenge. *Enough was enough*, he told himself. He put his hand on Magnos' shoulder and stopped him. He handed Magnus the encyclopedia and stood up. Aubrey pulled the crystal from his pocket and swung it over his head, faster and faster, until it formed a circular blur. "You will let us go," he demanded.

Ms. Thistlewood cackled maniacally. Her loud laughter bounced off the stone walls around the room. She crossed her arms and thrummed her fingers against her lips. "Now let me think…where have I seen this scene play out before?!" Devilish euphoria laced her tone. The color in her eyes faded briefly and, for a moment, Aubrey thought they turned pearly white. The spinning rock in his hand shattered. Small slivers of crystal sprayed across the room. Aubrey was twirling a string.

A sneer spread across her face. "You should have minded your own business, like the Old Widow told you." Ms. Thistlewood walked forward and towered over Magnos. "Now give me the book and get in that cage." She bent over and gripped the golden box on either side. Magnos pulled it closer to himself with his last ounce of strength.

The ceiling cracked and whined overhead. Everyone stared upwards as the boards glowed orange with the heat from upstairs. The wood buckled and smoked. Suddenly, the wood-burning stove crashed through the ceiling and shattered on the dirt floor in the back of the root cellar. Molten bits of metal and fiery ash plumed through the basement. All but Buzz covered their heads under the explosion.

Buzz lifted himself off the ground and at a full sprint hurled his weight at Ms. Thistlewood's rump. He plowed into her with all of his hurdling weight, and she flew headlong over Magnos into the cage, landing splayed onto the floor. Buzz fell to the side and scrambled to regain his footing. He rolled over and closed the door to the metal enclosure.

Aubrey screamed, "THE CLAMPS!!! PUT THE CLAMPS ON THE CAGE!!" Magnos turned around and set the lock on the door. Buzz set the jumper cables on the cage as Aubrey gloved his hand with a burlap sack from the corner and jammed the plug into the socket.

Ms. Thistlewood twisted herself around in the cage, her clothes and face smeared with mud, and her hair sagging over her face. She glared at Aubrey, and he could see her eyes fade to white again.

"We gotta get outta here," yelled Buzz. Aubrey covered the book with the burlap sack and handed it back to Magnos. He and Buzz lifted Magnos under each arm and scurried to the stairs, dragging him along the floor of the root cellar as his feet clambered to grip the dirt. Orange flames glowed from around the corner upstairs and lit their way. The radiating heat seared their faces, and they choked and heaved in the smoky air. Magnos missed most of the steps as Buzz and Aubrey hobbled upwards under his weight.

Aubrey looked up through the ceiling in the foyer, and the roaring blaze raged through the roof thatching. Red, hot cinder rained down throughout the house. Blackened with ash, they burst through the front door into the yard, gasping for breath and.

"You were just supposed to distract her, not set her house on fire," screeched Aubrey.

"I didn't mean to," replied Buzz meekly.

The three boys plodded toward the street, exhausted from their ordeal. Buzz pulled back, halting their progress, and Magnos and Aubrey gawked at him quizzically.

"No, wait," Buzz muttered, "We left her in there. We can't do that." The three boys shared glances briefly. Magnos' will was spent. He looked down, unable to share Buzz's concern.

Aubrey nodded. "You're right." They leaned the delicate Magnos against a potted shrub and walked back toward the house. They paused at the entrance. Buzz walked in first.

The ceiling in the foyer spilled onto the floor, releasing a fiery thrash of burning wooden planks and twigs, blocking the basement door. Buzz tumbled backwards onto the threshold. Aubrey helped him up, and they tumbled backwards into the yard.

"We tried," Aubrey said, looking back at the house, now engulfed in flames.

Blue and red lights flashed behind them. An all too familiar shoddy muffler sputtered to a stop in the street. Fred Kluggard stepped out of the car and raised his sunglasses on his head. Ned opened the passenger door and remained seated, letting out a long, slow whistle in amazement.

"What happened here?" Fred shouted.

"What does it look like?" responded Buzz sarcastically. Aubrey and Buzz walked over to Magnos and picked him up off the stone planter.

"Don't give me any lip, boy! Where's Ms. Thistlewood?" Fred demanded.

Aubrey and Buzz carried Magnos to Buzz's bike and raised him onto the seat, balancing it with their hands. "Shouldn't you be doing something useful, like calling the fire department?" Aubrey heckled.

Fred marched toward them. "I've had enough of your shenanigans today," he threatened. "If I find out Ms. Thistlewood has been harmed or you two are responsible for this fire, then I'll make sure your truancy is the least of your worries."

Aubrey rolled his eyes. "Let's get out of here," he murmured to Buzz. They pushed the bicycle forward, away from Fred.

"You're not going anywhere," Fred snarled, slapping his hand on Aubrey's shoulder.

Aubrey swiveled and cried, "HOVIS TROTTLE!"

A black fog formed between Fred and Aubrey, expanding quickly into a cloaked figure with chains, taut to the ground. Fred fumbled back onto the hood of his police car. The scar-faced man raised its arms, stirring the dust around him. Then he faded in the wind, more quickly than he appeared.

Fred quaked like a frightened toddler, and Ned's chin fell to his chest. Aubrey turned around and pushed the bicycle forward.

"Was...that?" was all Buzz could ask.

"My ghost," Aubrey replied.

# Pride and Precedence

Aubrey and Buzz juggled the fatigued Magnos on the bicycle between themselves as they teetered away from his burning prison toward Aubrey's house. They could hear the Kluggards scrambling and shouting behind them as they flailed about trying to figure out what to do next.

"AUBREY!! COME HERE!!"

The boys stopped the bike in the road. Aubrey's heart sank when he saw his father standing at the edge of their lawn. The indignation in his dad's voice shook his confidence, which had been bolstered by their victory over Ms. Thistlewood. Aubrey had even grown a sliver of pride from all the emotional and mental obstacles he had overcome that day, but all of that withered before the anger of his father. He had forgotten how mad he would be when he discovered the bedroom was destroyed.

Mr. Taylor walked heavy-footed into the street. His face was red, and the veins in his neck bulged as he clenched his jaw tightly together. His cheek muscles strained under the pressure and contracted like steel bands against his teeth. His fists were clenched, and his arms were rigid at his sides.

"Where have you been?" Mr. Taylor hissed.

Aubrey stared at the ground, the evening's events swirling round and round in his mind. He wanted to answer, but the words weren't there.

"A lot has happened today. There's a lot to explain," Buzz interjected. Aubrey's dad ignored Buzz and glared at Aubrey.

"Answer me!" his father demanded, raising his voice.

Aubrey shook his head, angry and confused, not sure how to make sense of it all, but he knew he was tired of being the scapegoat. "None of this is my fault," Aubrey muttered.

"Really?! I got a call from the high school today informing me you had missed the second half of your classes. I come home to find your bedroom looking like a war zone and flowerpots broken and scattered across the front yard. Now, when I finally track you down, you're hobbling away from a burning house?!" Mr. Taylor's voice crescendoed from seething grunts to a roaring shout.

"Did you see the bones?" Aubrey asked impatiently, "Did you see them?"

"What bones?" his father demanded.

"Aubrey's a hero," Magnos said, lifting his head to look Mr. Taylor in the eye.

"And just who are you?!" asked Mr. Taylor.

"It's Magnos Strumgarten," reported Buzz. "The kid who's been missing for the past two months."

Mr. Taylor peered at Magnos, incredulous of Buzz's claim. Slowly, the familiarity of the pictures in the newspaper and from the flyers posted around town sank in. His eyes widened with billowing recognition, his jaw relaxed, and his lips parted as his anger was tempered by astonishment.

"He's been trapped in Ms. Thistlewood's basement," exclaimed Buzz. "Can you believe it?!"

"Caged would be a better word," said Aubrey.

Magnos nodded in agreement. "Aubrey saved my life."

Mr. Taylor furrowed his brow and examined Magnos from several angles, struggling with presence of the frail boy on the bike in front of him.

"How did you know he was in there?" asked Mr. Taylor.

"We didn't," muttered Aubrey.

"We sorta stumbled upon him," offered Buzz.

"How did you get him out?"

Aubrey looked at Buzz for help with this question. "We pulled him from the burning house," Buzz said blankly.

"Who started the fire?" Mr. Taylor's onslaught on questions was becoming more intrusive. Buzz stuttered and didn't offer an answer for this one.

"We need to call the police," Aubrey redirected him.

Aubrey's father looked over the boys at the remains of Ms. Thistlewood's smoldering abode. Flashing lights from a fire truck and an ambulance rounded the distant corner. "Looks like the Kluggards are already there," he replied. "Let's flag them down and tell them about Magnos." Mr. Taylor took a couple steps forward down the street.

Buzz grabbed Mr. Taylor's arm to stop him. "They're in on the kidnapping, Mr. Taylor. We need to call the precinct. So there's no more funny business."

He looked at Buzz, bewildered by his accusation. Aubrey and Magnos gave him an affirming look, acknowledging that Buzz was right. Aubrey's dad stared back and forth between the boys.

"Well, if you think that's best," he said. The three of them nodded.

Aubrey decided to remind him, "Besides, Ms. Thistlewood is still in there."

## *Silenced Night*

Jordana jolted awake in her bed. Panicked, muffled screams shattered her sleep. She raised herself up and listened intently over her heart hammering in her ears. Painful yelling bellowed from her father's bedroom. She jumped out of bed, flipped her bedroom light on and stared into the hallway. A red, flickering light glowed from underneath his door.

"Dad, are you okay?" she whimpered, her throat closing tightly with dread. The screaming softened into bawling chokes and sputtered through tears. Jordana walked to his door and held her ear next to it.

"Dad, what's wrong?" she asked a little louder. There was no response. She heard shuffling from the other side of the door.

Jordana knocked quietly. "Is everything alright?"

"Yes," her dad replied through a stifled sob.

Jordana turned the doorknob slowly, but it was locked.

She could hear him approach the door. "Daddy, I'm scared."

"Everything's fine," he whispered.

A rumbling howl roared from outside, and Jordana felt the hardwood floor gently vibrate with the noise. She knew it had to be close by. She darted back into her bedroom to her window and brushed back the linen curtains.

Everything outside appeared as shades of black while her eyes slowly adjusted to the dim light. She scanned the skyline, but she could only pick out a few of the brightest stars, which hung in the orange halo from the distant glowing lights of Asheville. The wind rustled through the evergreen trees in the yard, and slowly she could discern the individual boughs as they swayed.

Two red, dim lights bobbed up and down at the edge of the yard, almost floating as they moved closer to the house.

Jordana's vision sharpened and her heart dropped as she gasped in terror. The lights were eyes. A hulking form stopped several yards from the house and peered directly up at her window. It took a step toward her.

She backed up quickly, spun and ran back to her father's bedroom. She rapped her knuckles urgently on his door.

"Dad! The Tsul'kalu is outside!" She heard her father breathe out quick puffs of air, and the light from under his door went dark.

"Daddy, what are we going to do?" she asked in fainthearted dismay.

"Are you sure?" he whispered. His voice was inches away from her on the other side of the door.

"Yes," she replied anxiously. He didn't respond. She put her ear to the door and listened intently. It sounded as if her father were panting.

She turned and looked through the hallway into her room. The glare from her bedroom light painted her window, obscuring the darkness outside.

Jordana tiptoed back into her room, her eyes locked onto the window. Slowly she angled herself so the glare dissipated, but she still could only see the sable darkness of the night.

She glided up to the windowsill and lifted the edge of the curtain. The two red eyes glared directly at her through condensing fog against the window, flaring from the creature's breath. Glistening, jagged teeth pierced through the shaggy coat that covered its face, and it snarled menacingly at her.

Jordana squeezed her eyes tightly together and screamed frantically. Muscular hands squeezed her shoulders like a vice.

"JORDANA!"

She awoke in her bed scrambling to free herself as her father shook her.

"You're having a nightmare," he cried. She looked curiously at her father, processing the images that flashed through her head.

"NO!" she shouted as she sat up in bed. "It was real!"

"What was real?" he asked earnestly. She pushed him away and looked through the part in her curtains. All she could see was the star-lit night sky.

"What were you doing in your room?"

"Sleeping," he replied. "Until your screaming woke me up."

She kneaded her fists into her face, trying to dissect her consciousness. Her father sat next to her on her bed and held her hand.

"You're exhausted because you haven't been sleeping," he consoled her. "You were sleeping so hard, I'm sure whatever you saw seemed real."

She shook her head disagreeably.

"Do you want a glass of water?"

Jordana refused to look at him.

He unraveled the covers at the bottom of her bed and pulled them over her gently. "Try and get some rest. We both have to be up early in the morning."

He stood up and walked toward the door. At the doorway, he turned back to her and gave her a loving smile. In the glint of the lamplight, Jordana caught a bead of sweat slide down his forehead. He turned off the light and walked to his bedroom.

Fear, anger and derision welled in her stomach. She knew what she had seen was no dream. It was as real as any other waking moment. She untethered her covers and a small, round hard object rolled along her bedding. She picked it up and examined it between her fingers. It was another one of her missing rings.

# Clear As Tears

Aubrey stared aimlessly out the square school bus window as it pulled up to the high school. He sat nearly comatose the entire ride from his house to school, trying to ignore the world and hoping it would return the favor. His mind was numb and blank, overloaded with all that had happened.

Aubrey recalled the two previous times in more than nine years of school that he had been forced to ride the bus. The first time was in second grade, when Gaetan had lost his bike in a bet to a friend, and it had taken a couple days for his dad to get it back. The second time, in fourth grade, was after his mother had been hospitalized at a local psychiatric facility. There would have been nobody home that day to meet him after school, so he had to ride the bus to his uncle's house in Asheville. Now that his bicycle had been stolen, and his father was livid at all that had happened, he fearfully entertained the idea of being on intimate terms with the school bus every day for the remainder of high school.

The bus stopped in the lane in front of the school, and it took Aubrey's last strand of courage to stand up and walk down the narrow, student-filled walkway. He wobbled like a lump of gelatin to the front of the bus, and gravity pulled him down the stairs outside.

As he stepped onto the curb, Aubrey nearly fell into Buzz, meeting him nose to nose. Buzz was trembling from head to toe. Aubrey figured he was either bitterly cold, or he was about to have a seizure.

"Have you heard?" Buzz asked in a scratchy, high-pitched tone.

Aubrey murmured flatly, "Heard what?"

"We're heroes!" Buzz exclaimed. Aubrey stared away from him blankly, irritated at his excessively euphoric mood. He walked past him toward the school.

Buzz chased after him like an overzealous puppy. "Everyone is talking about how we saved Magnos! This is huge!" Aubrey kept walking, nonplussed. McCrayden Miller, Jon Harney and Pam Trank huddled on the front lawn, whispering amongst themselves as they gawked at Aubrey and Buzz striding passed them. Buzz waved wildly at the clique and stepped up his pace to walk next to Aubrey. He puffed out his chest and lifted his chin with pride as a smug grin crept across his face.

"Dude! Our stock has just skyrocketed! We could probably even have our pick of dates to the Homecoming dance." With this statement, Aubrey stopped. Buzz backtracked, as he had stepped ahead of Aubrey.

"The house is gone," Aubrey said stoically.

"What?" asked Buzz, still lost in delirious excitement.

"The lot was empty this morning when I checked. No stone cottage, no charred remains, no evidence of a fire. Only the grass lot with its the old dead tree stump."

"Huh?" asked Buzz, confused.

"I also went looking for Old Widow Wizenblatt under the overpass. She's gone, too, and all of her stuff."

Buzz looked at Aubrey, his ecstatic balloon of new-found popularity rapidly deflating. "How…is that possible?"

"I don't know," replied Aubrey. "But what I do know is this…as soon as Magnos comes back to school, and the details all come out, his disappearance will be seen as an incredible hoax, and we'll be at the center of the blame."

"But…but we didn't do anything wrong," Buzz argued.

"It won't matter. There won't be any explanation, and weeding through options for the Homecoming dance will be the least of our worries. We'll have no stock, and we'll probably be happy to still be in high school — that is, if they don't ship us off to juvey hall."

Buzz's ruddy cheeks washed to a pale gray. "Where's Ms. Thistlewood? Is she dead?"

"Who knows," murmured Aubrey. Aubrey walked up the steps to the front door and plodded in, after several upperclassmen opened the door for him. Buzz slumped through the door behind Aubrey, the gravity of what he had said sapping his energy.

"Certainly Magnos will tell everyone the truth," said Buzz.

Aubrey shrugged, "It's not like Magnos has ever been one of our friends. If the police can't substantiate his claims, I'm sure he'll have no heartache about throwing us under the bus."

They walked past the cafeteria through the central foyer and into the main hallway. Scores of students sitting at tables and leaning against the walls admired them warily from a distance. Andy Anacker ran down the hallway at them and tripped two students as he zigzagged against the flow of the crowd.

"Is it true?" Andy asked in a celebratory tone.

Buzz trembled with frenzied agony. He wanted to tell Andy all about it, but he was afraid Aubrey was right.

"We gotta get to class, Andy", replied Aubrey, and he motioned Buzz to move along.

Buzz trailed behind Aubrey, trying to collect his thoughts.

"Way to go, Buzz!" shouted May O'Klammer from behind. She gave him a congratulatory slap on the back, nearly knocking him to the ground.

"Thanks," murmured Buzz, and he sped forward, hoping to avoid her arm's reach.

"But there had to be other witnesses to fire." Buzz scrambled through his memories for possibilities. "Your Dad! He saw it!"

Aubrey snorted. "Yeah, I thought so, too. But as of this morning, he's convinced it was some optical illusion…a prank put on by the mine protesters to take some of the heat off them. That's the theory he came up with when the fire wasn't in the newspaper this morning, and the lot had returned to the way it was."

Aubrey turned into Mr. Vandereff's class and froze in the doorway. Buzz bumped into him and then looked around to see what the holdup was.

Magnos was sitting in his old seat in first period. His seat had been vacant for two months, and his return to class was brutally overt and surprisingly unexpected. His head was down, with his shaggy blonde hair draped over his eyes. He was pale, gaunt, stone-faced and motionless, but a shower and clean clothes made him look a little more human than Aubrey recalled from yesterday.

Feverish whispers scurried throughout the classroom. McCrayden sat in the seat next to Magnos, but spoke in an animated hush to the classmate on the opposite side with her upper body wrenched away from him.

Aubrey's throat tightened, and he struggled to swallow as he slid around the outside of the desks to his seat in the back, staring at the floor to avoid eye contact with anyone. He and Buzz sat down and kept their heads down. Aubrey was comforted that Jordana was already in her seat next to him. Out of the corner of his eye, Aubrey watched the kids throughout the class.

Lenny and Benny sat next Magnos, precariously shifting in their seats, each looking to the other for ideas. Lenny backhanded Magnos' arm and chuckled, playfully picking a fight. Magnos didn't flinch.

"What happened yesterday?" whispered Jordana to Aubrey. She had discreetly lifted herself out of her seat and leaned into the aisle.

"Long story. I'll tell you at lunch," Aubrey responded, keeping his head down. Jordana frowned disappointedly as she fell back into her seat.

The bell rang. "All right, settle down," Mr. Vandereff redirected the class as he straddled his tall chair behind the podium. "We're all glad Mr. Strumgarten is back. Let's try and give him some room to breathe today."

"Yesterday we left off at iodine, the second most productive halogen in the series…" he continued into his lecture.

Aubrey was relieved by the start of a class for the first time in his life. At least while Mr. Vandereff was teaching, he didn't have to think about what other people thought. He focused his attention on Mr. Vandereff's words, but the words themselves didn't flow together in his mind. It was not enough distraction. His brain flipped between Magnos, Ms. Thistlewood and Hovis, no matter how hard he concentrated on iodine.

A folded, triangular-shaped piece of paper hopped across Aubrey's desk into the floor, snapping him out of his perplexed trance. Aubrey looked up and saw Lenny leering at him. Aubrey searched the floor and picked up the saliva-free projectile. Instead of a spit wad, Lenny had flung a paper football at Aubrey today. He looked up again at Lenny, who responded with a stern insistence, goading him to open it. Reluctantly, Aubrey unwrapped and read the note.

### Is it true?

was scribbled across the inside. Aubrey looked up at Lenny, anxiety rising in his chest. Lenny glowered at him, expectantly awaiting an answer.

Aubrey wrote furiously under Lenny's writing,

## IS WHAT TRUE?

Aubrey watched Mr. Vandereff, and as soon as he turned toward the blackboard, Aubrey folded the note and flipped it back to Lenny.

Lenny read the note and quickly scrawled underneath Aubrey's writing. Mr. Vandereff faced the class, "Courtois of France was the first to isolate iodine, but he lacked the funds to explore the chemical properties himself." He returned to the blackboard. Lenny volleyed the note back to Aubrey. He opened the note, which read,

### Did you and Buzz find Magnos?

Aubrey simply wrote the word,

## YES

He rewrapped the paper and sent it soaring back to Lenny.

"Sir Humphrey Davy, discoverer of many of the alkali metals, which we have already discussed..." Mr. Vandereff pivoted his attention between the class and the board, "was in dispute with Joseph Guy-Lussac over who was the first to discover the element independently...."

Lenny read the note, replied and returned it to Aubrey. Aubrey opened it.

### Where's he been?

"Both were prominent scientists at that time, and poor Mr. Courtois didn't stand much of a chance academically speaking...." Mr. Vandereff walked over toward his desk in the corner, continuing his lecture.

Aubrey feigned taking notes as he responded to Lenny's question.

## HE WAS KIDNAPPED

Aubrey waited for Mr. Vandereff to look down and then slid the note along the floor with his foot toward Lenny's desk. Lenny raked it over into reaching distance with his shoe, read it and wrote on it again, sending it back to Aubrey.

Aubrey opened it.

### Did you kidnap him?

Aubrey's face flushed with both embarrassment and anger. The notion that he could overwhelm Magnos was preposterous, but he also knew there was little concrete evidence to dispute the claim. Aubrey shifted his gaze around the room, and he could tell most of the kids in the classroom had been spying on his and Lenny's tacit conversation. Frustrated and irritated, Aubrey hastily replied,

## NO WAY! IF YOU WANT TO KNOW WHAT HAPPENED, ASK MAGNOS!

He flung the note back at Lenny. Lenny glanced quickly at the note and smugly scribbled at the bottom. He handed it to the student behind him, who dropped it onto Aubrey's desk.

Aubrey held the note between his fingers, debating what he should do next. A hand swooped down from over his shoulder and plucked the note out of his hand.

"If it is so important it needs to disrupt my lecture, then perhaps the entire class is entitled to know more details regarding this scripted tête-à-tête between Mr. Taylor and Mr. Van Zenny," concluded Mr. Vandereff, holding the folded note in the air. "Do you agree?" He looked directly at Aubrey and Lenny, but the looked away. Several of their classmates nodded in eager agreement.

Mr. Vandereff unwrapped the note and addressed the class, starting from the top:

### Is it true?

## IS WHAT TRUE?

### Did you and Buzz find Magnos?

## YES

### Where's he been?

## HE WAS KIDNAPPED
### Did you kidnap him?
## NO WAY! IF YOU WANT TO KNOW WHAT HAPPENED, ASK MAGNOS!
### My dad said you did

Mr. Vandereff's voice trailed off as he read the last line, slightly embarrassed that he had read it out loud.

Nervous murmurings wisped hastily between the students. Benny giggled, and Lenny stared him down.

"Enough," commanded Mr. Vandereff. He crumbled the note in his fist and dropped it into the wastebasket. "When Mr. Strumgarten is ready to speak of his recent ordeal, I am certain he is fully capable of deciding what he wishes to share and with whom. And when he does, he should be allowed to do so without the interference of intrusive peers. Regardless, this issue will not result in further or future disturbances in my classroom without swift and severe penalty. Am I clear?"

The austere chill of his words gripped the room, and everyone in the class sat up straight in their seats with their mouths closed. Aubrey forced himself to stare at the blackboard, hoping Magnos would say something and end the controversy. He peeked at Magnos out of the corner of his eye. He hadn't moved an inch. But Aubrey could see a single tear slide down his cheek.

# Rough Day

Jordana slid into the cafeteria between two students who were holding the double wooden doors open for friends. She noticed Buzz was already sitting at their usual table, and Aubrey had his lunch tray in hand and was heading that way. She was eager to hear about yesterday, and lunch would be the best-undisturbed time to find out what really happened. Each of her morning classes had been rife with rumors about Magnos' alleged rescue, and since Aubrey left school early, she knew there were plenty of details to catch up on.

Jordana picked up a tray and gauged which food lines would be the easiest to skip through. She grabbed a banana and a packet of yogurt, slipped through the hot food line to get a hot dog, and lifted a can of root beer from a classmate who was being chastised by one of the lunch ladies for not having correct change. She walked back toward the front of the lines, reached over the top of the condiments kiosk for a spoon and napkin, and turned toward their table, deftly bobbing and weaving through columns of students coming from both directions.

A hand gripped her upper arm and swiveled her around mid-stride.

"Hey there." Jordana was engulfed by the deep, velvety voice before she saw his face. His wavy blonde hair curled in tiny toddler locks, perching in boyish innocence above his ears and temples. His lagoon-blue eyes were sorrowfully seductive, like a wayward puppy looking for a home. A verge of gleaming ivory teeth filled his smile, but they were too straight and too perfect, thought Jordana, much like the rest of Hamilton.

"Hello, Hamilton," responded Jordana in a controlled, nonchalant tone. She quivered on the inside, but forced her exterior to stiffen.

Hamilton leaned forward, his nose brushing her cheek. "You know, you don't have to sit at the table of misfit kids, if you don't want to," he whispered gently in her ear.

Jordana pulled away resentfully. "What bothers you more, Hamilton? The fact that the 'misfits' are my friends? Or that I actually *like* them?"

Hamilton grinned at the jibe and dropped his lower lip in the hint of a pout. "I'm sorry. I didn't mean to offend. I was just wanted the chance to tell you how beautiful you look today. Besides, any girl who can tame bullies like Benny and Lenny Van Zenny is certainly a force to be reckoned with." He ran his knuckle gently down her cheek.

Jordana feigned a smile. "Flattery is beneath you, Hamilton. It makes you look desperate." She slowly pried his fingers from her arm.

Hamilton forced a grin, but his eyes quivered. "I'll see you tomorrow at seven, gorgeous." He turned around quickly and disappeared into the crowd.

Aubrey nearly spilled everything on his tray as he dropped his book bag and food on the lunch table.

"Rough day?" said Rodriqa in a commiserative tone as she sat across from him.

"I think he has a lot on his plate," said Buzz, not really meaning to be funny. He picked up a French fry and shoved it in his mouth.

The lunchroom was full of students, and two of his best friends sat next to him, but Aubrey still felt isolated by the days' unfolding events.

"What happened last night?" asked Rodriqa.

Aubrey's head dropped, his exhaustion reaching its peak. He tried to distract himself and picked up a tater tot, but the thought of anything in his stomach nauseated him. Buzz took the hint and relayed to Rodriqa in between French fries the noteworthy day he and Aubrey had had yesterday.

Aubrey tried to pay attention, mostly to correct Buzz's inaccurate elaborations, but he was distracted by McCrayden Miller and Magnos, speaking to each other in the far corner of the lunchroom. He desperately wished he could hear what they were saying. They both had solemn looks on their faces, looking down as their lips moved. McCrayden held her books to her chest with her arms crossed in front of them, like a shield to protect her heart. Magnos had his hands in his pockets with his back against the wall.

Jordana sat down next to Aubrey, breaking his trance.

"Rough day?" she murmured to him.

"Yeah, that seems to be the general consensus," he replied.

Buzz stopped his story. "Boyfriend troubles?"

Jordana cringed. "He's *not* my boyfriend."

"Buzz was filling me in on what happened yesterday," interrupted Rodriqa.

"Oh, let me start over," said Buzz, his voice muffled by the mash of digesting potatoes sloshing around in his mouth.

Rodriqa looked at him scornfully. "How can you keep shoveling those things in your mouth?"

"I'm hungry." Buzz shrugged innocently. "Besides, I eat a lot when I'm stressed."

"You must stay stressed," quipped Rodriqa.

Aubrey and Jordana snickered quietly. Buzz curled his lips at Rodriqa, but then quickly returned to the story. Jordana and Rodriqa listened with wide eyes and rapt attention.

Aubrey's mind wandered quickly away from the tale. He looked up again toward the far corner, but McCrayden and Magnos where gone. He scanned the lunchroom for both of them, but amongst the throngs of students milling between the tables and the lunch line, he had lost them both.

"Lenny has some nerve," scolded Rodriqa. Her long, beaded hair swished around her neck as she spoke with fervent animation. "His dad's a loudmouth cop that has nothing better to do than start trouble. You should have stood up to him." Rodriqa switched between pointing her finger at Aubrey and Buzz.

"And say what?" retorted Buzz sarcastically. "Magnos was kidnapped by some kind of witch, whose existence we can't prove because she and her entire house have disappeared? Yeah, Aubrey, we should go ahead and make that our alibi, don't you think?"

"Don't get lippy with me," barked Rodriqa. "I'm on your side, even if your story is the most bizarre thing I've ever heard. You two need to stay out of trouble, and you need to get Magnos to talk." Jordana nodded in agreement.

"Like that will ever happen. He's *never* done anything close to kind for me or Buzz, *ever*," complained Aubrey as a torrent of feelings erupted. "He's *always* been a bully. He's even had to go out of his way to be mean to us, and *worst* of all, I think he enjoys it." Buzz and Rodriqa straightened their posture as they quietly listened to Aubrey's rant. They both looked beyond him as something large caught their eyes. "Now he is in the perfect position to be a bully and not have to lift a finger. As a matter of fact, the less he does, the more harmful it will be." Rodriqa and Buzz twitched their heads softly back and forth. "Maybe I should have just left him in that basement." Buzz and Rodriqa's chins dropped to their chests.

"Aubrey, can I speak to you?" Magnos grumbled from behind him. Aubrey felt like he'd been hit in the chest with a sledgehammer. The color drained from his face, and he almost blended in with the white lunchroom tabletop. He turned around slowly and met Magnos face to face. Magnos' hulking form was slighter than before, but his muscles were already filling out again, and he was already less pale than he was this morning. *Eighteen hours had given him a lot of life back*, Aubrey thought to himself. He stared at Magnos, uncertain what to do. The former bully's blue eyes were dark and sunken, and pain creased across his face, like a badge of wrinkled scars from his agonizing imprisonment. Magnos nodded in the direction of the cafeteria doors, and then he waited for Aubrey.

Aubrey pushed himself up from the table, his legs trembling beneath him. He marched toward the front of the cafeteria, certain he was about to experience the beating of a lifetime. Magnos followed behind at a distance.

Once outside, Aubrey kept walking, but Magnos stopped him in the hallway. Aubrey angled his body away from him, hoping he could escape quickly when the first blow came.

"I need to tell you something," murmured Magnos. He glared at the floor and scrunched his face together. Aubrey stood there silently.

"I never said thank you." Magnos' mouth twisted and trembled as he spoke.

Aubrey sighed heavily, and a tsunami of relief washed over him. "Don't worry about it," he replied, waving it off.

"No. You saved my life. And I should have stood up for you this morning in class. I'm sorry I didn't," said Magnos heavily.

"It's cool...I mean...it's fine. No big deal," replied Aubrey, now feeling slightly uncomfortable.

"I'm not sure how much longer I would have lasted down there." Pools of tears swelled up between Magnos' eyelids. "I know we've never been friends, and I realize you could have just left me down there...to die. Most people probably would have."

"No way," replied Aubrey. "You're one of the most popular kids in school. Anyone and everyone would have done anything and everything they could to save you."

"Popular or feared." It was the most profound statement Aubrey had ever heard Magnos make. He couldn't dispute it, but Magnos' self-deprecation melted Aubrey's reluctance and fueled an inquisitive confidence.

"Why are you here?" asked Aubrey.

Magnos looked at him, puzzled. "Huh?"

"You've been held captive for two months," Aubrey asserted a little too loudly. Several passing students stared as they walked by. Aubrey suppressed his tone. "And you just got home last night. Why did you come to school today?"

Magnos shrugged. "Because I wanted to." Aubrey stared at him, dumbfounded. "Last night after I got home, the police came by and took my statement. They told my mom to take me to the hospital to have some tests done, but I told them I didn't want to go. I just wanted to sleep in my own bed. I just wanted everything to be like it was. I thought if I came back to school today, things would be like normal, but it's not what I expected. Everything's sorta topsy-turvy."

"You're tellin' me," echoed Aubrey. "Did the police say anything about what you told them?"

"They said they were going to bring Ms. Thistlewood in for questioning, but Lenny told me after first period that they couldn't find her. Do you think she died in the fire?"

"No, I don't," said Aubrey. "Because as far as the investigation goes, there is no fire, there is no house, and I'm willing to bet there is no Ms. Thistlewood."

"What?"

Aubrey looked over Magnos' shoulder and saw Lenny and Benny approaching from behind him. He spoke quickly, hoping the Van Zenny brothers wouldn't hear him. "Look, I'm glad you're back and safe. I'm sorry what I said in the cafeteria, but honestly I have a lot to deal with right now too. If I were you, I would take some time off and just enjoy it, because I have a feeling things are gonna be rocky for a while."

"Could you not talk to me in riddles and tell me what's going on?"

"If they can't find your captor, then they'll be coming after me and Buzz, and since we don't really have an alibi, we're toast."

Magnos rubbed his forehead. "That doesn't make any sense. I wouldn't be here right now if you two didn't find me. Ms. Thistlewood has to turn up somewhere. A person can't just disappear."

"You did," stated Aubrey.

Aubrey turned away from Magnos as the twins approached. Aubrey walked back into the cafeteria, grateful his conversation with Magnos had been reasonably pleasant. He joined Rodriqa, Jordana and Buzz at their lunch table.

"What did he want?" asked Jordana.

"He apologized and said thanks," murmured Aubrey sarcastically, discounting Magnos' sincerity with his tone. "At this point the further I stay away from him, the better."

"He might make a good ally at this point," Rodriqa challenged him. "He might know something that would be useful."

"Doubtful," Buzz countered. "Like Aubrey said, he's never been particularly helpful before, and he's been locked in a cage for two months, so you know he can't be all there." Buzz swirled his finger at his temple, zanily illustrating his point.

"You never know. He might have heard something in the basement that might clue you in to Hovis, or the Bigfoot, or the dam," replied Rodriqa.

"But getting info from him means I have to talk to him," responded Aubrey. "I don't want to do that. I've spent my whole life working hard to avoid him, and maybe it should stay that way." Buzz nodded in agreement.

"He won't be at the dance tonight. Maybe you two should come," interrupted Jordana.

"How do you know?" asked Buzz.

"Hamilton told me McCrayden was asked by Teton Bailston to the dance over a month ago, and she was supposed to tell Magnos at lunch today that she was still planning on going with Teton."

Rodriqa whistled solemnly. "Rough day for Magnos. That's a low blow to the ego."

"Yeah, Buzz, we could still go to the dance tomorrow with any number of girls lining up to ask us out," Aubrey harped sarcastically.

"What happened to your invites from this morning?" Rodriqa asked Buzz.

Aubrey answered for Buzz. "Stephanie now has a sore throat, Tonya has to babysit, all of a sudden, but I'm sure May O'Klammer is still available." Buzz hung his head mournfully.

"No doubt," cackled Rodriqa.

"You two could go stag," offered Jordana.

"I'm grounded for at least a month," sulked Aubrey. "My dad has me cleaning up my room every evening until it's back to normal, and then he said he would find other projects for me to work on so my 'idle hands' don't get into any more trouble."

"Bummer," sympathized Rodriqa.

"That's not the worst of it," continued Aubrey. "My dad threatened to send me to military school if I don't shape up. He thinks I'm more disturbed than the average teenager. He thinks I'm crazy, like my mom." Aubrey's words trailed off in embarrassment.

Everyone looked down at the table, sad for Aubrey and uncertain what to say.

"But I'm not crazy," Aubrey raised his voice angrily. "And I'm gonna prove it."

"How?" asked Buzz hesitantly.

"I'm digging up Hovis' grave and ending this madness once and for all."

# Shingle in the Coffin

Aubrey pulled the end of his comforter over his nose like a rudimentary gas mask as he lay in his bed. The stinging fumes from industrial-strength cleaners and stain-proof paint bit at the back of his throat, and he wondered whether he might wake up intoxicated after a night's sleep drenched in overwhelming odors. At least his dad let him keep his window open to dilute out the fumes.

Aubrey looked around his bare room, surprised and nearly proud of its remarkable transformation over the past day and a half. The soapy, charcoal-stained carpet was gone, leaving only unfinished hardwoods underneath. His walls were a fresh new hue of tan, and it only took four coats of paint to erase all of Hovis' messages. His dad had removed all of Aubrey's furniture, except his bed. Mr. Taylor had even taken the bedroom door off its hinges and stored it in the shed in the backyard so he could keep a closer eye on Aubrey. At first, Aubrey was angry about this final, demeaning slight, but with no door to close, he felt less like he was being imprisoned, and he was hopeful it would keep Hovis away.

With a single cover to top the mattress and a comforter to keep him warm, he wrapped himself up tightly, eager to dream in a carefree rest. The excesses of the day's manual labor drove his mind to wander through all the bizarre events that had happened this past week. He wanted to ignore it. *Was it too late to take the widow's advice*, he thought. He tossed and turned as he imagined himself freeing Hovis and himself.

The glow of light from downstairs dimmed into darkness, and Aubrey heard the tromping footsteps of his dad coming up the stairs.

His father peered in his room. "No funny business tonight," he said as he continued down the hallway. "There's plenty of work left to do tomorrow." Aubrey heard his parents' bedroom door click shut.

Darkness and loneliness engulfed him, and his thoughts ran wildly through his head. Would Hovis come back tonight? Is it over? What's happened with Magnos and the investigation of his kidnapping? Was Jordana having a good time with Hamilton at the dance? At least his grounding provided him adequate excuse not to go.

"*Aubrey.*" His name echoed in a low, soft voice throughout his empty room. Every muscle stiffened, and he nearly jerked off the side of his bed. He closed his eyes and slowly raised his head, scanning his bedroom for the supernatural. If Hovis was here, he could run to his parent's bedroom and finally prove to his dad he wasn't crazy. As the phosphenes faded, all that remained was the darkness behind his eyelids.

"*Get up*," muttered the voice in a harsh whisper. Aubrey squinted through his eyelashes at a figure peering through his window, the round face, thick glasses and curly locks squashed under a bike helmet were all too familiar.

Aubrey sighed loudly. "You really need to figure out a better way of getting my attention," he chided.

"Sorry," whispered Buzz dejectedly, "but I called you like a dozen times today, and you never answered."

"Yeah, I'm grounded. No phone. No friends. No fun." Aubrey fell back onto his bed, relieved that Buzz was not Hovis.

"I came to get you," offered Buzz.

"I'm not going to the dance," grumbled Aubrey.

"No," said Buzz, reassembling his thoughts. "I'm not either. Let's go free Hovis."

"I can't. I'm grounded," reiterated Aubrey.

"Are your parents in bed?"

"Yeah."

"Then we can do it tonight. I have everything we need. We'll be back before Gaetan gets home from the dance, and no one will ever know."

The honest possibility of Buzz's plan working sank in, and Aubrey's heart raced with excitement. He could end this all tonight, and tomorrow could be a brand new day. Aubrey jumped out of bed and tore off his pajamas. He grabbed a pair of jeans and a shirt from his closet and tiptoed toward the windowsill, redressing as he slunk to freedom.

Buzz pedaled down the cyclevator and hopped off at the bottom. Aubrey leaned outside his window and strained out a muted shout, "How am I supposed to get down?"

Buzz retracted the cyclevator, flipped it around and extended it toward Aubrey's window with the pedals resting near the top. "Oh, ye of little faith," Buzz smirked.

"Good thinkin'," Aubrey relented. He crawled out of his window, steadying himself against the side of his house, and placed his shoes in the pedals one at a time. Aubrey precariously wound his hands and feet in circles until he reached the ground.

"You didn't have to help me with my plan," Aubrey said apologetically. Buzz folded up the cyclevator and heaved it onto his shoulder.

"How else were you gonna sneak out of your room?" Buzz replied. "Have you had a chance to look at that golden book?"

"Not really. My dad's been keeping me busy the past two days, so I've had to hide it under the house."

"Do you remember the poem?" Buzz walked toward Rodriqa's backyard, waving Aubrey in his direction. Aubrey looked back at the house, afraid he would be caught, but all the windows were dark, and he decided he was safe for now.

"All of it," replied Aubrey. "Down to every minor detail."

"What do you think it's talking about?"

"I'm not quite sure, but I think the symbol on the bottom of the page looks just like the symbol at top of the gate to the cemetery and the front of the rock lodged in the dam."

"Really?" exclaimed Buzz.

"And the last verse is the key to tell you how to open it, but I don't know what it means."

"What's the last verse again?"

Aubrey recited it from memory.

> "The arm of wine, an ivy thread
> Slowly opens the sepulcher's head.
> The cipher grows but does not truly eat,
> Except to sift the dirt beneath its feet.
> Winding its arms toward the beckoning light,
> This be the key to free the buried night."

Buzz pondered the rhyme. "Hmmm," he said. "I'm not sure what it means, either. What happens if it's opened?"

"I guess it releases all the people trapped inside, but you would think they'd all be dead by now."

"Maybe that's where Hovis is buried," Buzz exploded excitedly.

Aubrey shook his head. "I don't think so. The things trapped inside were put there a very long time ago. Ancient times, I'm guessing, since it mentions Noah. Hovis was alive one hundred and fifty years ago. Plus, it seems that all of them were trapped completely, like body, spirit and all, so I don't think he could be haunting me if he were in there."

"Ah, good points," Buzz agreed.

Aubrey stopped in the middle of the Auerbach's backyard. "Where are we going?"

Buzz pointed to the rear of the Auerbach house. Aubrey could make out the faint outline of a shopping cart hitched with thick twine to the back of Buzz's bike. Buzz laid the cyclevator into the cart and walked over to his bike. He struck a match, lit the propane tank under its seat, and climbed on.

"Get in," said Buzz.

Aubrey shifted the cyclevator, two shovels and a lantern to the periphery of the cart and squatted down in the center. He found a helmet in the cart and put it on. Buzz turned on the headlight and stood up on the pedals to force them to move, but the weight of his cargo was too great for him to counteract. The pistons, attached to the pedals, jerked in circles as the steam pump roared to a boil. The wheels spun in the wet grass several times, until finally the bike lurched forward in a jerking motion; a few inches at first, then faster into a smooth momentum. They rounded Rodriqa's side yard and hit the pavement with a jarring thud. The wheels on the cart spun in circles with the asphalt's friction, and Aubrey braced himself with hands wrapped tightly around the front bar of the shopping cart.

Buzz turned onto the Asheville Highway at the top of the street without slowing down, his brakes a minor inconvenience to the power of the pistons. The centrifugal force edged the cart onto its outside wheels, and Aubrey leaned inward to keep from tipping.

A few cars passed them as they climbed to the dam road, but Aubrey hid from the oncoming headlights behind the shovels. Past the dam, Buzz veered off the road, and bike and cart soared up the hill toward the cemetery.

Buzz bent his head over his shoulder and shouted, "Which part of the graveyard should we head to?"

Aubrey edged up on his knees and squinted through the dimly lit darkness. He pointed toward the edge of the cemetery at the rounded Trottle family plot. Buzz nodded and angled the front of the bike along the edge of the graveyard. As they approached the grave of interest, Buzz leaned over and extinguished the propane tank's pilot light, coasting to a stop.

After Aubrey took off his helmet and hopped out of the cart, he lifted a shovel over his head and threw it into the grave plot. Buzz dropped his helmet in the cart, turned on the lantern, and carried it over the to the plot's stone wall.

"Sure you're up for this?" asked Aubrey.

"If Hovis wants out, then let's show him the way," replied Buzz with a confident smile, as he pulled the second shovel from the shopping cart.

Aubrey stared across the cemetery, closed his eyes and concentrated. The dull flickering phosphenes washed away, but the inky night remained.

"What are you doing?" interrupted Buzz.

Aubrey opened his eyes. "Nothing," he said. He walked onto the plot and raised the lantern to eye level, holding it close to the ruddy, rough-hewn cross. "Trottle" flashed across its arm, assuring Aubrey of their correct location.

Buzz walked up behind him. "Is this it?" he asked.

Aubrey nodded. Buzz fiddled with his shovel uneasily. "We can always rebury him when we're done," he said, nervously justifying their plan.

Aubrey shrugged. Buzz looked at him decisively and asked," We are going to put the coffin back after we've opened it, right?"

"I don't know," said Aubrey quietly. "I'm not sure what we're going to find."

Aubrey looked down at the three stone pots at the base of the cross and kicked them over, spilling their contents across the plot.

"What are you doing?" asked Buzz with a frantic edge to his tone.

"Pre-emptive strike," replied Aubrey. He scattered the dirt with his feet, exposing several human phalanges and a vertebra.

"Yuck," remarked Buzz with a disgusted grimace. "Who would leave someone's poorly cremated ashes lying about in open jars?"

"And why would Ms. Thistlewood have them in her house and outside her yard?" countered Aubrey.

Buzz's face brightened with comprehension. "The shoulder blade in the pot during the fire...."

"Exactly. And at least one of the flower pots on my porch, which were a gift from her, had bones buried in it."

"But why?"

"I think they're a way to ward something off that Ms. Thistlewood doesn't want around."

"Maybe they're meant to keep us away. I'm fairly freaked out by it," said Buzz, shaking his head as he batted around a humerus with his foot.

"Maybe, but I don't think so," replied Aubrey slowly.

Aubrey picked up the lantern and walked around the edge of the plot, reading the headstones. He stopped at 'Father' and placed the lantern next to the stone on the ground. "This is it," he told Buzz. Aubrey raised his shovel high and buried its flange deep into the dirt over the grave. He jumped on the edge of the scoop, pushing it deeper into the earth, levered it upwards, and flung a divot of dirt to the side.

"We're already heading to jail for kidnapping, not like adding a misdemeanor grave robbery charge will make much difference overall," chuckled Buzz pragmatically, trying to calm his own nerves. Aubrey grinned at him. Buzz dug his shovel into the ground next to his partner-in-crime and lifted a pile of dirt to the side.

"So what is the rock that shattered the dam?" asked Buzz as he heaved another mound off the top of the grave.

"A tomb," said Aubrey, already slightly winded from digging. "Built by an angel to imprison some surly characters, it sounds like."

"Do you think Ms. Thistlewood wants to open it?" Tiny beads of sweet were growing on Buzz's forehead.

"Most likely," strained Aubrey.

"I wonder what she wants to let out." A twig snapped violently in the darkness in front of them from outside the cemetery. They both froze in mid shovel-swing.

"Did you hear that?" whispered Buzz.

"Yeah," replied Aubrey through a heavy gulp. "Probably just a squirrel...or maybe a raccoon." Aubrey sunk his shovel into the dirt again and resumed digging.

Buzz squinted his eyes and scanned the distant forest, but the lantern's light obscured his vision in the darkness of the trees. "Do you think Ms. Thistlewood will come back?" asked Buzz with a trembling trepidation in his voice.

"I doubt she gives up easily," replied Aubrey darkly.

A pile of leaves thrashed in the forest as if something large skidded through them. Aubrey dropped his shovel and both of them hunkered down into the small pit they had dug.

"Turn off the light," whispered Aubrey. Buzz reached forward and extinguished the lantern. The murky night cloaked them with a blinding solitude. Their eyes refocused in the gray glimmer of moonlight, which swept through the tree tops and scattered bits of light across the cemetery in dim patches of broken shadows. One by one the insects of the forest ceased their nighttime chirps and squeaks, and an anxious silence settled over the boys.

A horn blared from the lake below. Both of them jumped.

"Mr. Osterfeld," they both whispered to each other with a sigh of relief.

"That man needs a new watch," remarked Buzz quietly.

Aubrey closed his eyes and looked at the forest behind his eyelids, but after the initial dance of lights had faded, only darkness remained.

Footsteps tromped outside the forest, each one closer than the one before.

"I think it's coming our way," whispered Buzz manically.

"Shhh," scolded Aubrey through rapid, wispy breaths. He felt his chest pound feverishly as the stomping feet marched toward them.

"Who's there?" cried Buzz with a crack in his voice. Aubrey smacked his shoulder to quiet him.

A tall form blotted out the moonlight from the trees in front of them as the footsteps stopped. Aubrey held his breathe and scrambled along the ground to find his shovel. Buzz dropped backward against the edge of the pit and crawled slowly back.

The form stooped over them. Aubrey lifted his shovel, ready to swing. The lantern flashed alight, illuminating the plot and burning Aubrey and Buzz's eyes.

Magnos stood upright, a crooked smile etched across his face. He waved a simple hello.

"Hoaker Croaker!" Buzz shouted. "You scared me silly!" His voice swelled with relief. Aubrey released a haggard sigh and dropped his shovel.

"What are you doing here?" grumbled Buzz and Aubrey simultaneously.

"I thought I might be able to help," said Magnos. His face flattened at their less than enthusiastic response.

"Why aren't you at the dance?" asked Buzz.

"Why aren't you at home?" rebutted Aubrey.

"I didn't have anyone to go with, and I needed to get out," mumbled Magnos.

"So you're stalking me now? I think I liked you better when you were a bully," said Aubrey in a petulant tone as he pulled his inhaler out of his pocket, placed it in his mouth and pressed the cartridge.

"Yeah, it's worse than having a jealous ex-girlfriend," sympathized Buzz as he shook his head in frustration.

Magnos stiffened at the shoulders. "Like either of you would know anything about having a jealous ex-girlfriend."

Aubrey and Buzz let Magnos' quip sink in, and they quietly decided not to respond, as they couldn't disagree. They stood up, and Aubrey resumed digging, ignoring Magnos in the hopes he would disappear. Buzz smiled at Magnos grimly, unsure of what to say.

"How did you find us?" asked Buzz, uncomfortable with the silence.

"I called Rodriqa before she left for the dance. She said I might find you two here."

"I always knew Rodriqa would sell us out, if she got the chance," replied Buzz, hoping to evoke a response from Aubrey. Aubrey continued shoveling.

"I came to warn you," said Magnos urgently.

Aubrey stopped digging and slowly turned toward Magnos. "Warn us about what?"

"The police came and interviewed me again today," answered Magnos. "They said they couldn't corroborate any of my story. In a round-about they way tried to accuse me of being a runaway. And they wanted to know how you two became involved. I told them what happened again, but they wouldn't let me finish. They said they wanted the truth this time, and if they couldn't get it from me, they'd get it from you."

Aubrey scowled. "I told you so." He glanced between Buzz and Magnos.

Buzz's glance drifted downward with despair. "Thanks for the warning," he muttered.

Magnos marveled at Aubrey. "Why are you digging up this grave?"

"None of your business," murmured Aubrey quietly as he lifted another divot of dirt from the pit.

"Does this have something to do with your ghost?" asked Magnos, point blank.

Aubrey ignored him.

"How did you know about Aubrey's ghost?" asked Buzz.

"It's a small town. Word gets around."

Aubrey gripped the handle of the shovel tightly at the exposure of his secret.

"It'll take you all night to dig six feet down, if you don't pass out from exhaustion first," determined Magnos.

Buzz rubbed his neck as he examined the small carter in the grave. "He has a point, Aubrey," said Buzz timidly.

"I'll make you a deal," said Magnos firmly. "You tell me what's going on, and I'll help you dig, so you two can take breaks."

Aubrey stopped digging and looked at Buzz. Buzz nodded affirmatively at Aubrey. "And you'll tell us everything we want to know about Ms. Thistlewood," countered Aubrey.

"Deal!" Magnos stepped into the pit, hoisted Buzz's shovel into the air, and dropped it deep into the earthy hollow.

"Who is Ms. Thistlewood?" asked Magnos, heaving a large mound of dirt to the side of the grave. Aubrey shrugged.

"We're not so sure," offered Buzz, since Aubrey was being tight-lipped. "She seemed pretty innocent. Would give us food and watch out for us."

Aubrey grunted in disagreement.

"But obviously she had ulterior motives," added Buzz.

"How long had she lived there?" asked Magnos.

"Oh, nuh-uh," said Buzz litigiously. "Quid pro quo."

Magnos understood. "Your turn."

"Were you locked in that cage in her basement for two months straight?" asked Buzz.

"Yes," snarled Magnos.

"Two months and one week," interjected Aubrey.

"Huh?" Magnos uttered.

"Aubrey was answering your previous question," Buzz redirected. "But we disagree on this issue. I think she's been there for years, but Aubrey insists-"

"Two months and one week," quipped Aubrey stoically.

Buzz rocked his head back and forth, confused by their time discrepancy. "What did she do to you while you were kidnapped?"

Magnos grimaced as he sifted through his memories. "It's hard to say. She kept me trapped in the dark mostly. Not much else. She fed me and, from time to time, even asked what I wanted to eat. She was nice in some ways, but if I ever asked to speak to my family, she tuned me out and I wouldn't see her for a while."

"That's so odd," said Buzz. "Then what was the point of keeping you down there?"

"I don't know," said Magnos choking back his tears. "The only time I was really scared was when she would get close to me. If her arm grazed my shoulder or she put her hand on my arm...."

"What happened?" asked Buzz softly.

"I don't know. It didn't hurt but...it felt like I was dying. Almost like she was sucking the life out of me."

Buzz furrowed his brow and peered at Magnos with a puzzled wince.

Magnos shuddered and took a deep, repressing breath. "What's up with the golden box?"

Buzz chuckled. "I was gonna ask you the same question. Aubrey knows more about it than I do."

Aubrey frowned at Buzz's candor. He shoveled a couple more piles of dirt out of the growing pit before answering. "It has the same poem in it written over and over again. I don't know what it really means."

"What did Ms. Thistlewood do with it?" asked Buzz.

"Don't know. I'd never seen it before two days ago," replied Magnos.

"Did she ever have any visitors?"

Magnos heaved a large rock out of the pit and wiped the sweat from his forehead. "Most of the time, no. She was by herself when she came downstairs, but a few times she held what sounded like séances with some guy named Hovis."

Aubrey slammed down his shovel and marched toward Magnos. "Who put you up to this?" demanded Aubrey. "Was it Lenny? Or was it Lenny's *dad*?" Aubrey nearly collided with Magnos, shoulders to chest.

Magnos flinched backwards and held his hands and shovel to his sides in surrender. "Whoa! Dude! Why are you freaking out?"

"Is this some cruel joke to you? Is this some fun bully game you're playing? Let me tell you something, Magnos Strumgarten. You don't know the half of what's going on. And if you did, you'd be happy to be back in your cage in Ms. Thistlewood's basement." Aubrey glowered at Magnos, his chest heaving with anger and his fists clenched white.

Buzz jumped into the pit in between Aubrey and Magnos, gently playing referee. "I don't think he knows," retorted Buzz thoughtfully.

"Knows what?" asked Magnos.

Buzz turned to face Magnos. "Aubrey is being haunted by a ghost named Hovis Trottle. And I'm not talking about a simple specter that just walks around your house casting shadows and making the floors creak. I'm talking about a ghost that invades your home, destroys your things, and threatens your sanity."

"So Hovis is a ghost and not a real person?" asked Magnos solemnly.

"He's a ghost, and we're standing a few feet over his grave," retorted Aubrey.

"What does he want?"

"For me to free him," replied Aubrey, nearly inaudibly. His face dropped, and he stared into the pit they had dug. "That's why we're here...doing this."

Magnos resumed digging. Buzz glanced at Aubrey, who turned away from him and returned to shoveling also. Buzz climbed out of the pit, assured everyone was on the same page.

"Did Hovis ever speak to Ms. Thistlewood?" asked Buzz.

"Yeah," replied Magnos. "I mean...I never saw him. I was always behind the curtain, but they talked a lot."

"Then if Ms. Thistlewood and Hovis Trottle are allies, the last thing we should be doing is helping Hovis out. Don't you think, Aubrey?" Buzz leaned over with the lantern in his hand, shining the light in Aubrey's direction.

Aubrey kept his face down, but his head quivered in agreement.

"I'm not so sure they were friends," said Magnos.

Buzz swayed the lantern toward Magnos' face. "So they were enemies?"

Magnos squinted at the bright light. "I don't know for sure, but more often than not, she screamed at him and he sounded unhappy with her. They talked about all sorts of crazy things that didn't make any sense."

**THUNK!!** Aubrey's shovel collided with a solid, hollow object beneath the soil. Aubrey and Magnos bent down and scooped dirt away from where the shovel hit. Buzz crouched along the edge of the pit, lowering the lantern down further so he could see what they had found.

"It's wood!" cried Aubrey triumphantly. Magnos flung handfuls of dirt over the edge, spraying particles of earth into Buzz's face. Buzz stood up, coughing slobbery bits of graveyard out of his nose and mouth.

"Watch it," Buzz said. Aubrey and Magnos raked more soil to the sides, revealing decaying planks of wood, fitted side by side. The more of the coffin he exposed, the harder he scrambled to clean off its top.

Buzz's cell phone chimed a love ballad from the 1980s. He wiped the debris from his face, looked at the number on the display and answered, "Hey, Rodriqa, how's the dance?"

"How does he have cellphone service up here?" questioned Magnos.

"Buzz fixed a signal amplifier to his phone," replied Aubrey nonplussed. Magnos nodded slowly, duly impressed. Aubrey and Magnos continued scraping earth to find the edges, sending more dirt soaring from the pit.

"You left?! Why?" asked Buzz into the phone.

Aubrey stood up and surveyed the coffin and its position in the bottom of the pit. "Something's not right," he murmured.

"Hamilton did *what* to Jordana?" exclaimed Buzz, enthralled by Rodriqa's story.

Aubrey glanced at Buzz worriedly. He picked up his shovel and dug at the front of the pit, where the hole seemed deepest. Magnos moved forward, cleaning more soil from the wood.

"I guess he was only after one thing then," continued Buzz. "Where's Andy?"

Aubrey waved at Buzz and pointed into the pit to get his attention, but Buzz held up his finger to delay him.

"Is Jordana all right?" asked Aubrey. Buzz ignored him.

"At the hospital," squalled Buzz. Aubrey's eyes widened and his stomach rolled. Buzz bent over at his waist, convulsing with laughter.

*"IT'S NOT FUNNY,"* screeched Rodriqa through the phone. Buzz yanked the phone away from his ear; her shrieking rebukes momentarily derailing his fit of explosive glee. He hugged his cell to his chest so Rodriqa couldn't hear him.

"Hey, Aubrey, get this," Buzz labored to breathe between talking and snorting. "Andy and Rodriqa went with a group to this seafood place, right. Well, come to find out, Andy is allergic to seafood, and he never told anybody. Ever since they've been at the dance, he's been vomiting violently, and he can't stop. Rodriqa said he hurled in the punch bowl and it splattered all over Mrs. Kapodophalous. They had to call 9-1-1 and take him to the hospital."

"That's awful," replied Aubrey with relief. "I hope he and Jordana are both okay." Aubrey waved his hand downward. "Can you look at this for a sec? I think we've got a problem." Aubrey stood away from the middle of the pit and pounded the dirt with his shovel.

Buzz waved him off and pulled the phone back to his ear. "Hey Rodriqa, did you hold Andy's head back by his ears as he blew chunks? There should have been plenty to grab onto."

More screeching reverberated through the phone. Buzz laughed even harder. Aubrey rolled his eyes impatiently.

"Is he always so easily distracted?" asked Magnos.

"Yeah, unfortunately," said Aubrey. "I think it's part of his epilepsy."

"Come get you where?" inquired Buzz, confused by Rodriqa's subject change.

"Yeah, we're at the cemetery," replied Buzz.

"Rodriqa and Jordana are at the bottom of the hill," Buzz told Aubrey and Magnos.

"Buzz, I need you to look at this," said Aubrey sternly. "The coffin is buried at an angle and we can't find the edges."

Buzz flipped his cell phone closed and swung the lantern deep into the pit, examining the bottom. A series of rotting, overlapping boards ran parallel, high toward the front of the pit and steep into the ground at the back. It was wider than any coffin he had ever seen. "That's weird," Buzz muttered. "The girls left the dance and they wanna join us. They're waiting for me to come get them. They're not far." He stood up and walked away. The light quickly drifted from the pit, leaving Aubrey and Magnos in complete darkness.

"Wait," hollered Aubrey.

"What's wrong?" Buzz replied from outside the cemetery.

"We need the light. We can't work without it," said Aubrey, trying to stifle the fear in his voice.

"I can't go get the girls in the dark," rebutted Buzz obstinately. "You're not going anywhere. I'll be right back."

Aubrey stared up at the night sky far above. Moonlight peered over the top of the pit, but the bottom remained in a shadowy vacuum. Crickets and roaches squirmed through the loosened soil at the top. Aubrey crouched down, careful not to touch the inside of the grave. The singing of cicadas filled the night air, and Aubrey considered this a hopeful sign that they were alone.

"Pretty creepy," murmured Magnos.

"You got that right," said Aubrey quietly.

"Reminds me of the cage," said Magnos in a hollow tone.

Aubrey sighed sympathetically, uncertain how to respond.

"Cold, dark, wet. Nobody else around. For hours. For weeks."

"I can't imagine how difficult it must have been."

Magnos grunted, nearly laughing sorrowfully. "Makes you wonder how someone could torture another person like that."

"Yes, it does," replied Aubrey, suppressing his own thoughts of karma.

Galloping footsteps crunching through dead leaves and withering grass approached the grave, as the lantern light streamed back into the pit.

"Can you believe the nerve of Hamilton," preached Rodriqa in a castigating tone. "Just because he's rich and pretty, he thinks he can do whatever he wants. I, for one, am proud of Jordana. She's a strong woman and a better person for standing up to him. Most girls would have let him have his way."

Aubrey stood up in the pit, grateful to see Buzz, Rodriqa and Jordana standing at the grave's edge. "What happened?"

Rodriqa ignored his question. "Why are you two hiding down there?"

"We're not hiding," grumbled Magnos.

"Buzz left us down here," Aubrey sulked.

Rodriqa smacked Buzz's arm. "That wasn't very nice."

"Owww," grimaced Buzz as he gingerly rubbed his injured arm. "I had to come get you two, and I only have one lantern."

"You should have thought ahead," bit Rodriqa.

Aubrey jumped up and gripped the edge of the grave, but the dirt crumbled through his fingers, and he slid against the pit wall back to the bottom. Magnos leaned over and formed a stirrup with his hands. Aubrey reluctantly raised his foot and placed it in Magnos' entwined palms, and Magnos heaved Aubrey over the edge of the graveside. Magnos hurdled out behind him with a single leap.

"How's the grave robbery going?" asked Rodriqa.

Aubrey brushed himself off and stood up. "Well, we found the coffin, but it's buried crooked, and we can't figure out a way to open it."

Aubrey took his first direct look at Rodriqa and Jordana, and he lost his breath. "Rodriqa...your hair," he squeaked.

Rodriqa's hair was absent of beads and braids and was wrapped in waves high around her head, like a woven brown tiara. Her strapless, knee-length pink taffeta dressed hugged her torso, subtly showing off her gentle curves.

Jordana's slight frame was barely hidden by her dress' layers of ever more translucent opal blue chiffon. Glints of light reflected from the lantern off her glossy, black hair and, to Aubrey, it looked like she had a halo. He had never thought of Rodriqa as pretty before, until tonight. Her usual sporty attire hid most of her femininity. And Jordana was stunning. Aubrey's stomach churned with an embarrassed excitement. He forced himself to look at Rodriqa; looking at Jordana was more than he could handle.

Magnos whistled. "Now I can see why Hamilton made a move," he said candidly.

Jordana squeezed her lips together and looked down. Rodriqa put her hands on her hips and glowered at him. "Excuse me?!"

Magnos blushed. "I mean…you both look really nice." He hung his head apologetically.

Rodriqa ignored their gawking. "So you were serious about digging up Hovis' grave?" She stared at Aubrey warily, as he seemed to have lost his words. "You might be a little off your rocker."

Her accusation shocked him, and he furrowed his brow.

"Don't get me wrong," said Rodriqa, amending her statement. "I'm not calling you crazy, but you're not quite right either."

"I hope you're never haunted," replied Aubrey bitterly.

"Or stalked by a Tsul'kalu," interjected Jordana in Aubrey's defense. Aubrey grinned with satisfaction.

Rodriqa ignored the jibe. "Okay, you've unearthed his coffin. Now what are you going to do? String him up on a float in the Paddling Pumpkin Festival and hope he does a dance so everyone can see he's still around?! *HE'S A CORPSE!!* And it's time you came to your senses!" Aubrey's eyes drooped and his mouth slowly opened at Rodriqa's verbal pummels. "I know it's not nice to say, but let your dad help you get your act together. Look at what you've done. You've dug up a grave! This insanity has to stop."

Everyone else was quiet as Rodriqa ended her tirade. Tears welled up in Aubrey's eyes, and he rubbed his nose along his forearm. "He wants out. If I let him out, maybe he'll leave me alone, and things will return to normal."

"What's so great about normal?" said Buzz. "Normal is boring. Like any one of us has stock in normal." Buzz glanced from friend and friend, and no one argued with him. "No sense in beating anyone up over this. We're already at the coffin. Let's see what's inside, rebury it, then leave. No harm done," offered Buzz in compromise.

"Then open it, so we can get out of here. I'm getting cold," said Rodriqa dryly.

The five of them stared into the grave, uncertain how to proceed. Aubrey kicked clumps of the dirt hopelessly along the edge.

Rodriqa peered into the pit and her eyes widened. She picked up a shovel and jumped into the pit, landing with a hollow *thud* on the wooden planks. She sprang upwards about a foot from the recoil before resting firm on the coffin lid. Rodriqa held the shovel high, bevel down, and thrust the tip into the lid. The planks cracked under its weight.

"What are you doing?" asked Buzz in shock. Rodriqa lifted the shovel and slammed it with all her might against the coffin again.

"I don't think that's a good idea," muttered Magnos.

"It's not very respectful either," added Jordana.

Rodriqa assaulted the wood again and again, the timbers giving way a little more each time. "You know why I don't feel bad about breaking open the coffin?" She lifted her shovel again and flung it against the planks. The wood shattered and the shovel slipped through her fingers and fell through a hole, disappearing into darkness. "Because it's not a coffin...." The shovel clanged distantly against a firm surface below. Rodriqa crouched down and pulled a thick clay square from between the overlapping boards. "It's a roof." She examined the piece of baked earth intently. "And this is a shingle." She held the clay-monogrammed plaque high in the pit for all of them to see.

"Whoa," wondered Buzz in amazement. He slipped into the grave with the lantern. Magnos, Aubrey and Jordana slowly followed, dumbfounded. Magnos pulled at the wood at the hole's edge, creating a greater opening to see through. The five of them crowded around the hole as Buzz dipped the lantern inside and peered down.

"Rodriqa might be right," said Buzz. "I think there's a room down there." They could hear his voice echo below.

"I think I see a door in the corner," said Jordana, looking around Buzz's head to gain a better view through the hole.

"I can see the shovel lying on the floor," added Aubrey.

Jordana stood up. Magnos ripped another shingle from the roof and dropped it inside. It plummeted deep into the room and then somersaulted across the floor.

"I can see a trunk," exclaimed Buzz excitedly.

"What if this is just the top floor...or an attic," proposed Rodriqa.

"Holy Yatsa balls! Aubrey, I see a stained glass window, and it's in the shape of the Circle of Circles," said Buzz.

"Really," Aubrey replied, craning his neck around Buzz's massive head to catch a glimpse.

"I don't feel right," murmured Jordana. Aubrey tore his eyes away from the hole and looked at her.

"Is there any way to get down there?" asked Magnos.

"I'm not sure," said Buzz. "I don't see any stairs, and it's about a fifteen foot drop."

"What's wrong?" whispered Aubrey in a startled tone to Jordana.

"I don't know," she replied. She lifted her head, and her eyes widened as if she was gazing at something distant. "My legs are numb…and so cold."

Aubrey shut his eyes and stared at Jordana's feet. The phosphenes swirled away behind his lids. He saw a shimmering, serpentine form curling up her legs, constricting and pulsating as they inched upwards from out of the roof.

"OUT! GET OUT!" screamed Aubrey. He shook Jordana's shoulders, urging her to move. Jordana was ghostly white, and her eyes were fading to gray as she looked through him.

"What's wrong with you?" snapped Rodriqa.

"Magnos, lift Jordana out of the grave," Aubrey ordered.

"What's wrong?" asked Buzz, puzzled.

"Why?" asked Magnos.

"Just trust me," pleaded Aubrey. "We all have to get out of here! NOW!!"

"Jordana can leave when she wants to," replied Rodriqa.

"NO! She can't!"

They looked at Jordana, the blood drained from her face and darkness creeping under her eyes and into her cheeks. Jordana fell to her knees, and she gasped for breath.

"My fingers are all tingly," said Buzz.

"Mine too," added Magnos.

Aubrey grabbed Magnos by the arm and pulled him toward Jordana. Magnos reluctantly took the hint and lifted her by the waist over the edge of the pit. She was dead weight.

"Everyone, out of the cemetery," ordered Aubrey.

"Okay, okay," relented Rodriqa. "So pushy."

They climbed out slowly, the loose dirt making it difficult for them to gain ground. Buzz lugged the lantern with him.

At the top, Aubrey backed out of the cemetery toward the edge of the forest. Jordana remained limp at the side of the grave. "Pull her over here."

Magnos picked her up and flung her over his shoulder as he walked toward the trees.

As he stepped down out of the family plot, Jordana stiffened. "What are you doing?" she asked angrily. "Put me down!!" She pounded Magnos' chest with her fists. He dropped her on her bottom outside the cemetery.

Aubrey raced to her side. "Are you okay?"

She wiped her face, straightened her dress and stood up. "I was fine until the gorilla started carrying me," she replied.

"No, you weren't," retorted Magnos.

"What did you see?" asked Rodriqa, leaning over Jordana.

"Something's not right," replied Aubrey. "We're not alone." He closed his eyes and faced the grave.

"There's no one down there," chuckled Buzz. "And whatever is in that room has been down there for a hundred years, and smells like it too." Buzz waved his hand in front of his nose.

Behind his eyelids, Aubrey watched as the snake-like creatures wriggled back toward the pit. "There's no one *alive* down there," corrected Aubrey.

"Why do you keep closing your eyes?" asked Buzz.

Aubrey opened his eyes. Before them, the dark, shimmering serpentine creatures appeared to all five of them, twisting down into the pit out of sight.

Rodriqa gasped in horror.

"What's that?" exclaimed Buzz.

"That's what I've been trying to warn you about," answered Aubrey.

"They look like fat, massive worms," said Buzz disgustedly.

"Or snakes," added Magnos. The others stood solidly still, shocked by the sight of the ethereal vermin.

Aubrey closed his eyes again, scanning the plot for other hidden figures. Thick, gray fingers curled over the lip of the grave. A shrouded form rose up with his wide jaw' clenched tightly. Chains clinked at his sides, pulling his arms taut to the ground. The deep-set eyes and face-long scar were unmistakable to Aubrey.

Hovis stood in the plot and raised his arms, with dust swirling around him. Aubrey opened his eyes and Hovis appeared, plainly visible to every eye.

Aubrey backed up into Magnos. "Do…you…see…him?" he asked in a frightened whisper.

"Yes," whimpered Magnos.

Rodriqa spewed a deafening, operatic scream that echoed over the hillside. The other four flinched in fear. Aubrey covered his ears. Hovis cringed and covered his face, the chains swarming at his sides, throwing the dust around him into a frenzied storm. Rodriqa spun on her heels and bolted down the hill with her scream in tow.

Buzz fell to his side, his legs failing him. He scrambled along the ground until he regained his posture, and then he ran after Rodriqa. Jordana reached for Buzz as he passed her, flaccidly clawing at him. She swung herself around and chased after him. Hovis stretched his arms outward and stepped toward Aubrey.

"Time to go," muttered Magnos. He took several large steps backward, turned, and launched into a full sprint after the others.

Aubrey stood there frozen, wanting to say his name and force Hovis to disappear, but he was unable to draw a breath.

"Whyyyyyyyyyy diiiiiiiiid yooooooouuuuuu dooooooo thiiiiiiissssss?" hissed Hovis in a nearly inaudible seethe, as he floated toward Aubrey.

Aubrey closed his eyes again, turned, and ran.

# *It's Not My Party, But I'll Spy If I Want To*

odriqa sprinted through twigs and brush, which sliced across her face and arms. With growing momentum from the steepening grade, gravity pulled her down the hill, her strides lengthening, as her pace quickened. She hurdled out of the woods onto the highway below. Bright yellow headlights streamed across the road from both directions, blinding her as she bounded across the road. She blocked the light with her arms and hurdled forward.

The two oncoming cars screeched wildly as their brakes slammed down hard, forcing them to fishtail, barely missing Rodriqa. She didn't flinch and dashed down into the forest beyond the opposite curb.

Magnos easily passed both Buzz and Jordana as they ran down the hill. He spotted Rodriqa in the headlights just before she disappeared down the hillside on the other side of the road. He slowed down as he crossed the highway and followed Rodriqa's path of trampled vegetation into the deepening woods.

Buzz and Jordana ran neck and neck through the dark forest. Buzz heaved hard in the night air, and Jordana kept her head down, fearful to look back.

Aubrey ran as hard as he could to catch up, but his legs protested in cramps after his two days of manual labor. He stopped half way down the hill to relieve his exhaustion, but his fear and uncertainty forced him onward. He turned around quickly, looking for Hovis, but he couldn't see him.

Aubrey opened his eyes and trotted down the hillside onto the highway. It was brighter than he expected, and two cars were stopped at odd angles in their lanes over the yellow middle line. Drivers of both cars were standing outside next to their cars with bewildered expressions.

"Did you hit her?" hollered the driver to Aubrey's right.

"I don't think so," replied the other driver.

"Where did they go?" interjected Aubrey.

The driver to his right pointed down the hillside.

"Hey! What's going on?" he asked.

Aubrey ignored the driver and picked up his pace into the woods below. The path was easy to follow, but it was steep, and Aubrey pushed back with his feet to avoid stumbling. He skidded downward in the darkness, and tree limbs whipped against his face. He listened for sounds of his friends, and followed their trail.

After several hundred yards, the grade of the hill leveled out, and distant lights peeked through the forest in front of him like stars in a woody night sky. He walked out of the forest, breathing heavily and sapped of stamina. He could see Magnos, Buzz, and Jordana huddled together behind tarp-covered trailer in the backyard of a two-story house with every window ablaze with lights.

Aubrey plodded up to his friends and rested his hands on his knees. "Where's Rodriqa?" he asked breathlessly.

"Inside," replied Magnos with an icy tone that matched his vacant gaze.

"Was that...Hovis?" asked Jordana, frightened by her own question.

Aubrey wagged his head up and down. He flopped down cross-legged on the damp grass, resting his legs.

"Dude! How could you put up with *that* haunting you all this time?" asked Buzz incredulously. "That's some serious scary."

"I guess he wasn't happy to see us digging up his grave," remarked Jordana.

Aubrey shook his head, still winded. "Is Rodriqa okay?" he asked.

"We're not sure," replied Jordana. She glanced quickly around the edge of the trailer toward the house.

"We should go find out," said Aubrey, pushing himself up. He stepped around the side of the trailer. Suddenly, he slid backwards in the dewy lawn. Magnos had caught him by the back of his shirt, pulling him behind the trailer.

"There's a small problem," added Buzz.

"What problem? We'll just knock on the door and ask if she's okay," Aubrey said. This dilemma was easy solved in comparison to his other quandaries.

"It's my house," said Magnos.

"Even easier," responded Aubrey.

Two cars screeched to a halt in the side yard, and another car followed them into the driveway, as if they had been racing for the best position. Nearly a dozen people, dressed in a mismatch of formal wear and street clothes, poured out of the cars, yelling and laughing gregariously at each other as they walked up to the house. A short scream pierced the night air from a girl in the middle of the group of students. A large glass bottle shattered against the brick walkway. Chuckles and guffaws followed as they bumbled into the front door of the house.

"Fayla is throwing a party for the seniors," added Magnos.

"Your sister?" asked Aubrey in a fog, as he watched the new arrivals' antics.

"Yeah," replied Magnos. "She warned me if I came home tonight, she'd make sure I was kidnapped again."

"How awful," said Jordana.

"You have no idea," Magnos replied. Aubrey recalled a time when Gaetan had dated Fayla briefly a couple of years ago, and after they had broken up,

Fayla had attempted to frame Gaetan by slipping a cheat sheet under his desk during a test in Mr. Vandereff's class. It was not difficult for Aubrey to believe that Fayla was just as much of a bully as Magnos, if not worse.

"Are you parents home?" Aubrey asked.

"No," said Magnos.

"Then if Rodriqa is in there, she might be in trouble," Jordana worried.

"Jordana's right," agreed Aubrey. "We have to go get her. Magnos, you stay out here."

"But Aubrey, it's a *senior* party, which means the Joxters and the Rowdys probably planned it," argued Buzz anxiously. "We'll get plowed if we go in there."

"We'll rush in, grab Rodriqa and leave," replied Aubrey. "We'll be in and out before anyone notices us."

"Won't Gaetan be there?" asked Buzz.

A jolt of fear stunned Aubrey for a moment. He examined each of the cars around the house, but he didn't see Gaetan's.

"He's not there yet," retorted Aubrey, gulping down the lump in his throat. "Let's get Rodriqa out while we still have time."

Magnos briefly explained to them the layout of his house while Aubrey pulled Buzz and Jordana by the elbow toward the back door. The three of them slunk closer to the ground as they neared the Strumgarten residence.

The two-story dwelling appeared to swell as they approached it from the backyard. It towered over them like a menacing Carnival Fun House, eagerly waiting to release its tricks and pranks on any wayward visitor. The lights from the windows of both floors blanketed the lawn with light, leaving few shadows for the kids to hide in as they scurried up to the back door. The top of the door had four small rectangular windows set in its top half, so they squatted behind its bottom metal section.

Thoughts of Hovis, Gaetan, Rodriqa, his father, and the deep trouble he would be in tomorrow flitted through Aubrey's head, but the adrenaline rush helped keep his distracted mind at bay.

Aubrey held his breath and peeked his head over the edge of the bottom window. He released a quiet sigh as he viewed the empty Strumgarten kitchen. The large rectangular room was neatly organized, with a wide, central cabinet-laden island that was surrounded by an outer ring of appliances, with a small dining nook set within a bay window to the left. Two hallways led in different directions at the opposite end of the kitchen.

Aubrey gripped the doorknob, but it was stiffly locked. He groaned and slipped down below the windows dejectedly.

"What's wrong?" whispered Buzz.

"It's locked," sniveled Aubrey as he pulled at the knob.

The door edged out slightly. "No, it's not," said Buzz. Although the knob wouldn't turn, the door opened easily.

"There's no one in the kitchen. Five minutes...in and out...okay," Aubrey directed them. Jordana and Buzz nodded. Aubrey slid around the edge of the door past the frame and hobbled to the back of the island stealthily. Jordana followed and sat beside him, out of sight. Buzz had to open the door wider to fit through. He rolled his body into a ball, like a curled-up armadillo, and somersaulted into Aubrey and Jordana. Buzz was proud of his awkwardly sly move, but he was hard to miss from any angle in the kitchen.

They heard laughing and chatter echo from the other rooms, and listened intently for Rodriqa or talk of her. Most of the words were conversation centered around partying and happenings at the Homecoming dance.

Aubrey slowly leaned his head out from behind the island and looked down the left-hand hallway. Instantly, he pulled back.

A gallivanting drove of galloping tromps rumbled down the hallway and into the kitchen. Screams erupted, and the scrambling of feet scattered around the island behind them. A thin, jagged line of red plastic shot over top of Aubrey and Jordana, crumpling into a gooey pile as it splattered against Buzz's back. The kitchen's upper atmosphere burst into a squiggly rainbow of neon colors.

The cavalcade of aerosol can-armed seniors, clad in nests of wispy string, battled back and forth toward the rear of the kitchen.

"Go," whispered Jordana. Aubrey slid around the left side of the island and raced on his hands and knees into the hallway. Jordana glided along the right-hand edge of the island and crawled into the other hallway. Buzz jerked his head up from underneath his chest and realized he was alone amidst the war of boisterous partiers, who were spewing their ammunition at each other relentlessly. He watched Aubrey disappear around the hallway's corner. He bolted after him.

Buzz scurried through a half-dozen pairs of legs, hustling frantically around the island. Two slight-framed senior girls tripped over his thick torso and face-planted on the tile. The other four seniors tripped over the two prone girls, and the putty string melee collapsed with walloping thuds into a sticky clump of colorful students.

The polychromatic fray ceased.

"What happened?" asked one of the girls at the bottom of the pile.

"Does Fayla own a pot-belly pig?" replied another senior girl, "'cause I think I tripped over it."

Buzz scooted along the corner of the hallway on all fours. He stopped as he ran into Aubrey, who was standing in the middle of the open hallway, completely exposed. Buzz nestled against the wall and lifted himself upwards to face Aubrey.

"We've got less than four minutes," whispered Buzz. "And you're not exactly being covert."

"The key..." mumbled Aubrey in a daze as he stared at the wall. His mouth was moving but no more words came out.

"They key to what?" asked Buzz sarcastically, "getting us killed?"

Aubrey glanced at Buzz and then looked back at the wall. "The key to the tomb. The key to free the buried night."

"Now you're just trying to be confusing," shrewed Buzz.

Aubrey looked down and twisted his fingers together. "The rock in the dam is a tomb, a tomb which holds monsters trapped long ago. It's the Tomb of Enoch."

Buzz faced the wall and pushed his thick glasses up on his nose. An antique nickel vine hung diagonally along the hallway, with delicate winding tendrils wrapping around amber and burgundy bottles of wine, which hung in various directions off the main stem. Clusters of vein-etched leaves decorated the length of the stem, supporting the metal decoration against the wall.

"It's a wine rack," said Buzz flatly.

"No," replied Aubrey distantly. He rattled his head, shaking himself out of his stupor. "Yes, it's a wine rack. But don't you see?" Aubrey repeated the poem. "*The arm of wine, an ivy thread, slowly opens the sepulcher's head. The cipher grows but does not truly eat, except to sift the ground beneath its feet.*"

"Ah yeah, it's a plant. It gets minerals and water from the soil," Buzz agreed.

"Buzz, do you remember what the rock in the dam was covered in?" asked Aubrey.

"Kudzu," Buzz whispered, his mind wheeling from his buddy's discovery.

"Someone's already trying to open it, and if they do all those things within it will be released," argued Aubrey.

"Ms. Thistlewood?" asked Buzz softly, afraid to speak her name.

Aubrey nodded. "Most likely. We have to get back down there and keep the tomb from opening."

"What if it's already opened?" asked Buzz warily.

"I have a feeling things would be much worse after it's open."

"You're probably right," agreed Buzz darkly.

"Let's find Rodriqa. Maybe she can get us in the dam tonight."

Jordana slipped silently down the opposite hallway with her back against the wall. She sidled up next to a column of built-in shelving, which provided a small recess for her to hide in. Combing the clumps of green string from her hair, she turned her head left and right and felt a small twinge of comfort that she was alone.

At the end of the hallway, the foyer opened up in front of an ornate, wooden front door with a large chandelier above. A set of stairs led upwards from where the foyer and hallway met. *I bet Rodriqa ran upstairs*, Jordana thought to herself. Suddenly, the front door swung open, so she skinnied herself deep into the corner and peered around the edge of the shelving.

Gaetan stepped into the foyer. Jordana gasped, then clamped her lips together so she wouldn't be heard. Gaetan rubbed his feet against the entry mat and pulled his date inside from behind him. He glanced down the hallway as if he saw something, but was pulled away by another party-goer.

Jordana sighed and fretted over what to do next. She needed to find Rodriqa, but should she warn Aubrey that Gaetan was here first? She decided Rodriqa was a little tougher than Aubrey. She turned back toward the kitchen.

"I think we just found our fly on the wall." A deep, rowdy voice stunned her from the end of the hallway. Wearing jeans and their jerseys with the names 'Compton' and 'O'Dant' lettered in block across their shoulders, two football players approached Jordana, filling the hallway's entire width from the kitchen.

Jordana spun on her heels and took a lengthy stride down the opposite way. Her feet skidded along the hardwood floors as she stopped.

"Hey there, little lady, where you headin' off to in such a hurry?" Another similarly dressed football player, with the name 'Rontimer' on the back of his jersey, walked toward her from the foyer.

The three seniors were more than a head taller than Jordana, and each of their legs had more girth than her waist. They cornered her against the built-in shelving.

Jordana stiffened her lip. "If you'll excuse me, I need to find my friends." She tried to lever the Compton out of the way, but he refused to yield. She shoved harder against his stomach, but he wouldn't budge. He laughed at her attempt to move him. A tight semi-circle of meatheads swaddled her against the wall.

"Who's your friend?" asked Rontimer as he touched her shoulder. She slapped the back of his hand with a resonating crack. He jerked it away quickly, scowling at her.

"Guess she's a rough and tumble kinda gal," crowed O'Dant.

"Leave me alone," she growled.

Rontimer shook the sting out of his hand. "We heard how you treated Hamilton tonight. You should be more appreciative, considering you're new and all. You're lucky he even asked you to the dance."

"Totally," chuckled the Compton.

O'Dant rested his hand on the wall behind her, his palm flat next to her head. His thick arm locked tightly, caging her in. He leaned in toward her. "We were sorta curious if you'd treat us the same way you treated Hamilton."

He gazed menacingly at her eyes through her honey-colored glasses, his nose and lips barely an inch from Jordana's face.

A lump rose in her throat, and she trembled as chill bumps raced down her arms and legs. She thought of her mother and wondered if this was how she had felt before she died. Jordana remembered promising herself this would never happen to her. She swallowed her fear, intent on keeping that promise.

Jordana tilted her head down and stared at the football player over her glasses. "And I was curious if I could ask a teensy, weensy favor."

In a brief moment Jordana's pupils faded out, and almost imperceptibly her eyes gleamed a brilliant white.


Raucous laughter drifted around the corner toward Aubrey and Buzz.

"Let's find Rodriqa," Buzz said. He poked Aubrey in the ribs.

Aubrey blinked out of his enlightened delirium and turned away from the wall. "Yeah, let's go."

They peered around the edge of the hallway into the living room. The cavernous room was scattered with groups of seniors clumped together chattering. A large screen television hung on the left wall with an open cabinet below it, holding multiple pieces of entertainment equipment. Several guys, kneeling down in front of the cabinet, punched various buttons and confidently instructed each other on how to use it. A series of leather sofas and a chaise lounge in a horseshoe arrangement occupied much of the center of the room. Along the far wall, three glass hutches held a variety of ceramic and crystal pieces, from dishware to statuettes. The foyer was at the opposite end, and Aubrey was grateful he could see the front door, just in case Gaetan walked in.

Aubrey and Buzz leaned back into the hallway. Aubrey and Buzz were hopeful that there was enough activity that they could find Rodriqa without notice.

"I think the fastest way to find Rodriqa would just be to ask someone," offered Buzz.

"Okay," agreed Aubrey, lost in thought.

Buzz stepped out into the living room and tapped on one of the seniors squatting next to the cabinet on the shoulder. The crouched senior brushed off his shoulder and ignored Buzz, immersed in the figuring out the sound system.

Aubrey saddled up next to Buzz and whispered, "Maybe you should ask someone...less involved."

Buzz nodded. Aubrey scanned the room and watched as Jordana ran through the foyer and up the stairs.

Suddenly, music rang loudly from the speakers throughout the room. The walls thrummed with the bass, and many of the seniors bobbed their heads to the beat. Two guys in front of the entertainment center gave each other a victorious high-five.

"ANYONE SEEN RODRIQA AUERBACH?!" shouted Buzz over the music.

Aubrey elbowed him sharply. "How about we be a little bit more subtle?"

Buzz would have responded, but amidst this treacherous sea of celebrating seniors, his eyes had encountered an oasis of beauty. The modelesque Fayla turned out of the crowd and locked eyes with Buzz. Her straight, silvery blonde hair cascaded around her swan-like neck and fanned down the middle of her back. She winked at him with her sky-blue eyes, and the corners of her mouth blossomed upward into a welcoming smile. Her features were both alluringly frail and angelically intimidating. To Buzz, Fayla's beauty was the kind men fought ancient wars over, and traded medieval kingdoms for.

Buzz felt dizzy, like he was melting into the floor and falling toward her at the same time. Aubrey grabbed Buzz's arms from behind, partly hiding, but mostly holding him upright.

Fayla approached them. "Aren't you two a little young for a senior party?" she asked, giggling at him childishly. Buzz grinned at her, enjoying her attention, but stood there, rapturously speechless.

Another senior approached Fayla from behind. One of the guys looked around Fayla and gawked at Aubrey and Buzz. Aubrey winced at the attention they were drawing.

"Hey! Who invited Dork and Mindy?" echoed a voice from the back of the room. Every head in the room turned toward Buzz and Aubrey. And Gaetan glared straight at Aubrey.

"YOU!" shouted Gaetan. He bounded from across the room, around Fayla, and grabbed Aubrey's ear, twisting it. "You are in so much trouble!"

"OWWWWW!" squalled Aubrey. Gaetan wrenched his ear clockwise and pulled it downward, like a vice grip squeezing a tomato. Searing pain swept across Aubrey's face, and his ear throbbed like someone had driven a railroad spike through his head. "You're hurting me!" Aubrey cried.

"Why are you crashing my homecoming party?" demanded Gaetan. "Aren't you supposed to be grounded?!"

"Yes, but I can explain," begged Aubrey. Tears bulged from his eyes as he fell to his knees, his head following Gaetan's pull.

"Oh, you'll explain all right. Wait till Dad hears about this. He'll chain you to your room for a year, at least. Or better yet, he'll send you away to boarding school."

"Gaetan, let him go," said Fayla glibly. "He's not hurting anything."

"Please don't tell Dad," begged Aubrey. "I'll do anything!"

"Why? Are you gonna cry?" asked Gaetan cruelly.

"I think he *is* gonna cry," replied Gaetan's best friend, Leon Hagwell, a stringy-haired senior with a nose shaped like a conch shell, who was laughing at the spectacle.

*THUD!!!* The house shuddered with a boom from outside. The music stopped as the CD player skipped and sputtered from the impact. Leon ran to one of the front windows, parted the drapes and looked outside.

"Dude," he exclaimed. "There's a huge dent in your hood!" Leon turned around and stared at Gaetan incredulously. Gaetan released Aubrey and marched toward the window. Aubrey fell on his hands, and a single teardrop dripped onto the carpet as blood rushed back into his ear.

"Hey, let's go!!" Husky-voiced shouts echoed from the foyer's hallway, and rhythmic clapping followed.

The back door slammed. "Aubrey?" a voice called from the kitchen.

"What the," muttered Gaetan as he looked out front.

"There's someone outside," cried Leon, looking out the window.

Suddenly, guttural cheering blared out from the hallway behind the foyer. "B-E starts off BEST, which is what we're gonna be..."

"My car," whimpered Gaetan as he looked outside. The hood of his Pontiac GTO was a concave crater, and the headlights were busted open. A large, crooked crack ran through the center of his windshield. Gaetan's ears and face flushed red with anger.

Another partier walked into the room from the kitchen and said, "There's a guy in a bear suit tearing up the shrubs outside."

"Let's grab that guy," growled Leon.

Gaetan ran toward the foyer, flung open the front door, and hurdled outside. An angry torrent of seniors followed Gaetan.

Magnos ran into the living room and stopped behind Aubrey. Magnos lifted him up and turned him around by the shoulders, so he could look him in the eyes. "Hovis is here."

Aubrey's eyes watered. He was bewildered as to what he should say or do.

Fayla glowered at Magnos, both surprised and disgusted. Her gentle smile curled into a vicious snarl, and she gritted her teeth as she yelled. "What are you doing here?! I thought I told you I was having a party tonight!" She flipped hair about her head with a commanding swish of her neck. Her face wrinkled around her nose, which flared wildly, as if she was about to breathe fire. Her Aphrodite-like appearance now reminded Buzz more of Medusa.

A muffled wail reverberated from outside. Aubrey thought it was probably Gaetan lamenting over his injured car.

Compton, O'Dant, and Rontimer skipped from the foyer's hallway into the living room. They wore their jerseys wrapped around their loins like adult-diapers, and their jeans were draped around their necks and tied in a knot like a sweater. Their cheer continued as if they were in a trance. "L-U, the Loser is You, and that's all you're gonna see."

Aubrey heard rattling at the back of the living room. He turned and watched in horror as one by one the glass-faced cabinets shook, as if something invisible was trying to pry them open. One of the cabinets flipped open, and a porcelain teacup flew across the room and shattered into a thousand tiny shards against the near wall. Several senior girls screamed and covered their faces from the flying shrapnel. Fayla's rage melted into fear, and she ran into the kitchen.

More cheering boomed throughout the room as the three football players pranced in a ring around the sofa, flailing their arms at the elbows in a disynchronous flurry of fist pumping. "G-A, Go AWAY, 'cuz you'll never measure up. B-E-L-U-G-A team is gonna mess you up!!"

Fine cups, ornate bowls and silver-lined saucers erupted from the hutch along the wall at once and blasted across the room in an explosion of fine dining ware. Some of the party-goers ducked and scattered to the exits to avoid the derelict dishes. Others dove under furniture for cover. A heavy porcelain ladle struck Compton in the temple and knocked him to the floor.

Magnos and Buzz cowered behind Aubrey, who faced the center of the room, straightened his shoulders and closed his eyes. "Show yourself," he murmured into the ether. The light from the room faded behind his eyelids and the phosphenes swirled like a kaleidoscope. Slowly, Aubrey could make out the shrouded figure of Hovis at the back of the room, his chains waving under his arms as he concussed the cabinets. Somehow Hovis knew he was being spied upon. He turned and looked directly at Aubrey, and stepped toward him.

"Look!! It's Rodriqa," shouted Buzz. Aubrey opened his eyes, and amongst the crawling and dodging horde of seniors, he saw Jordana guiding Rodriqa by her shoulders down the stairs. Aubrey smiled and waved, grateful to see Rodriqa and Jordana safe, and grateful their mission had been accomplished.

A gray mist swirled in front of Aubrey, and the room darkened. Terrified screams tore through the air as the few remaining students in the living room watched Hovis materialize into an opaque, solid form. He raised his arms over his head and swung them at Aubrey. Aubrey could feel Hovis pass through him, but Aubrey didn't budge, and it didn't hurt.

"FREEEEEEE MEEEEEEE," Hovis shrieked. His chains swiveled and clattered, spewing a murky cloud of dust spinning into the space around him. He lifted a lamp off an end table and launched it across the room. It skimmed the top of Aubrey's head and shattered against the cabinets.

Jordana and Rodriqa disappeared into the foyer's hallway.

"Time to split," said Magnos. Buzz spun and ran into to the kitchen. Magnos pulled Aubrey by the shirt, and they both followed Buzz.

The three of them were passed by seniors running both ways. They rounded the corner into the kitchen and met Rodriqa and Jordana on the near side of the island.

Huddled together in a jittery silence, a throng of seniors crowded around the kitchen's back door and stared through the windows.

"Are you okay?" whispered Aubrey to Rodriqa. She was pale and stiff, and her head shook up and down like a cogwheel in response.

"She's fine," answered Jordana for her. With her arm wrapped around Rodriqa's back supportively, she rubbed her arm, comforting her. "She's just scared. And honestly, right now, who isn't?" She smiled morosely at Aubrey, making light of the situation. Aubrey couldn't help but smile back. Jordana, more than anyone else, knew what he was feeling.

The seniors at the other end of the kitchen parted down the middle, and the back door burst open. Leon barreled through the door and screamed, "Call 9-1-1!!! Call 9-1-1!!!" He dodged several students in his way and disappeared into the hallway next to Magnos.

A low-pitched, thrumming growl resonated through the kitchen from outside. Several other party-goers shot through the backdoor, weaving around their peers, and followed Leon into the living room. The kids shrank into a tight bundle. The group of seniors around the door ran *en masse* from the kitchen into the hallways, most of them screaming frantically.

Another senior girl stumbled in to the kitchen and leaned against the wall next to Magnos and Buzz. "In…the…living room…there's…a…a…a…." She sputtered, looking blankly at Buzz.

"A ghost," replied Buzz, finishing her sentence. Her head trembled yes.

"We know," said Buzz matter-of-factly as he stepped away from her. Screeches sounded at various times throughout the house. She slumped to the floor, catatonic.

"We have to get out of here," Buzz said to his friends. They shared a tacit nod of agreement.

The five of them shimmied toward the now vacant opposite end of the kitchen and leaned against the wall on either side of the back door. They could hear running and shouting echo from the front and side yards. No one was brave enough to peer around the corner and look outside.

"Where are we gonna go?" asked Jordana.

"Maybe someone will give us a ride," whispered Buzz hopefully.

"Let's sneak around front," offered Aubrey, his voice cracking with fear.

"On the count of three," said Magnos. "One…two…."

Rodriqa flew into full sprint out the door and around the corner, disappearing into the night.

"Three," finished Magnos.

"Rodriqa, wait," cried Jordana, but it was too late.

The kids hurriedly slunk into the shadows next to the house outside and stole their way to the side yard.

Jordana turned back and saw Magnos watching them from the threshold of the door. "Hurry up, Magnos," she whispered. Aubrey and Buzz stopped and looked back at the door.

Magnos shook his head. "I should stay and help Fayla clean up. Maybe she won't hate me as much."

"There's a *ghost* in your *house*," Buzz reminded him in a patronizing tone.

Suddenly, they were all nauseated by an overpowering smell that was sharp and stinky, like a steamy cloud of evaporating, sun-baked cow dung.

"Oh, no," muttered Jordana, stunned by the odor.

A pair of red glowing eyes flashed in the darkness next to the house. They could hear the footsteps approaching, the figure moving faster as it got closer.

Out of the shadows, the eight-foot-tall, hairy monster stepped into the yard, fully visible in the light from the house. The creature bared its railroad spike-like fangs and howled a deep, throaty growl.

Buzz turned and ran with all his might into the side yard, hurdling into O'Dant, who was chanting the school fight song.

"BIGFOOT!" Buzz screamed in his face, and O'Dant's trance left him. O'Dant stopped cheering and shuffled off into the woods.

Buzz ran into the front yard where cars where spinning out as they accelerated up the driveway. Groups of seniors were running to their cars and pilling in as quickly as they could. Gaetan's car was packed with seven students all clamoring and jostling in the compact bucket seats. Gaetan repeatedly and forcefully turned the key, but the car would rev up and die, over and over again.

Buzz beat on the driver's side window. "Let me in," he pleaded.

"Go away!" shouted Gaetan from inside the car. He avoided Buzz's gaze as he turned the key harder.

Aubrey and Jordana followed Buzz toward the front of the yard. Aubrey felt the moist heat from the creature's foul breath warm his neck and shoulders. Jordana dashed to the nearest car as it heaved into reverse, abandoning Aubrey. A stiff arm looped under Aubrey's shoulder and flipped him upside down. Every one of his vertebrae popped as he landed face up on the ground.

Old Widow Wizenblatt towered over him, her eyes wide and darting from corner to corner as she examined him. She stuffed her boney finger into his equally boney breastbone. "You should have listened to me, boy," she squalled judgmentally. "This is one can of beef jerky you can't reseal. The spirit shards will never leave you alone now."

"The what?" squealed Aubrey.

"Spirit shards, son," snapped the Widow. "Those black snakes you saw in the graveyard. Once they get a hold of you, they'll never stop chasing you."

Aubrey trembled, and although air was rushing in and out of his lungs, he couldn't catch his breath. The dirt under him shuddered with the advance of heavy footsteps. Red glowing eyes leered over him, and the Tsul-kalu's massive frame eclipsed the night sky. Old Widow Wizenblatt held up her hand, and the creature growled, but backed up and walked away. Mrs. Wizenblatt turned away and left Aubrey's sight.

Aubrey slowly rose up on his elbows and swiveled his head around. The Widow and the Bigfoot had both disappeared. In front of him, seniors continued to scurry from car to car, looking for empty slots. Buzz was doing the same, and Jordana chased after Rodriqa, trying to calm her down.

The Strumgarten's ornate front door opened and closed, seemingly of its own accord. Timing the cycle, party-goers leapt outside, hoping to dodge being smashed between the door and the frame. Aubrey shook his head in disbelief. At least now he wasn't the only target of Hovis' mischief.

The last remaining cars peeled out of the yard and raced out of sight. Only Gaetan's car remained behind. Aubrey watched as Buzz implored Gaetan through the window. Jordana pulled Rodriqa away from the edge of the road and into the driveway.

Aubrey stood up and ran toward his brother's mangled car.

"Please, Gaetan, let us go with you," Aubrey begged, standing with his hands on the cratered hood.

The engine roared to life. Gaetan shuttled the car into reverse, and barreled backwards onto the road, driving away.

Jordana, Buzz and Aubrey looked at each other helplessly. Blue and red flashing lights bounced off the house's windows. A police car drove up alongside the driveway.

"Is it the Kluggards?" asked Aubrey, squinting through the night.

Buzz shook his head. "Nuh-uh. It's much worse."

Two police officers stepped out of the car, and Aubrey lost all remaining hope.

A pear-shaped man in police uniform stood next to the police car with one hand on his gun and the other clasping his belt buckle. He scratched his stubbly chin as he surveyed the house and the ensuing chaos outside. Notorious father of Benny and Lenny, Sergeant Van Zenny pulled out his nightstick and waved the kids over toward him. Aubrey was convinced he would most likely spend the rest of his life in prison.

"Go check inside the house," Van Zenny ordered the other officer, who eagerly drew his pistol and marched up to the front door. It stopped banging of its own accord as he approached.

Aubrey, Buzz, Jordana and Rodriqa walked slowly up the driveway and formed a semicircle around the Sergeant.

"I have somethin' I want to show ya's," he said. He turned around, walked to the rear of the police car, and opened the trunk. The kids followed him reluctantly.

"Does this belong to any of ya's," he asked. Van Zenny reached into the trunk and lifted up a crumpled pile of twisted metal. He dropped the mangled mess on the asphalt. The bike chain was coiled around the steam pump, separating the shattered ends of its cricket-legged pistons.

Buzz gasped, "My bike!" His eyes fluttered, and his arms and legs twitched. Aubrey and Jordana grabbed him and slowly lowered him to the ground as he fainted at the end of his seizure.

# Confidence and Consequence

"Did you have a nightmare?"

The voice frightened Aubrey, and he jerked awake. The light burned his eyes, and he wiped the sleep away from his blurry gaze. His father stood over him with a scowl on his face.

"Yeah, sorta," Aubrey replied sleepily.

Mr. Taylor walked away, his voice trailing behind him. "When did you move to the couch?"

"Around three A.M., I think." Aubrey lifted his head and looked around the living room. He hid his mud-caked arm under his blanket.

"Ahh," replied his Dad with a dry tone. He stood at the kitchen counter and pulled two coffee cups from the cabinet. "That would explain why I didn't hear you." He poured coffee in both cups and spooned several mounds of sugar into one of them.

Aubrey smiled at him weakly. He wrapped the blanket around him and stood up.

"Where are you going?"

Aubrey paused for a moment; his head spinning from lack of sleep. "I need to go to the bathroom."

"You have company coming in a few minutes," replied Mr. Taylor. He carried the two cups of coffee into the dining room and placed them on the table, sipping from the one full of sugar.

"Really," replied Aubrey, a little confused. "Who?"

Three strong knocks rapped against the front door.

"Here he is now." Mr. Taylor strode quickly over to the door and opened it. "Hello, sir. Please come in."

Sergeant Van Zenny gripped Mr. Taylor's hand and shook it brusquely. "Thank you, Dan. I appreciate ya's help wit' all this mess." He spoke with a thick, long draw, that to some was an odd combination of Italian mobster and redneck. To Aubrey, it sounded like he had a mouth full of molasses.

The Sergeant tipped his cap as Mr. Taylor showed him in and pulled out a chair for him at the dining room table. Van Zenny nodded in appreciation.

Mr. Taylor pointed at the coffee. "It's a little strong. I made it earlier this morning after you called."

"That's how I's likes it," the Sergeant replied with a grin.

The adrenaline suddenly reached Aubrey's bloodstream, and the stuporous remains of slumber finally burned off like fog on a hot July morning. His dry throat pushed hard against a rising lump, and his gut and fingers trembled nervously. Sergeant Van Zenny had dropped him off early this morning, and at the time, hadn't said much. Now he knew the precarious rubber was about to meet the suspicious road without a believable alibi.

"Why don't you join us?" his father asked cordially, looking at Aubrey. Dropping the blanket onto the couch, Aubrey tromped slowly over to the table and sat down across from Van Zenny.

"Up front, I'd just like to apologize for any problems Aubrey may have caused," started off Mr. Taylor. "I've tried to be firm with him, but he seems to have an unruly streak that's been difficult to control."

Aubrey furrowed his brow and gazed down at the table, feeling slightly abandoned by his dad through frustrating circumstances outside of his control.

"No need to apologize," returned Sergeant Van Zenny. "But there's a few things I need to gets to the bottom of." He pulled a leather-bound note pad and pen from his side pouch and flipped through several pages to the top. "Aubrey, do ya's mind if I ask y'all a few questions?"

"No," replied Aubrey weakly.

Van Zenny cleared his throat as he read his notes. "Were ya's present at Lake Julian High School's first football game this season?"

"Yes," replied Aubrey softly.

"And were ya's aware that this was the last place Magnos Strumgarten was seen prior to his disappearance two months ago?"

"Yes."

"And what did ya's do after the aforementioned football game?"

Aubrey thought for a moment, recalling that night. He was grateful when the memory popped into his mind. "I spent the night at Buzz's house".

"And by Buzz, ya's means Virgil Reiselstein?"

"Yes, sir."

"And can anyone else confirm ya's whereabouts besides you and Virgil?"

Aubrey paused. "I'm not sure. It was late, and I don't remember talking to his parents."

"Mmmmhmmm." The Sergeant scribbled furiously in his notebook as he sipped his coffee. "And what did y'all do that night."

"What we always do...played video games until we fell asleep."

"Did you go snooping around the Circle of Circles cemetery?" His tone changed from curious to accusatory.

"No," exclaimed Aubrey, startled by his question. "Not that night," he stammered, hoping to walk the fine line between being honest and avoiding punishment.

"There's evidence and witness accounts that indicate that ya's and Virgil spend a lot of time at the cemetery. Is that true?"

"No...I mean we've been up there a couple times, but it's close to the dam, and another one of our friends' parents works at the dam, so we walk through there all the time." Aubrey fidgeted with his fingers and rubbed his forehead. Mr. Taylor glared at him sharply.

"A little odd for a couple of teenagers to be hanging out at an old, abandoned cemetery, don't ya's think?" asked Van Zenny.

Aubrey shrugged. "We don't hang out there, really," he whimpered.

"How long have ya's been *visiting* the cemetery, then?"

"Only about a week or so, not long."

"About the same period of time since Mr. Strumgarten has miraculously returned?"

"What does that have to do with anything?"

"I'll ask the questions here, young man."

"Answer the Sergeant," his father demanded.

"I guess so," Aubrey replied meekly.

"Are you responsible, or in part responsible, for the disappearance of Magnos Strumgarten?"

"What?!" Aubrey had expected the question, but was off put by how blatantly he asked it. "No!!!"

"Then why are we unable to verify not only the identity of anyone named Ms. Thistlewood, but also her reported place of residence, which has been nothing but more than an empty lot for more than a decade?"

"How am I supposed to know?!"

"Sergeant, I agree that Aubrey has been a little troubled lately, but I find it highly unlikely that he possesses the ability to kidnap anyone," interjected Mr. Taylor.

"Is Magnos Strumgarten's kidnapping a hoax?" asked the Sergeant bluntly.

Aubrey shook his head and bit his lip.

"Seems like wherever there is trouble, ya's are involved, Aubrey."

"Trouble follows me," Aubrey murmured.

"Maybe ya's are trouble," countered the Sergeant. Mr. Taylor frowned at him warily, and Van Zenny changed his line of questioning. "What was your role in the disturbance at the Strumgarten residence last night?"

"One of our friends…g-g-g-got scared, and we chased her to Magnos' house," stuttered Aubrey frantically. All the events of last night stormed through Aubrey's mind, and his thoughts were impossible to distill succinctly.

"Were ya's at the cemetery beforehand?"

"Yeah," replied Aubrey dejectedly.

Mr. Taylor scowled at Aubrey, but he spoke to Sergeant Van Zenny. "He's supposed to be grounded."

"Really," chuckled Van Zenny as he took more notes. "And Aubrey, are you responsible for vandalizing the grave?"

Aubrey hung his head. "It's not a grave. There's something else under there."

The Sergeant shook his head. "Dan, have you noticed anything odd lately in Aubrey's behavior, or any major changes in how he acts?"

Mr. Taylor glared at his son, torn between loyalty and truth. "Not really," he mumbled.

"Mmmmmm," The Sergeant took another swig of coffee. "Well, I've spoken wit' a few of ya's neighbors, and they've noticed several irregularities recently."

"Like what," Dan questioned tersely.

The Sergeant turned another page of his notebook and stared at Aubrey with ice-cold eyes. "Do you know anything about the disappearance of the circus?"

Mr. Taylor slapped his hand on the table. "If you're gonna accuse my son of something, you better go ahead and do it!"

Sergeant Van Zenny flipped his notepad shut and scooted his chair away from the table. "I appreciate ya's time. I's be in touch." He stood up, pocketed his notepad, and walked quickly out the door.

A sterile silence hung in the air like dark clouds before a thunderstorm.

"Aubrey, you need to tell me what's going on," insisted his father.

Aubrey squeezed his forehead and searched for the right response. His world was spinning wildly wayward, and he had no idea how to rein his life back into reality. He wanted to share everything that had happened with his father. He would tell him every detail, if his father would only listen. But the story was crazy, even to Aubrey. He tried to construct a fib that made sense, but anything that was believable wouldn't fit the circumstances. Finally, he decided on the truth. He bolstered his courage deep in his stomach and released it in words. "Dad...there is this ghost, and he's been haunting my room."

Mr. Taylor stood up and walked into the kitchen. He picked up his keys and walked back toward the front door. "Talk to me when you've decided to grow up and be a man, Aubrey." He stormed outside and slammed the door shut.

# Have Hope, Will Travail

Aubrey marched upstairs and ran into his room, fuming with delirious frustration. Life was stumbling into a crumbling chaos. The starkness of his bedroom only fueled his anger; a naked, personal reminder of the unseen's invasion into his mundane life. Aubrey squeezed his fists tightly as he recalled Hovis' words last night. He kicked the corner of his bed in a burst of rage, scuttling the warbling, wooden frame across the room.

The bitter frenzy burning in his heart melted into a canyon of helplessness. He trusted his friends, but they were almost as pathetically clueless as he was. Aubrey needed advice, and it needed to be more reliable than the meandering counsel of a homeless widow or the written rantings of a vandal ghost. He searched his thoughts for an adult who was shrewd, dependable, and would believe him. He came up blank.

He slid open his window and leaned outside, breathing the crisp, autumn morning air, hoping it would clear his muddled mind. His tiny, simple, suburban world was now a swirling, unpredictable and dangerous universe.

Aubrey looked across the yard, and he could see Rodriqa sleeping soundly on her bed. He yawned wildly and rubbed his shoulder as his own exhaustion crept back into his bones. The excitement from last night flooded back in a sloppy wash of images and reactions: the appearance of Hovis to his friends, the Sasquatch's harassment in front of so many people, the chaos at the party, the widow's warning in the middle of it all, the mangling of Buzz's bike. Thought by thought, he teased the erratic events apart, and a glint of clarity flashed in his head. Hovis and the Sasquatch are linked…but why are they after the tomb?

And then Aubrey recalled his moment of insight at the party…the Strumgarten's elaborate wine rack…the kudzu on the rock under the dam…the poem.

Aubrey raced out of his room, down the stairs and stopped in the living room to peek out the side window. His dad's truck was missing from the driveway. Excitedly, he barreled through the back porch door, hopped down the stairs in two steps, and rounding the corner, clung to the latticework on the side of the porch.

Aubrey had fond memories of playing under the porch when he was younger. The sheltered, dirty darkness enclosed by all the treated lumber provided the perfect space for a lunar moon base, colonial frontier fort and Wild West train depot, depending on what the play called for that day. But no one had been under the porch for years, which is why Aubrey knew it would be the ideal hiding place for Ms. Thistlewood's golden book.

He snaked his hand through a splintered diamond in the lattice and reached up, pulling a small metal pin up and out of its stock. A rectangular crease formed in the latticework, and the part of the porch siding opened up like a small door. He pulled it open slowly and bent over, examining the dim crawl space closely for critters.

Aubrey knelt down and wriggled through the dirt under the house. A droning buzz rhythmically crescendoed as he squirmed further in. The late morning light diluted in the shadows, and Aubrey felt, more than saw, his way through the damp, dusty darkness.

In the middle of the crawlspace, a gray, humming cube of metal stretched from the ground into the bottom of the house. He pressed flush against its side, and a panel slid open, exposing the guts of the house's centralized HVAC unit. He reached within the cube and grunted as he pulled out a heavy burlap sack. Closing the panel, Aubrey scurried back out into the dim recess under the porch, dragging the sack behind him.

He squatted behind the lattice door, afraid to reveal his secret hiding place. Warmth filled his heart as he suddenly felt eight-years old again, hiding under the porch with his secret, buried treasure. He pulled the golden box from the sack and placed it in his lap. Its luster had faded, and small areas flaked with corrosion. Aubrey worried that the hot, humid HVAC unit under the house had damaged this obviously expensive and ornately crafted book.

He opened the book and flipped through the foil-thin pages. The insides were blemished with specks of rust, and squiggles of water stains twisted across the metal. And worst of all…there were no more words.

Aubrey had ruined the book, and the poem was lost forever. Sweat beaded on his forehead. He desperately needed to read the poem again. Even though he remembered a great deal of it, he couldn't cite each refrain verbatim anymore, and he wasn't sure what it all meant.

He thought back to Ms. Thistlewood's basement and how he found the book. So many events had occurred over such a short time, from the fire to finding Magnos and trapping Ms. Thistlewood, the details blurred incomprehensibly.

He wadded the end of his sleeve in his hand and wiped it against the rust and smudges. The stains remained. He spit on his sleeve and rubbed more furiously. Nothing changed. He jerked one of the thin, metal pages, hoping to rip it from the spine. It didn't budge. He folded it in half and creased it down the middle. The crease popped out, and the page returned to its original form.

Aubrey's frustration exploded, and he kicked the lattice door. The metal lock on the back of the wood glinted in the sunlight, and reflected rays flitted across the stubborn, golden book. A tingling sensation tickled his hands, and the golden page glimmered for less than an instant.

Aubrey dropped the book suddenly, startled by the return of the book's electric feel. He kicked the book into the daylight. The letters S-O-L-L-U-N-A scrolled diagonally down the front cover, and the image of the moon inset in the sun glistened next to it. He picked up a twig and turned the front cover over gently. Gracefully, the poem scrawled in heavy cursive across the page.

He read the words intently and, like reading a book after seeing the movie, the pieces fit together easily. He lowered his head and examined the shimmering page more closely. The Circle of Circles was carved into the front of the jagged stone below the words. The rock lodged in the dam was clearly the Tomb from the poem. The kudzu was its key. And someone was already unlocking it.

Aubrey scooped *Solluna* up in the burlap sack and scrambled back into the crawl space. He hid it in the HVAC unit's innards and hustled back out from underneath the house. He locked the lattice door and ran into the shed in the backyard. He brushed through shovels, brushes and tools hanging on the wall, and found what he was looking for buried under a grill cover.

Aubrey strapped Buzz's WASER to his back and ran across the yard to the Auerbach's house.

He knocked furiously at the front door. He only waited a few seconds before he banged impatiently on the frame.

The front door flew open. "WHAT do you want?" Rodriqa scowled at him as she rubbed the sleep out of her eyes.

"Hovis and the Tsul'kalu are trying to open the Tomb." Aubrey rattled wildly, forcing all his thoughts out at once. "I have to stop them...that's why they're here...that's why Hovis is haunting me...."

"What *tomb?*" questioned Rodriqa in perturbed confusion.

"The rock stuck in the bottom of the dam...the book I took from Ms. Thistlewood's basement...there's a picture and a poem...the kudzu on front of it is meant to open it...I have to cut the vines...."

Rodriqa rubbed her head, which was pounding from both lack of sleep and Aubrey's relentless prattle. "I really don't get what you're talking about."

"If I keep the tomb closed, then we win, and everything will return to normal."

Rodriqa curled her lips around her tightly clenched teeth. "You're telling me that if you cut the overgrowth on the front of the rock causing the leak in the dam, your ghost and Jordana's Bigfoot disappear like diets during Thanksgiving?"

"YES!"

Rodriqa pointed her finger into his chest. "That makes not one lick of sense."

"Please, I just need to get access to the bottom level of the dam. I cut the weeds and I leave. If nothing happens, no harm done."

"Even if I wanted to help you, I can't. There's a specialized 'dam leak repair crew' or something in today from California, and they're in the bottom level working, so your bizarre, dangerous and ridiculous request...yay for me...is a no go."

"No," insisted Aubrey, "that's even better." His words and ideas spun from his mouth giddily. "I can slip in while the crew is working, cut the kudzu and leave. No one will be the wiser!"

"But you'll stick out like a sore thumb," argued Rodriqa.

"I'll wear one of the waterproof suits, the whole thing. They'll be busy and I'll blend in," countered Aubrey.

"What about all the crazy stuff we saw when we were down there? Doesn't that scare you?"

"No," asserted Aubrey. "It's a trick. The tomb is booby-trapped. Anyone who gets near it experiences the 'threat of death's fire.' The poem explains it."

Rodriqa shook her head. "You could get hurt!"

"I could be haunted to the point of insanity!"

"Too late," murmured Rodriqa.

Aubrey scrunched up his face and tilted his head to the side. He looked up at her with wide eyes and sniffled.

Rodriqa shook her head. "The things I do for the people I love."

# Tomb Doom

In the dam, Aubrey rounded the corner at the bottom of the metal stairs and slowly sneaked into the brick room beyond the concrete wall. Bundles of wires and plastic tubes snaked from the spillway into the room through the submarine door and down the stairs. He flipped open the black box next to the door, noting that only two green bars were alight. *One foot deep*, Aubrey thought to himself, *easier than before*.

Only two waterproof suits hung against the wall. He set the WASER next to him on the floor and dressed himself in the yellow rubber pants, coat, helmet, and face guard. He felt more prepared to go into outer space than the abandoned, leaking level of a hydroelectric dam. And nothing fit appropriately. The boots portion of the pants was twice the size of his feet. The helmet drape touched his waist, and the gloves dangled off his arms, nearly a foot away from his wrists. He shoved the helmet back so he could look through the face guard, but it fell back forward and everything went dark. He flopped his head back and slid the helmet to the side, so he could see out of the corner. He picked up the WASER, ran it through a belt loop, and plodded down the stairs to the bottom floor.

Men in yellow, waterproof suits walked hurriedly through the antechamber at the end of the stairs. To Aubrey, it didn't even look like the same room. The old equipment was gone, only a small amount of water flooded the floor, and Aubrey could see his feet. Bright florescent lights blared from every angle, and a conveyer belt stood half a foot above the water and ran both ways down the corridor. A black, corrugated pipe hung from the middle of the ceiling with small globs of liquid concrete dribbling out onto the conveyer belt.

Aubrey took off in the direction they had followed before. He tracked through the hallways, and the conveyer belt guided him along the way. Even the ballasts weren't frightening this time, as crew members had placed tall, plastic braces under each one to prevent it from falling.

"Hey!" shouted a voice from behind him. "What are you doing?!"

Aubrey picked up his pace and ignored the voice. Hurried splashing echoed down the corridor. A large, meaty hand grasped Aubrey's shoulder and spun him around.

"I was talking to you." A broad-shouldered man with a gruff voice leered over him, fully dressed in the yellow rubber suit. The glare from the lights made it impossible to see the man through his face guard. A white nametag that read "Supervisor Kerigun" hung on the left side of his waterproof chest-piece.

Aubrey opened his throat to deepen his own voice. "Sorry, sir, I didn't hear you."

"What is that?" growled Kerigun, pointing to the WASER.

Aubrey stuttered and stumbled, uncertain what to say.

"Does it have metal in it?" interjected Kerigun impatiently.

"No, I don't think so."

"You better *know* so! You know better than to bring any metal near the conveyer belts. It'll ruin the magnet!"

"Ah, yes, sir," replied Aubrey with feigned understanding. He turned away and lumbered down the hall, hoping the conversation was over.

He zigzagged though the corridors, and the expansive room holding the Tomb opened up ahead. He stopped and stared in awe. The entire wall was laced with a forest of kudzu. He closed in on the room and looked for the glint of the quartz or the rubble underneath the Tomb, but it was all completely obscured by the tendrils and leaves of the growing weeds.

A single worker stood in front of the bed of hanging kudzu, garbed fully in his yellow rubber suit, his helmet shifting up and down and side to side as if he were scanning the wall.

Aubrey walked slowly up to the lakeside dam wall, careful to slosh through the knee-high water so he wouldn't startle the crew member.

He walked up beside the seemingly occupied worker and deepened his voice again. "Supervisor Kerigun sent me."

The worker turned toward him and looked Aubrey up and down. "Aren't you violating child labor laws?" A muffled woman's voice bellowed from within the helmet. She leaned her head forward and pulled off the helmet. She shook her bright, flowing red hair free from the lining of her suit.

Aubrey felt the blood rush out of his head and flood his quivering stomach. The world spun, and his vision darkened like a tunnel around him. He fell into the water onto his rear and angled his head between his knees to keep from passing out. He felt his coat pulling against his neck. Ms. Thistlewood pulled off his helmet and stood over him, her lips curling upwards.

"You...survived?" Aubrey said through waves of shallow breath. She raised her eyebrows high and nodded her head slowly.

"How?" Aubrey asked.

Ms. Thistlewood chuckled and threw his helmet into the water. "I've survived worse," she said tersely. A devilish smile swept across her face, and she chuckled loudly.

"What are you doing here?"

Ms. Thistlewood held her hands up and stared at the wall. "I'm simply here to appreciate this ancient feat of natural and spiritual union. It's marvelous." She bowed her head reverently. "Simple. Effective. Formidable."

Aubrey gulped. "Yeah, it's very pretty." He felt stupid for his childish reply.

"Hopefully it will remain here for a very long time as a symbol of strength to those who have fought so hard. And maybe for those who war against us, it will act like a scarecrow to the prudish, obstinate miscreants who refuse to accept reality as it is."

Aubrey's heart swelled. Maybe he had misjudged Ms. Thistlewood. Was she here to witness the continued existence of the Tomb, despite the interference of Hovis and the Tsul'kalu? Aubrey propped himself forward and stood up. "Thank goodness," he mumbled with relief.

Ms. Thistlewood smiled graciously at him. "This Tomb will remain as a searing reminder of the pervasive potency of will."

Aubrey nodded fastidiously. "I couldn't agree more. I'm here for the same reason."

"You are?" Her luscious tone washed over Aubrey like the smell of fresh, baked cookies. "How lovely. Then I guess I'll have to forgive you for your previous misdeeds." She ran her fingers through his hair wryly. "Us cherry tops have to stick together."

Aubrey's insides shuddered. "Would you like to do the honors?" he stuttered as he slowly stepped to the side.

Ms. Thistlewood sighed softly. "The honor is in simply being here."

Aubrey nodded and took a step forward. He unlooped the WASER out from his belt and nudged its lever all the way forward on the boxy top of the pole. Light escaped from the cracks in the box as it hummed to life.

"What's that?" Ms. Thistlewood asked, her demeanor hardening.

Aubrey chuckled. "It's a souped-up weed whacker...so I can kill the kudzu."

Ms. Thistlewood snarled. She shoved Aubrey back, her hands bashing into his chest. He fell into the water and skidded across the floor, coming to a stop a dozen yards behind her. Aubrey inhaled air as quickly as he could. He felt as if he was suffocating, even though he could feel his lungs filling with air.

Ms. Thistlewood sloshed through the water angrily and leered over him. "The Tomb will open, and you won't stop it!"

"But...you...can't," Aubrey sucked in chest-fulls of air. His heart pounded in his ears, and his fingers went numb.

Ms. Thistlewood cackled menacingly. "You silly child! I have wasted lifetimes waiting for this moment. What a pity you don't understand what a monumental occasion this is." She turned and bowed her head before the Tomb. "Today, the tide of war will change. Eons of unrequited treachery will at last succumb to justice, and the restless wranglers of order will know a new master."

"But...the Watchers...weren't nice...people," Aubrey was struggling to remain conscious, and he forced himself to breath slower.

"Being nice doesn't make you worthy," Ms. Thistlewood growled. "Fate hands us all a meager plate, and you either take more or live hungry."

Flashes of Magnos' rescue, the bones in the pots and Hovis' chained form bombarded Aubrey's brain. "Why...are you collecting...spirits?"

"You presume to know what I'm doing because you've caught a glimpse of what has been happening in your little world," she shouted, and the room reverberated with her rage. "In your feeble adolescent arrogance you decided to intervene...*ALONE!*"

Aubrey closed his mouth and eyes, hoping to calm himself so he could decide what to do next. Phosphenes swirled behind his eyelids as the darkness overtook the shimmering, remnant of light from the room.

Ms. Thistlewood watched him curiously. "Honestly, I was a little worried at first. Could there be a modest, yet significant, threat in my midst? Fortunately, a few small obstacles and a tincture of time have revealed the incompetent buffoon you really are."

The darkness behind his eyelids telescoped into the center of his vision, but the figure of Ms. Thistlewood remained. She glowed green, and small dark waves churned over her body. Aubrey couldn't believe it. He had never seen a living person behind his eyes before.

"You are no seer, Aubrey Taylor." Her tone was crisp and pointed as she removed her glove.

Aubrey's eyes snapped open, astonished by what she had said. "What do you mean?"

"Don't worry," she explained softly as she reached down for his hand, pulling off his glove. "If confusion is the last emotion you feel, consider yourself fortunate." She laced her fingers between his, and a sharp, tingling sensation marched up his forearm. "I'd let you witness the opening of the Tomb. It's supposed to be a magnificent sight, but I'm afraid keeping you around that long would be in poor judgment."

Aubrey went blind. He couldn't smell or taste anything, and he felt like he was floating. He tried to move, but his limbs wouldn't respond. He heard Ms. Thistlewood humming a soft, melodious lullaby, and the song drowned his mind. His head fell forward, and he felt as if he was tumbling through the floor of the dam.

The standing water trembled, and an electric buzz filled the air. The end of the conveyor belt at the opening of the room shuddered to life.

Suddenly, Aubrey was sitting in the water again. He could feel his arms and legs move again, and light flooded back into his eyes.

Ms. Thistlewood moaned and wrapped her arms around her chest.

"Hey!" hollered a familiar gruff voice. "You two need to clear out! We're pouring the mortar in!"

Aubrey turned his head, and Supervisor Kerigun was standing at the edge of the room next to the end of the spinning, conveyor belt. He waved furiously at them to move.

Ms. Thistlewood screamed as the static electricity in the air snapped around her. Green mist evaporated from around her arms, leaving blackened skeleton remnants of her hands and wrists. Black, twisting forms shrank back to her neck, and she doubled over in agony. Aubrey scrambled fearfully back away from her.

*CLUNK!* The Tomb's face quivered, and a green mist spewed through the kudzu from the top of the rock in the dam's face.

"No matter," seethed Ms. Thistlewood as she looked down at herself. "The Tomb is open." She ran out of the room with lightning speed and fled past Kerigun before he could stop her.

Aubrey hopped up out of the water. He ran over to the kudzu-covered wall, picked up the WASER, and flipped open the round base's cover. Searing beams of light burst through the room. He slashed the WASER across the cascading vines of kudzu. Smoke sizzled in the air as vines fell and withered in the water. Aubrey cut a swathe across the front of the Tomb, and the brilliant, polished pebbles gleamed like diamonds under the laser light.

Aubrey exposed the entire face of the Tomb with the WASER, and suddenly he could now see the complete Circle of Circles carved in its face. A dark green haze hissed from above the face of the Tomb, leaking into the room. Aubrey could see the top of the Tomb was slowly opening.

He smashed the base of the WASER against the Tomb and levered himself against the floor of the dam. The glass of the WASER's mirrors shattered, and shards pelted the water below. The laser beams died, and Aubrey pushed with all his might against the Tomb.

The Tomb suckled air from around its edges, and the dark green haze faded. The massive rocks clicked and sputtered, and then shook as the Tomb closed shut.

Aubrey sighed heavily and dropped the broken WASER into the water.

"Get out of there!" shouted Kerigun. Liquid cement poured into the room off the conveyer belt.

Aubrey closed his eyes and scanned the room. Nothing appeared. The thick mortar crawled around his feet under the water. He opened his eyes, pulled his helmet over his face, and plodded back toward Kerigun.

B uzz, Jordana, Magnos and Rodriqa sat huddled around the lunch table in the cafeteria whispering manically to one another. Each one was leaning in so far toward the middle their foreheads nearly touched. No matter how secretive they were trying to be, everyone who passed by the table knew that something was afoot, including Aubrey.

Aubrey walked over to his friends and slid his tray on the table in front of his seat. His four friends lurched back into their seats, their mouths abruptly clamping shut.

Aubrey sat down slowly, scrutinizing each of his friends' faces. Magnos looked healthier every day, and had nearly returned to his prior thickness. Rodriqa's hair had returned to its usual state, lined with tight rows of beads that hung down her neck. All four of them garnished awkward smiles, but their eyes glanced at each other, avoiding Aubrey. None of them said a word.

Aubrey was a little hurt by their silence, especially after all they had been through over the past couple of days, but he swallowed his pride, looked down, and forked a dollop of his mashed potatoes.

A digital crackle buzzed from the P.A. system overhead. The background hum of conversation in the cafeteria dimmed as most students' attention awaited an announcement. "Isaac Boyle, Asher Donnelly, Elizabeth Johns, and Jill Ann Besser, please report to the front office immediately." A collective sigh of relief heaved over the tables.

Magnos cleared his throat with a loud, scouring cough. Aubrey glanced in Magnos' direction out of the corner of his eye, but Magnos stared at the table. A swift kick from under the table jarred its top.

"OOOOWWWwww is your day," asked Buzz, his cry fading into a greeting. Aubrey glanced up at him. Buzz was rubbing his injured leg and looking back at Aubrey with an overzealous grin.

Aubrey shifted his focus back to his lunch. "Nothing unusual, I guess…which is a good thing these days."

"Good, good," replied Buzz automatically as if he wasn't listening. "How are things with your dad?"

Aubrey raked his mashed potatoes into a gooey, swirling mound. "My dad spent most of Sunday helping Gaetan get his car fixed so we haven't really talked much. And Gaetan's been preoccupied, which has saved me some heat from him."

"That's good, right?" remarked Jordana, a little too cheerily. Aubrey watched her expression, and although her smile forced him to let down his guard, the ashy gray circles under her eyes revealed her underlying exhaustion.

"But who knows how long I'll be grounded for," Aubrey added. "Sergeant Van Zenny showed up Sunday morning and interviewed me and my dad."

Buzz's grin shrank. "What did he want to know?"

"He's hunting for a reason to blame Magnos' kidnapping on me...and maybe you," Aubrey said solemnly. "And finding us at Magnos' house Saturday night only gave him more reason to be suspicious."

"Oh, boy," said Magnos.

"I think I'm a tail feather shy of being a jailbird," joked Aubrey darkly. The other four feigned a dwarfed chuckle out of sympathy. "You'd think people would start to believe me after everything that happened at the party Saturday night."

"No such luck," countered Magnos. "Fayla is blaming us for all the commotion. She's accused us of putting something in the punch, and she's convinced everyone who was at the party that's what caused them to see a ghost and a Bigfoot...and the crazy cheerleading performance of the football players."

"Tsul'kalu," interjected Jordana.

"Whatever," murmured Magnos. "Anyway, all the seniors think we're responsible for their 'hallucinations'. And rumors are starting to spread about us crashing the party. I doubt anyone there will be on our side now."

"So not only do the police have Aubrey and Buzz pegged as your captor, but soon the entire student body will think we're all responsible for drugging the most popular kids at Lake Julian High," commented Rodriqa with a sarcastically hopeless tone.

Aubrey shoved his tray to the middle of the table, folded his hands and laid his head face down. "It's hopefully finished anyway," he muttered.

"No, it's not," said Rodriqa with a pound of fortitude.

"I figured out what the poem in the golden book meant Saturday night at Magnos' house. The kudzu on the front of the Tomb was grown there to open the Tomb. Rodriqa got me back into the basement level, and I took Buzz's WASER. Ms. Thistlewood was there, but something about the dam worker's equipment scared her off. I killed the kudzu, and the Tomb will stay closed for now. Besides the workers filled in the bottom level with cement."

Everyone stared at him, a little confused, but mostly concerned for his sanity.

"You went back down into the basement of the dam without us?" asked Buzz incredulously.

Aubrey nodded with his head against the table. Rodriqa gave Buzz a confirmatory nod.

"And Ms. Thistlewood was there, and you escaped without a scratch?"

Aubrey nodded again.

"How can you rely on what you saw down there?" insisted Rodriqa. "We all thought Jordana drowned and the whole bottom level flooded, when it was really just some dream."

Aubrey thought for a moment and realized he couldn't disagree. "Something about the Tomb...I think it makes people see things, but as long as it's closed, everything should be okay."

"Everything is not okay," murmured Jordana. Aubrey's stomach soured, wondering if Jordana considered him insensitive.

"We have a plan," whispered Buzz as he leaned inward.

"No more plans," replied Aubrey. He slid his head back and forth against the table with resolute determination.

"The chain," whispered Rodriqa. "Hovis wants you to release him, but obviously not from his grave or his house. He must mean those chains that bind his arms to the ground."

Rodriqa tapped her forehead with her index finger. "I've heard my grandmother talk about curses, but they're called something else. I've heard her mention a kind of curse where someone who did something bad while they were alive could be cursed for it, and as a result, becomes confined to the physical world after death, denying them eternal rest."

"Your grandmother must be one weird woman. She knows way too much about freaky stuff," chided Buzz.

"Hush it, *geek-zilla*," barked Rodriqa. "Like you're one to talk about knowing too much." Buzz's jaw dropped in mock offense.

"But why me?" moaned Aubrey. "I don't know how to free him."

"Who knows?" shrugged Rodriqa. "But for some reason, he thinks you can break his chains and free him from an eternity of wandering the earth, I bet. And until you do that, none of us are gonna be free from him."

"No," whimpered Aubrey. "You guys should stay away from me. I'm so tired of all this that having it end, regardless of the heat I catch, would be best."

"I think we're pretty much in it one for all at this point," said Magnos softly.

"I know what you mean, Aubrey" sympathized Jordana as she hung her head. "I'm tired too."

Guilt pummeled Aubrey's feelings. "But every step I take, I just get us in more trouble," said Aubrey with frustration.

"Which is why we need to search Hovis' room. There's a stained-glass window of the Circle of Circles down there. So there has to be more clues as to why Hovis is haunting you, too. The room has to be the key to figuring on what's really going on. I can feel it! Let's go down there and end this," ordained Buzz.

"The front of the tomb was also a Circle of Circles," said Aubrey.

"Really?" asked Jordana. "That's what was behind all the kudzu?"

"Yes," replied Aubrey staunchly, lifting his head to address his friends. "And there'll be another Circle of Circles somewhere else, and we'll destroy more property. Or worse, someone will get really hurt!"

"You don't know that," said Rodriqa. "Honestly, the fact that the tomb is embossed with the Circle of Circles is quite peculiar, and may mean we're onto something."

"I agree," added an animated Buzz.

"It doesn't matter," argued Aubrey. "Besides, I'm sure the police have already filled in the grave."

"Nope," said Buzz triumphantly. "I checked yesterday. They covered it with a blue tarp, and there's still the hole in the roof. I hid some supplies in the grave for when we go back."

"What about the spirit worms?" Aubrey pointed out.

"We have a secret weapon," said Buzz, his grin widening mischievously.

"What?" asked Aubrey blankly.

"Not a what, Taylor," responded Rodriqa.

"Didn't you notice how Rodriqa was the only one of us that wasn't attacked by the worms Saturday night, and how Hovis cringed when she screamed?" analyzed Buzz out loud.

Aubrey pondered what Buzz said and nodded slowly in reticent agreement.

"I think it must be the aegis beads my grandmother gave me at the end of summer," added Rodriqa. She pulled the swathe of entwined strings of rainbow-colored and multi-sized beads up from underneath her shirt. "She told me I was gonna need them. Maybe this is what she was talking about."

Buzz rolled his eyes. "Regardless of the reason, Rodriqa has a knack for keeping the scary stuff away. It'll give us time to explore Hovis' buried room."

"This is beyond crazy," decided Aubrey. He laid his head back on the lunch table, exhausted and frustrated.

"What else can we do?" asked Magnos, prodding him.

"Ignore it! Like I was told at the start!" Aubrey asserted.

"It's too late for that," replied Jordana. "We need Hovis and the Tsul'kalu to leave us alone, and we're the only ones who can figure out what they want. Until we do, it's hopeless." A quivering tide of desperation rolled through her tone and tugged at Aubrey's heart. He turned his head to the side to look at her. She was looking down, but through her glasses. Tears billowed up along her eyelids. She wanted his help, and Aubrey was prepared to tell everyone no, except her.

"Maybe you guys should go without me," murmured Aubrey softly.

"No deal," countered Magnos. "You know Hovis better than anyone. We need you down there."

Aubrey slammed his hands against the table. The crisp slap echoed throughout the cafeteria. "I'M GROUNDED!! REMEMBER?!" Several students from nearby tables stopped talking and turned over their shoulders toward the source of the ruckus. Aubrey slid his hands under the table and slunk down into his chair with his nose nearly touching the table's edge.

"We can all go," whispered Buzz low to the table, "if we go now."

Aubrey sneered at Buzz like he was a pinecone shy of a manifesto shack in Montana.

"Don't look so incredulous," rebuffed Buzz. "It's not like you've never skipped school before."

"Those were my pre-fugitive days," groaned Aubrey.

The overhead speaker squalled to life again. "Gaetan Taylor, Leon Hagwell, Fayla Strumgarten and Romie Rachelle, please report to the principal's office immediately."

"But today is the best day of the school year for truancy, if you're not a senior," continued Buzz. "For starters, the Paddling Pumpkin Raft Race is today, which means a lot of folks will be leaving early to get ready for the race. And since it's race day, everyone knows that it's also senior skip day."

"But every senior knows," interjected Rodriqa, "if they get caught skipping, they can't walk for graduation. So the random, loudspeaker witch hunt has the administrators focused on twelfth grade and no one else."

"Giving us the perfect window to escape," rounded out Buzz.

Aubrey couldn't argue, and decided that since his defeat had been total so far, losing this battle was simply to be expected.

Buzz reached into his pocket and pulled a crumpled piece of green paper out of his jeans, smoothing it out on the table. "I got a pass from the Torquetum Club to leave for the race! We're golden! No one can stop us!"

Buzz looked down at his watch. He stood up and lifted his book bag onto his shoulder. "We have to leave now. We're wasting time." He glanced at Jordana, Magnos and Rodriqa. "Remember the plan and stick to it."

The three of them nodded. Aubrey was annoyed at being excluded. Buzz marched aloofly toward the cafeteria door. Rodriqa stood up and paused as she took in a panoramic view of the cafeteria. Then she turned and walked toward the door.

Magnos waited a few seconds, then jumped up abruptly and stood behind Aubrey. Jordana raked her packaged, unopened lunch into her knapsack and curled her body around in her seat. She touched Aubrey's arm. "Let's go," she whispered. Aubrey's arm tensed and his torso straightened. Jordana walked away.

Magnos yanked Aubrey out of his seat and placed him firmly on the tile floor, feet first. Magnos swiveled and headed for the door. Aubrey turned to watch them as one by one they exited the cafeteria. His feet felt as heavy as lead. He folded one foot in front of the other and followed Magnos into the hallway.

He pushed open the swinging double doors and turned out of the cafeteria. Each of his friends followed one another in a single-file line with some distance between them. They snaked through the hallways, passing groups of other students and an occasional teacher. Aubrey avoided all eye contact and kept his face to the ground, with only Magnos' feet at the top of his field of view.

Magnos rounded a distant corner, and Aubrey worried that he was alone. Behind him he heard the squeaking wheels of a rolling mop bucket shimmy closer toward him. He looked over his shoulder and could see Griggs out of the corner of his eye. He launched into a full run around the corner to escape his notice.

*THUD!* Aubrey skidded to an abrupt halt. The middle of his face smacked square into Magnos' back. Stunned by the blow, he backed up and shook off the pain. He felt a warm, wet dribble trickle down his upper lip. He wiped his nose with his hand and was nauseated by the scarlet stain smeared across his fingertips. His four friends stood side by side in front of him, blocking his view. "What's going on?" he whispered.

An oddly familiar voice from in front of his friends spoke, "Where are you kids heading off to?"

Aubrey pinched his nose and peeked through the slit of open space between Magnos' shoulder and Buzz's curly hair. Hamilton Miller, dressed in his typical bright, pastel button-down and seamless khakis, was leaning with his hand against the wall, facing them and flipping a shiny, metal object in his hand.

Jordana took a step forward, "Leave us alone, Hamilton," she demanded in a shrill voice.

Hamilton chuckled, and his eyes followed the shiny item he was tossing up and down. "First, it was leave *me* alone. Now, it's leave *us* alone," he jeered in a sing-song tone. Hamilton pushed himself off the wall and walked toward them. "I just have one question for you guys." He stopped in front of Jordana and caught the gleaming gold object brusquely. "Who is really bothering *whom*?"

Jordana lifted up her hands slowly up to her face, but Hamilton gripped her fingers in between his, squeezing tightly. Jordana stared at him through her glasses.

Hamilton looked away and caught Buzz's eye. "Am I bothering you, chubs?"

Buzz shook his head back and forth quickly in fearful denial.

"Am I bothering you, cornrows?" Hamilton asked Rodriqa.

Her jaw dropped. "My braids are *not* cornrows!"

Hamilton ignored her as he looked up at Magnos. "How about you, runaway?"

Magnos sneered disdainfully. He clenched his jaw and fists tightly.

Hamilton snapped his neck from shoulder to shoulder, his vertebra popping with machismo. He took a step back and looked down at Jordana. "Doesn't sound like I'm bothering anybody. You just have a *nasty* habit of turning me into the bad guy."

"Back off, Hamilton," snarled Magnos.

Hamilton slid the metal item onto Jordana's ring finger and curled her hand around it. He took another step back and released her hands. "You left that at the party Saturday night. The same party where you embarrassed some of my friends. So they thought today would be a good time to remind *you* to leave *them* alone." Hamilton took a few more steps backwards. He pulled a pair of dark sunglasses from his pant's pocket and covered his eyes.

From around the corner behind Hamilton, three football players, Compton, O'Dant and Rontimer, dressed in their jerseys and jeans, swaggered forward, also wearing sunglasses. They crossed their arms and stood in a line behind Hamilton, like a row of meathead mercenaries.

"You and your goons don't scare us," barked Magnos as he puffed up his bulbous chest.

"You had such potential, Magnos," derided Hamilton parentally. "You were feared and respected, even as a freshman." The three football players marched around Hamilton and formed a solid block around Magnos. "It's a wasted shame really. After your stupendous flub at the opening football game and your little disappearing act, you're little more than a memory now…among those who count, anyway." Hamilton snickered, "And just like his newfound friends, Magnos Strumgarten has become a misfit. Pathetic." The three football players echoed Hamilton's jeering laughter.

"And as payback for your little stunt Saturday night," continued Hamilton, as he glared at Jordana, "today will be a day you will never forget."

Hamilton took a step back. "This year's Paddling Pumpkin race comes with the expectation that each raft will have a unique design. There are five rafts entered in the competition from Lake Julian High and five of you. Isn't that convenient? They will speak of this year's 'living figureheads' for decades to come."

The football players wrenched Magnos' arms behind him as he scuffled his feet in circles to free himself. Rodriqa wrapped her arms around one of the players' shoulders and hung on, hoping to pull him down, while Buzz and Jordana grabbed each of Magnos' arms to help him struggle loose. Aubrey backed up slowly to avoid the swirling melee. His ankle clinked back against solid metal.

"Bit early to head out for the race, isn't it?" the craggy voice reverberated down the hallway and everyone froze in various postures of skirmish. Aubrey looked over his shoulder as Griggs slopped his soapy mop from his bucket to the floor and pushed it in a line down the tile.

Hamilton pulled down his sunglasses. "This doesn't concern you, old man!"

Griggs stopped cleaning and leaned on his mop. He lifted his hat and wiped his forehead with a handkerchief. "Pardon my objection, but if you're about to make a mess, then it will be my concern very soon." Griggs grinned wryly at Hamilton.

Hamilton marched over to Griggs and kicked his mop bucket mercilessly, dousing the hallway with suds and soiled water. "Move along, or you'll share the fate of your handmaid's pail." The three football players chuckled derisively.

Griggs looked down at the mess, and his shoulders slumped. He ran his mop through it and patted the floor forlornly. "I can take a hint," he muttered.

"Wise choice," snapped Hamilton.

Griggs soaked up some of the loose suds and squeezed them back into the bucket. "Except there's a chance you might be needed elsewhere," he said mysteriously.

"Doubtful," said Hamilton assuredly. "My calendar is clear for the day."

"You never know what might pop up," rebutted Griggs, looking at Hamilton with a clouded expression.

One of the football players snickered and said, "You've been hanging out in your supply closet too long. All those chemicals have gone to your head."

Hamilton chortled at the dig.

The P.A. system snapped and sizzled with static. "Hamilton Miller, Treywick Compton, Hank O'Dant and Ty Rontimer, report to the office immediately."

"What?" defied Hamilton incredulously. "That's impossible! I paid off the front secretary so she wouldn't call our names." He stared at the football players with dumbfounded eyes for some understanding.

"Maybe you should have paid off Principal Lequoia instead," harped Hank O'Dant, the middle football player.

"Or else you didn't pay her enough, and you got played," surmised Trey Compton.

Ty ripped off his sunglasses and marched passed Aubrey and Griggs down the hallway toward the front office.

"This isn't over," scowled Hamilton. He and the other two football players followed Ty.

The kids huddled together, bewildered at their own luck and grateful for the roundhouse reprieve.

"Amazing," said Griggs. "The power of a name." He looked down at Aubrey and winked with his bushy, white wooly-worm eyebrow.

Aubrey grinned at him. "Thanks," he muttered softly.

"Come on, guys! We're losing daylight," Buzz reminded them. The five of them took off down the hallway toward the side entrance.

Griggs returned to cleaning up the soapy floor. "Sonya is allergic to cheese," whispered Griggs as the kids walked by.

"Huh?" asked Aubrey. Griggs' softly spoken words didn't completely register. Griggs shook him off. Aubrey turned and chased after his friends.

"Oh! And watch out for any pretty stones you might find…they'll cut you."

Aubrey barely heard him as he rounded the corner to the outside door.

"Get down," whispered Rodriqa harshly as she yanked Aubrey suddenly from standing to the floor. The other four kids squatted in front of the heavy metal doors of the side entrance.

"What's wrong?" Aubrey asked quietly.

"Mr. Berdun," whispered Magnos, pointing toward the outside. Aubrey slowly edged his head upwards to peek through the wired-enmeshed, slit windows at the top half of the door. Mr. Berdun marched up and down the side lawn with his faithful pooch, Sonya at his side, his readied posture more akin to a guard at Leavenworth than to a medium-sized high school in the suburban Southeast.

"There's no way we can get past that dog," said Rodriqa. "As soon as we open the side door, she'll come running for us."

"We could wait for them to walk around," said Buzz.

"We're sitting ducks here," replied Rodriqa. "More teachers will be by any minute. That is, if Griggs doesn't rat on us."

Aubrey watched as Mr. Berdun walked in and out of view of the window, patrolling the side lawn. "Maybe we should go to class," conceded Aubrey. Mr. Berdun stopped his overzealous procession, turned and looked toward the door. His eyes met Aubrey's.

"Oh, no," moaned Aubrey as he sunk to the floor.

"What now?" asked Rodriqa.

"I think he saw me."

Hard-soled footsteps approached from the other side of the door along the sidewalk. Rapid, slobbering sniffs snorted through the crack of the metal doors.

"I have an idea," whispered Jordana confidently. "Aubrey, tell Mr. Berdun you heard your bike was stolen, and you need to go look for it."

"What about the dog?" he asked.

"I'll deal with her," Jordana replied. "Everyone else move back behind the corner." The other three nodded and slunk backwards out of sight.

Jordana stood up and motioned for Aubrey to stand. Aubrey straightened from his crouched position on the floor, and she shoved him against the door into the open air.

Aubrey squinted as the transition from the darkened foyer to the bright sunlight blinded him.

"What are you doing out of class?" commanded the squeaky, high-pitched voice of Mr. Berdun. He stepped forward from around the corner, his shot-putter frame blocking the sun overhead as he stared down at Aubrey. Aubrey lost his words and stiffened his mouth to regain composure. Jordana nudged him forward.

"Uh...hello...sir," he stammered.

"School is still in session, young man and young lady," chided Mr. Berdun effeminately, changing his stance to address both of them. "Back inside! NOW!" His scraggly mustache snarled as he spoke.

Aubrey cleared his throat to jump-start his vocal cords. "Yes, sir," he eked out, a little uncertain as to whether he should say ma'am or sir. "I came outside to find my bike."

"Your bike?" Berdun screeched, his voice rising nearly an octave in question. "You can check on your bike when school is out."

His dog murmured a warning growl and Mr. Berdun pulled back on her leash. Aubrey and Jordana looked down at the bulldog, whose droopy, incessantly teary eyes made you almost feel sorry for her, until she bared her drool-embossed razor-sharp incisors.

Jordana knelt down gently in front of the dog. The dog launched at Jordana, her chubby claws ripping through the air and her teeth snapping wildly.

"That's a bad idea, Missy! HEEL, SONYA!" ordered Mr. Berdun as he tightened her chain, preventing her from attacking Jordana by only a couple of inches. "Sonya is a viscous predator, especially when she encounters miscreants who like to break the rules."

Jordana smiled weakly. "Then I bet she'll like me. I'm pretty good with animals." She lowered her glasses and stared intently at Sonya's eyes. Sonya flailed on her corpulent haunches and whimpered quietly. She set her front paws on the ground and let out a short yelp, and then panted calmly. Mr. Berdun stared at Jordana and Sonya, bewildered at their interaction. Large slops of drool splattered onto the concrete.

"No...um...I heard my bike was stolen," interjected Aubrey.

"This has never happened before," mused Mr. Berdun, befuddled. "Sonya usually only tolerates me. I've never seen her be friendly to anyone." Jordana slid forward along the sidewalk and slipped her right hand behind Sonya's ear. Mr. Berdun focused his attention back to Aubrey. "And why do you think your bike has been stolen? There have been no unauthorized students on the grounds during my watch," he asserted defensively.

Jordana dug her fingers into Sonya's neck rolls, and the bulldog grunted and moaned blissfully, leaning sideways into Jordana's hand.

"Um...the office secretary...yeah," thought Aubrey through his fabrication, "she found me during lunch and told me someone might have stolen my bike."

Sonya rolled onto her side, and her back foot reflexively pedaled round in the air as Jordana scratched her belly. Jordana furtively wound her left hand into her knapsack and pulled out a cylindrical piece of mozzarella. She tore a tiny piece off the end and held it between her fingers.

"Did the office secretary give you a pass?" barked Mr. Berdun.

Aubrey's face flushed with the thinning transparency of his ruse. "Um...well, she did, but...I lost it."

Sonya panted heavily, and her tongue fell out of the corner of her mouth and draped the ground. Jordana dropped a couple of bite-sized chunks of cheese into the back of her throat, and she swallowed all of it with a large, easy gulp.

"You lost a hall pass between here and the cafeteria in less than five minutes?" questioned Mr. Berdun skeptically. Aubrey swallowed down the dry lump in his mouth and nodded quietly in agreement.

Mr. Berdun stepped forward and grabbed Aubrey by the collar. He leaned down and glared at Aubrey nose to nose. His foul, spicy breath singed Aubrey's eyes. "I've been an officer at this school since before you were born," he seethed in anger. "I've heard every excuse there is and seen every trick in the book.

"I know what today is, and this is a T.I.P."

"A what?" murmured Jordana.

"A Truancy-in-progress," reprimanded Mr. Berdun. "And if you don't go back to class this very instant, I'll do everything in my power to ensure that every day after today will be the worst day of your life."

Aubrey held his breath and blinked rapidly to protect himself from Mr. Berdun's olfactory assault. Mr. Berdun's squinty eyes examined Aubrey's face for signs of fear and flitted back and forth between his eyes. "What's wrong with you?" Mr. Berdun demanded.

"Mr. Berdun," interrupted Jordana, "something is wrong with Sonya." Sonya lay perfectly still on her back with all four legs stiffened skyward, as frothy, white foam guzzled out of her mouth.

"SONYA!" squealed Mr. Berdun frantically. He leaned down and shook her. She didn't move. He placed his ear on her chest to listen for signs of life.

Sonya sighed heavily, and her face turned radish red. She flipped with a single, full-body jerk onto her feet. Her limbs quaked, and she looked up at Mr. Berdun and let out a feeble cry. She bolted into an all-out gallop across the lawn, yanking the leash out of her owner's hand.

"Oh, no," murmured Mr. Berdun. "Come back!" He leapt to his feet and chased after her.

Jordana stood up and opened the side door. "Let's go!" she shouted to the others. Buzz, Rodriqa and Magnos shuffled into the foyer. "The coast is clear," she declared.

The five kids fled across the school lawn, pausing every few seconds to look over their shoulders and watch the spectacle of Mr. Berdun pursuing his zigzagging and bloated, crimson bulldog. Mr. Berdun slid across the patches of grass that were coated with slimy mucus from her enlarged tongue as it drug the ground. Jordana chuckled, pleased with herself.

Aubrey glimpsed a form in the window of the door from which they had escaped. He stopped to look more closely, hopeful that someone hadn't been left behind.

Gaetan glared at Aubrey with a menacingly grin from the inside of the double metal doors. He put his index finger to the side of his throat and raked it around the front of his neck in a slicing motion. Aubrey knew there would be no amnesty this time.

## Reticent Descent

Aubrey, Buzz, Jordana, Magnos and Rodriqa weaved between loaded dump trucks and honking cars as they crossed the Asheville Highway and ducked into the forest that rose between the Berybomag Mining Company and Lake Julian Dam. Buzz led the pack up the hillside confidently, as he appeared to know the most direct route to the cemetery.

"Good show, Jordana," shouted Buzz. Everyone murmured in agreement as they traipsed through the forest.

"That was awesome!" exclaimed Magnos.

Rodriqa walked next to Jordana. "Yeah, I've never seen a bulldog run that fast before. She looked like a runaway tomato, she was so red." The others chuckled.

"What did Hamilton give you?" Rodriqa asked quietly.

Jordana pulled the metallic object off her finger and whispered in reply. "It's one of my rings. But it's weird. Most of my rings been missing for two months, and I wasn't wearing it at the dance or at Fayla's party."

Rodriqa looked at her with a puzzled expression. Jordana handed her the ring and pointed out the inscription with her name on it. She turned the ring on its edge, exposing its inner line, which was cut roughly with linear, blackened markings.

Aubrey trotted up next to them. "I hope Sonya is okay," he remarked. "We don't want any more trouble!"

"How can we be in trouble?" asked Jordana rhetorically. "There's no way to prove we did anything wrong." She smiled at Aubrey with a glibly righteous expression. He stiffened his lip, a little disturbed by her apathy, but trying not to show it.

They crossed the forest's edge into the round clearing of the cemetery. Buzz trudged through the graveyard directly toward the Trottle family plot. Aubrey was lost in thought most of the way up the hill. In the middle of the cemetery, Aubrey suddenly blurted out, "Hey! Why were Hamilton and the football players wearing sunglasses inside?"

"Maybe they were trying to be intimidating," replied Rodriqa.

"Yeah, that's probably it," murmured Jordana with her head down.

Buzz and the other four stopped in front of a square, bright blue tarp covering Hovis' grave. Aubrey felt like he was being watched. He looked up across the clearing to the opposite side of the cemetery. The shiny black, dagger-beaked raven glared at him, roosting on a white pine branch, halfway up the tree. A tingling chill raced down Aubrey's spine. He shook it off, hoping the others wouldn't notice.

Buzz picked up a rock holding down one of the corners of the tarp. He glanced at it quickly, and then winced as he dropped it, since it looked like a piece of broken tombstone. He pulled back the nearest corner of the tarp and flipped it over, revealing the untouched pit they had dug over Hovis' grave three nights ago. The five kids stared down into the darkness, aghast at the uninviting, splinter-edged hole at the bottom. A wrinkled heap of mud-laced canvas sat in a corner of the dirt walls.

"Aubrey. Eyes," commanded Buzz. Aubrey scowled in reply. Buzz nudged his head toward the pit, urging him on.

"What are you doing?" Aubrey muttered.

"Buzz told us how you can see Hovis and the worms," said Rodriqa. "If there's something bad down there, you'll see it before anyone else will."

Aubrey frowned and looked away, feeling slightly betrayed that Buzz would share his secret.

Jordana touched his shoulder. "Is it true? Can you see ghosts when you close your eyes?"

Aubrey sighed. "I can see Hovis, and I saw the worms, but that's all I've seen."

"It's so weird that he can make it so we can see them too," bragged Buzz, faking a haunting tone.

"Have you been able to do it before?" Jordana asked, interested that she may not be alone in having unusual talents.

Aubrey shook his head and looked down. "And honestly, I want it to go away. I don't want to see things that aren't there."

"But they are there," argued Buzz. Aubrey ignored him.

"Why do you think it started happening all of a sudden?" questioned Magnos.

Aubrey shrugged and stared down into the pit.

"Well, whatever you think about it," retorted Rodriqa firmly. "I'm not going down there until you...*look*!"

Aubrey's shoulders slumped forlornly. "It doesn't work all the time. I don't have much control over what I can and can't see."

"Just try it," said Buzz.

"Okay," agreed Aubrey begrudgingly. "But don't order me around like I'm your personal circus freak." Buzz relented with an obscured roll of his eyes.

Aubrey angled his head down toward the hole in the roof and closed his eyes. The sunlight cast a burgundy background to his vision behind his eyelids, and he crouched down along the edge of the grave to position his face in the shadow. The lights faded, and the phosphenes streamed from one side to the other. Slowly everything dimmed, and only darkness remained. Aubrey couldn't see a worm or a spirit, and he was grateful he didn't see Hovis. As he concentrated, the distant background writhed and folded on itself, but there was no glow or outline to the rolling mass. "I can't make anything out, but...." Aubrey paused, uncertain how to describe what he saw.

"But what?" asked Rodriqa.

Aubrey squeezed his eyes with his fingers and watched below. The movement stopped. "Nothing," he said. "I don't see anything." He opened his eyes.

Buzz looked into the pit and looked around up top. "And we don't see anything. Let's get started."

The five of them slid down along the dirt walls of the grave. Rodriqa bent over and examined the hole, but the darkness below was impenetrable. She sniffed the air and opened her hand over the hole. "It smells a little musty, but it's not too bad, and there's a breeze."

"Really?" asked Buzz. He leaned over with his hand above the hole. "She's right."

"Does that mean there's another entrance?" asked Jordana.

"Or at least a small hole someplace down there that's allowing air to circulate," replied Buzz. He flipped the canvas back from the corner of the dirt wall and uncovered three electric lanterns, a rope ladder, a crowbar, and a Swiss army knife. He ignited the electric lanterns, and the pit flashed to a brilliant fluorescent white. Jordana edged away from the dirt wall, which she could now easily see was teeming with a multitude of scurrying centipedes, crickets and cockroaches.

Buzz coiled the rope ladder and handed it to Magnos. "Could you tie this up top for me? You're probably the best knot tier." Magnos took the top of the rope and climbed the crumbling walls of the grave, sliding backward half as much as he gained headway with each stretching reach. He wound the cord and the top portion of the rope ladder around the sturdy base of the plot's rough-hewn cross and secured the ladder with a bowline knot.

"We should be good," Magnos said into the grave.

Buzz yanked on the ladder from below with several stiff tugs, and it didn't budge. "Try it out," he hollered back.

Magnos' size fifteen-foot nearly filled an entire rectangular rung of the ladder. He clumsily walked down the ladder back into the pit, with the toes of his shoes on the edge of the rungs as he slid his hands along the ladder's sides. The ladder twisted and squeaked under his weight, threatening to fling him off.

"I think I'd rather jump down than ride this squirrely thing," Magnos complained. He was out of breath when he reached the others.

"If it can take Magnos' weight, we should be good," said Buzz.

"Yeah, but can it take Magnos' weight and *your* weight," jeered Rodriqa.

Buzz flung the rest of the ladder into the hole, its end rungs smacking against the dark room's floor. "For that remark, you get to go first," he volleyed back at her.

"I kinda figured I was going first anyway, since I've been elected the ghost bodyguard," she replied.

"More like a *soul*-guard," Jordana returned. Rodriqa mused at her, pondering her new title. She was rather pleased with it. She pulled out her aegis beads from under her shirt and clutched them tightly in front of her.

"Aubrey should go second," said Buzz.

"Huh? Why?" Aubrey asked anxiously.

"Because I need you to keep doing your eye thingy," explained Rodriqa. "If one of those worms or some other nasty pops up, I need to know which direction to scream in."

Aubrey nodded timidly.

"I'll go after Aubrey, followed by Jordana, then Magnos," continued Buzz.

"Are you sure I shouldn't stay up here and...you know...be a lookout in case someone comes looking for us?" fumbled Magnos, his face a little paler than usual.

"I think it's better if we stick together," replied Rodriqa. Aubrey and Jordana murmured in agreement.

"Are you scared, Magnos?" Buzz asked.

"Whatever, dude," uttered Magnos, curling his lip at Buzz.

Buzz grinned haughtily back at him. "We won't be down there long. Let's find what we need to know and then get out in time for the rafting race."

Buzz handed the second lantern to Rodriqa, and she clutched it in the same hand with her beads. She held onto the rope ladder with her other hand and stuck her feet into the rungs just below the edge of the hole. She slowly stepped down one rung at a time as her lantern's light fading into the darkness below the roof.

Aubrey hugged the rope ladder edge-on, with both arms wrapped around it so his hand could grasp his opposing forearm. He stuck his feet in the rungs from each side and shimmied clumsily down the ladder.

Rodriqa stopped about six feet down and took in a panoramic view of the room. She saw the shovel next the bottom of the rope ladder that she had accidently lost three nights ago. Along with the shovel, several large chests of varying sizes were scattered along the floor. Dust-covered sheets draped over pieces of furniture and racks of clothes, like ghostly statues, frozen in time. From a distance the wooden floors and walls glistened with moisture, but appeared mostly intact. Clay bricks lined some of the walls, and from underneath she could now tell for certain she had just climbed through a roof. Splintered trellis beams braced the old, angled wood overhead.

As Buzz and Jordana stepped onto the rope ladder and added their weight and downward momentum, it twisted and jerked exponentially with each kid's movement. To Aubrey, it felt like he was riding an epileptic slinky.

A rung from the floor, Rodriqa looked up and shouted, "Hold up!" Her voice echoed around the dark, sooty room. Aubrey was grateful the ladder was still for a moment, but his arms and legs spasmed as he held on tightly. He stared down at the floor and closed his eyes, scanning the room for any movement behind his eyelids.

"I still don't see anything," he murmured down to Rodriqa. She let go of her beads and held the lantern inches from the bottom. The murky brown boards sparkled with moisture, and specks of dirt glittered along the surface amongst patches of mud and shreds of rotting cloth.

Rodriqa gingerly set the lantern on the floor. The boards held it easily. She pushed down on the top of the lantern with her foot to test the floor's strength. The boards creaked but kept their station.

"I'm stepping down," Rodriqa announced.

"Good," sighed Aubrey.

"Hurry up," exclaimed Buzz frantically. The rope ladder jolted up and down. "I...can't...hold on," he grunted, struggling to keep his hold. Rodriqa and Aubrey jerked their heads upwards and stared aghast at Buzz, who was floundering with the handle of the lantern pinning his hand into a rung of the ladder, squeezing it blood red. Buzz's shoes slipped out of the rungs and he bicycled his legs, trying to catch hold of the ladder with his feet.

Rodriqa jumped onto the floor and backed up, both to get a better view of Buzz and hopefully steer clear of his fall. Aubrey shimmied down the ladder behind her and shook the cramps out of his arms.

Jordana reached down to help Buzz, but lost her balance as she leaned sideways to grab his trapped hand.

Magnos anchored his lower legs on the topside of the hole in the roof and flipped upside down next to the ladder. He entwined his arm around Buzz's arm and lifted him. The lantern's handle released from the rung and fell to the floor. Rodriqa jumped behind the ladder and caught it between her arms and chest, like a football.

"It's hot," she murmured, dropping the lantern to the floor. It bounced along the boards. She tapped her foot on the floor. "Come on down. The floor seems pretty solid."

Magnos' face flushed and he groaned as he strained to raise Buzz up. Sweat dripped across his forehead and down his forearm. Buzz slipped slowly downward.

"Grab the ladder," grunted Magnos, out of breath.

"I'm trying," replied Buzz, his frustration rising. The two of them swung back and forth like a pendulum as Buzz repeatedly reached for the rope ladder and then accidentally batted it away in his attempts to hold on. Magnos clamped Buzz's arm in both of his, but the harder Magnos fought to hold on, the faster Buzz squeezed through Magnos' hands.

Buzz dropped to the floor, his arms and legs flailing wildly. He landed with a damp thud and a sharp crack against the boards as they buckled under his weight. Buzz rolled, hoping to dampen the energy of his fall.

Aubrey picked up the fallen lantern and ran over to Buzz. "Are you okay?"

Buzz popped up quickly and brushed himself off. "Yep," he said overzealously, avoiding further embarrassment. "I just couldn't hold onto the ladder any longer." He nonchalantly felt his body for unseen injuries, wincing at a couple of sore spots along his rump.

Jordana and Magnos scurried down the ladder. Feeling his lungs tighten in the dingy air, Aubrey pulled out his inhaler and used it.

"Sorry about that," said Magnos, as he handed Buzz the crowbar and the third lantern.

"No worries. I'm fine," Buzz replied.

"You're lucky you didn't fall through," Rodriqa said, holding her lantern over the battered board he had crashed into. The five of them stared downward. Buzz stepped on the edge of the damaged board, and its crack widened, exposing the darkness below.

"There's something down there," Rodriqa told them, angling her lantern for a better view. Dim reds and hollow yellows glinted as the light filtered through the broken floor's splinters to the bottom.

"There's another room down there," said Buzz. "So it's definitely a house...with at least two stories."

"How can these boards be this tough after so long, especially when they've been underground for more than a century?" asked Aubrey, bouncing on his tiptoes.

"Good point," agreed Rodriqa. "It should be falling apart, or at least warped by all the water after all this time, but they look to be in pretty good shape."

"Hmmm," said Buzz pensively. He carried his lantern close to the nearby wall, examining it methodically. He rubbed its shimmering, wet surface with his fingers, and tapped on it with his index finger. He scraped the wood with his fingernails vigorously.

"No splinters," he muttered.

"So?" said Rodriqa flippantly.

"It's not wood anymore," he mused. "It's petrified."

"Doesn't that take millions of years?" asked Aubrey.

"Under natural circumstances, yes," replied Buzz.

Jordana grazed the walls with her hands. "The earth in this area has a rich concentration of unusual salts, like Beryllium, Boron and Magnesium. That's why my dad was transferred here. His branch of the mining company specializes in harvesting minerals, not gold or silver."

"Could those have petrified the wood?" Aubrey asked.

"Possibly," replied Buzz, distant in thought.

"I wonder if they etched that stained glass window," asked Rodriqa, pointing to the far wall, which held a wire-framed clerestory window just below the ceiling. The circular window was beset with circles, a row at the periphery and joined by three circles in its center. Some of its panels were cracked. A couple of them were missing, and mud filled their empty facets. The glass that remained was scarred with deep jagged lines on its back surface.

"Most likely," said Buzz. "Large quantities of salts can dissolve glass of all kinds."

"Is that what we came down here for?" asked Rodriqa. "The Circle of Circles?"

"Not exactly," replied Buzz. "The Circle of Circles is more of a guide."

"Wrong," interrupted Aubrey. "It's not a guide. It's a recurring symbol that was obviously important to Hovis. It doesn't tell us anything, except that Hovis was interested in the Tomb for some reason."

"Then what are we looking for?" Rodriqa asked. She unlatched a leather-strapped, wooden chest on the floor with her shoe, and its lid sprang open, spewing dust into the air. "Ah, never mind. Found it!" She reached into the chest and pulled out two tattered, cloth dolls, each with braided twine for hair, and patchwork dresses that were riddled with tiny holes and stained with brown, snaking watermarks. She displayed them at arm's length. The leg of the right hand doll dropped to the floor. Aubrey and Buzz shook their heads at her. Magnos chuckled.

The kids slowly searched the room for clues, carefully unlocking chests, sifting through folded clothing and papers, and shuffling bits of scrap and dirt on the floor with their shoes.

Jordana uncovered a tawny wedding dress that hung on a female mannequin, its former brilliant white now a dull grayish brown. She marveled at the lacework and beads that decorated its layered fringes. "So beautiful," she murmured.

A yellowed cloth hung over the top of a large piece of furniture, which was at least a foot taller than Buzz at its sharpest point in the middle, and then lowered to the floor at four corners, under which the edges of the cloth were folded. To him, it looked like a pyramid under an aging sheet. He yanked the cloth at the corner, but it wouldn't give. It was trapped beneath the item it covered, and glued in place with a mire of mud and decaying threads. Buzz pushed against its base. Nothing happened. It was solid as stone, and he couldn't overcome its weight. He grabbed a wad of the cloth and tore and twisted the sheet at its edge. It ripped up the middle to the top.

A pair of dark oval eyes stared back at him, searching him back and forth from eye to eye. Buzz gasped quickly, then screamed a high-pitched shrill that shook the air in the room and echoed louder with each second. Startled, the other four kids jerked in their spots, turning to look at Buzz. Aubrey and Jordana covered their ears.

Magnos charged over to Buzz and clamped his beefy hand around Buzz's mouth, ceasing his squalling. "It's a mirror," he whispered to Buzz.

Rodriqa marched over to Buzz and shook her finger at him. "If Hovis didn't know we were already here, he does now," chided Rodriqa. She pinched the back of his arm.

"OWWWWCHMMM!" he cried, his muffled voice behind Magnos' fingers. "What was that for?!"

"For screaming like a girl," replied Rodriqa. "Don't do it again."

Magnos let Buzz go, and Buzz rubbed his arm to ease the pain as he looked mournfully at Rodriqa.

Aubrey closed his eyes and looked around the room. The darkness behind his eyelids didn't change. "Guys, this isn't the right place. Hovis was a priest. He probably kept his private stuff in an office or library or something like that. This looks more like an attic."

"Then how do we get to the rest of the house?" asked Buzz.

"Over here, I think," said Jordana. "I found a way out."

The other four kids turned around. Jordana's head barely peeked over the sheets and chests at the far end of the room, opposite the broken stain glass window. They walked over toward her. She stood in front of a door at the far end of the room.

Jordana turned the brass doorknob, but her hand slipped in circles around it. "It's locked or frozen shut. It won't move."

"It may be bolted from the other side," said Buzz. He walked over and fixed the crowbar into the thin space between the door and its frame just above the latch. He leaned his weight against the crowbar, slowly applying more and more pressure. The doorframe creaked but held its form tightly.

Buzz took a step back, put his hands on the crowbar and launched himself forward. He could feel the frame bend, but his arms cramped under the pressure, and he let go, heaving for breath.

Magnos stepped toward the door. "May I?" he asked.

Buzz tried to remove the crowbar, but he couldn't pull it out from the edge of the door. He gestured toward the door with a 'be my guest' roll of his hand and backed away.

Magnos wrenched the crowbar out of the door and handed it back to Buzz. He touched the door with his fingertips, feeling its weight, then leaned backwards and rammed his shoulder onto the middle of the door. It groaned under his weight, leaving a splintered dent in the middle, but it remained closed.

Magnos motioned for everyone to move back. Readying his weight, he took several calculated steps backwards and weaved back and forth. He turned around and squinted at the door, like a fullback eyeing his opponent. He leapt twice, and then launched himself face-first into the door. With a massive snap from his running head butt, the door flung open, ripping the rusted iron hinges from its frame. Craggy bits of wood flew across the room and the door swung open, pinned to the locked latch on its opposite side. Magnos shook off the hit, turned to the others, and smiled whimsically.

"Nice," said Buzz sarcastically. "This *is* someone's house you know." He leaned forward to survey the door's long, jagged crack.

Magnos' smile faded. "But the owner's dead."

"That doesn't mean he doesn't deserve a little respect," said Buzz.

"Remind me, when I'm older, to never lock my keys in my car," said Rodriqa flatly.

"Everyone's a critic," rebuffed Magnos.

"Thanks for opening the door," said Jordana as she grinned at him. He smiled back at her sheepishly.

A feverish scratching drifted up from the other side of the broken door.

"What is that?" whispered Rodriqa and everyone listened. The clawing intensified as it moved closer toward the door, as if something was in a hurried struggle. The kids felt the wood beneath them vibrate from the scratching.

"There's something digging into the floor," said Buzz. He looked at Aubrey with a desperate grimace. Aubrey got the hint.

Aubrey closed his eyes and stared through the door, squinting his eyelids tightly together.

"Nothing there," said Aubrey, still searching the darkness.

Magnos stepped next to the latch and levered the door open, holding the top of the broken door. The door's top scraped against an angled ceiling and wedged itself along the ceiling's slats, fully open. The scratching stopped.

Magnos took a lantern from Buzz and held it beyond the door. A small landing turned down into a thin, winding staircase that led into darkness.

"I feel the breeze again," said Rodriqa.

Magnos stepped through the broken door and peered down the stairs.

"Oh, look," he said, slightly amazed. He waved the others forward. He took several steps down and squatted over a step. A tiny, furry creature shivered in the corner of one of the steps, its snout fearfully sniffing the air around its head. Magnos thought about cupping it into his palm, and then decided against it, considering where they were.

"It's a mouse," Magnos remarked.

Buzz leaned down and took a closer look. "No, it's a mole. You can't see its eyes and its nose is different. Not unexpected this far underground, I suspect."

"Yuck," replied Rodriqa with a snarled lip. "Ghosts I knew about, but nobody mentioned anything about the possibility of rodents down here."

Magnos stood up and shrugged. "Whatever it is, it's obviously not dangerous. It's kinda cute." He took another step down and looked down the stairwell. "Looks clear."

The five of them huddled together in the narrow stairs and slunk slowly toward the bottom. The boards protested with moans and creaks as they stepped, each one bowing with their weight. Aubrey closed his eyes and held his head up, scanning the space around behind his eyelids. He grasped tightly to the back of Rodriqa's shirt for guidance and felt each step with his feet so he wouldn't trip.

The stairs turned sharply like a corkscrew. Magnos stepped off the final step, and a spacious hallway opened up in front of them. An ornate banister ran along their left side, interrupted by a grand staircase that led to another floor below. A high wall with peeling, brown wallpaper bordered their right, in which two finely crafted, closed doors were set. More than thirty feet in front of them the hallway turned to the left and continued, with a railing on one side and a wall interrupted by several shut doors on its opposite side.

"Uh, oh," murmured Aubrey from the middle of the pack of kids. The other four turned anxiously to look at him.

Aubrey opened his eyes. "Trouble."

# Hovis Undone

Aubrey opened his eyes, and everyone could see what was troubling him.

Three glinting, over-sized worms, black as a starless night, writhed up the grand staircase in the middle of the hallway with their thick tube-like bodies undulating toward the five kids. Each serpentine slide of their torsos propelled their rotund bodies several feet forward, their shimmering coats absorbing any light as if they were coiling the night around them. The worms sniffed the air along the hallway, silently inching toward their prey.

The five kids scrambled backwards in a pack and wedged themselves into the corner, forcibly nudging Rodriqa out in front. Aubrey closed his eyes again and squeamishly inspected the threatening onslaught from behind his eyelids, over Rodriqa's shoulder.

The worms squeezed against the wood more quickly as they drew closer to the kids. Rodriqa held firmly to her beads and rattled them in front of her, hoping to ward off the approaching menace. The middle worm reared its head, like a cobra ready to strike, and flashed a ring of glistening, sharp teeth. It lunged past Rodriqa and clamped down on Jordana's foot, swallowing it in darkness. She squealed with fright and shook her leg to fling the creature off. It held its grip tightly.

"Do something," pleaded Jordana through a terse cry. The trembling kids pinned themselves against the wall, each rigid with fear. The other two worms encircled them from either side, hunting voraciously for exposed flesh. They latched on to Aubrey's arm and Magnos' leg, sliding slowly up their limbs.

Jordana stopped squirming. Aubrey watched the color drain from her face as he felt his arm tingle with fiery pricks. "Scream," he whispered harshly to Rodriqa.

Rodriqa inhaled deeply to scream, but her vocal cords only sputtered, stiff with terror. Jordana's eyes glazed over, and Aubrey and Magnos shook their limbs as the numbness crept up further.

Buzz pulled an inch of skin from the back of Rodriqa's arm and crushed it between his thumb and index finger.

"AAAWYYYAAWYYYYAWYAWYA!" screamed Rodriqa. The walls hummed with her excruciating yell. The three worms let go of their sinewy meals and twisted backward, growling at Rodriqa. She turned around and slapped Buzz's hand. "THAT HURT!"

"Who cares! It's working," exclaimed Buzz, pointing at the floor. She looked down as the worms edged away from her. She leaned forward and screamed again with all the air in her chest. She scrunched her face tightly together to open her mouth as widely as she could. The worms whimpered and edged backwards. After emptying her lungs, she took another full breath and hollered again. She stomped her feet against the boards, adding more fervor to her ruckus.

The worms shivered and squirmed over top of each other, their oily, black bodies churning in disarray. They fled up the small winding staircase behind them.

Jordana's face trembled as her color returned. "What happened?" she asked, unnerved by Rodriqa's shrieking.

"You did it," hollered Buzz excitedly. "That was *awesome*!"

"What was *not* awesome, was *you* pinching me," retorted Rodriqa, pointing a parental finger at him.

"I don't believe it," murmured Aubrey.

"Sometimes individual sacrifices need to be made for the good of the whole. You're our ghost tamer. I merely found a way to tap into your talents," said Buzz with a devilish grin. Rodriqa rolled her eyes.

"So the beads worked?" asked Jordana.

"I don't think the beads have anything to do with it," replied Aubrey.

"Are those things ghosts?" asked Magnos.

The other four looked at him, puzzled. "What do you mean?" asked Aubrey.

"What if they aren't ghosts? What if they're something worse?"

A high-pitched squeal echoed from the top of the staircase to the attic. The kids turned toward the stairs and listened intently. Claws scraped clumsily against the wood, louder than before. Gnarling chirps peeped in shuddering bursts from upstairs.

The mole jumped onto the bottom step, its form now nearly the size of small dog. Its beady eyes glowed faint red, and its fur spiked in sharply twirling mats. It flashed a ring of pointy teeth as it huffed the air ravenously.

The mole slipped down onto the hallway floor and snapped its jowls at the kids. They shifted out of the corner, separating from each other as they moved carefully down the hallway. Buzz braced himself against the railing as he stepped backwards, which creaked with the strain of his grip.

The mole sprinted down the hallway, its head and rear swishing back and forth as it ran. Rodriqa screamed and pounded her feet against the floor, but the mole kept coming toward her.

Buzz turned and hobbled down the grand staircase, dodging holes and crevices. The boards crumbled and snapped as each rotting step groaned under his weight.

Magnos pulled Rodriqa back by her arms and tried to crush the mole under his foot. The mole scurried from side to side and bit at his ankles.

Aubrey, Jordana and Rodriqa chased after Buzz down the stairs. Magnos heard them flee behind him, and he kicked the mole and ran after them. The mole flew through the air like a shaggy football and squeaked a brief cheep when it smacked against the far wall. It rolled itself over and roared angrily with an acerbic screech as it launched forward toward the top of the staircase.

The kids scrambled awkwardly down the dilapidated stairs, following Buzz's path. The mole sniffed the air at the top of the stairs and climbed downward after them.

Buzz reached the bottom and tested the boards under his feet. They were sturdy again, like the floor in the attic. He looked up at the door opposite the bottom of the stairs, and his eyes widened. He turned around and scanned the bottom floor for an escape route. He was standing in the middle of an open space, and at its far end, a hallway angled behind the grand staircase. Under the grand staircase was a set of smaller, darkened stairs. An open doorway to the left of the stack of staircases led into another dark room.

Buzz watched as his friends clumsily wavered from step to step. Magnos was trailing the pack, taking extra caution, as each board he stepped on squealed in protest at his size. The mole was gaining on Magnos, its pace quickening as he followed behind him.

"Hurry up!" shouted Buzz.

Magnos looked at Buzz, taking his eyes off the stairs. The step beneath him cracked and dissolved into tiny, wooden shards. Buzz cringed at the snap. Magnos' right leg slipped through, and he fell straight down, his hefty hip locked within the broken board. The mole scurried faster and aimed its teeth for Magnos' head.

"GET UP!" Buzz yelled. Magnos grabbed the bottom ledge of the railing and levered himself upward. The splintered board, trapping his leg, pierced his skin, and he moaned with the searing pain in his thigh. He released the railing and pushed the wooden barbs around his pinned leg downward, hoping to widen the hole.

Rodriqa, Jordana and Aubrey stepped off the stairs and turned around at Magnos, aghast that he was stuck. Magnos grunted and strained to free himself from the step. He winced as the board ripped through his jeans and dug deeper into his flesh.

"The mole is right behind you!" cried Jordana.

Magnos wrenched his torso around as the mole fell onto the step behind him. He gave the mole an uppercut with his beefy fist, and the mole soared up halfway up the stairs and landed against the railing. It shook of the hit, growled at him, and sped forward.

Magnos lifted himself off the step on his hands and rocked his body forward and backward. He curled his head down and reached for the step below him. He gripped the step, pulled and let go, jettisoning his torso backwards. He reversed his momentum and thrust himself forward again, pulling again on the lower step to catapult himself downward. The board beneath him crinkled, and his body sank forward. His right leg snapped loose from the step. The mole jumped after him, its snout biting the air furiously. The mole fell into the hole left by Magnos' leg and plummeted into the darkness. Its terrified shrieks dampened as it dropped further down into the deep. A quiet thud echoed upward, and the shrieking suddenly stopped.

Magnos somersaulted down the remaining steps and bowled into Aubrey and Jordana at the bottom, knocking them over. Aubrey's lantern bounced along the floor and its light went out. Buzz and Rodriqa jumped to the side, and Magnos rolled to a stop against the door behind them.

Buzz leaned forward and reached his hand toward Magnos. "That gives a new meaning to stop, drop and roll," he mused with chuckle. Rodriqa rolled her eyes. Aubrey and Jordana brushed themselves off as they regained their feet.

"Are you okay?" asked Jordana in a worried tone as she looked over Magnos. "You're jeans are all ripped up."

"I'm fine," grunted Magnos as he stood up. The jeans over his right leg were shredded, and he pushed away the scraps of denim to examine his leg for injury. "No harm done," he said glibly, even though he could feel something wasn't right.

"You're lucky you weren't hurt," said Jordana.

"Yeah, that was one feisty mole," Magnos replied jokingly.

"I think the worms had something to do with it," said Aubrey. He closed his eyes and looked up the stairs. "But I think they're gone now."

"And, hopefully, so is the mole," added Buzz.

Jordana rubbed her arms as a chill ran down them. "Much colder down here." She picked up Aubrey's lantern and tested it. With a grateful sigh, she turned it back on.

"Yeah," agreed Rodriqa as she held up her lantern to look around the stairs. The blinding darkness absorbed the fluorescent light each way she looked. She watched her breath mist in the frigid air around the lantern, and a chilling wind tingled against her cheek. "I think there's an open door on the other side of the stairs."

"Maybe that's where the draft is coming from," replied Jordana.

"I'm not sure where we need to go, but I'm not going down another set of stairs in here today," said Rodriqa firmly.

"I don't think you have to," replied Buzz. He rapped his knuckles against the door behind them, and the other four turned around. Emblazoned on the top half of the door was an intricately carved relief of the Circle of Circles. Buzz turned the doorknob, and it twisted easily, the door squeaking as he edged it open. He lifted up his lantern and peeked through the crack into the room.

"Wow!" exclaimed Buzz, as he levered the door fully open.

The tall, thin room filled with his white lantern light. Oaken bookshelves lined the entire room, and the ceiling extended beyond the darkness above. The edges of the shelves were decorated with rusting, wrought iron vines that curved along the wood, and thick, half-burnt candles were ensconced at the shelving borders. A wind chime of sculpted wooden and glass figures hung down from an iron rod jutting out from the wall. It seemed oddly out of place, but blended in with the other stately accoutrements in the room.

"Why is there a wind chime here of all places?" asked Aubrey. "Why would you need a wind chime *inside*?"

Buzz mused at him. "Ms. Thistlewood had one in her house too," he said thoughtfully. "And so did Mrs. Wizenblatt under the bridge, but that was outside."

"Old European superstition," Magnos replied. The other four kids stared at him, a little confused. "The saying goes:

> Bodes well the breeze
> That the windows seize
> But avoid the draft
> Which Nature didn't craft.

"It's a way to monitor for ghosts and other unwelcome, unseen visitors. When the chimes move without the wind, it's called a 'spirit draft.'"

"Creepy," murmured Aubrey.

The kids stepped slowly inside and marveled at the room's elegant detail. Unlike the rest of the house, the floor here was metal and solid. Rows of encyclopedic-sized tomes filled every shelf, their spines lettered with liquid, metal ink that hadn't lost its shine. Over two sets of shelves the metal vines wound upward across the bookcase, creating a cage with a small door, but both of these were open, and several books appeared to be missing. A rolling ladder leaned against a set of shelving, rusted in place. Except for a few small round objects, covered with fine, yellow linen, the floor was mostly open and clear, yet covered with a fine layer of dust.

Magnos sat down on one of the covered objects and sighed, rubbing his leg comfortingly. Rodriqa left her lantern next to Magnos, and then joined the others as they took their time staring at the books in the shelves, trying to read the loopy cursive writing on the outside covers.

"Why the metal floor?" Aubrey asked, as it was obviously out of place.

Buzz and Magnos shrugged.

"A solid foundation always keeps you from stumbling," muttered Rodriqa.

The others looked at her curiously. Rodriqa shook her head. "Just something my grandmother used to say."

"Maybe it's to protect all the books," guessed Buzz.

"And it looks like Hovis liked to read," Rodriqa said flatly.

Buzz's fingers ran from spine to spine of the books as he mouthed the words to himself, with his head cocked to the side for easier reading. "Plus, it looks like he had a particular interest in the occult." He read another title to himself, then wiped his fingers on his pants and snarled his lip disgustedly, as if he felt dirty simply for touching the book.

Magnos squirmed around on his makeshift seat to watch the others as they perused the library. Jordana passed a dozen columns of shelves and, holding her lantern high, walked into the darkness at the back of the room. Her feet shuffled along the metal floor before she bumped into something solid with a quiet grunt. "Look at this."

Rodriqa, Aubrey and Buzz followed her to the room's end. Wedged in a corner between sets of shelves was a slanted architect's desk. Its elevated portion rested against the wall and was lined with half-burnt candles. It sloped outward with several smaller shelves on either side. Open books were strewn up and down the desk's face with other closed books resting on the smaller side shelves. Jordana sat down on a wooden stool in front of the desk. She picked up a smaller black book lying on the center bottom part of the desk's pitched surface and thumbed through its pages.

"Interesting choice for a reading desk," critiqued Rodriqa, as she looked underneath the desk and shook its corner to check for sturdiness.

"I thought desks like these were usually for drawing or drafting," asked Aubrey.

"Usually," murmured Buzz in agreement. Rodriqa leaned over the desk and felt one of the book's rough and durable pages.

"These books aren't made with paper. They're all leather." Rodriqa turned the pages and ran her fingertips along the book's bumpy face. "And the writing isn't in ink. They've been etched."

"That's bizarre," remarked Aubrey.

"Except for this one," retorted Jordana. Her eyes didn't leave the page she was reading. "The paper is yellowed. And it's definitely been scribed with a pen."

Buzz slid his hands underneath the leading brim of the desk. He jerked his arm back quickly and squinted through a silent ouch. He reached under the desk again and pulled out a metal pin with a pointed tip. "It's a stylus. He must have transcribed older paper texts into these leather formats."

"That must have taken a great deal of time," added Aubrey. "Why would he go to that much trouble?"

"Hovis wanted these books to stay around a while," surmised Rodriqa, her eyebrows raised in deduction. "He must have planned on using them for decades…maybe centuries."

"He knew that he was going to need them later," agreed Buzz.

"What are the books for?" asked Magnos from across the room.

Aubrey, Buzz and Rodriqa thumbed through the pages of the books in front of them.

"This one reads like a cookbook for herbal remedies," said Aubrey, reading line after line of floral ingredients and their appropriately measured proportions and simmering times.

Buzz eyed the pages and twiddled the embedded lettering in the leather between his fingers, like a blind man reading Braille. "This book doesn't make any sense. It's talking about capturing stones and controlling spirits in the same sentence. Must be a reprint of some silly magic book."

A glint of gold ink caught Rodriqa's eye near the top of the slanted desktop. She closed the book she was reading and pulled the book scribed with gold out from under several other tomes. She rubbed the dust off of its spine and examined it closely. "I know this book."

"What is it?" asked Aubrey.

Rodriqa mouthed the syllables slowly. A decade's old memory flooded her brain. "Anath...Anathagraphia...my grandmother has this book in her house." She turned the pages, looking for something familiar. Diagrams and illustrations were cut into most of the leather leaflets. "Her copy was in color, and I was fascinated by all the pretty pictures when I was little. When I got older, she took it away from me. She forbade me to even touch it. So naturally when I would visit, I did what any kid would do...I snuck downstairs at night to read it."

The name of the book resounded in Jordana's head as the memory of the word reminded her of the night when her uncle and father fought openly in the yard. She gulped down the dry lump in her throat and clamped her teeth tightly together to keep herself from adding any details.

"What does that word mean?" Aubrey asked.

"I'm not exactly sure, but the book is about curses and their repercussions." Rodriqa scrambled through sections, hunting for a page she remembered.

"Like voodoo doll hocus pocus?" Buzz asked.

"Not really," Rodriqa said thoughtfully, as she searched her memory. "More like...enabling dire consequences to happen to people when they make bad decisions."

"So a curse with a sense of justice?" asked Aubrey in a puzzled tone.

"Kind of," Rodriqa replied, wavering in thought as her attention was absorbed by the book "But you can't curse just anybody on a whim. If someone breaks a promise or a rule, then they're at risk for receiving a curse."

"Like when you tell your parents you're gonna take out the trash, but you forget, and then they take away your online gaming privileges for a week?" Buzz queried.

Rodriqa sneered and shook her head at Buzz. "Not really. It has to be a little more substantial than that."

"Like a punishment for creating unnecessary harm or mischief for unsuspecting, undeserving individuals," asserted Magnos. The other four looked at him, a little unnerved at his erudite example. Rodriqa frowned but nodded slowly, unsure how best to respond.

"Or a sort of supernatural detention," Aubrey added, trying to make the connection and breaking the brief, awkward silence.

"Hammer...nail." Rodriqa tapped her closed fists together to point out that he was spot on. "But," she paused thoughtfully, paging through the book, "it's more complex than that. There are variations to the rules. You can curse yourself to contrive an unexpectedly good outcome in an otherwise hopeless situation, and you can curse yourself to remove a curse from someone else."

Rodriqa's finger landed soundly on a page. "Ah, ha," she exclaimed. "Found it!" She turned the open book around to face Aubrey and pointed at the top of the page.

Aubrey strained to read the etched heading at the top edge of the leather. "The Sandman Anathem?"

"Yep," affirmed Rodriqa. She set the book on the table and pointed to a picture buried within the text of the page. "Does this look familiar?"

Carved into the middle of the leather page was a cloaked human figure with outstretched arms, manacled to the ground with taut, bulky chains, which forced the form to stoop under their weight. A hazy particulate billowed up from the ground, surrounding the image in a cloud of blurring dust.

"It's a picture of Hovis," said Buzz, astonished by the similarity between the pictograph and what he had seen this past weekend in the cemetery.

"Or someone cursed, just like Hovis," confirmed Rodriqa. She read the passage underneath the picture aloud.

"In the retributive series of commensurate responses to terrestrial covenant offenses, the Sandman Anathem executes an inordinately indolent and insufferable reckoning for the accursed. Accordingly, the adjudicating victim must have succumbed to an extraordinarily heinous injury by the meditative intent or reckless inaction of the recipient for the anathem to inculcate and manifest appropriately.

Whereas, upon the anathem's recitation, the post-corporeal existence of the imbued becomes eternally bound to the Earth, regardless of prior history or future attainment of spiritual reconciliation. The irrevocable constraint does not preclude interaction with other spirits, whether human, shade or shinar.

As with any anathem, abrogation can be achieved. One means of supplantive resolution resides in direct interjection from an authority of the Divine. Such authorities can include a highly gifted shinar, any spirit endowed with more than a score of stones, or a sanguinous seer. Other methods of anathemic reversal may exist, but are otherwise cryptogenic.

Attempts at circumventing the anathem have been undertaken without proven success. Theoretically, migration of an affected spirit from its original vessel to an equally tellurian surrogate might sustain carnal proclivity, thus delaying both celestial matriculation and the anathem's incarcerating effect."

"Could you read the first sentence again," asked Magnos from across the room. Rodriqa reread the passage slowly for everyone to hear again. Magnos' face crinkled into a tight ball while his brain strained through a verbosity-induced migraine.

"There's that stone reference again. I don't understand what that means," said Buzz as he read over Rodriqa's shoulder.

"None of it makes any sense," added Aubrey.

Rodriqa brooded over the book, repeating the lines over and over again in her head.

"It makes perfect sense," she whispered.

"To whom?" chuckled Buzz arrogantly.

"Okay, Hovis was cursed. We know that now, but the rest of the text might as well have been written by a barrel of blind monkeys," replied Aubrey.

"Maybe he's been after the Tomb of Enoch because that's a way he can get free," surmised Buzz clumsily. "Didn't it say something in *Solluna* about Enoch being 'one who once knew blood?' Maybe he's the 'sanguinous seer' he needs to break the curse."

"That doesn't explain why he's been haunting Aubrey," Rodriqa said, lost in thought.

Aubrey stared at them with a puzzled expression.

"He needs someone to free him," continued Rodriqa slowly, "not from his grave and not from the Tomb, but from his chains. And he needs an authority of divinity. Shade and shinar are archaic terms for demons and angels. I'm guessing he's had access to those. And they've not been helpful. He needs a seer who is sanguinous, someone through whom blood still runs."

"And what is a seer, and where would he find one?" asked Buzz, annoyed at her seemingly clear understanding of the passage.

"Aubrey," said Rodriqa, nearly inaudibly.

Aubrey shook his head and raised his eyebrow derisively at her suspected jab. "Not funny, Rodriqa." Then suddenly, he remembered what Ms. Thistlewood had said in the bottom of the dam. His expression dulled, and his thoughts fogged with the vague recollection of conversation under duress.

Buzz laughed heartily. "I think the lack of oxygen down here is getting to you."

Rodriqa slammed the book closed. "It makes perfect sense! How else do you explain how Aubrey could see Hovis... and the worms?! And how he could not only see them, but make *us* see them! Aubrey must be able to release him from his chains! That's why he's after you!"

Buzz's jaw slowly dropped as his mind digested what she had said.

Aubrey shrugged incredulously, his feelings of misfit uselessness fighting against what Rodriqa was proposing.

"And you can read that book," added Magnos. "*Solluna*. I don't think many people can. I think Hovis tried to read it once...when I was trapped in the basement. He got really angry when he couldn't."

Jordana lifted her face from the book she had been reading. "Rodriqa's right," she said firmly. "Aubrey, you need to read this." She turned to him and handed him the smaller, black, unlabeled book she had been reading. "I know why Hovis was cursed and why this house is buried under a cemetery."

"How?" asked Aubrey barely able to articulate his monosyllabic question.

"Because I found his diary," Jordana replied. She flipped back several pages and pointed to a paragraph in the middle of the inky manuscript. "Start here."

Aubrey's eyes scampered across the page, yearning to learn more about Hovis.

"What's it say?" asked Rodriqa.

"You're dead on about the anathem," replied Jordana, recounting what she read. "He came to the States from England to start life anew. It sounds like he was a bit of an outcast there. He gathered what little he had and bought a ticket on a ship across the Atlantic. All he could afford was fare on a ship carrying slaves.

"The conditions on the ship were reprehensible, and something awful happened...something out of his control, but he never forgave himself for it...and he was cursed for it. He spent the rest of his life dreading the Sandman Anathem.

Jordana pushed up her glasses and rubbed the chill out of her hands. "For decades he hunted for a means to release himself from the curse, but he became desperate. The search turned dark. His faith crossed the line from exploring religion to experimenting with sorcery. He lost himself in the black places of this world, and it affected the people around him.

"The locals noticed that their preacher had been swayed by alternative beliefs. A drought hit the area, and it was followed by waves of illness. They felt Hovis was to blame. They took matters into their own hands. They decided the only way to rid themselves of their spiritual menace and cleanse the land of Hovis' misdeeds was to cleanse the Trottle family.

"The townsfolk found some way to exact atonement and punish Hovis. They buried Hovis and his family alive in their own house. A marker was placed in the ground over the grave to remind future generations of Hovis' crimes. A symbol for the redemption of the fallen."

"The Circle of Circles," muttered Aubrey in a weary voice.

Jordana nodded slowly in agreement.

"Just like the Watchers," continued Aubrey, "from the poem in *Solluna*. They were bound by the Tomb of Enoch as reparation."

Magnos stood up and moved toward the desk, their discussion engaging his curiosity. The sheet underneath his rear clung to the back of his injured leg, and the shifting cloth bunched together around his feet. He tripped forward and fell to his knees onto the metal flooring. He muttered under his breath and brushed off his hands as he pushed himself off the ground.

"You're bleeding," remarked Jordana. She walked over toward him and pointed to where the blood from his wounds had trickled down his jeans and dried on the sheet.

Buzz's eyes widened and his cheeks tightened in disbelief as he looked behind Magnos. "That's what we saw from the attic." He marched over to the object on which Magnos had been sitting and held the lantern directly over top of it.

Sparkling, pale yellow and hearty red stones twinkled from the bejeweled lid of the gritty pot on the floor. The five kids stared silently at the intricate detail and arrangement of the jewel-encrusted sandstone pot. Rectangular and triangular gems embedded in its cover and around the sides sent rays of reflected light across the room, and cast shimmering rainbows on the books and shelving.

"It's the most beautiful thing I've ever seen," said Buzz whimsically, hypnotized by the lights.

"It's pretty amazing, all right," agreed Magnos, unsettled that he had been sitting on it for so long. He separated the sheet from his jeans and searched his leg for the source of his bleeding.

Jordana and Aubrey stood behind Buzz and marveled at the pot's beauty. Rodriqa remained at the desk, lost in thought.

Buzz squatted down on his knees and caressed the top of the lid with his fingertips, admiring its craftsmanship and opulence. He pried the lid upwards, but it refused to move. "It's locked,' he remarked. He pressed down on the stones firmly and turned his hand sideways. The outer circle of stones slid easily along the sandstone.

Buzz's eyes lit up gleefully. Now he could see how the gems were grouped together on plates of sandstone that could glide past each other. "It's a puzzle!"

Aubrey watched him examine the lid, unnerved that Buzz was so enamored by it. "Maybe we should leave it alone."

"Are you kidding? I wonder if there is any way we could get it up the stairs," asked Buzz.

Magnos bent over and wrapped his arms around the sandstone jar's base. He strained against its weight. It didn't budge. "There must be something heavy inside of it."

Jordana held her lantern over the pot. With both hands Buzz cupped the edge of the round lid and swept sections left and right, up and down, searching for a familiar pattern. Crescents, ellipses and circles slid past one another, creating new shapes within the larger circle. Suddenly he realized the form the stones were supposed to take. His hands flew across the lid, moving section after section into various configurations, hoping to find the correct positions.

"What are you doing?" asked Aubrey, his insides quivering with dread the faster Buzz worked.

"I know what the puzzle is," snipped Buzz, annoyed by the distraction, his hands scurrying in a frenzy to reach their goal.

Aubrey's skin twitched, and a chill ran down his spine. "I don't think you should do this," he spat out quickly, the words running together.

"Too late," said Buzz, abounding with pride. Buzz was right. Aubrey peered over his shoulder as the lines and curves of the gems were now in the shape of the Circle of Circles.

The lid jerked upwards, and dust spewed from underneath it. A sharp, white and blinding light spun from the edge of the lid's perimeter, shredding the front of Buzz's shirt into thin, ragged strips.

Aubrey clutched Buzz's shoulders and yanked him backwards. Magnos and Jordana jumped several feet back, startled by the jar's whirring blades. The mechanism within the pot ground against metal and sputtered along the sandstone, as the circular rows of countercurrent turning knives twitched to a halt. Aubrey looked down at Buzz as he stared back from the floor, his eyes wide with terror. A small rivulet of blood trickled down Buzz's chin and around the side of his neck. Aubrey reached out his hand to help him up.

"Thanks," whimpered Buzz, his body trembling in shock as he regained his feet.

"Griggs tried to warn me," said Aubrey contemplatively. "I missed it, but he knew this would happen somehow."

"Guys!" shouted Rodriqa as she marched toward the middle of the room. "We're not alone down here." The other four stared at her blankly, still recovering from Buzz's near-beheading. "The sheet was not over the pot when we were in the attic. We couldn't have seen it if it were covered." She held her lantern high and peered at the ceiling, barely able to make out the broken wood in the attic's floor. "And look," she continued as she pointed to the floor. "There's a path of dust missing from the floor next to the pot. It's been moved."

Magnos examined the floor and scuffed his foot along the metal, cleaning away a fine swathe of dust. "She's right," he said solemnly.

The lid of the jar floated slowly up, exposing two tiny, metal hinges within the jar that were extending it skyward. Jordana glanced inside the open pot and turned her head immediately. She gagged and covered her mouth. Tears swelled in her eyes, and her throat burned with a dry ache of oncoming bile. She ran for the door and disappeared into the hallway.

Rodriqa looked into the pot and snarled her lip. "Let's go, you all. We've found out what we needed to know." She chased after Jordana. At the door to the library, she turned her head back into the room and watched Buzz, Magnos and Aubrey moving closer toward the pot, marveling at its contents. Her gut rolled in revulsion. "Hurry up! If there's someone else down here, we don't need to be running into them." Rodriqa passed through the door and rushed up the grand staircase.

The three boys ignored Rodriqa and slowly approached the pot, unable to take their eyes off of what was inside.

"Is it dead?" asked Aubrey.

"It must be," replied Magnos.

"I don't think it was ever alive," argued Buzz softly.

A crumpled body was stuffed into the large pot, its arms and legs folded like a deflated balloon and its head limp on its shoulder like a puppet cut from its strings. There was no decay, and the skin was wrinkled and gamey in appearance. Its face had a nearly imperceptible grin, but its other features were perfectly formed…too perfect.

"It doesn't smell bad," said Aubrey, uncertain of his evaluation, as the entire house was musty.

"Maybe it's a mummy," suggested Magnos.

"Not quite," murmured Buzz. He ran over to the desk and picked up the stylus from its ledge. He walked back to the pot and pricked the body's face with the metal tip of the pen, tracing a line along its skin. Magnos and Aubrey cringed as fleshy bits curly-cued up the stylus. Buzz chuckled deliriously.

"What's funny?" asked Magnos with a disgusted bite to his question.

"It's wax," replied Buzz. He reached into the pot and lifted up an arm and squeezed it. "And the limbs are made of burlap and leather."

"That's just freaky," decided Magnos, still disgusted.

"Is it a toy?" asked Aubrey in a confused tone.

"Doubtful," replied Buzz. "I think it's a golem." Magnos and Aubrey stared at him, awaiting an explanation. "In ancient Jewish traditions, it's a way to trap a spirit. But after what Rodriqa just read, I'm guessing this was Hovis' way to escape his curse, if his other plans failed."

"Aubrey! Help me!" The distant, echoing cry from Jordana snapped the three of them out of their morbidly curious investigation of the pot.

"Aubrey! I need you!"

## *Jock Shock and Peril*

Aubrey picked up the lantern on the floor and launched himself toward Jordana's cry for help, bolting out the library door with Magnos and Buzz close behind him. Aubrey retraced his steps up the grand staircase, his feet touching the rotting boards just long enough to push himself to the next step. His significantly lighter weight gave him a sizeable speed advantage. The distance between Aubrey and the other two widened quickly. Magnos and Buzz had to be a great deal more careful, testing every step with a guarded touch of their shoe.

"Aubrey! Hurry!" Jordana's voice drifted through the house, sounding more urgent each time. Aubrey's heart filled with dread and fueled his legs to climb more quickly.

Aubrey avoided the weaker boards and holes and rounded the top of the staircase. In a frenzy, he scrambled up the narrow, spiral stairs and dodged the cloth-covered furniture in the attic.

"I'm coming," he cried up to the ceiling as he latched both hands on the rope ladder. He concentrated on Jordana as he struggled upward, hoping to ignore the searing pain from his arms and legs. His feet slipped out of the rungs with each step, and he knew he'd fall if he didn't hurry with spasms gaining pressure in his calves.

He rolled his upper body onto the top of the roof, his chest heaving to breathe. "Almost... there," he panted, his voice barely audible. The dust from the drying grave-wall dirt choked him and stuck to the inside of his cheeks and tongue. He spit on the ground to clear the grime from his mouth.

Aubrey looked out of the grave, and the afternoon sun burned his eyes. He squinted, peering through his lashes, and raised his hand to his brow to shade them, like a blinded salute. He wondered how long they had been in the dark, underground house.

"Jordana? Where are you?" Aubrey pushed his hands against his knees so he could stand. A long empty pause followed his inquiry to the cemetery above.

A long, lean arm reached down over the edge of the grave, stopping only a couple of feet from Aubrey's face. Its hand opened and wiggled its fingers welcomingly. Aubrey placed his palm in the outstretched hand, and the fingers clamped down hard around his palm, squeezing the blood from his hand into his fingertips. Aubrey reached up to pry his fingers loose, but the hand crushed Aubrey's fingers even harder. The pads of his fingers felt as if they would burst, and they were turning bright red, like cherry tomatoes.

"Ouch! Not so hard," squeaked Aubrey. The hand suddenly pulled Aubrey up and out of the grave. He felt like his shoulder might pop out of its socket.

He landed front-first on the mossy weeds of the Trottle family plot. Specks of dirt and the sharp edges of grass scratched face, and he could taste the bitter, warm tincture of blood in his mouth. A heavy weight pressed against the middle of his back, forcing the air out of his lungs and pinning him to the ground.

Large sneakered feet sloppily stampeded the ground around him. Two hands grabbed each of his arms and crossed them behind him. His wrists burned as they were wrenched together. The pressure in his back eased and he sucked in a breath. "What's going on?" he whimpered.

His arms cramped tightly as someone stretched them backwards, and his head and torso jerked skyward. Gaetan smirked at him with a deeply devilish grin and lifted up his sunglasses briefly to catch Aubrey eye to eye, as he stood Aubrey upright. "Do you find your ghost, you little freak?" He took out a pocketknife and flashed it open within an inch of Aubrey's nose. Aubrey tried to pull his hands in front of him to protect himself. It was then he realized they were tied together.

"Why are you doing this?" squalled Aubrey.

Gaetan leaned in and whispered into Aubrey's ear. "Did you think I would forget about Saturday night?" Aubrey shuddered at his icy words. Gaeten bent down and cut through the cord tethering the rope ladder to the plot marker, which skidded across the grass and dropped into the grave. Leon Hagwell, with his conch-shaped nose and stringy hair, stepped around in front of Aubrey with a handful of tawny, braided rope coiled around his arm. Aubrey's gut sunk with dread. Leon adjusted his sunglasses and handed the frayed end of the rope to Gaetan, who tied a figure eight knot around Aubrey's ankles.

Behind Gaetan, Treywick Compton, who was still wearing his sunglasses, held Rodriqa off the ground, his trunk-like legs scissored around hers to stop her from kicking and his thick arms wrapped around her torso, clasping her body to his chest, with a hand wrapped around the bottom-half of her face. Rodriqa squirmed within her muscled cage and only faint, muffled moans escaped her throat.

"Leave Rodriqa alone," whined Aubrey. Aubrey felt the coarse, prickling strands of the rope tightening against his skin as Leon and Gaetan wound it upwards, weaving him into a threadbare mummy.

Next to Treywick and Rodriqa, the Strumgarten trailer bed, resting only a few yards outside of the cemetery, was loaded with a mammoth, fire-engine red canoe with carved and painted wooden totems bolted to its bow and stern, each rising ten feet high, mimicking the appearance of a Viking long boat. A wooden, rectangular box was also attached to the bow of the canoe, unsanded and undecorated, out of place with the rest of the ornately embellished canoe. Gaetan's newly fixed Pontiac GTO was hitched to the trailer a few yards down the hill. Wearing football jerseys and sunglasses, Hank O'Dant and Ty Rontimer carried large wooden oars from trunk the of Gaetan's car and threw them into the canoe's hull.

"Where's Jordana?" squealed Aubrey.

Jordana walked up to Aubrey from behind him. Tears swelled along her eyelids, and her lower lip trembled. Her eyes glanced quickly at him through her honey-colored glasses, and then she dropped her head, unable to bear his stare.

"Are you okay?" Aubrey asked, desperately confused as to why she had cried for help, but elated she was safe. Jordana didn't answer. She turned away from and yelled at Gaetan, "You promised not to hurt him!"

Gaetan waved her off. "Looks like neither one of us is good at promises."

Jordana glowered in reply, crossed her arms, stared at the ground.

Gaetan stood up, spiraling the rope around Aubrey's chest and chuckling arrogantly. "Are you okay?" he mocked in a childish tone. "Dude, she's the one that led you into this trap." Gaetan tied the rope off at Aubrey's shoulders. He pinched Aubrey's cheek and winked at him, faking fraternal affection. Then he angled his head toward Jordana. "You might want to let this one be. I think she still has feelings for Hamilton."

"Speaking of Hamilton," grunted Treywick. "After you found Aubrey, Hamilton wanted us to bring Jordana to him."

Gaetan turned around quickly and scowled at Treywick. "You don't answer to that yuppie toad thrower or any other spoiled, little rich kid. Man it up, Compton! We have a race to win."

Treywick scowled in reply. Gaetan softened his face and smirked back. "Besides, I need you to be in charge of our secret weapon." The corner of Treywick's lips curled up with excitement, and he quickly forgot about Hamilton.

Gaetan put two of his fingers in his mouth and whistled. Ty and Hank lifted Aubrey over their heads and tossed him effortlessly into the canoe. Treywick flung Rodriqa to the ground and kept his heels up as he ran away, fearing a rear attack. Rodriqa grasped handfuls of dirt and threw them at the escaping Treywick.

"Aubrey, I'm sorry," whimpered Jordana.

Compton, O'Dant, and Rontimer boarded the canoe, and Gaetan and Leon hopped in the GTO and sped off down the hill toward Lake Julian, pulling the canoe and Aubrey behind them.

Fuming mad, Rodriqa pushed herself up and brushed the dirt off her knees.

"Where are they taking him?" Jordana asked, too embarrassed to look at her.

"The river race," replied Rodriqa tersely. "It starts soon."

"I'm so sorry," cried Jordana.

"We can talk about it later," Rodriqa replied sternly.

Distant shouting rose out of the open grave. Rodriqa climbed into the pit and stuck her head through the splintered hole in the roof. Buzz and Magnos were standing in the middle of the attic, staring upwards with lanterns and rope ladder in hand.

"What's going on?" hollered Buzz.

"Throw me the ladder!" shouted Rodriqa. "We need to hurry!"

## The Paddling Pumpkin Raft Race, Part 1

Buzz, Magnos, Jordana and Rodriqa raced out of the cemetery and down the hill toward Lake Julian. Rodriqa led them through the park along the water's edge, explaining to Buzz and Magnos what had happened to Aubrey as they changed pace from a steady jog to a hurried walk.

At the head of the lake, where the Wontawanna Creek fed Lake Julian, a lively throng of several hundred people milled about at the bank. A low, mumbling roar of friendly chatter and cheerful banter wafted from the swarming crowd. Balloons and poster boards, scribed with praises and quirky phrases, dotted the tops of several clumps of rallying groupies. Most folks were dressed in brightly colored T-shirts and shorts, still clinging to the last ounces of summer weather.

"Why are all these people here?" Jordana asked in a winded voice.

"To watch the Paddling Pumpkin Raft Race," answered Buzz. "It's popular tradition for the whole community. It takes place every fall after the Homecoming Dance, but before the Paddling Pumpkin Festival and parade."

"I didn't realize it was such a big deal," replied Jordana, a little bewildered at the unique local custom's impressive turnout. Her mind kept returning to Aubrey, but she didn't know where to start looking for him in the massive mess of people.

"Huge," replied Buzz gleefully. "It's almost as big as Christmas."

"Who's in the race?" asked Jordana.

"Students from the local schools mostly," replied Magnos.

"And some nearby organizations. The Lake Julian V.F.W. is usually in it every year," added Buzz.

"Yeah," giggled Rodriqa. "Those old men always look so cute in their uniforms riding down the creek."

Magnos chuckled. "It's kinda sad, though. Their Pump*king* is always the first to get knocked off."

"Their what?" asked Jordana, trying to stay focused on the conversation.

"*Pumpking*," Buzz reiterated.

Jordana shook her head in confusion.

"It's not just a rafting race," explained Rodriqa. "First off, the craft you're riding in can't be a regular raft. It has to be modified in some way. Second, each group has one person in the raft dressed in pumpkin shells, their designated *Pumpking*. The goal of the race is to get your raft's Pumpking to Lake Julian first."

"That doesn't sound too hard," Jordana retorted.

"Except that every other raft is trying to knock your Pumpking off your boat," added Buzz. "If your Pumpking touches the water, your teams out."

"Sounds dangerous," replied Jordana, a little unnerved by his description.

"Not really," said Buzz. "Wontawanna Creek is pretty shallow and slow for most of the race, and there aren't really any obstacles except for Pyramid Rock, which is at the end anyway. Besides, you can be disqualified for unnecessary roughness by the judges. But the winning Pumpking and their crew get to be grand marshals at the parade and win a nice lump of cash.

"The Lake Julian Torquetum Club entered a raft this year, and they have a secret weapon! They even consulted me on some of the design modifications." Buzz rubbed his hands together with a smugly mischievous grin.

"Mr. Congeniality is also awarded for the Pumpking with the best costume," added Magnos.

"It's a stupid tradition," discounted Rodriqa. "A barbaric display of testosterone-fueled ingenuity and elitism."

"It's not stupid. It's gravy," countered Magnos. Rodriqa rolled her eyes.

The four kids walked up to the back of the mingling crowd. There were lots of groups mulling around blankets with picnic baskets, most close to the bank, who had been waiting there most of the afternoon, since they had the best seats. Most folks were laughing and talking with neighbors about work and school, killing time until the race started. Some people walked through the crowd, hunting for the best place to watch the race. Others continued to join the crowd from behind, searching for friends and eagerly looking up the creek for signs of the first rafts.

"Where do you think Aubrey is?" asked Jordana worriedly.

"They must have taken him to the starting point," said Magnos.

"Where's that?"

Magnos looked to their right, and Jordana followed his gaze. He raised his hand and pointed over the crowd. Jordana stretched her neck, searching for Aubrey's bright red hair. For several hundred yards before it reached Lake Julian, Wontawanna Creek flowed through a wide, straight bed before disappearing around a sharp bend shrouded by dense woods. At the right edge of the horde of spectators, a fence separated the people from a stretch of narrow land that ran along the bank where the forest pressed closer in.

"Gaetan has most likely taken Aubrey with them to the starting point," surmised Rodriqa. "The race begins about two miles upstream, around the bend and out of sight. We won't be able to see the initial part of the race, but most people don't care since, the end is the most exciting. It's usually a photo finish."

"Then let's go get him," pleaded Jordana.

"We can't," Rodriqa replied. "Only rafters are allowed at the start. There's limited space for them to put in. And it looks like Principal Lequoia is in charge of keeping the dodgy dawdlers out."

Jordana examined the barbed wire fence perpendicular to the creek, separating the crowd from upriver. A wide, metal cattle gate at the fence's outer edge was the only way through. A lump rose in her throat as she saw her uncle staring directly at her from behind the gate.

Magnos could see the angst in Jordana's face, compelling him to help. "Maybe they'll let me back, since I'm on the football team..." Magnos paused for a moment and reconsidered his words, "...was on the football team." His voice trailed off as he turned and walked through the crowd.

Magnos marched toward the gate along the rim of the crowd with his head down. He dodged young children playing tag as they chased each other in circles, and wound between the lines of folks waiting in front of the tiny, but popular, make-shift concession stand. Principal Lequoia was opening the gate for a couple of kids leaving the starting area to join the audience. Seeing his window of opportunity, Magnos stepped up his pace.

Magnos grabbed the top bar of the cattle gate just before it closed. "Hello, sir," he spoke steadily.

Mr. Lequoia measured him with his with stern, black eyes. "Hello, Magnos. How are you feeling?" Lequoia pushed the gate to close it the last few inches, but it didn't move.

"I'm fine, sir," replied Magnos, with an edge to his voice. "I need to speak with the football team before the race starts." Magnos tightened his grip on the gate.

"You know the rules," stated Lequoia administratively. "No visitors before the race." Lequoia jerked the gate with a stiff arm, but it didn't budge.

Magnos leaned in toward his principal and set his ankle against the gate's lower rung. "It's urgent, sir. I need to go back there."

Lequoia furrowed his brow and placed his other hand on the gate. "The race will be starting momentarily. You won't make it in time."

A flicker of anger flashed across Magnos' face. "They have something...that I need to retrieve."

"It'll have to wait until after the race," asserted Lequoia staunchly. He heaved the gate against the latch with all his weight and it clicked with authoritative finality.

Magnos sighed deeply, trying to control his temper. A sweetly soft, melodic voice twirled in his ears. "Did you lose something, Magnos?"

An ear-ringing squelch of radio feedback echoed over the crowd as Buzz, Rodriqa and Jordana walked closer to the creek.

**"Ladies and Gentleman! Welcome to the Tenth Annual Paddling Pumpkin Rafting Race."**

Everyone erupted in applause around them as the booming, twangy voice vibrated through speakers around the creek's edge. A round man dressed in a stark, white suit with a black bowtie stood several feet above the crowd at the edge of the lake. His black, overgrown mustache matched his thick, matted eyebrows, and his eyes danced with each word he spoke. **"We are truly blessed with this crisp and sunny fall afternoon, apropos for a pumpkin festival, to watch these brave men and women compete for one of Lake Julian's finest honors."**

"Who is that?" asked Jordana, covering her ears to buffet the sound.

"FAGAN MCELORY," yelled Buzz over the loudspeakers. "HE'S THE EDITOR OF THE *LAKE JULIAN MOUNTAIN LYRE*." Several people around them turned to give Buzz a curious yet disapproving look, as he hollered a little too loudly.

**"We have an illustrious cadre of contestants for today's race, both new and old. They have sacrificed much of their time and skills to bring you this uniquely daring sport. It takes a heart overflowing with courage to fight to be the first down Wontawanna Creek. Share your jubilee and praise by welcoming each athlete and their organization as I introduce them. Representing...."**

"Jordana, isn't that your dad?" asked Rodriqa, a little surprised. Next to the mouth of the creek stood a long, spindly table draped in banners and advertisements. At the table, three well-dressed men and women sat facing the creek as Fagan McElory stood on his chair with microphone in hand. Scanning the crowd, Jordana recognized the profile of her father's injured face in the seat next to Mr. McElory.

"Yeah, it is," said Jordana, slightly bewildered at first. Then she remembered her father's reminder before she left for school. "He said he had an event at the lake this afternoon, but I didn't really know what he was talking about. The lack of sleep is catching up with me." Sputters of applause resounded along the creekside as Mr. McElory announced the racers.

"He must be one of the judges for the race," Rodriqa replied. "Quite an honor." Mr. McElory finished listing each participant and tapped the microphone to ensure everyone was looking at him.

**"A formidable group, I must say. This year's race will undoubtedly go down in the record books, not only for the size of the crowd, but also for the fierceness of the competition. Now I would like to introduce this year's august panel of judges for the race.**

**"To my right, last years Pumpking or more appropriately, Pumpqueen, Kiki Januzweski."**

Kiki rose to her feet and turned to the crowd, rotating her hand in the air with beauty pageant flare. Her blonde curly hair was wrapped high on top of her head, and her hoop earrings swayed as she smiled and greeted the crowd.

**"Also to my right, the distinguished Sergeant Alec Van Zenny with the Poage County Police Department."**

Van Zenny only turned halfway around in his chair and smirked at the crowd. He raised two fingers to acknowledge that he had been acknowledged, but he wasn't happy to do so.

**"To my left, Mr. Arturo Galilahi, chief foreman of the Berybomag Mining Operations, Lake Julian Division."**

Jordana's dad stood up and took a modest bow. He wore a cap with the mining logo emblazoned on the front, but he didn't take it off, hoping to hide his scarred features under the shadow of its bill.

**"And of course, your very own, Fagan McElory, editor-in-chief of the Lake Julian Mountain Lyre, the proportioned yet unhampered voice of the Eastern Pisgah Valley.**

**We'd also like to thank our sponsors for today's race...."**

"This guy sure does like to hear himself speak," commented Jordana.

Rodriqa nodded. "No kidding."

"Mr. McElory is known for his colorful manner and his unduly unabridged speeches," added Buzz, "but he's well-thought of around town. He keeps the mucky-mucks in line."

"Speaking of mucky-mucks," whispered Rodriqa as they walked up behind McCrayden Miller, Jon Harney and Pam Trank, who were gossiping in a tight group. Jordana marveled at how they dressed similarly from cap to heel. They were even each wearing the same blue silk scarf around their necks.

Jon was looking through a pair of binoculars while Pam was chewing her gum, hand on her hip, and clinging adoringly to McCrayden's every word.

"...Teton and his crew have worked so hard on their raft, I mean, I hardly ever get to see him after school, they've been so busy working on it, and he keeps mentioning this secret weapon they have, but he won't tell me what it is, he just keeps teasing me, you know, but he'll say these really mysterious things out of the blue like, 'it'll cause a huge stink, but it won't matter 'cuz we're gonna win anyway,' but then I heard some of the band geeks talking and they're up to something too, and Daddy and the guys in the Mount Camelot Home Owner's Association, they have a raft entered too, and they've been practicing for months, so who knows what's really gonna happen...." McCrayden never took a breath.

Rubbing its hide against the bristly fibers of McCrayden's sweater, Prissy rolled around and stretched in her crossed arms while she spoke. Jordana peeked over McCrayden's shoulder and noted how calm the kitten was while it was purring with its long wispy, cotton-candy-like fur twirled in patched bundles of beiges, charcoals and creams.

Pam noticed Jordana watching McCrayden. She straightened up, put her fingertips to lips, and twisted her fingers, like turning a key in a lock. McCrayden flipped her head around and glared at Jordana. "Riffraff should be more grateful when they receive a gift," she growled.

"Excuse me?" stumbled Jordana.

McCrayden turned back to Pam. "I told Hamilton he was taking a huge gamble asking out a misfit, but he insisted she was different."

Pam nodded emphatically.

"I told him he shouldn't be throwing scraps to pigs," continued McCrayden. "Because then all you get is an ornery pig."

"Pig?" questioned Jordana timidly.

McCrayden turned back to Jordana. "You have no idea how good you could have had it. He did you a favor, sister."

Jordana's sullen face tensed up. She was unable to speak.

"You're a bigger snail shucker than your brother is," blasted Rodriqa as she stepped in between Jordana and McCrayden. "You need to learn to mind your own business and keep your big mouth shut, *sistah*." Rodriqa's head swiveled as she glowered at McCrayden, and the beads in her hair bounced against her neck and shoulders.

Jon lowered his binoculars, aghast at the twist the conversation had taken. McCrayden squinted her eyes at Rodriqa and leaned against Jon. "Let's find a new place to watch the race. There's too much trash nearby. It's stinking up the place." McCrayden, Jon and Pam turned and walked away. Rodriqa fumed with her fists clenched tightly, glaring at their backs. Buzz watched the veins in her neck pulsate.

"It's ok, Rodriqa," Jordana said, downplaying McCrayden's acrid remarks. She pulled Rodriqa by the arm, and they took several steps into the crowd.

Buzz took a couple of steps back, distracted by his own thoughts. "I'm gonna go check on Magnos."

# The Paddling Pumpkin Raft Race, Part 2

The yammering din of the crowd gathering along the mouth of Wontawanna Creek echoed upstream and around the forested bend that hid the competitors. A dull brown pier, lined with planks splintering around rusting nails and bolts, stretched several hundred yards across the slow-moving waters. Next to the pier, a wide and cracked concrete boat landing dove below the creek's surface at the bank, like a drowning driveway.

Gaetan and the other football players drug their makeshift Viking long boat through the water from the landing up to the edge of the pier as Leon, driving Gaetan's GTO, pulled the trailer out of the creek and up to a weed-infested gravel lot a few hundred feet from up the bank. Ty Rontimer and Hank O'Dant tied the mooring lines to a tiny bollard on the pier while Gaetan pulled himself into the thirty-foot canoe. He lifted a cooler with both hands from the middle of the boat and stepped over a tarp with a child-sized lump wriggling underneath it. Balancing himself toward the aft of the canoe, Gaetan jumped out onto the pier with cooler in hand and plopped himself down on the edge with his feet dangling in the water.

Gaetan pulled off his water-soaked T-shirt and snapped open the lid to the cooler. Pushing around the ice on top, he gently lifted a pumpkin carved into the shape of a football helmet out from the bottom and slid it slowly onto his head. He dug through the ice and pulled out two more pumpkin shells carved into football shoulder pads, which were woven with dangling wet shoelaces, and rested them cautiously on the tops of his shoulders.

"I think you're chances are 2 in 3," said a light, cheerful voice from behind him.

Gaetan slowly turned his torso stiffly to the side and glanced up. Out of the corner of his eyes, Fayla Strumgarten stood behind him, grinning sweetly, her light blonde hair dancing in the breeze around her long neck.

Gaetan chuckled and faced forward to a position of comfort. "For what?"

"That you'll win the race," said Fayla as she sat cross-legged behind him. She brushed the dirt and a few dead leaves off his back and knotted up the top lace of his pumpkin shoulder pads. "Of course, you have some grueling competition."

"Like who?" Gaetan asked, tying the together the front section of his shoulder pads.

Fayla tied another knot. "Hamilton Miller's dad for one. And all his buddies from Mount Camelot. They've been training for six months."

Gaetan snorted. "They're all old."

"But they used to be top athletes themselves," returned Fayla.

"Yeah," countered Gaetan. "A century ago."

Fayla knotted the bottom of his pads. "And then there's the Torquetum Club."

Gaetan guffawed, his head rocking backwards. "You're not serious. Look at us," bragged Gaetan as he lifted his hand toward the canoe. "We're all the toughest guys in the county. No one stands a chance."

Fayla knotted the last lace and patted his back gingerly. She raised herself up on his pumpkin-shrouded shoulders and leaned over with her head next to his. "Tough isn't enough in this game," she whispered in his ear. "But cunning is stunning." She kissed him lightly on the cheek and walked up the pier.

Gaetan tried to look at her, but the confinement of his outfit forbade him from moving too quickly without breaking it. He glimpsed toward the bank as Leon waddled toward him, carrying another cooler.

Gaetan cocked his head to side, feigning oversight of the other football players, who were securing the totems to the canoe and testing out the oars. Out of the corner of his eye, Gaetan carefully watched as Maximillian Miller and his group from the Mount Camelot Home Owner's Association launched their long yellow raft, which was lashed flush on either side with Ivy League rowboats. Maximillan Miller stood on shore in lycra bicycle shorts and a matching tank top, stretching every limb of his tall, thin frame with his oar trapped under his feet. Each muscle group Mr. Miller pulled and flexed popped taut under his skin like a sinewy strap. To Gaetan, he kinda looked like a cheetah preparing to track down his evening meal. Truly, the only giveaway to Mr. Miller's advancing age was the small ring of thinning gray hair looping his temples below his shiny baldness. Several other gentlemen in their mid-forties joined Mr. Miller and plied and pressed their own bodies through a series of warm-ups. For a split second, Gaetan questioned his chances of winning.

Leon Hagwell dropped a cooler on the pier next to Gaetan.

"Careful!" scolded Gaetan.

"Sorry, boss," said Leon. "It's heavy."

Gaetan pushed himself to his feet and slipped off his gym shorts, revealing his damp, plaid boxer shorts. Gaetan flipped open the lid and pulled out of the tumbling pieces of ice a kilt of pumpkin shards neatly strung together with plastic twist-ties. He wrapped the kilt around his waist and fastened it together.

"I'm gonna go check out the competition," said Gaetan as he checked out his outfit. "Get everyone ready to go. We're only accepting a 'W' on this one. And make sure the secret weapon stays hidden."

"Yep. You got it, man," agreed Leon, turning to the canoe and shaking the aft totem for snugness.

Gaetan strutted down the pier, like a gourded gladiator ready for battle. The chilled pumpkin shells warmed in the afternoon sun, and he could feel the sticky, stringy lining of his suit melt and mush against his skin. He kept his head forward, peeking at the rafts to his right along the pier as he evaluated the contending entries.

The Grandfather Rock High School cheerleaders had borrowed a *blob* from a local summer camp as their raft. The *blob* was a ridiculously large and flimsy cylinder of polyvinyl chloride that summertime campers would jump onto, catapulting another kid, like a piece of newborn popcorn, into a lake. It reminded Gaetan of a giant, inflatable pillowcase. He gave a quick raise of his fingers to one of the cheerleaders, who was nervously tying her oversized life vest to loops in her jean shorts.

Further down the pier, Gaetan wasn't sure if the craft next to the *blob* was a raft at all. A ring of overturned shopping carts with sawed-off under car-riages, each filled with multiple, inflated industrial strength garbage bags, pro-viding buoyancy, were bound together with bungee cords. The upside-down carts surrounded a hull of plywood scraps, water-sealed with duct tape. Steadying himself precariously in the middle of the raft, Teton Bailston, who wore sunglasses, a tiny pirate hat made of pumpkin shards and a leather over-coat with bits of pumpkin guts glued to it, ordered his fellow Mafisito broth-ers around in his best buccaneer impression as he pulled a long pair of orange kitchen gloves up to this elbows. The words *Ghetto Gondola* were scrawled in wire through the cage of the shopping carts.

Gaetan sneered at them as he wondered if their boat would make it around the first bend.

Like a step pyramid, the next raft rose up out of the water from a series of stacked inflatable tubes, which narrowed with each level. Gaetan recognized several Chimney Falls High School football players clambering around inside the raft, who were following orders from their Pumpking who sat at the very top. Gaetan knew him well, since he had been a rival quarterback for the past two years. The Chimney Falls Pumpking was dressed in a toga, composed of pumpkin guts, to look like the Roman god Neptune, complete with pumpkin pulp and seed beard and trident.

"Hey…ey…ey…ey, Taylor. You're…re…re…re going down!" shouted the Chimney Falls quarterback.

"In your dreams, Pu…Pu…Pu…Poisedon!" heckled Gaetan at the quar-terback and his speech impediment. Gaetan could hear Teton and several other Mafisito members laughing at his jab as he walked away proudly.

Something odious caught Gaetan's eye. He stormed past the Lake Julian Marching band's pontoon boat, and Stew Parsons and Snakes McWhorter, who were setting up camouflage netting in the Junior Rifle Association jon boat. Glaring at pier's end, Gaetan's heart pounded furiously at the potential risk to his championship.

A hexagonal yellow raft bobbed in the slowly drifting creek. At each apex of the raft, a jointed wooden arm sprouted from within the raft, bent twice, straightened out and then dove down, with hinges and pulleys joining each section. The ends of the wooden arms plunged into the water and two lines of ropes ran counter to each other along the shaft and joints of the arms. The top joints of the six arms were connected above the raft by a series of curved bamboo, grooved tubes with rope running in them and wound tight in a star-like pattern by gears to a heavy metal spring, suspended and spinning over the middle of the raft. To Gaetan, the mechanical monster of a raft looked like a massive wooden water spider or a floating scrambler ride from an amusement park.

Adorned in shards of pumpkin shells linked together with metal notebook rings, like a silvery orange shirt of chainmail, Bates Hindenberg squatted unsteadily in a raised swivel office chair in the middle of the raft, adjusting the gears fastened to the spring above him. His helmet was a gruesomely carved pumpkin with a jagged open mouth and triangular eyes, through which his own eyes could be seen.

Gaetan marched toward the end of the pier, examining the raft more closely with every step.

Behind each wooden arm, modified bicycles rested upright within the boat, with the handlebars attached to the wooden arms and the ropes running down around the pedals. Lake Julian High students sat on each of the bicycles, preoccupied with calibrating the bikes' gears and pulling levers next to them, which shifted the bicycles side to side within the raft. Each of the students wore a white T-shirt with a single number from '1' to '6' crudely painted on the front. Gaetan recognized several of the kids as Wi-chromes from the Torquetum Club.

Gaetan bent down at the edge of the pier and heaved his large hands against the side of the hexagonal raft. The raft spun wildly in circles, and the Wi-Chromes jerked to secure their balance.

Bates plopped himself in his swivel chair and pulled the lever to his left so he's chair spun the opposite direction. Bates faced Gaetan, pumpkin shell to pumpkin shell.

"Come to ask for mercy?" challenged Bates in a haughty, video-game pantomimed tone.

"No, but you probably should," countered Gaetan, as he pushed the raft again.

"POSITIONS!" shouted Bates. "PEDAL CLOCKWISE!" The other six students climbed onto their bikes and pedaled swiftly. They turned their bicycle handles to the right, and in a fluid synchronized motion, the six spidery wooden arms shifted under the command of the handles, slanting sideways in the creek.

Gaetan took a step back, slightly unnerved. Bubbles rose from the water around the sides of the raft in the water, and the raft slowly stopped spinning, as if halted by an unseen force. The kids stopped pedaling and turned to look at Gaetan's squeamish expression.

"Are you afraid?" bantered Bates.

"Afraid of what?" growled Gaetan. "A bunch of geeks in an overgrown merry go round."

"You will behold the power of the *Ben-Zing*, and you will tremble!"

"The power of *what*?" exclaimed Gaetan.

"*Ben-zing*," said Jafar Gungandeep from atop a bicycle in the raft in front of Gaetan. Jafar's dark eyes peered curiously at Gaetan underneath disheveled swatches of wavy black hair, and he had the number '3' painted on his shirt. "Our boat's a hexagon with a ring on top of it, like a benzene molecule. And it goes really fast, so we call it *Ben-zing*."

Gaetan's brain stalled out. He had no idea how to respond. He raised his hands and shook his head.

"Gaetan!" shouted a voice from behind him. Gaetan turned around, and the corner of his lip curled. Hamilton's curly toddler locks of dark blonde hair unfurled in the breeze. Lifting his sunglasses to the top of his head, he smiled with his rack of gleaming white teeth and waved happily at Gaetan. Gaetan muttered several unmentionables under his breath and walked slowly up the pier.

Hamilton patted Gaetan on his pumpkin shoulder pad. "Ready to win the day?"

"Yeppers," grunted Gaetan annoyed at Hamitlon's overly joyous demeanor.

"Where's my girl?" Hamilton's blinding bite widened across his cheeks.

"I don't know. Where did you put her?" Gaetan walked swiftly past Hamilton up the pier.

"I thought we had a deal?" asked Hamilton with a worried expression as he chased Gaetan.

"No, you offered me information and expected something in return. I don't remember making a deal." Gaetan quickened his pace with his face set forward.

Hamilton jumped in front of Gaetan with his hand out. Gaetan stopped abruptly and glowered at Hamilton. "I'm a Rowdy. You're a Joxster," said Hamilton as his smile returned. "We help each other out."

Gaetan turned his head to the side. "I heard what you tried to do."

Hamilton popped his neck, and his grin faded. "And I know what your freakish brother and his little friends have been up to."

"Yeah, you've told me, and now I know." Gaetan looked back at Hamilton and crumpled his brow tightly. "Move. Or I'll move you."

"Ready for second place," came a voice from off the pier. Gaetan and Hamilton turned toward the water. The Mount Camelot raft-row boat combo drifted up to the pier with Maximillian Miller perched with a foot on the edge of the raft's bow.

"Hardly," scoffed Gaetan. "I don't know why anyone else is bothering to try to win the raft race. We've got this."

Mr. Miller adroitly hopped onto the pier and faced Hamilton and Gaetan, who both toddled backwards slightly from the intrusion. "You may be the best quarterback in western North Carolina," said Mr. Miller, "but that doesn't make you the best athlete."

"I'll remember that when you come in second place," rebutted Gaetan.

"Where are my manners," spoke Mr. Miller as he patted his son's shoulder and squeezed it firmly. "Was I interrupting something?"

Hamilton smiled broadly. "Gaetan and I were in the middle of an exchange, but I always welcome input from someone as experienced and insightful as you, Dad."

Mr. Miller rolled his head backwards and laughed loudly with pride. "What kind of exchange?"

Hamilton's smile quickly shrunk into a sneer. "I gave Gaetan a gift, hoping for a kindness in return. Unfortunately, the favor has turned cold."

Gaetan rolled his eyes. "This was all in your head, Hamilton. We never agreed on anything."

"You understood what my expectations were."

Gaetan smirked. "You should never assume anything. It's bad for your complexion."

"Now, now, boys." Mr. Miller clamped down on Gaetan's pumpkin shoulder pad and squeezed it. Gaetan could feel it crack under the pressure of Mr. Miller's bony fingers. "Certainly two gentleman like yourselves can work all this out amicably…and fairly."

"Define gentleman," jabbed Gaetan.

Hamilton rolled out of Mr. Miller's grasp and stormed up the pier.

Mr. Miller smiled gently and stepped nose to nose with Gaetan.

"Be a good lad, and do the right thing."

Gaetan furrowed his brow. "I'll do…what I want." Gaetan pushed Mr. Miller's hand off his shoulder and marched up the pier.

Mr. Miller turned around and shouted after Gaetan. "I hate to embarrass you. Seems like your popularity might be the only thing keeping you sane, these days. Certainly your family isn't. From what Hamilton has told me, another one of your kin has gone off the deep end?"

The words pierced Gaetan like envenomed spears. *My brother is fair game and deserves whatever he gets*, thought Gaetan to himself. *But my mother is not.*

"Everything's ready, boss," announced Leon as Gaetan approached their Viking longboat. Mr. McElory's introductions were reverberating off the water and trees, like a poorly produced song.

Gaetan shoved Leon out of the way and launched himself off the pier and into the canoe. He straddled the tarp and tore down its corner. Aubrey squirmed underneath.

Aubrey stopped moving instantly as the light flooded his eyes, and the bleary sight of Gaetan's sneering face focused into view.

Gaetan leaned down next to Aubrey and whispered into his ear. "This isn't just for my car, or for crashing the party, or even for being the biggest dork on the planet." Aubrey's eyes widened as he listened to Gaetan. "It's for mom. Ready to go for a ride?"

## The Paddling Pumpkin Raft Race, Part 3

Buzz scanned the crowd for Magnos. Mr. Lequoia stood guard behind the closed cattle gate, staring blankly at the festivities along the sore. Buzz followed the narrow creek bank behind the gate and examined the faces of the people roaming around it, but he couldn't see Magnos.

Buzz knew something was wrong. He walked behind the main section of spectators and headed for the gate, slowly investigating each person more carefully.

Behind the mass of onlookers swarming in front of the concession stands and Paddling Pumpkin merchandise vendors, Buzz glimpsed the shaggy blonde hair he was looking for. He trotted around the lines of customers to take a better look.

Magnos stood in the distance, separated from the crowd. His pale face was beaded with sweat, and he stood rigidly, staring blankly at a woman in front of him, who was holding his hand. Her tall, shapely frame and head were wrapped in a sheer sarong of subtle pastels. Buzz couldn't see her face, but her head moved as if she was speaking to Magnos.

Watching Magnos' face intently, Buzz walked slowly toward them. Magnos' lips curled down and his brow furrowed fretfully.

"Magnos!" shouted Buzz, hoping to grab his attention.

Magnos didn't move. The woman's head turned, and her pale green eyes glared at Buzz. Bright red hair fell from underneath her head covering. She twisted the dial on the stone watch bound to her wrist.

"Oh, no," uttered Buzz with forlorn recognition. "HELP!" he screamed, waving his arms, and he launched into a sprint toward Magnos.

"**Enough delay!**" announced Mr. McElory. "**I hear our competitors are in position. Good luck to them all.**" He lifted his hand skyward, holding a miniature plastic gun. "**Let the Paddling Pumpkin Raft Race begin!**" A startling pop rang through the valley, and a tiny, red comet arced through the air overhead. The crowd cheered and raised their binoculars to watch for the first rafts.

Ms. Thistlewood dropped Magnos' hand and disappeared into a group of folks rushing toward the bank. Buzz quickly lost sight of her.

Buzz ran up to Magnos and shook him by the shoulders. His skin was cold, and chill bumps covered his arms and legs. Magnos shivered uncontrollably, while his clothes dripped wet from sweat as if he was both freezing and burning up at the same time.

"Is...she...gone?" shuddered Magnos. His glazed eyes were distantly lost and twitched from corner to corner. Spittle oozed around his chin from his open mouth, while his teeth chattered violently.

"What did she do to you?" asked Buzz.

Unable to put his thoughts into words, Magnos rubbed his face vigorously with his hands, straining against the torment of her lasting touch.

"We've got to find her!" urged Buzz. "This has to stop!"

"I need to rest," begged Magnos as he kneeled to the ground.

"Get up!" entreated Buzz as he pulled up on Magnos' oversized arm. "It's time to make her pay for what she's doing. We have to catch her!"

"You go ahead," whispered Magnos, folding his legs under himself. He lowered his head as his chest heaved, his lungs happily exchanging poison for air.

"I can't leave you!"

"I'll be okay."

Buzz squatted down and met Magnos eye to eye. "It's now or never." Buzz turned and wrapped Magnos' arm over his neck. Wobbling to a standing position, Buzz forced the half-limp Magnos to his feet. "Look for the red hair."


Jordana and Rodriqa pushed through the tightly knit gangs of friends and family, scouring the bank for a spot they could occupy. Most people completely ignored them, their binoculars and their attention fully attuned to the distant bend in the creek. Jordana was somewhat grateful for being mostly invisible, and Rodriqa appreciated the restored quiet since the start of the race.

"I wonder when we'll see Aubrey," murmured Jordana.

"Probably not till the end of the race without binoculars," replied Rodriqa.

Rodriqa squirmed up next to a teacher she recognized from Lake Julian High. "Excuse me, ma'am. Can you tell me what's happening?"

"No one's rounded the bend yet," the woman replied. Her lips moved, but the binoculars remained fixed to her face.

Rodriqa looked around for someone else who might be more helpful. She spotted a familiar hat, royal blue with a white, capital 'K' above the bill, and spindles of silver, twirling hair peeking out from underneath. She sidled up next to the elderly gentleman.

"Mr. Jennings?" asked Rodriqa. "Do you remember me?"

Ray Gene pulled the binoculars off his eyes and looked down at her. His face brightened joyfully. "Bless my soul," he remarked, his voice full of surprise. "I haven't seen you in a spruce's age." He rested his hand on her shoulder as he marveled at her. "You're all grown up! Time passes too quickly for my liking any more. How have you been?"

Rodriqa's smile grew, and her face flushed slightly. "Good," she replied quickly, moving directly to the point. "Mr. Jennings, I'm sorry to bother you, but my friend Aubrey might be in the race, and I'd really like to look for him. Is there any way I could share your binoculars?"

"Aubrey Taylor?" said Mr. Jennings thoughtfully. "That's exciting! I saw Aubrey the other day. Seemed like he had a lot on his mind. I always liked that boy, although I think he's a bit misunderstood. I'm glad things are looking up for him." Rodriqa nodded exuberantly with each sentence, anxious for him to answer her question.

"I have an idea," he continued. "I'm an old man, and my eyesight's not what it used to be. Even with these binoculars, I really can't see much. If I let you use my binoculars, will you give me a play-by-play of the race?"

"Deal," said Rodriqa happily.


Dragging Magnos around had Buzz as out of breath as Magnos was. Buzz hunted from group to gaggle, looking for telltale signs of Ms. Thistlewood with no success.

Suddenly, a hundred feet in front of him through a scattering of lawn chairs and balloons, Buzz noticed a woman standing in the midst of half a dozen children who were laughing and skipping around her. She face away from him, but was turning her head from side to side, staring intently at the children. She had no binoculars, and she was wrapped from head to toe in a multi-colored sarong. The colors of her covering were darker than he remembered. *A trick of the late afternoon sun, no doubt*, Buzz thought to himself.

Buzz lowered Magnos to the ground. "Wait here," Buzz told him. Magnos gratefully dropped to his rear and rested.

Buzz slowly approached the woman from behind, examining her moves and interactions with the children. *So this is how she lures her victims*, Buzz surmised. The breeze floated along the creek, and Buzz saw several red wisps of hair unfurl from her underneath her head covering. He crept up behind, carefully avoiding the children.

Buzz grappled the woman about the waist and clenched his forearms together, sealing her tightly against his chest.

"Gotcha!" he announced triumphantly.


**"And here comes the first raft around the bend,"** announced Mr. McElory. **"No wait...make that...rafts!"**


"POLICE! I NEED THE POLICE!" Buzz screamed, but no one could hear him over the din of the people's cheers and the reverberation of the loud-speakers.

The woman twisted in Buzz's arms and pulled at his hands, trying to wrench herself free. Buzz clamped down harder, sucking air into his chest to tighten his grip. The children around them pointed and laughed, amused at the bizarre tussle between the chunky teenager and the tall, thin woman.

The woman turned her shoulders and smacked Buzz on top of his head several times with the palm of her hand. "Let me go!" she insisted in a thick Asian accent.

Buzz eased his grip slightly and looked up. Her head covering had fallen onto her shoulders, and suddenly Buzz realized he had a captured a dark-skinned, dark-eyed, dark-haired woman with auburn highlights.

Buzz released her and stepped backwards. "I'm sorry, ma'am. I thought you were someone else."

"Rude boy! You must be punished!" the woman shouted with a turbulent 'R'. She grabbed a whiffle bat from one of the children and beat Buzz about the head and shoulders. Buzz guarded his face with his hands and begged loudly for forgiveness.

Magnos watched the spectacle from behind and couldn't help but grin, despite his exhaustion.

"Why can't you all just leave well enough alone?" uttered a crotchety voice from behind Magnos.

Magnos turned around, and an elderly woman dressed in a tattered floral dress was picking at her teeth. Her curly white hair looped wildly about her face, and she smelled as if she hadn't bathed for years.

"You all are in a heap of trouble," she continued, flicking bits of food from her gums. "And especially after all you've been through, son, you'd think you'd know better."

"Know better?" asked Magnos.

"Mmmmhmmm," she replied.

"The trouble finds us," Magnos said.

Mrs. Wizenblatt rolled her eyes. "Well, you all are gonna need some help soon. I hope you all know where to find it." She picked up a dirt-speckled tote bag at her feet and lumbered off into the crowd.


"It's a three-way tie for first! The Torquetum Club is running high in the outside current in their *Ben-Zing* raft. In the middle, the Mount Camelot Home Owner's Association are holding fast, and running along the inner edge, here comes the *Ghetto Gondola*!"


"What's happening?" asked Jordana anxiously. Mr. Jennings nodded excitedly, waiting for Rodriqa's report.

Casting his gaze up the creek, Bates Hindenberg spun in his chair in the middle of *Ben-Zing*, plotting his strategy for victory. The six other Wi-Chromes pedaled furiously on their makeshift bikes. Instead of being spread out as before. All six cyclists were controlling the long spindly wooden arms, clumped together at the back of *Ben-Zing*. Bates glared at the Mount Camelot rowers, scrutinizing their orderly, methodical strokes.

In the Mount Camelot raft, Maximillian Miller leaned out of the rowboat he sat and shouted at the *Ben-Zing*. "Geeks are like Tootsie Rolls®. They may seem tough at first, but give 'em a couple licks and they melt on ya!" The other Mount Camelot rowers laughed in reply.

Bates swiveled to face the Mount Camelot raft and scowled at Mr. Miller through his pumpkin helmet. "Time to show these antique jocks who the new big man on campus is!" Bates yelled at his fellow Wi-Chromes. "Number '4'! Number '5'! UNLEASH HADES!!"

The Torquetum Club kids with the numbers '4' and '5' on their shirts stopped pedaling and pulled back the levers to the right of their bikes. The heavy, metal spring overhead jerked and moaned, and Number '4' and '5' slid on their bicycles in a semicircle within the raft portside, swinging their wooden arms through the water with them. The two kids returned the levers to the forward position, and the bicycles stopped inside *Ben-Zing* perpendicular to the Mount Camelot rowing team.

Number '4' and Number '5' pulled back on their handlebars and then pushed them outwards. Their attached jointed, wooden arms craned out of the water like arachnidesque tentacles and reached out across the creek, hovering mechanically over the Mount Camelot rowers. Number '4' and '5' resumed pedaling. The rope running up and down each arm moved quickly. Each tentacle of lumber bore a shining, stainless steel propeller at its tip, which glinted in the sunlight as they spun furiously.

Maximillian Miller, seated in the back of the Mount Camelot raft, was visibly startled by the two arms bearing down over his vessel. He pushed his pumpkin shell hat backward on his head and shouted at his fellow rowers. "POWER TWENTY!! CATCH! DRIVE! FINISH! HARD LEFT!"

The men in the rowboats looked up and twitched with fright at the sharp propellers slicing through the air only a few feet above their heads. The rowers leaned forward and dug hard into the water with their paddles. The Mount Camelot raft lurched forward ahead of *Ben-Zing*.

Mr. Miller reached up with his oar and batted at the second propeller as he passed it. Number '5' spun hard on his bike, and the spoon of the wooden oar splintered into toothpicks.

Number '5' cackled ominously at his minor victory, turning the handlebars to and fro and forcing the long arm to dance through the air wildly.

Mr. Miller looked portside and screamed, "Teton! Help us!"

Teton Bailston threw down his oar into the *Ghetto Gondola* and yelled, "Paddle faster and to the right!" at the other four Mafisito gang members. Teton opened a makeshift side door in one of the shopping carts and pulled one of the garbage bags into the middle of the raft.


"MORE SPEED!" commanded Bates as the Mafisito drove closer toward them.

Number '4' pulled her left hand lever and slid to the back of the raft and drove her wooden arm into the water, pedaling her bicycle faster.

"Number '5'! Finish them off!" Bates shouted.

A sinister grin crept across the face of Number '5'. He dropped his head and spun his bike pedals with every ounce of his strength. The wooden arm winched forward, and the propeller dove between the rowboats into the central Mount Camelot raft, shredding it like paper in a blender. The force of the raft turned the rowboats inward, dumping most of the Mount Camelot crew into the creek.

Number '5' lifted his hands into the air triumphantly, banging his head up and down to his own internal heavy metal beat. The other Wi-Chromes cheered.

A slimy, steaming ball of red and green refuse soared across the creek, smacking Number '5' squarely in the face. Mealy bits of putrid meat and souring, oily leaves of brown lettuce dripped off his chin onto his shirt. The stagnant, surly smell singed his nose, and he choked in a breath and held it. He wiped his face off and looked at his hands. Fat, squirming maggots crawled in the grimy waste between his fingers.

Number '5' wretched violently, hurling his lunch over the edge of the raft.

"We'll avenge you, Mr. Miller!" shouted Teton at the defeated Mount Camelot team. Maximillian stepped out of his swamped rowboat into the creek and headed for shore. Teton reached into the garbage bag and flung handfuls of rotten fruit and mounds of weeks-old cat litter at the *Ben-Zing*. Within moments, every member of the Torquetum club in the raft had been pelted with fetid rubbish.


**"Our first defeat of the race! Mount Camelot falls victim to the *Ben-Zing*! Coming around the bend on the Ghetto Gondola's tail is the Lake Julian Marching Belugas in their inflatable pontoon, rafts from Chimney Falls High School, Grandfather Rock High School and the Lake Julian Junior Rifle Association. And trailing the pack is the Lake Julian High School Football Team."**

"Ummm…I see Aubrey," said Rodriqa darkly.

"Where?" asked Jordana frantically. "Is he okay?" She jerked the binoculars away from Rodriqa and scanned the creek for him.

## *The Paddling Pumpkin Raft Race, Part 4*

Aubrey clutched desperately to the totem pole behind him. His fingers and toes were splayed widely against the bow of the football team's massive canoe, gripping it with the last of his strength. Despite the thick braided rope wound around him, binding him to the bow, with every slosh of the canoe down the creek he was afraid he would slip through and be dragged underneath.

Fortunately, until now they had only been drifting through the water. Aubrey heard his brother and the football team razzing each other and cutting up behind him. If Aubrey looked up, he could see all the rafts in the race battling in front of him, but he kept his gaze turned downward as waves of bile rolled in his stomach.

Aubrey heard his brother's voice shouting from behind him "Enjoying the view, little brother?" Roaring laughter echoed along the creek from within the boat.

"Okay," hollered Gaetan. "Time to expose the losers." He sat down on a ledge high in the stern of the boat and spouted orders. "Oars in the water! Release the destroyer! Full steam ahead! Chimney Falls and Grandfather Rock first!"

Hank O'Dant climbed to the front of the boat and slid the box at the bottom of the bow off into the creek. Aubrey looked below and witnessed a dull, metallic, screw-shaped harpoon emerge, jutting six feet forward into the water. The canoe accelerated swiftly. Aubrey closed his eyes and hoped it would be over soon.

"Hamilton wasn't joking about using one of us as a living figurehead," said Rodriqa. She slowly lifted the binoculars from Jordana and looked for herself.

"How could anyone be that mean?" exclaimed Jordana.

"You don't know Gaetan," replied Rodriqa. "He totally resents Aubrey's existence."

"Enough to lash him to the front of a canoe?" Jordana asked.

Rodriqa tilted her head from side to side, unsure how best to answer.

"Is Aubrey okay?" Jordana demanded.

"He doesn't look hurt," answered Rodriqa. "Aubrey should make it through safely. There's no reason for the other teams to target him. They're after the Pumpkings."

"Unless they use him for a shield," interjected Mr. Jennings.

Rodriqa and Jordana looked at each other. Jordana bit her lip.

"Hey, boss!" hollered Leon back toward Gaetan as he stroked. "The *blob* should be easy pickings." The Grandfather Rock cheerleaders clung to the side of the *blob* with their oars barely reaching the water.

"Naaaawww," groaned Gaetan. "It's too easy a kill...unless...." He looked across the creek and examined the Chimney Falls pyramid raft. "Pull up next to the *blob*," ordered Gaetan. "I've got an idea."

"Of course it's your fault! Aubrey will never ignore it!"

The voice behind Rodriqa caught her ear, and she angled her head slightly to the side so she could better hear the conversation, while still reporting the events of the race to Jordana and Mr. Jennings as she looked through the binoculars.

"No, Hovis! That's an even worse idea. He needs to be removed from the picture. He's only a liability now."

The mention of both Aubrey and Hovis' name by the same person in consecutive sentences was too much to be coincidence in Rodriqa's mind. She handed the binoculars to Jordana, who eagerly looked through them. Rodriqa focused her attention on the source of the voice behind her, while staring at the creek.

"No! That is no longer any of our concern...when will you realize your need for revenge has been your undoing from the start?"

Rodriqa turned her head and pretended to look through the crowd, so she could inconspicuously view the woman speaking in partial conversation.

"That will draw too much attention."

In her peripheral vision, Rodriqa saw a tall, curvaceous woman draped in a lightly colored chiffon tunic, with matching culottes and a sheer scarf, which hung loosely about her face, obscuring her mouth. Her creamy, porcelain skin was without blemish, and her full, red hair cascaded over her pale green eyes. She looked familiar. Her beauty was almost supernatural, and particularly out of place for Lake Julian. Yet her behavior was petulantly childlike. Rodriqa was perplexed by the unduly important conversation she seemed to be sharing with someone, yet she stood all by herself.

"What?! Where?!"

Rodriqa noticed that the lines of anger on her face lightened into simple joy.

"Time to eliminate our problem."

Rodriqa turned nonchalantly to Jordana, interrupting her commentary on the race. "Would you know Ms. Thistlewood if you saw her?" she asked.

Jordana pulled her eyes away from the binoculars and looked at Rodriqa, confused. "No," she replied. "Why?"

"Because I think she is standing behind us."

Jordana jerked her torso around and scrutinized the people behind them. Her eyes were drawn to the woman hiding within her pastel sarong. The woman snapped her head and glared directly at Jordana, her eyes squinting menacingly at her.

"I have an idea," scowled the woman as she pulled her scarf tightly around her face. She turned and disappeared into the crowd.

"Oh, no," said Jordana under her breath. "Where are Buzz and Magnos?" Rodriqa's eyes widened.

The football team's canoe torpedoed through the water. The players rowed with exacting precision like a mechanized army. They swiftly saddled up next to the *blob*. Some of the cheerleaders waved flirtingly, others made rude hand gestures as the canoe easily careened in the front of their massive plastic barge.

"What's the word, boss?" asked Leon over his shoulder.

"Starboard, full reverse! Port, full forward!" ordered Gaetan, bracing himself against the inside hull.

The canoe spun ninety degrees counterclockwise on the creek's surface in only a second, shooting sprays of water onto the blob.

"NOW! ALL FORWARD!" yelled Gaetan, standing up and waving both arms manically.

The *blob* convulsed down its entire length as the harpoon pierced the skin of its bow. A bubbling plume spewed from its shredding fuselage like a geyser, as the pressure from the weight of the craft squeezed its inflated air into the creek. Cheerleaders popped and bounced from the leaking raft, landing face and rear down in the rapids.

"Don't stop! Keep going!" commanded Gaetan. The force of the canoe strung the remnants of the dying *blob* transversely across the creek bed. The football players rowed harder as they strained against the growing load of weight.

The harpoon threaded through the *blob* while it deflated and poked out the opposite side, and the canoe rammed into the bottom tubes of the Chimney Falls' raft.

The rowers inside the pyramid structure floundered, and several rowers splashed into the creek within the raft. The towering rafts swayed above, and their Pumpking aloft teetered from side to side. The Chimney Falls craft crumpled under the sideward push from the football team, hurling their Pumpking onto the blob. His trident punctured the blob in the middle, and more air swooshed upwards like a whale's blowhole.

**"From out of nowhere, the Lake Julian Football Team is back in the race with an amazing double bump, skewering both the Grandfather Rock and Chimney Fall teams!  And now there's a traffic jam!"**

Wrinkled, plastic flotsam from the two injured boats floated down the creek bed.  And the carnage blocked the rafts from behind from moving forward.

Ty Rontimer, Hank O'Dant and Treywick Compton jumped into the creek and ripped the deflating shreds of the blob off the end of their harpoon.  The two victimized teams limped out of their boats into the shallow creek, moaning and cursing at their decisive loss.  Aubrey looked down at them and whimpered, "Sorry about that," hoping not to be the object of their derision in his exposed position.

Tittering clicks tapped at the top of the bow's totem.  Aubrey craned his neck upwards.  A dark, gleaming eye peered down at him from above the totem's head.  Aubrey's heart pounded fearfully.  The razor-beaked raven glared oppressively at him with its wings stretched aloft and claws dug deeply into the carved wood.

The raven jabbed at his head, and Aubrey barely dodged the sharp point of his beak.  He squirmed within the rope, trying to inch his way down the totem.  The raven flapped its wings and hopped down, gripping the hefty, braided rope.  Aubrey could feel the end of its talons pierce the spaces between the rope and graze the skin of his chest.  Aubrey flailed wildly but the raven clung more tightly, thrashing its wings for balance.  The raven thrust its beak forcefully toward Aubrey.  He screamed in terror as the raven pecked over and over again.  The harder Aubrey fought, the more fervently the raven dove its beak down at him.  Suddenly Aubrey realized he wasn't feeling any pain, and there was no bleeding.  The top ring of rope across his chest had split, its frayed ends unwinding.  The raven was trying to free him.

"Get a move on! We're losing ground!" yelled Gaetan, his mouth twitching with competitive fervor.  The three football players climbed frantically back in the boat, and the team soared swiftly through the water.


Ms. Thistlewood stepped gingerly between the clusters of onlookers who were intently watching the race.

"Perfect," she said, as she stopped behind McCrayden, Pam and Jon.  She lifted her arm from beneath her sarong and slid her bulky stone watch down to her wrist.  She turned the prong of the sundial, and a hiss sighed from underneath the stone.

"Bring me the seer."

The air around her arm darkened slightly, like a shadow passing slowly next to her, but there was nothing to block the light. The twirling dimness snaked down her hand and over McCrayden's shoulder, slowly engulfing Prissy as she rolled in McCrayden's arms.

Prissy froze. Her eyes fluttered and her whiskers twitched. The corners of her mouth peeled backwards in a grimaced mixture of agony and confusion, and she raked her front paws along her snout. All four limbs stiffened and her long, angora hairs stood straight on end.

McCrayden squeezed the cat tightly, trying to calm her down. "I think Prissy has a hairball."

Prissy vaulted out of her arms and onto Jon's head, her back arched high with her tail shooting straight up.

Jon screamed in frantic fits with his hands on the sides of his face, too fearful to push the cat off. McCrayden and Pam backed away. Jon fell to his knees.

Prissy leapt five feet skyward and landed on a bald man standing next to them. The man yelped and ducked. Prissy hopped into a bushel of curly locks on the head of the bald man's wife. The woman brushed at the sides of her hair and squealed, "Oh my…get it off me!"

Prissy erupted into a parabolic gallop, leaping from one head to another through the crowd upstream. Bobby pins and wigs spun through the air, and hands and shoulders flailed in protest amid screeches and squalls as Prissy's pace accelerated from crown to crown.

The commotion spread quickly upwind, and the throngs slowly scattered away from the flying, fuzzy fur ball springing over the crowd. Prissy dropped to the creek bank and exploded into a dauntless dash through the wet grass and slippery mud. At the fence she jumped into the water, bounding from rock to rock toward the rafters.


"Get your propellers in the water!" yelled Bates.

"I'm trying," replied Number '4', who was using a screwdriver to scrape drying cheese and eggshells from the ball bearings connecting her handles to the long, wooden arm. Her screwdriver broke off at the hilt, wedging the metal tip in the bearing of the joint. The wooden arm of Number '4' was frozen in mid-air.

Number '4' looked at Number '5'. "Push the arm!"

"What?" asked Number '5'.

Number '4' climbed on her bicycle and pointed at her wooden arm. "Push my arm over and shove the screwdriver out!"

Number '5' took a deep breath and flung another glop of pungent waste off his handlebars.

Suddenly, a cream and gray comet of fur exploded out of the creek and grappled the end of Number '4's frozen wooden arm. Prissy was now the size of a bobcat and completely soaked, her twirling hair spiking out like a sea urchin. Her dagger-like claws splintered the wood she clung to, as she slowly pulled herself upwards.

Number '5' grappled his handlebars and swung the wooden arm wide through the air. He dropped his head and pedaled with all his strength.

Prissy shook her torso, showering the air with droplets of water. The spinning propeller dove at Prissy. Prissy squalled and jumped onto the bamboo ring on top of *Ben-Zing*. She swatted the wooden arm of Number '5'. It snapped with a crack at its second joint and dangled in the water, flailing in the creek bed, completely disabled.

Two heads of rotting cabbage whizzed past Bates' head, who was preoccupied with the antics of their feline stowaway. "Number '6'," ordered Bates, "Starboard! Give it all you got! Number '5', leave the cat alone. Everyone else, pedal harder!"


Jordana handed the binoculars back to Mr. Jennings and thanked him.

"But the race isn't over," said Mr. Jennings. There was no reply. Rodriqa and Jordana had slipped around behind him and had already disappeared into the crowd, sifting through faces for anyone familiar.

Jordana spotted Buzz between blankets and picnic baskets, stumbling to support Magnos on his shoulder. Buzz waddled low to ground to avoid the wrath of gazers whose binocular line of sight he might obscure. Jordana hollered over the crowd for Rodriqa and ran up to Magnos and Buzz.

Jordana thought it was an odd sight. Buzz's face was red and swollen, and although Magnos looked pale and tired, he had a smile that stretched from sideburn to sideburn.

Rodriqa rushed up behind them. "Are you okay?"

"Yeah," replied Magnos and Buzz simultaneously. They looked at each other precariously. Buzz unloaded Magnos on to the grass, where he rolled onto his back and exhaled deeply.

"What happened to you two?" demanded Jordana.

"No time," huffed out Buzz. "Ms. Thistlewood is here."

"I knew it," exclaimed Rodriqa. "We saw her a few just a few moments ago, I think." She searched Jordana's eyes for acknowledgment. "That's why we started looking for you."

Buzz looked at her, puzzled. "How did you know it was her?"

"I think I overheard her talking to Hovis about Aubrey," replied Jordana.

"You saw Hovis," asked Buzz with heightened surprise.

Jordana shook her head, looking at Rodriqa warily.

"How did you all find her?" asked Rodriqa.

Buzz looked at Magnos as if he was about to tell a nasty secret. "I saw Magnos in front of her behind the crowds."

"You talked to her?" asked Jordana.

Magnos shook his head and strained to put images to words. "I don't remember what really happened. I was talking to Principal Lequoia and then…all of a sudden…I blanked out."

"When I found him, he looked like he was in some sort of trance," added Buzz.

"How's Aubrey?" interrupted Magnos.

"Not good," replied Rodriqa soberly. "He's tied to the front of the football team's canoe as their 'living figurehead'. I'm afraid he's gonna get hurt. The competition is intense this year."

"I figured as much from all the cheering from the spectators," said Buzz.

The corners of Jordana's mouth rumpled as her lips tightened when she thought about Aubrey. She lowered herself onto her knees next to Magnos and leaned over him. "How do you feel?"

"Like I did when I was kidnapped," he replied quietly.

"What did she do to you?" Jordana asked Magnos, glancing at Buzz for input.

"Better still, what has she done to this whole town," asked Rodriqa sternly. "All this craziness *can't* be coincidence!"

Slow hand-clapping snapped rhythmically from behind them. The four kids turned their heads to the side. Ms. Thistlewood stood over them with an unearthly grin of simmering satisfaction.

**"Three boats are in the lead, racing neck and neck into the final quarter-mile of the race. Pyramid rock is their only remaining obstacle to victory!"**

Prissy prowled along the top portions of the *Ben-Zing*, pacing slowly as the raft advanced forward. Bates kept a close eye on her, but his mind was focused on winning the race.

The Lake Julian High Football team rowed easily past the Marching Band's float and plowed forward. Gaetan plunged his oar into the water from his seat at the stern and spun the canoe's aft portside. He knew exactly what his next target would be.

Bates watched carefully as the Lake Julian Football Team's Viking longboat approached.

"Number '3'," bellowed Bates in a deranged, giddy tone. "Tear me up some Joxster! Show the football team that the Wi-chromes are the new kings in town. Everyone else, pedal like the wind!"

Jafar Gungandeep pounded the number '3' on his chest and pulled his handlebars back. His propeller shot out of the water, and he wound it wildly through the air in large waving circles, as if taunting the canoe to come near. Prissy grappled the bamboo on top of *Ben-Zing* tightly and watched the action behind her.

Aubrey's shoulders were free, and he was able to shimmy his hands around to his stomach. With the raven's continuous pecking and his own attempts to both dodge the saber-like beak and dagger-like talons, Aubrey had completely forgotten about the race, despite all the commotion around him. A few more minutes of this and Aubrey could slip through the turns of rope and try to get away through the creek.

The raven stopped and turned his head, his coal-black, shimmering eye peering directly at Aubrey. It launched into the air, its wings flapping violently.

A sharp, glimmering propeller, attached to a wooden arm, spun forward at Aubrey's face, its blades fanning him with a sour breeze. It sliced through the air only inches from his nose.

With its wings, shifting in the wind, the raven perched on the wooden tentacle attached to the propeller. The weight of the bird forced the propeller downward, spinning just shy of Aubrey's chin.

"Stop!" screamed Aubrey. Jafar looked around the jointed arm he controlled.

"Aubrey?" he questioned, yelling downstream. "Why are you on the football team's raft?"

"I'm not!" answered Aubrey. "They strapped me to this thing."

Jafar looked at the wooden arm and the raven perched aloft. He looked at his handlebars and then back to Aubrey.

"Aubrey, do you trust me?" hollered Jafar.

Aubrey didn't answer and acted like he didn't hear the question.

"If I freed you, could you get into the boat and disrupt their rowing?" Jafar got to the point.

Aubrey thought for a moment. He didn't know if he really could, or would, hop into the canoe after he was free, but he decided he had at least considered it, and that was good enough. "Sure thing," he replied with a crack in his voice.

Jafar grinned widely and steered the propeller toward Aubrey's chest. The buzzing whirl of the curled blades vibrated in Aubrey's ears as they approached his mid-section.

Prissy leapt from the top of *Ben-Zing* with her limbs slashing through the air and landed on the end of Jafar's wooden arm. The propeller sunk below Aubrey and shaved splinters off the front, bottom section of the Viking longboat's stern totem. The raven unfolded its wings and with a single flap nipped the cat's nose and floated gracefully forward onto the circular bamboo stabilizer at the top of the *Ben-Zing*.

Prissy caterwauled as she clung to the arm, jostling with the raft's sway in the rapids. She yanked herself backwards and glowered at the raven with her dark, red eyes. She cantered up the next section of the arm and howled savagely, throwing herself back onto the ring of bamboo where the raven perched. The raven sauntered sideways with its good eye on the cat. Prissy gripped the wood with her naked paws and exploded into a sprint along the ring after the raven. The raven flapped its wings in a half-flight, half-jog and stayed ahead of Prissy on the bamboo. The cat chased the bird round and round, and the *Ben-Zing* spun under the torque.

Jafar's propeller swung off to the side, and Aubrey sighed with relief.

"Row harder!" ordered Gaetan, and Aubrey watched the harpoon move closer to the inflatable lower section of the Torquetum's raft.

The Wi-chromes flailed within the uncontrollably rotating Ben-Zing. Number '1', '2', and '6' twisted their handlebars sideways, trying to force their propellers to counter the boat's spinning motion. Jafar waved his propeller up and down. Number '4' sat on the first joint of her wooden arm, forcing her propeller into the water and pedaled backwards. Number '5' held tightly to his flailing, fractured wooden arm as it dipped in and out of the creek.

"Congratulations," scoffed Ms. Thistlewood, "on your less than accurate conclusion." Her voice was bitterly raspy, like she was at the zenith of her anger. Rodriqa, Buzz, Magnos, and Jordana shrank at her words, completely caught off guard that she was standing directly behind them.

"Despite what you *think* you know, your bungling attempts to get in my way have failed miserably. I *cannot* be stopped! And in a few moments, Aubrey will pay for his treachery with his life." Ms. Thistlewood looked out over the creek at the race, and the kids' faces followed.

The raven teased Prissy by stalling as she clambered within inches of its tail feathers, and then with a single, full beat of its wings would lift itself to the opposite side of the bamboo. Prissy didn't tire with the countless revolutions she ran, but became more fervently agitated at the raven's game.

A harsh breeze blew from the forest on the opposite bank of the creek. The raven jerked its head upwards, and its taunting disposition shriveled as its instincts sensed a looming danger. It flew off the *Ben-Zing* and perched on the totem above Aubrey. It peered through the trees, searching for the source of the smell. With a foreboding squawk, it announced its displeasure and soared quickly into the sky above the trees and out of sight.

Prissy climbed clumsy down the broken wooden arm of Number '5' and jumped into the hull of the canoe. She prowled through the disarray of football players' legs. Ty Rontimer smacked at Prissy with his oar like a massive fly-swatter, but she adeptly dodged his swing. She hissed at him and landed several swift smacks against the oar's blade. Prissy leapt paw-first into the rapids and swam for shore.

The football player's canoe angled starboard and the harpoon slipped through the broken wooden arm of Number '5', jerking the raft out of its spin and pulling it alongside the canoe. Bates fell out of his seat and landed face first in the bottom of *Ben-Zing*. The football players dug their oars in the water to stabilize their canoe.

"Hey Bates! Watch out!" shouted Leon at the *Ben-Zing*. "You're gonna hit Pyramid Rock!"


"You witch!" exclaimed Buzz as he barreled for Ms. Thistlewood. He grappled her arm and ripped the phylactery from her wrist. He flung it to the ground and stomped on it with both feet. The stone crumbled into tiny chunks under his weight.

Ms. Thistlewood screeched in anguish as she reached down for her broken sundial. "How dare you?!"

"The gig is up!" shouted Rodriqa. She ran at Ms. Thistlewood.

A black haze flickered behind Rodriqa and snaked around her ankles. Rodriqa tripped face forward onto the grass, landing flat on her chest. The darkness flowed next to Buzz and grazed the back of his legs. Buzz slipped backwards, his rear end smacking the ground.

Ms. Thistlewood stepped forward and placed her hands on Buzz's and Rodriqa's foreheads. "Now you shall understand your insignificance." Buzz and Rodriqa went limp.


"Get us off these geeks!" hollered Gaetan. The football players dug deep into the water with their oars, trying to pull away from *Ben-Zing*.

Wooden arms scrambled wildly in the air around Aubrey, the sharp-edged propellers nicking the rope and totem as they swung past him. He looked up, and Pyramid Rock was directly in front of him. The massive boulder in the middle of the rapids was aptly named with its sharply cornered sides adjoined with broad, flat faces of jagged rock fusing together to a point at that top. It was the size of a semi, and it was quickly encompassing Aubrey's entire field of view.

"Everyone, slide port side," ordered Bates. Number '1' and '2' guided their propellers into the water and pedaled in reverse.

Jafar jumped off his bike and snapped his feet down with all his weight on the bike of Number '5'. The bike cracked loose, and Jafar flung the bike and its disabled arm into the creek. *Ben-Zing* broke free from the football players' canoe, and the Wi-chromes cheered loudly.

The weight of the bike and wooden arm of Number '5' drug along the bottom of the creek and strained against the harpoon of the Viking longboat, slowing the canoe to a creep. Aubrey breathed a short sigh as Pyramid Rock's approach halted only a few yards from his face.

"Row harder!" yelled Gaetan. The football players flexed their oars aft with all of their strength. The canoe broke free, rending the harpoon from the front of the canoe. The boat lurched swiftly forward through the water, and Aubrey clamped his eyes tightly closed, preparing for the impact with Pyramid Rock.

A tall, dark brown shaggy figure walked out of the edge of the forest and onto the creek bank opposite the crowds. Its dim, red eyes glinted through the unshorn hair draping down over its face. It bounded into the rapids and stood only a few feet starboard of the canoe, towering over the rowers. The Tsul'kalu howled fiercely across the water with arms outstretched and claws spread bare. The gut-gnarling roar echoed loudly throughout the valley. Every football player in the canoe shouted and cowered to the back of the canoe, clumping together in a huddled, shivering mass. Aubrey winced in fear, twisting his head for a better look at the noise behind him.

With the weight of the football team concentrated at a small spot at the stern, the canoe tipped backwards, its bow lifting out of the water. Aubrey felt as if he was tumbling head over heels as the canoe titled backwards and the full dome of the sky filled his view. The canoe jolted to a stop as the bottom of its bow smashed into Pyramid Rock. Gaetan, Leon and Ty were thrown aft into the creek, and the canoe pivoted against the rock and spun lengthwise through the water.

As the canoe turned and drifted sideways, Aubrey could see the Tsul'kalu without hindrance. Its full-body mane of thick scraggly fur covered its massive human-like frame. Jagged fangs protruded through its gaping mouth, and the stench of burning flesh singed the inside of Aubrey's nose.

The Tsul'kalu howled again and marched through the water toward the crowd. Anxious mutterings drifted through the groups of onlookers, who were previously fixed with their binoculars to the race. Now most were grabbing their children, tripping over each other and hurriedly rushing away from the bank. The judges stood up from the table, quickly preparing their exits.

**"Uhhh, folks it appears that we have uhhhh ...that we should ummm...please stay calm...HEY! HEY! NO PUSHING!"**

Ms. Thistlewood glanced up at the race. She clenched her fists and stepped away from Buzz and Rodriqa. A shiver chilled both Buzz and Rodriqa, and they shook it off. Buzz blinked as he tried to focus his eyes from the blurring loss of concentration. Rodriqa rubbed the numbness out of her arms.

Officers Ned and Fred Kluggard ran up from behind her, Ned's torso jiggling as much out of fear as out of sprinting a dozen yards.

"This is bad," whispered Fred ominously.

Ms. Thistlewood scowled at him. "Hovis! Time to go," she ordered. She turned away and ran.

Jordana looked at the creek bed and murmured, "Oh, no!"


The Tsul'kalu snarled at the blaring announcement from the P.A. system as it squelched downstream. It scanned the bank from the creek, searching for the cause of the noise. It glowered at the corner of land at the mouth of the creek.

In two giant leaps, it sprang from the middle of the water to the grassy edge in front of the judge's table. Fagan McElory trembled and threw his microphone at the Sasquatch. It growled and slammed its massive forearm on the judge's table, snapping it in two. Mr. McElroy slid onto the bank in a quivering heap.

Mr. Galilahi fell out of his chair and scrambled backwards on his arms and legs. Kiki Januszewski squealed and climbed under one side of the broken table. Sergeant Van Zenny fumbled with the holster of his gun, his sweaty fingers shaking violently at the leather, unable to unsnap its latch.

The Tsul'kalu stepped over Mr. McElory with a single stride and looked down at Mr. Galilahi. It bent over and sniffed him, and low rumbling tones throbbed from its chest.

The fervid Prissy pounced onto the Sasquatch, raking at its fur and biting its shoulders. The Bigfoot took a step back and spun in circles, wrenching the cat from its torso and lobbing her high overhead into the creek. The Tsul'kalu glared at Mr. Galilahi. It howled loudly and ran back across the creek, disappearing into the forest.

# Unsettled Scores

**Two days later.**

"Principal Lequoia, please."

Aubrey overheard his father speaking into the phone downstairs. Aubrey lay in bed, buried in twisted covers and stared at the walls and ceiling of his starkly furnished room.

His dad had finally allowed him to have more than one sheet on his bed and a bedside table with a mechanical alarm clock, since there had been no further destruction in his room recently. But these small rewards were little comfort.

No one had called for two days. No one had visited or checked up on him. He hadn't even received homework instructions from his teachers.

Aubrey felt sick even though he wasn't ill. He felt totally abandoned, but he was surrounded by a cadre of accusers, bullies and naysayers. His mood had been swallowed in dire contemplation for nearly forty-eight hours since he returned home from the rafting race. Images of his kidnapping, figurehead entrapment and Jordana's betrayal had tumbled through his head, immobilizing him with grief and confusion. He wished he could simply disappear.

His father had said little to him since yesterday, but he had also not been angry with him, for which Aubrey was thankful. Aubrey continued eavesdropping while Mr. Taylor spoke on the phone.

"Yes, sir. I wanted to let you know I decided to keep Aubrey home for a couple days."

"He's doing fine. Resting mostly."

"It really wasn't all that bad. He wasn't hurt. Gaetan brought him home after the race and explained what happened."

Aubrey frowned at his father's lack of compassion for his ordeal. He lifted himself out of the covers and stood up.

"He's had a rough first few months of high school."

*That's an understatement*, thought Aubrey. He walked into the hallway and peered down the stairs.

"No," said Mr. Taylor, surprised by the question. "Everything is fine at home."

*Oh yeah. Everything is perfect*, fumed Aubrey to himself.

"His behavior has been a little difficult to manage."

Aubrey was stunned by his father's allegation. Whatever self-loathing inertia had drowned him for two days erupted into fervent determination. He marched down the stairs and sat on the couch in the living room. On the coffee table lay a copy of the **Lake Julian Mountain Lyre**. The headline read *Pumpkin or Bumpkin: Has the Raft Race Raced its Last?* Aubrey wanted to read the story, but he needed to listen to the phone conversation.

"Perhaps he needs more structure."

Aubrey scoffed silently as he watched his father in the kitchen.

"I've managed to plan something a little more significant, but I appreciate the advice."

"Yes, sir, I'll be at the meeting tonight."

"Thank you. I will."

Mr. Taylor hung up the phone and walked into the living room. Aubrey pulled his knees to his chest and wrapped his arms around his legs. He peered at his father over his knees. His father slapped a pamphlet on the coffee table. The rectangular glossy page depicted rows of lush green trees lining a white graveled road, which led up to an opulent, plantation-style house. The words *St. Pinnetackwah Military School for Boys* scrolled across the top in alternating red, white and blue block letters.

"So this is what I deserve?" asked Aubrey with his voice muffled behind his knees. "I get tortured in front of the entire town, and you decide to send me away."

Mr. Taylor looked away and shrugged. "Aubrey, you need more than I can give you here at home. Especially since I'm...." He stopped short, uncomfortable with continuing his train of thought.

"Since what?" insisted Aubrey.

"Since...it's just me."

"I'm not mom," sputtered Aubrey.

"I never said you were," his dad whispered as he wrung his hands.

"And Gaetan blames me."

"Blames you for what?"

"For mom being...like she is."

Mr. Taylor frowned. "If he said that, he doesn't mean it."

Aubrey snorted derisively. "Then how is Gaetan tying me to a canoe and making a spectacle of me my fault?"

Mr. Taylor sighed and raised his arms. "It was a joke, Aubrey. You take things too seriously, and I think it stems from the fact the strain of high school has been too much for you." Mr. Taylor looked at the floor as he spoke in a premeditated tone. "You're emotionally immature. You need some focused time to grow up in a place that's safe and secure, yet motivating in a positive way."

"Nice way of telling me I need to man up, Dad." Aubrey covered his face with his hands and held his breath.

"Maybe a change of scenery will give you a new perspective."

Tears rolled down Aubrey's bright red face, but he was exhausted by arguing with his father. He was forced to consider that maybe his father was right. Besides, did he really have any friends anymore? If he went back to high school now, wouldn't he be teased without mercy? And if he moved away, maybe Hovis would leave him alone for good.

Mr. Taylor walked into the kitchen and picked up the phone. He paused, staring at the receiver, and then replaced it on its hanger gently.

"There's a town council meeting tonight." His father's tone resumed its usual evenly administrative tone. "I'm not sure when I'll be home. No phone calls and no leaving the house. Understood?"

Aubrey nodded with his head down. "What's the meeting about?"

Mr. Taylor ignored him. He grabbed his coat and walked briskly out the back door. Aubrey turned and looked through the window behind the couch. He watched as his dad's pickup truck rolled down the driveway.

Suddenly, a thought struck Aubrey. He stood up and stepped lightly to the door. Listening as the truck sped away down Dalton Circle, he bolted through the door and down the stairs from the back porch. Careful to stay close to the house, Aubrey rounded the porch and thrust his hand through the lattice work, unlocking the small door into the crawl space. He knelt down and wriggled through the dirt, pulled the burlap sack from its hiding place in the thrumming HVAC unit, and hurriedly escaped the deafening darkness.

Aubrey slowly crept from under the porch and found a patch of sunlight sifting through the treetops in the back yard. He sat in the middle of the glimmering, late afternoon beam and collected his thoughts. He removed *Solluna* from the coarse, dusty sack and opened it in the sunlight. The dull, filmy plates twinkled brilliantly as the sun washed away their grimy sheen and revealed the gleaming, engraved plates underneath. He rubbed his fingers over its front cover, both a little frightened and invigorated by its tingly feel.

Aubrey flipped through the foil-like pages, examining each for any minor change in detail. Each golden sheet was the same, the same as the next and the same as before, when he had first opened the book in Ms. Thistlewood's basement.

Aubrey rubbed the pages between his hands, creating heated friction against the engravings. Nothing changed. He opened his throat and exhaled slowly on a page. A misty fog bloomed on the surface of the metal from his humid breath, but then quickly evaporated. The golden plate was no different. He smacked the page hard with his hand. Nothing happened.

Aubrey gripped *Solluna's* spine and pulled one of the pages at its insertion point. The thin, wiry metal warbled under the strain, but it didn't budge. His frustration grew. The book refused to give up any more information, and nothing he could do to the book could change that.

Aubrey raised the book over his head, and his arms buckled under its weight. He partly flung, but mostly dropped, *Solluna* on the ground, its cover's corner gouging out a small hole in the lawn. He angrily kicked the book out of the circle of light. Its metal luster faded into a tarnished rusty coat.

"Stupid book," groaned Aubrey.

"They do offer anger management classes after school," uttered a voice from behind him. "It's mostly for kids who get in fights or have outbursts in class, but I'm sure for you they might make an exception."

Aubrey jerked his head around, both surprised and embarrassed. Magnos was leaning against the corner of the house, smiling at him. Aubrey turned back around quickly. He grabbed *Solluna* and stuffed it back into the burlap sack. "What are you doing here?" he murmured.

"I was told to come get you," Magnos replied.

"By whom, Gaetan or Hamilton?" asked Aubrey darkly.

"Neither. We were worried about you."

Aubrey snorted, unimpressed. "Whatever."

"You haven't been at school for two days."

"Can you blame me? Besides if you all were so worried, someone could have called."

Magnos walked over toward Aubrey and squatted down next to him, facing the same direction he was, so as not to be intrusive. "Jordana's dad ran into your father yesterday. He asked how you were doing and your dad said you were fine. That you wanted to be left alone. Mr. Galilahi mentioned that we had all tried to call you, but the phone was disconnected. Your dad said he had changed the number to prevent prank calls to the house."

Aubrey furrowed his brow and glared at Magnos in disbelief.

"Are you okay?" Magnos asked with genuine concern.

"What do you think?" Aubrey scorned.

"I know the bruised ego hurts, but are you injured?"

Aubrey looked down at the ground and shook his head.

"Jordana is sick, because she thinks you hate her."

Aubrey rolled his eyes. "Why does it matter?"

"Because she cares about you. You're her friend."

Aubrey laughed derisively. "She sold me out to Gaetan! How could she have done that if she cares about me?!"

"It wasn't all her fault."

"I know the pressure Hamilton has put her under has to be intense, and part of me doesn't blame her for choosing to side with the popular kids...but I can't trust her anymore."

"Jordana didn't sell you out," replied Magnos sternly.

Aubrey slammed his fist into the ground. "YES, SHE DID!"

"Gaetan threatened to hurt you, if she didn't draw you out of Hovis' house."

Aubrey stewed in his own contemplative frustration as he considered what Magnos had said. He bit his upper lip irritably, unsure of what to think.

Magnos turned and looked directly at Aubrey. His tone increased in urgency. "I know you don't want to hear this, but we need your help. The Bigfoot has been showing up at Jordana's house every night for more than a week. Buzz has a plan to catch to it."

Anger rippled across Aubrey's face. He stood up and loomed over Magnos. "Don't you all get it?! Every time we come up with some crazy plan to fix things, we only make it worse!"

"So then we should just lie down and take it? We should put up with being bullied by things we think we can't control? Ignore it like nothing ever happened?"

Aubrey marveled at Magnos' conviction. Two months ago, it would have been the most hypocritical statement Magnos could have made, but now, with all they had been through together, Aubrey couldn't deny his sincerity. The anger fell out of his voice. "That's what I was told to do from the beginning. I should have taken the advice."

"From who? Old Widow Wizenblatt?"

Aubrey studied Magnos' face, perplexed by his question. "How did you know?"

"She found me in the crowd after Buzz rescued me from Ms. Thistlewood. She told me we should have left well enough alone, but since we hadn't, we would need help."

"Help?" questioned Aubrey. "Whose help?"

Magnos shrugged. "All I know is that the five of us are in way too deep. We have to help each other. We have to fight."

"Speak for yourself."

Magnos stood up. "I speak for all of us. We need you, Aubrey. We have to get to the bottom of all this. You didn't abandon me, and I'm not going to abandon you."

# The Prod that Binds

Aubrey and Magnos strode through the dense woods on the shortcut to Jordana's house. Twilight had stolen most of the evening light, and the dense canopy above absorbed the rest of dusk's dissolving glow. The bushes and tree trunks were buried in darkness until they were only a few feet away. Aubrey followed Magnos' steps closely on the foot-wide path.

Aubrey twitched with a start as Magnos' voice shattered the darkness. "Did *Solluna* tell you anything different?"

"Nope," said Aubrey decisively. "Same poem, every page...without variation. Did it sound like Mrs. Thistlewood read something different?"

Magnos thought carefully. "It seems so, but I wasn't really paying much attention."

The forest cleared into a round patch of open land with a large, white Victorian house towering in the middle. Magnos whistled like a whippoorwill and Buzz, Rodriqa and Jordana turned to face the two of them from the back porch.

"Be careful where you step," hollered Buzz.

"Oh, right," said Magnos, stopping abruptly.

"Why?" asked Aubrey as he peered around Magnos.

"Buzz has set netted snare traps all around the yard. I think I remember where most of them are."

"You *think?*" asked Aubrey in an unnerved tone.

"Just follow me." Magnos sidestepped and pivoted his way through the yard, much like a treasure hunter skulking his way through a maze of hidden booby traps.

Aubrey looked up above Jordana's house, and a thick ring of curved bamboo and braided rope encircled the roof. The contraption balanced high in mid-air, except for a few strands of heavy cord tying it to outstretched boughs of evergreens.

"What's Buzz's plan?" asked Aubrey, as they shimmed precariously through the yard.

Magnos hesitated. "It's a little complex. Buzz would explain it better."

"Greeeaaat," murmured Aubrey.

Aubrey and Magnos lumbered up the stairs of the back porch, where Buzz, Rodriqa and Jordana huddled around a piece of white poster board.

Rodriqa walked over to Aubrey and gave him a crushing hug. "How you doin', little man?"

Aubrey shrugged, hoping to create some room to breathe. "All right, I guess." He looked at Jordana, but she kept staring at the floor.

"What is all this?" asked Aubrey, bewildered by the mess of broken wood, frayed rope and rusted metal strewn across the porch.

"The Torquetum Club let me have the wreckage from *Ben-Zing*. I used it and a few more odds and ends from my dad's scrap yard to create a trap for Jordana's Bigfoot." Buzz raised his hands reverently in the air. "I call it the Trap-Eaze." He glanced around the group, ready for their awestruck appreciation. They all looked back at him with flat and underwhelmed expressions. Buzz frowned, slightly annoyed that his friends didn't think his plan's name was clever.

"I'd call it a full week's worth of labor slapped together in a couple hours," remarked Rodriqa in an annoyed tone. Aubrey could see the exhaustion in her face as she fanned herself with her hand.

"Here's the plan." Buzz pointed to the white poster board lying on the floor of the porch, which displayed a crude drawing of Jordana's house with a large circle around it and several hashed areas scattered around the house. Stick figures were drawn standing on top of the house and inside it.

"The first line of defense is the hidden nets. I've countered each of them with heavy weights, so if that catches the Bigfoot, or Tsul'kalu, then we're done...game over...and we're famous." Buzz grinned slyly. "If it's smart enough to avoid these traps, then we engage defense line two."

"Wait a sec," interrupted Aubrey. "What makes you think it's gonna be here tonight?"

Buzz looked knowingly at Jordana. She kept her head down as she spoke softly. "The Tsul'kalu has been here every night this week. It seems to be on a mission. I don't think it'll give up till it gets what it wants."

"From what Jordana has said, this thing could be on top of us right now, and we wouldn't even know it," argued Aubrey.

"Dude, if you can see ghosts, then I'm willing to bet you can see it coming," countered Buzz.

"But the Bigfoot is *not* a ghost!"

"How do you know?" Everyone paused and thought about what Buzz had said. Aubrey opened his mouth in rebuttal, but his mind couldn't craft a reasonable riposte.

"Part two." Buzz resumed debriefing the plan. "Me, Magnos and Rodriqa will be on the roof."

"Let me guess...you're gonna tackle it from above," squawked Aubrey, feeling a little more feisty, the more ridiculous Buzz's plan seemed.

"No," responded Buzz condescendingly. He reached around behind him and dug through the junk scattered over the porch. He pulled out three long metal tubes, each with two sharp prongs on their tips.

"Cattle prods?!" challenged Aubrey.

"Yep," replied Buzz proudly. "I found these in my dad's garage a few years back. I honestly didn't think I'd ever come up with a need for them, but I hid them under my bed for a special occasion."

Rodriqa and Magnos glared at Buzz with sternly puzzled expressions.

"Anyway," continued Buzz. "I supped them up a bit." He flipped one of the cattle prods around, exposing the top end, which was wired together with a re-engineered motherboard of microchips and a battery the size of his fist. "They should deliver enough current to stun an adult elephant. That'll give our Bigfoot a kick in the pants. It's no longer a cattle prod. I call it the *battle* prod!"

"But how are you gonna run after it?" asked Aubrey. "The beast leapt across the mouth of the Wontawanna Creek in about three steps."

"Not run...ride," replied Buzz. "That's where the Trap-Eaze comes into play."

Aubrey pointed at Magnos and Rodriqa. "You two are going along with this?" asked Aubrey incredulously.

Magnos and Rodriqa looked at each other and nodded grimly.

"Severe circumstances require severe intervention," Buzz spoke with the authority of a colonial revolutionary. "Besides, we can't let *you* be the only swashbuckler in the group."

Aubrey frowned. "And where will I be?"

"Inside. Protecting the bait," said Buzz with a sinister grin.

Aubrey sighed deeply. Anger, fear and frustration were gnawing a pit in his stomach.

Buzz peered out from underneath the porch at the night sky. "Nighttime has arrived. Let's finish setting up and get into position." Magnos, Rodriqa and Buzz lifted various items from the porch and flung them over their shoulders.

"Where are the flashlights?" asked Aubrey.

"No flashlights. We won't need them," replied Buzz.

"But how are you gonna be able to see anything? It's pitch dark out here."

"The moon should rise before too long. It's full tonight. It should give us all the light we need."

Aubrey paused in thought as Buzz's words spoke to him unexpectedly. He tucked away his contemplation into the corner of his mind and promised himself he would remember it later.

"How can we get to the roof without a flashlight?" asked Rodriqa.

"Through the attic," directed Buzz. "There's a dormer window on the roof large enough for the three of us to fit through."

Buzz motioned everyone inside. He stopped Aubrey before they walked inside. "Here. You'll need this." He handed Aubrey a video game headset with an attached microphone.

"What's this for?"

Buzz smiled widely.

## *Trap-Eaze*

Buzz, Rodriqa and Magnos plodded through the kitchen, each with coils of rope wrapped around a shoulder as they hauled their equipment up the stairs and into the attic. Jordana followed them into the living room and sat down. Aubrey dawdled in the kitchen and fiddled with his headset, hoping to avoid talking to Jordana. He swiveled in circles, staring with feigned interest at the sink and the table.

Aubrey genuinely liked Jordana's house, which was simultaneously rustic and state-of-the-art. Many of the wooden objects had been meticulously carved out of oak and pine and looked as if they had been handed down for generations, yet the appliances were stainless steel and very modern.

Aubrey looked up toward the living room. Jordana was staring at him. He turned his head and sighed. His stomach gnashed against broken heart. Aubrey wanted to know why Jordana did what she did, but he wasn't sure he could ever trust her. He swallowed his pride, his desire overwhelming his ego. Deciding it was time to get the uncomfortable part over with, Aubrey walked slowly with his eyes toward his feet into the living room.

Three linen couches formed a triangle around a central oval coffee table, which was topped with a fogged piece of glass that was clutched within a cage of sculpted, varnished tree limbs underneath. Latticed, double-faced windows were set in each wall, which were decorated with dream-catchers, ceremonial pipes, chiseled gemstones and decorated animal hides. Aubrey felt like he was in a Native American museum.

On the right-hand wall, underneath the stairs, a sparkling rock nailed to a wooden frame caught Aubrey's attention. He walked over to the wall and examined it. Tiny purple and yellow quartz crystals spiked out from a hollow stone shell that had been sheered in half. At first, it looked a geode, a common tourist shop trinket. Then he realized the quartz was on the outside. It was a miniature version of the Tomb of Enoch.

"Incredible," murmured Jordana. She was standing next to him, and he hadn't realized it.

"Yeah, it is," replied Aubrey solemnly.

"No. I mean everything that's happened." Jordana's soft voice made Aubrey's heart beat quickly. "The marching band has taken on hero status, now that they won this year's rafting race," she said happily. "You should see May O'Klammer. She's so proud of herself. She's even louder and more obnoxious than she was before." Jordana chuckled uncomfortably.

"Wait," replied Aubrey. "I thought Teton and the Mafisito had won the race."

"They were in the lead," commented Jordana, "but they got disqualified for throwing garbage."

Aubrey nodded quietly.

Jordana twisted her lip as she searched for the right words. "You're a hero too, Aubrey."

"Yeah, right," replied Aubrey sourly.

"No, really! Everyone is talking about you like you're some adrenaline-thirsty daredevil. No one can believe how brave you had to be to be tied to the football team's canoe...to be a living figurehead."

Aubrey snorted unconvincingly.

Jordana stared at her feet and shifted her body closer Aubrey's. "I'm really sorry about what happened. If Gaetan hadn't made me-"

"It's okay," said Aubrey reluctantly.

"No, it's not okay," insisted Jordana. "It was wrong of me. But Gaetan said he'd convince your dad to send you away to boarding school, if I didn't help him."

Aubrey nodded. "I know Gaetan can be very intimidating."

Jordana smiled appreciatively at him.

"Where's your dad?" asked Aubrey, hoping to change the subject to more mundane matters.

"He's upstairs in his room," Jordana answered sadly. "He barely comes out anymore. Except to go to work."

"And he's okay with all of Buzz's craziness?"

"Yeah, can you believe it?" Jordana chuckled. "He even wished Buzz good luck."

Aubrey's headset whined and crackled. "This is Billy Goat 1. Come in Ground Hog. Do you read me? Over." The headset squawked through static as the voice relayed words over the airwaves.

Aubrey rolled his eyes. "Ground Hog," he murmured, and glanced apologetically at Jordana. She shook her head, and a grin broke through her insomnia-beaten face.

"Yes, Buzz, I can hear you," Aubrey responded with an artificially obligatory tone. Audio snow hummed before and after each communication.

"The puppeteer is ready to dance. I repeat, the puppeteer is ready to dance," Buzz replied in his best mission control voice.

"What?" Aubrey asked. Buzz's secret code was becoming less transparent. Aubrey looked to Jordana for clarification, but she shrugged in agreement with his confusion.

Rodriqa's voice busted over the intercom, "He means, we're finally tethered to the ropes of this death machine! Oh, and just to be crystal clear...I will NOT be answering to Billy Goat 3!"

Aubrey and Jordana grinned, wondering how many of Rodriqa's buttons Buzz must have pushed today.

"But what if the enemy is listening? We need to keep our identities hidden," explained Buzz. "Besides there are multiple safety mechanisms installed to ensure no harm comes to anyone!"

"Being tied to a tree limb by my ankle is HARDLY a safety measure," interrupted Rodriqa, her anxiety reaching its zenith. The static snapped and sputtered into a soft shush of audio snow. Rodriqa had thrown her headset onto the roof.

"They're going to argue all night, aren't they?" Jordana turned the volume on the intercom down to the minimum setting, diminishing Rodriqa and Buzz's jeering prattle to distant background mumbles and screeches.

"Most likely," Aubrey remarked, "which should keep the Bigfoot away. If we're lucky, we'll just all tire out and fall asleep without a peep from anyone…or anything."

Jordana's mood drifted downward, and a despondent shadow darkened her face as she looked down. Her mournful eyes struck him sharply, and he scrambled to correct himself, "Or maybe we'll scare them away?"

She shook her head, breaking off his attempt to backpedal. "If nothing happens tonight, then this is just the most bizarre slumber party ever," Jordana replied in frustration.

*Poorly played*, Aubrey thought to himself. He tried again. "Good point. We should ask them to keep it down."

"I doubt that will help. Driqa rarely keeps her thoughts to herself," responded Jordana. Aubrey agreed silently, feeling defeated.

"This has to work. We can't live like this anymore." Jordana's raw emotions rose to the surface. "My grades have tanked, because I'm constantly falling asleep in class. My dad sleeps at work, since we can't get more than a couple hours of sleep here. Why else would my dad agree to let Buzz do something so crazy? We're desperate! And there are only so many nights I can stay at Driqa's house before I become a huge nuisance. Her family has been unbelievably kind. I've been staying over twice a week for more than a month now. That's the only break I get from this insanity." Every word was wrapped in exhaustion, and her shoulders hung low at her sides.

Aubrey nodded understandingly. Empathy for what she was going through was not hard for him to find. His own nightly visitor had tortured away his rest as well. He couldn't decide which was worse, a ghostly invader who was incessant but harmless or a threatening, tangible vandal.

"Do you have any other family nearby?" offered Aubrey, searching for solutions.

Jordana sighed deeply, "Only an uncle, my dad's brother, but he's not very sympathetic to our situation."

"Why?"

"He thinks the nightly Tsul'kalu assaults are our fault," Jordana exclaimed angrily.

"What? Really?!" Aubrey was shocked at the suggestion.

"It's a long, stupid family story. Suffice it to say old legends and baseless superstitions are the bane of my existence right now."

"Mine too," Aubrey muttered nearly inaudibly.

"Some people refuse to accept reality and only believe what they have been told." Jordana whimpered as her voice cracked. Tears, which had formed more and more easily over the past year, leaked down her face. Aubrey sensed her tender frailty as she spoke, like a vine beaten by summer storms, withered by loss of time to heal. She seemed ready to give up.

"You must feel pretty lonely sometimes." Aubrey gulped back on the last part of his sentence. Jordana's silence remitted her acceptance of Aubrey's assessment of her situation. Her head dropped beneath her shoulders in surrender. She was surrounded by her closest friends in a final, pathetic effort to protect her, yet she still felt helpless and alone.

Fearful he had crossed the line, Aubrey tried to explain his perspective. "Really, it makes sense…brand new school, not much family around, your dad buries himself in his work. You've lost your mom, and now your small band of close-knit, misfit friends are turning a complicated series of circumstances into a circus. And no matter what anyone says to try and comfort you, it never cools the ache that burns in your heart, especially when this new life is neither what you wanted nor hoped for, and what you want most now is your old life back."

Jordana couldn't move, stupefied by the gunfire of veracity that clearly outlined the crux of her grief. A sledgehammer to the forehead would have been subtler.

Aubrey bit his lip, convinced he had upset her. He wanted to kick himself for opening his mouth. "I said too much. I can go overboard sometimes. Sorry." Aubrey turned his head away from her, expecting an onslaught of verbal retribution, or worse, silent pouting.

"No," Jordana replied softly. She leaned her shoulder against his to keep him in the conversation. She chuckled unexpectedly and then balled both of her hands, holding them apart in front of Aubrey. "Hammer…nail." She pounded one fist on top of the other, acknowledging that he was exactly right. Aubrey faced her and smiled, thankful she wasn't mad.

"For a quiet guy, you're certainly perceptive. I guess all that time everyone else is talking, you're busy listening." Her tone was nearly congratulatory.

Aubrey laughed, "I think I just see things a little easier than most."

"Obviously," Jordana replied with a twinge of annoyance in her voice.

Aubrey's smile shortened, worried that his intrusive welcome had ended. He shoved a verbal foot in her mind's door before it closed. "I wish the Tsul'kalu had come after me instead of you. Hovis was already visiting me at night. My dad would have heard them, too, and couldn't just call me nut case and forget about it."

"I hope you don't have to go away to boarding school," Jordana responded apologetically.

"Yeah, well, I'm still hopeful my dad will realize I'm not as crazy as he thinks."

"We're all in the crazy boat at this point," replied Jordana. A smirk danced across her face. Aubrey snickered in agreement. "But I wouldn't wish this on my worst enemy. I'm really sorry you all have gotten involved in this. It's not like everybody doesn't have enough to deal with. Magnos was kidnapped and tortured by some crackpot who is still on the loose. Your house is haunted, and you're his only target. We're all in a big mess!"

Aubrey leaned in toward her. "What are friends for?" He smiled at her, entranced by her delicate features. "Misery loves company, right? And I think this is the best company I've had in a long time."

Jordana stared at Aubrey's eyes, fully appreciating their uniqueness for the first time. "How did you learn to see behind your eyelids?" she asked as she studied his pupils within his dark green irises.

Aubrey shifted his gaze toward the floor. "I'm not sure," Aubrey replied. "I've never been able to do it before. It just started happening when Hovis came around." Aubrey's enthusiasm waned. "Maybe I should join the circus. I could be part of the freak show."

Jordana leaned in toward him. "Nah," she offered, staring at him more intently. "They're special. Just like you." Aubrey lifted his head, and his nose nearly touched hers. His eyes drifted down toward her lips, partly open with a small dark sliver between them. Aubrey closed his eyes and leaned in.

"THE FOX IS OUTSIDE THE HEN HOUSE! BOGEY SPOTTED AT FOUR O'CLOCK!" blasted the hurried, muffled screech from the headset.

Aubrey and Jordana's postures straightened rigidly, blitzed out of their languid silence by Buzz's announcement.

"Where's four o' clock?" asked Jordana.

Aubrey stood up and spun in circles, looking at the house's layout as he tried to regain his bearings. "Twelve o' clock is most likely the porch."

*TWING!* The loud pinging noise sang from outside, followed by a breezy swoosh.

Aubrey turned forty-five degrees to his right and ran to the window in front of him. Jordana chased after him.

"WE CAUGHT IT! WE CAUGHT IT!" squalled Buzz over the airwaves.

Aubrey and Jordana's jaws dropped as they looked outside. The hulking, hairy Tsul'kalu swung from a white pine in the fetal position, swaddled by the coarse net of one of Buzz's traps. The beast struggled, rocking its torso side to side. It squeezed a foot and a hand through the latticed threads, and then suddenly all its movement stopped. The trap slowly swayed to a standstill, with the monster's arms and legs hanging limply out of its ropey cage.

"Hoaker Croaker! That smells bad," exclaimed Rodriqa distantly through Buzz's microphone.

"I think it's dead," said Buzz morosely.

"Let's head down and check," Magnos suggested.

"No, wait," interrupted Rodriqa. "Something's happening!"

The Tsul'kalu didn't move, but its shaggy coat lengthened slightly, and its entire body appeared grainy, like a smudge on a photograph. The Sasquatch dropped like a ton of rocks to the ground.

"Oh, no! The net broke," whined Buzz.

Aubrey shook his head as he stared outside. He pulled the headset to his mouth. "No, look! The net is still intact."

The beast lay on its back, still in the grass

"It looks dead," repeated Magnos.

"Uhhh…no! It's still breathing. I can see its chest rising from here," baulked Aubrey.

The Tsul'kalu sat straight up and turned toward the window. Its dim red eyes glowered at Aubrey, and the creature pushed itself to its feet. Aubrey gulped against the dry fear in his throat. The beast craned its head to the sky and howled an air-battering roar that shook the windows. The Bigfoot bolted around the back corner of the house, its cry diminishing as it ran.


"'Tis the season for breezin'!" Buzz yanked one of the ropes strapped to his harness and balanced himself between the edge of the roof and its gutter. The first spring overhead zinged into a high-pitched whistle, corkscrewing along its axis and forcing ropes and pulleys to shudder and swing from side to side. The heavy cords attaching Buzz, Magnos and Rodriqa to the circular bamboo truss tightened as the Trap-Eaze shimmied to life. Three metal clips raced swiftly along a groove inside the bamboo ring above and caught the rope holding Buzz's harness.

The rope jerked Buzz off the roof, and he soared through the air into the yard. The second metal clip approached, and the second spring whirred into motion.

"Wait!" yelled Rodriqa. "My headset!" It was out of reach, and the harness was pulling her quickly closer to the edge of the roof.

Magnos steadied himself on the brim of the house. "Hurry up!" he shouted. "Your clip is coming!" The second metal clip caught his rope, and it flung him off the roof.

Rodriqa knew she only had a few seconds until the third metal clip pulled her from the roof. She dove for her headset and clutched it tightly between her fingers. The third spring rang to life, and her harness snapped snuggly around her waist.

"Noooooooooooo!" she screamed, as the Trap-Eaze drug her along the roof. She pulled at the shingles, trying to gain leverage to right herself. The roof dropped out from underneath her, and she spiraled through the air face down toward the yard. Her headset fell to the grass.

"Billy Goat 1 is aloft and flying high!" exclaimed Buzz into his headset as he rounded the back porch. He tugged on the rope on his right and swung outward, clearing the corners of the porch easily. The wind fluttered against his cheeks, and he giggled gleefully, enjoying the speed as the ground passed effortlessly six feet below him.

Aubrey and Jordana observed the chaos outside through the living room window and watched in awe as Buzz and Magnos sped around the house. They both looked at each other and moaned, "Oh, no," as they watched Rodriqa flailing upside down in flight.

"Billy Goat 2, come in," ordered Buzz.

"Psssshhhh...Billy Goat 2 here...pssssssshhhh... right behind you."

"Fantastic, Billy Goat 2," replied Buzz. "Billy Goat 3?"

There was no response.

As Buzz swung around another corner toward the front of the house, he pulled his battle prod out from beneath his belt. "Bogey spotted. I'm hot on his trail!"

The Tsul'kalu lumbered in front of Buzz as he rapidly approached it. The Sasquatch growled at Buzz over its shoulder, its glowing red eyes squinting as he flew at the beast. Buzz's jaw dropped in wonder. The Sasquatch launched into a sprint, staying well ahead of Buzz in the Trap-Eaze. It jumped over the nets and traps and climbed along the outside walls of the house, avoiding every snare. It rounded the next corner, and Buzz was close behind, but he knew he was losing ground.

"Wow! It's fast," Buzz reported into the headset. He reached for his belt and untied a knot of rope. Buzz jerked it free, and it fell into the yard. The fourth spring in the center of the bamboo ring above the roof whirred in circles, and the metal clips along the bamboo accelerated forward.

Aubrey and Jordana ran from window to window, trying to glean a glimpse of the action, but as the Tsul'kalu passed, Buzz flew by a moment later and turned another corner of the house. Following the action, Aubrey and Jordana could only pause for a fleeting moment at each window before they had to move onto the next one.

Jordana pulled Aubrey's headset to her face and squeezed the speaker button. "Buzz, you've gotta stop that contraption," shouted Jordana rapidly into the receiver.

"That's a negative, Ground Hog. There wasn't enough daylight to install a brake," relayed Buzz mechanically.

"Rodriqa isn't in her harness!" Jordana's voice screeched frantically over the airwaves.

"Is Billy Goat 3 down?"

Aubrey and Jordana looked at each other, uncertain how best to reply. Aubrey leaned into the receiver. "Billy Goat 3 is toe up and not going to be much help…to herself or anyone else," he answered.

"I secured the harnesses myself," announced Buzz. "She should be fine. We only have a couple more passes around the house before the springs lose all their kinetic energy, anyway."

The force of the increasing momentum from the spinning metal clips jerked Buzz, Magnos and Rodriqa forward.

The gap between Buzz and the Tsul'kalu tightened, and he clicked the power switch to his battle prod. It crackled to life, and sprigs of electricity zipped into the air from its tip.

Buzz rounded another corner, and the Sasquatch turned to look behind him. Buzz leaned forward and poked the prod into the monster's face.

*ZAAAAAPPP!!* The Tsul'kalu growled barbarically, and the corners of its mouth flared open, exposing two racks of raggedly sharp fangs. Its jaw clenched under the electrical current, and its dull red eyes bulged from its sockets. The creature slumped to the ground in a heaping hulk of singed hair and twitching flesh.

Buzz flew over the creature and hollered, "WOOOOHOOOOO! BOGEY DOWN. REPEAT, BOGEY IS DOWN! BILLY GOAT 2, GIVE IT ANOTHER TASTE OF BATTLE PROD FURY!"

Magnos watched Buzz's back round the corner of the house, and he looked down as the Tsul'kalu shook its head and scrambled to move its arms and legs with coordination. The rotting smell thickened in the air and turned even more sour. Magnos had to close his mouth to keep the stench from burning his throat, but he couldn't swallow the taste of rancid vinegar out of his mouth. The monster shuddered, and its hair shortened. Magnos was amazed at how it looked more fuzzy than hairy, almost as if the creature was out of focus. He rubbed his eyes with his fists and looked again, but nothing changed.

The Sasquatch arched its trunk up on all fours. Magnos whipped out his battle prod, turned it on and swiveled his body downward to reach the beast. The prod sparkled and snapped against its fur, but nothing happened. The monster was undaunted by the shock. As Magnos swung overhead, the creature stood up and batted at Magnos' legs.

"Something's wrong with my battle prod," reported Magnos into his headset.

"All three of them were in perfect working order before sunset," chided Buzz.

"It went off, but it didn't do anything," replied Magnos.

"Impossible. I'll shock it again next pass. Is it still down?"

"No. It was trying to stand up when I passed by."

Buzz frowned incredulously at Magnos' report. The wind was stinging his face, and he knew the Trap-Eaze was now at full velocity. He flew quickly around the porch and turned the back corner of the house.

The Tsul'kalu was gone. Buzz wrenched his body from side to side, searching for the beast, hoping to find it captured in one of his nets, scampering through the yard, or hiding in the trees. Buzz saw no sign of the Bigfoot. And the Trap-Eaze was slowing down.

"Where is it?" exclaimed Buzz angrily into the headset.

There was a long pause over the airwaves as the Trap-Eaze continued to hurl the three kids around the house.

"I don't know," replied Aubrey. "We can't find it."

"It's not here," Magnos agreed.

"ARRGGHHHH!" cried Buzz. His frustration peaked as more yard passed beneath him without any clue as to where the Sasquatch was.

To be so close to capturing such a creature of austere legend, to have the animal subdued and within moments of complete submission, and yet instantly lose all hope of finding it. It was exasperation to the nth degree for Buzz.

"Help," sputtered Magnos briefly over his headset. "Pssssssssshhhhhhh-hhh!" Static filled the frequency. The bamboo ring over the house moaned and pivoted erratically. Buzz swung forward to a halt as the line holding his harness to the Trap-Eaze quivered to a stop.

"What's going on?" asked Buzz over the headset. "Why did we stop so suddenly?"

No one answered. The metal clips in the bamboo ring clicked and clacked as the springs continued to turn, despite the clips' lack of forward movement. Buzz's side of the ring tilted skyward, and Buzz was yanked up above the roof.

Buzz's legs flailed, and he gripped the rope above the harness tightly. "GROUND HOG?! BILLY GOAT 2?! WHAT'S HAPPENING?!"

"The Tsul'kalu has Magnos," whispered Jordana through crumbling static.


On the other side of the house, the Bigfoot's massive hand grappled both of Magnos' ankles between its palm and fingers. The rope above him stretched Magnos' pelvis away from his legs as the Trap-Eaze towed the harness forward. Magnos grunted in agony as he stiffened his muscles to hold his body together. He felt like he was being drawn and quartered. The Tsul-Kalu's mouth vibrated softly, like a curious coo, as he examined Magnos and the harness he was tied within. The creature pulled Magnos downward, and Magnos screamed in pain. Their side of the bamboo ring tilted down and was only a few feet above the ground. The Tsul'kalu stared at Magnos' face, which was drenched with sweat and crunched tightly together. The beast took a step away and released Magnos.

The bamboo ring zipped quickly forward, and Buzz was catapulted toward the ground, his knees scraping along the grass. Specks of dirt pelted his face as the night raced by him. Buzz twisted his arm around the rope and heaved himself upwards.

*TWING!* A net engulfed Buzz's entire body and cinched tightly around him. It jerked him out into the yard, and he swung helplessly in circles underneath the limbs of a white oak, trapped in his own snare.

The bamboo ring above the roof cracked, and the springs snapped free. Magnos shot into the air and flew high above the roof until his rope pulled tight from the net below. He was flung back down around the corner of the house toward the porch.

Rodriqa spun upside down in disabled orbit in her harness toward the backyard, with the release of the metal clips from the bamboo ring. The rope holding her harness caught the fork of a tree limb, and she swung like a pendulum beneath it.

*CRAAAAAAAAASSSSSSHHH!*

The kitchen door exploded in a supernova of shattered lumber and glass shards, showering debris across the kitchen as Magnos hurled through the rear entryway and face planted on the hard kitchen floor.

Aubrey and Jordana covered their ears and fell to the floor with the explosion of Magnos' impact. Shiny slivers and wooden crumbs tinged and twitched across the hardwoods into the living room. Everything went silent. Aubrey and Jordana crawled through the living room and squatted behind the couch closest to the kitchen, peering over its back. Magnos lay prone next to the kitchen table, covered in reddening scraps and bumps, and moaning in agony. The gaping oval hole in the back of the kitchen wall was surrounded by shredded siding and sheetrock and exposed the entire landscape of the backyard.

Jordana ran into the kitchen and stooped over Magnos. Aubrey stood up and reached for her, but she was fast out of his grasp. Jordana reached down for Magnos in despair, wavering between pulling him up and checking for a pulse.

The Tsul'kalu walked up the back porch steps and growled. The porch groaned under its massive weight. It stopped at the top and stared at Jordana and Magnos. Jordana backed up slowly, and fled behind the couch.

The Tsul'kalu pivoted its neckless head from side to side as it examined the creviced exterior of the house and the destruction of the kitchen inside. Its fingers twitched, and its torso jerked unevenly. For the first time, the monster seemed almost nervous.

Aubrey and Jordana shifted further back into the living room slowly and pinched their noses to avoid the smell. The Tsul'kalu walked past the dining room table and leered over Magnos, with its feet on other side of his body. It bent over, and soppy drool from its fangs dripped onto the back of Magnos' neck. It sniffed the air around his back like a wild animal claiming its kill. The creature reached down with its fist closed and placed a golden ring next to Magnos.

An echoing scream bellowed from outside. Aubrey and Jordana looked at each other and murmured in fear, "Rodriqa."

The Tsul'kalu erected itself quickly and turned toward the outside. Aubrey and Jordana looked beyond the beast into the backyard. Eleven more Tsul'kalu appeared at the edge of the yard out of the forest and were slowly striding toward the house.

Rodriqa scrambled helplessly in her corded confinement in the tree, and she gawked at the clan of Sasquatch moving quietly beneath her. Each creature was different than the next. They were various heights and sizes and colors, some fatter, others shorter, some burgundy, others black, and one appeared childlike, although it was only slightly smaller than Magnos. The forest around the house was coldly quiet, and the air was swimming with dumpster-like odors.

A barrage of baying hounds burst through the tree line in the yard. Dressed in orange safety vests and camouflage and armed with guns, Stew Parsons and Snakes McWhorter ran into the yard next to the clan, holding onto the leashes of a half-dozen dogs, which snapped and barked at the Tsul'kalu. Several members of the clan hunkered down and hissed at the intruders, bearing their jagged fangs.

Snakes pulled his rifle to his chest and took quick aim with one of his beady eyes. He pulled the trigger. The rifle exploded. The nearest Tsul'kalu, who appeared more feminine with slightly rounded torso and hips, lurched backwards and stumbled clumsily from side to side. She stabilized herself and defiantly pulled a dented metal bullet from her fur. Flinging the tiny projectile into the forest, she raised her head and growled at Snakes. Snakes cocked his gun and aimed again. In two great leaps, the female Tsul'kalu was standing over top of Stew and Snakes. She had both of their guns in one hand and the leashes to the crop of hounds in the other. The dogs barked and bit at her ferociously, but she held them out at arm's length so they couldn't reach her.

She howled fiercely, and the blast of her hot, moist breath washed over Stew and Snakes. Snakes turned and dashed into the forest. Stew passed out. The dogs quickly switched to yelping and whining. She released them, and the hounds disappeared into the darkness.

From the living room, Aubrey and Jordana watched the odd scene take place in the backyard through the kitchen's massive hole. The Tsul'kalu in the kitchen ran outside of the house and met the others, bounding a hundred feet in only a few steps. It lifted up its chin repeatedly and grunted and squawked in short, stunted bursts. The family returned its greeting.

The three largest Tsul'kalu stepped out in front toward the porch. These three were a head taller than the others, and their hair lighter in color. The oldest was almost graying, another one was dirty blonde, and the third a glowing auburn. They sniffed the air and grunted and snorted at each other as they surveyed the yard.

Cautiously viewing the movements of the Sasquatch, Aubrey and Jordana hunkered down and scampered into the kitchen. Jordana held a hand over her mouth as she squatted down to touch Magnos, hoping to comfort him and to see if he was breathing. Aubrey couldn't stand to look at Magnos. At the sight of all his injuries, his stomach was racked with nausea, and he locked his teeth together to keep himself from vomiting. Magnos' left arm had an S-like curve at the elbow, and Aubrey turned away quickly from the site of the fractures.

Aubrey sidled against the inside wall of the kitchen and scooted over to the phone. He picked up the receiver and dialed 9-1-1.

"Is he still alive?" he whispered.

Jordana nodded.

"What is the nature of your emergency?" squeaked the woman's voice through the phone.

The house shook violently. The inside walls pounded with the force of a dozen battering rams, and the floor pushed Aubrey and Jordana off their feet. Aubrey dropped the phone and covered his ears.

The three largest Tsul'kalu had jumped onto the roof of the back porch and were climbing the outside walls of the second story, smashing hand and foot-sized holes through the siding. They scurried along the walls, like ants on a trail, hunting for their prey, smelling each opening that was made. They crawled to the front of the house and bashed more holes with their fists in a circle around a window.

CRRAAAAAACCCKKKK! The house rattled, and its trusses and support beams staggered. Aubrey thought the house was being ripped in two. A heavy, baritone scream filtered down the stairs and echoed from the outside.

Jordana stood up and jerked her head toward the second floor. "Daddy," she whimpered. She hopped a couple of steps toward the bottom of the stairs, but her fear caught up with her.

The Tsul'kalu had torn off an outer section of the house, exposing Arturo Galilahi's bedroom. The blonde Tsul'kalu wrapped his ape-like hands around Arturo and flung him over his shoulder. They leapt to the ground from the second story and strode toward the forest of the backyard.

Arturo flailed and yelled, beating his fists against the hairy creature's back, but the three beasts maintained their slow walk toward the rest of their clan. Jordana ran to the hole in the kitchen and yelled for her father.

One by one, the Tsul'kalu disappeared into the forest.  The three largest Sasquatch faded into the darkness behind the rest and Arturo Galilahi with them.

The childlike Bigfoot was the last to step through the trees.  Before it walked away, it looked up at Rodriqa and pointed directly at her.  Even through the night, Rodriqa thought she saw it wave.

## *Controlling Stones*

Blue and red flashing lights flickered in a rhythmic glimmer across Jordana's house, with an eerie glaze of urgent doom. Sergeant Van Zenny was speaking with Rodriqa in the backyard as she retold the night's events with animated gestures and raucous squeals. Aubrey couldn't bear staying inside the broken house, and so had wandered into the yard in the guise of inspecting the damage and searching for clues. Deep down, it was a way for him to evade the emotional aftermath.

Jordana stood in the yard with a blank stare as two paramedics loaded Magnos, strapped to a gurney and moaning in pain, into the back of an ambulance. As the ambulance drove off, Jordana walked over to the back porch steps, sat down, and buried her head in her lap with one fist securely clenched tight by her side.

Aubrey surveyed the scene of the near war-like destruction, awestruck. The Galilahi home creaked with residual fallout of sheetrock and lumber from the gaping crevice in the second floor. Siding and two-by-fours littered the yard like the remnants of a construction explosion. Shards of bamboo track and shreds of knotted rope swung from the trees in the nighttime breeze. Another police officer was cutting one thread of net at a time with his pocketknife in an attempt to free Buzz from his own snare. And Stew Parsons sat on a rock in the yard, holding the side of his swollen head.

Lost in his thoughts, Aubrey looked up to the sky, hoping for answers. Maybe a big, booming voice from the heavens was an unreasonable request, but was a hint, a whisper, a tiny spark of direction too much to ask? The full round moon glowed down at him, silently mocking him.

Then he remembered what he told himself to remember. And he remembered he wasn't supposed to leave the house.

Aubrey ran up to Jordana, leaned over and embraced her tightly. "I'm sorry, but I have to go." Jordana nodded understandingly.

He interrupted Rodriqa's report to the Sergeant. "Will you take care of her?"

"Of course," Rodriqa replied. "She can stay with me tonight."

Aubrey nodded and raced away from the house.

"Hey! Where ya's goin'?" asked Van Zenny.

"There's something I have to check on immediately." He cut off his reply to the Sergeant and ignored him. "Do you think Magnos would mind if I borrowed his bicycle?" he asked Rodriqa.

She pursed her lips together sympathetically. "From the looks of it, I don't think he's gonna be riding a bike any time soon." Aubrey told her and Jordana goodbye and waved to Buzz in the tree as he pedaled with all his strength across the yard and onto the street.

Aubrey rode down Dalton Circle in the dim glow of the streetlights, slowly rolling along the brim of the asphalt. Most of the homes along the road were dark, since midnight was approaching. He craned his neck to look down the street and was grateful the inside of his house was dark, too.

He pedaled into the driveway and dropped Magnos' bike next to the porch. He sighed deeply with relief, as his father's truck was still gone. Like most town council meetings convening for a serious issue, it could be expected to ramble on into the wee hours of the morning.

Aubrey crawled under the porch and pulled the bagged *Solluna* from its basement metallic crypt. He looked up at the sky, and the full moon shone brightly back at him. He sat on the ground, clear of the murky shade from the trees, and pulled *Solluna* from the sack.

Its grimy surface faded, and the lustrous gold cover shimmered to silver in the moonlight. The pictograph on the front twisted and swirled, and the crescent moon forced its shaped over top of the sun. The full moon on the cover matched the round orb in the sky, except for the pair of eyes, the nose, and the face that snarled grimly back at Aubrey. Unnerved by the cover, he opened the book, and the pages warbled and moaned as words curled and coiled into the metal.

*Before a Word broke the Clockmaker's lips*
*And First Light spread from sun to sun,*
*The Darkness spooled in hidden, whirling wisps,*
*Festering to tease growing hope undone.*

*The Clockmaker feared his handiwork displayed*
*And mourned his children's loss before their birth.*
*Vacuum's teeth dripped remains of worlds remade,*
*Its belly bloated with decaying sister earths.*

*The Clockmaker struck a seal in all He would create*
*A stamp to return the children to the fold*

By branding each spirit with a stone, gilded by divine
fate
And bridging His mind with every heart and soul.


But as all children tend to do,
They fight to break their parent's hold,
To cut the bonds and unhinge the glue,
Releasing their slavery to the mold.


The Watchers toyed with human stones,
Merging and taunting their spirit's creep
By severing sons' minds from skin and bones
And dulling daughters' hearts into restless sleep.


Yet to the Clockmaker all eventually returned
Save one experimental expire;
When the spherical space around the stone burned
With the crackle and spark of raining heaven's fire.


Aubrey read through the phrases over and over again. He placed *Solluna* gently on the ground, ran inside and hurried back into the yard with pen and paper. He scrawled the poem down quickly, not trusting his frayed mind to remember it. He had learned the first poem by heart simply by repetition, but time was no longer a friend on his side.

He wrapped *Solluna* in its burlap sack and tied the drawstring around his waist.

Aubrey considered his time restraints and decided his father would not be home for at least another hour. That was all he needed to find some answers. He picked up Magnos' bike and rode quickly back up Dalton Street. Passing Rodriqa's house and the empty lot, he turned down the dirt hill next to the overpass.

Aubrey skidded out as he stopped in the middle of the dusty, barren space. There was no stove, no garbage bags overflowing with collected items, and no wind chimes hanging from the supporting beams overhead. Every trace of the Widow Wizenblatt was gone.

The darkness of loneliness closed in on Aubrey. Who else could he turn to? Who else might give him an ounce of direction in these awry matters of the unseen? He reread the scribbled poem in his hand.

Suddenly, another person popped in his head. He crammed the paper into his pocket and raced out of the underpass.

# Meddling Mischief

Aubrey rode into the empty Lake Julian High School parking lot, apprehensively studying every corner and shadow for any unwelcome nightly visitors: ghostly, hairy, or otherwise. The streetlights stood like tall, silent soldiers on guard, flooding spotted sections of the asphalt with a dull, orange glow. Rectangular fluorescent lights blared stark, white beams down from underneath school's ledge awning, easily cleaning the walls and doors of night's darkness.

Aubrey coasted up to the front door and leaned Magnos' bike on an entrance column as he went afoot. He placed his forehead against one of the windowed double doors and cupped his hands around his forehead to occlude the glare. Inside, the foyer and atrium were dimly lit by fluorescent lights and a foggy, red glint from the fire alarms. It was too dark to see down any of the hallways, and he saw no evidence of any activity, human or otherwise.

Aubrey jogged around to the side of the school and looked into the next set of doors. The hallways were dark in the middle, but better lit at their intersections. Out of the corner of his eye, he thought he saw a flicker of movement. He focused his gaze to the far right, and a dark figure floated into another hallway.

Aubrey raced to the next set of doors and cautiously peered through the window. He found what he was looking for.

Griggs tromped through the hallway, dredging his mop along the tile slowly and methodically.

Aubrey knocked feverishly on the window. Griggs paused and looked outside, then turned back to his mop and resumed cleaning.

Aubrey beat his fist against the door. Griggs ignored him.

Aubrey untied the top of the sack around his waist and pulled out *Solluna*. He slammed the rusty book against the window so Griggs could see it.

Griggs faced Aubrey slowly, and his wooly worm-like eyebrows scrunched up along his forehead. He dropped his mop and walked toward the door.

Griggs pressed the door open. "You shouldn't be here. It's late," scolded Griggs. "Don't you have a curfew?!"

"Yes, but I need your help," replied Aubrey earnestly.

"Help with what? Cleaning your rusty, metal box?"

"It's not a box," replied Aubrey quietly. "Please look at it." Aubrey opened the tarnished, brown *Solluna* and flipped the pages, hoping Griggs would see something.

"You should take better care of your things," he criticized. "It's beyond repair. Looks like its only fit for the dump...or smelting." He pulled an oily rag from his back pocket, bunched up a corner of cloth and spit on it. Griggs rubbed an area of rust on one of the crusty, metal pages.

*Solluna* burst into a fiery, brilliant gold. The electric tingle zapped Griggs' fingers, and he jerked his arm back. Aubrey felt the tingle, too. Startled, Aubrey jumped backwards and dropped the book to the floor. It clanged heavily along the tile, quickly resuming its blemished appearance.

"Sorry," mumbled Aubrey. "I should have warned you that it feels weird when you touch it." He scrambled to recover the book off the floor.

Griggs resheathed his rag and sniffled, squiggling his whiskers.

"Do you know what this is?" Aubrey asked meekly.

Griggs glowered at him and frowned. "Simply asking a question doesn't guarantee an answer," snapped Griggs. "You should take that back to where it belongs!"

Aubrey wilted, confused and embarrassed. He briefly considered trying to give it back to Ms. Thistlewood, then shuddered at the thought. "I…can't."

"I know you stole it," accused Griggs. "No one would willingly give it to you."

"Yeah, but-"

"Yeah, but, what," mocked Griggs. "Do you know how much trouble this *book* is?"

Of all the things that had caused Aubrey trouble recently, this book seemed pretty low on the list. He didn't know how to respond.

"Do *you* know what this is?" interrogated Griggs.

Aubrey thought for a moment. "It's a book of poetry?"

Griggs cackled wildly. "It's not even a book." He looked at *Solluna* disgustedly.

"It is an incarnation of meddling mischief. It's been here since the beginning of time. And it has rarely been a book."

Aubrey grimaced at his puzzling words. Griggs collected his thoughts and sighed heavily. "It's been known by many names: the fire of Prometheus, the book of Raziel, Pandora's box, Solomon's key, the string of Ariadne, and even Captain Kid's buried treasure.

"It is a prize soaked in myth and exalted by fairy tales. Kings and queens have wasted entire national stores of gold questing to possess it. Sages, knights, and saints have spent lifetimes searching for it. Countless others have sacrificed sanity, fame, wealth and security, only to be disappointed."

"But I wasn't trying to find it. I just did," rebutted Aubrey.

"Transfer of possession rarely occurs willingly or easily," asserted Griggs. Aubrey stared at his feet and swallowed the huge lump in his throat. "So either by thievery or murder, it found its way into your hands." Griggs softened his tone and asked, "Can you read what it says?"

"Yeah…I guess, but there was only one poem, the same poem on every page and I could only read it in the daylight, but just now…in the moonlight, there was something different."

"Most people who want to understand it, cannot. And those who can, have met sorrowful ends. It chooses to whom it speaks and always in riddle. It displays its knowledge in a way that seems to impart significance or indispensable aid, when, in reality, what it has to offer is mostly confounding and elusive."

Aubrey struggled with Griggs' explanation. "I was able to decipher the first poem. I just need a little help with the second one."

"And the information you gleaned from the first poem, did it make things better or worse?"

Aubrey mused for a moment, recalling his encounter with Ms. Thistlewood in front of the Tomb of Enoch under the dam. Better or worse weren't the right words to describe the outcome. What might have happened if Ms. Thistlewood had opened the tomb? Aubrey didn't really know. He stammered and sputtered looking for a way to explain the details.

"Bury the book, Aubrey. It will only bring more trouble. If you follow what it says, even if it does bring you success, the darkness of this world and its minions will chase you ceaselessly for control of it."

"But if *Solluna* is known to be so tricky, why would anyone want it?"

Griggs leaned slowly back against the wall, crossed his arms and closed his eyes. "In a time before time, it was a gift between former friends, which brokered a promise of peace. That promise was forgotten. Our world has long suffered the consequences of the collapsing covenant. Some think if the gift is returned to its owner, then all that suffering would be reversed. Others believe that it was a gift of great power, and they wish to wield its secrets. Regardless of what it really is, ignore it."

Aubrey sighed, tired of hearing this advise. "What if you read the poem for me and tell me what you think, then I'll never read the book again," pleaded Aubrey.

"I can't! Only its owner can read what it says."

"I wrote the poem down." Aubrey pulled the crumpled piece of paper from his pocket and smoothed it out with his hands against his thigh. He handed it to Griggs.

Griggs sighed heavily, disgruntled at this request. He pulled a pair of bent, wire-rimmed bifocals from his pocket and read the paper through the lenses.

"It's mostly gibberish," decided Griggs hastily. "The reference to stones is highly suspect. Everyone knows you can't kill a spirit, but you can send it back to where it came from."

A spark of intuition flashed inside Aubrey's mind.

"It means little to me, but I can see by the expression on your face, it means the world to you," mused Griggs.

"YES!"

"Of course it does," mumbled Griggs.

"Of course it does! That's it," exclaimed Aubrey with heightened enlightenment.

"Exactly! That's what it does," growled Griggs. "It seemingly provides immense insight, but without context! Misinterpretation leads to poor decisions and loss of judgment, and then the bearer's life is worse off than if he or she hadn't bothered seeking its wisdom in the first place."

"But you don't understand!" countered Aubrey.

"I know. That's why I'm immune to it."

"I've been haunted by a ghost since the beginning of school, and one of my closest friends, her dad was taken tonight by the Tsul'kalu...I mean Bigfoot...I mean Bigfeet...there's a whole clan of them. The same ones who have been attacking the mine."

"Yes...yes...I read the newspaper," grumbled Griggs.

"You don't understand! Bigfoot isn't what everyone thinks they are...it's a spirit too...like a ghost almost...and this is what I need to fix the entire situation. We can send the Tsul'kalu back to where they came from and free Hovis from his Sandman anathem, and everything will return to normal."

Griggs guffawed loudly.

"A victim of the Sandman anathem can't haunt anyone, boy! They can't move at all. That's the point of the curse. They're fixed in place, bound to their old world...their past life, unless your ghost is linked to another spirit, and that can only happen if that person is willing to accept terrible, personal loss. No one in their right mind would ally themselves to a ghost suffering the Sandman curse. You are greatly mistaken, and I suspect this book is at the heart of your delusion."

Aubrey's mind whirred and twisted into an odd, new reality. He grabbed *Solluna* and shoved it back into the burlap sack. He turned and walked away toward the front of the school. The door slammed behind him.

Griggs pushed open the door. "Aubrey," he shouted after him.

Aubrey kept walking.

"AUBREY!"

He picked up his pace with determination as he approached the front corner of the school.

"NAWBEY!!"

Aubrey stopped instantly, his knees locking in place. A chill prickled down his spine. Only one other person had ever called him by that name. He snapped his head around and glowered at Griggs.

"Hide the book. Beware its deception. Cling tightly to your friends. Your compassion for each other has brought you all this far! Don't ignore the bond you have."

Aubrey nodded his head in agreement. For the first time, the fog around his universe parted, and he understood that the contention over the Tomb of Enoch was not simply a treasure hunt or a squabble over stolen goods. This battle was a portion of a greater struggle. Battle lines had been drawn, and there weren't only two sides warring for primary authority. There were likely scores of invested parties, each with a sword to bear and a place to fight, and he and his friends had been thrust into the middle of the fray.

There was much Aubrey didn't know, but of one thing he was perfectly clear. He would no longer be a casualty. If fate had chosen to include him in the battle, then he would choose to fight!

## The Rift that Keeps on Giving

Flickers of blurry blue lightning highlighted sheets of rain that cascaded down the glass panes of the spare bedroom window. The storms raging outside were sympathetically calming to Jordana, as the drops of rain pelting the roof broke the eerie silence of the murky early morning, and the rumbling thunder mirrored her heart's tumult of sorrow and dread.

Jordana thought sleep might embrace her easily tonight after her marathon of fretful insomnia. Despite her comfort in the Auerbach's home, the destructive invasion of the clan of Tsul'kalu and the loss of her father stole all rest from her mind. She lay on the bed on top of the blankets, unable to bury herself under a single sheet without oppressive thoughts of coerced restriction. Her eyes blinked quickly and twitched from the open door to the window and around the room to each wall in strict surveillance. She had decided to leave the bedroom light off, for if the Tsul'kalu hunted for her along Dalton Circle, the glow from the window would only make it easier to find her.

Jordana twiddled the ring that she found next to the injured Magnos between her fingertips, hoping to absorb from its smooth metal surface some understanding of why the Tsul'kalu had stolen all of her rings and then returned them one by one.

"Jordana," whispered a soft moan from the hallway. She stiffened and sat up straight as she focused every sense on the sound.

"Jordana," echoed the voice again, and this time it was unmistakable. The voice belonged to her father.

"Dad?" she whispered in reply, but there was no response. She slid out of bed and crept cautiously over to the door. "Hello?" she asked, but her greeting was lost in the darkness.

Jordana flipped the light switch but nothing happened. She groaned with frustration as she realized that the storm must have interrupted the power to the house. She stepped into the hallway, and her mind spun and twisted in confusion. She was not standing in the upstairs of Rodriqa's house. She was standing in the hallway in front of her father's bedroom.

The lightning flashed through the window in her father's room, and she peered around the threshold, expecting to see a gaping, mangled breach in the side of the house. The walls were whole, with the beams and trusses unscathed, and even the wallpaper completely intact, but the floor was bare. There was no bed, no dresser, no chairs and the rugs were all missing.

"Jordana!" cried her father with greater urgency. She turned and stared down the stairs. It sounded more like he was calling her from the kitchen.

She leaned over the banister and yelled, "Dad?! Where are you?!"

All the furniture in the living room, including the antiques, the tribal wall hangings and couches were missing. Jordana walked several steps down and craned her neck to view more of the downstairs. "What's going on?" she yelled in confusion.

"JORDANA?!" Her dad screamed. The voice roared from the spare bedroom. She bolted back upstairs.

Suddenly, the lightning and thunder cracked together above the roof. Arturo hung outside the window, his hands gripping tightly to the ledge above. The rain washed over his face and shoulders and dribbled off the tips of his doused hair. He struggled to keep from falling, raking his feet along the siding to gain footing in the downpour.

"DAD?!" Jordana shrieked and rushed over to the window. She clawed at the lock, but it wouldn't move.

"JORDANA! LOOK INSIDE!" Arturo struggled to speak as the rainwater poured down the front of his face and into his nose and mouth.

"How do I fix this?!" Jordana sobbed with fright and frustration. She slapped her hand against the window, and it shattered. Shards of glass flew toward her.


Jordana woke up. The faint early morning light kindled the dawn outside, and the dew clung to the window. Her sheets were damp and disheveled with sweat, and her arms and legs ached with exhaustion. Tears filled her eyes, and she held her head and cried. Not only was her mind unraveling, but now her world was being ripped to ragged tatters. Her dreams were circling the event horizon of insanity, the Tsul'kalu had robbed her of sleep and stability, and now her father, her only parent, and her last anchor to reason, was gone.

Jordana needed to throw something. She grabbed her ring off the nightstand and cocked her arm. An odd darkness between her fingers caught her eye, and she stopped in mid-throw. She opened her hand, and the ring tumbled down into her lap. Black marks had been scratched inside the inner edge of the ring, just like the other reclaimed rings. But these markings were more distinct, more organized.

She angled the ring between her fingers, and her lips rounded and curled as she realized the scraped lines were letters, forming words. And they were written in ancient Cherokee.

Aubrey's eyes twitched to and fro, looking at his alarm clock every few minutes. He tried to distract himself by counting cracks in the ceiling. He tried to bore himself to sleep by staring at a single spot in the window. He hadn't slept for more than twenty-two consecutive minutes all night. His anxiety was forcing him to keep track. He glanced at the alarm clock again.

# 6:47

He had lain in his bed since returning from his late night rendezvous with Griggs, and his thoughts raced with hypotheticals and suppositions. His heart spiraled from self-pity to disbelief, and finally to despair. But at some point around 4:41 am, his internal jumble of heartache and uncertainty reached critical mass, forging a fury of resolute determination within him.

Aubrey knew his days at Lake Julian High were numbered. His time to disprove his insanity had evaporated. His chances to protect those who had suffered with him were fleeting, and he had one final opportunity to unveil the culprit behind the madness. Griggs had given him the final pieces of information he needed to fit everything together. After a few hours of uninterrupted mental mulling and neurotic kneading, he had a simple, straightforward plan. All he needed was a little help. He read the clock's face again.

# 6:49

However, subtlety would be a necessity, with his recent infamous shenanigans placing him high on most people's suspicion radar. He knew he couldn't call Buzz on a Saturday morning until the hour was a little more decent.

The dull, gray glare of early sunrise edged its way through the valley, and for the first time over the long night, Aubrey could make out the bleak outline of the Auerbach house through his window. He sat up in bed and curled his legs against his chest, lost somewhere between his mind and his heart.

Never had he wanted to visit Rodriqa's house so badly in all his life. Jordana was a dozen yards away from him, lying in bed, engulfed in another sleepless night, tormented by beasts and the loss of her father. Aubrey was helpless to comfort her, and he knew he was the best person for the job. Who else had suffered like the two of them had over the past couple of months?

He ran through scenario after scenario of how he could ring Rodriqa's front doorbell and explain to Mr. and Mrs. Auerbach that he had to speak to Rodriqa and Jordana right away because…he knew they were still in danger…or perhaps because he needed to share with them the battle which he now understood, that all five of them were caught in the middle of. But regardless of the reasoning he would provide, without a novel crisis or divine interference, going over to see Jordana in the middle of the night would exhibit an unacceptable degree of desperation, and he already had enough going against him. He looked at the alarm clock again.

# 6:55

Aubrey decided he had waited long enough. He stood up out of bed and tiptoed into the hallway. Both Gaetan's and his parents' bedroom doors were closed, and he couldn't hear a sound. He knew he would only need a few minutes of privacy to set his plan into motion.

Aubrey hurriedly slid down the stairs and turned the corner into the kitchen. He reached for the phone. It rang loudly. He jerked the receiver off its stand, hoping the ring hadn't woken anyone, and slowly put the speaker to his ear.

"Aubrey?" questioned his best friend's familiar voice.

"Buzz! I was just about to call you," Aubrey replied. "How did you get my new number?"

"One of the guys I online-game with works for a branch of one of the local phone companies. He was able to sleuth out your number in no time," exulted Buzz. "I've got info. Good news or bad first?"

"Good news," chose Aubrey.

"The police found Jordana's dad."

"Is he okay?"

"That's the bad news. They found him at the mine, tied to the top of an excavator, sitting in a carved, oak wooden chair with a red 'X' painted across his chest.

"How bizarre," interjected Aubrey.

"No doubt. Supposedly he was totally delirious, and he couldn't tell the police what had happened."

"Where is he now?" asked Aubrey

"They took him to the hospital," replied Buzz. "Do you think we should go visit him?"

"No," asserted Aubrey. "He'll have enough visitors today with everything else going on, and I'm sure Jordana will want to see him alone. Besides I need your help. *Solluna* said something different last night, and I found out a few things that change up the score."

"Really?! Tell me!"

A tingle raced down Aubrey's spine, and the hairs on his arms stood to attention. He felt like he was being watched. "Meet me at Hovis' in half an hour, and call Rodriqa. We'll need her help, too," spewed Aubrey as quickly as he could into the phone, and then he hung up the receiver. Aubrey closed his eyes and turned around slowly, scanning the downstairs. The phosphenes faded quickly, and only darkness remained behind his eyelids. He looked up and down, left and right, certain something was there.

"Problem with your eyes?" asked his father from in front of him. Aubrey opened his eyes up suddenly and scrambled for the words to explain his behavior. Mr. Taylor didn't let him get much mumbling out. "Hovis?" he questioned authoritatively.

"It's a project for school," returned Aubrey, righting his train of thought. "Buzz and I need to finish it this weekend, and it's the only time we have to work together."

"I don't think you really need to worry too much about homework from Lake Julian," countered his father. "We meet with the Dean of St. Pinnetack-wah early Monday. It shouldn't take long to get you transferred after that."

Aubrey's face hardened with resolution. "Until everything is final, I don't think I should let any of my work here slip."

Mr. Taylor considered his response. "Be home by sundown. I'll be at the electric plant late. I'll have Gaetan check-in on you."

## Nosey Ring

Rodriqa walked quietly into the spare bedroom, hoping not to disturb any sleep the dream-starved Jordana might be getting. Yet, she wasn't surprised to see her sitting upright in bed, fully awake.

"Did you rest at all?" Rodriqa asked. Jordana shrugged. She turned her golden ring round and round between her fingers, and seemed to be concentrating on it.

"They found your dad," Rodriqa said quietly as she sat on the edge of the bed.

"Is he okay?" Jordana didn't look up.

"He's alive," replied Rodriqa carefully. "They've taken him to the hospital."

Jordana continued staring blankly at the ring.

"My parents offered to take you down there, whenever you want to go."

Jordana didn't respond.

Rodriqa scratched her head, unsure of the best thing to say. "I'm sure you're exhausted. Maybe you should try and get some rest, and we could go later. My parents said you're welcome to stay here as long as you like."

Jordana looked straight at Rodriqa as heavy tears dripped down Jordana's cheeks. She handed the ring to Rodriqa. "The Tsul'kalu has been leaving behind one of my rings each time it comes to my house." She choked through each word as sobs welled up in her throat. Rodriqa took the ring and examined it briefly. She shook her head, completely confused.

"It stole a bunch of my rings the first time it broke into my house and, one by one, it has been returning them." Jordana sniffed back her tears and rubbed her eyes and nose with the sleeve of her shirt.

"I don't get it," replied Rodriqa.

"I didn't either…until this morning. This ring has marks etched on the inside of it, which were not there before it was stolen."

Rodriqa looked along the inner rim and saw the irregular cuts and dashes scoured into the metal. "Looks like it's been scraped up pretty badly. Maybe the Sasquatch was trying to use it as a nail file?" Rodriqa smiled, but Jordana's mood didn't change.

"It's writing, and I can read it."

Rodriqa looked at the ring more closely. "How? It looks like a mess," she said warily.

"It's in ancient Cherokee." Jordana took the ring back from her and angled it between her index finger and thumb. She turned the ring slowly, and her lips moved before she spoke. "Do not let Hovis open the tomb, but avoid him without fail."

"Sounds like good advice," replied Rodriqa. "Did any of the other rings ever say anything?"

"I don't know. I never knew it was writing before."

"Too bad our friends won't be heeding the Tsul'kalu's warning."

"What do you mean?" Jordana's tears of grief were slowing from worry.

"Buzz left me a message a little bit ago. Aubrey figured something out, and the two of them are headed back to Hovis' house. They wanted us to meet up with them. It didn't make much sense, really."

Jordana jumped out of bed and hurriedly changed into her street clothes.

"What are you doing?" asked Rodriqa, slightly confused by her abrupt change in attitude.

"We have to stop them!"

Rodriqa sighed, almost annoyed. "I think you should be with your dad right now and let Aubrey and Buzz do their thing."

Jordana glared at Rodriqa, her face taut with determination. "No! Don't you see, Rodriqa? The Tsul'kalu was never after me…it was after my dad! It was trying to help me!"

Rodriqa's eyes widened with the revelation.

Jordana wiped her face and slid the ring on her finger. "We have to stop Aubrey and Buzz. My dad can wait. *This* is all his fault."

## Stealthcare

Magnos squinted through blinding whiteness as he slowly opened his eyes. For a moment, he thought he was in heaven. Then he tried to move, and a stabbing pain nettled him inside and out from head to toe. His eyes adjusted to the bright light, and his ears tuned into a repetitively monotonous shrill beep that jabbed at his eardrums every few seconds.

He pushed himself up in his hospital bed. His left arm wouldn't move. He leaned down and examined himself. His left arm was casted in white plaster from his shoulder to his fingertips. He methodically wiggled his toes and fingers and decided everything else seemed to be functioning, despite most of his body surface being patched with swathes of gauze and bandages.

The white curtain next to his bed flew back quickly, and a portly nurse in green scrubs glowed at him with a welcoming smile. She stood in the doorway, holding a small plastic cup. "I'm surprised you're awake so early," she said. "I figured you'd sleep most of the day." She had brown tight curly hair, and her bright blue eyes eased a bit of Magnos' pain. She walked over to his bed and pulled the pillows from around him to the top of the bed so he could sit up.

"I have some medicine for you," she said happily as she pushed the button on the side rail, angling the head of the bed upward.

"What kind of medicine?" grunted Magnos, one syllable at a time.

"It's for pain. It will help you rest." She slid a large white pill onto his tongue, and handed him the plastic cup of water. Lifting his chin up, he swallowed the pill and upturned the cup into his mouth.

"Good boy," she said, and patted him gently on the shoulder. "Do you need anything?"

"Maybe more visitors?" drifted a kind and comforting tone from the door, like a mother singing a lullaby. The tall and modelesque Fayla leaned against the threshing with her straight blonde hair cradling her neck. Magnos' eyes widened at the sight of his sister, and the monotonous beep in the background pinged more quickly.

"The perfect medicine for an ailing patient," replied the nurse. She turned and motioned for Fayla to come inside. The nurse scurried toward the foot of the bed and lifted the chart hanging from the railing. She retuned to the head of the bed, watching his chest closely. Placing the bell of her stethoscope over Magnos' heart, she squeezed his wrist while looking at her watch. After half of a minute, she scribbled a few numbers on the chart and replaced it on the end of his bed.

Fayla took a couple of steps into the room and smiled broadly at the nurse. "Thank you so much for taking care of him." Her words were soppingly sweet.

The nurse nodded at Fayla appreciatively. "He's been the perfect patient," she said. The nurse smiled at Magnos and walked out of the room.

Fayla pulled the curtain closed and scowled at Magnos. She dropped a bag full of clothes at the end of the bed. "I can't believe you're wasting my time!"

"You didn't have to come," he stammered.

"I wouldn't be here if I didn't have to be," she chided brusquely. "Mother told me to come see you and bring you some clothes. She'll be back in town tonight."

"Thanks," he murmured.

"You can thank me by *not* trying to be the center of attention all the time. Did you know I was supposed to be at a party for the Paddling Pumpkin Parade right now? But instead I'm here with you, because you continue to hang out with those misfits."

Magnos shifted his eyes to the far side of the room. "Have you heard anything?"

"About what?" she replied in a petulant tone.

Magnos looked down and closed his lips, immediately sorry he'd asked the question.

"You mean about your crazy friends? Yeah," she chuckled cruelly as she glanced in a small mirror on the wall and fixed her hair. "They found that Jordana girl's dad. Actually he's down the hall. He was hung up in a chair at the mine. So weird! They should put the two of you in a room together and call it the loony ward."

Magnos perked up. "Is her dad okay?"

"How should I know? I'm just glad you'll be out of my hair and stuck in here for a few more days. Tell Mother I said hello." Fayla turned on her heels, with her silky blonde hair swishing behind her, and strode out the door.

Magnos listened as her heels clicked down the hallway and disappeared around a corner. Sighing with relief, he pushed himself up in the bed, and his calves shuddered with spasms. He gently dragged one leg to the side of the bed, followed by the other, and sat up. The room spun for a moment. He took a couple of deep breaths, and the world righted itself.

Magnos stood up and balanced himself slowly. He could feel the pain medication start to work. He took a step forward, and something pulled and poked inside his right elbow. Looking down, Magnos could see a coil of clear, plastic tubing taped to his forearm arm, with a needle piercing his skin just above it. He traced the tubing with his eyes and found the bag of I.V. fluids hanging from a metal pole a few feet away. Magnos grabbed the pole and rolled it toward him.

With his casted hand holding his hospital gown closed, and the other hand directing the I.V. pole, Magnos waddled out into the hallway. His stiff feet slapped against the frigidly sterile tile floor. He inspected both directions of the spacious corridor, which appeared to be nearly mirror images of each other, except for a few varying pieces of medical equipment resting outside of patient rooms.

Magnos didn't need to ask anyone which room Mr. Galilahi was in. There was a flurry of policemen, nurses, miners and reporters buzzing in and out of a room at the end of the hall, next to the nurse's station. He turned the pole and his torso to face the room, hoping he wouldn't need to make any turns until he reached the doorway, and lurched forward. He was met by nodding smiles and curt greetings from staff who were carrying breakfast trays and personal hygiene items to other patients on the floor, each clearly aware of the source of his injuries, yet unwilling to expose too much of their intrigue.

Sergeant Van Zenny stormed out of Mr. Galilahi's room, chased by several newspaper reporters barraging him with 'whats' and 'whys' and begging him for a statement. He waved his hands authoritatively in front of them and cut their questions short. "What's important is that Mr. Galilahi is safe, and now he needs privacy to mend and be with his family. In the meantime, we'll investigate this attack, just as vigorously as we have the others and bring justice to those responsible. Perhaps a township-wide curfew is in order, with all that's been happening lately." His arms snapped to his sides, forcefully closing any opportunity for further discussion, and he disappeared around the corner. The rumor-hungry flock chased after him.

Magnos shuffled into the doorway, and his stomach dropped as he stared at Mr. Galilahi in his hospital bed. The craters in his face wrinkled up tightly from the surrounding swelling of his face, and the distended bags under his eyes propped up his lower lids, shutting them flush, nearly to his eyebrows. Purple and blue hues of bruises discolored his arms and legs, and his chest was wrapped in gauze.

Magnos walked over to the bed and stood over Jordana's dad, awestruck at the beating his body had taken. Magnos felt his own physical pain ebb as his mind absorbed the composite of all of the injuries of Jordana's dad.

"Mr. Galilahi," Magnos addressed him formally in a soft and somber tone. "I know you can't hear me, and I know that this probably isn't the right time to tell you this, but," Magnos swallowed hard against his dry throat, "I'm sorry I demolished your kitchen."

Magnos traced the multiple lines of plastic tubing that crisscrossed the bed, from the I.V.'s in Mr. Galilahi's arms to the oxygen prongs taped into his nose, and other tubes hanging from the edge of the sheets, which drained bodily fluids. He reminded Magnos of a modern-day Frankenstein.

"I'm sorry I couldn't save you and Jordana from the Tsul'kalu," Magnos murmured gently.

"It wasn't Jordana who needed saving." Magnos' eyes widened as Mr. Galilahi's jaw twisted to speak.

"I'm sorry, sir…I didn't mean to disturb you." Magnos spoke with quiet urgency.

"Don't worry about it. I'm not really in any condition to be resting," replied Jordana's father. His pupils rolled within the thin slit his eyelids could hold open. Shifting his weight in the bed, he clutched his chest to ease the searing pain, caused by the slightest movement.

"Do you want me to call your nurse?" asked Magnos.

Mr. Galilahi took short, shallow breaths until the pain subsided. "No, I'm okay."

"What did the Tsul'kalu do to you?"

Mr. Galilahi hissed a chuckle through his swollen jowls. "It feels like they tried to rip out my stomach through my spine."

"I don't understand. I thought the Sasquatch was after Jordana."

"No, it's always been me they were after."

"But why?" asked Magnos.

Mr. Galilahi snorted, both a little amused and annoyed. "I gave a ghost new life."

Magnos thought carefully about what Mr. Galilahi said. "Hovis Trottle?"

Mr. Galilahi turned his head slowly and eyed Magnos warily. "How do you know that name?"

"Hovis is Aubrey's ghost," replied Magnos. Mr. Galilahi continued glaring at Magnos, awaiting explanation. "Aubrey…Aubrey Taylor…our friend…Jordana's friend….Aubrey's been haunted by Hovis since the beginning of school. We found his house under the cemetery, and he was at the raft race…Wait! What does Hovis have to do with the Tsul'kalu?"

Mr. Galilahi closed his eyes and sighed, hoping to exhale the grief as he recalled the memories. "The Tsul'kalu wish to protect what I have allowed Hovis to fight for."

"I don't understand," murmured Magnos.

"Few do," agreed Mr. Galilahi. "I only wanted to protect Jordana. Please understand me. I never intended evil upon anyone. But Hovis offered Jordana and I a new life."

"What do you mean?"

"Jordana and her mother, Lilliana, have always been the two most important people in my life. Lilliana was the most beautiful woman I had ever met, the woman of my dreams, the woman I never deserved."

Mr. Galilahi stared away from Magnos. "Lilliana was murdered, but her killers were never convicted, and what little Lilliana and I had been able to save during her young career as a musician was slowly eaten away. Her manager stole everything. In less than a year after her death, I was jobless, poor and nearly homeless, with my precious daughter to care for, and the only skill I had ever learned was mining. The problem was I hadn't been in the bottom of a mine in over a decade, thanks to Lilliana and her incredible voice.

"But I was out of options, so I returned to the mines." Mr. Galilahi squeezed his face taut through another wave of pain. "I resented the 16 hour-days of hard labor making next to nothing. Instead of being thoughtful and patient, I took matters into my own hands."

"What did you do?" asked Magnos with a steely expression.

"I had heard so many folk tales as a child about how thin the layer between worlds was, that penetrating one from the other was dangerously easy and as humans, we were uniquely part of both worlds. As the Clockmaker is, so we were made to be.

"Beings in the spirit world were constantly acting either on our behalf or to our detriment, and a whole man or woman would be aware of these influences, and could even manipulate them, if they were careful.

"As I wallowed in my loss and self-pity, Cherokee fables replayed in my mind. Eventually I decided I had to do what was best for Jordana.

Mr. Galilahi stretched his shoulder and winced. "I went searching for a spirit to help us. I hunted for weeks in my dreams, in prayer circles, but I never found anything. It was like I was completely out of touch with the other world.

"Then one day, I was walking home, when a woman came up to me from out of nowhere. Until that day I thought Lilliana was the most beautiful woman I'd ever seen, but this woman was entrancing in a way that seemed divinely spellbinding. Her red hair and pale green eyes locked up my mind, and I almost couldn't move.

"She told me she had an uncle who had died suddenly, and he had some unfinished personal business that had to be reconciled quickly, or else the fall-out among her family would be catastrophic. She offered fame and fortune beyond belief for a simple request...she asked me to link my soul to his and allow him to complete what he had left undone. The link would only last a few days, but the rewards would last a lifetime."

"Who could offer something like that?" asked Magnos with a curl to his lip.

"I don't know, but I was desperate and hardly in a position to turn down such a generous offer for what seemed a small inconvenience."

"How did she do it?"

"She spoke an oath and touched my forehead as I knelt. Quickly, I realized the mistake I had made. The physical explosion that fused the link between the ghost," Mr. Galilahi paused and rethought his choice of words, "...Hovis' spirit and my own claimed a great deal of the flesh from my face and my right hand and foot. I needed a cover story. I blamed my disfigurement on a mining explosion to keep suspicions low.

"After my recovery, things went well for a while. I got some insurance money and the mining company offered me a top foreman's position at the new mine here in Lake Julian. It was a fresh start for me and Jordana, and that was all I had hoped for."

"How did the Tsul'kalu get involved?" questioned Magnos.

Mr. Galilahi thought for a moment. "At first, I didn't make the connection between the Sasquatch attacks and my link to Hovis. In the Cherokee tradition, the Sasquatch is a forest guardian, and I thought that they were simply disturbed by the mine and would eventually relocate someplace else. But when they showed up at my house, I realized this was personal, and they were after me.

"You see, there's a good reason why no one's ever found Bigfoot bones or Sasquatch droppings in the forest. The Tsul'kalu are neither animal nor spirit. They live in the collapsed space between the natural and the supernatural, guarding both from the other. Consequently, neither world can ever be their home, which is why they are so elusive. And that's also why they had a problem with me. My link to Hovis was an unacceptable anomaly that pulled the two worlds too close together, and it was their place to remedy it.

"I stole a book from my brother and tried to break the bond myself, but the link with Hovis was too strong."

Mr. Galilahi dropped his head to his chest and closed his puffy eyelids. Magnos stood frozen and speechless. His brain was numb from Mr. Galilahi's words.

"Did they do it?" asked Magnos.

"Do what?" replied Arturo.

"Did the Tsul'kalu break the link between you and Hovis?"

Mr. Galilahi tenderly caressed the bandages on his chest. "It's weaker, but I can still feel Hovis, like a nagging nightmare. He's always there."

"So this," Magnos swallowed hard, "all of this…is your fault."

Mr. Galilahi sighed and closed his eyes. "I'm afraid so."

Fury billowed in Magnos' heart. Suddenly he realized, the reason for his imprisonment, the impetus behind Jordana's torment and Aubrey's hauntings, lay in front of him, in a man who should have known better, but chose the easy path. Bile rose to Magnos' lips. "If the link is weakened, then Hovis should be fragile, and he'll leave Aubrey alone. The Tsul'kalu will leave you all alone, and everything will return to normal?"

"Except that Hovis' plans are incomplete. The Tsul'kalu will be after Hovis next."

"Then they'll leave everyone else alone and go after Hovis?"

"But they can't get to him."

"Why not?"

"Hovis and that woman have a plan. They'll surround themselves with other creatures from the darkness that will keep the Tsul'kalu at bay."

"What creatures?"

"The Tsul'kalu aren't the only beings stuck in between worlds. When most of us leave the physical realm, sometimes we shed those parts of ourselves, which aren't so desirable. Jealousy, rage, and revenge aren't especially welcome qualities when you're soon to meet the Clockmaker. Those abandoned attributes can simply leave behind an imprint on the spiritual world, or they can mass together and form a spirit shard that spends its days scouring the Earth with unquenchable hunger, wanting nothing more but to ravage the life from other spirits so they can be whole again."

"Do they look like big black worms?" asked Magnos.

"Maybe. Why?"

Magnos shook off the question. "What will the Tsul'kalu do next?"

"They'll go after anyone else associated with Hovis Trottle."

"Oh, no," murmured Magnos.

Mr. Galilahi looked Magnos directly in the eye. "Your friend Aubrey is in danger."

Magnos clenched his fists, tortured by what he had learned. "I have to go." Magnos pushed his I.V. pole out of the room and shuffled as quickly as he could down the hallway. The adrenaline rush of information propelled him forward and dulled the aches from his wounds. Wound dressings and the edges of his gown flapped in the air around him as he picked up speed. He turned into his room and picked up the telephone. His mind went blank. He suddenly realized he had never learned the phone numbers of any of his new friends. He looked around the room, desperate for a way to get in touch with someone. The bag of clothes on his bed was the only invitation to freedom he needed.

Magnos jerked the tape off his arm and yanked the tiny catheter inserted under his skin. He kinked his elbow to stop the bleeding and shoved a piece of gauze from another bandage that was already falling off in his elbow's crease. He ripped open the bag of clothes and shed his hospital gown and, with two disabled hands, dressed himself as best he could.


Mr. Galilahi watched Magnos leave the room and closed his eyes. He tried to clear his mind, hoping to release some of the pain, both from the damage to his body and from the ache in his heart. He was angry, but he knew that retaining his ill temper would only lead to more destruction. He was sad, but he knew his grief would only consume him further if he continued to make the wrong decisions.

The room darkened, and the door shut quietly at the end of his bed. Arturo opened the slits of his eyes, and a tall, hazy figure approached him.

"Nurse?" His voice cracked hesitantly.

"Mr. Galilahi, how are you feeling?" The gentle, inviting voice eased his pain simply with its question.

"I've been better," he joked half-heartedly.

"Yes, you have," agreed the voice. A tall, shapely woman sat on his bed and touched his hand softly. "Unfortunately, your further assistance is required, Arturo."

# Missing Ink

Buzz chugged up the hill toward the cemetery at more of a trot than a run. His backpack and belly bobbed up and down like a seesaw, threatening to throw him off balance with each step.

Aubrey sat on Magnos' bicycle next to the Trottle plot. Annoyed, Aubrey eyed Buzz with a stern and weary face. "Dude! What took you so long?!"

Buzz flung himself down on the short plot stone wall and panted between each responding word. "I...had...to...wait...for...my...mom...to... drop... me...off... there's...no...way...I... was...walking...the... entire...way... from...my...house."

Aubrey took note of his demeanor. "Does she know why you're here?"

"No way! I made up some story about the Paddling Pumpkin Parade."

"How's Jordana?" asked Aubrey.

Buzz shrugged. "I couldn't get a hold of anybody." Aubrey frowned, hoping for more information.

"What did the book say?" asked Buzz.

Aubrey handed him the crumpled piece of paper, its ink smudged from its repeated handling. Buzz skimmed it quickly.

"So what does it mean?"

Aubrey grabbed the paper back impatiently and shoved it in his pocket. "It means that you can't really kill a spirit, but you can send it back to where it came from, and in some puzzling way the poem tries to tell you how to do that. But that's not the important part. Besides from what I've found out, the book is a little on the loony-side itself.

"After some investigating, I've learned that the Sandman Anathem binds the ghost to where they are...not just to the earth itself, but also to the same spot where it left its body."

"Then how does Hovis walk around?"

"That's just it. We didn't read enough about the anathem from the book in Hovis' library. From what I've gathered, it goes on to say that only by linking itself to another living soul could the cursed spirit have enough power to move about."

"Then Hovis must have somehow linked himself to Ms. Thistlewood," surmised Buzz.

"I don't think so," rebutted Aubrey tersely.

"Why not? It's the most logical answer."

"Because linking your soul to a ghost comes at a terrible price."

"What price?"

"I'm not sure. That's why we have to read more in the book. We have to find out who is empowering Hovis and then stop them."

"And didn't it mention something about stones?" added Buzz.

Aubrey shook his head. "I'm not sure."

"If the book changed what it's saying, I'm sure it did so for a reason," surmised Buzz.

Aubrey hopped off the bike and walked over to Hovis' grave, his mind focused on his goal. Buzz crawled over to the blue tarp and pulled back the corner.

A wave of hot air rolled out from the grave, like opening a car door on a warm summer's day. Aubrey backed up and blinked quickly, his eyes drying from the heat.

"Whoa," said Buzz. "It was cold down there before. Can you see anything?"

Aubrey nodded, understanding what Buzz was asking. He closed his eyes and stared down into the grave. The phosphenes danced, and the lights slowly disappeared, until all that remained was a shifting darkness, the same distant, undulating pitch he had seen before.

"Nothing there," said Aubrey, hoping his voice sounded certain.

"I'm not sure we can tolerate that kind of heat," added Buzz.

"We won't be down there long," replied Aubrey.

Buzz pulled an electric lantern out of his backpack and handed it to Aubrey. Next out of the bottom of his pack he retrieved a latticed, rectangular cube of thin, metal strips with multiple hinges at either end.

Aubrey turned on the lantern. "What's that?"

Buzz opened the hinges one by one. "Watch this." The thin metal strips formed a long solid pole, lengthening about a foot with each strip he unhinged. Buzz climbed down onto Hovis' roof and took the lantern from Aubrey. He formed a hook with the two end sections, threading them through the lantern's handle. Slowly Buzz lowered the lantern down into the hole as he opened the device piece by piece.

Buzz stared down into the attic as sweat beaded up on his forehead. Everything looked the same as before, and he could see the rope ladder coiled chaotically off to the side. He dropped the lantern onto the floor and unhooked it. He shifted the metal pole over and carefully threaded the hook through one of the ladder's rungs.

"Got it," he said triumphantly, as he pulled the ladder up out of the attic and onto the roof. Buzz climbed clumsily out of the grave and snapped portions of the metal strips together, locking a section around the top rung of the ladder. He wrapped the pole around the base of the rough-hewn cross and locked another section back into the rung.

"We're good to go," reported Buzz. Aubrey was genuinely impressed, although he knew he shouldn't be. Buzz always came through.

The two boys climbed precariously down into the attic. The smothering heat enveloped them, and they were drenched as they stepped onto the attic floor.

"Eyes," Buzz murmured softly, trying not to anger Aubrey.

Aubrey closed his eyes and looked around. He scratched his head, both confused and a little concerned. "There's something I didn't tell you all last time."

"What?" exclaimed Buzz, more surprised than curious.

"Well," said Aubrey needing time to form the words in his mind. "There's nothing close by, but last time I saw movement in the distance, which I didn't think was a big deal, but…"

"BUT?!" Buzz trembled with hint of fear and a dash of anger.

"Now it's a lot of movement and they're…shiny."

"What's shiny?!"

"It's these black *things*, kind of like the worms but really small, and they're just twisting around each other, but they weren't shiny before."

"What does shiny mean?!"

"I have no idea."

"How many of them are there?"

Aubrey shrugged.

"Maybe we should go back."

"No," replied Aubrey firmly as he opened his eyes. "There is nothing nearby. We can grab the book and get out of here in no time." Aubrey picked up the lantern and walked toward the stairs. Buzz scurried after him, hurrying away from the darkening attic.

They carefully climbed down the narrow spiral staircase. Aubrey would close his eyes every few steps to check for the unseen. They tiptoed across the hallway and stood over the grand staircase.

"I'll go first," offered Aubrey. "Step where I step." Buzz agreed easily.

Aubrey zigzagged down the stairs, aiming for the safest way down. Buzz followed several steps behind, wincing every time the wood creaked under his weight.

Aubrey waited for Buzz at the bottom landing. Buzz looked at the closed door in front of them. "I think we all hurried out of here without closing the door," he whispered.

"Maybe the change in the temperature pulled it shut," offered Aubrey.

Buzz couldn't disagree. They stepped toward the door, marveling at the intricately carved Circle of Circles on its face. Aubrey turned the handle and shone the light inside.

Aubrey couldn't believe what he saw. He ran frantically inside and hovered the lantern in front of the stacks of floor-to-ceiling shelves. Buzz edged his way inside, and his chin fell to his chest, awe-struck.

"They're gone," said Buzz quietly.

Aubrey ran to the end of the room and stood over the architect's desk. "No!" he shouted. It was bare. The shelves were empty, the locked sections were clean, and not a single book remained in the entire library. Buzz and kicked the metal floor. Even the bejeweled jar and the other sheet-covered items were missing.

Aubrey felt under the desk and pulled at its drawers. Nothing was there.

"How can this be?" asked Aubrey incredulously.

Buzz shrugged, searching his mind for possibilities.

A hand clasped tightly over Buzz's mouth, and he inhaled deeply, readying a scream.

# Widow Smack

The pain medication had kicked in. Magnos barreled down Dalton Circle, carrying his casted left arm concealed under his jacket, and he didn't feel a thing. He had run through high-grass fields, cut across busy intersections, and hoofed it over the Lake Julian Dam, and he barely felt winded. At first the cast had weighed him down a bit, but over the five miles or so, he had grown used to it.

Magnos turned into the Auerbach's empty driveway and raced up to the front door. He pounded frantically on the glass, anxious for someone to answer. No one came to the door. He covered his eyes with his hand to shade the glare from the sun, but he couldn't see anyone inside.

Magnos ran through the yard to Aubrey's house. He hopped up the porch steps and raised his hand to knock on the front door. The door flung open. Gaetan met Magnos eye to eye.

"Where's Aubrey?" they asked each other simultaneously with an equal amount of disdain. Gaetan gawked at the broken and wounded Magnos. "By the looks of it, you've seen him more recently than I have."

"I need to talk to him. Where is he?" demanded Magnos.

"Not a clue," rebutted Gaetan. Magnos clamped his good hand against the doorframe, intentionally blocking Gaetan's path. Gaetan sighed with annoyance. "My dad let him go work on some project with Buzz for school. He supposedly said something about meeting up with some guy named 'Hovis', but I don't know who he's talking about."

Magnos grimaced at the mention of Hovis' name. That was exactly what he was most fearful of hearing. He took a step back and made room for Gaetan to pass.

"Does Aubrey need help?" A dreamy voice echoed from behind Gaetan.

Gaetan turned quickly and replied, "No, Mom. Aubrey is fine." Magnos stole a glance over Gaetan's shoulder of the frail woman, dressed in worn pajamas, with a glazed look in her eyes. Gaetan stepped outside and slammed the door behind him. He shouldered Magnos out of his way and strutted down the porch stairs.

Magnos' grimace flattened, and his eyes widened with enlightenment. *Help.* That was exactly what Aubrey needed, what all five of them needed. And someone had already offered it.

"The bag lady! Where does she live?" hollered Magnos at Gaetan. Gaetan had opened his car door and had one leg in the foot well.

He swiveled back toward the porch. "You mean Old Widow Wizenblatt? She lives under the bridge overpass near the top of the street." Gaetan waved his hand toward the head of Dalton Circle. He titled his head to the side and squinted his eyes, almost examining Magnos. "What happened to you, dude? You could have been the most popular freshman ever and now…now, you're crazier than my brother." Gaetan sank into his car seat and shut the door.

For a moment, Gaetan's jab stung Magnos' ego. Honestly, a large part of Magnos missed his former popularity. He wanted to be one of the cool kids again, and there was some security in being the bully. But with all that had happened, from curses to cages, ghost to Bigfoot, his world had become a bigger, darker place. And he knew his place in the world would never be the same, could never be the same. And the only others who had any right to judge him were the ones who had experienced all of it with him.

Gaetan's Pontiac GTO fishtailed out of the driveway and rocketed up the street. Magnos trotted out of the yard and walked up the sidewalk toward the overpass. He cringed as he passed the empty lot that had once been his prison. He followed the brown clay dirt trail off the side of the bridge.

Magnos stepped quietly toward the bottom, as he could hear the Widow humming to herself. He peered around the concrete abutments, marveling at her odd collection of items: the shopping cart, the refrigerator pond, the wood-burning range, and her own personal spirit-draft wind chimes. The Widow sat on a bench wrapped in plastic, and from his point of view, it looked like she was polishing a bicycle seat.

The humming stopped. "You know it's rude to stare." Finished with the bicycle seat, she picked up a steering wheel and dabbed her rag with more black polish. Mrs. Wizenblatt resumed humming.

Magnos walked into the clearing under the overpass. The mallard in the waterlogged fridge quacked unhappily at his intrusion. "I need your help," he told the Widow.

"Uh-huh, you do." She looked up at him. "But do you know why you need my help?"

Magnos frowned, not in the mood to play games. "The Tsul'kalu are after Aubrey. I'm afraid what they did to Mr. Galilahi, they'll do to him."

The Widow cackled wildly. "Try again."

Magnos cocked his head, fully annoyed. "It's true," he demanded. "Mr. Galilahi is lying in a hospital bed, nearly torn apart by those hairy devils, and they're after anyone else who has anything to do with Hovis Trottle!"

Mrs. Wizenblatt returned to her polishing. "Mr. Galilahi is lying in a bed of his own making." Her dark tone bit back at Magnos.

Magnos uncovered his cast. "So this is my fault too, then, is it?"

"You were told to stay away."

Magnos' frustration mirrored the increasing pitch of his voice. "And my being kidnapped, that was also my fault?"

"No," replied the Widow with a calculated tone. "Sometimes *bad* things just happen to *bad* people."

Magnos stormed toward the Widow. She dropped the steering wheel and curled her fingers around her palm, twisting her hand in the air.

Magnos lifted off the ground and spun in circles in front of her, like a floating top. Magnos felt a crushing grip around him and his eyes widened with astonishment.

"Go home, boy," grumbled the Widow. "I'm clean out of patience today."

"But...what...about...Aubrey?" he grunted as he twirled in mid-air.

"To my knowledge, Aubrey hasn't helped Hovis," snapped the Widow. "And is in no danger from being harmed by the Tsul'kalu." She folded her hands under her arms, and Magnos dropped like a stone to his knees.

"Then help us free Hovis." Magnos spoke on the cusp of a cry. The jarring fall sparked a cascade of incising pain, which shot up his legs and back.

"The Tsul'kalu would have done that a long time ago...if they could find him. He can't be allowed to open the tomb. I've been tracking him for months myself. He has an exceptionally nasty habit of disappearing, even for a ghost."

Magnos stiffly shoved his right leg forward and planted his foot firmly on the ground. He moaned as he pushed himself up. "I know where Hovis is."

"Sure you do," she chuckled, resting her steering wheel next to her.

"I've seen Hovis, and I know where he's staying," heaved Magnos. "I've even seen his books."

"What?" she asked, straightening up in disbelief. "Where?!"

"The Circles of Circles Cemetery."

The old Widow bellowed with full amusement. "I've been to that cemetery a dozen times. I've combed through every plot and canvassed every grave. Hovis isn't there."

Magnos took a step back as his aching body relaxed. He cocked his head to the side in thought.

"Did you look *under* the cemetery?"

## *A House Divided*

**B**uzz screamed with all of his diaphragmatic might. All that echoed through the wiry fingers was a muffled yawp. After he finished, the hand released him and spun him around forcefully. Buzz came nose to nose with Rodriqa.

"Man, it's hot down here," she said, as she fanned herself with the top of her shirt.

Buzz took a step back and gawked at Rodriqa and Jordana, standing in the door of the empty library with flashlights in hand, as his wits reconfigured reality. He gritted his teeth and howled, "You nearly gave me an aneurysm!"

"I owed you one," replied Rodriqa.

Aubrey ran toward the front of the library. His demeanor churned from disappointment and frustration quickly into basking wonder as he saw Jordana.

"How are you feeling?" Aubrey leaned forward to hug her, but she seemed too fragile. Her eyes were puffy from crying, and the corners of her mouth edged downward slightly.

Jordana brushed a lock of her hair back behind her ear and smiled weakly at his greeting.

"That's a stupid question," interjected Buzz brashly. "Of course, she feels like snail spit."

Aubrey frowned at Buzz bitterly, but ignored him. "Any word about your dad?"

"Not yet," answered Rodriqa. "We headed here as soon as I got your message."

"What we need isn't here," fumed Aubrey.

Rodriqa surveyed the room, slightly disturbed at the vacant shelving. "Where did all of the books go?"

Aubrey and Buzz shrugged.

"I was looking for *Anathagraphia*," explained Aubrey. "Hovis' curse should bind him to where he is. He shouldn't be able to move around. The only reason he can is because someone has linked their spirit to him. Once we figure out who that is...then we can break the link. Hovis will be powerless again, and this all ends! But we need to read the rest of the section of the Sandman Anathem to figure out how."

Jordana looked up at Aubrey and bit her lip.

"Jordana's made a little discovery of her own," replied Rodriqa. "The Tsul'kalu have warned her about having anything to do with Hovis. That's the only reason we came down here was to get you two to leave!"

"You saw the Tsul'kalu again," asked Buzz.

"No…it's a long story and we can tell it later." Rodriqa grabbed Buzz by the ear and twisted. Buzz doubled over and hollered in pain, swiveling the direction Rodriqa pulled. "Ghostly recess is over, boys. Time to let the dead deal with their own issues."

Jordana propped open the door to the library as Rodriqa maneuvered the squirming Buzz to the bottom of the stairs like a cat on a leash.

"But we can't leave yet," protested Aubrey. "We have to find that book!"

"Yes, we can, and no, we don't," insisted Rodriqa. Jordana cupped Aubrey's elbow with her hand and tugged him gently forward. Aubrey leaned toward her, and he felt he had no choice but to relent to her tacit request.

Rodriqa stopped abruptly in front of the library, the sniveling Buzz writhing beside her.

"What's wrong?" asked Aubrey as he and Jordana stepped into the hallway. Rodriqa's brow was heavy, and her right lower eyelid twitched. She pointed off to the side with her flashlight, its hazy beam shimmering through the entranceway into the room off to the right of the bottom of the grand staircase.

"I see a light," she said timidly.

"Where?" asked Aubrey.

Rodriqa nodded in the direction her light was shining.

"We can't see a light if your flashlight is stronger than the light in question," grunted Buzz as he wrenched his ear free from her hand and rubbed the pain away.

Rodriqa angled her flashlight downward.

"It doesn't matter, Driqa. We need to go," murmured Jordana.

Rodriqa bobbed her head quickly up and down, but was unable to take her eyes off the next room.

The darkness had quickly engulfed any light from their lanterns before, but now in the far corner a dim, orange glow suffused softly along the wooden wall. The light crept forward slowly into the next room and then retreated, just as it grew.

"Look," said Buzz, pointing into the next room. "There's a wind chime in there. I think it's the same one that was in the library before."

An aching moan echoed from around the corner in the room.

"Time to go," said Buzz. Aubrey and Rodriqa agreed, and they stumbled over each other as they scurried for the stairs.

"Wait," cried Jordana, shuttering behind them. The other three turned around, confused. "It sounds like my dad," she murmured.

"But he's in the hospital, isn't he?" asked Buzz, looking to Aubrey and Rodriqa for confirmation.

Rodriqa turned her head to the side to listen. "That's what my parents had said."

Aubrey stepped down, took a deep breath and lifted his chin. "I'll go check." He held the electric lantern neck-high and tiptoed into the entranceway toward the orange glow.

Jordana grabbed the back of Aubrey's shirt and peeked around him. Rodriqa and Buzz walked behind them, keeping a distance of several strides in between.

Aubrey rounded the corner, careful to dodge the wind chimes, which hung from the ceiling in deadly stillness. The others followed his lead.

A hefty, oval table ran the length of the room, and a cankerous brass chandelier dangled precariously in pieces over the table's center. Except for the missing chairs, it reminded Aubrey of a dining room. Puddles of dark moisture pooled on the table between craters of insect-noshed holes. The walls were lined with empty bookshelves, and the edges of the aging wood were flaking off into softened splinters onto the cracking floor.

Aubrey noticed the closer he was to the light, the hotter the air was. He could see the glow burn brighter through an open doorway into the next room. He looked down at Jordana, whose head was at his elbow, and she nodded, urging him forward. Aubrey closed his eyes and examined the darkness. The swirling, shimmering mass he had seen before seemed to boil beneath them, but he was unsure how close it was.

Rodriqa and Buzz crept into the dining room, but Rodriqa stopped at the bookshelf across from the oval table. "Wait, I think I see something," she whispered. Rodriqa knelt down next to the shelf abutting the wall behind them. She scooped her hands underneath the bottom shelf.

"Ouch!" she yelped. "It scratched me."

"What are you doing?" asked Jordana, frantic and a little miffed.

"There's a cat under here," replied Rodriqa. She groped under the shelf again, and a tan and cream-colored mat of fur slid to the side. Balls of hair wound tightly around dried clumps of mud, and its paws shivered at its hid its eyes. "I think it's Prissy," said Rodriqa. "Shouldn't we try to take it back to McCrayden?"

Its tail whipped from side to side, and it raked its paws down its face.

"I'd leave it be," added Buzz warily. "It's probably rabid."

"There are more pressing matters at hand, Rodriqa," chided Jordana. She turned around and nudged Aubrey forward into the next room.

Aubrey and Jordana stepped around the edge of the open doorway into the next room, and Jordana covered her mouth with her hand, quieting her own gasp. The open space in front of them was more like a cave than another room in the house. Most of the lumber from the walls had been torn away, splintered at their edges, revealing the damp, compacted dirt and rock surrounding the house. The top of the cave formed a hanging dome of earth, reaching two stories high. The floor had been ripped open, forming a cavernous shaft, from which flashed a brilliant, fiery beam radiating outward from the wide crevice, and spilling over into the dining room.

Aubrey closed his eyes again and looked down at his feet. The oscillating mass of gleaming blackness was directly below them, and it was suddenly clear to Aubrey what he had been seeing all along. Several stories below the house squirmed a massive nest of spirit shards.

"Listen," whispered Jordana. "I hear voices." She pointed into the cave. Aubrey opened his eyes and turned his head toward the center.

"There is nothing more I can do." The voice was crisp and precise as it floated up from the pit below. Jordana and Aubrey scampered quietly to the edge of the crater and allowed their eyes to adjust to the bright light as they gazed down below.

A black, rusty metal staircase crisscrossed down into the pit, like a fire escape, and reached a grated landing four stories down. Through the landing several hundred yards below, Aubrey and Jordana witnessed a terrifying sight. Hordes of large worms rolled clumps of dirt down hundreds of yards along the pit's walls, scraping rocks and debris as they squirmed deeper toward a molten globe of lava that was swirling and popping from its internal heat. The bubbling fiery sphere was slowly growing with the added mass from the worms, rising inside the pits.

On the landing stood Ms. Thistlewood, dressed in her multi-colored pastel sarong, next to the clearly visible Hovis, who stooped achingly over as his chains pulled him tautly to the earthy walls. And there was another form standing with them. A figure neither Jordana nor Aubrey had seen before. He looked like a man, but he was translucent and dull gray in color, draped in shreds of gray cloth that danced at his feet as the heat billowed up from below. He had long spindly arms, which were folded as if he was addressing an audience, and his baldhead was held stubbornly high. Where his right eye should have been was gray haziness, but his left eye absorbed the light in total darkness, fully blackened. Jordana clutched Aubrey's arm as Hovis hovered closer to Ms. Thistlewood. Another figure appeared as Hovis moved along the grate. Jordana's father lay limply underneath him, seemingly suspended with his body floating and his legs crumpled beneath him. A shimmering cord of light ran straight from Hovis to Mr. Galilahi's chest, tethering them together. A scalded 'X' blistered the torso of Jordana's father from shoulder to hip. Bruises darkened his arms, and his hospital pajamas bottoms clung to his legs, wet with sweat.

"Release me now," crowed Hovis hoarsely.

"Your obligations to our contract remain unfulfilled," tersely replied the transparent, gray man.

"Now," hissed Hovis ethereally as he turned to Ms. Thistlewood. "Make him do it!"

"Enough bickering," she barked. "The tomb will be open within the hour, and soon enough we'll have our war, Zaks. No one can stop us now. The plan is foolproof, and your request is complete in all *but* deed."

"So hot," moaned Mr. Galilahi in agony.

"Silence," wheezed Hovis.

Ms. Thistlewood pressed her foot against Mr. Galilahi's chest. "Quiet, Arturo," she whispered. "Don't worry. I'll release you from your service soon. You've performed your role nicely."

"The Tsul-kalu are more strategic than you credit them. They disrupted Hovis' link easily, and they still have time to interrupt your directed task," stated Zaks formally.

"They'd never last more than a moment down here," challenged Ms. Thistlewood. "With the army of shade shards I created from that circus troupe, I could fend off ten clans of forest guardians."

"How about the children?" asked Zaks petulantly.

"What children?" she scowled.

"Don't underestimate their divinoi. I've seen them use it, and they've yet to discern their own strength."

"You're speaking of the red-haired scrawny brat and his fat, loud-mouthed friend?!" Ms. Thistlewood chortled arrogantly. "They are a minor inconvenience...nothing more."

Zaks twisted his head from side to side and mumbled, "Inconveniently close." He raised his long, thin arm and sliced it like a sword across Hovis' robe. A blinding flash of light erupted from the landing, accompanied by a thunderous snap. Hovis' chains cracked in two, releasing him. Hovis raised his elbows over his head, and he bellowed victoriously. The glimmering cord between Hovis and Mr. Galilahi dissipated, and Arturo fell silently back onto the landing.

Aubrey pulled back from the edge as Jordana looked over his shoulder. "We should go," he whispered. A series of rapid tappings rattled against the metal staircase out of the crater.

"What's happening?" asked Rodriqa from a few feet behind them.

"Someone's coming," whispered Aubrey.

A blackened skeletal hand, swarmed by a soupy green haze, rose out of the crevice immediately in front of Jordana and Aubrey.

"The seer has seen enough," Ms. Thistlewood exclaimed as she ascended the stairs. She flicked her dark, boney hand at Aubrey.

Aubrey's gums tingled and sharp pricks jabbed at his lips. He felt his mouth being stretched out of shape. Mangled silvery wires sprang from his braces and wrapped around his head almost instantly. Two stray wires twirled beyond Aubrey's head and lashed themselves around Jordana's head, strapping her face to the back of Aubrey. The aluminum tendrils grew out of control, sending spurts of wires in every direction and coiling Aubrey and Jordana in a cocoon of metal mesh.

Ms. Thistlewood stepped onto the dirt floor of the cave and smiled at the creation of her wiry enclosure. She waved her black boney hand at Rodriqa and Buzz. They screamed and scurried back into the dining room. Ms. Thistlewood followed after them.

As she passed into the dining room, Ms. Thistlewood flicked her hand at Rodriqa as she rounded the corner into the hallway. The bookshelves lurched forward, and wooden arms broke from the molding at various levels along the insets. Rodriqa reached for her necklace. A stick-like arm, protruding from the shelf, tripped her. She fell face forward, and her hand jerked to the side. The string snapped, and a shower of multi-colored beads scattered across the floor. Two more wooden arms picked her up and pulled her back against the shelving. Three more arms cuffed her elbows and knees like a stockade. Rodriqa was swaddled in timber. Prissy clawed her way out from underneath the shelves and climbed up into Rodriqa's pants pocket.

Buzz bumbled into the hallway, heading straight for the grand staircase. Ms. Thistlewood flicked her hand again. The stairs and railing disintegrated into bits and pieces. A rain of toothpicks showered the hallway and the stair-well beneath it. Buzz jerked back from the crumbling stairs and looked up at the second floor hopelessly, which was now completely disconnected from the level he was standing on. Ms. Thistlewood grinned menacingly at him. He turned and ran into the empty library.

"There's no place left to run." Her voice was consoling and kind. Buzz poised himself tactically in the middle of the room, searching the metal floor and corners for a way to escape. "I never meant to hurt you or Aubrey. You two were always my favorites." Her inviting, syrupy tone comforted Buzz, and he slowly turned to face her.

Ms. Thistlewood leaned against the door and smiled peacefully at him with her skeleton arm behind her. "I wish things could have been different. I wish I could have saved you from all this torment." She took several smooth steps into the room and Buzz stood completely still, paralyzed by her melodic words and lost in her beautiful face. She lifted her skeletal hand to eye level, and the bile-colored mist foamed around it. "I know it looks gruesome, but it will only hurt for a second." She took a few more fluid steps closer to Buzz. "Then all your cares will fade away." She touched her hand to his face.

Buzz's look of blithe enchantment melted away, and his eyes went hollow and widened in horror. His flesh turned pale, and he felt his life leaving him.

*CRRAAAAAAAAAASSSHHHH!* The ceiling crumpled overhead as bits of decayed wood fell to the floor. Jordana's Tsul'kalu burst through the ceiling and dropped through the air with Magnos' clinging to its back. The Bigfoot's feet dented the metal floor, but it easily landed upright.

Magnos jumped from the beast's shoulders. "Back off, Witch!" he yelled at Ms. Thistlewood. The Tsul'kalu's red eyes brightened, and it bared its fangs at her. The creature opened its jowls and howled fiercely, and the metal floor trembled.

Ms. Thistlewood stumbled backwards, releasing Buzz. His color quickly returned to his face, and he shook off his daze. One after another, the entire clan of Tsul'kalu hurled from the attic above, like a flurry of furry comets zooming into the empty library, pounding the metal flooring.

"HOVIS!" screamed Ms. Thistlewood as fled out of the library. "I NEED THOSE WORMS UP HERE NOW!" She disappeared into the hallway.

Hovis floated up the stairs and out of the fiery crater, his chains dangling freely from his arms. His thin craggy lips turned upward in a devilish smile. "As you wish, my Queen."

Magnos ran up to Buzz and shook him by the shoulders. "Are you hurt?"

Buzz flapped his head as he tried to regain his wits.

"We can't let Hovis open the tomb," Magnos told him.

Buzz stared at Magnos. "The tomb," queried Buzz. "The tomb is cemented up under the dam. There's no way to get to it."

"Ms. Thistlewood will find a way," demanded Magnos.

Buzz came to. "Uh-oh," he said, looking around at the previously empty library, which was now full of the entire clan of Tsul'kalu.

"They're on our side," announced Magnos.

The Tsul'kalu gathered together and walked one by one out of the library after Ms. Thistlewood. The first few ducked through the doorway and squeezed themselves through. The large blonde one hammered the headboard and walls with his fists, busting a Bigfoot-sized hole through the doorway.

Rodriqa screamed from the dining room.

"Where are the others?" asked Magnos worriedly.

"Come with me," replied Buzz. Buzz led Magnos through the hallway and into the dining room. They wove their way between the legs of the marching Tsul'kalu who were fanning out through the underground house, searching rooms and hallways.

Rodriqa had stopped screaming and was quaking violently in fear as the blonde Tsul'kalu ripped her wooden shelving trap to pieces, releasing her.

"It's okay," comforted Magnos, giving Rodriqa a tight hug with his bulky cast.

"Aubrey and Jordana are in the next room," directed Buzz. The wind chimes overhead clanged and whipped wildly as if they had been smacked, but nothing they could see was anywhere close to the chimes.

Magnos stared at Buzz and muttered, "Spirit draft."

Buzz rushed into the cave. The gray-haired Tsul'kalu stood over the metallically conjoined Aubrey and Jordana, stripping clumps of wire from around them. Buzz walked slowly behind the Sasquatch, trying not to interrupt him, and addressed his two friends. "Now, when we get you out of there, don't scream."

The Tsul'kalu broke off several of the wires connected to Aubrey's braces, and the remaining cage tumbled to the floor. Jordana clambered away on all fours, desperately trying to flee. Magnos caught her at the entranceway to the cave. He picked her up and held her. Aubrey shuddered on the floor, frozen in fear.

"Aubrey! EYES!" yelled Buzz.

Aubrey closed his eyes. *Hurry up! Hurry up! Hurry up!* he murmured to himself frantically. The darkness overtook the phosphenes, and worms, just like the ones he and his friends had seen atop the staircase, crawled everywhere. He opened his eyes, and the room flashed with a shimmering darkness. The army of serpentine spirit shards could be seen by everyone.

Brandishing their ring of sharp, shiny teeth, the large, tube-like worms climbed on every surface of the cave, their oily black bodies writhing toward the kids and the clan.

The gray-haired Bigfoot hobbled backwards. He reached behind over his shoulder, raking his back. His body trembled, and his hair shortened and lengthened, as if he was forcing himself to focus out of reality. He spun in circles. Three worms clung with a frenzy to his expansive back, gnawing deeply into the shaggy flesh of the Tsul'kalu. His outline smeared around him, his skin was evaporating into an ashy smoke.

The Sasquatch fell forward onto the cave floor with a deadening thud. He twitched for a moment, and then was still. The worms huffed in the foggy remains as the Tsul'kalu dissolved into the air.

The murderous shade shards tripled in size, and a dark pink hue gleamed around them. They flashed their razorous teeth at Aubrey.

Hovis floated over the pit from the far side, waving his arms freely. He scooped up the worms in his hands and swallowed all three of them whole. Hovis grinned as he looked down greedily at Aubrey, his dark shroud now imbued with the same pink glow.

Buzz grabbed Aubrey by the shirt collar and drug him back toward the dining room. "Scream! Rodriqa! Scream!"

"My beads broke!" hollered Rodriqa frantically.

"Forget the beads!" yelled Buzz. "SCREAM!"

Two worms had wrapped their bodies around the arms of the blonde Tsul'kalu and were corkscrewing their way to his torso. He moaned and pulled at his arms, attempting to rake the spirit shards off of him, but they dodged his clawed hands. Rodriqa stood next to the blonde Bigfoot and screamed with her lungs fully loaded with air. The two worms convulsed and fell to the floor, squalling in spine-shattering agony. The Sasquatch smashed both of them under his massive foot, and they burst into a puff of soot.

Jordana's Tsul'kalu stormed into the dining room, swatting worms falling on top of him from the ceiling. The rest of the clan followed, batting at more shade shards attached to their own hairy bodies. One by one Rodriqa shouted louder at the worms, knocking them all to the ground.

Rodriqa clipped her nose between her fingers and gulped air through her mouth. "I don't know which smells worse," she shouted and then screamed at another worm. "The hairy monsters or the dying demon snakes!"

The blonde Bigfoot yawped several staccato cries and shoved the large oval table to the side. It shattered against the far, petrified wall. The Sasquatch clicked his tongue and swiveled his head, and the entire clan of Tsul'kalu formed a ring, facing outwards, around the kids. Rodriqa stood in the middle, stomping her feet and bellowing as loudly as her vocal cords would vibrate.

The army of worms converged on them from every angle. Soot powdered the air with the battered death of more shade shards. As more worms died, more filed in to fight in their places. The light from the kids' flashlights and electric lantern couldn't pass beyond the thick blanket of shadow from their serpentine assailants.

"We have to get outta here!" yelled Magnos. The other kids nodded in agreement. Magnos tugged on the blonde fur of the Tsul'kalu's back. The creature turned and bent down to look at him. Magnos pointed to the ceiling with his thumb and fist. "UP!" he shouted. "We need to go UP!"

Rodriqa's voice was straining to project more sound, and yet she was losing the battle as the worms moved closer into the ring. The blonde beast cried several somber thrills and lifted Magnos over his shoulder. The red Bigfoot flung Buzz over his shoulder, wincing slightly at the weight. The smallest Tsul'kalu kneeled down in front of Rodriqa and offered her a piggyback ride. She reluctantly climbed on and wrapped her arms around his neck. The feminine-shaped Sasquatch raised Aubrey up with her hands under his armpits and rested him on her hip.

Jordana's Tsul'kalu presented Jordana with his open palm and stared down at her, the red glow in his eyes nearly extinguished. She took a step back. "I'm not leaving without my father," she shouted. The creature angled his head to the side and stretched his arm closer toward her. She swatted his hand away. "Ta Kenahisda Adoda!"

The Tsul'kalu picked Jordana up by the waist and cradled her in his arms. He stooped over, and in a couple of steps they were both staring into the pit of the cave where her father's motionless body lay on the metal grating below. Jordana covered her eyes at the sorrowful sight and cried.

The Tsul'kalu set Jordana on the ledge gently and leapt into the crevice, swinging adeptly down along the fire escape railing to the landing. The beast straddled Arturo, scrutinizing his wounds, and rested his hand on the man's chest.

Jordana shrieked in fear from above. The Sasquatch jerked his head upwards. Hovis dropped from above and swung his arms at the Bigfoot, knocking him off his feet.

The Tsul'kalu growled as he sat upright. Hovis turned in the air and floated back toward the beast. From shoulder to fingers, the Tsul'kalu's right arm shivered, wavering in the light from below. His arm turned nearly transparent. He reached into the air and cinched Hovis by the neck.

Hovis gasped and choked, clawing at the Tsul'kalu's mighty grip. The creature pitched Hovis into the pit's rock wall, and the ghost passed through it, vanishing instantly.

The Bigfoot slid Mr. Galilahi's body under his arm. It jumped high into the air and out of the pit.

# The Song of the Tsul'kalu

Jordana's Tsul'kalu handed Mr. Galilahi over to another Sasquatch who was standing behind Jordana. Jordana reached for her father, but the transition was too quick. She couldn't tell if he was alive. Suddenly, she was being cradled again in the arms of her own personal Bigfoot and was being rushed from room to room, while the empty-handed Tsul'kalu around them beat off the attacking worms.

Once in the library, Jordana looked up, and she could see her friends being carried aloft by the other Tsul'kalu. They climbed like spiders up the empty bookshelves to the floor of the upstairs attic through several of a dozen holes. She felt the world turn on end as her Tsul'kalu crawled vertically, upside and upwards behind his family. Daylight broke from above as they squeezed into the attic. Again the room slanted with their advance up the attic wall. They hurried through the grave, and she was upright again as they bounded onto cemetery ground.

Air rushed over her. The chest of the Tsul'kalu vibrated with a rhythmic hum. Jordana peered over his hefty arm and watched in awe as the grass, trees, water and sky slid by in a blur. The clan was running as a pack. Any slight deviation, to the left or right, was made in unison, like a flock of birds or a school of fish.

Within a minute they had reached the mouth of the Wontawanna Creek and were heading further upstream, faster than Jordana thought she had ever moved before. Jordana looked at her friends and couldn't help but snicker. Buzz, who was hunched over the shoulder of the red Tsul'kalu with his rear facing forward, grinned wildly and fanned his fingers through the air while he enjoyed the ride of a lifetime. Aubrey was green and paler than usual. He buried his head in the chest of the female Sasquatch he was riding. And Magnos in front with the blonde Bigfoot in the lead held tightly to the beast's back with his good arm, as his legs flopped like a windsock behind him.

Jordana took a double-take at Rodriqa. She was riding piggyback on the childlike Tsul'kalu, and her arms were blurry and nearly transparent. Rodriqa angled her head backwards and bayed at the sky, like a wolf to the moon.

The river and surrounding forest returned to focus. Instantly, the five kids were sitting next to each other on the riverbank, and the Tsul'kalu were gathering several yards away from them next to the edge of the forest.

Aubrey clutched the damp carpet of moss and grass beneath him, grateful to be on solid ground. Rodriqa, Buzz and Magnos high-fived each other, astounded at their unworldly ride and thankful for their narrow escape from Hovis' house. Jordana stared at her father solemnly, who lay next to the female

Tsul'kalu quietly breathing, while she wiped his forehead and rubbed mud on his chest.

"Wasn't that incredible," crowed Buzz. "Saved by the Tsul'kalu!"

"Simply amazing," marveled Rodriqa.

"I'm just glad we landed on the metal floor," added Magnos. "I thought we might fall through to the middle of the earth when they decided to crash the house."

"A solid foundation always keeps you from stumbling," repeated Rodriqa cheerfully. Magnos and Buzz laughed.

"How did you find them?" Buzz asked.

"The Widow," replied Magnos. "She and the Tsul'kalu have been hunting Hovis for months."

Aubrey's face lost all expression. "And to think, all we needed to do was introduce the two and this all would have been over."

Magnos patted Aubrey on the back with his good hand and grinned at him.

Aubrey pointed at the clan, watching them group together.

The Tsul'kalu formed two circles and kneeled down on one knee. The inner circle of beasts faced outward, and the outer circle, inward, so that they were looking at each other.

The blonde Bigfoot hummed alone at first, but slowly, one by one, the creatures added their voices to the low, somber rumbling. An occasional squeak erupted from deep in one's throat that seemed random, but with time, squeaks slipped through the hum more regularly. A couple of the Tsul'kalu cooed. The feminine one whined in a finely high-pitched squeal. And a few others moaned quietly until the sounds all spread together into a harmonious din.

"What are they doing?" asked Buzz.

"I think they're mourning," answered Magnos soberly. "For their fallen family member...the gray-haired one. He died to save us." The other kids gathered around him and listened.

To Aubrey, it sounded too simple a cry for raw despair, too composed for tears of sudden loss, and too beautiful for protests of unjust agony. At the very least it was a song. Their song. Aubrey knew that only one word summed up what he heard. Their song was a prayer.

"They've created a protected tunnel," added Jordana, tracing an invisible circle in the air with her finger, "made up of their own spirits to provide the dead with safe passage to next world."

Magnos folded his hands together and hung his head. He bent down on one knee in mimicked respect, and his friends followed his example.

The smallest Tsul'kalu broke from the circle and walked deliberately over toward the kids. Its movements were fluid but direct and clear. It eyed them cautiously as it kneeled down in front of Rodriqa. She leaned back, a little uncomfortable with how close it was. The smaller Bigfoot tilted its head from side to side and raised and lowered the corners of its mouth, exposing its glistening canines. Rodriqa couldn't decide if it was trying to growl or smile. The ember of red light in the center of its coal-black eyes was difficult to look at, but she couldn't pull herself away.

The junior Tsul'kalu raised its hand and unrolled its fingers until its flat palm faced Rodriqa. Rodriqa watched him warily, unnerved by the tiny, sharp claws projecting from the tips of its fingers and the thick, heavily creased skin of a hand that was flush with hair. It bobbed its head up and down and grunted softly.

Rodriqa got the hint, but she wasn't excited about it. Slowly, she raised her hand and placed her palm against his. Rodriqa's fingers tingled as if her hand had fallen asleep, which didn't bother her, since she had felt the same sensation when she was riding piggyback. But as her hand blurred out of focus, she pushed herself up and stepped away from the little Tsul'kalu.

Within a few moments, every inch of Rodriqa, her face, her arms, and her legs, all were translucent. Startled by her rapid transformation, she raised her hand to her face and stared wondrously at her friends through her own skin. She was not the only one who had transformed. Instead of the small Tsul'kalu, a boy, clad in deer hides, stood in front of her. His smooth, sorrel skin glinted in late morning sun, and his shiny, straight black hair formed a ring on the top of his head. He covered his mouth and giggled as he waved to Rodriqa in her new form.

Jordana stood up abruptly, mesmerized by both of them.

"Cool," said Buzz as stood up and walked over to the new Rodriqa. "You look like a *GHOST*!" He pulled a bit of her hair to check and see if she was tangible. She squawked and backhanded the broad side of his face.

"Ouch!" hollered Buzz as he rubbed his cheek. "Except you're still real."

"Ulu Adahasada...Ulu Ohusdava Ayale Elaho," said the Cherokee boy to Jordana.

"What's he saying?" asked Aubrey.

Jordana replayed the words in her mind and thought carefully. "He said, 'She's also a guardian...that's why she can fit in between worlds, too.'"

"Can we do that?" asked Buzz excitedly.

"I don't think so," replied Jordana.

The boy waved at Jordana then sped off toward the circle of Tsul'kalu, weaving through the grass with his arms outstretched like he was flying. He was clearly enjoying being a boy again. The blonde Sasquatch stepped out from the circles and walked over to the kids. He kneeled before Rodriqa and clasped her forearm in his hand. She returned the greeting.

The Tsul'kalu spoke in the unfamiliar ancient Cherokee. Jordana translated.

"We are proud to have another guardian in our midst. Your task will be difficult, but you are brave and honorable. Stand strong. Force out your fear. That will enliven your spirit." Rodriqa nodded, although she was confused yet humbled by his kind and thoughtful words.

"Is my father okay?" asked Jordana in ancient Cherokee.

The Tsul'kalu turned briefly back to the circles of his clan and replied, "Hopefully he will be."

Jordana swallowed a great deal of her fear and grief. "Who are you?"

The blonde Bigfoot kneeled stood up and addressed the friends.

"We were once human like you. Several millennia ago, an angel-man visited our village here in these hills and told us of a time before the Great Flood. He reminded us that humans were the youngest and most precious children of the Clockmaker, and as such, our race had been assigned special caretakers, a unique regimen of sentinels, known as Watchers, to guide our paths and lead us from insolence after our fall from perfection.

"In the beginning, the accord between humans and the Watchers was benevolent and fruitful, but greed blossomed in both hearts. Curiosity consumed our forefathers, and they desired greater knowledge and power. The Watchers grew tired of babysitting and expected special recognition for their earthly toil. The Grand Clockmaker refused both requests.

"In return, the Watchers taught humans ideas they were not ready to know and corrupted their place in the universe. As punishment for their crimes, the Watchers were entombed indefinitely in the Earth, and humanity's perversions were washed away."

The Tsul'kalu raised his hands skyward. "Humanity was reborn, and the Clockmaker insisted humanity develop without invasive assistance. Over time the Shade, the light-starved spirits of the world, attempted to free the Watchers for their own gain, hoping to build an allegiance against the Clockmaker. Although they were repeatedly unsuccessful, they had come uncomfortably close in achieving their goal.

"The angel-man realized his Tombs had weaknesses, and he needed emissaries who would be unyieldingly guards until the end of time. He chose three families from among our tribe, who he felt were the most stalwart of heart. It was a tremendous honor with a lonely price.

"As guardians we would be separated from both worlds, living in the recess between the spiritual and the natural. That made us better soldiers against anyone or anything who might try to open the Tomb. Humans would seek to know us, but we would have to avoid them, except when necessary to ensure the security of the Tomb."

The blonde Tsul'kalu took a step forward and stared downriver. "In these recent days, the Tomb has rested in peril, and it has escaped our reach to protect it. Now we must ask for your help."

"But how can anyone open the Tomb when it's buried at the bottom of the dam and encased in cement?" asked Buzz impertinently.

"Part of it is buried," replied the blonde Tsul'kalu. "The rest of it lies at the bottom of the lake, fully exposed. "The Tomb is quite ornate, but its engineering is very simple. It consists of two interlocked casings of bedrock, one bound within the other, yet they do not touch. They are separated by a layer of sand and punctured with scores of quartz crystals. The crystals produce heaven's fire as the Earth slowly shifts, perpetually holding the Watchers within their soily prison."

"Brilliant," interjected Buzz. "It works by the piezoelectric effect...like we talked about before. The Tomb is just a giant Leyden jar. As tectonic plates force it to move through the crust, electricity is generated over time in the inner lining, trapping the Watchers inside."

The Tsul'kalu continued. "The tomb is nearly indestructible when buried deep underground, but above ground it is much more vulnerable."

"How can *we* help?" asked Jordana, incredulous and almost amused. "We're just kids."

The Bigfoot's eyes glowed a brighter red. "Hovis Trottle has one final hope to achieve his ends. If the sphere of molten salts underneath the cemetery dissolves within the lake, it will disrupt the crystals, and the Tomb will fall to pieces."

"How do we keep it from reaching the lake?" asked Aubrey.

The Tsul'kalu fell silent.

"We can't," replied Buzz as he thought carefully. "The ball of magma has already reached critical mass. It will erupt soon despite anything we can do."

The Tsul'kalu stared at Buzz knowingly.

"There's only one option left," continued Buzz.

"What's that?" asked Aubrey.

"We have to empty the lake."

Aubrey chuckled. "We can't *empty* Lake Julian."

Buzz looked back over his shoulder downriver. "We can't...but Rodriqa can."

"W hat was it like?" asked Buzz with fanatic perkiness.

"Like being trapped in clear helium balloon," replied Rodriqa, who was now back to her usual self in every regard. "I could still see and feel everything. I just felt a little…separated."

"It had to be totally weird," gushed Buzz. "To be caught between both worlds….to be the only contemporary human to *know* what it's like to actually *be* a ghost! Do you feel any different now?"

"For a bit it was like being on a merry-go-round that I couldn't let go of, but now it just itches." She kept scratching her neck and arms as if there was a part of the transformation she couldn't quite shake.

Rodriqa reached down in her pocket and quickly jerked her hand back out.

"Wait a sec," she told the others as she stopped and pried open the top of her pocket. "There's something sharp in my pants."

"Maybe the Tsul'kalu left you something," replied Buzz excitedly.

"I don't think so." The five kids watched as the tiny bulge at the bottom of her pocket squirmed and writhed between the fabric of Rodriqa's pants. A furry round ball popped out from inside and crawled up Rodriqa's shirt and onto her shoulder, shivering and clawing at its face as it nuzzled her neck.

"It's Prissy," announced Aubrey in a disturbed tone.

"Why did you bring that cat?" accused Buzz.

"I didn't," refuted Rodriqa. "I left it alone after it scratched me. It must have crawled inside my pocket during the fight."

"Put it down," said Magnos. "That cat's a nuisance."

"I can't just leave it out here!"

"Have it your way," said Buzz, rolling his eyes. Rodriqa handed the cat to Buzz, and he carefully placed it in the bottom of his backpack. The feline squirmed and quivered for a moment, but then lost all desire to fight and went limp.

The five of them resumed lumbering their way down the banks of the Wontawanna Creek to Lake Julian. They alternated between jogging, trotting and walking as they trekked toward the dam, already exhausted by the morning's events.

Jordana moved more slowly than the others. Magnos and Aubrey walked alongside her, both to keep her company and hoping to keep her heading forward. Magnos cradled his casted arm, its constant heavy weight cramping his shoulder.

"I'm sure the Tsul'kalu will take good care of your dad," comforted Aubrey. "They seem to know more about what's happening than anyone else. They're best equipped to help him at this point."

Jordana nodded her head fleetingly and sniffed back her tears, but she never looked up. "This is all his fault," she whimpered sadly. "I can't believe he would do this to me."

Everyone walked a little more slowly, unsure of what to say.

Magnos cleared his throat. "I spoke with your dad while we were in the hospital this morning."

Jordana glared at him crossly, warning him with her eyes.

"A lot of what he told me was none of my business," Magnos continued thoughtfully, "But two things are without a doubt true...he loved your mother with all his heart...and he loves you more than he loves his own life." Magnos paused for a moment. "What I wouldn't give for family like that." His voice was barely audible.

Aubrey bit his lip fretfully, searching for the right words to say. He opened his mouth, but Rodriqa cut him off.

"Sometimes our minds are in the right place, but our hearts go crazy trying to make things happen, and when our hands and our mouths listen to a runaway heart, things just get all messed up." Rodriqa looked at Jordana gently and smiled. Jordana smiled back as she wiped her face.

"One thing is for sure, Rodriqa...you make a *mean* lookin' ghost," chortled Magnos, trying to lighten the mood. Rodriqa sneered amusingly back at him.

"You all realize this is never gonna work," chided Rodriqa, taking up the charge to change the subject. She cleared her crackly voice after she spoke.

"It has to," retorted Buzz. "There's no other way."

"My parents will not empty the lake simply because I ask them to," insisted Rodriqa. Her voice cracked again mid-sentence, and she cleared her throat to emphasize her point.

"Then you'll tell them the entire, outrageous story of the past two months, and they'll have to believe us."

"No one would believe any of us! It's too crazy!"

"Yeah, totally crazy," grumbled Aubrey. "Just like my mother...just like me."

Silence fell over them as they trudged toward the dam.

Buzz stopped suddenly and held out his arms. The other four stopped as well and stared at him curiously.

"Feel that," Buzz said.

"Feel what?" asked Rodriqa, her voice waning quickly.

"Look where we are," added Buzz.

The other four looked around. They were within a hundred yards of the dam and were standing at the foot of the hill between the dam and the mine.

They looked at each other in amazement. They felt the rumbling of the earth beneath their feet. It was like standing on a bridge when a heavy truck was driving past, yet they were standing on solid ground.

"We don't have much time," said Buzz.

All five of them took off in a sprint toward the dam.

# Dam.age Control

The late morning sunlight streamed through the panels of steel-trimmed glass doors into the spacious marble foyer of the Lake Julian Dam. Particles of dust drifted through the air, glinting in the warm glow from outside. No tourists had wandered through the Visitor's entrance as of yet, which Jaime Kontrearo found highly unusual for a Saturday morning in autumn. So he decided the security cameras would probably need little tending, and today's shift was going to be a relaxing one. Propping up his feet on the security desk, Jaime pulled out his phone. He frowned. No service. He put his phone away and clicked on the web browser on the security computer. It was blocked. Jaime grunted and rested his head on his hands on the desk and grabbed a magazine.

Jaime glanced up quickly and noticed a pack of familiar faces barreling toward the entrance doors from outside. He buried his face in the magazine, hoping that it was a mirage.

Rodriqa flung open one of the glass doors, yanking with all her weight to lever it backwards, and all five kids raced into the foyer. They bounded quickly to the security desk, and each of them landed hard against the waist-high counter top.

"Jaime, I'm so glad you're here," puffed Rodriqa through her heavy breaths.

Jaime kept his eyes on his magazine. "Oh, no," he said determinedly as he waved them off. "No excitement today, folks. I'm not in the mood."

"I need to ask you a favor," she asked urgently.

Jaime shook his head.

"We have to release the water from the dam."

Jaime's eyebrows arched upwards and he glared snidely at her from under his forehead. "Rodriqa, go home. I got in enough trouble last time."

"Don't you want to help out your little sis number two?" Rodriqa's tone was syrupy sweet.

"This is not a good time," growled Jamie.

"This is serious," growled Rodriqa back.

"Yeah," chuckled Jaime. "Just as serious as the Bigfoot and the ghost."

"Exactly!" All five kids nodded in agreement.

Jaime leaned forward and flipped the magazine closed. "I guess there's no hope in me ignoring you all, is there?"

"Not a chance," Rodriqa replied.

"Look. They've tightened up security around here," explained Jaime. "Even the tour groups have to have a security guard accompany them. And I suspect that the changes have something to do with you hooligans. So no trouble today, get me?"

"You have to let us into the control room," demanded Rodriqa. "Something bad is about to happen."

"Really bad," Magnos reiterated.

"Like *end of the world* bad," added Buzz ominously.

"Like I need to call Homeland Security bad?" asked Jaime sarcastically.

"We don't have time to explain," insisted Rodriqa, cutting him off. "The lake has to be emptied...NOW!"

"Do I look like I can afford to lose my job? Besides your dad is downstairs. He's not gonna let you open the dam."

Rodriqa's heart sank, and her eyes shifted back and forth as she tried to think things through. "Why is he here on a Saturday?"

Jaime cocked his head and curled his lip. "He's working."

"What's going on?" she begged.

"That's official information for official use only, and you're *not* official."

Rodriqa snarled her mouth and twisted her neck. "Is there another way to advance the turbines other than from the control room?"

Jaime shrugged and opened the cover to the magazine. "Not my department."

"You have to help us," growled Rodriqa. "This is *serious*!"

"No," Jaime responded tersely.

"If you don't help us, we'll figure it out on our own!"

Jaime picked up the red security phone next to him and dialed three numbers. "Yeah, Charlie, I need some help up here. I have a couple of unruly visitors."

Charlie Buckswaine herded the kids together simply by stretching his long, muscular arms out and forward. All five of them fit neatly within his wingspan and Jaime stood behind them to secure the fold. Charlie turned around, and the group marched slowly down the back stairs in a tight group with Charlie in the lead. They stepped out onto the turbine level, and Aubrey held his chest as the whirring hum from the massive metal blocks jarred his insides.

Charlie stepped up to a steel door with a keypad on the wall next to it. He turned around and bent over, facing Rodriqa nose to nose. "Not...a...word," he whispered to her loudly. Charlie turned back to the door and hurriedly punched several numbers on the keypad. The door released its lock with a brisk snap.

Charlie led them into the control room. Various scientists and engineers in white lab coats scurried from banks of flashing screens to blinking panels of buttons, recording data on clipboards and adjusting calculations. Another group of men and women hovered quietly around the central console.

"Dr. Auerbach," called Charlie in a military tone. "I have detained a testy group of rabble rousers who were creating a ruckus in the Visitor's Center. What would you like me to do with them?"

"Call the police, of course," barked Dr. Auerbach from within the crowd.

"Sir, I mean no disrespect, but perhaps with the recent increase in seismic activity *these* visitors should be escorted quickly from the premises."

Dr. Auerbach stood up and turned toward Charlie. The five kids cowered in front of Jaime as they stared blankly toward the center of the room. A scowl crinkled across Dr. Auerbach's face. "Bring them here, Charlie," he replied, waving them forward.

The kids moved in a pack toward the central console. Dr. Auerbach eyed each one of them with a sternly raised eyebrow.

"Jordana, did you go see your father?" he asked, his gruff voice, softening slightly.

Jordana thought for a moment, and mumbled, "Yes, sir," knowing she wouldn't be lying.

He eyed her warily and then gazed at Aubrey. "I feel certain your father intends for you to be home today," accused Dr. Auerbach, the edge to his voice cutting Aubrey to the heart. Aubrey hung his head silently.

"Buzz," Dr. Auerbach nodded in greeting. "Burn down any more houses lately?"

Buzz opened his mouth to speak, but then thought better of it.

Dr. Auerbach angled his head and stared at Magnos. "You, I don't know."

"Magnos, sir," he replied. "Magnos Strumgarten."

"Ah, yes," he recalled. "The kidnapped boy who wasn't really kidnapped."

Magnos shot a disdainful glance at Rodriqa.

Rodriqa looked at up her father with pleading eyes, but he refused to look back at her.

"The dam is not a playground," ordered Dr. Auerbach. "You're lucky I don't call your parents. You all need to go home immediately."

"Dad, I need to ask a favor," squeaked out Rodriqa.

Dr. Auerbach raised his hand and cut her off. "It's not safe here."

"I need you to drain the lake." Her dry, shaky voice was barely audible.

"ENOUGH!" His voice echoed off the sterile, steel walls. Everyone in the room grew uncomfortably quiet and turned toward Dr. Auerbach. "Why is your voice hoarse?" he asked.

"I don't have time to explain. You have to reverse power to the turbines and empty Lake Julian."

"Rodriqa, I don't have time for this," uttered her father in a dismissive tone. He turned back toward the central console and resumed his seat.

Rodriqa grabbed his arm. "You don't understand!"

"No," he interrupted harshly. "You don't understand!" He pointed to the seismograph atop of the central console. Its thin, straight needle jumped and jiggled erratically, scratching sharp black squiggles up and down on the piece of paper running next to it. "Something very bad is about to happen. I need everyone out of the dam *now*!"

"That's exactly why you have to remove the water from Lake Julian," strained Rodriqa.

Her father shook his head. "That doesn't make any sense!"

"It doesn't matter. Please, just trust me!"

"Draining the lake won't stop another earthquake!"

Rodriqa clenched her fists in frustration, searching for the words that would make her father understand.

Jordana stepped up next to Rodriqa and touched her arm gently. "Can I speak to him?'

"He's more stubborn than I am," squawked Rodriqa under her breath.

Jordana angled herself next to his chair and stood nearly eye-to-eye with him, although he was sitting.

"Jordana, you have been through enough. You need to be with your father now." He spoke to her, but kept his attention tuned to the seismograph in front of him.

"Mr. Auerbach," she addressed him kindly, with a genteel confidence that commanded respect in return. "You and your family have been so generous and thoughtful toward me, and there is nothing I could ever do to pay you back. I'm really sorry to have to do this."

Dr. Auerbach turned slowly toward her, unnerved by her words. Jordana inhaled deeply and mustered all the anguish and fear that had plagued her for the past two months. She compressed it tightly into a ball in her mind and plunged it down deeply into the pit of her stomach. She glared at Dr. Auerbach, eye to eye, and slid her honey-colored glasses down her nose. "I need you to drain the lake immediately."

The five kids burst out of the emergency exit door from the side of the observation tower at the highway level of the Lake Julian Dam. They raced down the embankment and precariously dodged the oncoming cars across the four-lane road. On the opposite side they clung to the tall chain-linked fence and marveled at the turbines' full power.

Like horizontal geysers, three massive plumes of white water surged from the dam's face, raining millions of gallons into the ravine below. The clamorous fracas of the turbines in overdrive and the walloping whoosh of rushing water filled the air with a reverberating roar.

Buzz heard Aubrey mumble something.

"WHAT?" screamed Buzz over the din.

"IT'S BEAUTIFUL!" Aubrey screamed back, admiring the view.

Buzz turned to Jordana. "HOW DID YOU DO THAT?"

"DO WHAT?" replied Jordana nonplussed.

"MAKE DR. AUERBACH REVERSE THE TURBINES."

Jordana shrugged and kept looking at the raging water below.

"I'VE NEVER SEEN ANYONE CHANGE THEIR MIND THAT QUICKLY BEFORE," insisted Buzz.

Rodriqa moved over in between Jordana and Buzz. "MY DAD HAS A SOFT SPOT FOR JORDANA. SHE'S BEEN THROUGH A LOT." Rodriqa's voice scratched through the noise. Buzz grimaced at her, unhappy with her muddling answer.

"I WONDER HOW FAR THE WATER HAS GONE DOWN IN THE LAKE," asked Aubrey.

"LET'S WATCH THE LAKE DROP FROM THE TOWER," suggested Magnos.

"GOOD IDEA," agreed Rodriqa.

They turned around and trotted one by one through the traffic to the lakeside of the dam.

Jordana paused at the double-yellow line and held her hands to her face. A man lay very still with his chin to his chest in the side corner next to the observation tower. She recognized him instantly.

"DADDY!" she squealed.

Jordana ran over to her father and kneeled down beside him. She touched his face, and relief washed over her as she watched him breathe. His arms and torso were plastered with cracked, drying mud festooned with bits of rolled up leaves and broken twigs. The other four kids gathered around Jordana and her father, hovering worriedly over them.

"Dad, please wake up," pleaded Jordana. She shook his face gently and squeezed his fingers. His eyes rolled behind their lids, and slowly he squinted them open.

"Jordana," he sighed breathlessly. "I'm so sorry."

"Don't," she whispered as she leaned her face to his scarred forehead. "I understand." Magnos gritted his teeth to keep quiet.

"You've been through the wringer, Mr. G," said Buzz. Aubrey and Rodriqa nodded thoughtfully.

"Being alone and helpless changes a person," grumbled Magnos.

Mr. Galilahi looked up at Magnos and nodded slowly. "You know more than anyone."

"Weren't you in the hospital this morning?" asked Aubrey with a clueless expression.

"He was," replied Magnos. "And I'll give you three guesses as to who stole him out."

"Ms. Thistlewood," answered Rodriqa in an enlightened tone.

Mr. Galilahi slowly raised his fisted hands and smacked one on top of the other. Hammer. Nail.

"I know I've never met that woman," spoke Rodriqa decisively, "but I have grown to dislike her greatly."

A loud foghorn blasted from over top of the embankment.

"It's Mr. Osterfeld," announced Aubrey.

"He never blows his horn this early," added Buzz.

Magnos walked over to the tall concrete wall at the edge of the dam. He interlaced his fingers, forming a stirrup with his hands. He nodded at Aubrey.

Aubrey planted his foot in Mangos' hands, and Magnos vaulted him to the top of the wall. Aubrey pumped his fists in the air gleefully. "Mr. Osterfeld's tugboat has run aground in the middle of the lake! I can see the lakebed!"

"Woohooo," cheered Buzz as he high-fived Rodriqa.

Tears dripped down Jordana's smiling face. "We did it, Dad!"

Her father looked at her stiffly. "Did what?" he asked in an uncertain, raspy voice.

"We kept the Tomb from being opened!" She gripped his hand consolingly. "We won! The Tsul'kalu won't bother us anymore." Jordana wiped the tears from her face and laughed in overwhelming relief. Aubrey fell onto Magnos' shoulder, and he rode him around as they jostled and pranced around the embankment with jubilation. Rodriqa and Buzz slashed at each other playfully, and Buzz pretended to take an imaginary sword to the heart, mimicking how Hovis must be feeling at this very moment.

"How?" Mr. Galilahi's question was as stern as his rigid face.

"We emptied the lake. The turbines to the dam drained all the water. The ball of salt under the cemetery won't reach the Tomb now, and it'll never be opened."

Mr. Galilahi waved his hand angrily. He tried to talk quickly, but he could only sputter, choking on the unformed words.

"Everything is going to be all right," Jordana said soothingly.

"That won't stop Hovis," he wheezed through a shuddering cough. He inhaled deeply, garnishing all his remaining strength to speak. "He'll eliminate the power to the dam and the whole city if he has to. He'll do anything to open the Tomb. He has a score to settle, and his anger outweighs all reason."

Jordana chuckled incredulously. "But how can he shut off the power? He's just a ghost."

Mr. Galilahi shook his head. "Now that he's free from his curse, he's not just a ghost. He's a Shade...a creature of darkness. He'll ingest the worms and become more powerful. He'll also take on all their grief and anger, fueling his own desire for retribution. He'll destroy the electric plant if he has to. I overheard them talking about it." Suddenly, the kids stopped celebrating and stared in horror at Mr. Galilahi's words.

"But...that's...impossible," muttered Jordana.

The dam rumbled violently, shaking everyone who was standing to their hands and knees. The earth shook, and within a few moments all of Lake Julian convulsed on top of the moving earth. Birds squawked fearfully as they fled trembling trees. Cars swayed to skidding stops on the bucking asphalt.


In the cemetery on the hill, tombstones lurched skyward, and statues sank into the earth with the crescendoing shudder of the ground beneath. The rusted, wrought iron gate embossed with the Circle of Circles ripped in two and fell forward into the quivering grass.

The Trottle family plot dropped into the darkness below, forming a ravenous sinkhole that devoured dirt and stone as its edges expanded. Steam and smoke fumed from the underground house's entrails, billowing into a dusky mushroom cloud over the town.

Erupting from deep within the earth, a massive ball of fiery exploded from the cemetery and soared skyward. White pines alighted with flame and fell into the residual crater.

The terrestrial meteorite arced overhead, nearly reaching the lowest levels of clouds. It singed the atmosphere, dissipating any moisture that it approached. Hanging in mid-air for only a moment, the bolder of lava plummeted back toward the earth. The flaming sphere battered the air as it fell faster and faster. The kids hunkered down and covered their ears. It sounded like an out of control train barreling toward them.

The dam shook again in one last great spasm. The magma ball collided with the swampy lakebed, throwing waves of mud and clay across the full length and width of the lake. Fluffy clouds of steam rolled off the sinking pile of solidifying salts and ash. Its outer layer cooled, encasing its contents within.

The kids scrambled to regain their feet, and Magnos hoisted Aubrey to the top of the wall again.

"It barely missed Mr. Osterfeld's boat," Aubrey reported with amazement.

"Is it dissolving?" asked Buzz manically.

Aubrey shook his head. "No, it's cooling off, but it hasn't lost its shape…it's still just a giant ball of rock."

A low, aching moan echoed from the cemetery, reverberating off the empty lakebed and down the valley.

Aubrey closed his eyes and looked through his eyelids. "Oh, no," he murmured. While the phosphenes faded into darkness, he scanned the valley and hillside cautiously. He gasped in alarm and his eyes flipped open. He tilted backwards, tumbling off Magnos' shoulders. Magnos caught him and slowly lowered him to the ground.

"What is it?" asked Rodriqa.

The pale Aubrey pointed to the sky over the cemetery. A large red-hued phantom twirled and spun through the air, his undulating ghostly form phasing in and out through shades of black and white. His loosened chains sliced wildly around him, and he groaned angrily, growing in size the further he writhed above the treetops.

"Hovis is free," whimpered Buzz.

"How do we stop him?" asked Magnos.

The super-sized Hovis Trottle floated over the lakebed like a snake through the clouds of steam evaporating from the boiling bog, his fullness clearly comparable to the size of a two-story house.

"Where's he going?" asked Buzz.

"To the power plant," chided Jordana. "Weren't you listening?!" She pointed toward her father. Buzz nodded his head slowly as he watched Hovis overhead.

"The power plant is miles away," Buzz mumbled in thought.

"It's on the other side of Lake Julian," corrected Rodriqa.

"We have to call them and warn them," cried Jordana.

"Who's gonna believe us," replied Aubrey flatly. "Everyone thinks we're crazy."

"They'll believe it when they see Hovis," argued Magnos.

Buzz looked at his friends and shook his head. "And how are they going to see Hovis without Aubrey."

Everyone stopped for a moment, each glancing at Aubrey, who was pale with defeat. The deeply sinking sting of failure pierced everyone's heart.

"Someone will have to drive us there," insisted Rodriqa. "We can't let Hovis win."

"Who's gonna drive us anywhere?" quipped Aubrey. "We're all misfits."

Jordana grabbed her father's hand and clenched it tightly.

Rodriqa jumped up repeatedly, catching glimpses of the lakebed. "Hovis has already crossed the lake. We'll never catch him on foot," surmised Rodriqa.

"It's over," murmured Aubrey. "We've done all we can do."

Buzz gripped his forehead in thought. He tapped his finger on his forehead, urging his mind to come up with a plan. Rodriqa kicked the concrete beneath her angrily. Aubrey just stood there, numb with limp futility.

An ear-strafing screech broke the silence. "YOU STOLE MY HOUSE!"

## Buggin'

"**Y**OU STOLE MY HOUSE!"

Everyone turned around, completely unsettled by the shouting.

"THAT"S *MY* HOUSE AND IT WAS IN *YOUR* GARAGE!!" Old Widow Wizenblatt stormed up from the highway onto the sidewalk, waving her finger at Buzz. Parked half on the sidewalk, a dark blue, rusted 1970s Volkswagen Beetle was perched behind her, hovering on tiny wheels only a few inches off the pavement.

The blood drained from Buzz's face and his mouth gaped open widely.

"YOU HAD NO RIGHT!" hollered the Widow as she marched toward Buzz. "NOW YOU'VE RUINED IT!"

"It didn't belong to anybody! It was trash laying alongside the road," sputtered Buzz. He shuffled backwards, huddling behind his friends. No one else moved.

"I TOLD YOU IT WAS MINE!"

Buzz was cornered between the between the observation tower and the concrete wall. "How did you find it?!" Buzz questioned her through incredulous stutters. "How did you get it here?!"

Mrs. Wizenblatt scowled at him as she corralled him into a single spot along the wall. She planted her fists on her hips and huffed furiously under her breath about nefarious hooligans that stole shopping carts, derelict neighborhood gardeners, and children's relentless unruliness these days.

"I'm sorry," squeaked Buzz, flinching as if he anticipated an oncoming blow. "You can have it back. It was just something I was fiddling with."

"Well then," accused the Widow sullenly, "are you going to use it or not?!"

"Excuse me?" murmured Buzz warily.

"You don't have all day," she retorted. "Are you stopping Hovis, or do you just plan on moping around, hoping someone else takes care of it for you?" She spun on her heels and pointed her fingers at the other kids. "Because up to this point, you seemed determined to fix things yourselves...now here's your chance!"

Buzz slipped around Mrs. Wizenblatt and raised his arms to his sides, motioning everyone to the sidewalk. All five of them clumped up together and walked toward the Volkswagen.

"What's she talking about?" asked Rodriqa.

"Just get in the car," replied Buzz quietly, pushing them all forward.

"That's not a car, it's just the chassis," protested Aubrey.

On the outside, the Volkswagen was nearly the same as when Aubrey and Buzz had encountered it abandoned on the edge of the overpass along Dalton

Circle, a stripped-down aluminum shell. As the five kids stepped up to the car and looked inside, they gawked in awe.

Five unicycles, two in the front, one dead center and two in back, were linked to a large counter-weighted, thick metal spring in the open trunk. One set of bicycle chains ran from pedals under the seats to one side of the spring, and a second set of chains connected the opposite side of the spring to the thin, round wheels of the unicycles.

Each unicycle had a small chair back, which resembled a miniature bucket seat, with the addition of small handlebars jutting out from underneath. A vinyl steering wheel protruded from a kitchen countertop dashboard, with two upside-down spatulas rising from below, which took the place of the accelerator and brake pedals. On the dash sat a dented, brass-plated alarm clock and a globe with a map taped around it, with a tangled mess of gears attached to its belly. The tip of a sharp needle touched the north pole of the globe.

"Holy ravioli," spouted Rodriqa in bewildered amazement.

"Thanks...I think," said Buzz reluctantly. "I've been working on it for several weeks. It was ultimately meant to be a replacement for my steam-powered bike."

"Where did you get all this stuff?" Rodriqa asked.

"My dad's junkyard mostly. I pilfered some stuff from the circus grounds after they disappeared." Buzz puffed out his chest and announced proudly, "I call it the 'Buzz Bug'." The others continued staring inside, underwhelmed by his proclamation.

"So it actually works," asked Jordana.

"Theoretically, yes," replied Buzz. "But there are still a few kinks to work out, and I haven't been able to take it for a test drive yet."

"Congratulations! Today we test drive it." Rodriqa opened the door and crawled in.

"Wait," said Buzz. "I'm not sure it's safe."

"We have to catch Hovis," asserted Rodriqa. "You have any better ideas?" She looked at the other four, and they stared back at her blankly. "Then get in and let's go!" Rodriqa took the driver's seat. Magnos hunched over and took the seat in the middle, since it had the most room, gripping one handlebar with his uninjured hand and holding his casted arm in his lap. Aubrey and Jordana climbed into the back.

"It's a pretty tight fit in here," grunted Jordana as she squeezed around Magnos.

"No joke," Magnos agreed.

Buzz stood at the open door with a disdainful grimace. "I'm driving," he insisted.

"I'm older," countered Rodriqa, gripping the wheel.

"By two days," replied Buzz dryly.

"I have driving experience," continued Rodriqa.

"Once…this summer…in an open field!"

"I'm still the most qualified."

"The Buzz Bug is mine!"

Rodriqa cocked her head to the side and squinted her eyes. "If you can pull me out of this seat, then you can drive."

Buzz sighed heavily. He plopped his rear in the front passenger seat and closed the door. He secured his backpack around the back of his seat, cinching the straps down tightly. He pulled a small, thin belt from underneath him and slid the prong into its buckle on the opposite side of his seat. The other four watched him and followed suit.

Rodriqa released the emergency brake lever next to her seat. The unicycle pedals snapped to life and the bicycle chains jostled back and forth. Magnos spun his feet in the pedals.

"We're not moving," Magnos protested.

"At least let me explain how it works," shouted Buzz.

"Save it for later. We're losing time," replied Rodriqa. She pushed down on the accelerator spatula, and the Buzz Bug lurched forward.

"Pedaling winds the spring in the back," continued Buzz in an annoyed tone. "Then the person driving controls the release of the spring when they push down the accelerator, causing the car to move forward. So there's a top bike chain that transfers energy from pedaling to the spring and then the bottom chain drives the wheels."

"So the more we pedal, the more energy we have to move faster?" asked Aubrey.

"Precisely," answered Buzz.

"Aubrey! EYES!" interrupted Rodriqa.

All five of them pedaled. Aubrey gripped the handlebars at the edges of his seat and closed his eyes tightly.

The Bug jumped forward off the sidewalk and onto the highway. A prolonged honk blared at them from a car from behind. Rodriqa hit the brake spatula, and the car jerked to a stop.

"You're supposed to yield to oncoming traffic," reprimanded Buzz.

"There aren't any rearview mirrors," argued Rodriqa.

"I told you the Buzz Bug wasn't finished," reminded Buzz.

Rodriqa sighed with an annoyed huff and turned her head over her shoulder. As best she could tell, the highway was clear, so she eased her foot down on the accelerator spatula.

The car moved forward slowly at first, but gained speed quickly. Aubrey clenched his face together, hunting for Hovis in the distance. Rodriqa tested the wheel, turning it a little bit each way, and the car swerved slightly in the lane.

"Seems to handle well," Rodriqa offered.  Buzz grunted unapologetically.

Rodriqa shoved the accelerator spatula down further, and the wheels spun furiously as the asphalt past swiftly by below them.

"Won't we be in deeper trouble if we ride in this thing," asked Jordana worriedly.  "None of us has a license to drive a car!"

"It's technically not a car," replied Buzz pedantically.  "There's no engine…no gas tank…no gear shift…it's simply a modified bicycle. If the cops pull us over, we're untouchable."

Rodriqa slammed on the brake spatula, and the car heaved to a stop.

"*WHAT* are *you* doing?" yelled Buzz.

"There's a red light," replied Rodriqa.

"It's a hundred feet in front of us!"

Rodriqa let off the brake and the car crept toward the stoplight.  "Aubrey, have you found Hovis yet?"

"There," shouted Aubrey in triumph.  He opened his eyes and pointed at the red glow in the distant sky off to their right.  It seemed so harmless, so far away, a twinkling, rose-colored wave above the horizon.

"We need to hurry up," commanded Rodriqa.  She forced the accelerator spatula to the floor and turned right, toward Hovis.  The globe on the dashboard spun 90 degrees to the right.

"What is this thing?" asked Rodriqa as she nodded toward the globe.

"It's my citywide version of a GPS," answered Buzz proudly.

"You're kidding me," replied Rodriqa.

"No, seriously," replied Buzz.  "I made a map of the city and laid it over the globe.  The needle points to the position we are currently.  The gears are attached to a small wheel below that move when the car moves and changes the position of the globe.  So we always know where we are…as long as we're in Lake Julian."

Rodriqa rolled her eyes at him.  "You really need a normal hobby."

"We're not going fast enough," interrupted Aubrey.  He pointed toward the sky at Hovis, whose form was shrinking in the distance.

Rodriqa pushed down harder on the accelerator spatula, and everyone pedaled faster.  She sped through several stop signs, slowly only briefing to look for opposing traffic.  Jordana looked out her window as the houses and yards whipped by faster and faster.

"How do we know how fast we're going?" asked Jordana nervously.  "We might be exceeding the speed limit."

"The brass clock on the dashboard acts like a speedometer," replied Buzz.  "Each number represents approximately five miles per hour.  So if it's at '3', we're going fifteen miles per hour."

The other four kids leaned forward and stared at the old-fashioned, dented brass alarm clock.  Its face was cracked and a single, bent hand wavered around six o'clock.

"Red light," barked out Buzz.

Rodriqa jerked her foot over to the brake spatula and pushed down hard. The car squealed to a stop. She held her left foot just above the accelerator, eager to keep moving. The red, glowing swathe of Hovis disappeared behind the tree line.

"Dang, we lost him," fumed Rodriqa. "Aubrey, can you find him again?"

"I'll try," replied Aubrey. He closed his eyes and clenched his jaw together, concentrating on the darkness.

The rhythmic thud of vibrating bass rang from a set of overly-amped car speakers, pelting the Bug with sonic thumps from behind. A rumbling engine pulled up beside them. Annoyed by the noise, Aubrey opened his eyes. He sank backwards against his seat.

"Oh, no," he muttered through the noise. The other four kids turned away, sharing his anxious sentiment.

The red Pontiac GTO's tinted passenger window slowly slid down into the door. Gaetan leaned over into the passenger seat and gawked at the Volkswagen as he dialed the volume down on his stereo. He snapped open his cell phone and punched in three, quick numbers. "Poage County Police Department…I've spotted a group of underage, unlicensed drivers in an antique Volkswagen Beetle on the north end of Lake Julian…."

The light turned green.

"Punch it!" yelled Buzz. Rodriqa floored the accelerator, pushing all five kids against their seatbacks.

"Maybe we should be on the sidewalk, since this is technically a bicycle," Jordana said as she gripped her handlebars tightly.

"But bikes are allowed on the road," countered Buzz.

"If the cops catch us, there is no way we'll catch up to Hovis," Magnos added, breathing heavily from cycling.

Rodriqa swerved onto the sidewalk, and the Bug fit perfectly between the curb and the grass. She cornered the Bug, tracing the path of the concrete.

"This is taking too long," said Aubrey frantically.

"What do you want me to do?" asked Rodriqa.

"Avoid the pedestrians," hollered Buzz, and he grabbed the wheel. An elderly couple dove into the grass in front of them as Buzz turned the car onto the grassy lawn.

"We're driving on church property," announced Jordana, and all five of them stared upward as a stone nave and steeple reached skyward in front of them.

Rodriqa scowled and pointed her finger at Buzz. "Don't you *ever* grab the steering wheel again!"

"You were about to run people over," hollered Buzz.

"I was totally going to give them the right of way," retorted Rodriqa.

"Let's just get back on the road and head for the power plant," suggested Magnos in a stern voice.

Rodriqa steered the car through the churchyard and took a hard right at the corner of the building's stone wall. White lace zipped through the air. Stark black and shiny pink figures raced back and forth across the lawn. Grains of rice pelted the windshield. The Buzz Bug mowed down a row of folding chairs and clipped the leg of a long, cafeteria table. Flatware and plastic utensils slid to the ground, littering the lawn. Rodriqa swerved to avoid as much of the chaos as she could.

The other four kids sat still and pedaled, unable to speak. They covered their eyes and glanced through their fingers as men, women and children, dressed in their Sunday's finest scattered across the church's front yard. Feminine squeals and gruff, masculine expletives echoed off the rough stone entranceway.

"I can't believe…we just drove through a wedding party," whimpered Jordana.

Buzz leaned forward and glowered at Rodriqa. She held up her hand, palm out, with her lower lip as stiff as her fingers. With this gesture, the others remained silent.

Rodriqa maneuvered the car through the empty side lot next to the church and steered onto the street. No one uttered a word. A mixture of shock and embarrassment hung in thick silence in the car. Jordana leaned out the window and examined the car for damage. All she could see was that the Buzz Bug had a new accoutrement…a tablecloth pinned within the doors' creases and draped around the car's bottom like a skirt.

*WEEEEYYYYYYYOOOOOUUUUUU*!! A blue light flashed at the Buzz Bug from behind. Aubrey turned around in his seat.

"It's the police," Buzz said in a flat, accusing tone as he stared straight ahead.

Rodriqa glared over towards him. She lifted her foot off the accelerator and pulled up to the curb. She jerked the emergency brake back tersely. It snapped off in her hand. Buzz shook his head and covered his eyes with his hand.

"It's worse," replied Aubrey. "It's the Kluggards." Aubrey instantly recognized the shoddy muffler of their Poage County Police Car, stopping several yards behind them. Ned wobbled out of the passenger seat as Fred's lanky form straightened out from under the driver's side.

"Joyride's over," muttered Magnos.

"Maybe if we'd stayed on the sidewalk," seethed Buzz.

Rodriqa sighed angrily.

"Guys, look!" Aubrey pointed out his window, drawing everyone's attention outside. The car was parked along the sidewalk in front of the entrance walkway into Lake Julian Square.

Both the judicial center for the town as well as its historic birthplace, this rustic street's cobblestone road was lined with carefully restored and preserved nineteenth-century brick buildings, which housed both the civic and bureaucratic heart of Lake Julian. Centuries-old houses, which had been converted into trendy, boutique shops, huddled haphazardly in between commercial and governmental offices. Wooden-latticed markets held locally harvested fruits and vegetables, and antique gas lampposts and recently painted benches dotted the sidewalk. Usually the Square was littered with vehicles during the week, the choicest spots for the office and managerial staff members to park. On the weekends the road was closed to cars, allowing more foot traffic for tourists and shoppers.

Today was different. The street was lined with over-sized sawhorses bearing warnings of "DO NOT CROSS" along their outer edges. Throngs of people crowded together along the sidewalk. The Lake Julian Marching Band filed out of City Hall, and the uniformed, instrument-adorned students organized themselves into a perfectly symmetrical block.

"It's the parade," remarked Aubrey.

"Duh," mocked Buzz sarcastically.

"No, you don't understand. We can't let the Kluggards catch us," protested Aubrey.

"They're the police," refuted Rodriqa. "What are we supposed to do?! Run?!"

"Precisely," replied Aubrey. The other four turned toward Aubrey and looked at him like he'd grown toenails for eyelids.

"I don't think the Kluggards are really police officers," continued Aubrey. "I think they're Ms. Thistlewood's henchmen." Aubrey looked at Buzz pointedly. "Think about it. How they conveniently appeared when Old Widow Wizenblatt was terrorizing Ms. Thistlewood, and how quickly they showed up when her house was burning down."

"And how they ushered her away from the Raft Race when the Tsul'kalu scared everyone off," replied Buzz as he continued Aubrey's thought. The other four stared between the two of them thoughtfully, their words striking a familiar chord. Aubrey glanced behind the car. The Kluggard brothers sauntered closer toward them.

"If we don't go now, they'll detain us, and we'll never stop Hovis in time," asserted Aubrey.

"Go where?" asked Rodriqa. The marching band's sonorous sound blanketed the Square in rich tones and synchronized melodies. The crowd cheered wildly as the band entered the Paddling Pumpkin Parade.

"Into the Parade," he replied.

Rodriqa guffawed loudly.

"He's right! Do it!" ordered Buzz. He reached over and grabbed the steering wheel. "If you don't, I will!"

Rodriqa scoffed at him as she brushed his hand away. She slammed on the accelerator spatula, and the car jumped onto the sidewalk. Fishtailing between the lampposts and benches, the Buzz Bug rolled onto the cobblestone street.

"STOP!" yelled Officer Fred as his thin, rubbery legs launched into a dead-on sprint. Ned scampered quickly after him, but tripped over the curb when he waddled onto the sidewalk.

Rodriqa edged the car behind the marching band. The kids kept their heads down and pedaled slowly. The pomp and ruckus from the band shrouded them, and no one seemed to be paying any attention to the low-riding Volkswagen that had slipped into the parade.

"It's working. Maybe we can disappear," whispered Jordana.

"I'm not sure that's the best tactic," countered Buzz.

"Why not?" questioned Rodriqa.

"If we don't act like we're part of the parade," said Buzz, "someone will figure out we don't belong here. If we blend in, then no one will know the difference, and we can zip through the parade and get to the power plant."

Aubrey looked behind them, and the next entry into the parade pulled into the Square. A house-sized cornucopia, filled with pumpkins whose spookily carved faces glowed eerily from inside their shells, rolled onto the street with men and women dressed in Pilgrim outfits, sitting on rumpled sections of the horn and waving banners that read "Mount Camelot brings you Prosperity!"

McCrayden Miller peered through a mesh windshield at the bottom of the mechanized cornucopia, glaring the Volkswagen in front of her.

"Ugh, McCrayden is behind us," reported Aubrey.

Jordana took a quick peek behind her and shuddered at the massive float bearing down on them.

"Maybe Buzz is right," offered Magnos. "Let's blend in."

A white-faced clown with a bulbous, red rubber nose and rainbow-painted wig weaved between the marching band members on inline skates. He taunted them by threatening to push a button on their instruments while they were playing, or by sticking his pointed finger only a few millimeters away from their eyes. Rodriqa was disturbed by two things; the carelessness with which he barely avoided the band students, and that he was wearing fluorescent green, Lycra biker shorts. The clown exited the rigorously regimented lines of tuba players and bolted straight for the Buzz Bug.

The clown grabbed the bottom ledge of Rodriqa's driver side window and wheeled himself in a semicircle to a stop. He leaned in the car and glared at each of the kids. Rodriqa pulled herself into the middle of the car.

"You're not in the parade," exclaimed the clown.

Rodriqa closed her eyes and looked away, trying to pretend he wasn't there. The sharp smell of acetone from his makeup burned her nose, and she started breathing heavily in the midst of her clown claustrophobia.

"We're a late entry," improvised Buzz. "The parade committee just approved our application for our toy Volkswagen float a couple days ago."

"There are no toy Volkswagen Beetles registered for the parade," insisted the clown. "I know. I'm co-chair of the parade committee."

Sweat dripped down Rodriqa's forehead. Magnos recognized the clown's voice and cringed as it brought back a flood of memories. He examined the clown's face, forcing himself to see the features behind the grotesque white face cream, bright baby blue eye shadow and rainbow-colored tears.

"Mr. Miller, is that you?" asked Magnos.

"Yes, and haven't you all caused enough trouble for the time being? I'm making a citizen's arrest and pulling this vehicle over."

"Wait! Let us explain," pleaded Buzz. Mr. Miller grabbed the wheel and turned it all the way to the passenger side. His wig brushed Rodriqa's cheek. She exhaled wildly, and her eyes flipped open suddenly. She slapped her hand over his on the windowsill and yanked the wheel the opposite direction. She pushed the accelerator spatula down and steered around the side of the band.

"What are you doing?" hollered Mr. Miller frantically. He raked his skates clumsily along the road, trying to stay upright and pull himself free. Between the changing momentum of the car and Rodriqa's tight grip, he helplessly fumbled along next to the Buzz Bug in true clown slapstick splendor.

The crowd clapped and laughed at the shtick of the gangly clown stuck on the low-riding Volkswagen with a partial drape around its bottom, racing down the bumpy, cobblestone street.

The car whipped in front of the band, and the Bug sped forward, passing the next float in front of them, the Lake Julian Quilting Club's "Menagerie of Pumpkin Quilts." Clotheslines, strung together on a flat bed covered in straw, carried quilts of various shapes and sizes, all with Halloween or Thanksgiving themes.

"Rodriqa, stop!" yelled Jordana. "You're making a scene."

Rodriqa released Mr. Miller as she slammed on the brake spatula. He spun wildly like a rainbow-colored disco ball into the crowd and disappeared into a maelstrom of flailing hands and feet.

Rodriqa breathed heavily. "I *hate* clowns." She felt her heart pounding like a bass drum inside her chest. She looked up. Most of the crowd was cheering at them. Some onlookers where staring sternly at the Bug. Others were eagerly awaiting the cars next trick. She looked behind the car, and the elderly women from the Quilting Club glowered down on them with bewilderment from underneath white, acorn-shaped bonnets.

"Time for plan B," said Rodriqa. "Everyone wave."

Aubrey, Jordana, Buzz and Rodriqa stuck their hands out of the windows and plastered their faces with broad smiles. Rodriqa eased the car forward, riding the small tract of road between the floats in the center and the crowd on the sidewalk. They passed by the Local Merchants float, where Mr. Jennings stood at the back among five mechanized skeletons bearing cell phones, MP3 players and flashy tennis shoes. Buzz hung out of the window and waved over the top of the car at him. Mr. Jennings waved exuberantly back with a wide grin. He shifted the ball cap bearing the large white 'K' on top of his head, and the corners of his mouth turned down as he realized who was waving at him and what the kids were riding in. Unnerved by Mr. Jennings' change in disposition, Buzz shrunk back into the car.

"We need to get back on the surface roads," urged Aubrey. "We're wasting time."

"What's the quickest way to the power plant?" asked Rodriqa.

Aubrey tried to regain his bearings. The Square was not usually this crowded, and the masses and floats blocking most points of interest was slightly disorienting. He looked out his window and wobbled his head around Magnos, who took up most of the mid-section of the car's interior. "Take the next right," directed Aubrey.

Rodriqa continued her careful commute past several more floats and turned between two sawhorses onto the next side street. Everyone in the car stopped waving and pulled their arms in the car as she sped up and raced away from the Square.

"At least we lost the police," offered Buzz apologetically.

"I wonder if Hovis has already made it to the plant," asked Magnos gloomily.

"Until the lights go out, we've still got time," encouraged Aubrey. "The central power station supplies all of Poage County."

Jordana and Buzz looked outside at the houses and buildings passing by. The local folks appeared to still have electricity, and the kids breathed a little more easily.

"Still, I have no idea how we're gonna stop him once we get there, though," added Aubrey.

"He definitely seems stronger than before," agreed Magnos.

Rodriqa pulled up to a traffic light. "Which way?" she asked.

Aubrey examined the road ahead. A wide green street sign laced with white reflector buttons stood to the right of the road, signaling the onramp to the Interstate Highway.

Aubrey thought for a moment as he looked ahead. "The Interstate would be faster. It's just a couple exits up."

Jordana glowered at him. "We can't get on the Interstate with this thing. We'll get pulverized."

"I think we'd be okay," interjected Buzz. "The lowest speed acceptable on the highway is 40 miles per hour. The Buzz Bug can definitely handle it."

"There's no way these unicycles can handle forty miles an hour," argued Jordana.

"I agree with Jordana," said Magnos. "There's not even a floorboard in here. What if one of us falls off our seats?"

*WEEEEYYYYYYYOOOOOUUUUUUU*!! Bursts of blue, flashing lights pelted the car from behind. All the kids jerked around to look behind them. Two police cars were closing in on them quickly.

"Interstate it is," barked Rodriqa. She shoved the accelerator spatula to the ground and hugged the corner tightly. The Buzz Bug raced up the onramp.

"This is crazy," murmured Jordana.

"PEDAL!" ordered Rodriqa.

Rodriqa held the accelerator down, eager to see what Buzz's creation could really do. She watched as the bent hand on the broken alarm clock shuddered as it passed the '8' and approached the '9.' The car careened into the rightmost lane of the Interstate as the merge lane ended.

Aubrey looked through the back window. The two police cars peaked over the horizon in the merging lane with flashing lights and blinking headlights.

"The cops are after us," reported Aubrey.

"Look for Hovis," redirected Rodriqa. She glanced over her shoulder and merged into the next lane. The clock's hand winnowed to '10'.

Magnos stopped pedaling and placed his feet on the foot rests below his seat. He struggled for deep breaths. "Sorry, but I'm worn out. It's been a long couple days."

"It's okay," replied Jordana sympathetically. She touched his arm and smiled gently at him. Aubrey grimaced. He closed his eyes and stared at the darkness behind his eyelids as he pedaled harder.

"Untidy Heidi!" exclaimed Rodriqa with frustration. Red brakes lights popped on brightly in the cars ahead.

"What's going on?" asked Magnos.

Buzz craned his neck around, hoping to get a better view. "I can't tell. Must be an accident or something. Move over another lane."

Rodriqa weaved over between two cars in the left-hand lane. "This lane isn't moving any faster," argued Rodriqa.

"Ahhhhh…it's construction," replied Buzz disgustedly. A heavy concrete barrier separated makeshift lanes as the opposite lanes of traffic were funneled down into a single lane. A semi, loaded with half a house, vied with a hazardous materials truck for best position in the shrinking roadway, halting progress by anyone.

"Ugh!" Rodriqa smacked the steering wheel angrily as they stopped only a few inches away from the bumper of the next car.

The flashing lights of the police cars illuminated the inside of the Buzz Bug like strobes in a discothèque. The heavy door of the cruiser slammed shut. The kids froze with terror and regret. They kept their heads forward and their hands clasped around their handlebars.

With one hand on his gun and another on his belt buckle, Sergeant Van Zenny strode up to the Volkswagen. He stopped at the first window and gripped the top of the car, almost examining it to see if it was real. The Sergeant leaned over and leered at Aubrey over his silvery sunglasses.

"You kids are in a whole mess a' trouble," he grumbled in his thick, slow draw. He pulled out his note pad and flipped several pages through. "I've been keepin' track of each of ya's. And I've been tryin' to be the good guy...give ya a benefit of the doubt, but ya's pushed me too hard now."

He gazed down at his notepad and turned a page back. "Here's what I've got ya's on so far. Multiple counts of Trespassing, Destruction of Private Property, Truancy, and Obstruction of Justice. There's still the question of Kidnapping, Conspiracy to Commit a Crime and Unlawful Imprisonment." Aubrey scowled at the last charges. "And today I add to the list Vehicular Assault and Underage Driving."

"We haven't hit anyone," insisted Buzz.

"Your little trick wit' Mr. Miller...that's assault."

Buzz sighed heavily. "But there's not a motor. We're not in a car. It's a glorified bicycle."

Sergeant Van Zenny crumpled his forehead. "Son, you been drivin' this vehicle down the highway at nigh on 50 miles an hour. I know...I clocked ya's. You can't make a bike go 50 miles an hour, and I think the judge will agree wit' me."

"You don't understand, sir," said Magnos

"No, I'm afraid it's y'all who don't understand. Today, I don't have a choice in the matter. I need to take y'all downtown."

"Something bad is about to happen at the power plant," pleaded Rodriqa forlornly. "We need you to take us there as soon as possible. We can explain everything on the way."

"Your time for bargaining has long passed, Missy," replied Van Zenny.

Ned and Fred Kluggard walked up behind the Sergeant, their heads held high. "What can we do to help, sir?" offered Fred in his most official tone.

"Watch these characters. I needs to grab some more handcuffs, and I needs to call for more backup." The Sergeant lurched away from the Bug and walked back to his cruiser.

A car to the left and just a few feet in front of them moved up, and Buzz saw a space in the barrier ahead.

Fred squatted and, with his long torso, met the kids eye to eye outside the car. He scanned the vehicle from hood to wheels, doors to spring. He shook his head and glared at Aubrey. The kids kept still and silent.

"Looks like the kiddies are a bit out of their league today...wouldn't you agree Ned?" giggled Fred. Ned answered with a jiggling bellow from his globular belly.

"Man! I have been waiting for this day for a long time now," continued Fred. He rested his hands on his thighs and settled in. "You all have been the biggest thorn in my backside for weeks, but I knew as long as I was patient, I'd be rewarded."

Buzz whispered inaudibly to Rodriqa. Her eyes widened as she looked ahead. Magnos overheard them.

Fred wiped his forehead. "It's kinda sad, really. All you all had to do was nothing. All you had to do was simply stay out of the way. Let nature take its course. Let things happen as they should happen...but no. You had to pick things apart. You had to get in there and make a difference. Add your own little spice to the stew."

Rodriqa whispered to Buzz. Buzz nodded and whispered back.

"What blows my mind is how you all got this far. Powers beyond your imagination have been scheming for centuries for this very day, and you all come along and mess everything up." Ned chortled heavily at Fred's comment.

Buzz motioned at the spatulas slowly with his hands. Rodriqa nodded.

"And in case you haven't realized it yet, you all are really, really pathetic." Fred turned up to Ned and addressed him directly as he berated the kids, gesturing at each of them as he spoke about them. "You've got this fat nerd who thinks he's Thomas Edison, but couldn't crawl his way out of a wet sleeping bag...the misplaced loner whose dad brought her halfway across the country just to stir up trouble, and says he cares about her when all he ever cared about was himself...the tough girl with the attitude of a cage wrestler who's afraid of her own shadow...and the skinny, red-headed misfit who couldn't do anything right if he tried." Jordana and Aubrey stiffened their lips.

"And you," Fred eyes widened with realization. He stood up and pointed to Magnos excitedly. "You're the kid who screwed up in Lake Julian's first football game...you cost the Lake Julian Belugas their winning season."

Rodriqa gripped the steering wheel and pointed to the left with her right index finger. Buzz tightened his hands around his handlebars.

"The kid who was supposedly kidnapped and whose parents wouldn't even come see him in the hospital," continued Fred. "You know, football players and fathers of football players will talk about you for *years*. When they're hanging around the fire pit or talking after Christmas dinner, reminiscing the past...they'll remember *you*. They'll remember what a mistake it was to have a freshman start on the Varsity football team. They'll remember how you ruined their kids' most promising year of football...they'll remember the only tactic you could employ after your painful mistake was to disappear...but you didn't disappear long enough."

Magnos grit his teeth and furrowed his brow. He set his feet on the pedals and balled his fists tightly together. His rage rose like a taunted dragon, and his chest heaved waves of air in and out of his lungs.

"The name Magnos Strumgarten will be worse than any swear word ever uttered around these parts, and you'll be considered a wretch the rest of your pitiful life. You should have just stayed gone."

Magnos' eyes flashed white. He had had enough.

"RODRIQA! DRIVE!" shouted Magnos. He gripped the handles on the ceiling of the car and spun his wheels so quickly the pedals and chain below his seat were swallowed in a blur.

Rodriqa slammed down the accelerator spatula. She edged the Buzz Bug between the car in front of her and the space to the left and zipped between the break in the concrete barrier.

"What are you doing?" asked Aubrey frantically.

"They can't follow us on the wrong side of the road," replied Buzz in a clever tone.

Magnos bent over and pedaled with all his might. The spring in the trunk warbled and moaned under the increasing tension of stored potential energy. Rodriqa hugged the barrier wall and whipped past cars driving the opposite direction. The lanes opened up, and Rodriqa drove along the makeshift shoulder, gaining speed with every second.

"That's a great plan," said Jordana flatly. "What happens when the shoulder is blocked?"

"We'll stop," replied Buzz condescendingly.

A white SUV pulled over onto the shoulder, dark smoke rolling from underneath its hood. Rodriqa pushed hard with both feet on the brake spatula. It broke off, tinging and bouncing along the asphalt below. The gears whirred wildly and the car sped forward faster.

Rodriqa yelled at Magnos, "STOP PEDALING!" Magnos was lost in frenzy. He pulled against the handlebars in the ceiling, and the metal crumpled in around them, creating tiny craters in the roof.

"WE'RE GONNA CRASH!" squalled Buzz, and he placed his hands on the dash and lowered his head.

Aubrey and Jordana screamed.

Rodriqa's insides stiffened. The SUV seemed to grow in size as they raced toward it. She knew this was the end. She closed her eyes to await the impact.

In the darkness, she saw the Cherokee boy, who this morning had stood in front of her, so darling and unafraid, and she remembered what the Tsul'kalu had told her. *Force your fear out.*

Rodriqa opened her eyes and clasped her hands around the steering wheel. She turned it to the left, barely missing the SUV.

Cars barreled toward the car in the oncoming lanes. Buzz covered his face and screamed. Magnos continued to pedal. Jordana and Aubrey put their heads down and leaned into the car.

*Fear out*, Rodriqa told herself, and a calm washed over her quivering stomach. She shifted lanes, dodging a blue coupe. She shifted back, avoiding a black sedan. Horns honked madly, decrescendoing as they passed by.

Buzz peered timidly through his fingers as the car leap-frogged sideways from lane to lane, each movement only inches from the next car. Buzz stared at Rodriqa in amazement. Her gaze was fixed, and her knuckles were transparent. Her ghostly form was returning as her forearms slowly faded.

Maroon convertible. Beige hatchback. Violet hybrid. Cars were swerving into other lanes, but Rodriqa had already turned the car out of the way before they reached them.

"PULL OFF THE ROAD!" yelled Jordana as she pointed ahead. Three Semi-trailers filled each of the three lanes ahead at nearly the same distance, like a wall of chrome and steel hurtling toward them.

Rodriqa veered around two more cars and aimed the Buzz Bug for the middle semi.

"STOP!" hollered Buzz savagely. The blowing horns from the semis echoed along the highway, and smoke billowed from their skidding wheels as they braked hard. The three trucks bore down on the Buzz Bug swiftly.

Rodriqa twisted the steering wheel all the way to the right, and the Bug slid past the rightmost semi's cabin and under its bed less than a yard beyond the massive charcoal-colored wheels. The semi blasted its horn again. Sparks flew as the top of the Buzz Bug scraped against the bed of the trailer. The semis swerved as the momentum of their heavy cargo pushed them forward. Smoke poured through the windows of Volkswagen. Rodriqa banked the steering wheel hard left, and the car fishtailed under the trailers of the other two semis across the Interstate. The Buzz Bug emerged from beneath the leftmost semi, barely missing its set of double rear wheels.

Rodriqa angled around another oncoming SUV, which nearly T-boned the Buzz Bug, and weaved up onto the onramp on the far side of the Interstate. She rode the shoulder, passing three more cars, which drove by slowly, shocked at the makeshift Volkswagen heading the wrong way.

"I can't believe it," sputtered Aubrey. "We survived."

Several more cars swerved and honked at them as the kids sped through the intersection.

"AUBREY! EYES!" shouted Rodriqa. She cornered the car onto the road and straightened out into the correct lane. Aubrey scrunched his face together and searched the darkness behind his eyelids. Jordana and Buzz held their breaths, stunned by the wayward detour up the Interstate.

"THERE!" Aubrey shouted as he opened his eyes. The writhing, red form appeared on the horizon down the road, larger than they had ever seen it before. It hovered over the trees and dipped slowly down below the canopy.

"The power plant is just up ahead on the left," cheered Aubrey. "We can still make it!"

"Magnos! Stop!" cried Rodriqa. Magnos shook his head and raised his feet to the footrest, with the empty pedals beneath him still spinning wildly. The spring whizzed furiously as it unwound, and the chains strained and jerked under the deceleration. Everyone sighed heavily, grateful to be slowing down.

Rodriqa turned into the long, steep driveway at the entrance to the Central Poage County Electrical Power Station. The car rolled quickly down the hill toward the chain-link security gate at the bottom. Rodriqa jostled the metal nub left behind from the brake spatula, but the car was regaining speed.

"Looks like we'll have another couple of felonies to add to our rap sheet," remarked Rodriqa sarcastically. She stiffened her arms and aimed the car for the gate.

The Buzz Bug soared down the driveway. A security guard in a tight-fitting, green uniform with bright buttons walked out of the boxy gatehouse and waved his arms dissuasively overhead. Rodriqa steadied the wheel and the others covered their faces as they barreled toward the entrance. The security guard shouted at them and then jumped out of the way.

Like a runaway comet, the car bulleted through the chain-link gate, ripping one side from its hinge and mangling the other side into crumpled scrap of tin foil.

Rodriqa swerved along the asphalt, trying to slow their speed as they approached the industrial complex of the plant. She turned away from a parking lot full of cars to the left and aimed the car for an empty graveled area on the right. They were racing toward the external metal wall of the plant, which was protected by three large concrete barriers several feet out from it.

"We're gonna hit!" yelled Buzz.

Rodriqa jerked the steering wheel to the right, and the Buzz Bug skidded violently. It bounced off one of the barriers and then slowly rolled to a stop.

Aubrey scurried hastily out of his window. Buzz flung open his door and fell to his knees. He kissed the gravel, thankful to be on solid, stationary ground, unharmed. Magnos and Jordana crawled out quickly, heaving sighs of relief. Rodriqa tried to open her door, but it was jammed from its beating by the concrete barrier. She stepped out of Buzz's door, head held high with pride.

"You...should never...be allowed...behind the wheel...of a car... ever...AGAIN!" insisted Buzz.

"What are you talking about?" she balked. "I thought I did an amazing job!"

"I give you an 'A' for effort, skill and luck," said Magnos, "but a 'D' in judgment."

"I'd flunk her," reprimanded Buzz.

Exhausted, Magnos rubbed his face with his good hand and then cradled his broken arm. Jordana walked around to the passenger side of the car and kneeled down next to Aubrey, who was lying face down in the gravel. She turned him over. He was a pale green, and he stared up at her in shock.

"I know we're not still moving," Aubrey said breathlessly, "but it feels like we are."

"Sit up. You'll feel better," Jordana said, raising the back of his head with her hand. He leaned forward and put his head between his knees.

"We need to get inside," Rodriqa said urgently.

"Where's Hovis?" asked Jordana.

"I'm not sure, but we need to find him now." Rodriqa pointed back toward the entranceway. A half-dozen police cars, flashing their lights, turned down the hill toward them.

# The Electron's Edge

Aubrey, Jordana, Magnos, Buzz and Rodriqa raced toward the side entrance of the power plant. Rodriqa flung open the heavy metal door. Magnos ducked as a folding chair flew over the threshing and tumbled into the parking lot, leg over back along the asphalt. Blasts of heated air rushed through the door. The kids looked at each other, and then peered warily inside.

Dressed in blue cleanroom suits and electrician uniforms, workers and foremen scurried panic-stricken through the warehouse-sized room. Some clutched to desks, which were scooted across the concrete floors under the force of the gushing wind. Others gripped pipes and wires to gain their footing along the metal walls. The hot waves of wind whirled through the room, and papers, pens and small tools flew through the air like a hurricane of debris. A chalkboard toppled backwards and landed flat against the concrete with a loud crack, and bullet-sized pieces of chalk zipped through the room. A canopy of broad, fluorescent lights flickered overhead, swinging violently from the ceiling, and glass doors at the rear of the room vibrated furiously under the strain of the spinning gale.

The kids hugged the wall, dodging flying bits of plastic and metal. Magnos helped one of the workers brace a set of lockers from tipping over.

The swirling squall of hardware frightened away Aubrey's nausea. He knew what was causing the maelstrom, and he was also certain he was the only person who could stop it. He couldn't ignore his place in this battle any longer. He pooled his remaining, anemic courage into the pit of his stomach and decided that this madness would stop now.

"Wait here!" yelled Aubrey through the din of the industrial tempest. He marched cautiously into the middle of the room. He held his hands out and closed his eyes as screws and wrenches clanged against the walls, and voices screamed warnings and expletives across the plant floor.

"HOVIS TROTTLE!" Aubrey's voice echoed off the metal walls and aluminum lighting above. Slowly, the whirlwind died. Filing cabinets and benches skidded to a stop, and debris fell from the air, banging against the floor. Dazed by the ethereal onslaught, the workers stared at each other and Aubrey in amazement and confusion.

One man, dressed in a button-down shirt and tie, stomped angrily into the center of the room. "AUBREY! WHAT ARE YOU DOING?!" Mr. Taylor clenched his fists and shouted in fuming frustration as he approached Aubrey. "WHY DO YOU *REPEATEDLY* DISOBEY ME?!" Aubrey kept his eyes closed tightly and concentrated on the darkness behind his eyelids, calmly focusing on breathing deeply and slowly.

"Oh, no," whimpered Buzz. He ran toward the middle of the room. "Mr. Taylor...we can explain."

"Save it, Buzz," snapped Mr. Taylor as he held up his hand to cut him off. "You all shouldn't be here. You should leave...NOW!"

"But," Buzz tried to argue.

Mr. Taylor scowled at him. "HUSH IT!"

Dan Taylor marched over and stopped inches away from his son's face. "For once, can you *not* do as you're told!" Aubrey didn't move. He barely breathed. His eyes were closed, and his father's rage exploded.

"DON'T *TUNE* ME OUT!"

Aubrey opened his eyes. They were white from corner to corner, like a blank sheet of paper. Mr. Taylor took a step back, startled by the lack of color to his eyes.

"I'm not trying to *tune* you out," asserted Aubrey. "I'm simply trying to show you what I've been going through for the past three months." Aubrey raised his arm and pointed with his index finger beyond his father. Mr. Taylor turned around slowly. Aubrey's father lost his breath, and every muscle locked itself in place.

A gray mist of a man hovered over the floor with thick locks of hair shrouding his face, like the hood of a cloak. His deep-set eyes glowed faintly red and studied Aubrey's dad intensely. His wide jaw and scarred cheek clenched together tightly, and his chains swung from underneath his arms, no longer shackled to the ground. Hovis Trottle had resumed his usual shape and leaned forward to meet Mr. Taylor eye to eye.

Aubrey could no longer see dust swirling around Hovis. He knew the Sandman Anathem had been broken.

Hovis howled menacingly through his hollow mouth. Mr. Taylor dropped to his knees and scrambled backwards on all fours behind Aubrey. Now nothing stood between Hovis and Aubrey.

"Freeeeeeee theeee Waaaatcheeeeeers," hissed Hovis indignantly.

Aubrey shook his head determinedly and clenched his teeth.

"Ooooopeeen theeeee Toooomb," Hovis growled louder.

"You won't win," commanded Aubrey, his white eyes gleaming with conviction.

"FREEEEEZZZZE!" A loud, shrill command echoed from the back of the plant. Everyone in the room turned to look instantly. A battalion of police officers lined the fore wall, pistols readied and pointed into the middle of the room. Flanked by the Kluggards, Sergeant Van Zenny stepped slowly forward, sweeping his head from side to side.

Aubrey faced the officers and moved out of the way to give the policemen a clear view of the phantom in the background. The Sergeant approached warily, confused by the entire scene. He considered every angle quickly. *Why is this plant such a wreck? Did those kids make all of this mess? Why does everyone seem to be afraid of the red-head? Why were his eyes white? And who is the joker standing behind him?*

"Who's the guy in the costume?" Van Zenny waved his gun in the direction of the ghostly figure.

"Hovis Trottle," said Aubrey with an authoritative snap to his jaw.

Hovis roared like a firing cannon, vibrating the floor and shattering fluorescent bulbs above. Red swirls glowed around him, and his body twisted and wretched in a boiling fury of wavy ether as he grew in size. The full monstrosity of the new Hovis hovered over everyone as his head reached the ceiling. He lifted a metal cabinet leaning against the wall behind him and threw it across the power plant. Van Zenny dove to the floor. Alarmed, the other policeman scurried to either side of the room. The cabinet crashed into the glass doors behind the authorities, and shards of glass shrapnel exploded through the air.

Everyone scattered to edges of the room. Most of the policemen and utility workers ran out of the building. Aubrey didn't move.

The whirling tempest of spiraling hardware and electronic flotsam resumed. Workers covered their heads and ducked. Hovis glided past Aubrey over to the shattered glass doors.

Hovis paused for a moment, studying what he saw in the next room. Columns and rows of generators posted on tiers of metal frames spun and sparked, forcing electricity into massive metal transformers. Sparks of lightning flashed from wire to wire, and the smell of ozone leaked through the plant.

With Hovis on the other side of the plant, Buzz, Magnos, Jordana and Rodriqa ran up behind Aubrey, carefully watching Hovis' movements.

Buzz glanced three times at Aubrey, each time looking at him a little harder. "Aubrey...your eyes." His voice was full of wonder.

Hovis reared his massive translucent head and roared again. He floated through the back wall next to the glass doors and disappeared into the generator room.

Van Zenny popped up behind the kids, hiding behind them. His face was as white as Aubrey's eyes. "What is that thing?" he asked with a shaky voice.

"That *thing* is what's responsible for a great deal of the trouble around here," replied Aubrey boldly. "Care to question him? He might be able to give you the answers you're looking for."

Van Zenny shook his head and stared warily at Aubrey.

"Let's get out of here," whispered Jordana.

"We are way out of our league," agreed Rodriqa quietly.

"We can't let him turn off the power," Aubrey said with a steady tone of determination.

"But we can't stop him," insisted Jordana.

Hovis screamed in agony and tumbled back through the wall and onto the floor. The churning wisps of his injured spirit writhed helplessly throughout the plant and his red hue faded to a dull pink. Everyone in the room flinched in fear.

"Oh, no," murmured Buzz.

"What is it?" asked Magnos.

"I'm about to have a seizure," Buzz stuttered.

Buzz clenched his teeth, and drool seeped down his chin. His eyes fluttered wildly, and Rodriqa grabbed his arm to brace his fall. It lasted only a few seconds.

Buzz's eyes open and his posture straightened. "I've got an idea," he said excitedly.

Hovis slumped over, and his flailing strands surged toward his center. His red glow brightened, and he stood up straight, whole once more. Hovis picked up the desk next to the wall and flung it through the broken glass doors into the generator room. Chasing after the desk, he disappeared through the back wall again.

Buzz ran after Hovis, but stopped just outside of the generator room a few yards in front of the mangled glass doors. The other kids ran up behind him. Inside the generator room, Hovis kicked the desk and it skidded across the floor, knocking a washing machine-sized generator lop-sided out of its socket. Sparks singed insulation, and the fluorescents in the plant flickered like strobe lights for several seconds.

"The electromagnetic field from the generators," murmured Buzz. "It's tearing Hovis apart. He can't get too close to it." Buzz turned and scanned the room. "Hey you! I need your suit!" he shouted at a worker dressed in a cleanroom suit, who was laying in the fetal position in the corner. The worker shook his head, drawing his knees closer to his chest.

Magnos stepped over to a closet, the doors of which swung back and forth in the gusting swells from Hovis. He grabbed a cleanroom suit and carried it over to Buzz.

"Were there coat hangers in the closet?" Buzz yelled over the noise from the wind and electrical discharges.

Magnos nodded affirmatively.

"Bring me all of them," Buzz ordered. "Jordana, run outside and find all the jumper cables you can!"

"From where?" she asked.

"Ask anybody who has a car here. I need as many as you can get."

"But how?" Jordana trembled with reticence.

"Take Van Zenny with you. He can help."

Jordana gasped slightly at Buzz ordering the Sergeant around. Van Zenny agreed without hesitation, and both he and Jordana bolted through the tornado of debris and ran out through the side entrance.

Hovis floated back into the plant room. The kids backed up slowly, watching each move cautiously.

Buzz pointed to Rodriqa. "Rodriqa, I need you to hold Hovis off. Keep him from damaging any more generators."

"You're crazy," Rodriqa replied. "What am I supposed to do? Sing to it?"

Buzz frowned at her. "You know what to do. I saw your knuckles in the car."

Rodriqa thought for a moment. "But I don't know how to make it happen."

"Today, you get a crash course," announced Aubrey.

Hovis flipped the metal closet over. Carrying an armload of intertwined coat hangers, Magnos jumped out of the closet's way just as it toppled to the floor, and ran back to Buzz.

Hovis threw the closet through the shattered glass doors, ripping the remaining shards of glass from the edges of its threshing and ripping portions of the entranceway's metal frame.

"Don't be afraid," consoled Aubrey, as he touched Rodriqa's shoulder.

Rodriqa's eyes widened. "You're wrong," she shouted in a sudden burst of enlightenment. "I have to be afraid for it to happen." She hung her head and focused her thoughts. She jogged lightly in place and blew into her fists to dry off the sweat from her palms.

"What do I do with these?" Magnos asked, clumsily sifting the coat hangers out of their wiry knot.

Buzz was dressing into the cleanroom suit. "Unbend them, and then I'll show you."

Hovis lifted the metal closet into the air and launched it into the middle of the generators. It landed square against the second level, knocking two offline. The lights overhead flickered wildly.

Hovis swayed back into the plant and pulled a long metal pole from off the opposite wall. With the glass doors clear, Rodriqa raced into the generator room. She looked around for a weapon, but the only thing at her feet was a piece of chalk. Her heart beat fiercely faster, and she could feel her chest fill with indomitable fear.

Hovis hurled the metal pole across the room. It bounced in front of Buzz, Magnos and Aubrey and then rolled against the bottom frame of the broken glass doors. Rodriqa picked up the chalk and stepped forward slowly out of the generator room. She planted her foot on the metal pole, pinning it to the ground. She inhaled deeply, focused her attention, and bellowed loudly at Hovis.

Perturbed by her wailing, Hovis flew across the room and roared back at her angrily. The wind washed past Rodriqa's face, blowing her beaded braids behind her. Rodriqa leaned over and scraped the chalk along the floor in a straight line. She pointed the chalk at Hovis. "This far shall you come and *NO FARTHER!*"

Hovis swung his arms and chains through the air viciously at her. Rodriqa ducked, and a tingling sensation prickled along her spine. She raised her head and saw her arms blur out of focus. Her legs and torso fuzzed into smudges, and her ghostly form rippled from head to toe. Within moments, she had recalled the spirit of the Tsul'kalu. Rodriqa was completely transparent.

"Unbelievable. She did it," observed Magnos.

Rodriqa yanked one of Hovis' broken chains and spun him around. Hovis growled at her and slapped her face with his free hand, and she released him and staggered backwards. Rodriqa regained her footing and charged Hovis. She rammed him at full sprint and then body checked him to the ground. Hovis snapped a broken chain like a whip and grappled her legs. He flung his arm overhead and Rodriqa flew through the air, head over foot, into the middle of the plant. Hovis recoiled skyward and flipped his arms above his head.

"No time to gawk," barked Buzz. "Start bending the coat hangers at right angles."

Magnos put his head down and picked up a straightened coat hanger, fashioning it under Buzz's direction.

"Aubrey, you have to find Hovis' stone," Buzz shouted to Aubrey through the mask of his cleanroom suit.

"His what?" questioned Aubrey in confusion, as he watched Hovis throw Rodriqa across the plant floor. He wanted to help her, but he was no match physically for Hovis.

"His *stone*," reiterated Buzz. "Like from *Solluna*...the second poem...the only way we can get rid of Hovis is by isolating his stone."

Aubrey shook his head in confusion. "But I don't know how to do that."

"Today, you get a crash course!" Buzz smiled wryly at him. "Don't you see...Ms. Thistlewood shrinking away from the magnetic conveyer belt...Hovis unable to get near what he wants to destroy most...it's heaven's fire...electromagnetism...but that's not enough...you have to find his stone. You have to make us see it."

Aubrey looked up helplessly. He didn't know where to look. Seeing shadows and ghosts behind his eyelids was one thing, but finding something he didn't even know for sure existed was beyond comprehension. In the far corner of the room, a small window in the top corner caught his eye. He thought he saw movement. He looked more closely. The saber-beaked raven was perched on the sill outside, staring in at him with its black eye.

Magnos handed Buzz several newly bent coat hangers.

"Aubrey, you have to try," Buzz begged.

Rodriqa gritted her teeth as she flipped herself onto her feet. Hovis swooped down and raised the metal pole to the ceiling. Slinging the long pole at Rodriqa, he cried out in fierce rage. She somersaulted forward and dodged the metal pole as it clanged and bounced along the floor.

Aubrey closed his eyes and stared at Hovis. Familiar phosphenes careened in circles and bobbed back and forth behind his eyelids. Darkness dissolved the edges of his sight, and the lights twinkled into an opaque twilight. Hovis in melee sparkled red in front of him. His ghostly arms and chains flailed from side to side as he tussled with Rodriqa. Aubrey squeezed his eyelids more tightly together and concentrated on Hovis. The ghost's form brightened, and the red haze sharpened into shimmering tufts of darkness that orbited his body.

Aubrey held his breath and clenched his fists, focusing all his thought on Hovis. His hearing faded, and the din of madness around him softened. Hovis was as bright and distinct behind his eyelids as ever. Aubrey could see the ghost's every detail, but Aubrey couldn't search within the phantom's haze.

Next to Aubrey, Buzz and Magnos continued fiddling with coat hangers. Buzz smacked Magnos' hand. "No, that doesn't fit right. Bend it this way!"

"Okay…okay," sulked Magnos.

"Have you found Hovis' stone yet?" Buzz called impatiently.

Aubrey pursed his lips in concentration. He wanted to tell Buzz he couldn't do it, but he refused to derail his focus. He bit his lip and looked harder. He had never seen Hovis so clearly before, but beyond his specter shell, nothing else was there.

"Hurry up!" shouted Buzz. "Hovis is wearing Rodriqa out!"

*This is impossible*, Aubrey thought to himself. Futility gripped his gut, and he desperately fought the urge to join the fray.

*Don't you want to ignore it?* a calm, gentle whisper stirred in his mind.

Aubrey tried to ignore the voice, and heaved his gut into chest, grunting to muster more focus.

*How can I ignore any of this anymore?* Aubrey thought to himself.

*Then do you believe?* whispered the same serene voice in reply.

Sharp pains racked Aubrey's chest and back. He wanted to stop, but he refused to fail.

*Yes…I believe*, he answered within his mind.

Warmth gushed from his stomach, filling his lungs and rushing into his head and arms.

*Find your own stone*, instructed the voice, *then you can find the stone of another*.

Aubrey groaned inside. He was tired of riddles, exhausted by mystery and impatient with hidden truths. At this moment, he needed direction, not obscure and fanciful proverbs.

*How?* Aubrey asked. In his heart, he shackled his hate and questioned boldly with the intention of receiving the answer he needed.

*Follow me*, the voice replied.

Hovis faded from his view, and a ring of spangling radiance grew from the middle of Aubrey's vision. Ring after glimmering ring chased the next, and he followed the blazing tunnel behind his eyelids.

The tunnel twisted and turned downward. Deeper and deeper Aubrey was drawn in. The rings evaporated slowly, and at the end, only a single, white stone encircled by a single spinning point of light remained.

His vision cleared. The background glowed a crisp white. His eyes were closed, but Aubrey could see every person in the room: workers cowering in the corners, Magnos and Buzz bent over in front of him, Rodriqa wrestling with Hovis. And all of them had the same white stone embedded in their chests, with a single bright light hovering in circles around it.

Magnos and Buzz gawked at each other with wide eyes. In the other's torso, a white stone glimmered orange with a pinpoint of light in orbit around it. The stone and its miniature satellite reminded Buzz of a living Bohr model of an atom.

Magnos and Buzz stood up and scanned the plant. Everyone in the room had the same fist-sized glowing stone, spinning inside them, except for Hovis.

Jordana and Sergeant Van Zenny ran back into the plant from the side door, hurdling and ducking flying screwdrivers, pencils and needle-thin pieces of glass.

"Here ya's go," Van Zenny said, handing Buzz a tangled nest of jumper cables.

"Perfect," hollered Buzz. "Link them together. Black clamp to black, red to red. And leave one spare."

Van Zenny's jaw dropped. "What's going on? Why's everyone's chest glowing?"

Jordana looked down at herself in amazement. She tried to touch the white stone glowing within her, but her skin was in the way.

"Now's not the time for questions," squawked Buzz. "Get to work!"

Buzz glanced at Aubrey and furrowed his brow. Blood trickled from Aubrey's nose, and his hands were white from squeezing his fingers forcefully into his palms.

In front of the generator room, Rodriqa collapsed forward and landed on her hands. The stinging that had needled her skin was replaced with cramping shudders and aching sores. She looked at her hands, and they were normal again. She pushed herself up and moaned under the strain of her contused muscles. The spirit of the Tsul'kalu had left her. Darkness crept in around her, and she passed out.

Hovis floated across the room, hunting for more projectiles.

"Hovis' stone!" Buzz yelled at Aubrey. "Hovis' stone!" Buzz waved his hand in front of Aubrey's eyes, but Aubrey's gaze was distant and undaunted.

Aubrey saw Buzz move in front of him, but that was only because his stone moved as well. He could also see Jordana and Van Zenny off to the side, and their stones spinning within them. Aubrey stared at Hovis. He washed the rest of his view away and pierced the ghostly hide with his eyes.

Suddenly, Hovis' stone flashed like a star in the middle of his rosy, undulating translucent form. The orange glow from inside him flooded the plant with light. From the remaining workers to Van Zenny and the kids, everyone paused and marveled at the myriad of spinning colors within the phantasm's heart.

"You did it!" shouted Buzz, who had readied his plan. Entangling the outer layer of his cleanroom suit, precisely bent coat hangers intertwined into a cage around his entire body, conforming to each of his extremities and wrapping spirally around his torso and head. Linking it all together, Magnos twisted the final loose ends of coat hangers together in the center of Buzz's back, like a twist tie on a bag of bread.

"Look out!" shouted Buzz as he flinched at an oncoming projectile.

Magnos bolted toward Jordana and Van Zenny and tackled them both to the ground. A wooden desk flew overhead and pelted the wall adjacent to the generator room, splintering into shredded sticks and crumbling panels.

Van Zenny sat up, rubbing his head. "You saved my life," he murmured incredulously to Magnos. Jordana lay flat and still against the floor with her eyes closed.

Buzz looped the conjoined jumper cables in his left hand and held a single pair in his right. In his metal-woven contraption, he waddled into the generator room. He climbed the metal stairs clumsily to the third floor of generators and clamped the long set of jumper cables to a pair of electrical leads up top. A charged snap jolted his fingers through his glove as he made the connection, and he could feel the air sizzle around him. A filing cabinet rolled along the floor into the generator room, but stopped shy of the lowest bank of generators.

Hovis' form filled the generator room, his bright red billowing exterior illuminated by the gleaming white stone within him. Avoiding the magnetic fields, the ghost edged his way cautiously toward the filing cabinet and kicked at it with his feet, hoping to pull it away from the generators.

Buzz leaned over the railing above Hovis.

"Hey, Hovis!" Buzz shouted. Hovis' head rolled backwards. His eyes widened, as he looked skyward.

"HAUNT THIS!" yelled Buzz as he jumped from the landing. In midfall, Buzz threw the end of the single set of jumper cables into the row of generators. The coat hanger cage flashed a brilliant blue and, like a human-sized light bulb, and electricity crackled around Buzz from wall to wall.

Everything went white.

# Victory Chimes

Hundreds of shimmering shadows snaked around the room and scurried into nothingness. The raven unfurled its wings and soared off the edge of the windowsill.

Then everything was still. The static hum from the cranking generators had died. The air hung softly without a draft or hurling ballastics. All the light bulbs were dark, and nothing moved. The interior of the power plant resembled a field of war between the inanimate, with casualties of battered furniture and crippled appliances bearing open wounds of steel and glass.

Footsteps echoed along the concrete floor of the generator room. The breaker snapped loudly, and the uninjured generators sparked to life. Power spun through their wires. The fluorescent lights overhead glowed bright white again.

Mr. Taylor stepped timidly through the gaping remnant of the devastated glass doors, surveying the damage.

Sergeant Van Zenny pushed his paunchy frame upright. His wonder-filled eyes met Mr. Taylor's gaze. Neither one could speak.

Aubrey raised himself up on his elbows and blinked in confusion, the bright lights blinding him. Mr. Taylor ran over to his son and lifted him up from underneath by his shoulders. He righted Aubrey on his feet. Aubrey rubbed his temple with the flat of his hand, trying to regain his senses.

"Are you okay?" his father asked.

Aubrey nodded. "Best day all year," he said with an impish grin. His father laughed heartily and grabbed him around the shoulders.

Magnos scooted himself over toward Jordana on his rigid, casted arm and slid his hand under her head. She was quiet and limp, but he couldn't see any signs of injury. Even her honey-colored glasses remained on her nose, clear and intact. Magnos fretted over the best thing to do next. He gently pulled her head forward, and her eyes opened slightly. She gazed at him with weepy eyes.

"You saved me," Jordana whispered. Magnos' cheeks knotted up and blushed a bright red as a grateful grin squirreled across his mouth. He looked down at her and nodded slowly.

Rodriqa rolled herself forward, shook her head, and stood up. "Oh, no," she muttered as she stared into the generator room. Everyone followed her gaze. Surrounded by the singed and mangled wire cage, Buzz laid face down, motionless on the concrete. Tiny rivulets of smoke billowed up around him. Black streaks lacquered the floor. But there were no signs of Hovis.

Aubrey ran into the generator room and fell down next to him, pulling apart the fried coat hangers and tearing open his burnt and shredded clean-room suit.

Buzz jerked, and a muffled voice cried, "That tickles."

Aubrey reeled Buzz's rotund body onto his back with all his might, grunting as he pushed against the ground for leverage. He yanked off the plastic headgear. Buzz's eyes were closed, and a smile quivered at the bottom of his face.

Buzz shot both arms in the air and screamed, "THAT WAS *AWESOME* !!!"

"I thought you were dead," huffed Aubrey sternly. Buzz chortled manically. Aubrey stormed away, half-angry, but mostly grateful that his best friend was alive.

"That thing was a *ghost?*" the Sergeant asked as he patted his frizzled hair down with his fingers.

"Yes," asserted Aubrey. He closed his eyes and stared around the room. "And hopefully now he's gone for good."

Mr. Taylor shook his head and tried to refocus on reality. "Looks like there's a twist in your investigation, Officer."

"Ya's ain't kiddin'," murmured Van Zenny. "And look at this mess! Think the plant can be salvaged?"

"Fortunately, the main breaker kicked off when Buzz…when Buzz…when the short circuit flashed, so most of the generators are back online. Should be enough to keep the town going. The rest will take some time. We need to find out if anyone is hurt."

One by one, plant workers stood up and brushed themselves off. Several crept in from side doors cautiously, marveling at the destruction.

Mr. Taylor gathered the kids together. "Is anyone injured?"

Magnos held up his cast. "Yeah, but I have this to blame on the Tsul'kalu." Magnos smiled and the other four chuckled.

"Huh?" queried Aubrey's dad confusedly.

"Never mind," muttered Magnos. "Inside joke."

"I'm good, Mr. Taylor," replied Rodriqa as she popped her shoulder and stretched her hamstrings.

"Me too," echoed Jordana.

"Same here," said Buzz gleefully, with a twitch in his charcoal-smudged cheeks.

Mr. Taylor addressed one of the workers wearing a cleanroom suit who had taken off his helmet to examine the scattered debris more clearly. "Can you handle things for a bit? I need to get the kids out of here." The worker nodded through a daze of shock.

"Sergeant, I should run the kids home and talk to their parents. I'll call the central office when I get back. Do you need any information from me right now?"

Van Zenny scratched his head. "I can't think of anything at the moment. I'll get your statement later. I should get back to the office. I'll be in touch."

"Okay, let's go. Your parents are all probably worried," ordered Mr. Taylor as he herded the kids toward the side entrance.

"Dad, can we make a pit stop before we head home?" Aubrey asked softly.

"Sure thing," replied his father with a musing grin. "Everyone in my truck."

"What about the Buzz Bug?" Buzz asked anxiously.

"I'm impounding it," boasted the Sergeant.


"Thanks again, Mr. Jennings," yelled Aubrey into the **Smart Mart & Finer Diner** as he held the door open for his four friends. Mr. Taylor leaned against the open door of his truck, puzzled by what they had purchased. Each of them held aloft a set of wind chimes, admiring the hanging trinkets of shaped metal and sculpted glass as they swayed and tinkled in the breeze.

Buzz, Rodriqa, Jordana and Magnos climbed into the back seat of the truck, cradling their new acquisitions delicately. Aubrey walked up to his dad behind his friends.

"We already have a set of wind chimes hanging from the porch at home," remarked Mr. Taylor calmly.

"This set is for my bedroom," Aubrey notified him without hesitation.

"Spirit draft," mumbled Magnos, as he squirmed to fit in between Jordana and the side of the truck.

Mr. Taylor gave a quick nod and acquiesced. Today, he had learned better than to argue with his son any further in matters of the spirit.

Aubrey stepped up onto the runner board, but his father halted him with a hand on his stomach, blocking his way. Aubrey rocked back to the ground, and Mr. Taylor closed the truck door.

Dan Taylor curled his mouth and stared at the ground. "I have something I need to say to you...man to man."

Aubrey nodded slightly and listened carefully.

"I don't really understand everything that's happened, but what I do know is that you tried to be honest with me and I didn't give you a fair shot." A lump welled up in his throat as his voice thickened. "Things have been rough lately...you know that."

Aubrey shook his head meekly.

"I wanted to make Gaetan's last year of high school a year he could remember, and I felt like maybe you were trying to steal attention from him."

Aubrey forced himself to hold a snarl.

"And everything with your mother hasn't made things easier." His father rubbed the corner of his eye to hide a tear. "Then with all the craziness surrounding you, I felt out of control, like my world was falling apart." He snickered to conceal a sob.

"Both of our worlds were falling apart," corrected Aubrey sullenly.

His dad nodded. "I know that now." He cleared his throat.

"And another thing," continued Aubrey, as he stiffened his lower lip. "I'm...not...mom."

His father shook his head and cupped his hands around Aubrey's shoulders. He glared lovingly at his son, as if he hadn't truly seen him for months. "You are so much like her," he spoke through a clenched jaw. He sighed deeply through pursed lips. "But the one thing you are *not*...is crazy."

Dan Taylor wrapped his arms around his son and held him tightly. It was a hug Aubrey had needed for a very long time.

Tears streamed freely from both their eyes. Aubrey's heart floated.

"I'm sorry," Mr. Taylor said softly.

All Aubrey could do was nod his head against his father's shoulder, grateful for his father's understanding.

"Now let's get home and redo your room," Mr. Taylor said. They both chuckled through sniffles. Aubrey walked around the front of the truck and crawled into the passenger seat.

Aubrey glanced into the back cab, and his heart dropped into his stomach. Magnos' calloused, beefy fingers were wrapped around Jordana's hand, and a soft smile creased her lips as she looked down and combed strands of her black straight hair behind her ear. Aubrey sighed quietly. Although he had hoped to be the one to win Jordana's heart, her bond with Magnos wasn't completely unexpected. *He had saved her life, after all*, Aubrey thought to himself. Being in second place wasn't fun, but he had won two out of three battles today. *Not too shabby*.

"OUCH!" screeched Rodriqa as she swatted at Buzz.

Buzz raised his arms to guard himself from her palmy wrath. "Leave me alone!"

"Something is poking me," she snapped.

"I didn't touch you!"

Rodriqa looked down at the small space in between them. "Something in your backpack did!" She lifted Buzz's backpack off the seat and ripped its zipper open.

"Hoaker Croaker!" she exclaimed as she peered inside. She reached in and pulled out a trembling ball of cream and charcoal-colored fur. "It's McCrayden's cat!!"

She laid the forgotten feline in the floorboard, and everyone in the back pulled their feet upwards warily to avoid touching it. The timid beast jerked and clawed at the floor. It whined and meowed, and then raked its paws down its face.

"Do you think we should take her back to McCrayden?" Aubrey asked.

"I don't think she'll want her now," replied Magnos. "That cat is damaged goods."

"I think it's a crime she named a boy cat Prissy," commented Rodriqa.

Everyone in the truck gave her a strange look. She rolled her eyes and turned the cat over onto its back. Its legs spun in the air, and everyone stared at its belly. A collective, comprehending *Ahhh* echoed between them.

"Aubrey, I know it's been a rough day, but a cat is the last thing we need," remarked Mr. Taylor.

"No worries," quipped Rodriqa. "I'll take him home." Rodriqa cradled the cat into her lap, and even though he was obviously agitated and distressed, the cat relaxed just slightly. Jordana scooted closer to Magnos.

"I think he needs a new name," said Rodriqa in a musical tone.

"I think it needs some medicine," Buzz sarcastically replied.

Rodriqa glowered at him for his lack of sympathy.

"How about Whimperfidget?" interjected Jordana.

Aubrey, Magnos, Buzz and Mr. Taylor cackled loudly, but Rodriqa frowned at her.

"No, I'm serious," Jordana insisted. "It's a perfect description of him."

Silence filled the truck for a moment, and then Buzz crowed in exploding hilarity with his fist over his mouth. "That's the craziest name for a cat I've ever heard!"

Rodriqa glared at him as she rubbed her new cat's neck. "Whimperfidget it is."

Mr. Taylor shifted the truck into gear and pulled out onto the highway. "Buzz, I'll take you home first since you live the furthest away," he stated matter-of-factly.

"I'm sure I'll have a lot of explaining to do," replied Buzz in a depressed tone.

"I called your dad while you were in the store. He seemed a little confused." Mr. Taylor glanced over at Aubrey and smiled. Aubrey grinned knowingly back.

They drove over the dam, and everyone leaned over to look out at Lake Julian, which was still nothing more than a swamped pit of muck. The gray ball of condensed rock stood firmly in the mud, a testament to shadow's defeat. Clusters of locals had parked at the sides of the dam and had climbed the observatory tower to view the unusual spectacle.

"I still have a question," stated Rodriqa with a hint of didactic superiority.

The other four kids turned toward her inquisitively.

She stared at each of her friends individually. "Why us?"

Buzz leaned forward to stare at Magnos, who looked at Jordana, who refused to look at anyone. Aubrey titled his head to the side. He really wanted to know the answer to her question.

"Maybe we're superheroes," Buzz prattled nonchalantly.

"Maybe so," replied Magnos, smiling grandly.

Rodriqa shook them off. "Why were our collective set of gifts unified against Hovis?"

"Maybe it's magic," replied Buzz in a spooky tone.

Magnos chuckled, Aubrey giggled, and Jordana rolled her eyes.

"No, sprain brain," chided Rodriqa. "There's no such thing as magic!"

Magnos and Jordana stared out the window. Buzz rubbed smudges of burnt plastic off his arm. Aubrey looked at Rodriqa.

Rodriqa shrugged. "There has to be a reason!"

Aubrey agreed with her wholeheartedly. But with all they had seen and in all the ways their world had changed, he only knew one thing for certain. Simply asking a question doesn't guarantee you'll receive an answer.

# *Cruxtaposition*

A ragged smile cracked the Old Widow Wizenblatt's face as she listened to the sputtering rush of the dam's turbines. She stood on the banks of the empty Lake Julian, admiring the mucky earth of the lakebed with satisfaction. Despite the sloppiness of the kids' role, she was grateful that both Hovis' elemental wrecking ball and Mrs. Thistlewood's grand plan had completely fizzled out.

She stepped into the boggy bed and walked toward the dam. Her bare feet sank shin-deep into the mire, and her tattered dress fringe was soiled by the mud as it sloshed along the ground. A trickle of water from Wontawanna Creek meandered through the swampy muck, but, except for a few larger murky pools, the entire bottom of Lake Julian was exposed.

Lodged into the back of the dam, the Tomb of Enoch jutted over the mud in full view. Its jagged shards of pastel-colored quartz sparkled in the sun, and its finely hewn rock glistened with trickling rivulets of receding lake water. Mrs. Wizenblatt paused for a moment in reverence of its majestic craftsmanship, but she kept her distance.

The widow lifted her hands toward tomb like she was embracing it from afar. She closed her eyes and squeezed her face tightly in concentration. The breeze spun through her curly white hair, flipping locks to and fro, and the veins in her arms popped up under the strain of her focus. The wind whipped violently around her, rippling the soggy earth at her feet away from her.

Her eyes snapped open and flashed fully white. The tomb rocked from side to side, twisting and creaking against the concrete face of the dam. With a resounding crack it pulled away, revealing the dam's filled-in lower level as the rocky cocoon slid backwards across the mud. An imprint of the tomb's face, the Circle of Circles, remained in the solidified cement, like a monument to recent events, scarring the bottom of the dam.

Mrs. Wizenblatt thrust her hands toward the ground, her palms parallel to the mud. The tomb shifted under a great invisible weight. Its face tipped skyward, and its oblong rear sank into the boggy lakebed. Like a sinking ship, Enoch's tomb slowly squeezed itself through the earth until the thick, gurgling silt lapped over the last quartz shard. The bedrock convulsed underneath the widow's feet for a few seconds before calmly and peacefully shuddering to stillness.

A tiny tingle trickled down her spine. She felt like she was being watched. She whipped her neck around and glared at Mr. Osterfeld several hundred yards away, who was spying on her with binoculars from the deck of his stranded, sludge-drenched tugboat. She waved happily at him. Startled, Mr.

Osterfeld took a step backward, refusing to remove his binoculars from his face. He slipped forward on the angled deck of his vessel and fell into the muck below.

The widow sighed deeply, and her shoulders slumped forward in exhaustion. The blueness returned to her eyes as she wiped the sweat from her forehead. She fiddled with her disheveled hair, only improving it from a complete mess to mildly disarrayed. She rubbed her hands together to relieve the aching cramps in her joints.

The saber-beaked raven soared out of the sky and landed on a rock in the mud several yards from Mrs. Wizenblatt. The raven folded it wings and angled its head to the side to gain full view of her. With a staccato cackle, he greeted her.

She scowled at the raven and pointed her finger at it. "You're responsible for a great deal of this trouble." She grunted in disdain to show her displeasure.

The raven opened its beak and a low rumble choked out of its throat.

"You should be the one replacing the Tomb," she chided.

The raven hissed at her.

She walked through the mud and swung her foot toward its head. The raven jaunted into the air with its wings flailing wildly, barely avoiding her foot. Flapping his wings with full force, it launched itself skyward and glided along the breeze toward the safety of the opposite bank.

The raven landed in the grass and composed itself, preening its feathers of splatters of mud. It rubbed its wings along patches of moss as if it was preparing itself for the arrival of someone important.

The autumn wind abruptly stopped, and the noises of the forest one by one became silent. The raven stood motionless, anxious amidst the calm.

Three silvery mists floated through the woods and hovered toward the edge of the lake. The translucent, smoky spheres appeared as a blur that was slowly coming into focus. Faces formed above them with sharply angled cheeks and diamond-faceted eyes. Their individual hazes shrank, and arms and legs formed at the edges until torsos precipitated out of each cloud. The three shimmering beings had mirror-like skin, and their bodies took humanoid shape, trembling from head to toe with minute vibration.

The raven turned his body perpendicular to them and ruffled his feathers upwards in a territorial display. Looking at them directly was difficult for the bird, as the sunlight glinted brightly off their skin, obscuring most details. Through the brilliant radiating and reflecting light, the raven watched as three pairs of wings fluttered on each of the beings, one on the back of each upper arm, one on the back of each lower leg and two at their backs. A less adept creature would mistake the wings for an illusion, as they smeared the air around them like a hummingbird's wings.

As they approached the raven, it noticed the two left figures were more masculine in appearance and the right one was more feminine.

The form to the left bent down on one knee and examined the raven. "Clever," he said, pondering the bird in front of him. "Perhaps after someone has spent enough time on this dirt ball, they begin to take on the characteristics of some of its vermin." His words were crisp and elegantly articulated; complete perfection in every syllable and enunciation. He raised himself up and wiped his hands clean of any earthly contamination.

The raven chided him with an admonishing caw. The middle being spoke with the same beautiful diction as his compatriot. "Let us not be rude to our messenger, Yoyle."

The wind spun in erratic circles around the raven. Blades of grass gyrated violently, and the nearby trees leaned inward, their trunks creaking under the strain of the growing gale. The raven buried his beak under his wing, and one by one the strands of long, ebony plumage were pulled from its body and whipped around its head like a feathery black hurricane. The dark, rotating mass drew dirt and dead leaves into it, and the center of the turbulence grew in size, matching the height of the other three creatures.

Slowly, the wind relented, and the grass and trees returned to their resting positions. The swirling darkness materialized into a dull gray humanoid shape with long spindly arms and a baldhead, clothed in flowing robes that draped the ground. Unlike his counterparts in front of him, the sunlight was both partially absorbed and partially reflected by his translucent skin. His right was eye was flat and gray, but his left eye took the shape of a slanted dark oval, giving him a mournful expression. Several bits of rock and broken twigs slowly turned in orbit around his torso, ignoring earth's gravity. His transition from physical to soulful form had drained him, and he heaved his chest upwards to hide his exhaustion.

"Rest, Zaks," greeted the middle silvery creature.

"Rest, Grandmaster Starazor," Zaks replied, his lackluster voice crudely fashioned in comparison. "I trust you are enjoying your exile," he asked in a devilishly polite manner.

Starazor's thin lips curled around the edges at his distasteful question. "Not an exile," he reassured Zaks. "Simply a reassignment."

Zaks nodded respectfully. "Rest, Yoyle and Amana," he addressed the beings flanking Starazor.

They quietly nodded in return.

"Enoch's Tomb remains closed," reported Zaks in a disappointed, yet official, tone.

"Yes, we have already heard of your failure, Magi," quipped Yoyle.

"Not a failure, simply a defeat," Zaks replied slyly.

Starazor's smile widened slightly. "And thus no Watcher escaped bondage?"

"That is mostly correct," affirmed Zaks.

"Mostly?" questioned Yoyle.

"A single Watcher may have escaped. It is yet unclear. However, it is inconsequential. One Watcher provides minimal distraction and poses no threat."

Yoyle scoffed at his assessment.

"Then I should assume the forest guardians' efforts to protect the tomb were simply insurmountable?" asked Starazor methodically.

"Not entirely," reported Zaks. "There was also a significant amount of interference from a nearby group of puds."

"Really?" asked Starazor jeeringly. "A couple of humans undermined the flawless plan of the mighty Zaks?!" He chuckled airily, and Amana mimicked his amusement. "Please, entertain us with your story of the exceptionally cunning flesh dwellers."

Zaks squinted his stodgy eye and chose his words carefully. "There are half a dozen humans in the area who have demonstrated adept manifestations of the *divinoi*, and they used those skills in tandem with the aid of the forest guardians and a few other interlopers to prevent the opening of the tomb."

"Impossible," accused Yoyle, lunging forward. Starazor raised his hand to silence him as he contemplated Zaks' veracity.

"I agree with Yoyle's assessment," interjected Amana, with a sturdy balance in her tone. "It's not unheard of for one or two puds to appear in a region with an unusual penchant for manipulating their divinoi. But *six* would be very unlikely, especially this many millennia after the divinoi were separated."

"Exactly," added Yoyle tersely. "The divinoi are too diluted amongst the population for any one of them to be able to harness and control the power in any meaningful or perceptible way. Either Zaks is mistaken, or his lengthy vacation on this pitiful planet has polluted his judgment."

Zaks bowed his head humbly. "Grandmaster, under most prior circumstances I would agree with Yoyle and Amana, but I have seen it myself. I do not speak of rumor or conjecture. I am witness to the divinoi they have proficiently wielded in shaping the events around them. These children are remarkably gifted."

"Children?" exclaimed Yoyle incredulously. "It takes most puds a lifetime to-"

"It may be foolish, but the terminal prophecy may be at hand," interrupted Zaks as he raised his voice to drown out Yoyle.

The light around Yoyle flashed in a sparkling rage. "This is nonsense!"

"Perhaps patience poses itself as the most prudent action now," added Zaks, ignoring Yoyle. Starazor pondered his words carefully.

"Patience?" questioned Yoyle. "Grandmaster, now is the time to act! We have debated the Clockmaker's lack of intervention for eons. If we do not force closure to this perpetual war, who knows how long it will continue?"

Starazor spoke slowly. "Zaks has provided us with uniquely unexpected information that we must consider."

"The terminal prophecy is a myth, a device to keep those of us, who are beyond exhaustion, trapped in a web of endless, misguided hope," insisted Yoyle. "We cannot disregard the undercurrent of discontent and dismay amongst all of the Clockmaker's progeny."

"Yoyle is right," interjected Amana steadily. "Many factions await to unravel the Clockmaker's plan. If we do not act first, others will, and our ability to maintain control will be compromised."

"How certain are your suspicions regarding the prophecy?" Starazor asked.

Zaks wrapped his arms around his chest as he recalled recent events. "The boy, this Aubrey Taylor, could see the ghost whose help I enlisted to open the tomb. He could see the spirit shards guarding his house, and he could see me. He could see the ghost and translate him into physical form so others around him could see. And he translated soul stones. I am convinced he is the Last Seer."

"Preposterous!" shouted Yoyle.

"If what you say is true, Magi, then perhaps we should wait and see how these events unfold," decided Starazor, his words wrapped in contemplation.

"No!" Yoyle roared. "We have waited long enough!"

Starazor turned toward Yoyle and glared at him studiously with his sharp, crystalline eyes glinting in the afternoon sun.

"Have we?"

# *Acknowledgments*

The love of my family and friends has always been my greatest gift.
Love expresses itself through a multitude of words and gestures; a stern rebuke, a whimsied chortle or a tear-stained face, each action tugging and prodding at the heart in their own unique ways. It is the complex mystery of the highest emotion which frames a network of caring and devotion that I cling to daily, driving me to be more thoughtful and enlivening me to action.

I am exceedingly grateful for all the support I have received over the past two-and-a-half years as I drowned myself in this seemingly purposeless dream. Bending ears, tender shoulders, and encouraging words carried me through the deeply personal challenge of writing my first novel.

Deserving exceptional distinction, below are the individuals who through selfless care and concern contributed to the completion of my goal.

**Chris Francis**, brother-in-arms and copy editor, who with unbridled tolerance has listened to my raving imagination for far too long.
**Sunny Fry**, sister-in-law, copy editor and the best universal perspective adjustor around.
**Eric Losh**, illustrator extraordinaire who brought visual life to my written concoction.
**Ryan Carr**, a friend whose support and purity of heart is never-ending.
**Jacob Fry**, for his priceless point of view.
**Thuy Bui**, for her support and mad football expertise.
**Michael Carlson**, for his comments, critiques, and thoughtful analysis in all things.
**Deb Lartigue**, friend and supporter from the beginning.
My mom, **Sandra Thompson-Fry**, my biggest cheerleader,
And my dad, **Bob Holder**, my newest best friend.

If I have inadvertently left someone out, I sincerely apologize and can hopefully make amends by including mention of you in future works. But please remember, I am new at this.

CPSIA information can be obtained at www.ICGtesting.com
Printed in the USA
237110LV00001B/2/P